WORDSWORTH CLASSICS
OF WORLD LITERATURE

*General Editor: Tom Griffith*

# THE PLAYS

# Christopher Marlowe
# The Plays

❖

*With Introductions by Emma Smith*

WORDSWORTH CLASSICS
OF WORLD LITERATURE

This edition published 2000 by Wordsworth Editions Limited
8b East Street, Ware, Hertfordshire SG12 9HJ

ISBN 1 84022 130 5

2 4 6 8 10 9 7 5 3 1

Typeset by Antony Gray
Printed and bound in Great Britain by
Mackays of Chatham, Chatham, Kent

# CONTENTS

# CHRONOLOGY

## CHRISTOPHER MARLOWE (1564–93)

1564 Christopher Marlowe born in Canterbury, son of a shoe-maker.

1579 Gained a scholarship to the King's School, Canterbury

1580 Obtained a scholarship to Corpus Christi College, Cambridge, where he studied divinity.

1584 Awarded the degree of Bachelor of Arts. There is some evidence that during his time at Cambridge he was also working as a spy for Sir Francis Walsingham, head of the Elizabethan secret service. While a student he translated from Latin Ovid's erotic lyrics, and probably wrote his first play *Dido, Queen of Carthage*.

1587 Awarded the degree of Master of Arts, following a letter from the Queen's Privy Council to the University of Cambridge authorities who, it seems, suspected him of being a Catholic spy.

1589 Marlowe arrested on the charge of murdering one William Bradley in a fight. In fact, Marlowe's friend Thomas Watson had delivered the fatal blow. Marlowe was imprisoned in Newgate for a fortnight until he was bailed by friends; Watson was eventually pardoned, having been judged to have acted in self-defence.

1590 *Tamburlaine the Great* published, including both Parts I and II. These are the only plays of Marlowe's to be published during his lifetime. The dating of his other plays is difficult to determine, but it is conjectured that *Tamburlaine* was probably first performed in 1587–8, *The Jew of Malta* in 1588–9,

*Edward II* somewhere between 1591–3 and *Doctor Faustus* in 1592.

1593   *The Massacre at Paris* performed at the Rose Theatre. Most of Marlowe's plays were probably performed here, but the *Massacre* is the only one which can be precisely dated. Marlowe was arrested after heretical papers were found in the room of Thomas Kyd, another playwright and one-time room-mate. Kyd insisted that the papers belonged to Marlowe, accusing him in a deposition of heresy, blasphemy and other 'monstrous opinions'. A government agent, Richard Baines, was given the task of investigating the case while Marlowe was on bail, and he produced a note detailing other treasonable and blasphemous opinions supposedly uttered by Marlowe. These included the claims that 'Christ was a bastard', that 'St John the Evangelist was bedfellow to Christ [and] used him as the sinners of Sodoma', 'that all they that love not tobacco and boys were fools', and that 'he has as good a right to coin as the Queen of England'. There was also the suggestion that some 'great men, who in convenient time shall be named' were also implicated in these opinions. Baines concluded that 'all men in Christianity ought to endeavour that the mouth of so dangerous a member may be stopped'. Before Marlowe could be tried, he was stabbed to death by a drinking companion, Ingram Frizer, in a tavern in Deptford, supposedly over a dispute about the bill. Two former secret service colleagues were the only witnesses, and the suggestion that this was a cover-up has often been made, most cogently by Charles Nicholl in his book *The Reckoning*.

# GENERAL INTRODUCTION

This chronology lists all the known facts about Marlowe's life, and some widely-accepted and informed conjecture about his activities. Fact and fiction – both his own creations and those of others – are peculiarly intertwined in responses to Marlowe's work. Since his violent death in a tavern brawl in Deptford at the age of twenty-nine, the playwright has become the stuff of literary myth, fuelled by speculation in fiction and scholarship about this mysterious man of the Elizabethan theatre. Variously identified as a spy, a double agent, a free-thinker, an atheist, a homosexual or all of these, Marlowe's bad-boy reputation threatens to distort our reading of the plays. Even where his role is incidental, as in the recent Oscar-winning film *Shakespeare in Love* which presents him as saturnine and brilliantly, morosely creative, he is portrayed as an enigma. We have no evidence other than self-interested hearsay to confirm his dangerous reputation – no evidence, for example, that any of his plays was ever censored – but it is striking that critics have been so unwilling to let go of this powerful myth. The response of the more morally orthodox strain of literary criticism was to castigate the author-sinner for what William Hazlitt described as 'a lust for power in his writings, a hunger and thirst after unrighteousness, a glow of the imagination, unhallowed by any thing but its own energies'. Recent criticism has, without significantly changing the terms of the commentary, radically revalued these qualities: 'millennial Marlowe', according to the editor of a recent collection of critical essays on the plays and poetry, 'will be canonised . . . not for pious orthodoxy but for the perversion, violence, cruelty and excess that formerly disqualified him from sainthood' (Richard Wilson, in *Christopher Marlowe*, Longman 1999).

The elision of the sensationalised accounts of his short life with the events and characters of the plays he wrote began soon after his death. As a satirical play produced in 1600 in Cambridge, Marlowe's alma mater, described him:

> Marlowe was happy in his buskind [i.e. tragic] muse,
> Alas unhappy in his life and end.
> Pity it is that wit so ill should dwell,
> Wit lend from heaven, but vices sent from hell.

Numerous critics have identified Marlowe's morally ambiguous heroes with their creator: Marlowe the atheist is thus figured by Faustus, who enters into a pact with the devil; Marlowe the amoral outsider merges with Barabas; Marlowe the homosexual is expressed in Edward; Marlowe the ambitious wordsmith is echoed by Tamburlaine. While it is impossible entirely to separate the colourful accounts of his life from the plays, such biographical readings are fraught with speculation. Marlowe's plays are distinctive for their shifting quality, their refusal to allow for moral certainties, and as such they may reflect the shadowy world in which their author moved. Beyond this association, it is as difficult to discover Marlowe's own opinions from the evidence of his writings as it is from those accusatory and moralistic contributions published just before and after his death. Marlowe's drama is characteristically challenging, unsettling and unconventional, and the introductions in this volume, which includes his entire dramatic corpus, will attempt to demonstrate these qualities. Marlowe's early death deprived the English theatre of a great talent. It is as if all we had of Shakespeare was the *Henry VI* plays, *Titus Andronicus*, *Romeo and Juliet* and *The Comedy of Errors*. Marlowe's particular legacy was linguistic: his gift for dramatic poetry, what Ben Jonson famously described as his 'mighty line', the iambic pentameter which was to transform theatrical writing. The scope of his plays and their characteristic mode of hyperbole and bombast, demonstrate the high aspirations of his dramatic imagination.

EMMA SMITH
*Hertford College, Oxford*

# THE FIRST PART OF
# TAMBURLAINE THE GREAT

# INTRODUCTION

The two parts of Tamburlaine were probably performed during 1587–8, by the Lord Admiral's Men at the Rose Theatre. They were published together in 1590, with the graphic extended title *Tamburlaine the great; who, from a Scythian shepherd, by his rare and wonderful conquests became a most puissant and mighty monarch, and for his tyranny and terror was termed the scourge of God.* There is no indication of authorship on this first printed version of the plays. The question of the relationship between the two parts will be considered in more detail in the introduction to Part II: the available evidence seems to suggest that Part I was originally conceived as a single, self-standing play, but it was so popular with the theatregoing public that a sequel was hastily commissioned and performed to cash in on this initial success. This introduction will consider Part I as it must have been experienced by Elizabethan playgoers: as a complete and completed dramatic narrative.

The Prologue to the play identifies it as a dramatic departure, away from 'jigging veins of rhyming mother-wits', Marlowe's disdainful reference to the doggerel rhythms and home-spun predictability of his fellow dramatists. Leaving such inconsequential forms behind, the audience is to be led 'to the stately tent of war', to hear Tamburlaine 'threat'ning the world with high astounding terms'. A sense of geographical scope is suggested in the phrase 'scourging kingdoms with his conquering sword'. This is a play of powerful, effective language, a blank verse drama of action, not of contemplation or reflection. We are invited to 'view but his picture in this tragic glass,/And then applaud his fortunes as [we] please'. As so often in Marlowe's plays, the prologue offers an immediate introduction to significant themes on which the play will discourse at more length. Firstly, this is a new kind of play – both in ideological and dramatic terms. Its subject matter, too, is a departure, and the play will be concerned with the theatre of war. Tamburlaine's character is defined in terms of his linguistic prowess, and this power over and through language is, of course, a highly theatrical one, analogous to the authority of the actor. The play is identified as a 'tragic glass', but here, too, Marlowe is innovative. Tragedies conventionally end in the death of their major protagonist, but Tamburlaine is not dead at the end of Part I, and thus the prologue alerts the generic expectations of tragedy only to frustrate them. Finally, the audience is invited, even commanded, to respond to the play as they see fit. Moral responsibility, the authority to endorse or criticise the play's actions and characters, is smartly devolved onto the audience. This is not a play which is going to give us the satisfaction of telling us what to think, but rather one which offers a thoroughgoing challenge to our expectations of genre, style, characterisation, and moral standpoint. Our active participation is demanded.

This typically Marlovian start is developed through the play. The play deals with the rise to power of Tamburlaine, a Scythian shepherd. Through an alliance with Cosroe who has rebelled against his brother Mycetes, King of Persia, Tamburlaine's power increases until he defeats Cosroe himelf. He conquers the Turkish emperor Bajazeth and humiliates him and his wife into a violent suicide by imprisoning and goading them in a cage. Only Zenocrate, Tamburlaine's captive and later his wife, can mediate his ruthless ambition; she persuades him to spare her father when he captures Damascus, slaughtering its population. From the outset, then, Tamburlaine refuses to acknowledge limitations. Elizabethan social hierarchy held that the upper classes were born to their rank and wealth because they were natural leaders. Tamburlaine discards this convention, proclaiming at his first appearance on stage, 'I am a lord, for so my deeds shall prove,/ And yet a shepherd by my parentage', drawing on the mythic iconography of Jove, the king of the gods who took the form of a shepherd on earth. And if Tamburlaine proclaims this, it must be so, for throughout the play he is characterised as a man whose words, however extravagant, are never empty, vainglorious delusions but firm prophecies we see enacted before our eyes. 'Forsake thy king,' he tells Theridamas, 'and do but join with me,/ And we will triumph over all the world.' Theridamas does, and they do. Like Zenocrate in the same scene, Theridamas is won over by Tamburlaine's rhetoric, and the play makes it clear that it is this control over language which both symbolises and enacts the hero's power. As he tells Theridamas, ' "will" and "shall" best fitteth Tamburlaine' (3.3): this purposive grammar is the means of his success. Even his name, repeated some eighty times in the play, takes on a talismanic power. Tamburlaine's words are literally irresistible, for characters onstage and for the audience in the theatre. Those who do not succumb to this seduction are summarily despatched, so there is small wonder that Elizabethan audiences fell for this hero. A play which seemed to offer ultimate moral judgement to the intellectually-engaged spectator of the play turns out to countermand this offer within minutes: perhaps the prologue, rather than inviting us to judge as we please, was issuing a challenge, daring us not to yield to its supremely powerful, charismatic hero. There is no room for us to dissent from this dramatisation of absolutism, and indeed, we may well be excited by its representation of power, wealth and excess. The characteristically Marlovian tension between revulsion and admiration, between identifying with and distancing from the major protagonist, is established.

What is so unorthodox about Tamburlaine's linguistic vaunting is that it does not undergo any setback. In the second scene of the play, he boasts:

> I hold the Fates bound fast in iron chains,
> And with my hand turn Fortune's wheel about;
> And sooner shall the sun fall from his sphere
> Than Tamburlaine be slain or overcome.

Conventions of tragedy lead us to expect that any man who so clearly sets himself above the control of fortune is going to be brought low. Tamburlaine's cosmic words seem like an archetypal instance of hubris – that pridefulness which, according to Aristotle's theory of classical tragedy, was always and inevitably followed by a fall. But Tamburlaine's supreme force of will does seem, in this play at least, to control his destiny. He is untouchable, both by the mortals he encounters in his sweep across half the globe, and by the unseen forces thought to control human existence. Tamburlaine acknowledges no such limitations, either physical or metaphysical, and it is as if by not believing in them, he renders them impotent. There is no nemesis in the form of divine or human intervention. Opponents of Tamburlaine's expansion are expeditiously killed, or, sometimes, as in the case of Bajazeth who brains himself to death in his cage, put to a brutal and bloody death. While we may feel repelled by this summary brutality, even these actions do not fundamentally fix our response to Tamburlaine himself, since none of these challengers is dramatically or morally worthy of our respect – from the ineffectual Mycetes, whose impotence is tellingly revealed by his own initial admission that he is not good with words, to Cosroe, whose dying curse on Tamburlaine is bathetic in its ineffectiveness. The play ends not with the expected reversal of Tamburlaine's fortunes according to the tragic model, but with a conclusion more akin to the structures of contemporary comedy: a marriage. The 'dead bodies' borne off in the final stage direction do not, as they might in Shakespearean tragedy, include that of the eponymous hero.

All this is not to say that Marlowe's portrait of his hero is entirely favourable. Tamburlaine is presented as pitiless and tyrannical. Moments of uncharacteristic tenderness – his feelings about Zenocrate in Act 5, for example – are quickly erased by the force of his brutality, in the murder of the innocent virgins of Damascus. The banquet before the gates of Damascus dramatises the excesses of his appetite for power, as he serves up crowns to his captains and carves up the world with his dagger. Tamburlaine is terrifyingly irresistible, both within the play and within the theatre, not least because his power, as in this banquet scene, is preeminently theatrical: his greatest acts are *coups de theatre*. His is not a story of inner psychology but of external self-presentation, of declaiming rather than musing, of action, including linguistic action, rather than contemplation. If we look for realist or three-dimensional characterisation in Marlowe's works, we look in vain, for the concern of the plays is in developing action and poetry rather than personality.

A decade after *Tamburlaine* was performed at the Rose, the rivals of the Admiral's Men, the Lord Chamberlain's Men, associated with Marlowe's most famous contemporary, William Shakespeare, opened a new theatre on London's Bankside. They called it the

Globe. Marlowe, however, anticipates this analogy between the theatre and the world by bringing the world on to the stage of *Tamburlaine*. Part of the play's triumphant appeal, then, is to the armchair traveller, the Elizabethan hungry for fantastic news of farflung and unfamiliar places. Thomas Platter, a German who visited the Globe theatre during his tour of England in 1599, observed that the English enjoy 'learning at the play what is happening abroad . . . since for the most part they do not travel much, but prefer to learn foreign matters and take their pleasures at home'. *Tamburlaine* seems to fit this role perfectly. The play's rhetoric is a gazetteer of place-names, rather like the contemporary catalogues of exotic locations mapping out the newly opening trade routes which contributed to London's prosperity and England's increasing international ascendancy. It has been suggested that in his subjugation of the world, Tamburlaine prefigures and triumphantly symbolises the emerging practice of colonisation through trade and conquest. The 'scourge of God' is, seen in this light, the ideal Englishman, and the ambivalence of the audience to this figure who is at once barbarously foreign and also recognisable, even admirable, is considerable. Tamburlaine is untrammelled by geographical place. He scorns the 'blind geographers' who seek to divide the world into the 'three regions' of Europe, Africa and Asia. He reduces the world 'to a map', inscribing it with his power to name: 'Calling the provinces, cities, and towns/ After my name and thine, Zenocrate' (5.1). At the end of Part I he is instructing his noblemen how to rule over these newly acquired dominions, taking 'truce with all the world' – a truce declared, of course, on his own terms.

## CHARACTERS IN THE PLAY

MYCETES, *King of Persia*

COSROE, *his Brother*

MEANDER  
THERIDAMAS  
ORTYGIUS } *Persian lords*  
CENEUS  
MENAPHON

TAMBURLAINE, *a Scythian shepherd*

TECHELLES } *his followers*  
USUMCASANE

BAJAZETH, *Emperor of the Turks*

KING OF FEZ

KING OF MOROCCO

KING OF ARGIER

KING OF ARABIA

SOLDAN OF EGYPT

GOVERNOR OF DAMASCUS

AGYDAS } *Median lords*  
MAGNETES

CAPOLIN, *an Egyptian*

PHILEMUS, BASSEOS, *Lords, Citizens, Moors, Soldiers and Attendants*

ZENOCRATE, *daughter to the Soldan of Egypt*

ANIPPE, *her maid*

ZABINA, *wife to Bajazeth*

EBEA, *her maid*

*Virgins of Damascus*

# THE FIRST PART OF
# TAMBURLAINE THE GREAT

## THE PROLOGUE

From jigging veins of rhyming mother-wits,
And such conceits as clownage keeps in pay,
We'll lead you to the stately tent of war,
Where you shall hear the Scythian Tamburlaine
Threatening the world with high astounding terms,
And scourging kingdoms with his conquering sword.
View but his picture in this tragic glass,
And then applaud his fortunes as you please.

## ACT ONE

### SCENE I

*Enter* MYCETES, COSROE, MEANDER, THERIDAMAS,
ORTYGIUS, CENEUS, MENAPHON, *with others*

MYCETES    Brother Cosroe, I find myself agriev'd;
Yet insufficient to express the same,
For it requires a great and thundering speech:
Good brother, tell the cause unto my lords;
I know you have a better wit than I.

COSROE    Unhappy Persia – that in former age
Hast been the seat of mighty conquerors,
That, in their prowess and their policies,
Have triumph'd over Afric, and the bounds
Of Europe where the sun dares scarce appear     10
For freezing meteors and congealed cold –
Now to be rul'd and govern'd by a man
At whose birthday Cynthia with Saturn join'd,
And Jove, the Sun, and Mercury denied
To shed their influence in his fickle brain!

Now Turks and Tartars shake their swords at thee,
Meaning to mangle all thy provinces.

MYCETES   Brother, I see your meaning well enough,
And through your planets I perceive you think
I am not wise enough to be a king:                              20
But I refer me to my noblemen,
That know my wit, and can be witnesses.
I might command you to be slain for this –
Meander, might I not?

MEANDER   Not for so small a fault, my sovereign lord.

MYCETES   I mean it not, but yet I know I might –
Yet live; yea, live; Mycetes wills it so.
Meander, thou, my faithful counsellor,
Declare the cause of my conceived grief,
Which is, God knows, about that Tamburlaine,                    30
That, like a fox in midst of harvest-time,
Doth prey upon my flocks of passengers;
And, as I hear, doth mean to pull my plumes:
Therefore 'tis good and meet for to be wise.

MEANDER   Oft have I heard your majesty complain
Of Tamburlaine, that sturdy Scythian thief,
That robs your merchants of Persepolis
Trading by land unto the Western Isles,
And in your confines with his lawless train
Daily commits incivil outrages,                                40
Hoping (misled by dreaming prophecies)
To reign in Asia, and with barbarous arms
To make himself the monarch of the East:
But, ere he march in Asia, or display
His vagrant ensign in the Persian fields,
Your grace hath taken order by Theridamas,
Charg'd with a thousand horse, to apprehend
And bring him captive to your highness' throne.

MYCETES   Full true thou speak'st, and like thyself, my lord,
Whom I may term a Damon for thy love:                           50
Therefore 'tis best, if so it like you all,
To send my thousand horse incontinent
To apprehend that paltry Scythian.
How like you this, my honourable lords?

       Is it not a kingly resolution?

COSROE     It cannot choose, because it comes from you.

MYCETES    Then hear thy charge, valiant Theridamas,
       The chiefest captain of Mycetes' host,
       The hope of Persia, and the very legs
       Whereon our state doth lean as on a staff,     60
       That holds us up and foils our neighbour foes:
       Thou shalt be leader of this thousand horse,
       Whose foaming gall with rage and high disdain
       Have sworn the death of wicked Tamburlaine.
       Go frowning forth; but come thou smiling home,
       As did Sir Paris with the Grecian dame:
       Return with speed; time passeth swift away;
       Our life is frail, and we may die today.

THERID.     Before the moon renew her borrow'd light,
       Doubt not, my lord and gracious sovereign,     70
       But Tamburlaine and that Tartarian rout
       Shall either perish by our warlike hands,
       Or plead for mercy at your highness' feet.

MYCETES    Go, stout Theridamas; thy words are swords,
       And with thy looks thou conquerest all thy foes.
       I long to see thee back return from hence,
       That I may view these milk-white steeds of mine
       All loaden with the heads of killed men,
       And, from their knees even to their hoofs below,
       Besmear'd with blood that makes a dainty show.     80

THERID.     Then now, my lord, I humbly take my leave.

MYCETES    Theridamas, farewell ten thousand times.

                               *[exit Theridamas*
       Ah, Menaphon, why stay'st thou thus behind,
       When other men press forward for renown?
       Go, Menaphon, go into Scythia,
       And foot by foot follow Theridamas.

COSROE     Nay, pray you, let him stay; a greater [task]
       Fits Menaphon than warring with a thief:
       Create him pro-rex of all Africa,
       That he may win the Babylonians' hearts,     90
       Which will revolt from Persian government,
       Unless they have a wiser king than you.

| | |
|---|---|
| MYCETES | Unless they have a wiser king than you! |
| | These are his words; Meander, set them down. |
| COSROE | And add this to them – that all Asia |
| | Lament to see the folly of their king. |
| MYCETES | Well, here I swear by this my royal seat – |
| COSROE | You may do well to kiss it, then. |
| MYCETES | Emboss'd with silk as best beseems my state, |
| | To be reveng'd for these contemptuous words!     100 |
| | O where is duty and allegiance now? |
| | Fled to the Caspian or the Ocean main? |
| | What shall I call thee? Brother? No, a foe; |
| | Monster of nature, shame unto thy stock, |
| | That dar'st presume thy sovereign for to mock! |
| | Meander come: I am abus'd, Meander. |

*[exeunt all except Cosroe and Menaphon*

| | |
|---|---|
| MENAPH. | How now my lord! What, mated and amaz'd |
| | To hear the king thus threaten like himself! |
| COSROE | Ah, Menaphon, I pass not for his threats! |
| | The plot is laid by Persian noblemen     110 |
| | And captains of the Median garrisons |
| | To crown me emperor of Asia: |
| | But this it is that doth excruciate |
| | The very substance of my vexed soul, |
| | To see our neighbours, that were wont to quake |
| | And tremble at the Persian monarch's name, |
| | Now sit and laugh our regiment to scorn; |
| | And that which might resolve me into tears, |
| | Men from the farthest equinoctial line |
| | Have swarm'd in troops into the Eastern India,     120 |
| | Lading their ships with gold and precious stones, |
| | And made their spoils from all our provinces. |
| MENAPH. | This should entreat your highness to rejoice, |
| | Since Fortune gives you opportunity |
| | To gain the title of a conqueror |
| | By curing of this maimed empery. |
| | Afric and Europe bordering on your land, |
| | And continent to your dominions, |
| | How easily may you, with a mighty host, |
| | Pass into Graecia, as did Cyrus once,     130 |

And cause them to withdraw their forces home,
Lest you subdue the pride of Christendom!

*[trumpet within*

COSROE     But, Menaphon, what means this trumpet's sound?
MENAPH.     Behold, my lord, Ortygius and the rest
         Bringing the crown to make you emperor!

*Re-enter* ORTYGIUS *and* CENEUS, *with others, bearing a crown*

ORTYGIUS    Magnificent and mighty prince Cosroe,
         We, in the name of other Persian states
         And commons of this mighty monarchy,
         Present thee with th' imperial diadem.
CENEUS     The warlike soldiers and the gentlemen,        140
         That heretofore have fill'd Persepolis
         With Afric captains taken in the field,
         Whose ransom made them march in coats of gold,
         With costly jewels hanging at their ears,
         And shining stones upon their lofty crests,
         Now living idle in the walled towns,
         Wanting both pay and martial discipline,
         Begin in troops to threaten civil war
         And openly exclaim against their kings:
         Therefore, to stay all sudden mutinies,        150
         We will invest your highness emperor;
         Whereat the soldiers will conceive more joy
         Than did the Macedonians at the spoil
         Of great Darius and his wealthy host.
COSROE     Well, since I see the state of Persia droop
         And languish in my brother's government,
         I willingly receive th' imperial crown,
         And vow to wear it for my country's good,
         In spite of them shall malice my estate.
ORTYGIUS    And, in assurance of desir'd success,        160
         We here do crown thee monarch of the East,
         Emperor of Asia and Persia;
         Great lord of Media and Armenia;
         Duke of Africa and Albania,
         Mesopotamia and of Parthia,
         East India and the late-discover'd isles;

Chief lord of all the wide vast Euxine Sea,
And of the ever-raging Caspian Lake.

ALL      Long live Cosroe, mighty emperor!

COSROE   And Jove may never let me longer live        170
Than I may seek to gratify your love,
And cause the soldiers that thus honour me
To triumph over many provinces!
By whose desires of discipline in arms
I doubt not shortly but to reign sole king.
And with the army of Theridamas
(Whither we presently will fly, my lords)
To rest secure against my brother's force.

ORTYGIUS We knew, my lord, before we brought the crown,
Intending your investion so near        180
The residence of your despised brother,
The lords would not be too exasperate
To injury or suppress your worthy title:
Or, if they would, there are in readiness
Ten thousand horse to carry you from hence,
In spite of all suspected enemies.

COSROE   I know it well, my lord, and thank you all.

ORTYGIUS Sound up the trumpets, then.        [*trumpets sounded*

ALL      God save the king!

[*exeunt*

## SCENE 2

*Enter* TAMBURLAINE *leading,* ZENOCRATE, TECHELLES,
USUMCASANE. AGYDAS, MAGNETES, *Lords
and Soldiers loaden with treasure*

TAMBUR.  Come, lady, let not this appal your thoughts;
The jewels and the treasure we have ta'en
Shall be reserv'd, and you in better state
Than if you were arriv'd in Syria,
Even in the circle of your father's arms,
The mighty Soldan of Aegyptia.

ZENOCR.  Ah, shepherd, pity my distressed plight!
(If, as thou seem'st, thou art so mean a man)

And seek not to enrich thy followers
By lawless rapine from a silly maid,     10
Who, travelling with these Median lords
To Memphis, from my uncle's country of Media,
Where, all my youth, I have been governed,
Have pass'd the army of the mighty Turk,
Bearing his privy-signet and his hand
To safe conduct as thorough Africa.

MAGNETES And, since we have arrived in Scythia,
Besides rich presents from the puissant Cham,
We have his highness' letters to command
Aid and assistance, if we stand in need.     20

TAMBUR. But now you see these letters and commands
Are countermanded by a greater man;
And through my provinces you must expect
Letters of conduct from my mightiness,
If you intend to keep your treasure safe.
But, since I love to live at liberty,
As easily may you get the Soldan's crown
As any prizes out of my precinct;
For they are friends that help to wean my state
Till men and kingdoms help to strengthen it,     30
And must maintain my life exempt from servitude –
But. tell me, madam, is your grace betroth'd ?

ZENOCR. I am, my lord – for so you do import.

TAMBUR. I am a lord, for so my deeds shall prove;
And yet a shepherd by my parentage.
But, lady, this fair face and heavenly hue
Must grace his bed that conquers Asia,
And means to be a terror to the world,
Measuring the limits of his empery
By east and west as Phoebus doth his course –     40
Lie here, ye weeds, that I disdain to wear!
This complete armour and this curtle-axe
Are adjuncts more beseeming Tamburlaine –
And, madam, whatsoever you esteem
Of this success, and loss unvalued,
Both may invest you empress of the East;
And these that seem but silly country swains

May have the leading of so great an host
As with their weight shall make the mountains quake.
Even as when windy exhalations,　　　　　　　50
Fighting for passage, tilt within the earth.

TECHELLES　As princely lions, when they rouse themselves,
Stretching their paws, and threatening herds of beasts,
So in his armour looketh Tamburlaine.

TAMBUR.　Methinks I see kings kneeling at his feet,
And he with frowning brows and fiery looks
Spurning their crowns from off their captive heads.

USUMCAS.　And making thee and me, Techelles, kings,
That even to death will follow Tamburlaine.

TAMBUR.　Nobly resolv'd, sweet friends and followers!　　60
These lords perhaps do scorn our estimates,
And think we prattle with distemper'd spirits:
But, since they measure our deserts so mean,
That in conceit bear empires on our spears,
Affecting thoughts coequal with the clouds,
They shall be kept our forced followers
Till with their eyes they view us emperors.

ZENOCR.　The gods, defenders of the innocent,
Will never prosper your intended drifts,
That thus oppress poor friendless passengers.　　70
Therefore at least admit us liberty,
Even as thou hop'st to be eternised
By living Asia's mighty emperor.

AGYDAS　I hope our lady's treasure and our own
May serve for ransom to our liberties:
Return our mules and empty camels back,
That we may travel into Syria,
Where her betrothed lord, Alcidamus,
Expects the arrival of her highness' person.

MAGNETES　And wheresoever we repose ourselves,　　80
We will report but well of Tamburlaine.

TAMBUR.　Disdains Zenocrate to live with me?
Or you, my lord, to be my followers?
Think you I weigh this treasure more than you?
Not all the gold in India's wealthy arms
Shall buy the meanest soldier in my train.

Zenocrate, lovelier than the love of Jove,
Brighter than is the silver Rhodope,
Fairer than whitest snow on Scythian hills,
Thy person is more worth to Tamburlaine          90
Than the possession of the Persian crown,
Which gracious stars have promis'd at my birth.
A hundred Tartars shall attend on thee,
Mounted on steeds swifter than Pegasus;
Thy garments shall be made of Median silk,
Enchas'd with precious jewels of mine own,
More rich and valurous than Zenocrate's;
With milk-white harts upon an ivory sled
Thou shalt be drawn amidst the frozen pools,
And scale the icy mountains' lofty tops,          100
Which with thy beauty will be soon resolv'd:
My martial prizes, with five hundred men,
Won on the fifty-headed Volga's waves,
Shall we all offer to Zenocrate,
And then myself to fair Zenocrate.

TECHELLES What now! In love?

TAMBUR.   Techelles, women must be flattered:
But this is she with whom I am in love.

*Enter a Soldier*

SOLDIER   News, news!

TAMBUR.   How now! What's the matter?                110

SOLDIER   A thousand Persian horsemen are at hand,
Sent from the king to overcome us all.

TAMBUR.   How now, my lords of Egypt and Zenocrate!
Now must your jewels be restor'd again,
And I, that triumph'd so, be overcome?
How say you, lordlings? Is not this your hope?

AGYDAS    We hope yourself will willingly restore them.

TAMBUR.   Such hope, such fortune, have the thousand horse.
Soft ye, my lords, and sweet Zenocrate!
You must be forced from me ere you go –          120
A thousand horsemen! We five hundred foot!
An odds too great for us to stand against.
But are they rich? And is their armour good?

| | |
|---|---|
| SOLDIER | Their plumed helms are wrought with beaten gold, |
| | Their swords enamell'd, and about their necks |
| | Hang massy chains of gold down to the waist; |
| | In every part exceeding brave and rich. |
| TAMBUR. | Then shall we fight courageously with them? |
| | Or look you I should play the orator? |
| TECHELLES | No; cowards and faint-hearted runaways |
| | Look for orations when the foe is near: |
| | Our swords shall play the orators for us. |
| USUMCAS. | Come, let us meet them at the mountain-top. |
| | And with a sudden and an hot alarum |
| | Drive all their horses headlong down the hill. |
| TECHELLES | Come, let us march. |
| TAMBUR. | Stay, Techelles; ask a parle first. |

*The Soldiers enter*

Open the mails, yet guard the treasure sure:
Lay out our golden wedges to the view,
That their reflections may amaze the Persians;        140
And look we friendly on them when they come:
But, if they offer word or violence,
We'll fight, five hundred men-at-arms to one,
Before we part with our possession;
And 'gainst the general we will lift our swords,
And either lance his greedy thirsting throat,
Or take him prisoner, and his chain shall serve
For manacles till he be ransom'd home.

| | |
|---|---|
| TECHELLES | I hear them come: shall we encounter them? |
| TAMBUR. | Keep all your standings, and not stir a foot:        150 |
| | Myself will bide the danger of the brunt. |

*Enter* THERIDAMAS, *with others*

| | |
|---|---|
| THERID. | Where is this Scythian Tamburlaine? |
| TAMBUR. | Whom seek'st thou, Persian? I am Tamburlaine. |
| THERID. | Tamburlaine! |
| | A Scythian shepherd so embellished |
| | With nature's pride and richest furniture! |
| | His looks do menace heaven and dare the gods; |
| | His fiery eyes are fix'd upon the earth, |
| | As if he now devis'd some stratagem, |

130

Or meant to pierce Avernus' darksome vaults     160
To pull the triple-headed dog from hell.

TAMBUR.    Noble and mild this Persian seems to be,
If outward habit judge the inward man.

TECHELLES His deep affections make him passionate.

TAMBUR.    With what a majesty he rears his looks!
In thee, thou valiant man of Persia,
I see the folly of thy emperor.
Art thou but captain of a thousand horse,
That by characters graven in thy brows,
And by thy martial face and stout aspect,     170
Deserv'st to have the leading of an host?
Forsake thy king, and do but join with me,
And we will triumph over all the world:
I hold the Fates bound fast in iron chains,
And with my hand turn Fortune's wheel about;
And sooner shall the sun fall from his sphere
Than Tamburlaine be slain or overcome.
Draw forth thy sword, thou mighty man-at-arms,
Intending but to raze my charmed skin,
And Jove himself will stretch his hand from heaven
To ward the blow, and shield me safe from harm.
See, how he rains down heaps of gold in showers,
As if he meant to give my soldiers pay!
And, as a sure and grounded argument
That I shall be the monarch of the East,
He sends this Soldan's daughter rich and brave,
To be my queen and portly emperess.
If thou wilt stay with me, renowmed man,
And lead thy thousand horse with my conduct,
Besides thy share of this Egyptian prize,     190
Those thousand horse shall sweat with martial spoil
Of conquer'd kingdoms and of cities sack'd:
Both we will walk upon the lofty cliffs;
And Christian merchants, that with Russian stems
Plough up huge furrows in the Caspian Sea,
Shall vail to us as lords of all the lake;
Both we will reign as consuls of the earth,
And mighty kings shall be our senators.

Jove sometimes masked in a shepherd's weed;
And by those steps that he hath scal'd the heavens  200
May we become immortal like the gods.
Join with me now in this my mean estate
(I call it mean, because, being yet obscure,
The nations far-remov'd admire me not)
And when my name and honour shall be spread
As far as Boreas claps his brazen wings,
Or fair Boötes sends his cheerful light,
Then shalt thou be competitor with me,
And sit with Tamburlaine in all his majesty.

THERID.     Not Hermes, prolocutor to the gods,          210
Could use persuasions more pathetical.

TAMBUR.     Nor are Apollo's oracles more true
Than thou shalt find my vaunts substantial.

TECHELLES   We are his friends; and if the Persian king
Should offer present dukedoms to our state,
We think it loss to make exchange for that
We are assur'd of by our friend's success.

USUMCAS.    And kingdoms at the least we all expect,
Besides the honour in assured conquests,
Where kings shall crouch unto our
                              conquering swords,   220
And hosts of soldiers stand amaz'd at us,
When with their fearful tongues they shall confess,
These are the men that all the world admires.

THERID.     What strong enchantments tice my yielding soul
To these resolved, noble Scythians!
But shall I prove a traitor to my king?

TAMBUR.     No; but the trusty friend of Tamburlaine.

THERID.     Won with thy words, and conquer'd with thy looks,
I yield myself, my men, and horse to thee,
To be partaker of thy good or ill,                       230
As long as life maintains Theridamas.

TAMBUR.     Theridamas, my friend, take here my hand,
Which is as much as if I swore by heaven,
And call'd the gods to witness of my vow.
Thus shalt my heart be still combin'd with thine
Until our bodies turn to elements,

And both our souls aspire celestial thrones –
Techelles and Casane, welcome him.

TECHELLES Welcome, renowmed Persian, to us all!

USUMCAS. Long may Theridamas remain with us!          240

TAMBUR.  These are my friends, in whom I more rejoice
Than doth the king of Persia in his crown;
And, by the love of Pylades and Orestes,
Whose statues we adore in Scythia,
Thyself and them shall never part from me
Before I crown you kings in Asia.
Make much of them, gentle Theridamas,
And they will never leave thee till the death.

THERID.  Nor thee nor them, thrice-noble Tamburlaine,
Shall want my heart to be with gladness pierc'd,          250
To do you honour and security.

TAMBUR.  A thousand thanks, worthy Theridamas –
And now, fair madam, and my noble lords,
If you will willingly remain with me,
You shall have honours as your merits be;
Or else you shall be forc'd with slavery.

AGYDAS   We yield unto thee, happy Tamburlaine.

TAMBUR.  For you, then, madam, I am out of doubt.

ZENOCR.  I must be pleas'd perforce – wretched Zenocrate!

                                        [exeunt

## ACT TWO

### SCENE I

*Enter* COSROE, MENAPHON, ORTYGIUS, *and* CENEUS, *with Soldiers*

COSROE    Thus far are we towards Theridamas,
And valiant Tamburlaine, the man of fame,
The man that in the forehead of his fortune
Bears figures of renown and miracle.
But tell me, that hast seen him, Menaphon,
What stature wields he, and what personage?

MENAPH.    Of stature tall, and straightly fashioned
Like his desire, lift upwards and divine;
So large of limbs, his joints so strongly knit,
Such breadth of shoulders as might mainly bear   10
Old Atlas' burden; 'twixt his manly pitch,
A pearl more worth than all the world is plac'd,
Wherein by curious sovereignty of art
Are fix'd his piercing instruments of sight,
Whose fiery circles bear encompassed
A heaven of heavenly bodies in their spheres,
That guides his steps and actions to the throne
Where honour sits invested royally;
Pale of complexion, wrought in him with passion,
Thirsting with sovereignty and love of arms;   20
His lofty brows in folds do figure death,
And in their smoothness amity and life;
About them hangs a knot of amber hair
Wrapped in curls, as fierce Achilles' was,
On which the breath of heaven delights to play,
Making it dance with wanton majesty;
His arms and fingers long and sinewy,
Betokening valour and excess of strength –
In every part proportion'd like the man
Should make the world subdu'd to Tamburlaine.   30

COSROE    Well hast thou pourtray'd in thy terms of life
The face and personage of a wondrous man:

Nature doth strive with Fortune and his stars
To make him famous in accomplish'd worth;
And well his merits shew him to be made
His fortune's master and the king of men,
That could persuade, at such a sudden pinch,
With reasons of his valour and his life,
A thousand sworn and overmatching foes.
Then, when our powers in points of swords
         are join'd,  40
And clos'd in compass of the killing bullet,
Though strait the passage and the port be made
That leads to palace of my brother's life,
Proud is his fortune if we pierce it not;
And, when the princely Persian diadem
Shall overweigh his weary witless head,
And fall, like mellow'd fruit, with shakes of death,
In fair Persia noble Tamburlaine
Shall be my regent, and remain as king.

ORTYGIUS In happy hour we have set the crown  50
Upon your kingly head, that seeks our honour
In joining with the man ordain'd by heaven
To further every action to the best.

CENEUS He that with shepherds and a little spoil
Durst, in disdain of wrong and tyranny,
Defend his freedom 'gainst a monarchy,
What will he do supported by a king,
Leading a troop of gentlemen and lords,
And stuff'd with treasure for his highest thoughts!

COSROE And such shall wait on worthy Tamburlaine.  60
Our army will be forty thousand strong,
When Tamburlaine and brave Theridamas
Have met us by the river Araris;
And all conjoin'd to meet the witless king,
That now is marching near to Parthia,
And with unwilling soldiers faintly arm'd,
To seek revenge on me and Tamburlaine;
To whom, sweet Menaphon, direct me straight.

MENAPH. I will, my lord.

              [exeunt

## SCENE 2

*Enter* MYCETES, MEANDER, *with other Lords; and Soldiers*

MYCETES     Come, my Meander, let us to this gear.
            I tell you true, my heart is swoln with wrath
            On this same thievish villain Tamburlaine,
            And of that false Cosroe my traitorous brother.
            Would it not grieve a king to be so abus'd,
            And have a thousand horsemen ta'en away?
            And, which is worse, to have his diadem
            Sought for by such scald knaves as love him not?
            I think it would: well, then, by heavens I swear,
            Aurora shall not peep out of her doors,              10
            But I will have Cosroe by the head,
            And kill proud Tamburlaine with point of sword.
            Tell you the rest, Meander: I have said.
MEANDER     Then having pass'd Armenian deserts now,
            And pitch'd our tents under the Georgian hills,
            Whose tops are cover'd with Tartarian thieves,
            That lie in ambush, waiting for a prey,
            What should we do but bid them battle straight,
            And rid the world of those detested troops?
            Lest, if we let them linger here a while,             20
            They gather strength by power of fresh supplies.
            This country swarms with vile outragious men
            That live by rapine and by lawless spoil,
            Fit soldiers for the wicked Tamburlaine;
            And he that could with gifts and promises
            Inveigle him that led a thousand horse,
            And make him false his faith unto his king,
            Will quickly win such as be like himself.
            Therefore cheer up your minds; prepare to fight:
            He that can take or slaughter Tamburlaine,           30
            Shall rule the province of Albania;
            Who brings that traitor's head, Theridamas,
            Shall have a government in Media,
            Beside the spoil of him and all his train:

But, if Cosroe (as our spials say,
And as we know) remains with Tamburlaine,
His highness' pleasure is that he should live,
And be reclaim'd with princely lenity.

*Enter a Spy*

SPY     An hundred horsemen of my company,
Scouting abroad upon these champion plains,     40
Have view d the army of the Scythians;
Which make report it far exceeds the king's.

MEANDER     Suppose they be in number infinite,
Yet being void of martial discipline,
All running headlong, greedy after spoils,
And more regarding gain than victory,
Like to the cruel brothers of the earth,
Sprung of the teeth of dragons venomous,
Their careless swords shall lance their fellows' throats
And make us triumph in their overthrow.     50

MYCETES     Was there such brethren, sweet Meander, say,
That sprung of teeth of dragons venomous?

MEANDER     So poets say, my lord.

MYCETES     And 'tis a pretty toy to be a poet.
Well, well, Meander, thou art deeply read;
And having thee, I have a jewel sure.
Go on, my lord, and give your charge, I say;
Thy wit will make us conquerors today.

MEANDER     Then, noble soldiers, to entrap these thieves
That live confounded in disorder'd troops,     60
If wealth or riches may prevail with them,
We have our camels laden all with gold,
Which you that be but common soldiers
Shall fling in every corner of the field;
And, while the base-born Tartars take it up,
You, fighting more for honour than for gold,
Shall massacre those greedy-minded slaves;
And, when their scatter'd army is subdu'd,
And you march on their slaughter'd carcasses
Share equally the gold that bought their lives,  .   70
And live like gentlemen in Persia.
Strike up the drum, and march courageously:

Fortune herself doth sit upon our crests.

MYCETES  He tells you true, my masters; so he does —
Drums, why sound ye not when Meander speaks?

*[exeunt, drums sounding*


## SCENE 3

*Enter* COSROE, TAMBURLAINE, THERIDAMAS, TECHELLES,
USUMCASANE, *and* ORTYGIUS, *with others*

COSROE  Now, worthy Tamburlaine, have I repos'd
In thy approved fortunes all my hope.
What think'st thou, man, shall come of our attempts?
For, even as from assured oracle,
I take thy doom for satisfaction.

TAMBUR.  And so mistake you not a whit, my lord;
For fates and oracles [of] heaven have sworn
To royalise the deeds of Tamburlaine,
And make them blest that share in his attempts.
And doubt you not but, if you favour me,                    10
And let my fortunes and my valour sway
To some direction in your martial deeds,
The world will strive with hosts of men-at-arms
To swarm unto the ensign I support.
The hosts of Xerxes, which by fame is said
To drink the mighty Parthian Araris,
Was but a handful to that we will have:
Our quivering lances, shaking in the air,
And bullets, like Jove's dreadful thunderbolts,
Enroll'd in flames and fiery smouldering mists,            20
Shall threat the gods more than Cyclopian wars;
And with our sun-bright armour, as we march,
We'll chase the stars from heaven and dim their eyes
That stand and muse at our admired arms.

THERID.  You see, my lord, what working words he hath;
But, when you see his actions top his speech,
Your speech will stay, or so extol his worth
As I shall be commended and excus'd
For turning my poor charge to his direction:

|  | And these his two renowmed friends, my lord, | 30 |
|  | Would make one thirst and strive to be retain'd |  |
|  | In such a great degree of amity. |  |

TECHELLES  With duty and with amity we yield
Our utmost service to the fair Cosroe.

COSROE  Which I esteem as portion of my crown.
Usumcasane and Techelles both,
When she that rules in Rhamnus' golden gates,
And makes a passage for all prosperous arms,
Shall make me solely emperor of Asia,
Then shall your meeds and valours be advanc'd          40
To rooms of honour and nobility.

TAMBUR.  Then haste, Cosroe, to be king alone,
That I with these my friends and all my men
May triumph in our long-expected fate.
The king, your brother, is now hard at hand:
Meet with the fool, and rid your royal shoulders
Of such a burden as outweighs the sands
And all the craggy rocks of Caspia.

*Enter a Messenger*

MESSENG.  My lord,
We have discovered the enemy          50
Ready to charge you with a mighty army.

COSROE  Come, Tamburlaine; now whet thy winged sword,
And lift thy lofty arm into the clouds,
That it may reach the king of Persia's crown,
And set it safe on my victorious head.

TAMBUR.  See where it is, the keenest curtle-axe
That e'er made passage thorough Persian arms!
These are the wings shall make it fly as swift
As doth the lightning or the breath of heaven,
And kill as sure as it swiftly flies.          60

COSROE  Thy words assure me of kind success:
Go, valiant soldier, go before, and charge
The fainting army of that foolish king.

TAMBUR.  Usumcasane and Techelles, come:
We are enow to scare the enemy,
And more than needs to make an emperor.

*[exeunt to the battle*

## SCENE 4

*Enter* MYCETES, *with his crown in his hand*

MYCETES    Accurs'd be he that first invented war!
They knew not, ah, they knew not, simple men,
How those were hit by pelting cannon-shot
Stand staggering like a quivering aspen-leaf
Fearing the force of Boreas' boisterous blasts!
In what a lamentable case were I,
If nature had not given me wisdom's lore!
For kings are clouts that every man shoots at,
Our crown the pin that thousands seek to cleave:
Therefore in policy I think it good          10
To hide it close: a goodly stratagem,
And far from any man that is a fool:
So shall not I be known; or if I be,
They cannot take away my crown from me.
Here will I hide it in this simple hole.

*Enter* TAMBURLAINE

TAMBUR.    What, fearful coward, straggling from the camp,
When kings themselves are present in the field!

MYCETES    Thou liest.

TAMBUR.    Base villain, darest thou give me the lie?

MYCETES    Away! I am the king; go; touch me not.      20
Thou break'st the law of arms, unless thou kneel,
And cry me 'mercy, noble king!'

TAMBUR.    Are you the witty king of Persia?

MYCETES    Ay, marry, am I: have you any suit to me?

TAMBUR.    I would entreat you to speak but three wise words.

MYCETES    So I can when I see my time.

TAMBUR.    Is this your crown?

MYCETES    Ay: didst thou ever see a fairer?

TAMBUR.    You will not sell it, will you?

MYCETES    Such another word, and I will have thee executed.
Come, give it me.

TAMBUR.    No; I took it prisoner.

MYCETES    You lie; I gave it you.

TAMBUR.   Then 'tis mine.

MYCETES   No; I mean I let you keep it.

TAMBUR.   Well, I mean you shall have it again.
          Here, take it for a while: I lend it thee,
          Till I may see thee hemm'd with armed men;
          Then shalt thou see me pull it from thy head:
          Thou art no match for mighty Tamburlaine.          [*exit*

MYCETES   O gods, is this Tamburlaine the thief?
          I marvel much he stole it not away.

                                        [*trumpets within sound
                                        to the battle: he runs out*


                          SCENE 5

*Enter* COSROE, TAMBURLAINE, MENAPHON, MEANDER, ORTYGIUS,
    THERIDAMAS, TECHELLES, USUMCASANE, *with others*

TAMBUR.   Hold thee, Cosroe; wear two imperial crowns;
          Think thee invested now as royally,
          Even by the mighty hand of Tamburlaine,
          As if as many kings as could encompass thee
          With greatest pomp had crown'd thee emperor.

COSROE    So do I, thrice-renowmed man-at-arms;
          And none shall keep the crown but Tamburlaine:
          Thee do I make my regent of Persia,
          And general lieutenant of my armies —
          Meander, you, that were our brother's guide,          10
          And chiefest counsellor in all his acts,
          Since he is yielded to the stroke of war,
          On your submission we with thanks excuse
          And give you equal place in our affairs.

MEANDER   Most happy emperor, in humblest terms
          I vow my service to your majesty,
          With utmost virtue of my faith and duty.

COSROE    Thanks, good Meander — Then, Cosroe, reign,
          And govern Persia in her former pomp.
          Now send embassage to thy neighbour kings,          20
          And let them know the Persian king is chang'd,
          From one that knew not what a king should do,

To one that can command what 'longs thereto.
And now we will to fair Persepolis
With twenty thousand expert soldiers.
The lords and captains of my brother's camp
With little slaughter take Meander's course,
And gladly yield them to my gracious rule –
Ortygius and Menaphon, my trusty friends,
Now will I gratify your former good,                        30
And grace your calling with a greater sway.

ORTYGIUS  And as we ever aim'd at your behoof,
And sought your state all honour it deserv'd,
So will we with our powers and our lives
Endeavour to preserve and prosper it.

COSROE    I will not thank thee, sweet Ortygius;
Better replies shall prove my purposes –
And now, Lord Tamburlaine, my brother's camp
I leave to thee and to Theridamas,
To follow me to fair Persepolis;                            40
Then will we march to all those Indian mines
My witless brother to the Christians lost,
And ransom them with fame and usury:
And, till thou overtake me, Tamburlaine,
(Staying to order all the scatter'd troops)
Farewell, lord regent and his happy friends.
I long to sit upon my brother's throne.

MEANDER   Your majesty shall shortly have your wish,
And ride in triumph through Persepolis.

*[exeunt all except Tamburlaine,*
*Theridamas, Techelles and Usumcasane*

TAMBUR.   And ride in triumph through Persepolis!             50
Is it not brave to be a king, Techelles!
Usumcasane and Theridamas,
Is it not passing brave to be a king,
And ride in triumph through Persepolis?

TECHELLES O, my lord, it is sweet and full of pomp!

USUMCAS.  To be a king, is half to be a god.

THERID.   A god is not so glorious as a king:
I think the pleasure they enjoy in heaven,
Cannot compare with kingly joys in earth –

To wear a crown enchas'd with pearl and gold,    60
Whose virtues carry with it life and death;
To ask and have, command and be obey'd;
When looks breed love, with looks to gain the prize,
Such power attractive shines in princes' eyes.

TAMBUR. Why, say, Theridamas, wilt thou be a king?

THERID. Nay, though I praise it, I can live without it.

TAMBUR. What say my other friends? Will you be kings?

TECHELLES Aye, if I could, with all my heart, my lord.

TAMBUR. Why, that's well said, Techelles: so would I —
And so would you, my masters, would you not?    70

USUMCAS. What, then, my lord?

TAMBUR. Why, then, Casane, shall we wish for aught
The world affords in greatest novelty,
And rest attemptless, faint, and destitute?
Methinks we should not. I am strongly mov'd,
That if I should desire the Persian crown,
I could attain it with a wondrous ease:
And would not all our soldiers soon consent,
If we should aim at such a dignity?

THERID. I know they would with our persuasions.    80

TAMBUR. Why, then, Theridamas, I'll first assay
To get the Persian kingdom to myself;
Then thou for Parthia; they for Scythia and Media;
And, if I prosper, all shall be as sure
As if the Turk, the Pope, Afric, and Greece,
Came creeping to us with their crowns a-piece.

TECHELLES Then shall we send to this triumphing king,
And bid him battle for his novel crown?

USUMCAS. Nay quickly, then, before his room be hot.

TAMBUR. 'Twill prove a pretty jest, in faith, my friends.    90

THERID. A jest to charge on twenty thousand men!
I judge the purchase more important far.

TAMBUR. Judge by thyself, Theridamas, not me;
For presently Techelles here shall haste
To bid him battle ere he pass too far,
And lose more labour than the gain will quite:
Then shalt thou see this Scythian Tamburlaine
Make but a jest to win the Persian crown —

Techelles, take a thousand horse with thee,
And bid him turn him back to war with us,          100
That only made him king to make us sport:
We will not steal upon him cowardly,
But give him warning and more warriors:
Haste thee, Techelles; we will follow thee.

                                        [exit Techelles

What saith Theridamas?

THERID.                    Go on, for me.

                                        [exeunt


## SCENE 6

*Enter* COSROE, MEANDER, ORTYGIUS
*and* MENAPHON, *with Soldiers*

COSROE   What means this devilish shepherd, to aspire
With such a giantly presumption,
To cast up hills against the face of heaven,
And dare the force of angry Jupiter?
But, as he thrust them underneath the hills,
And press'd out fire from their burning jaws,
So will I send this monstrous slave to hell,
Where flames shall ever feed upon his soul.

MEANDER  Some powers divine, or else infernal, mix'd
Their angry seeds at his conception;          10
For he was never sprung of human race,
Since with the spirit of his fearful pride
He dares so doubtlessly resolve of rule,
And by profession be ambitious.

ORTYGIUS What god, or fiend, or spirit of the earth,
Or monster turned to a manly shape,
Or of what mould or mettle he be made,
What star or fate soever govern him,
Let us put on our meet encountering minds;
And, in detesting such a devilish thief,          20
In love of honour and defence of right,
Be arm'd against the hate of such a foe,
Whether from earth, or hell, or heaven he grow.

COSROE   Nobly resolv'd, my good Ortygius;

And since we all have suck'd one wholesome air,
And with the same proportion of elements
Resolve, I hope we are resembled,
Vowing our loves to equal death and life.
Let's cheer our soldiers to encounter him,
That grievous image of ingratitude,                    30
That fiery thirster after sovereignty,
And burn him in the fury of that flame
That none can quench but blood and empery.
Resolve, my lords and loving soldiers, now
To save your king and country from decay.
Then strike up, drum; and all the stars that make
The loathsome circle of my dated life,
Direct my weapon to his barbarous heart,
That thus opposeth him against the gods,
And scorns the powers that govern Persia!               40

*[exeunt, drums sounding*

## SCENE 7

*Alarms of battle within. Then enter* COSROE *wounded,*
TAMBURLAINE, THERIDAMAS, TECHELLES,
USUMCASANE, *with others*

COSROE    Barbarous and bloody Tamburlaine,
Thus to deprive me of my crown and life!
Treacherous and false Theridamas,
Even at the morning of my happy state,
Scarce being seated in my royal throne,
To work my downfall and untimely end!
An uncouth pain torments my grieved soul,
And death arrests the organ of my voice,
Who, entering at the breach thy sword hath made,
Sacks every vein and artier of my heart –            10
Bloody and insatiate Tamburlaine!

TAMBUR.    The thirst of reign and sweetness of a crown,
That caus'd the eldest son of heavenly Ops
To thrust his doting father from his chair,
And place himself in the empyreal heaven,

Mov'd me to manage arms against thy state.
What better precedent than mighty Jove?
Nature, that fram'd us of four elements
Warring within our breasts for regiment,
Doth teach us all to have aspiring minds:          20
Our souls, whose faculties can comprehend
The wondrous architecture of the world,
And measure every wandering planet's course,
Still climbing after knowledge infinite,
And always moving as the restless spheres,
Will us to wear ourselves, and never rest,
Until we reach the ripest fruit of all,
That perfect bliss and sole felicity,
The sweet fruition of an earthly crown

THERID. And that made me to join with Tamburlaine,          30
For he is gross and like the massy earth
That moves not upwards, nor by princely deeds
Doth mean to soar above the highest sort.

TECHELLES And that made us, the friends of Tamburlaine,
To lift our swords against the Persian king.

USUMCAS. For as, when Jove did thrust old Saturn down,
Neptune and Dis gain'd each of them a crown,
So do we hope to reign in Asia,
If Tamburlaine be plac'd in Persia.

COSROE The strangest men that ever nature made!          40
I know not how to take their tyrannies.
My bloodless body waxeth chill and cold.
And with my blood my life slides through my wound;
My soul begins to take her flight to hell,
And summons all my senses to depart:
The heat and moisture, which did feed each other,
For want of nourishment to feed them both,
Are dry and cold; and now doth ghastly Death
With greedy talons gripe my bleeding heart,
And like a harpy tires on my life –          50
Theridamas and Tamburlaine, I die:
And fearful vengeance light upon you both!

*[Cosroe dies. Tamburlaine takes the*
*crown, and puts it on his own head*

TAMBUR.    Not all the curses which the Furies breathe
            Shall make me leave so rich a prize as this.
            Theridamas, Techelles, and the rest,
            Who think you now is king of Persia?
ALL        Tamburlaine! Tamburlaine!
TAMBUR.    Though Mars himself, the angry god of arms,
            And all the earthly potentates conspire
            To dispossess me of this diadem,                  60
            Yet will I wear it in despite of them,
            As great commander of this eastern world,
            If you but say that Tamburlaine shall reign.
ALL        Long live Tamburlaine, and reign in Asia!
TAMBUR.    So; now it is more surer on my head
            Than if the gods had held a parliament,
            And all pronounc'd me king of Persia.

                                           *[exeunt*

# ACT THREE

## SCENE I

*Enter* BAJAZETH, *the* KINGS *of* FEZ, MOROCCO
*and* ARGIER, *with others, in great pomp*

BAJAZETH  Great kings of Barbary, and my portly bassoes,
We hear the Tartars and the eastern thieves,
Under the conduct of one Tamburlaine,
Presume a bickering with your emperor,
And think to rouse us from our dreadful siege
Of the famous Grecian Constantinople.
You know our army is invincible;
As many circumcised Turks we have,
And warlike bands of Christians renied,
As hath the ocean or the Terrene sea          10
Small drops of water when the moon begins
To join in one her semicircled horns:
Yet would we not be brav'd with foreign power,
Nor raise our siege before the Grecians yield,
Or breathless lie before the city-walls
FEZ  Renowmed emperor and mighty general,
What, if you sent the bassoes of your guard
To charge him to remain in Asia,
Or else to threaten death and deadly arms
As from the mouth of mighty Bajazeth?          20
BAJAZETH  Hie thee, my basso, fast to Persia;
Tell him thy lord, the Turkish emperor,
Dread lord of Afric, Europe, and Asia,
Great king and conqueror of Graecia,
The ocean, Terrene, and the Coal-black sea,
The high and highest monarch of the world,
Wills and commands (for say not I entreat)
Not once to set his foot in Africa,
Or spread his colours in Graecia,
Lest he incur the fury of my wrath:          30
Tell him I am content to take a truce,

Because I hear he bears a valiant mind:
But if, presuming on his silly power,
He be so mad to manage arms with me,
Then stay thou with him – say, I bid thee so;
And if, before the sun have measur'd heaven
With triple circuit, thou regreet us not,
We mean to take his morning's next arise
For messenger he will not be reclaim'd,
And mean to fetch thee in despite of him.                    40

BAJAZETH  Most great and puissant monarch of the earth,
Your basso will accomplish your behest,
And shew your pleasure to the Persian,
As fits the legate of the stately Turk.                    [exit

ARGIER  They say he is the king of Persia;
But, if he dare attempt to stir your siege,
'Twere requisite he should be ten times more,
For all flesh quakes at your magnificence.

BAJAZETH  True, Argier; and trembles at my looks.

MOROCCO  The spring is hinder'd by your smothering host;        50
For neither rain can fall upon the earth,
Nor sun reflex his virtuous beams thereon,
The ground is mantled with such multitudes.

BAJAZETH  All this is true as holy Mahomet;
And all the trees are blasted with our breaths.

FEZ  What thinks your greatness best to be achiev'd
In pursuit of the city's overthrow?

BAJAZETH  I will the captive pioners of Argier
Cut off the water that by leaden pipes
Runs to the city from the mountain Carnon;                    60
Two thousand horse shall forage up and down,
That no relief or succour come by land;
And all the sea my galleys countermand:
Then shall our footmen lie within the trench,
And with their cannons, mouth'd like Orcus' gulf,
Batter the walls, and we will enter in;
And thus the Grecians shall be conquered.
                                                      [exeunt

## SCENE 2

*Enter* ZENOCRATE, AGYDAS, ANIPPE, *with others*

AGYDAS       Madam Zenocrate, may I presume
             To know the cause of these unquiet fits
             That work such trouble to your wonted rest?
             'Tis more than pity such a heavenly face
             Should by heart's sorrow wax so wan and pale,
             When your offensive rape by Tamburlaine
             (Which of your whole displeasures should be most)
             Hath seem'd to be digested long ago.

ZENOCR.      Although it be digested long ago,
             As his exceeding favours have deserv'd,                    10
             And might content the Queen of Heaven, as well
             As it hath chang'd my first-conceiv'd disdain;
             Yet since a farther passion feeds my thoughts
             With ceaseless and disconsolate conceits,
             Which dye my looks so lifeless as they are,
             And might, if my extremes had full events,
             Make me the ghastly counterfeit of death.

AGYDAS       Eternal heaven sooner be dissolv'd,
             And all that pierceth Phoebus' silver eye,
             Before such hap fall to Zenocrate!                         20

ZENOCR.      Ah, life and soul, still hover in his breast,
             And leave my body senseless as the earth,
             Or else unite us to his life and soul,
             That I may live and die with Tamburlaine!

*Enter, behind,* TAMBURLAINE, *with* TECHELLES, *and others*

AGYDAS       With Tamburlaine! Ah, fair Zenocrate,
             Let not a man so vile and barbarous,
             That holds you from your father in despite,
             And keeps you from the honours of a queen
             (Being suppos'd his worthless concubine)
             Be honour'd with your love but for necessity!              30
             So, now the mighty Soldan hears of you,
             Your highness needs not doubt but in short time

|              | He will, with Tamburlaine's destruction, |
|--------------|-------------------------------------------|
|              | Redeem you from this deadly servitude. |
| ZENOCR.      | Leave to wound me with these words, |
|              | And speak of Tamburlaine as he deserves: |
|              | The entertainment we have had of him |
|              | Is far from villany or servitude, |
|              | And might in noble minds be counted princely. |
| AGYDAS       | How can you fancy one that looks so fierce,      40 |
|              | Only dispos'd to martial stratagems? |
|              | Who, when he shall embrace you in his arms, |
|              | Will tell how many thousand men he slew; |
|              | And, when you look for amorous discourse, |
|              | Will rattle forth his facts of war and blood, |
|              | Too harsh a subject for your dainty ears. |
| ZENOCR.      | As looks the sun through Nilus' flowing stream, |
|              | Or when the Morning holds him in her arms, |
|              | So looks my lordly love, fair Tamburlaine; |
|              | His talk much sweeter than the Muses' song      50 |
|              | They sung for honour 'gainst Pierides, |
|              | Or when Minerva did with Neptune strive: |
|              | And higher would I rear my estimate |
|              | Than Juno, sister to the highest god, |
|              | If I were match'd with mighty Tamburlaine. |
| AGYDAS       | Yet be not so inconstant in your love, |
|              | But let the young Arabian live in hope, |
|              | After your rescue to enjoy his choice. |
|              | You see, though first the king of Persia, |
|              | Being a shepherd, seem'd to love you much,      60 |
|              | Now, in his majesty, he leaves those looks, |
|              | Those words of favour, and those comfortings, |
|              | And gives no more than common courtesies. |
| ZENOCR.      | Thence rise the tears that so disdain my cheeks, |
|              | Fearing his love through my unworthiness. |

                *[Tamburlaine goes to her, and takes her away lovingly*
                    *by the hand, looking wrathfully on Agydas, and says*
                          *nothing. Exeunt all except Agydas.*

| AGYDAS       | Betray'd by fortune and suspicious love, |
|--------------|-------------------------------------------|
|              | Threaten'd with frowning wrath and jealousy, |

Surpris'd with fear of hideous revenge,
I stand aghast; but most astonied
To see his choler shut in secret thoughts,          70
And wrapt in silence of his angry soul:
Upon his brows was pourtray'd ugly death;
And in his eyes the fury of his heart,
That shone as comets, menacing revenge,
And cast a pale complexion on his cheeks.
As when the seaman sees the Hyades
Gather an army of Cimmerian clouds,
(Auster and Aquilon with winged steeds,
All sweating, tilt about the watery heavens,
With shivering spears enforcing thunder-claps          80
And from their shields strike flames of lightning)
All-fearful folds his sails, and sounds the main,
Lifting his prayers to the heavens for aid
Against the terror of the winds and waves;
So fares Agydas for the late-felt frowns,
That send a tempest to my daunted thoughts,
And make my soul divine her overthrow.

*Re-enter* TECHELLES *with a naked dagger, and* USUMCASANE

TECHELLES See you, Agydas, how the king salutes you!
He bids you prophesy what it imports.
AGYDAS  I prophesied before, and now I prove          90
The killing frowns of jealousy and love.
He needed not with words confirm my fear,
For words are vain where working tools present
The naked action of my threaten'd end:
It says, Agydas, thou shalt surely die,
And of extremities elect the least;
More honour and less pain it may procure,
To die by this resolved hand of thine
Than stay the torments he and heaven have sworn.
Then haste, Agydas, and prevent the plagues          100
Which thy prolonged fates may draw on thee:
Go wander free from fear of tyrant's rage
Removed from the torments and the hell
Wherewith he may excruciate thy soul;

And let Agydas by Agydas die,
And with this stab slumber eternally.     [*stabs himself*
TECHELLES Usumcasane, see, how right the man
       Hath hit the meaning of my lord and king!
USUMCAS. Faith, and, Techelles, it was manly done;
       And, since he was so wise and honourable,     110
       Let us afford him now the bearing hence,
       And crave his triple-worthy burial.
TECHELLES Agreed, Casane; we will honour him.
                        [*exeunt, bearing out the body*

## SCENE 3

*Enter* TAMBURLAINE, TECHELLES, USUMCASANE, THERIDAMAS,
       *a Basso*, ZENOCRATE, ANIPPE *with others*

TAMBUR. Basso, by this thy lord and master knows
       I mean to meet him in Bithynia:
       See, how he comes! Tush, Turks are full of brags,
       And menace more than they can well perform.
       He meet me in the field, and fetch thee hence!
       Alas, poor Turk! His fortune is too weak
       T' encounter with the strength of Tamburlaine:
       View well my camp, and speak indifferently;
       Do not my captains and my soldiers look
       As if they meant to conquer Africa?     10
BASSO Your men are valiant, but their number few,
       And cannot terrify his mighty host:
       My lord, the great commander of the world,
       Besides fifteen contributory kings,
       Hath now in arms ten thousand janizaries,
       Mounted on lusty Mauritanian steeds,
       Brought to the war by men of Tripoly;
       Two hundred thousand footmen that have serv'd
       In two set battles fought in Graecia;
       And for the expedition of this war,     20
       If he think good, can from his garrisons
       Withdraw as many more to follow him.

TECHELLES  The more he brings, the greater is the spoil:
           For, when they perish by our warlike hands,
           We mean to set our footmen on their steeds,
           And rifle all those stately janizars.

TAMBUR.    But will those kings accompany your lord?

BASSO      Such as his highness please: but some must stay
           To rule the provinces he late subdu'd.

TAMBUR.    [to his Officers] Then fight courageously: their
                                    crowns are yours,   30
           This hand shall set them on your conquering heads
           That made me emperor of Asia.

USUMCAS.   Let him bring millions infinite of men,
           Unpeopling Western Africa and Greece,
           Yet we assure us of the victory.

THERID.    Even he that in a trice vanquish'd two kings
           More mighty than the Turkish emperor,
           Shall rouse him out of Europe, and pursue
           His scatter'd army till they yield or die.

TAMBUR.    Well said, Theridamas! Speak in that mood:   40
           For *will* and *shall* best fitteth Tamburlaine,
           Whose smiling stars give him assured hope
           Of martial triumph ere he meets his foes.
           I that am term'd the scourge and wrath of God,
           The only fear and terror of the world,
           Will first subdue the Turk, and then enlarge
           Those Christian captives which you keep as slaves,
           Burdening their bodies with your heavy chains,
           And feeding them with thin and slender fare;
           That naked row about the Terrene sea,   50
           And, when they chance to rest or breathe a space,
           Are punish'd with bastones so grievously
           That they lie panting on the galleys' side,
           And strive for life at every stroke they give.
           These are the cruel pirates of Argier,
           That damned train, the scum of Africa,
           Inhabited with straggling runagates,
           That make quick havoc of the Christian blood:
           But, as I live, that town shall curse the time
           That Tamburlaine set foot in Africa.   60

*Enter* BAJAZETH, *Bassoes, the* KINGS *of* FEZ,
MOROCCO *and* ARGIER; ZABINA *and* EBEA

BAJAZETH Bassoes and janizaries of my guard,
Attend upon the person of your lord,
The greatest potentate of Africa.

TAMBUR. Techelles and the rest, prepare your swords;
I mean t' encounter with that Bajazeth.

BAJAZETH Kings of Fez, Morocco, and Argier,
He calls me Bajazeth, whom you call lord!
Note the presumption of this Scythian slave!
I tell thee, villain, those that lead my horse
Have to their names titles of dignity;                     70
And dar'st thou bluntly call me Bajazeth?

TAMBUR. And know, thou Turk, that those which lead
                                          my horse
Shall lead thee captive thorough Africa;
And dar'st thou bluntly call me Tamburlaine?

BAJAZETH By Mahomet my kinsman's sepulchre,
And by the holy Alcoran I swear,
He shall be made a chaste and lustless eunuch
And in my sarell tend my concubines;
And all his captains, that thus stoutly stand,
Shall draw the chariot of my emperess,                     80
Whom I have brought to see their overthrow!

TAMBUR. By this my sword that conquer'd Persia,
Thy fall shall make me famous through the world!
I will not tell thee how I'll handle thee,
But every common soldier of my camp
Shall smile to see thy miserable state

FEZ What means the mighty Turkish emperor,
To talk with one so base as Tamburlaine?

MOROCCO Ye Moors and valiant men of Barbary,
How can ye suffer these indignities?                       90

ARGIER Leave words, and let them feel your lances' points,
Which glided through the bowels of the Greeks.

BAJAZETH Well said, my stout contributory kings!
Your threefold army and my hugy host
Shall swallow up these base-born Persians.

TECHELLES   Puissant, renowm'd, and mighty Tamburlaine,
            Why stay we thus prolonging of their lives?
THERID.     I long to see those crowns won by our swords,
            That we may rule as kings of Africa.
USUMCAS.    What coward would not fight for such a prize?      100
TAMBUR.     Fight all courageously, and be you kings:
            I speak it, and my words are oracles.
BAJAZETH    Zabina, mother of three braver boys
            Than Hercules, that in his infancy
            Did pash the jaws of serpents venomous;
            Whose hands are made to gripe a warlike lance,
            Their shoulders broad for complete armour fit,
            Their limbs more large and of a bigger size
            Than all the brats y-sprung from Typhon's loins;
            Who, when they come unto their father's age,      110
            Will batter turrets with their manly fists –
            Sit here upon this royal chair of state,
            And on thy head wear my imperial crown,
            Until I bring this sturdy Tamburlaine
            And all his captains bound in captive chains.
ZABINA      Such good success happen to Bajazeth!
TAMBUR.     Zenocrate, the loveliest maid alive,
            Fairer than rocks of pearl and precious stone,
            The only paragon of Tamburlaine;
            Whose eyes are brighter than the lamps of heaven, 120
            And speech more pleasant than sweet harmony;
            That with thy looks canst clear the darken'd sky,
            And calm the rage of thundering Jupiter;
            Sit down by her, adorned with my crown,
            As if thou wert the empress of the world.
            Stir not, Zenocrate, until thou see
            Me march victoriously with all my men,
            Triumphing over him and these his kings,
            Which I will bring as vassals to thy feet;
            Till then, take thou my crown, vaunt of my worth,  130
            And manage words with her, as we will arms.
ZENOCR.     And may my love, the king of Persia,
            Return with victory and free from wound!
BAJAZETH    Now shalt thou feel the force of Turkish arms,

Which lately made all Europe quake for fear.
I have of Turks, Arabians, Moors, and Jews,
Enough to cover all Bithynia:
Let thousands die: their slaughter'd carcasses
Shall serve for walls and bulwarks to the rest;
And as the heads of Hydra, so my power,                    140
Subdu'd, shall stand as mighty as before:
If they should yield their necks unto the sword,
Thy soldiers' arms could not endure to strike
So many blows as I have heads for them.
Thou know'st not, foolish-hardy Tamburlaine,
What 'tis to meet me in the open field,
That leave no ground for thee to march upon.

TAMBUR.    Our conquering swords shall marshal us the way
We use to march upon the slaughter'd foe,
Trampling their bowels with our horses' hoofs,            150
Brave horses bred on the white Tartarian hills.
My camp is like to Julius Caesar's host,
That never fought but had the victory;
Nor in Pharsalia was there such hot war
As these, my followers, willingly would have.
Legions of spirits, fleeting in the air,
Direct our bullets and our weapons' points,
And make your strokes to wound the senseless light;
And when she sees our bloody colours spread,
Then Victory begins to take her flight,                   160
Resting herself upon my milk-white tent —
But come, my lords, to weapons let us fall;
The field is ours, the Turk, his wife, and all.
                                        [*exit with his followers*

BAJAZETH   Come, kings and bassoes, let us glut our swords
That thirst to drink the feeble Persians' blood.
                                        [*exit with his followers*

ZABINA     Base concubine, must thou be plac'd by me
That am the empress of the mighty Turk?

ZENOCR.    Disdainful Turkess, and unreverend boss,
Call'st thou me concubine, that am betroth'd
Unto the great and mighty Tamburlaine?                    170

ZABINA     To Tamburlaine, the great Tartarian thief!

ZENOCR.     Thou wilt repent these lavish words of thine
            When thy great basso-master and thyself
            Must plead for mercy at his kingly feet,
            And sue to me to be your advocate.

ZABINA      And sue to thee! I tell thee, shameless girl,
            Thou shalt be laundress to my waiting-maid –
            How lik'st thou her, Ebea? Will she serve?

EBEA        Madam, she thinks perhaps she is too fine;
            But I shall turn her into other weeds,                    180
            And make her dainty fingers fall to work.

ZENOCR.     Hear'st thou, Anippe, how thy drudge doth talk?
            And how my slave, her mistress, menaceth?
            Both for their sauciness shall be employ'd
            To dress the common soldiers' meat and drink;
            For we will scorn they should come near ourselves.

ANIPPE      Yet sometimes let your highness send for them
            To do the work my chambermaid disdains.
                                    [they sound to the battle within

ZENOCR.     Ye gods and powers that govern Persia,
            And made my lordly love her worthy king,                 190
            Now strengthen him against the Turkish Bajazeth,
            And let his foes, like flocks of fearful roes
            Pursu'd by hunters, fly his angry looks,
            That I may see him issue conqueror!

ZABINA      Now, Mahomet, solicit God himself,
            And make him rain down murdering shot
                                              from heaven,
            To dash the Scythians' brains, and strike them dead,
            That dare to manage arms with him
            That offer'd jewels to thy sacred shrine
            When first he warr'd against the Christians!             200
                                    [they sound again to the battle within

ZENOCR.     By this the Turks lie weltering in their blood,
            And Tamburlaine is lord of Africa.

ZABINA      Thou art deceiv'd. I heard the trumpets sound
            As when my emperor overthrew the Greeks,
            And led them captive into Africa.
            Straight will I use thee as thy pride deserves;
            Prepare thyself to live and die my slave.

ZENOCR.     If Mahomet should come from heaven and swear
            My royal lord is slain or conquered,
            Yet should he not persuade me otherwise          210
            But that he lives and will be conqueror.

            *Re-enter* BAJAZETH, *pursued by* TAMBURLAINE

TAMBUR.     Now, king of bassoes, who is conqueror?
BAJAZETH    Thou, by the fortune of this damned foil.
TAMBUR.     Where are your stout contributory kings?

            *Re-enter* TECHELLES, THERIDAMAS *and* USUMCASANE

TECHELLES   We have their crowns; their bodies strow the field.
TAMBUR.     Each man a crown! Why, kingly fought, i'faith.
            Deliver them into my treasury.
ZENOCR.     Now let me offer to my gracious lord
            His royal crown again so highly won.
TAMBUR.     Nay, take the Turkish crown from her, Zenocrate,     220
            And crown me emperor of Africa.
ZABINA      No, Tamburlaine; though now thou gat the best,
            Thou shalt not yet be lord of Africa.
THERID.     Give her the crown, Turkess, you were best.
                                              [*takes it from her*
ZABINA      Injurious villains, thieves, runagates,
            How dare you thus abuse my majesty?
THERID.     Here, madam, you are empress; she is none.
                                              [*gives it to Zenocrate*
TAMBUR.     Not now, Theridamas; her time is past:
            The pillars, that have bolster'd up those terms,
            Are faln in clusters at my conquering feet.          230
ZABINA      Though he be prisoner, he may be ransom'd.
TAMBUR.     Not all the world shall ransom Bajazeth.
BAJAZETH    Ah, fair Zabina! We have lost the field;
            And never had the Turkish emperor
            So great a foil by any foreign foe.
            Now will the Christian miscreants be glad,
            Ringing with joy their superstitious bells,
            And making bonfires for my overthrow –
            But, ere I die, those foul idolaters
            Shall make me bonfires with their filthy bones;      240
            For, though the glory of this day be lost,

Afric and Greece have garrisons enough
To make me sovereign of the earth again.

TAMBUR.    Those walled garrisons will I subdue,
And write myself great lord of Africa:
So from the East unto the furthest West
Shall Tamburlaine extend his puissant arm.
The galleys and those pilling brigandines,
That yearly sail to the Venetian gulf,
And hover in the Straits for Christians' wreck,        250
Shall lie at anchor in the Isle Asant,
Until the Persian fleet and men-of-war,
Sailing along the oriental sea,
Have fetch'd about the Indian continent,
Even from Persepolis to Mexico,
And thence unto the Straits of Jubalter;
Where they shall meet and join their force in one,
Keeping in awe the Bay of Portingale,
And all the ocean by the British shore;
And by this means I'll win the world at last.        260

BAJAZETH    Yet set a ransom on me, Tamburlaine.

TAMBUR.    What, think'st thou Tamburlaine esteems thy gold?
I'll make the kings of India, ere I die,
Offer their mines, to sue for peace, to me.
And dig for treasure to appease my wrath –
Come, bind them both, and one lead in the Turk;
The Turkess let my love's maid lead away.

                                        [they bind them

BAJAZETH    Ah, villains, dare you touch my sacred arms?
O Mahomet! O sleepy Mahomet!

ZABRINA    O cursed Mahomet, that mak'st us thus        270
The slaves to Scythians rude and barbarous!

TAMBUR.    Come, bring them in; and for this happy conquest
Triumph, and solemnise a martial feast.

                                        [exeunt

# ACT FOUR

## SCENE I

*Enter the* SOLDAN OF EGYPT, CAPOLIN, *Lords, and a Messenger*

SOLDAN   Awake, ye men of Memphis! Hear the clang
         Of Scythian trumpets; hear the basilisks,
         That, roaring, shake Damascus' turrets down!
         The rogue of Volga holds Zenocrate,
         The Soldan's daughter, for his concubine,
         And, with a troop of thieves and vagabonds,
         Hath spread his colours to our high disgrace,
         While you, faint-hearted base Egyptians,
         Lie slumbering on the flowery banks of Nile,
         As crocodiles that unaffrighted rest                10
         While thundering cannons rattle on their skins.

MESSENG. Nay, mighty Soldan, did your greatness see
         The frowning looks of fiery Tamburlaine,
         That with his terror and imperious eyes
         Commands the hearts of his associates,
         It might amaze your royal majesty.

SOLDAN   Villain, I tell thee, were that Tamburlaine
         As monstrous as Gorgon prince of hell,
         The Soldan would not start a foot from him.
         But speak, what power hath he?

MESSENG.                          Mighty lord,         20
         Three hundred thousand men in armour clad,
         Upon their prancing steeds, disdainfully
         With wanton paces trampling on the ground;
         Five hundred thousand footmen threatening shot,
         Shaking their swords, their spears, and iron bills,
         Environing their standard round, that stood
         As bristle-pointed as a thorny wood;
         Their warlike engines and munition
         Exceed the forces of their martial men.

SOLDAN   Nay, could their numbers countervail the stars,   30
         Or ever-drizzling drops of April showers,

Or wither'd leaves that autumn shaketh down,
Yet would the Soldan by his conquering power
So scatter and consume them in his rage,
That not a man should live to rue their fall.

CAPOLIN   So might your highness, had you time to sort
Your fighting men, and raise your royal host;
But Tamburlaine by expedition
Advantage takes of your unreadiness.

SOLDAN   Let him take all th' advantages he can:                40
Were all the world conspir'd to fight for him,
Nay, were he devil, as he is no man,
Yet in revenge of fair Zenocrate,
Whom he detaineth in despite of us,
This arm should send him down to Erebus,
To shroud his shame in darkness of the night.

MESSENG.   Pleaseth your mightiness to understand,
His resolution far exceedeth all.
The first day when he pitcheth down his tents,
White is their hue, and on his silver crest        50
A snowy feather spangled-white he bears,
To signify the mildness of his mind,
That, satiate with spoil, refuseth blood:
But, when Aurora mounts the second time,
As red as scarlet is his furniture;
Then must his kindled wrath be quench'd with blood,
Not sparing any that can manage arms:
But, if these threats move not submission,
Black are his colours, black pavilion;
His spear, his shield, his horse, his armour, plumes,  60
And jetty feathers, menace death and hell;
Without respect of sex, degree, or age,
He razeth all his foes with fire and sword.

SOLDAN   Merciless villain, peasant, ignorant
Of lawful arms or martial discipline!
Pillage and murder are his usual trades:
The slave usurps the glorious name of war.
See, Capolin, the fair Arabian king,
That hath been disappointed by this slave

Of my fair daughter and his princely love,                    70
May have fresh warning to go war with us,
And be reveng'd for her disparagement.

                                                  [*exeunt*


## SCENE 2

*Enter* TAMBURLAINE, TECHELLES, THERIDAMAS, USUMCASANE,
ZENOCRATE, ANIPPE, *two Moors drawing* BAJAZETH *in a cage,
and* ZABINA *following him*

TAMBUR.    Bring out my footstool.
                              [*they take Bajazeth out of the cage.*
BAJAZETH   Ye holy priests of heavenly Mahomet,
           That, sacrificing, slice and cut your flesh,
           Staining his altars with your purple blood,
           Make heaven to frown, and every fixed star
           To suck up poison from the moorish fens,
           And pour it in this glorious tyrant's throat!
TAMBUR.    The chiefest god, first mover of that sphere
           Enchas'd with thousands ever-shining lamps,
           Will sooner burn the glorious frame of heaven      10
           Than it should so conspire my overthrow.
           But, villain, thou that wishest this to me,
           Fall prostrate on the low disdainful earth,
           And be the footstool of great Tamburlaine,
           That I may rise into my royal throne.
BAJAZETH   First shalt thou rip my bowels with thy sword,
           And sacrifice my heart to death and hell,
           Before I yield to such a slavery.
TAMBUR.    Base villain, vassal, slave to Tamburlaine,
           Unworthy to embrace or touch the ground          20
           That bears the honour of my royal weight;
           Stoop, villain, stoop! Stoop: for so he bids
           That may command thee piecemeal to be torn,
           Or scatter'd like the lofty cedar-trees
           Struck with the voice of thundering Jupiter.
BAJAZETH   Then, as I look down to the damned fiends,
           Fiends, look on me! And thou, dread god of hell,

With ebon sceptre strike this hateful earth,
And make it swallow both of us at once!

                  *[Tamburlaine gets up on him into his chair*

TAMBUR.   Now clear the triple region of the air,       30
And let the Majesty of Heaven behold
Their scourge and terror tread on emperors.
Smile, stars that reign'd at my nativity,
And dim the brightness of your neighbour lamps,
Disdain to borrow light of Cynthia!
For I, the chiefest lamp of all the earth,
First rising in the east with mild aspect,
But fixed now in the meridian line,
Will send up fire to your turning spheres,
And cause the sun to borrow light of you.       40
My sword struck fire from his coat of steel,
Even in Bithynia, when I took this Turk;
As when a fiery exhalation,
Wrapt in the bowels of a freezing cloud,
Fighting for passage, makes the welkin crack,
And casts a flash of lightning to the earth:
But, ere I march to wealthy Persia,
Or leave Damascus and th' Egyptian fields,
As was the fame of Clymene's brain-sick son
That almost brent the axle-tree of heaven,     50
So shall our swords, our lances, and our shot
Fill all the air with fiery meteors;
Then, when the sky shall wax as red as blood,
It shall be said I made it red myself,
To make me think of naught but blood and war.

ZABINA   Unworthy king, that by thy cruelty
Unlawfully usurp'st the Persian seat,
Dar'st thou, that never saw an emperor
Before thou met my husband in the field,
Being thy captive, thus abuse his state,      60
Keeping his kingly body in a cage,
That roofs of gold and sun-bright palaces
Should have prepar'd to entertain his grace?
And treading him beneath thy loathsome feet,
Whose feet the kings of Africa have kiss'd?

TECHELLES  You must devise some torment worse, my lord,
          To make these captives rein their lavish tongues.
TAMBUR.  Zenocrate, look better to your slave.
ZENOCR.  She is my handmaid's slave, and she shall look
          That these abuses flow not from her tongue —     70
          Chide her, Anippe.
ANIPPE  Let these be warnings, then, for you, my slave,
          How you abuse the person of the king;
          Or else I swear to have you whipt stark nak'd.
BAJAZETH  Great Tamburlaine, great in my overthrow,
          Ambitious pride shall make thee fall as low,
          For treading on the back of Bajazeth
          That should be horsed on four mighty kings.
TAMBUR.  Thy names, and titles, and thy dignities
          Are fled from Bajazeth, and remain with me,     80
          That will maintain it 'gainst a world of kings —
          Put him in again.          [they put him into the cage.
BAJAZETH  Is this a place for mighty Bajazeth?
          Confusion light on him that helps thee thus.
TAMBUR.  There, while he lives, shall Bajazeth be kept;
          And, where I go, be thus in triumph drawn;
          And thou, his wife, shall feed him with the scraps
          My servitors shall bring thee from my board;
          For he that gives him other food than this
          Shall sit by him, and starve to death himself:     90
          This is my mind, and I will have it so.
          Not all the kings and emperors of the earth,
          If they would lay their crowns before my feet,
          Shall ransom him, or take him from his cage:
          The ages that shall talk of Tamburlaine,
          Even from this day to Plato's wondrous year,
          Shall talk how I have handled Bajazeth:
          These Moors, that drew him from Bithynia
          To fair Damascus, where we now remain,
          Shall lead him with us wheresoe'er we go —     100
          Techelles, and my loving followers,
          Now may we see Damascus' lofty towers,
          Like to the shadows of Pyramides
          That with their beauties grace the Memphian fields.

The golden stature of their feather'd bird,
That spreads her wings upon the city walls,
Shall not defend it from our battering shot:
The townsmen mask in silk and cloth of gold,
And every house is as a treasury;
The men, the treasure, and the town are ours.          110

THERID.   Your tents of white now pitch'd before the gates,
And gentle flags of amity display'd,
I doubt not but the governor will yield,
Offering Damascus to your majesty.

TAMBUR.   So shall he have his life, and all the rest:
But, if he stay until the bloody flag
Be once advanc'd on my vermilion tent,
He dies, and those that kept us out so long;
And when they see me march in black array,
With mournful streamers hanging down their heads,
Were in that city all the world contain'd,
Not one should scape, but perish by our swords.

ZENOCR.   Yet would you have some pity for my sake,
Because it is my country and my father's.

TAMBUR.   Not for the world, Zenocrate, if I have sworn —
Come; bring in the Turk.

                                        [*exeunt*

## SCENE 3

*Enter* SOLDAN, KING OF ARABIA, CAPOLIN,
*and Soldiers, with streaming colours*

SOLDAN   Methinks we march as Meleager did,
Environed with brave Argolian knights,
To chase the savage Calydonian boar.
Or Cephalus, with lusty Theban youths,
Against the wolf that angry Themis sent
To waste and spoil the sweet Aonian fields.
A monster of five hundred thousand heads,
Compact of rapine, piracy, and spoil,
The scum of men, the hate and scourge of God,
Raves in Egyptia, and annoyeth us:          10

My lord, it is the bloody Tamburlaine,
A sturdy felon, and a base-bred thief,
By murder raised to the Persian crown,
That dare control us in our territories.
To tame the pride of this presumptuous beast,
Join your Arabians with the Soldan's power;
Let us unite our royal bands in one,
And hasten to remove Damascus' siege.
It is a blemish to the majesty
And high estate of mighty emperors,       20
That such a base usurping vagabond
Should brave a king, or wear a princely crown.

ARABIA    Renowmed Soldan, have you lately heard
The overthrow of mighty Bajazeth
About the confines of Bithynia?
The, slavery wherewith he persecutes
The noble Turk and his great emperess?

SOLDAN    I have, and sorrow for his bad success;
But, noble lord of great Arabia,
Be so persuaded that the Soldan is       30
No more dismay'd with tidings of his fall,
Than in the haven when the pilot stands,
And views a stranger's ship rent in the winds,
And shivered against a craggy rock:
Yet in compassion to his wretched state,
A sacred vow to heaven and him I make,
Confirming it with Ibis' holy name,
That Tamburlaine shall rue the day, the hour,
Wherein he wrought such ignominious wrong
Unto the hallow'd person of a prince,       40
Or kept the fair Zenocrate so long,
As concubine, I fear, to feed his lust.

ARABIA    Let grief and fury hasten on revenge;
Let Tamburlaine for his offences feel
Such plagues as heaven and we can pour on him:
I long to break my spear upon his crest,
And prove the weight of his victorious arm;
For fame, I fear, hath been too prodigal
In sounding through the world his partial praise.

SOLDAN     Capolin, hast thou survey'd our powers?       50
CAPOLIN    Great emperors of Egypt and Arabia,
             The number of your hosts united is,
             A hundred and fifty thousand horse,
             Two hundred thousand foot, brave men-at-arms,
             Courageous and full of hardiness,
             As frolic as the hunters in the chase
             Of savage beasts amid the desert woods.
ARABIA     My mind presageth fortunate success;
             And, Tamburlaine, my spirit doth foresee
             The utter ruin of thy men and thee.       60
SOLDAN     Then rear your standards; let your sounding drums
             Direct our soldiers to Damascus' walls –
             Now, Tamburlaine, the mighty Soldan comes
             And leads with him the great Arabian king
             To dim thy baseness and obscurity,
             Famous for nothing but for theft and spoil;
             To raze and scatter thy inglorious crew
             Of Scythians and slavish Persians.

                                             *[exeunt*


## SCENE 4

*A banquet set out; and to it come* TAMBURLAINE *all in scarlet,*
ZENOCRATE, THERIDAMAS, TECHELLES, USUMCASANE,
BAJAZETH *drawn in his cage,* ZABINA, *and others.*

TAMBUR.    Now hang our bloody colours by Damascus,
             Reflexing hues of blood upon their heads,
             While they walk quivering on their city-walls,
             Half-dead for fear before they feel my wrath.
             Then let us freely banquet, and carouse
             Full bowls of wine unto the god of war,
             That means to fill your helmets full of gold,
             And make Damascus' spoils as rich to you
             As was to Jason Colchos' golden fleece –
             And now, Bajazeth, hast thou any stomach?       10
BAJAZETH   Ay, such a stomach, cruel Tamburlaine, as I could
             willingly feed upon thy blood-raw heart.

TAMBUR.    Nay, thine own is easier to come by: pluck out that;
           and 'twill serve thee and thy wife – Well, Zenocrate,
           Techelles, and the rest, fall to your victuals.

BAJAZETH   Fall to, and never may your meat digest!
           Ye Furies, that can mask invisible,
           Dive to the bottom of Avernus' pool,
           And in your hands bring hellish poison up
           And squeeze it in the cup of Tamburlaine!                    20
           Or, winged snakes of Lerna, cast your stings,
           And leave your venoms in this tyrant's dish.

ZABINA     And may this banquet prove as ominous
           As Progne's to th' adulterous Thracian king
           That fed upon the substance of his child!

ZENOCR.    My lord, how can you suffer these
           Outrageous curses by these slaves of yours?

TAMBUR.    To let them see, divine Zenocrate,
           I glory in the curses of my foes,
           Having the power from the empyreal heaven                    30
           To turn them all upon their proper heads.

TECHELLES  I pray you, give them leave, madam; this speech is a
           goodly refreshing for them.

THERID.    But, if his highness would let them be fed, it would do
           them more good.

TAMBUR.    Sirrah, why fall you not to? Are you so daintily brought
           up, you cannot eat your own flesh?

BAJAZETH   First, legions of devils shall tear thee in pieces.

USUMCAS.   Villain, knowest thou to whom thou speakest?

TAMBUR.    O, let him alone. Here; eat, sir; take it from my sword's
           point, or I'll thrust it to thy heart.
                        [*Bajazeth takes the food, and stamps upon it*

THERID.    He stamps it under his feet, my lord.

TAMBUR.    Take it up, villain, and eat it; or I will make thee slice
           the brawns of thy arms into carbonadoes and eat them.

USUMCAS.   Nay, 'twere better he killed his wife, and then she shall
           be sure not to be starved, and he be provided for a
           month's victual beforehand.

TAMBUR.    Here is my dagger: despatch her while she is fat; for,
           if she live but a while longer, she will fall into a

consumption with fretting, and then she will not be worth the eating.

THERID.     Dost thou think that Mahomet will suffer this?

TECHELLES 'Tis like he will, when he cannot let it.

TAMBUR.     Go to; fall to your meat. What, not a bit! Belike he hath not been watered today: give him some drink.

> [*they give Bajazeth water to drink,*
> *and he flings it on the ground*

Fast, and welcome, sir, while hunger make you eat. How now. Zenocrate! Doth not the Turk and his wife make a goodly show at a banquet?

ZENOCR.     Yes, my lord.

THERID.     Methinks 'tis a great deal better than a consort of music.

TAMBUR.     Yet music would do well to cheer up Zenocrate. Pray thee, tell why art thou so sad? If thou wilt have a song, the Turk shall strain his voice: but why is it?

ZENOCR.     My lord, to see my father's town besieg'd,
The country wasted, where myself was born,
How can it but afflict my very soul?
If any love remain in you, my lord,
Or if my love unto your majesty
May merit favour at your highness' hands,
Then raise your siege from fair Damascus' walls,          70
And with my father take a friendly truce.

TAMBUR.     Zenocrate, were Egypt Jove's own land,
Yet would I with my sword make Jove to stoop.
I will confute those blind geographers
That make a triple region in the world,
Excluding regions which I mean to trace,
And with this pen reduce them to a map,
Calling the provinces, cities, and towns
After my name and thine, Zenocrate:
Here at Damascus will I make the point          80
That shall begin the perpendicular:
And wouldst thou have me buy thy father's love
With such a loss? Tell me, Zenocrate.

ZENOCR.     Honour still wait on happy Tamburlaine!
Yet give me leave to plead for him, my lord.

TAMBUR.     Content thyself: his person shall be safe,

And all the friends of fair Zenocrate,
If with their lives they will be pleas'd to yield,
Or may be forced to make me emperor;
For Egypt and Arabia must be mine —          90
Feed, you slave; thou mayst think thyself happy to be
fed from my trencher.

BAJAZETH  My empty stomach, full of idle heat,
Draws bloody humours from my feeble parts,
Preserving life by hastening cruel death.
My veins are pale; my sinews hard and dry;
My joints benumb'd: unless I eat, I die.

ZABINA  Eat, Bajazeth; let us live in spite of them, looking some
happy power will pity and enlarge us.

TAMBUR.  Here, Turk; wilt thou have a clean trencher?          100

BAJAZETH  Ay, tyrant, and more meat.

TAMBUR.  Soft, sir! You must be dieted; too much eating will
make you surfeit.

THERID.  So it would, my lord, 'specially having so small a walk
and so little exercise.

                    [a second course is brought in of crowns

TAMBUR.  Theridamas, Techelles, and Casane, here are the cates
you desire to finger, are they not?

THERID.  Ay, my lord: but none save kings must feed with these.

TECHELLES 'Tis enough for us to see them, and for Tamburlaine
only to enjoy them.

TAMBUR.  Well; here is now to the Soldan of Egypt, the King of
Arabia, and the Governor of Damascus. Now, take these
three crowns, and pledge me, my contributory kings. I
crown you here, Theridamas, king of Argier; Techelles,
king of Fez; and Usumcasane, king of Morocco — How
say you to this, Turk? These are not your contributory
kings.

BAJAZETH  Nor shall they long be thine, I warrant them.

TAMBUR.  Kings of Argier, Morocco, and of Fez,
You that have marched with happy Tamburlaine          120
As far as from the frozen plage of heaven
Unto the watery Morning's ruddy bower,
And thence by land unto the torrid zone,
Deserve these titles I endow you with

By valour and by magnanimity.
Your births shall be no blemish to your fame;
For virtue is the fount whence honour springs,
And they are worthy she investeth kings.

THERID.   And since your highness hath so well vouchsaf'd,
If we deserve them not with higher meeds                 130
Than erst our states and actions have retained,
Take them away again, and make us slaves.

TAMBUR.   Well said, Theridamas: when holy Fates
Shall stablish me in strong Aegyptia,
We mean to travel to th' antarctic pole,
Conquering the people underneath our feet,
And be renowm'd as never emperors were —
Zenocrate, I will not crown thee yet,
Until with greater honours I be grac'd.

                                                   [exeunt

## ACT FIVE

### SCENE I

*Enter the* GOVERNOR OF DAMASCUS *with three or four Citizens,
and four Virgins with branches of laurel in their hands*

GOVERNOR   Still doth this man, or rather god of war,
        Batter our walls and beat our turrets down;
        And to resist with longer stubbornness,
        Or hope of rescue from the Soldan's power,
        Were but to bring our wilful overthrow,
        And make us desperate of our threatened lives.
        We see his tents have now been altered
        With terrors to the last and cruel'st hue;
        His coal-black colours, everywhere advanc'd,
        Threaten our city with a general spoil;           10
        And, if we should with common rites of arms
        Offer our safeties to his clemency,
        I fear the custom proper to his sword,
        Which he observes as parcel of his fame,
        Intending so to terrify the world,
        By any innovation or remorse
        Will never be dispens'd with till our deaths.
        Therefore, for these our harmless virgins' sakes,
        Whose honours and whose lives rely on him,
        Let us have hope that their unspotted prayers,     20
        Their blubber d cheeks, and hearty humble moans
        Will melt his fury into some remorse,
        And use us like a loving conqueror.

I VIRGIN   If humble suits or imprecations
        (Utter'd with tears of wretchedness and blood
        Shed from the heads and hearts of all our sex,
        Some made your wives, and some your children)
        Might have entreated your obdurate breasts
        To entertain some care of our securities
        Whilst only danger beat upon our walls,        30
        These more than dangerous warrants of our death

Had never been erected as they be,
Nor you depend on such weak helps as we.

GOVERNOR Well, lovely virgins, think our country's care,
Our love of honour, loath to be enthrall'd
To foreign powers and rough imperious yokes,
Would not with too much cowardice or fear,
Before all hope of rescue were denied,
Submit yourselves and us to servitude.
Therefore, in that your safeties and our own,          40
Your honours, liberties, and lives were weigh'd
In equal care and balance with our own,
Endure as we the malice of our stars,
The wrath of Tamburlaine and power of wars;
Or be the means the overweighing heavens
Have kept to qualify these hot extremes,
And bring us pardon in your cheerful looks.

2 VIRGIN Then here, before the Majesty of Heaven
And holy patrons of Aegyptia,
With knees and hearts submissive we entreat          50
Grace to our words and pity to our looks,
That this device may prove propitious,
And through the eyes and ears of Tamburlaine
Convey events of mercy to his heart;
Grant that these signs of victory we yield
May bind the temples of his conquering head,
To hide the folded furrows of his brows,
And shadow his displeased countenance
With happy looks of ruth and lenity.
Leave us, my lord, and loving countrymen:          60
What simple virgins may persuade, we will.

GOVERNOR Farewell, sweet virgins, on whose safe return
Depends our city, liberty, and lives.

                    [*exeunt all except the Virgins*

## SCENE 2

*Enter* TAMBURLAINE, *all in black and very melancholy,*
TECHELLES, THERIDAMAS, USUMCASANE, *with others*

TAMBUR.　What, are the turtles fray'd out of their nests?
　　　　Alas, poor fools, must you be first shall feel
　　　　The sworn destruction of Damascus?
　　　　They knew my custom; could they not as well
　　　　Have sent ye out when first my milk-white flags,
　　　　Through which sweet Mercy threw her gentle beams,
　　　　Reflexed them on their disdainful eyes,
　　　　As now when fury and incensed hate
　　　　Flings slaughtering terror from my coal-black tents,
　　　　And tells for truth submission comes too late?　　10

I VIRGIN　Most happy king and emperor of the earth,
　　　　Image of honour and nobility,
　　　　For whom the powers divine have made the world,
　　　　And on whose throne the holy Graces sit;
　　　　In whose sweet person is compris'd the sum
　　　　Of Nature's skill and heavenly majesty;
　　　　Pity our plights! O, pity poor Damascus!
　　　　Pity old age, within whose silver hairs
　　　　Honour and reverence evermore have reign'd!
　　　　Pity the marriage-bed, where many a lord,　　　20
　　　　In prime and glory of his loving joy,
　　　　Embraceth now with tears of ruth and blood
　　　　The jealous body of his fearful wife,
　　　　Whose cheeks and hearts, so punish'd with conceit,
　　　　To think thy puissant never-stayed arm
　　　　Will part their bodies, and prevent their souls
　　　　From heavens of comfort yet their age might bear,
　　　　Now wax all pale and wither'd to the death,
　　　　As well for grief our ruthless governor
　　　　Hath thus refus'd the mercy of thy hand,　　　30
　　　　(Whose sceptre angels kiss and Furies dread)
　　　　As for their liberties, their loves, or lives!
　　　　O, then, for these, and such as we ourselves,

           For us, for infants, and for all our bloods,
           That never nourish'd thought against thy rule,
           Pity, O pity, sacred emperor,
           The prostrate service of this wretched town;
           And take in sign thereof this gilded wreath,
           Whereto each man of rule·hath given his hand,
           And wish'd, as worthy subjects, happy means     40
           To be investers of thy royal brows
           Even with the true Egyptian diadem!
TAMBUR.    Virgins, in vain you labour to prevent
           That which mine honour swears shall be perform'd.
           Behold my sword; what see you at the point?
I VIRGIN   Nothing but fear and fatal steel, my lord.
TAMBUR.    Your fearful minds are thick and misty, then,
           For there sits death; there sits imperious Death,
           Keeping his circuit by the slicing edge.
           But I am pleas'd you shall not see him there;    50
           He now is seated on my horsemen's spears,
           And on their points his fleshless body feeds –
           Techelles, straight go charge a few of them
           To charge these dames, and shew my servant Death,
           Sitting in scarlet on their armed spears.
VIRGINS    O, pity us!
TAMBUR.    Away with them, I say, and shew them Death!
                      [*the Virgins are taken out by Techelles and others*
           I will not spare these proud Egyptians,
           Nor change my martial observations
           For all the wealth of Gihon's golden waves,    60
           Or for the love of Venus, would she leave
           The angry god of arms and lie with me.
           They have refus'd the offer of their lives,
           And know my customs are as peremptory
           As wrathful planets, death, or destiny.

                *Re-enter* TECHELLES

           What, have your horsemen shown the virgins Death?
TECHELLES They have, my lord, and on Damascus' walls
           Have hoisted up their slaughtered carcasses.
TAMBUR.    A sight as baneful to their souls, I think,

As are Thessalian drugs or mithridate:                70
But go, my lords, put the rest to the sword.

*[exeunt all except Tamburlaine*

Ah, fair Zenocrate! Divine Zenocrate!
Fair is too foul an epithet for thee,
That in thy passion for thy country's love,
And fear to see thy kingly father's harm,
With hair dishevell'd wip'st thy watery cheeks;
And, like to Flora in her morning's pride,
Shaking her silver tresses in the air,
Rain'st on the earth resolved pearl in showers,
And sprinklest sapphires on thy shining face,      80
Where Beauty, mother to the Muses, sits,
And comments volumes with her ivory pen,
Taking instructions from thy flowing eyes;
Eyes, when that Ebena steps to heaven,
In silence of thy solemn evening's walk,
Making the mantle of the richest night,
The moon, the planets, and the meteors, light;
There angels in their crystal armours fight
A doubtful battle with my tempted thoughts
For Egypt's freedom and the Soldan's life,         90
His life that so consumes Zenocrate;
Whose sorrows lay more siege unto my soul
Than all my army to Damascus' walls:
And neither Persia's sovereign nor the Turk
Troubled my senses with conceit of foil
So much by much as doth Zenocrate.
What is beauty, saith my sufferings, then?
If all the pens that ever poets held
Had fed the feeling of their masters' thoughts,
And every sweetness that inspir'd their hearts,    100
Their minds, and muses on admired themes;
If all the heavenly quintessence they still
From their immortal flowers of poesy,
Wherein, as in a mirror, we perceive
The highest reaches of a human wit;
If these had made one poem's period,
And all combin'd in beauty's worthiness,

Yet should there hover in their restless heads
One thought, one grace, one wonder, at the least,
Which into words no virtue can digest.          110
But how unseemly is it for my sex,
My discipline of arms and chivalry,
My nature, and the terror of my name,
To harbour thoughts effeminate and faint,
Save only that in beauty's just applause,
With whose instinct the soul of man is touched;
And every warrior that is rapt with love
Of fame, of valour, and of victory,
Must needs have beauty beat on his conceits:
I thus conceiving, and subduing both,          120
That which hath stoop'd the chiefest of the gods,
Even from the fiery-spangled veil of heaven,
To feel the lovely warmth of shepherds' flames,
And mask in cottages of strowed reeds,
Shall give the world to note, for all my birth,
That virtue solely is the sum of glory,
And fashions men with true nobility —
Who's within there?

*Enter Attendants*

Hath Bajazeth been fed today?
ATTEND.  Ay, my lord.          130
TAMBUR.  Bring him forth; and let us know if the town be
         ransacked.          [*exeunt Attendants*

*Enter* TECHELLES, THERIDAMAS, USUMCASANE, *and others*

TECHELLES  The town is ours, my lord, and fresh supply
          Of conquest and of spoil is offer'd us.
TAMBUR.   That's well, Techelles. What's the news?
TECHELLES  The Soldan and the Arabian king together
          March on us with such eager violence
          As if there were no way but one with us.
TAMBUR.   No more there is not, I warrant thee, Techelles.

*Attendants bring in* BAJAZETH *in his cage, followed by* ZABINA
                                        [*exeunt Attendants*
THERID.   We know the victory is ours, my lord;          140

But let us save the reverend Soldan's life
For fair Zenocrate that so laments his state.

TAMBUR.    That will we chiefly see unto, Theridamas,
For sweet Zenocrate, whose worthiness
Deserves a conquest over every heart –
And now, my footstool, if I lose the field,
You hope of liberty and restitution?
Here let him stay, my masters, from the tents,
Till we have made us ready for the field –
Pray for us, Bajazeth; we are going.                    150

                    [exeunt all except Bajazeth and Zabina

BAJAZETH   Go, never to return with victory!
Millions of men encompass thee about,
And gore thy body with as many wounds!
Sharp forked arrows light upon thy horse!
Furies from the black Cocytus' lake
Break up the earth, and with their fire-brands
Enforce thee run upon the baneful pikes!
Vollies of shot pierce through thy charmed skin,
And every bullet dipt in poison'd drugs!
Or roaring cannons sever all thy joints,                160
Making thee mount as high as eagles soar!

ZABINA     Let all the swords and lances in the field
Stick in his breast as in their proper rooms!
At every pore let blood come dropping forth,
That lingering pains may massacre his heart,
And madness send his damned soul to hell!

BAJAZETH   Ah, fair Zabina! We may curse his power,
The heavens may frown, the earth for anger quake;
But such a star hath influence in his sword
As rules the skies and countermands the gods           170
More than Cimmerian Styx or Destiny:
And then shall we in this detested guise,
With shame, with hunger, and with horror stay,
Griping our bowels with retorqued thoughts,
And have no hope to end our ecstasies.

ZABINA     Then is there left no Mahomet, no God,
No fiend, no fortune, nor no hope of end
To our infamous, monstrous slaveries.

Gape, earth, and let the fiends infernal view
A hell as hopeless and as full of fear                    180
As are the blasted banks of Erebus,
Where shaking ghosts with ever-howling groans
Hover about the ugly ferryman,
To get a passage to Elysium!
Why should we live? O wretches, beggars, slaves!
Why live we, Bajazeth, and build up nests
So high within the region of the air,
By living long in this oppression,
That all the world will see and laugh to scorn
The former triumphs of our mightiness                    190
In this obscure infernal servitude?

BAJAZETH  O life, more loathsome to my vexed thoughts
Than noisome parbreak of the Stygian snakes,
Which fills the nooks of hell with standing air,
Infecting all the ghosts with cureless griefs!
O dreary engines of my loathed sight,
That see my crown, my honour, and my name
Thrust under yoke and thraldom of a thief,
Why feed ye still on day's accursed beams,
And sink not quite into my tortur'd soul?                    200
You see my wife, my queen, and emperess,
Brought up and propped by the hand of Fame,
Queen of fifteen contributory queens,
Now thrown to rooms of black abjection,
Smeared with blots of basest drudgery,
And villainess to shame, disdain, and misery.
Accursed Bajazeth, whose words of ruth,
That would with pity cheer Zabina's heart,
And make our souls resolve in ceaseless tears,
Sharp hunger bites upon and gripes the root                    210
From whence the issue of my thoughts do break!
O poor Zabina! O my queen, my queen!
Fetch me some water for my burning breast,
To cool and comfort me with longer date,
That, in the shorten'd sequel of my life,
I may pour forth my soul into thine arms
With words of love, whose moaning intercourse

Hath hitherto been stay'd with wrath and hate
Of our expressless bann'd inflictions.

ZABINA  Sweet Bajazeth, I will prolong thy life          220
As long as any blood or spark of breath
Can quench or cool the torments of my grief.     [*exit*

BAJAZETH  Now, Bajazeth, abridge thy baneful days,
And beat the brains out of thy conquer'd head,
Since other means are all forbidden me
That may be ministers of my decay.
O highest lamp of ever-living Jove,
Accursed day, infected with my griefs,
Hide now thy stained face in endless night,
And shut the windows of the lightsome heavens!          230
Let ugly Darkness with her rusty coach,
Engirt with tempests, wrapt in pitchy clouds,
Smother the earth with never-fading mists.
And let her horses from their nostrils breathe
Rebellious winds and dreadful thunder-claps,
That in this terror Tamburlaine may live,
And my pin'd soul, resolv'd in liquid air,
May still excruciate his tormented thoughts!
Then let the stony dart of senseless cold
Pierce through the centre of my wither'd heart,          240
And make a passage for my loathed life!
                    [*he brains himself against the cage*

                *Re-enter* ZABINA

ZABINA  What do mine eyes behold? My husband dead!
His skull all riven in twain! His brains dash'd out,
The brains of Bajazeth, my lord and sovereign!
O Bajazeth, my husband and my lord!
O Bajazeth! O Turk! O emperor!
    Give him his liquor? Not I. Bring milk and fire, and
my blood I bring him again — Tear me in pieces — Give
me the sword with a ball of wild-fire upon it — Down
with him! Down with him! Go to my child; away,
away, away! Ah, save that infant! Save him, save him! I,
even I, speak to her — The sun was down — Streamers
white, red, black — Here, here, here! Fling the meat in

his face – Tamburlaine, Tamburlaine! Let the soldiers be
buried – Hell, death, Tamburlaine, hell! Make ready my
coach, my chair, my jewels – I come, I come, I come!

           [*she runs against the cage, and brains herself*

          *Enter* ZENOCRATE *with* ANIPPE

ZENOCR.    Wretched Zenocrate! That liv'st to see
           Damascus' walls dy'd with Egyptians' blood,
           Thy father's subjects and thy countrymen;
           The streets strow'd with dissever'd joints of men,    260
           And wounded bodies gasping yet for life;
           But most accurs'd, to see the sun-bright troop
           Of heavenly virgins and unspotted maids
           (Whose looks might make the angry god of arms
           To break his sword and mildly treat of love)
           On horsemen's lances to be hoisted up,
           And guiltlessly endure a cruel death;
           For every fell and stout Tartarian steed,
           That stamp'd on others with their thundering hoofs,
           When all their riders charg'd their quivering spears,
           Began to check the ground and rein themselves,
           Gazing upon the beauty of their looks.
           Ah, Tamburlaine, wert thou the cause of this,
           That term'st Zenocrate thy dearest love?
           Whose lives were dearer to Zenocrate
           Than her own life, or aught save thine own love.
           But see, another bloody spectacle!
           Ah, wretched eyes, the enemies of my heart,
           How are ye glutted with these grievous objects,
           And tell my soul more tales of bleeding ruth!      280
           See, see, Anippe, if they breathe or no.

ANIPPE    No breath, nor sense, nor motion, in them both:
           Ah, madam, this their slavery hath enforc'd,
           And ruthless cruelty of Tamburlaine!

ZENOCR.    Earth, cast up fountains from thy entrails,
           And wet thy cheeks for their untimely deaths;
           Shake with their weight in sign of fear and grief!
           Blush, heaven, that gave them honour at their birth,
           And let them die a death so barbarous!

Those that are proud of fickle empery 290
And place their chiefest good in earthly pomp,
Behold the Turk and his great emperess!
Ah, Tamburlaine my love, sweet Tamburlaine,
That fight'st for sceptres and for slippery crowns,
Behold the Turk and his great emperess!
Thou that, in conduct of thy happy stars,
Sleep'st every night with conquest on thy brows,
And yet wouldst shun the wavering turns of war,
In fear and feeling of the like distress,
Behold the Turk and his great emperess! 300
Ah, mighty Jove and holy Mahomet,
Pardon my love! O, pardon his contempt
Of earthly fortune and respect of pity;
And let not conquest, ruthlessly pursu'd,
Be equally against his life incens'd
In this great Turk and hapless emperess!
And pardon me that was not mov'd with ruth
To see them live so long in misery!
Ah, what may chance to thee, Zenocrate?

ANIPPE    Madam, content yourself, and be resolv'd, 310
Your love hath Fortune so at his command,
That she shall stay, and turn her wheel no more,
As long as life maintains his mighty arm
That fights for honour to adorn your head.

*Enter* PHILEMUS

ZENOCR.    What other heavy news now brings Philemus?
PHILEMUS    Madam, your father, and the Arabian king,
The first affecter of your excellence,
Come now, as Turnus 'gainst Aeneas did,
Armed with lance into the Aegyptian fields,
Ready for battle 'gainst my lord the king. 320
ZENOCR.    Now shame and duty, love and fear present
A thousand sorrows to my martyr'd soul.
Whom should I wish the fatal victory,
When my poor pleasures are divided thus,
And rack'd by duty from my cursed heart?
My father and my first-betrothed love

Must fight against my life and present love;
Wherein the change I use condemns my faith,
And makes my deeds infamous through the world:
But, as the gods, to end the Trojans' toil,                          330
Prevented Turnus of Lavinia,
And fatally enrich'd Aeneas' love,
So, for a final issue to my griefs,
To pacify my country and my love,
Must Tamburlaine by their resistless powers,
With virtue of a gentle victory,
Conclude a league of honour to my hope;
Then, as the powers divine have pre-ordain'd,
With happy safety of my father's life
Send like defence of fair Arabia.                                    340

    [*they sound to the battle within; and Tamburlaine enjoys*
    *the victory: after which, the King of Arabia enters wounded*

ARABIA    What cursed power guides the murdering hands
Of this infamous tyrant's soldiers,
That no escape may save their enemies,
Nor fortune keep themselves from victory?
Lie down, Arabia, wounded to the death,
And let Zenocrate's fair eyes behold,
That, as for her thou bear'st these wretched arms,
Even so for her thou diest in these arms,
Leaving thy blood for witness of thy love.

ZENOCR.    Too dear a witness for such love, my lord!                  350
Behold Zenocrate, the cursed object
Whose fortunes never mastered her griefs;
Behold her wounded in conceit for thee,
As much as thy fair body is for me!

ARABIA    Then shall I die with full contented heart,
Having beheld divine Zenocrate,
Whose sight with joy would take away my life
As now it bringeth sweetness to my wound,
If I had not been wounded as I am.
Ah, that the deadly pangs I suffer now                               360
Would lend an hour's licence to my tongue,
To make discourse of some sweet accidents
Have chanc'd thy merits in this worthless bondage,

And that I might be privy to the state
Of thy deserv'd contentment and thy love!
But, making now a virtue of thy sight,
To drive all sorrow from my fainting soul,
Since death denies me further cause of joy,
Depriv'd of care, my heart with comfort dies,
Since thy desired hand shall close mine eyes.          370

[dies

*Re-enter* TAMBURLAINE, *leading the* SOLDAN; TECHELLES,
THERIDAMAS, USUMCASANE, *with others*

TAMBUR.   Come, happy father of Zenocrate,
A title higher than thy Soldan's name.
Though my right hand have thus enthralled thee,
Thy princely daughter here shall set thee free:
She that hath calm d the fury of my sword,
Which had ere this been bath'd in streams of blood
As vast and deep as Euphrates or Nile.

ZENOCR.   O sight thrice-welcome to my joyful soul,
To see the king, my father, issue safe
From dangerous battle of my conquering love!          380

SOLDAN   Well met, my only dear Zenocrate,
Though with the loss of Egypt and my crown!

TAMBUR.   'Twas I, my lord, that gat the victory;
And therefore grieve not at your overthrow,
Since I shall render all into your hands
And add more strength to your dominions
Than ever yet confirm'd th' Egyptian crown.
The god of war resigns his room to me,
Meaning to make me general of the world:
Jove, viewing me in arms, looks pale and wan,          390
Fearing my power should pull him from his throne:
Where'er I come the Fatal Sisters sweat,
And grisly Death, by running to and fro,
To do their ceaseless homage to my sword:
And here in Afric, where it seldom rains,
Since I arriv'd with my triumphant host,
Have swelling clouds, drawn from
                                        wide-gaping wounds,

Been oft resolv'd in bloody purple showers,
A meteor that might terrify the earth,
And make it quake at every drop it drinks:                    400
Millions of souls sit on the banks of Styx,
Waiting the back-return of Charon's boat;
Hell and Elysium swarm with ghosts of men
That I have sent from sundry foughten fields
To spread my fame through hell and up to heaven:
And see, my lord, a sight of strange import –
Emperors and kings lie breathless at my feet;
The Turk and his great empress, as it seems,
Left to themselves while we were at the fight,
Have desperately despatch'd their slavish lives:            410
With them Arabia, too, hath left his life:
All sights of power to grace my victory;
And such are objects fit for Tamburlaine.
Wherein, as in a mirror, may be seen
His honour, that consists in shedding blood
When men presume to manage arms with him.

SOLDAN    Mighty hath God and Mahomet made thy hand,
Renowmed Tamburlaine, to whom all kings
Of force must yield their crowns and emperies;
And I am pleas'd with this my overthrow,                    420
If, as beseems a person of thy state,
Thou hast with honour us'd Zenocrate.

TAMBUR.   Her state and person want no pomp, you see;
And for all blot of foul inchastity,
I record heaven, her heavenly self is clear:
Then let me find no further time to grace
Her princely temples with the Persian crown;
But here these kings that on my fortunes wait,
And have been crowned for proved worthiness
Even by this hand that shall establish them,                 430
Shall now, adjoining all their hands with mine,
Invest her here the Queen of Persia.
What saith the noble Soldan, and Zenocrate?

SOLDAN    I yield with thanks and protestations
Of endless honour to thee for her love.

TAMBUR.   Then doubt I not but fair Zenocrate

Will soon consent to satisfy us both.

ZENOCR.    Else should I much forget myself, my lord.

THERID.    Then let us set the crown upon her head,
That long hath linger'd for so high a seat.                    440

TECHELLES My hand is ready to perform the deed;
For now her marriage-time shall work us rest.

USUMCAS. And here's the crown, my lord; help set it on.

TAMBUR.    Then sit thou down, divine Zenocrate;
And here we crown thee Queen of Persia,
And all the kingdoms and dominions
That late the power of Tamburlaine subdu'd.
As Juno, when the giants were suppress'd,
That darted mountains at her brother Jove,
So looks my love, shadowing in her brows             450
Triumphs and trophies for my victories;
Or as Latona's daughter, bent to arms,
Adding more courage to my conquering mind.
To gratify thee, sweet Zenocrate,
Egyptians, Moors, and men of Asia,
From Barbary unto the Western India,
Shall pay a yearly tribute to thy sire;
And from the bounds of Afric to the banks
Of Ganges shall his mighty arm extend –
And now, my lords and loving followers,               460
That purchas'd kingdoms by your martial deeds,
Cast off your armour, put on scarlet robes,
Mount up your royal places of estate,
Environed with troops of noblemen,
And there make laws to rule your provinces:
Hang up your weapons on Alcides' posts;
For Tamburlaine takes truce with all the world –
Thy first-betrothed love, Arabia,
Shall we with honour, as beseems, entomb
With this great Turk and his fair emperess.           470
Then, after all these solemn exequies,
We will our rites of marriage solemnise.

                                                    [exeunt

# THE SECOND PART OF
# TAMBURLAINE THE GREAT

## INTRODUCTION

Part II of *Tamburlaine* was apparently written in response to the overwhelming popularity of Part I: 'the general welcomes Tamburlaine received,/ When he arrived last upon our stage,/ Hath made our poet pen his second part'. The language of the prologue suggests that the stage was one further piece of territory over which the conqueror has asserted his inexorable power. It seems likely that it was written within months of the first play, although the events it represents are separated by some span of years from those of Part I: Tamburlaine's sons, unborn in the previous play, are now grown men. As with many sequels, it may be thought to suffer by contrast with its inevitably more arresting predecessor, overshadowed by the memory of previous success but unable quite to reconstruct the winning formula. Some critics, however, have attempted to run the plays together as one epic ten-act drama, in which a conventional providential order asserts itself in the downfall of its vaunting protagonist. The title page of the 1590 edition of both plays gives some support to this conception of a single play, as it gives one title, *Tamburlaine the Great*, and describes the work as 'divided into two tragical discourses, as they were sundry times showed upon stages in the city of London'. But while the prologue to this play tells us what is going to happen as the 'murd'rous Fates throws all his triumphs down', it is not, in fact, ultimately clear that Tamburlaine's eclipse is managed by such powers. At the beginning of the second play, Tamburlaine's subordinates are reintroduced, now crowned kings of parts of his vast empire, offering troops for his latest offensive. Most of the play is concerned with the continuation of his conquests, including the memorable image of his ride through Babylon in a chariot

dragged by the defeated monarchs, in a stage picture which was
often evoked in contemporary literature by the quotation 'holla,
ye pampered jades of Asia' (4.3). Zenocrate dies, and the play
ends with the death of Tamburlaine himself. This is not
necessarily the fulfilment of Part I's frustrated tragic momentum,
however. He dies a noble death, with the body of Zenocrate at
his side, in the mirror image of their departure towards their
marriage at the end of Part I, and the play's final words are his
fitting epitaph: 'let earth and heaven his timeless death deplore,/
For both their worths will equal him no more.' The end of the
play proves that Tamburlaine was in fact mortal, rather than that
his proud challenge to fate was his downfall. It is only death, not
any other human, which can defeat him.

Tamburlaine's self-proclaimed status as the 'scourge of God'
encapsulates a contradiction in his character: is he acting as the
mechanism of a deity or in challenge to that deity – scourging on
behalf of God or scourging God himself? This conflict is contained
in Part I, but becomes increasingly evident in Part II. Now
Tamburlaine's enemies are not the lords of exotic Eastern provinces but European monarchs, and the counter-attack is figured as
a Christian battle against barbarous forces. Tamburlaine's inner
contradictions threaten to sap his invincibility. Key to this is
the death of Zenocrate, who acted as a stabilising and tempering
influence in Part I, proposing an alternative of compassion to his
ruthless self-assertion. Her first speech in the second play is to
beseech her husband to give up war. Tamburlaine cannot accept
her death, encasing her body in a shroud of sheet gold and bearing
it on his conquests. It seems that her death brings an awareness of
mortality: Tamburlaine seems more careworn, simply older, in this
play, and it is significant that his efforts at self-projection turn to his
three sons. Late Elizabethan culture was preoccupied by the question of succession, and the ageing Tamburlaine is, in this respect at
least, a kind of Elizabeth. Celebinus and Amyras are in their father's
mould, but what seemed awe-inspiring in him seems puppyish in
them: 'I would strive to swim through pools of blood [ . . . ] Ere I
would lose the title of a king', (1.3), states Amyras, and the rhetoric
is ratcheted up to be more terrifying, succeeding instead in relaying
its hollowness. The rebellion of Calyphas, the third son, is a refusal
to live by the father's lights, rather than an opposition to his power

on the same terms, and for this, he is killed by Tamburlaine. However, in a departure from his source material, Marlowe has the succession proceed without dissent: Tamburlaine bequeaths the spoils of his depredations to his sons without dispute, and sees his son crowned before he dies. It is difficult, then, to read into Tamburlaine's death a punishment for his earlier ambition.

It is only death which halts his progress. Zenocrate's death marks a turning point, as his great war train is deployed in her funerary procession – the might that roared unimpeded across half the world could not keep one woman alive, nor, ultimately, keep death from Tamburlaine himself. Tamburlaine's death, however, like that of Zenocrate, is from natural causes: having lived by the sword, he refuses to fulfil the proverbial logic. But through his sons, as well as through his plays, he has achieved a kind of immortality: 'My flesh, divided in your precious shapes,/ Shall still retain my spirit, though I die,/ And live in all your seeds immortally.' (5.3) It may be that Tamburlaine's last advice to his heir Amyras, urging him not to 'bar thy mind that magnanimity/ That nobly must admit necessity' (5.3.), represents a change in his philosophy, since admitting of necessities – social, political, physical – has been a notable absence in Tamburlaine's own behaviour. Amyras' actions, however, do not suggest that there will be such a change of emphasis, and the play ends with him on his father's imperial throne. Tamburlaine's triumph is undimmed, as he passes on his empire to his eldest son.

# CHARACTERS IN THE PLAY

TAMBURLAINE, *King of Persia*

CALYPHAS
AMYRAS, } *his sons*
CELEBINUS

THERIDAMAS, *King of Argier*

TECHELLES, *King Of Fez*

USUMCASANE, *King of Morocco*

ORCANES, *King of Natolia*

KING OF TREBIZON

KING OF SORIA

KING OF JERUSALEM

KING OF AMASIA

GAZELLUS, *Viceroy of Byron*

URIBASSA

SIGISMUND, *King of Hungary*

FREDERICK } *Lords of Buda and Bohemia*
BALDWIN

CALLAPINE, *son to* BAJAZETH, *and prisoner
to* TAMBURLAINE

ALMEDA, *his keeper*

GOVERNOR OF BABYLON

CAPTAIN OF BALSERA

HIS SON

ANOTHER CAPTAIN

MAXIMUS, PERDICAS, *Physicians, Lords, Citizens,
Messengers, Soldiers and Attendants*

ZENOCRATE, *wife to* TAMBURLAINE

OLYMPIA, *wife to the* CAPTAIN OF BALSERA

*Turkish Concubines*

# THE SECOND PART OF
# TAMBURLAINE THE GREAT

## THE PROLOGUE

The general welcomes Tamburlaine receiv'd,
When he arrived last upon the stage,
Have made our poet pen his Second Part,
Where death cuts off the progress of his pomp,
And murderous Fates throw all his triumphs down.
But what became of fair Zenocrate,
And with how many cities' sacrifice
He celebrated her sad funeral,
Himself in presence shall unfold at large.

## ACT ONE

### SCENE I

*Enter* ORCANES *king of Natolia,* GAZELLUS *viceroy of Byron,*
URIBASSA, *and their train, with drums and trumpets*

ORCANES    Egregious viceroys of these eastern parts,
Plac'd by the issue of great Bajazeth,
And sacred lord, the mighty Callapine,
Who lives in Egypt prisoner to that slave
Which kept his father in an iron cage –
Now have we march'd from fair Natolia
Two hundred leagues, and on Danubius' banks
Our warlike host, in complete armour, rest,
Where Sigismund, the king of Hungary,
Should meet our person to conclude a truce:    10
What! Shall we parle with the Christian?
Or cross the stream, and meet him in the field?
GAZELLUS  King of Natolia, let us treat of peace:
We are all glutted with the Christians' blood,

And have a greater foe to fight against –
Proud Tamburlaine, that now in Asia,
Near Guyron's head, doth set his conquering feet,
And means to fire Turkey as he goes:
'Gainst him, my lord, you must address your power.

URIBASSA Besides, King Sigismund hath brought from
                                        Christendom 20
More than his camp of stout Hungarians –
Sclavonians, Almains, Rutters, Muffs, and Danes,
That with the halberd, lance, and murdering axe,
Will hazard that we might with surety hold.

ORCANES Though from the shortest northern parallel,
Vast Grantland, compass'd with the Frozen Sea
(Inhabited with tall and sturdy men,
Giants as big as hugy Polypheme),
Millions of soldiers cut the arctic line,
Bringing the strength of Europe to these arms,          30
Our Turkey blades shall glide through all their throats,
And make this champion mead a bloody fen:
Danubius' stream, that runs to Trebizon,
Shall carry, wrapt within his scarlet waves,
As martial presents to our friends at home,
The slaughter'd bodies of these Christians:
The Terrene main, wherein Danubius' falls,
Shall by this battle be the bloody sea:
The wandering sailors of proud Italy
Shall meet those Christians, fleeting with the tide,     40
Beating in heaps against their argosies,
And make fair Europe, mounted on her bull,
Trapp'd with the wealth and riches of the world,
Alight, and wear a woful mourning weed.

GAZELLUS Yet, stout Orcanes, pro-rex of the world,
Since Tamburlaine hath muster'd all his men,
Marching from Cairo northward with his camp,
To Alexandria and the frontier towns,
Meaning to make a conquest of our land,
'Tis requisite to parle for a peace                      50
With Sigismund, the king of Hungary,
And save our forces for the hot assaults

Proud Tamburlaine intends Natolia.
ORCANES  Viceroy of Byron, wisely hast thou said.
My realm, the centre of our empery,
Once lost, all Turkey would be overthrown;
And for that cause the Christians shall have peace.
Sclavonians, Almains, Rutters, Muffs, and Danes,
Fear not Orcanes, but great Tamburlaine;
Nor he, but Fortune that hath made him great.　　60
We have revolted Grecians, Albanese,
Sicilians, Jews, Arabians, Turks, and Moors,
Natolians, Sorians, black Egyptians,
Illyrians, Thracians, and Bithynians,
Enough to swallow forceless Sigismund,
Yet scarce enough t'encounter Tamburlaine.
He brings a world of people to the field,
From Scythia to the oriental plage
Of India, where raging Lantchidol
Beats on the regions with his boisterous blows,　　70
That never seaman yet discovered.
All Asia is in arms with Tamburlaine,
Even from the midst of fiery Cancer's tropic
To Amazonia under Capricorn;
And thence, as far as Archipelago,
All Afric is in arms with Tamburlaine:
Therefore, viceroy, the Christians must have peace.


SCENE 2

*Enter* SIGISMUND, FREDERICK, BALDWIN,
*and their train, with drums and trumpets*

SIGISMUND  Orcanes, (as our legates promis'd thee)
We with our peers, have cross'd Danubius' stream,
To treat of friendly peace or deadly war.
Take which thou wilt; for, as the Romans us'd,
I here present thee with a naked sword:
Wilt thou have war, then shake this blade at me;
If peace, restore it to my hands again,
And I will sheathe it, to confirm the same.

ORCANES     Stay, Sigismund; forgett'st thou I am he
            That with the cannon shook Vienna-walls,                      10
            And made it dance upon the continent,
            As when the massy substance of the earth
            Quivers about the axle-tree of heaven?
            Forgett'st thou that I sent a shower of darts,
            Mingled with powder'd shot and feather'd steel,
            So thick upon the blink-ey'd burghers' heads,
            That thou thyself, then County Palatine,
            The King of Boheme, and the Austric Duke,
            Sent heralds out, which basely on their knees,
            In all your names, desir'd a truce of me?                     20
            Forgett'st thou that, to have me raise my siege,
            Waggons of gold were set before my tent,
            Stampt with the princely fowl that in her wings
            Carries the fearful thunderbolts of Jove?
            How canst thou think of this, and offer war?
SIGISMUND   Vienna was besieg'd, and I was there,
            Then County Palatine, but now a king,
            And what we did was in extremity.
            But now, Orcanes, view my royal host,
            That hides these plains, and seems as vast and wide  30
            As doth the desert of Arabia
            To those that stand on Bagdet's lofty tower,
            Or as the ocean to the traveller
            That rests upon the snowy Appenines;
            And tell me whether I should stoop so low,
            Or treat of peace with the Natolian king.
GAZELLUS    Kings of Natolia and of Hungary,
            We came from Turkey to confirm a league,
            And not to dare each other to the field.
            A friendly parle might become you both.                       40
FREDERICK   And we from Europe, to the same intent;
            Which if your general refuse or scorn,
            Our tents are pitch'd, our men stand in array,
            Ready to charge you ere you stir your feet.
ORCANES     So prest are we: but yet, if Sigismund
            Speak as a friend, and stand not upon terms,
            Here is his sword; let peace be ratified

On these conditions specified before,
Drawn with advice of our ambassadors.

SIGISMUND Then here I sheathe it, and give thee my hand    50
Never to draw it out, or manage arms
Against thyself or thy confederates,
But, whilst I live, will be at truce with thee.

ORCANES But, Sigismund, confirm it with an oath,
And swear in sight of heaven and by thy Christ.

SIGISMUND By Him that made the world and sav'd my soul,
The Son of God and issue of a maid,
Sweet Jesus Christ, I solemnly protest
And vow to keep this peace inviolable!

ORCANES By sacred Mahomet, the friend of God,    60
Whose holy Alcoran remains with us,
Whose glorious body, when he left the world,
Clos'd in a coffin mounted up the air,
And hung on stately Mecca's temple-roof,
I swear to keep this truce inviolable!
Of whose conditions and our solemn oaths,
Sign'd with our hands, each shall retain a scroll,
As memorable witness of our league.
Now, Sigismund, if any Christian king
Encroach upon the confines of thy realm,    70
Send word, Orcanes of Natolia
Confirm'd this league beyond Danubius' stream,
And they will, trembling, sound a quick retreat;
So am I fear'd among all nations.

SIGISMUND If any heathen potentate or king
Invade Natolia, Sigismund will send
A hundred thousand horse train'd to the war,
And back'd by stout lanciers of Germany,
The strength and sinews of the imperial seat.

ORCANES I thank thee, Sigismund; but, when I war,    80
All Asia Minor, Africa, and Greece,
Follow my standard and my thundering drums.
Come, let us go and banquet in our tents:
I will despatch chief of my army hence
To fair Natolia and to Trebizon,
To stay my coming 'gainst proud Tamburlaine:

Friend Sigismund, and peers of Hungary,
Come, banquet and carouse with us a while,
And then depart we to our territories.

[*exeunt*


### SCENE 3

*Enter* CALLAPINE, *and* ALMEDA *his keeper*

CALLAPINE  Sweet Almeda, pity the ruthful plight
　　　　　Of Callapine, the son of Bajazeth,
　　　　　Born to be monarch of the western world,
　　　　　Yet here detain'd by cruel Tamburlaine.

ALMEDA  My lord, I pity it, and with my heart
　　　　Wish your release; but he whose wrath is death,
　　　　My sovereign lord, renowmed Tamburlaine,
　　　　Forbids you further liberty than this.

CALLAPINE  Ah, were I now but half so eloquent
　　　　　To paint in words what I'll perform in deeds,      10
　　　　　I know thou wouldst depart from hence with me!

ALMEDA  Not for all Afric: therefore move me not.

CALLAPINE  Yet hear me speak, my gentle Almeda.

ALMEDA  No speech to that end, by your favour, sir.

CALLAPINE  By Cairo runs –

ALMEDA  No talk of running, I tell you, sir.

CALLAPINE  A little further, gentle Almeda.

ALMEDA  Well, sir, what of this?

CALLAPINE  By Cairo runs to Alexandria-bay
　　　　　Darotes' stream, wherein at anchor lies      20
　　　　　A Turkish galley of my royal fleet,
　　　　　Waiting my coming to the river-side,
　　　　　Hoping by some means I shall be releas'd:
　　　　　Which, when I come aboard, will hoist up sail,
　　　　　And soon put forth into the Terrene sea,
　　　　　Where, 'twixt the isles of Cyprus and of Crete,
　　　　　We quickly may in Turkish seas arrive.
　　　　　Then shalt thou see a hundred kings and more,
　　　　　Upon their knees, all bid me welcome home.
　　　　　Amongst so many crowns of burnish'd gold,      30

          Choose which thou wilt, all are at thy command:
          A thousand galleys, mann'd with Christian slaves,
          I freely give thee, which shall cut the Straits,
          And bring armadoes, from the coasts of Spain,
          Fraughted with gold of rich America:
          The Grecian virgins shall attend on thee,
          Skilful in music and in amorous lays,
          As fair as was Pygmalion's ivory girl
          Or lovely Iö metamorphosed:
          With naked negroes shall thy coach be drawn,      40
          And, as thou rid'st in triumph through the streets,
          The pavement underneath thy chariot-wheels
          With Turkey-carpets will be covered,
          And cloth of arras hung about the walls,
          Fit objects for thy princely eye to pierce:
          A hundred bassoes, cloth'd in crimson silk,
          Shall ride before thee on Barbarian steeds;
          And, when thou goest, a golden canopy
          Enchas'd with precious stones, which shine as bright
          As that fair veil that covers all the world,      50
          When Phoebus, leaping from his hemisphere,
          Descendeth downward to th'Antipodes –
          And more than this, for all I cannot tell.

ALMEDA      How far hence lies the galley, say you?

CALLAPINE      Sweet Almeda, scarce half a league from hence.

ALMEDA      But need we not be spied going aboard?

CALLAPINE      Betwixt the hollow hanging of a hill,
          And crooked bending of a craggy rock,
          The sails wrapt up, the mast and tacklings down,
          She lies so close that none can find her out.      60

ALMEDA      I like that well: but, tell me, my lord, if I should let you
          go, would you be as good as your word? Shall I be made
          a king for my labour?

CALLAPINE      As I am Callapine the emperor,
          And by the hand of Mahomet I swear,
          Thou shalt be crown'd a king, and be my mate!

ALMEDA      Then here I swear, as I am Almeda,
          Your keeper under Tamburlaine the Great
          (For that's the style and title I have yet),

> Although he sent a thousand armed men                    70
> To intercept this haughty enterprise,
> Yet would I venture to conduct your grace,
> And die before I brought you back again!

CALLAPINE  Thanks, gentle Almeda: then let us haste,
> Lest time be past, and lingering let us both.

ALMEDA    When you will, my lord: I am ready.

CALLAPINE  Even straight – and farewell, cursed Tamburlaine!
> Now go I to revenge my father's death.

> > > > > *[exeunt*


## SCENE 4

*Enter* TAMBURLAINE, ZENOCRATE, *and their three sons,* CALYPHAS,
AMYRAS, *and* CELEBINUS, *with drums and trumpets*

TAMBUR.   Now, bright Zenocrate, the world's fair eye,
> Whose beams illuminate the lamps of heaven,
> Whose cheerful looks do clear the cloudy air,
> And clothe it in a crystal livery,
> Now rest thee here on fair Larissa-plains,
> Where Egypt and the Turkish empire part
> Between thy sons, that shall be emperors,
> And every one commander of a world.

ZENOCR.   Sweet Tamburlaine, when wilt thou leave these arms,
> And save thy sacred person free from scathe,       10
> And dangerous chances of the wrathful war?

TAMBUR.   When heaven shall cease to move on both the poles,
> And when the ground, whereon my soldiers march,
> Shall rise aloft and touch the horned moon;
> And not before, my sweet Zenocrate.
> Sit up, and rest thee like a lovely queen.
> So; now she sits in pomp and majesty,
> When these, my sons, more precious in mine eyes
> Than all the wealthy kingdoms I subdu'd,
> Plac'd by her side, look on their mother's face.    20
> But yet methinks their looks are amorous,
> Not martial as the sons of Tamburlaine:
> Water and air, being symbolis'd in one,
> Argue their want of courage and of wit;

Their hair as white as milk, and soft as down
(Which should be like the quills of porcupines,
As black as jet, and hard as iron or steel),
Bewrays they are too dainty for the wars,
Their fingers made to quaver on a lute,
Their arms to hang about a lady's neck,     30
Their legs to dance and caper in the air,
Would make me think them bastards, not my sons,
But that I know they issu'd from thy womb,
That never look'd on man but Tamburlaine.

ZENOCR. My gracious lord, they have their mother's looks,
But, when they list, their conquering father's heart.
This lovely boy, the youngest of the three,
Not long ago bestrid a Scythian steed,
Trotting the ring, and tilting at a glove,
Which when he tainted with his slender rod,     40
He rein'd him straight, and made him so curvet
As I cried out for fear he should have faln.

TAMBUR. Well done, my boy! Thou shalt have shield and lance,
Armour of proof, horse, helm, and curtle-axe,
And I will teach thee how to charge thy foe,
And harmless run among the deadly pikes.
If thou wilt love the wars and follow me,
Thou shalt be made a king and reign with me,
Keeping in iron cages emperors.
If thou exceed thy elder brothers' worth,     50
And shine in complete virtue more than they,
Thou shalt be king before them, and thy seed
Shall issue crowned from their mother's womb.

CELEBINUS Yes, father; you shall see me, if I live,
Have under me as many kings as you,
And march with such a multitude of men
As all the world shall tremble at their view.

TAMBUR. These words assure me, boy, thou art my son.
When I am old and cannot manage arms,
Be thou the scourge and terror of the world.     60

AMYRAS Why may not I, my lord, as well as he,
Be term'd the scourge and terror of the world?

TAMBUR. Be all a scourge and terror to the world,

Or else you are not sons of Tamburlaine.

CALYPHAS  But while my brothers follow arms, my lord,
Let me accompany my gracious mother:
They are enough to conquer all the world,
And you have won enough for me to keep.

TAMBUR.  Bastardly boy, sprung from some coward's loins,
And not the issue of great Tamburlaine!          70
Of all the provinces I have subdu'd
Thou shalt not have a foot, unless thou bear
A mind courageous and invincible;
For he shall wear the crown of Persia
Whose head hath deepest scars, whose breast
                                        most wounds,
Which, being wroth, sends lightning from his eyes,
And in the furrows of his frowning brows
Harbours revenge, war, death, and cruelty;
For in a field, whose superficies
Is cover'd with a liquid purple veil,          80
And sprinkled with the brains of slaughter'd men,
My royal chair of state shall be advanc'd;
And he that means to place himself therein,
Must armed wade up to the chin in blood.

ZENOCR.  My lord, such speeches to our princely sons
Dismay their minds before they come to prove
The wounding troubles angry war affords.

CELEBINUS No, madam, these are speeches fit for us;
For, if his chair were in a sea of blood,
I would prepare a ship and sail to it,          90
Ere I would lose the title of a king.

AMYRAS  And I would strive to swim through pools of blood
Or make a bridge of murder'd carcasses,
Whose arches should be fram'd with bones of Turks,
Ere I would lose the title of a king.

TAMBUR.  Well, lovely boys, ye shall be emperors both,
Stretching your conquering arms from east to west –
And, sirrah, if you mean to wear a crown,
When we shall meet the Turkish deputy
And all his viceroys, snatch it from his head,          100
And cleave his pericranion with thy sword.

CALYPHAS  If any man will hold him, I will strike,
          And cleave him to the channel with my sword.
TAMBUR.  Hold him, and cleave him too, or I'll cleave thee;
          For we will march against them presently.
          Theridamas, Techelles, and Casane
          Promis'd to meet me on Larissa-plains,
          With hosts a-piece against this Turkish crew;
          For I have sworn by sacred Mahomet
          To make it parcel of my empery.        100
          The trumpets sound; Zenocrate, they come

*Enter* THERIDAMAS, *and his train, with drums and trumpets*

          Welcome Theridamas, king of Argier.
THERID.  My lord, the great and mighty Tamburlaine,
          Arch-monarch of the world, I offer here
          My crown, myself, and all the power I have,
          In all affection at thy kingly feet.
TAMBUR.  Thanks, good Theridamas.
THERID.  Under my colours march ten thousand Greeks,
          And of Argier and Afric's frontier towns
          Twice twenty thousand valiant men-at-arms,    110
          All which have sworn to sack Natolia.
          Five hundred brigandines are under sail,
          Meet for your service on the sea, my lord,
          That, launching from Argier to Tripoly,
          Will quickly ride before Natolia,
          And batter down the castles on the shore,
TAMBUR.  Well said, Argier! Receive thy crown again.

*Enter* USUMCASANE and TECHELLES

          Kings of Morocco and of Fez, welcome.
USUMCAS.  Magnificent and peerless Tamburlaine,
          I and my neighbour king of Fez have brought,    120
          To aid thee in this Turkish expedition,
          A hundred thousand expert soldiers;
          From Azamor to Tunis near the sea
          Is Barbary unpeopled for thy sake,
          And all the men, in armour under me,
          Which with my crown, I gladly offer thee.
TAMBUR.  Thanks, king of Morocco: take your crown again.

TECHELLES And, mighty Tamburlaine, our earthly god,
Whose looks make this inferior world to quake,
I here present thee with the crown of Fez,                    130
And with an host of Moors train'd to the war,
Whose coal-black faces make their foes retire,
And quake for fear, as if infernal Jove,
Meaning to aid thee in these Turkish arms,
Should pierce the black circumference of hell,
With ugly Furies bearing fiery flags,
And millions of his strong tormenting spirits:
From strong Tesella unto Biledull
All Barbary is unpeopled for thy sake.

TAMBUR.   Thanks, king of Fez: take here thy crown again.    140
Your presence, loving friends and fellow-kings,
Makes me to surfeit in conceiving joy:
If all the crystal gates of Jove's high court
Were open'd wide, and I might enter in
To see the state and majesty of heaven,
It could not more delight me than your sight.
Now will we banquet on these plains a while,
And after march to Turkey with our camp,
In number more than are the drops that fall
When Boreas rents a thousand swelling clouds;               150
And proud Orcanes of Natolia
With all his viceroys shall be so afraid,
That, though the stones, as at Deucalion's flood,
Were turn'd to men, he should be overcome.
Such lavish will I make of Turkish blood
That Jove shall send his winged messenger
To bid me sheathe my sword and leave the field;
The sun, unable to sustain the sight,
Shall hide his head in Thetis' watery lap,
And leave his steeds to fair Boötes' charge;               160
For half the world shall perish in this fight.
But now, my friends, let me examine ye;
How have ye spent your absent time from me?

USUMCAS.  My lord, our men of Barbary have march'd
Four hundred miles with armour on their backs,
And lain in leaguer fifteen months and more;

For, since we left you at the Soldan's court,
We have subdu'd the southern Guallatia,
And all the land unto the coast of Spain;
We kept the narrow Strait of Jubalter,   170
And made Canaria call us kings and lords:
Yet never did they recreate themselves,
Or cease one day from war and hot alarms;
And therefore let them rest a while, my lord.

TAMBUR. They shall, Casane, and 'tis time, i'faith.

TECHELLES And I have march'd along the river Nile

To Machda, where the mighty Christian priest,
Call'd John the Great, sits in a milk-white robe,
Whose triple mitre I did take by force,
And made him swear obedience to my crown.  180
From thence unto Cazates did I march,
Where Amazonians met me in the field,
With whom, being women, I vouchsaf'd a league,
And with my power did march to Zanzibar,
The western part of Afric, where I view'd
The Ethiopian sea, rivers and lakes,
But neither man nor child in all the land:
Therefore I took my course to Manico,
Where, unresisted, I remov'd my camp;
And, by the coast of Byather, at last   190
I came to Cubar, where the negroes dwell,
And, conquering that, made haste to Nubia.
There, having sack'd Borno, the kingly seat,
I took the king and led him bound in chains
Unto Damascus, where I stay'd before.

TAMBUR. Well done, Techelles! What saith Theridamas?

THERID. I left the confines and the bounds of Afric,

And made a voyage into Europe,
Where, by the river Tyras, I subdu'd
Stoka, Podolia, and Codemia;   200
Then cross'd the sea and came to Oblia,
And Nigra Silva, where the devils dance,
Which, in despite of them, I set on fire.
From thence I cross'd the gulf call'd by the name
Mare Majore of the inhabitants.

Yet shall my soldiers make no period
Until Natolia kneel before your feet.

TAMBUR.   Then will we triumph, banquet, and carouse;
Cooks shall have pensions to provide us cates,
And glut us with the dainties of the world;                210
Lachryma Christi and Calabrian wines
Shall common soldiers drink in quaffing bowls,
Ay, liquid gold, when we have conquer d him.
Mingled with coral and with orient pearl.
Come, let us banquet and carouse the whiles.

                                                    [exeunt

# ACT TWO

## SCENE I

*Enter* SIGISMUND, FREDERICK, *and* BALDWIN, *with their train*

SIGISMUND  Now say, my lords of Buda and Bohemia,
What motion is it that inflames your thoughts,
And stirs your valours to such sudden arms?

FREDERICK  Your majesty remembers, I am sure,
What cruel slaughter of our Christian bloods
These heathenish Turks and pagans lately made
Betwixt the city Zula and Danubius;
How through the midst of Varna and Bulgaria,
And almost to the very walls of Rome,
They have, not long since, massacred our camp.        10
It resteth now, then, that your majesty
Take all advantages of time and power,
And work revenge upon these infidels.
Your highness knows, for Tamburlaine's repair,
That strikes a terror to all Turkish hearts,
Natolia hath dismiss'd the greatest part
Of all his army, pitch'd against our power
Betwixt Cutheia and Orminius' mount,
And sent them marching up to Belgasar,
Acantha, Antioch, and Caesarea,                       20
To aid the kings of Soria and Jerusalem.
Now, then, my lord, advantage take thereof,
And issue suddenly upon the rest;
That, in the fortune of their overthrow,
We may discourage all the pagan troop
That dare attempt to war with Christians.

SIGISMUND  But calls not, then, your grace to memory
The league we lately made with King Orcanes,
Confirm'd by oath and articles of peace,
And calling Christ for record of our truths?          30
This should be treachery and violence
Against the grace of our profession.

BALDWIN   No whit, my lord; for with such infidels,
          In whom no faith nor true religion rests,
          We are not bound to those accomplishments
          The holy laws of Christendom enjoin;
          But, as the faith which they profanely plight
          Is not by necessary policy
          To be esteem'd assurance for ourselves,
          So that we vow to them should not infringe          40
          Our liberty of arms and victory.

SIGISMUND Though I confess the oaths they undertake
          Breed little strength to our security,
          Yet those infirmities that thus defame
          Their faiths, their honours, and religion,
          Should not give us presumption to the like.
          Our faiths are sound, and must be consummate,
          Religious, righteous, and inviolate.

FREDERICK Assure your grace, 'tis superstition
          To stand so strictly on dispensive faith,          50
          And, should we lose the opportunity
          That God hath given to venge our Christians' death,
          And scourge their foul blasphemous paganism,
          As fell to Saul, to Balaam, and the rest,
          That would not kill and curse at God's command,
          So surely will the vengeance of the Highest,
          And jealous anger of his fearful arm,
          Be pour'd with rigour on our sinful heads,
          If we neglect this offer'd victory.

SIGISMUND Then arm, my lords, and issue suddenly,          60
          Giving commandment to our general host,
          With expedition to assail the pagan,
          And take the victory our God hath given.

                                                  [exeunt

## SCENE 2

*Enter* ORCANES, GAZELLUS, *and* URIBASSA, *with their train*

ORCANES   Gazellus, Uribassa, and the rest,
Now will we march from proud Orminius' mount
To fair Natolia, where our neighbour kings
Expect our power and our royal presence,
T' encounter with the cruel Tamburlaine,
That nigh Larissa sways a mighty host,
And with the thunder of his martial tools
Makes earthquakes in the hearts of men and heaven.

GAZELLUS   And now come we to make his sinews shake
With greater power than erst his pride hath felt.   10
An hundred kings, by scores, will bid him arms,
And hundred thousand subjects to each score:
Which, if a shower of wounding thunderbolts
Should break out of the bowels of the clouds,
And fall as thick as hail upon our heads,
In partial aid of that proud Scythian,
Yet should our courages and steeled crests,
And numbers, more than infinite, of men,
Be able to withstand and conquer him.

URIBASSA   Methinks I see how glad the Christian king   20
Is made for joy of our admitted truce,
That could not but before be terrified
With unacquainted power of our host.

*Enter a Messenger*

MESSENGER   Arm, dread sovereign, and my noble lords!
The treacherous army of the Christians,
Taking advantage of your slender power,
Comes marching on us, and determines straight
To bid us battle for our dearest lives.

ORCANES   Traitors, villains, damned Christians!
Have I not here the articles of peace   30
And solemn covenants we have both confirm'd,
He by his Christ, and I by Mahomet?

GAZELLUS  Hell and confusion light upon their heads,
          That with such treason seek our overthrow,
          And care so little for their prophet Christ!

ORCANES   Can there be such deceit in Christians,
          Or treason in the fleshly heart of man,
          Whose shape is figure of the highest God?
          Then, if there be a Christ, as Christians say,
          But in their deeds deny him for their Christ,          40
          If he be son to everliving Jove,
          And hath the power of his outstretched arm,
          If he be jealous of his name and honour
          As is our holy prophet Mahomet,
          Take here these papers as our sacrifice
          And witness of thy servant's perjury!
                         [*he tears to pieces the articles of peace*
          Open, thou shining veil of Cynthia,
          And make a passage from th' empyreal heaven,
          That he that sits on high and never sleeps,
          Nor in one place is circumscriptible,                  50
          But everywhere fills every continent
          With strange infusion of his sacred vigour,
          May, in his endless power and purity,
          Behold and venge this traitor's perjury!
          Thou, Christ, that art esteem'd omnipotent,
          If thou wilt prove thyself a perfect God,
          Worthy the worship of all faithful hearts,
          Be now reveng'd upon this traitor's soul,
          And make the power I have left behind
          (Too little to defend our guiltless lives)             60
          Sufficient to discomfit and confound
          The trustless force of those false Christians —
          To arms, my lords! On Christ still let us cry:
          If there be Christ, we shall have victory.
                                                   [*exeunt*

## SCENE 3

*Alarms of battle within. Enter* SIGISMUND *wounded*

SIGISMUND Discomfited is all the Christian host,
And God hath thunder'd vengeance from on high,
For my accurs'd and hateful perjury.
O just and dreadful punisher of sin,
Let the dishonour of the pains I feel
In this my mortal well-deserved wound
End all my penance in my sudden death!
And let this death, wherein to sin I die,
Conceive a second life in endless mercy!          [*dies*

*Enter* ORCANES, GAZELLUS, URIBASSA, *with others*

ORCANES  Now lie the Christians bathing in their bloods,          10
And Christ or Mahomet hath been my friend.

GAZELLUS See, here the perjur'd traitor Hungary,
Bloody and breathless for his villany!

ORCANES  Now shall his barbarous body be a prey
To beasts and fowls, and all the winds shall breathe,
Through shady leaves of every senseless tree,
Murmurs and hisses for his heinous sin.
Now scalds his soul in the Tartarian streams,
And feeds upon the baneful tree of hell,
That Zoacum, that fruit of bitterness,          20
That in the midst of fire is ingraff'd,
Yet flourisheth as Flora in her pride,
With apples like the heads of damned fiend.
The devils there, in chains of quenchless flame,
Shall lead his soul, through Orcus' burning gulf,
From pain to pain, whose change shall never end.
What say'st thou yet, Gazellus, to his foil,
Which we referr'd to justice of his Christ
And to his power, which here appears as full
As rays of Cynthia to the clearest sight?          30

GAZELLUS 'Tis but the fortune of the wars, my lord,
Whose power is often prov'd a miracle.

ORCANES   Yet in my thoughts shall Christ be honoured,
          Not doing Mahomet an injury,
          Whose power had share in this our victory;
          And, since this miscreant hath disgrac'd his faith,
          And died a traitor both to heaven and earth,
          We will both watch and ward shall keep his trunk
          Amidst these plains for fowls to prey upon.
          Go, Uribassa, give it straight in charge.          40
URIBASSA  I will, my lord.                              [exit
ORCANES   And now, Gazellus, let us haste and meet
          Our army, and our brothers of Jerusalem,
          Of Soria, Trebizon, and Amasia,
          And happily, with full Natolian bowls
          Of Greekish wine, now let us celebrate
          Our happy conquest and his angry fate.

                                                      [exeunt


                        SCENE 4

          *The arras is drawn, and* ZENOCRATE *is discovered*
          *lying in her bed of state;* TAMBURLAINE *sitting by her;*
          *three physicians about her bed, tempering potions; her*
          *three sons* CALYPHAS, AMYRAS, *and* CELEBINUS;
          THERIDAMAS, TECHELLES *and* USUMCASANE

TAMBUR.   Black is the beauty of the brightest day;
          The golden ball of heaven's eternal fire,
          That danc'd with glory on the silver waves,
          Now wants the fuel that inflam'd his beams;
          And all with faintness, and for foul disgrace,
          He binds his temples with a frowning cloud,
          Ready to darken earth with endless night.
          Zenocrate, that gave him light and life,
          Whose eyes shot fire from their ivory brows,
          And temper'd every soul with lively heat,          10
          Now by the malice of the angry skies,
          Whose jealousy admits no second mate,
          Draws in the comfort of her latest breath,
          All dazzled with the hellish mists of death.

Now walk the angels on the walls of heaven,
As sentinels to warn th' immortal souls
To entertain divine Zenocrate:
Apollo, Cynthia, and the ceaseless lamps
That gently look'd upon this loathsome earth,
Shine downwards now no more, but deck the heavens
To entertain divine Zenocrate:
The crystal springs, whose taste illuminates
Refined eyes with an eternal sight,
Like tried silver run through Paradise
To entertain divine Zenocrate:
The cherubins and holy seraphins,
That sing and play before the King of Kings,
Use all their voices and their instruments
To entertain divine Zenocrate;
And, in this sweet and curious harmony,                    30
The god that tunes this music to our souls
Holds out his hand in highest majesty
To entertain divine Zenocrate.
Then let some holy trance convey my thoughts
Up to the palace of th' empyreal heaven,
That this my life may be as short to me
As are the days of sweet Zenocrate –
Physicians, will no physic do her good?

I PHYS.   My lord, your majesty shall soon perceive,
          And if she pass this fit, the worst is past.      40
TAMBUR.   Tell me, how fares my fair Zenocrate?
ZENOCR.   I fare, my lord, as other empresses,
          That, when this frail and transitory flesh
          Hath suck'd the measure of that vital air
          That feeds the body with his dated health,
          Wane with enforc'd and necessary change.
TAMBUR.   May never such a change transform my love,
          In whose sweet being I repose my life!
          Whose heavenly presence, beautified with health,
          Gives light to Phoebus and the fixed stars;       50
          Whose absence makes the sun and moon as dark
          As when, oppos'd in one diameter,
          Their spheres are mounted on the serpent's head,

Or else descended to his winding train.
Live still, my love, and so conserve my life,
Or, dying, be the author of my death.

ZENOCR.     Live still, my lord; O, let my sovereign live!
And sooner let the fiery element
Dissolve, and make your kingdom in the sky,
Than this base earth should shroud your majesty;     60
For, should I but suspect your death by mine,
The comfort of my future happiness,
And hope to meet your highness in the heavens,
Turn'd to despair, would break my wretched breast,
And fury would confound my present rest.
But let me die, my love; yes, let me die;
With love and patience let your true love die:
Your grief and fury hurts my second life.
Yet let me kiss my lord before I die,
And let me die with kissing of my lord.                70
But, since my life is lengthen'd yet a while,
Let me take leave of these my loving sons,
And of my lords, whose true nobility
Have merited my latest memory.
Sweet sons, farewell! In death resemble me,
And in your lives your father's excellence.
Some music, and my fit will cease, my lord.

                                    [*they call for music*

TAMBUR.     Proud fury, and intolerable fit,
That dares torment the body of my love,
And scourge the scourge of the immortal God!     80
Now are those spheres, where Cupid us'd to sit,
Wounding the world with wonder and with love,
Sadly supplied with pale and ghastly death,
Whose darts do pierce the centre of my soul.
Her sacred beauty hath enchanted heaven;
And, had she liv'd before the siege of Troy,
Helen, whose beauty summon'd Greece to arms,
And drew a thousand ships to Tenedos,
Had not been nam'd in Homer's Iliads –
Her name had been in every line he wrote;           90
Or, had those wanton poets, for whose birth

Old Rome was proud, but gaz'd a while on her,
Nor Lesbia nor Corinna had been nam'd –
Zenocrate had been the argument
Of every epigram or elegy.

[*the music sounds – Zenocrate dies*

What, is she dead? Techelles, draw thy sword,
And wound the earth, that it may cleave in twain,
And we descend into th' infernal vaults,
To hale the Fatal Sisters by the hair,
And throw them in the triple moat of hell,            100
For taking hence my fair Zenocrate.
Casane and Theridamas, to arms!
Raise cavalieros higher than the clouds,
And with the cannon break the frame of heaven;
Batter the shining palace of the sun,
And shiver all the starry firmament,
For amorous Jove hath snatch'd my love from hence,
Meaning to make her stately queen of heaven.
What god soever holds thee in his arms,
Giving thee nectar and ambrosia,                      110
Behold me here, divine Zenocrate,
Raving, impatient, desperate, and mad,
Breaking my steeled lance, with which I burst
The rusty beams of Janus' temple-doors,
Letting out Death and tyrannising War,
To march with me under this bloody flag!
And, if thou pitiest Tamburlaine the Great,
Come down from heaven, and live with me again!

THERID.   Ah, good my lord, be patient! She is dead,
And all this raging cannot make her live.             120
If words might serve, our voice hath rent the air;
If tears, our eyes have water'd all the earth;
If grief, our murder'd hearts have strained forth blood:
Nothing prevails, for she is dead, my lord.

TAMBUR.   *For she is dead!* Thy words do pierce my soul:
Ah, sweet Theridamas, say so no more!
Though she be dead, yet let me think she lives,
And feed my mind that dies for want of her.

Where'er her soul be, thou [*to the body*] shalt stay
                                             with me,
Embalm'd with cassia, ambergris, and myrrh,          130
Not lapt in lead, but in a sheet of gold,
And, till I die, thou shalt not be interr'd.
Then in as rich a tomb as Mausolus'
We both will rest, and have one epitaph
Writ in as many several languages
As I have conquer'd kingdoms with my sword.
This cursed town will I consume with fire,
Because this place bereft me of my love;
The houses, burnt, will look as if they mourn'd;
And here will I set up her stature          140
And march about it with my mourning camp,
Drooping and pining for Zenocrate.
                              [*the arras is drawn*

# ACT THREE

## SCENE I

*Enter the* KINGS OF TREBISON *and* SORIA, *one bringing
a sword and the other a sceptre; next,* ORCANES *king of
Natolia, and the* KING OF JERUSALEM *with the imperial
crown; after,* CALLAPINE; *and, after him, other lords and*
ALMEDA. ORCANES *and the* KING OF JERUSALEM *crown*
CALLAPINE, *and the others give him the sceptre*

ORCANES  Callapinus Cyricelibes, otherwise Cybelius, son and
successive heir to the late mighty emperor Bajazeth, by
the aid of God and his friend Mahomet, Emperor of
Natolia, Jerusalem, Trebizon, Soria, Amasia, Thracia,
Ilyria, Carmania, and all the hundred and thirty kingdoms late contributory to his mighty father – long live
Callapinus, Emperor of Turkey!

CALLAPINE  Thrice-worthy kings, of Natolia and the rest,
I will requite your royal gratitudes
With all the benefits my empire yields;                    10
And, were the sinews of th' imperial seat
So knit and strengthen'd as when Bajazeth,
My royal lord and father, fill'd the throne,
Whose cursed fate hath so dismember'd it,
Then should you see this thief of Scythia,
This proud usurping king of Persia,
Do us such honour and supremacy,
Bearing the vengeance of our father's wrongs,
As all the world should blot his dignities
Out of the book of base-born infamies.                    20
And now I doubt not but your royal cares
Have so provided for this cursed foe,
That, since the heir of mighty Bajazeth
(An emperor so honour'd for his virtues)
Revives the spirits of all true Turkish hearts,
In grievous memory of his father's shame,
We shall not need to nourish any doubt,

But that proud Fortune, who hath follow'd long
The martial sword of mighty Tamburlaine,
Will now retain her old inconstancy,                          30
And raise our honours to as high a pitch,
In this our strong and fortunate encounter;
For so hath heaven provided my escape
From all the cruelty my soul sustain'd,
By this my friendly keeper's happy means,
That Jove, surcharg'd with pity of our wrongs,
Will pour it down in showers on our heads,
Scourging the pride of cursed Tamburlaine.

ORCANES   I have a hundred thousand men in arms;
Some that, in conquest of the perjur'd Christian,          40
Being a handful to a mighty host,
Think them in number yet sufficient
To drink the river Nile or Euphrates,
And for their power enow to win the world.

JERUSALEM And I as many from Jerusalem,
Judaea, Gaza, and Sclavonia's bounds,
That on Mount Sinai, with their ensigns spread,
Look like the parti-colour'd clouds of heaven
That show fair weather to the neighbour morn.

TREBIZON  And I as many bring from Trebizon,                     50
Chio, Famastro, and Amasia,
All bordering on the Mare-Major-sea,
Riso, Sancina, and the bordering towns
That touch the end of famous Euphrates,
Whose courages are kindled with the flames
The cursed Scythian sets on all their towns,
And vow to burn the villain's cruel heart.

SORIA     From Soria with seventy thousand strong,
Ta'en from Aleppo, Soldino, Tripoly,
And so unto my city of Damascus,                             60
I march to meet and aid my neighbour kings;
All which will join against this Tamburlaine,
And bring him captive to your highness' feet.

ORCANES   Our battle, then, in martial manner pitch'd,
According to our ancient use, shall bear
The figure of the semicircled moon,

Whose horns shall sprinkle through the tainted air
The poison'd brains of this proud Scythian.

CALLAPINE Well, then, my noble lords, for this my friend
That freed me from the bondage of my foe,     70
I think it requisite and honourable
To keep my promise and to make him king,
That is a gentleman, I know, at least.

ALMEDA That's no matter, sir, for being a king; for Tamburlaine
came up of nothing.

JERUSALEM Your majesty may choose some 'pointed time,
Performing all your promise to the full;
'Tis naught for your majesty to give a kingdom.

CALLAPINE Then will I shortly keep my promise, Almeda.

ALMEDA Why, I thank your majesty.     80

           [*exeunt*


## SCENE 2

*Enter* TAMBURLAINE *and his three Sons,* CALYPHAS,
AMYRAS, *and* CELEBINUS; USUMCASANE; *four Attendants*
*bearing the hearse of* ZENOCRATE, *and the drums*
*sounding a doleful march; the town burning*

TAMBUR. So burn the turrets of this cursed town,
Flame to the highest region of the air,
And kindle heaps of exhalations,
That, being fiery meteors, may presage
Death and destruction to the inhabitants!
Over my zenith hang a blazing star,
That may endure till heaven be dissolv'd,
Fed with the fresh supply of earthly dregs,
Threatening a dearth and famine to this land!
Flying dragons, lightning, fearful thunderclaps     10
Singe these fair plains, and make them seem as black
As is the island where the Furies mask,
Compass'd with Lethe, Styx, and Phlegethon,
Because my dear Zenocrate is dead!

CALYPHAS This pillar, plac'd in memory of her,
Where in Arabian, Hebrew, Greek, is writ,

> *This town, being burnt by Tamburlaine the Great,*
> *Forbids the world to build it up again.*

AMYRAS     And here this mournful streamer shall be plac'd,
            Wrought with the Persian and th' Egyptian arms,     20
            To signify she was a princess born,
            And wife unto the monarch of the East.

CELEBINUS And here this table as a register
            Of all her virtues and perfections.

TAMBUR.     And here the picture of Zenocrate,
            To show her beauty which the world admir'd:
            Sweet picture of divine Zenocrate,
            That, hanging here, will draw the gods from heaven,
            And cause the stars fix'd in the southern arc
            (Whose lovely faces never any view'd     30
            That have not pass'd the centre's latitude),
            As pilgrims travel to our hemisphere,
            Only to gaze upon Zenocrate.
            Thou shalt not beautify Larissa-plains,
            But keep within the circle of mine arms:
            At every town and castle I besiege,
            Thou shalt be set upon my royal tent;
            And, when I meet an army in the field,
            Those looks will shed such influence in my camp,
            As if Bellona, goddess of the war,     40
            Threw naked swords and sulphur-balls of fire
            Upon the heads of all our enemies –
            And now, my lords, advance your spears again;
            Sorrow no more, my sweet Casane, now:
            Boys, leave to mourn; this town shall ever mourn,
            Being burnt to cinders for your mother's death.

CALYPHAS If I had wept a sea of tears for her,
            It would not ease the sorrows I sustain.

AMYRAS     As is that town, so is my heart consum'd
            With grief and sorrow for my mother's death.     50

CELEBINUS My mother's death hath mortified my mind,
            And sorrow stops the passage of my speech.

TAMBUR.     But now, my boys, leave off, and list to me,
            That mean to teach you rudiments of war.
            I'll have you learn to sleep upon the ground,

March in your armour thorough watery fens,
Sustain the scorching heat and freezing cold,
Hunger and thirst, right adjuncts of the war;
And, after this, to scale a castle-wall,
Besiege a fort, to undermine a town,     60
And make whole cities caper in the air:
Then next, the way to fortify your men;
In champion grounds what figure serves you best,
For which the quinque-angle form is meet,
Because the corners there may fall more flat
Whereas the fort may fittest be assail'd,
And sharpest where th' assault is desperate:
The ditches must be deep; the counterscarps
Narrow and steep; the walls made high and broad:
The bulwarks and the rampires large and strong,     70
With cavalieros and thick counterforts,
And room within to lodge six thousand men;
It must have privy ditches, countermines,
And secret issuings to defend the ditch;
It must have high argins and cover'd ways
To keep the bulwark-fronts from battery,
And parapets to hide the musketeers,
Casemates to place the great artillery,
And store of ordnance, that from every flank
May scour the outward curtains of the fort,     80
Dismount the cannon of the adverse part,
Murder the foe, and save the walls from breach.
When this is learn'd for service on the land,
By plain and easy demonstration
I'll teach you how to make the water mount,
That you may dry-foot march through lakes and pools,
Deep rivers, havens, creeks, and little seas,
And make a fortress in the raging waves,
Fenc'd with the concave of a monstrous rock,
Invincible by nature of the place.     90
When this is done, then are ye soldiers,
And worthy sons of Tamburlaine the Great.
CALYPHAS My lord, but this is dangerous to be done.
We may be slain or wounded ere we learn.

TAMBUR.  Villain, art thou the son of Tamburlaine,
         And fear'st to die, or with a curtle-axe
         To hew thy flesh, and make a gaping wound?
         Hast thou beheld a peal of ordnance strike
         A ring of pikes, mingled with shot and horse,
         Whose shatter'd limbs, being toss'd as high as heaven
         Hang in the air as thick as sunny motes,
         And canst thou, coward, stand in fear of death?
         Hast thou not seen my horsemen charge the foe,
         Shot through the arms, cut overthwart the hands,
         Dying their lances with their streaming blood,
         And yet at night carouse within my tent,
         Filling their empty veins with airy wine,
         That, being concocted, turns to crimson blood,
         And wilt thou shun the field for fear of wounds?
         View me, thy father, that hath conquer'd kings,     110
         And, with his host, march'd round about the earth,
         Quite void of scars and clear from any wound,
         That by the wars lost not a drop of blood,
         And see him lance his flesh to teach you all.
                                      [*he cuts his arm*
         A wound is nothing, be it ne'er so deep;
         Blood is the god of war's rich livery.
         Now look I like a soldier, and this wound
         As great a grace and majesty to me,
         As if a chair of gold enamelled,
         Enchas'd with diamonds, sapphires, rubies,          120
         And fairest pearl of wealthy India,
         Were mounted here under a canopy,
         And I sat down, cloth'd with a massy robe
         That late adorn'd the Afric potentate,
         Whom I brought bound unto Damascus' walls.
         Come, boys, and with your fingers search my wound,
         And in my blood wash all your hands at once,
         While I sit smiling to behold the sight.
         Now, my boys, what think ye of a wound?

CALYPHAS  I know not what I should think of; methinks 'tis a
          pitiful sight.

CELEBINUS  'Tis nothing – Give me a wound, father.

AMYRAS      And me another, my lord.

TAMBUR.      Come, sirrah, give me your arm.

CELEBINUS   Here, father, cut it bravely, as you did your own.

TAMBUR.      It shall suffice thou dar'st abide a wound;
             My boy, thou shalt not lose a drop of blood
             Before we meet the army of the Turk;
             But then run desperate through the thickest throngs,
             Dreadless of blows, of bloody wounds, and death;   140
             And let the burning of Larissa-walls,
             My speech of war, and this my wound you see,
             Teach you, my boys, to bear courageous minds,
             Fit for the followers of great Tamburlaine –
             Usumcasane, now come, let us march
             Towards Techelles and Theridamas,
             That we have sent before to fire the towns,
             The towers and cities of these hateful Turks,
             And hunt that coward faint-heart runaway,
             With that accursed traitor Almeda,                 150
             Till fire and sword have found them at a bay.

USUMCAS.     I long to pierce his bowels with my sword,
             That hath betray'd my gracious sovereign –
             That curs'd and damned traitor Almeda.

TAMBUR.      Then let us see if coward Callapine
             Dare levy arms against our puissance,
             That we may tread upon his captive neck
             And treble all his father's slaveries.

                                                    [exeunt


                          SCENE 3

             Enter TECHELLES, THERIDAMAS, and their train

THERID.      Thus have we march'd northward from Tamburlaine,
             Unto the frontier point of Soria;
             And this is Balsera, their chiefest hold,
             Wherein is all the treasure of the land.

TECHELLES    Then let us bring our light artillery,
             Minions, falc'nets, and sakers, to the trench,
             Filling the ditches with the walls' wide breach

   And enter in to seize upon the hold –
   How say you, soldiers, shall we not?
SOLDIERS Yes, my lord, yes; come, let's about it.    10
THERID. But stay a while; summon a parle, drum.
   It may be they will yield it quietly,
   Knowing two kings, the friends to Tamburlaine,
   Stand at the walls with such a mighty power.
      [*A parley sounded – Captain appears on the walls,*
        *with Olympia his wife, and his son*

CAPTAIN What require you, my masters?
THERID. Captain, that thou yield up thy hold to us.
CAPTAIN To you! Why, do you think me weary of it?
TECHELLES Nay, captain, thou art weary of thy life,
   If thou withstand the friends of Tamburlaine.
THERID. These pioners of Argier in Africa,    20
   Even in the cannon's face, shall raise a hill
   Of earth and faggots higher than thy fort,
   And over thy argins and cover'd ways,
   Shall play upon the bulwarks of thy hold
   Volleys of ordnance, till the breach be made
   That with his ruin fills up all the trench;
   And when we enter in, not heaven itself
   Shall ransom thee, thy wife, and family.
TECHELLES Captain, these Moors shall cut the leaden pipes
   That bring fresh water to thy men and thee,   30
   And lie in trench before thy castle-walls,
   That no supply of victual shall come in,
   Nor [any] issue forth but they shall die;
   And, therefore, captain, yield it quietly.
CAPTAIN Were you, that are the friends of Tamburlaine,
   Brothers of holy Mahomet himself,
   I would not yield it; therefore do your worst:
   Raise mounts, batter, intrench, and undermine,
   Cut off the water, all convoys that can,
   Yet I am resolute: and so, farewell.    40
      [*Captain, Olympia, and son, retire from the walls*
THERID. Pioners, away! And where I stuck the stake,
   Intrench with those dimensions I prescrib'd;
   Cast up the earth towards the castle-wall,

|  | Which, till it may defend you, labour low, |  |
|--|-------------------------------------------|--|

Which, till it may defend you, labour low,
And few or none shall perish by their shot.

PIONERS     We will, my lord.                    [*exeunt Pioners*

TECHELLES A hundred horse shall scout about the plains,
To spy what force comes to relieve the hold.
Both we, Theridamas, will intrench our men,
And with the Jacob's staff measure the height          50
And distance of the castle from the trench,
That we may know if our artillery
Will carry full point-plank unto their walls.

THERID.    Then see the bringing of our ordnance
Along the trench into the battery,
Where we will have gallions of six foot broad,
To save our cannoneers from musket-shot;
Betwixt which shall our ordnance thunder forth,
And with the breach's fall, smoke, fire, and dust,
The crack, the echo, and the soldiers' cry,            60
Make deaf the air and dim the crystal sky.

TECHELLES Trumpets and drums alarum presently!
And, soldiers, play the men; the hold is yours!

                                                  [*exeunt*


### SCENE 4

*Alarms within. Enter the Captain, with* OLYMPIA, *and his son*

OLYMPIA    Come, good my lord, and let us haste from hence,
Along the cave that leads beyond the foe:
No hope is left to save this conquer'd hold.

CAPTAIN    A deadly bullet gliding through my side,
Lies heavy on my heart; I cannot live:
I feel my liver pierc'd, and all my veins,
That there begin and nourish every part,
Mangled and torn, and all my entrails bath'd
In blood that straineth from their orifex.
Farewell sweet wife! Sweet son farewell! I die.       10
                                                  [*dies*

OLYMPIA    Death, whither art thou gone, that both we live?
Come back again, sweet Death, and strike us both!

One minute end our days, and one sepulchre
Contain our bodies! Death, why com'st thou not?
Well, this must be the messenger for thee:

*[drawing a dagger*

Now, ugly Death, stretch out thy sable wings,
And carry both our souls where his remains —
Tell me, sweet boy, art thou content to die?
These barbarous Scythians, full of cruelty,
And Moors, in whom was never pity found,                    20
Will hew us piecemeal, put us to the wheel,
Or else invent some torture worse than that;
Therefore die by thy loving mother's hand,
Who gently now will lance thy ivory throat
And quickly rid thee both of pain and life.

SON          Mother, despatch me, or I'll kill myself;
For think you I can live and see him dead?
Give me your knife, good mother, or strike home:
The Scythians shall not tyrannise on me:
Sweet mother, strike, that I may meet my father.     30

*[she stabs him, and he dies*

OLYMPIA     Ah, sacred Mahomet, if this be sin,
Entreat a pardon of the God of heaven,
And purge my soul before it comes to thee!

*[she burns the bodies of her husband and son,*
*and then attempts to kill herself*

*Enter* THERIDAMAS, TECHELLES, *and all their train*

THERID.     How now, Madam! What are you doing?

OLYMPIA     Killing myself, as I have done my son,
Whose body, with his father's, I have burnt,
Lest cruel Scythians should dismember him.

TECHELLES 'Twas bravely done, and like a soldier's wife.
Thou shalt with us to Tamburlaine the Great,
Who, when he hears how resolute thou wert,          40
Will match thee with a viceroy or a king.

OLYMPIA     My lord deceas'd was dearer unto me
Than any viceroy, king, or emperor;
And for his sake here will I end my days.

THERID.     But, lady, go with us to Tamburlaine,

And thou shalt see a man greater than Mahomet,
In whose high looks is much more majesty,
Than from the concave superficies
Of Jove's vast palace, the empyreal orb,
Unto the shining bower where Cynthia sits,     50
Like lovely Thetis, in a crystal robe;
That treadeth fortune underneath his feet,
And makes the mighty god of arms his slave;
On whom Death and the Fatal Sisters wait
With naked swords and scarlet liveries;
Before whom, mounted on a lion's back,
Rhamnusia bears a helmet full of blood,
And strows the way with brains of slaughter'd men;
By whose proud side the ugly Furies run,
Hearkening when he shall bid them plague the world;
Over whose zenith, cloth'd in windy air,
And eagle's wings join'd to her feather'd breast,
Fame hovereth, sounding of her golden trump,
That to the adverse poles of that straight line
Which measureth the glorious frame of heaven
The name of mighty Tamburlaine is spread;
And him fair, lady, shall thy eyes behold.
Come.

OLYMPIA     Take pity of a lady's ruthful tears,
That humbly craves upon her knees to stay,     70
And cast her body in the burning flame
That feeds upon her son's and husband's flesh.

TECHELLES     Madam, sooner shall fire consume us both
Than scorch a face so beautiful as this,
In frame of which Nature hath show'd more skill
Than when she gave eternal chaos form,
Drawing from it the shining lamps of heaven.

THERID.     Madam, I am so far in love with you
That you must go with us: no remedy.

OLYMPIA     Then carry me, I care not, where you will,     80
And let the end of this my fatal journey
Be likewise end to my accursed life.

TECHELLES     No, madam, but the beginning of your joy:
Come willingly, therefore.

THERID.   Soldiers, now let us meet the general,
          Who by this time is at Natolia,
          Ready to charge the army of the Turk.
          The gold and silver, and the pearl, ye got,
          Rifling this fort, divide in equal shares:
          This lady shall have twice so much again          90
          Out of the coffers of our treasury.

                                              [*exeunt*

## SCENE 5

*Enter* CALLAPINE, ORCANES, *the* KINGS OF JERUSALEM, TREBIZON,
*and* SORIA, *with their train*, ALMEDA, *and a Messenger*

MESSENGER  Renowmed emperor, mighty Callapine,
          God's great lieutenant over all the world,
          Here at Aleppo, with an host of men,
          Lies Tamburlaine, this king of Persia,
          (In number more than are the quivering leaves
          Of Ida's forest, where your highness' hounds
          With open cry pursue the wounded stag)
          Who means to girt Natolia's walls with siege,
          Fire the town, and over-run the land.

CALLAPINE  My royal army is as great as his,          10
          That, from the bounds of Phrygia to the sea
          Which washeth Cyprus with his brinish waves,
          Covers the hills, the valleys, and the plains.
          Viceroys and peers of Turkey, play the men;
          Whet all your swords to mangle Tamburlaine,
          His sons, his captains, and his followers:
          By Mahomet, not one of them shall live!
          The field wherein this battle shall be fought
          For ever term'd the Persians' sepulchre,
          In memory of this our victory.          20

ORCANES    Now he that calls himself the scourge of Jove,
          The emperor of the world, and earthly god,
          Shall end the warlike progress he intends,
          And travel headlong to the lake of hell,
          Where legions of devils (knowing he must die

         Here in Natolia by your highness' hands),
         All brandishing their brands of quenchless fire,
         Stretching their monstrous paws, grin with their teeth,
         And guard the gates to entertain his soul.

CALLAPINE  Tell me, viceroys, the number of your men,       30
         And what our army royal is esteem'd.

JERUSALEM  From Palestina and Jerusalem,
         Of Hebrews three score thousand fighting men
         Are come, since last we show'd your majesty.

ORCANES  So from Arabia Desert, and the bounds
         Of that sweet land whose brave metropolis
         Re-edified the fair Semiramis,
         Came forty thousand warlike foot and horse,
         Since last we number'd to your majesty.

TREBIZON  From Trebizon in Asia the Less,       40
         Naturalis'd Turks and stout Bithynians
         Came to my bands, full fifty thousand more
         (That, fighting, know not what retreat doth mean,
         Nor e'er return but with the victory),
         Since last we number'd to your majesty.

SORIA  Of Sorians from Halla is repair'd,
         And neighbour cities of your highness' land,
         Ten thousand horse, and thirty thousand foot,
         Since last we number'd to your majesty;
         So that the army royal is esteem'd       50
         Six hundred thousand valiant fighting men.

CALLAPINE  Then welcome, Tamburlaine, unto thy death!
         Come puissant viceroys, let us to the field
         (The Persians' sepulchre), and sacrifice
         Mountains of breathless men to Mahomet,
         Who now, with Jove, opens the firmament
         To see the slaughter of our enemies.

       *Enter* TAMBURLAINE *with his three sons,* CALYPHUS,
       AMYRAS, *and* CELEBINUS; USUMCASANE, *and others*

TAMBUR.  How now, Casane! See, a knot of kings,
         Sitting as if they were a-telling riddles!

USUMCAS.  My lord, your presence makes them pale and wan:  60
         Poor souls, they look as if their deaths were near.

TAMBUR.   Why, so he is, Casane; I am here:
          But yet I'll save their lives, and make them slaves –
          Ye petty kings of Turkey, I am come,
          As Hector did into the Grecian camp,
          To overdare the pride of Graecia,
          And set his warlike person to the view
          Of fierce Achilles, rival of his fame:
          I do you honour in the simile;
          For, if I should, as Hector did Achilles       70
          (The worthiest knight that ever brandish'd sword),
          Challenge in combat any of you all,
          I see how fearfully ye would refuse,
          And fly my glove as from a scorpion.

ORCANES   Now, thou art fearful of thy army's strength,
          Thou wouldst with overmatch of person fight:
          But, shepherd's issue, base-born Tamburlaine,
          Think of thy end; this sword shall lance thy throat.

TAMBUR.   Villain, the shepherd's issue (at whose birth
          Heaven did afford a gracious aspect,         80
          And join'd those stars that shall be opposite
          Even till the dissolution of the world,
          And never meant to make a conqueror
          So famous as is mighty Tamburlaine)
          Shall so torment thee, and that Callapine,
          That, like a roguish runaway, suborn'd
          That villain there, that slave, that Turkish dog,
          To false his service to his sovereign,
          As ye shall curse the birth of Tamburlaine.

CALLAPINE  Rail not, proud Scythian: I shall now revenge    90
          My father's vile abuses and mine own.

JERUSALEM  By Mahomet, he shall be tied in chains,
          Rowing with Christians in a brigandine
          About the Grecian isles to rob and spoil,
          And turn him to his ancient trade again:
          Methinks the slave should make a lusty thief.

CALLAPINE  Nay, when the battle ends, all we will meet,
          And sit in council to invent some pain
          That most may vex his body and his soul.

TAMBUR.   Sirrah Callapine, I'll hang a clog about your neck for

running away again: you shall not trouble me thus to
come and fetch you –
But as for you, viceroys, you shall have bits,
And, harness'd like my horses, draw my coach;
And, when ye stay, be lash'd with whips of wire:
I'll have you learn to feed on provender,
And in a stable lie upon the planks.

ORCANES    But, Tamburlaine, first thou shalt kneel to us,
And humbly crave a pardon for thy life.

TREBIZON    The common soldiers of our mighty host       110
Shall bring thee bound unto the general's tent.

SORIA    And all have jointly sworn thy cruel death,
Or bind thee in eternal torments' wrath.

TAMBUR.    Well, sirs, diet yourselves; you know I shall have occasion
shortly to journey you.

CELEBINUS    See, father, how Almeda the jailor looks upon us!

TAMBUR.    Villain, traitor, damned fugitive,
I'll make thee wish the earth had swallow'd thee!
See'st thou not death within my wrathful looks?
Go, villain, cast thee headlong from a rock,       120
Or rip thy bowels, and rent out thy heart,
T'appease my wrath; or else I'll torture thee,
Searing thy hateful flesh with burning irons
And drops of scalding lead, while all thy joints
Be rack'd and beat asunder with the wheel;
For, if thou liv'st, not any element
Shall shroud thee from the wrath of Tamburlaine.

CALLAPINE    Well in despite of thee, he shall be king –
Come, Almeda; receive this crown of me:
I here invest thee king of Ariadan,       130
Bordering on Mare Roso, near to Mecca.

ORCANES    What! Take it, man.

ALMEDA    [to Tamburlaine] Good my lord, let me take it.

CALLAPINE    Dost thou ask him leave? Here; take it.

TAMBUR.    Go to, sirrah! Take your crown, and make up the half
dozen. So, sirrah, now you are a king, you must give
arms.

ORCANES    So he shall, and wear the head in his scutcheon.

TAMBUR.    No; let him hang a bunch of keys on his standard, to

put him in remembrance he was a jailor, that, when I
take him, I may knock out his brains with them, and
lock you in the stable, when you shall come sweating
from my chariot.

TREBIZON  Away! Let us to the field, that the villain may be slain.

TAMBUR.  Sirrah, prepare whips, and bring my chariot to my tent;
for, as soon as the battle is done, I'll ride in triumph
through the camp.

*Enter* THERIDAMAS, TECHELLES, *and their train*

How now, ye petty kings? Lo, here are bugs
Will make the hair stand upright on your heads,
And cast your crowns in slavery at their feet!          150
Welcome, Theridamas and Techelles, both:
See ye this rout, and know ye this same king?

THERID.  Ay, my lord; he was Callapine's keeper.

TAMBUR.  Well now ye see he is a king. Look to him, Theridamas,
when we are fighting, lest he hide his crown as the
foolish king of Persia did.

SORIA  No, Tamburlaine; he shall not be put to that exigent,
I warrant thee.

TAMBUR.  You know not, sir –
But now, my followers and my loving friends,          160
Fight as you ever did, live conquerors,
The glory of this happy day is yours.
My stern aspect shall make fair Victory,
Hovering betwixt our armies, light on me,
Loaden with laurel-wreaths to crown us all.

TECHELLES  I smile to think how, when this field is fought
And rich Natolia ours, our men shall sweat
With carrying pearl and treasure on their backs.

TAMBUR.  You shall be princes all, immediately –
Come, fight, ye Turks, or yield us victory.          170

ORCANES  No; we will meet thee, slavish Tamburlaine.

*[exeunt severally*

# ACT FOUR

## SCENE I

*Alarms within.* AMYRAS *and* CELEBINUS *issue from
the tent where* CALYPHAS *sits asleep*

AMYRAS    Now in their glories shine the golden crowns
Of these proud Turks, much like so many suns
That half dismay the majesty of heaven.
Now, brother, follow we our father's sword,
That flies with fury swifter than our thoughts,
And cuts down armies with his conquering wings.

CELEBINUS Call forth our lazy brother from the tent,
For, if my father miss him in the field,
Wrath, kindled in the furnace of his breast,
Will send a deadly lightning to his heart.        10

AMYRAS    Brother, ho! What, given so much to sleep,
You cannot leave it, when our enemies' drums
And rattling cannons thunder in our ears
Our proper ruin and our father's foil?

CALYPHAS Away, ye fools! My father needs not me,
Nor you, in faith, but that you will be thought
More childish-valourous than manly-wise.
If half our camp should sit and sleep with me,
My father were enough to scare the foe:
You do dishonour to his majesty,        20
To think our helps will do him any good.

AMYRAS    What, dar'st thou, then, be absent from the fight,
Knowing my father hates thy cowardice,
And oft hath warn'd thee to be still in field,
When he himself amidst the thickest troops
Beats down our foes, to flesh our taintless swords?

CALYPHAS I know, sir, what it is to kill a man;
It works remorse of conscience in me.
I take no pleasure to be murderous,
Nor care for blood when wine will quench my thirst.

CELEBINUS O cowardly boy! Fie, for shame, come forth!
Thou dost dishonour manhood and thy house.

CALYPHAS   Go, go, tall stripling, fight you for us both,
           And take my other toward brother here,
           For person like to prove a second Mars.
           'Twill please my mind as well to hear, both you
           Have won a heap of honour in the field,
           And left your slender carcasses behind,
           As if I lay with you for company.

AMYRAS   You will not go, then?                                   40

CALYPHAS   You say true.

AMYRAS   Were all the lofty mounts of Zona Mundi
           That fill the midst of farthest Tartary
           Turn'd into pearl and proffer'd for my stay,
           I would not bide the fury of my father,
           When, made a victor in these haughty arms,
           He comes and finds his sons have had no shares
           In all the honours he propos'd for us.

CALYPHAS   Take you the honour, I will take my ease;
           My wisdom shall excuse my cowardice:                    50
           I go into the field before I need!
                  [*alarms within. Amyras and Celebinus run out*
           The bullets fly at random where they list;
           And, should I go, and kill a thousand men,
           I were as soon rewarded with a shot,
           And sooner far than he that never fights;
           And, should I go, and do nor harm nor good,
           I might have harm, which all the good I have,
           Join'd with my father's crown, would never cure.
           I'll to cards – Perdicas!

*Enter* PERDICAS

PERDICAS   Here, my lord.                                         60

CALYPHAS   Come, thou and I will go to cards to drive away the
           time.

PERDICAS   Content, my lord: but what shall we play for?

CALYPHAS   Who shall kiss the fairest of the Turks' concubines first,
           when my father hath conquered them.

PERDICAS   Agreed, i'faith.                                       [*they play*

CALYPHAS   They say I am a coward, Perdicas, and I fear as little
           their taratantaras, their swords, or their cannons as I do

a naked lady in a net of gold, and, for fear I should be
afraid, would put it off and come to bed with me.

PERDICAS   Such a fear, my lord, would never make ye retire.

CALYPHAS   I would my father would let me be put in the front of
such a battle once, to try my valour! [alarms within]
What a coil they keep! I believe there will be some hurt
done anon amongst them.

*Enter* TAMBURLAINE, THERIDAMAS, TECHELLES, USUMCASANE;
AMYRAS *and* CELEBINUS *leading in* ORCANES, *and the* KINGS
*of* JERUSALEM, TREBIZON *and* SORIA; *and Soldiers*

TAMBUR.    See now, ye slaves, my children stoop your pride,
And lead your bodies sheep-like to the sword —
Bring them, my boys, and tell me if the wars
Be not a life that may illustrate gods,
And tickle not your spirits with desire              80
Still to be train'd in arms and chivalry?

AMYRAS     Shall we let go these kings again, my lord,
To gather greater numbers 'gainst our power,
That they may say, it is not chance doth this,
But matchless strength and magnanimity?

TAMBUR.    No, no, Amyras; tempt not Fortune so:
Cherish thy valour still with fresh supplies,
And glut it not with stale and daunted foes.
But where's this coward villain, not my son,
But traitor to my name and majesty?                  90
                    [*he goes in and brings Calyphas out*
Image of sloth, and picture of a slave,
The obloquy and scorn of my renown!
How may my heart, thus fired with mine eyes,
Wounded with shame and kill'd with discontent,
Shroud any thought may hold my striving hand
From martial justice on thy wretched soul?

THERID.    Yet pardon him, I pray your majesty.

TECHELLES *and* USUMCASANE
Let all of us entreat your highness' pardon.

TAMBUR.    Stand up, ye base, unworthy soldiers!
Know ye not yet the argument of arms?                100

AMYRAS     Good my lord, let him be forgiven for once,
And we will force him to the field hereafter.

TAMBUR.    Stand up, my boys, and I will teach ye arms,
           And what the jealousy of wars must do –
           O Samarcanda, where I breathed first,
           And joy'd the fire of this martial flesh,
           Blush, blush, fair city, at thine honour's foil,
           And shame of nature, which Jaertis' stream,
           Embracing thee with deepest of his love,
           Can never wash from thy distained brows!        110
           Here, Jove, receive his fainting soul again;
           A form not meet to give that subject essence
           Whose matter is the flesh of Tamburlaine,
           Wherein an incorporeal spirit moves,
           Made of the mould whereof thyself consists,
           Which makes me valiant, proud, ambitious,
           Ready to levy power against thy throne,
           That I might move the turning spheres of heaven;
           For earth and all this airy region
           Cannot contain the state of Tamburlaine.        120
                                        [stabs Calyphas

           By Mahomet, thy mighty friend, I swear,
           In sending to my issue such a soul,
           Created of the massy dregs of earth,
           The scum and tartar of the elements,
           Wherein was neither courage, strength, or wit,
           But folly, sloth, and damned idleness,
           That hast procur'd a greater enemy
           Than he that darted mountains at thy head,
           Shaking the burden mighty Atlas bears,
           Whereat thou trembling hidd'st thee in the air,    130
           Cloth'd with a pitchy cloud for being seen –
           And now, ye canker'd curs of Asia,
           That will not see the strength of Tamburlaine,
           Although it shine as brightly as the sun,
           Now you shall feel the strength of Tamburlaine,
           And, by the state of his supremacy,
           Approve the difference 'twixt himself and you.

ORCANES    Thou show'st the difference twixt ourselves and thee,
           In this thy barbarous damned tyranny.

JERUSALEM Thy victories are grown so violent,                140

That shortly heaven, fill'd with the meteors
Of blood and fire thy tyrannies have made,
Will pour down blood and fire on thy head,
Whose scalding drops will pierce thy seething brains,
And, with our bloods, revenge our bloods on thee.

TAMBUR.    Villains, these terrors, and these tyrannies
(If tyrannies war's justice ye repute)
I execute, enjoin'd me from above,
To scourge the pride of such as Heaven abhors;
Nor am I made arch-monarch of the world,               150
Crown'd and invested by the hand of Jove,
For deeds of bounty or nobility;
But, since I exercise a greater name,
The scourge of God and terror of the world,
I must apply myself to fit those terms,
In war, in blood, in death, in cruelty,
And plague such peasants as resist in me
The power of Heaven's eternal majesty –
Theridamas, Techelles, and Casane,
Ransack the tents and the pavilions                    160
Of these proud Turks, and take their concubines,
Making them bury this effeminate brat;
For not a common soldier shall defile
His manly fingers with so faint a boy:
Then bring those Turkish harlots to my tent,
And I'll dispose them as it likes me best –
Meanwhile, take him in.

SOLDIERS                          We will, my lord.
                              [exeunt with the body of Calyphas

JERUSALEM  O damned monster! Nay, a fiend of hell,
Whose cruelties are not so harsh as thine,
Nor yet impos'd with such a bitter hate!               170

ORCANES    Revenge it, Rhadamanth and Aeacus,
And let your hates, extended in his pains,
Excel the hate wherewith he pains our souls!

TREBIZON   May never day give virtue to his eyes,
Whose sight, compos'd of fury and of fire,
Doth send such stern affections to his heart!

SORIA      May never spirit, vein, or artier, feed

The cursed substance of that cruel heart;
But, wanting moisture and remorseful blood,
Dry up with anger, and consume with heat!        180
TAMBUR.  Well, bark, ye dogs: I'll bridle all your tongues,
And bind them close with bits of burnish'd steel,
Down to the channels of your hateful throats;
And, with the pains my rigour shall inflict,
I'll make ye roar, that earth may echo forth
The far-resounding torments ye sustain;
As when an herd of lusty Cimbrian bulls
Run mourning round about the females' miss,
And, stung with fury of their following,
Fill all the air with troubles bellowing.        190
I will, with engines never exercis'd,
Conquer, sack, and utterly consume
Your cities and your golden palaces,
And, with the flames that beat against the clouds,
Incense the heavens, and make the stars to melt,
As if they were the tears of Mahomet
For hot consumption of his country's pride;
And, till by vision or by speech I hear
Immortal Jove say 'Cease, my Tamburlaine',
I will persist a terror to the world,        200
Making the meteors (that, like armed men,
Are seen to march upon the towers of heaven)
Run tilting round about the firmament,
And break their burning lances in the air,
For honour of my wondrous victories –
Come, bring them in to our pavilion.

                                        [exeunt

## SCENE 2

*Enter* OLYMPIA

OLYMPIA   Distress'd Olympia, whose weeping eyes,
Since thy arrival here, behold no sun,
But, clos'd within the compass of a tent,
Have stain'd thy cheeks, and made thee look
                         like death,
Devise some means to rid thee of thy life,
Rather than yield to his detested suit,
Whose drift is only to dishonour thee;
And, since this earth, dew'd with thy brinish tears,
Affords no herbs whose taste may poison thee,
Nor yet this air, beat often with thy sighs,       10
Contagious smells and vapours to infect thee,
Nor thy close cave a sword to murder thee,
Let this invention be the instrument.

*Enter* THERIDAMAS

THERID.   Well met, Olympia: I sought thee m my tent,
But, when I saw the place obscure and dark.
Which with thy beauty thou wast wont to light,
Enrag'd, I ran about the fields for thee,
Supposing amorous Jove had sent his son,
The winged Hermes, to convey thee hence;
But now I find thee, and that fear is past,       20
Tell me, Olympia, wilt thou grant my suit?

OLYMPIA   My lord and husband's death, with my sweet son's
(With whom I buried all affections
Save grief and sorrow, which torment my heart),
Forbids my mind to entertain a thought
That tends to love, and meditate on death,
A fitter subject for a pensive soul.

THERID.   Olympia, pity him in whom thy looks
Have greater operation and more force
Than Cynthia's in the watery wilderness;       30
For with thy view my joys are at the full,

|          | And ebb again as thou depart'st from me. |
| OLYMPIA  | Ah, pity me, my lord, and draw your sword, |
|          | Making a passage for my troubled soul, |
|          | Which beats against this prison to get out, |
|          | And meet my husband and my loving son! |
| THERID.  | Nothing but still thy husband and thy son? |
|          | Leave this, my love, and listen more to me: |
|          | Thou shalt be stately queen of fair Argier; |
|          | And, cloth'd in costly cloth of massy gold,     40 |
|          | Upon the marble turrets of my court |
|          | Sit like to Venus in her chair of state, |
|          | Commanding all thy princely eye desires; |
|          | And I will cast off arms to sit with thee, |
|          | Spending my life in sweet discourse of love. |
| OLYMPIA  | No such discourse is pleasant in mine ears, |
|          | But that where every period ends with death, |
|          | And every line begins with death again: |
|          | I cannot love, to be an emperess. |
| THERID.  | Nay, lady, then, if nothing will prevail,     50 |
|          | I'll use some other means to make you yield: |
|          | Such is the sudden fury of my love, |
|          | I must and will be pleas'd, and you shall yield. |
|          | Come to the tent again. |
| OLYMPIA  | Stay now, my lord; and, will you save my honour, |
|          | I'll give your grace a present of such price |
|          | As all the world can not afford the like. |
| THERID.  | What is it? |
| OLYMPIA  | An ointment which a cunning alchymist |
|          | Distilled from the purest balsamum     60 |
|          | And simplest extracts of all minerals, |
|          | In which the essential form of marble stone, |
|          | Temper'd by science metaphysical, |
|          | And spells of magic from the mouths of spirits, |
|          | With which if you but 'noint your tender skin, |
|          | Nor pistol, sword, nor lance, can pierce your flesh. |
| THERID.  | Why, madam, think you to mock me thus palpably? |
| OLYMPIA  | To prove it, I will 'noint my naked throat, |
|          | Which when you stab, look on your weapon's point, |
|          | And you shall see't rebated with the blow.     70 |

THERID.    Why gave you not your husband some of it,
               If you lov'd him, and it so precious!
OLYMPIA   My purpose was, my lord, to spend it so,
               But was prevented by his sudden end;
               And for a present easy proof thereof,
               That I dissemble not, try it on me.
THERID.    I will, Olympia, and will keep it for
               The richest present of this eastern world.
                                          *[she anoints her throat*
OLYMPIA   Now stab, my lord, and mark your weapon's point,
               That will be blunted if the blow be great.      80
THERID.    Here, then, Olympia –            *[stabs her*
               What, have I slain her? Villain, stab thyself!
               Cut off this arm that murdered my love,
               In whom the learned Rabbis of this age
               Might find as many wondrous miracles
               As in the theoria of the world!
               Now hell is fairer than Elysium;
               A greater lamp than that bright eye of heaven,
               From whence the stars do borrow all their light,
               Wanders about the black circumference;      90
               And now the damned souls are free from pain,
               For every Fury gazeth on her looks;
               Infernal Dis is courting of my love,
               Inventing masks and stately shows for her,
               Opening the doors of his rich treasury
               To entertain this queen of chastity;
               Whose body shall be tomb'd with all the pomp
               The treasure of my kingdom may afford.
                                          *[exit with the body*

## SCENE 3

*Enter* TAMBURLAINE, *drawn in his chariot by the* KINGS
*of* TREBIZON *and* SORIA, *with bits in their mouths, reins
in his left hand, and in his right hand a whip with which
he scourgeth them;* AMYRAS, CELEBINUS, TECHELLES,
THERIDAMAS, USUMCASANE; ORCANES *king of Natolia,
and the* KING OF JERUSALEM, *led by five or
six common soldiers; and other soldiers*

TAMBUR.    Holla, ye pamper'd jades of Asia!
            What, can ye draw but twenty miles a-day,
            And have so proud a chariot at your heels,
            And such a coachman as great Tamburlaine,
            But from Asphaltis, where I conquer'd you,
            To Byron here, where thus I honour you?
            The horse that guide the golden eye of heaven,
            And blow the morning from their nostrils,
            Making their fiery gait above the clouds,
            Are not so honour'd in their governor            10
            As you, ye slaves, in mighty Tamburlaine.
            The headstrong jades of Thrace Alcides tam'd,
            That King Aegeus fed with human flesh,
            And made so wanton that they knew their strengths,
            Were not subdu'd with valour more divine
            Than you by this unconquer'd arm of mine.
            To make you fierce, and fit my appetite,
            You shall be fed with flesh as raw as blood,
            And drink in pails the strongest muscadel:
            If you can live with it, then live, and draw            20
            My chariot swifter than the racking clouds;
            If not, then die like beasts, and fit for naught
            But perches for the black and fatal ravens.
            Thus am I right the scourge of highest Jove;
            And see the figure of my dignity,
            By which I hold my name and majesty!
AMYRAS     Let me have coach, my lord, that I may ride,
            And thus be drawn by these two idle kings.

TAMBUR.   Thy youth forbids such ease, my kingly boy:
         They shall tomorrow draw my chariot,      30
         While these their fellow-kings may be refresh'd.
ORCANES   O thou that sway'st the region under earth,
         And art a king as absolute as Jove,
         Come as thou didst in fruitful Sicily,
         Surveying all the glories of the land,
         And as thou took'st the fair Proserpina,
         Joying the fruit of Ceres' garden-plot,
         For love, for honour, and to make her queen,
         So, for just hate, for shame, and to subdue
         This proud contemner of thy dreadful power,      40
         Come once in fury, and survey his pride,
         Haling him headlong to the lowest hell!
THERID.   You majesty must get some bits for these,
         To bridle their contemptuous cursing tongues,
         That, like unruly never-broken jades,
         Break through the hedges of their hateful mouths,
         And pass their fixed bounds exceedingly.
TECHELLES Nay, we will break the hedges of their mouths
         And pull their kicking colts out of their pastures.
USUMCAS. Your majesty already hath devis'd      50
         A mean, as fit as may be, to restrain
         These coltish coach-horse tongues from blasphemy.
CELEBINUS How like you that, Sir King? Why speak you not?
JERUSALEM Ah, cruel brat, sprung from a tyrant's loins!
         How like his cursed father he begins
         To practice taunts and bitter tyrannies!
TAMBUR.   Ay, Turk, I tell thee, this same boy is he
         That must (advanc'd in higher pomp than this)
         Rifle the kingdoms I shall leave unsack'd,
         If Jove, esteeming me too good for earth,      60
         Raise me, to match the fair Aldeboran,
         Above the threefold astracism of heaven,
         Before I conquer all the triple world —
         Now fetch me out the Turkish concubines:
         I will prefer them for the funeral
         They have bestow'd on my abortive son.

                          *[the Concubines are brought in*

|              |                                                        |     |
|--------------|--------------------------------------------------------|-----|
|              | Where are my common soldiers now, that fought          |     |
|              | So lion-like upon Asphaltis' plains?                    |     |
| SOLDIERS     | Here, my lord.                                          |     |
| TAMBUR.      | Hold ye, tall soldiers, take ye queens apiece –         | 70  |
|              | I mean such queens as were kings' concubines;          |     |
|              | Take them; divide them, and their jewels too,          |     |
|              | And let them equally serve all your turns.             |     |
| SOLDIERS     | We thank your majesty.                                  |     |
| TAMBUR.      | Brawl not, I warn you, for your lechery;               |     |
|              | For every man that so offends shall die.              |     |
| ORCANES      | Injurious tyrant, wilt thou so defame                  |     |
|              | The hateful fortunes of thy victory,                   |     |
|              | To exercise upon such guiltless dames                  |     |
|              | The violence of thy common soldiers' lust?             | 80  |
| TAMBUR.      | Live continent, then, ye slaves, and meet not me       |     |
|              | With troops of harlots at your slothful heels.         |     |
| CONCUBINES   | O pity us, my lord, and save our honours!              |     |
| TAMBUR.      | Are ye not gone, ye villains, with your spoils?        |     |

                      *[the Soldiers run away with the Concubines*

|              |                                                        |     |
|--------------|--------------------------------------------------------|-----|
| JERUSALEM    | O, merciless, infernal cruelty!                        |     |
| TAMBUR.      | Save your honours! 'Twere but time indeed,             |     |
|              | Lost long before ye knew what honour meant.            |     |
| THERID.      | It seems they meant to conquer us, my lord,            |     |
|              | And make us jesting pageants for their trulls.         |     |
| TAMBUR.      | And now themselves shall make our pageant,             | 90  |
|              | And common soliders jest with all their trulls.        |     |
|              | Let them take pleasure soundly in their spoils;        |     |
|              | Till we prepare our march to Babylon,                  |     |
|              | Whither we next make expedition.                       |     |
| TECHELLES    | Let us not be idle, then, my lord,                     |     |
|              | But presently be prest to conquer it.                  |     |
| TAMBUR.      | We will, Techelles – Forward, then, ye jades!          |     |
|              | Now crouch, ye kings of greatest Asia,                 |     |
|              | And tremble when ye hear this scourge will come        |     |
|              | That whips down cities and controlleth crowns,         | 100 |
|              | Adding their wealth and treasure to my store.          |     |
|              | The Euxine sea, north to Natolia;                      |     |
|              | The Terrene, west; the Caspian, north northeast;       |     |
|              | And on the south, Sinus Arabicus;                      |     |

Shall all be loaden with the martial spoils
We will convey with us to Persia.
Then shall my native city Samarcanda,
And crystal waves of fresh Jaertis' stream,
The pride and beauty of her princely seat,
Be famous through the furthest continents;          110
For there my palace royal shall be plac'd,
Whose shining turrets shall dismay the heavens,
And cast the fame of Ilion's tower to hell:
Thorough the streets, with troops of conquer'd kings,
I'll ride in golden armour like the sun;
And in my helm a triple plume shall spring,
Spangled with diamonds, dancing in the air,
To note me emperor of the threefold world;
Like to an almond-tree y-mounted high
Upon the lofty and celestial mount          120
Of evergreen Selinus, quaintly deck'd
With blooms more white than Erycina's brows,
Whose tender blossoms tremble every one
At every little breath that thorough heaven is blown.
Then in my coach, like Saturn's royal son
Mounted his shining chariot gilt with fire,
And drawn with princely eagles through the path
Pav'd with bright crystal and enchas'd with stars,
When all the gods stand gazing at his pomp,
So will I ride through Samarcanda-streets,          130
Until my soul, dissever'd from this flesh,
Shall mount the milk-white way, and meet him there.
To Babylon, my lords, to Babylon!

                                        [*exeunt*

# ACT FIVE

## SCENE I

*Enter the* GOVERNOR OF BABYLON, MAXIMUS
*and others, upon the walls*

GOVERNOR What saith Maximus?

MAXIMUS My lord, the breach the enemy hath made
Gives such assurance of our overthrow,
That little hope is left to save our lives,
Or hold our city from the conqueror's hands.
Then hang out flags, my lord, of humble truce,
And satisfy the people's general prayers,
That Tamburlaine's intolerable wrath
May be suppressed by our submission.

GOVERNOR Villain, respect'st thou more thy slavish life          10
Than honour of thy country or thy name?
Is not my life and state as dear to me,
The city and my native country's weal,
As any thing of price with thy conceit?
Have we not hope, for all our batter'd walls,
To live secure and keep his forces out,
When this our famous lake of Limnasphaltis
Makes walls afresh with every thing that falls
Into the liquid substance of his stream,
More strong than are the gates of death or hell?          20
What faintness should dismay our courages,
When we are thus defenc'd against our foe,
And have no terror but his threatening looks?

*Enter above, a Citizen, who kneels to the* GOVERNOR

CITIZEN My lord, if ever you did deed of ruth,
And now will work a refuge to our lives,
Offer submission, hang up flags of truce,
That Tamburlaine may pity our distress,
And use us like a loving conqueror.
Though this be held his last day's dreadful siege,
Wherein he spareth neither man nor child,          30

Yet are there Christians of Georgia here,
Whose state he ever pitied and reliev'd,
Will get his pardon, if your grace would send.

GOVERNOR How is my soul environed!
And this eternis'd city Babylon
Fill'd with a pack of faint-heart fugitives
That thus entreat their shame and servitude!

*Enter, above, a Second Citizen*

2 CITIZEN My lord, if ever you will win our hearts,
Yield up the town, and save our wives and children;
For I will cast myself from off these walls,　　40
Or die some death of quickest violence
Before I bide the wrath of Tamburlaine.

GOVERNOR Villains, cowards, traitors to our state!
Fall to the earth, and pierce the pit of hell,
That legions of tormenting spirits may vex
Your slavish bosoms with continual pains!
I care not, nor the town will never yield
As long as any life is in my breast.

*Enter* THERIDAMAS *and* TECHELLES, *with Soldiers*

THERID. Thou desperate governor of Babylon,
To save thy life, and us a little labour,　　50
Yield speedily the city to our hands,
Or else be sure thou shalt be forc'd with pains
More exquisite than ever traitor felt.

GOVERNOR Tyrant, I turn the traitor in thy throat.
And will defend it in despite of thee –
Call up the soldiers to defend these walls

TECHELLES Yield, foolish governor; we offer more
Than ever yet we did to such proud slaves
As durst resist us till our third day's siege.
Thou seest us prest to give the last assault,　　60
And that shall bide no more regard of parle.

GOVERNOR Assault and spare not; we will never yield.
*[alarms: and they scale the walls*

*Enter* TAMBURLAINE, *drawn in his chariot (as before) by the*
KINGS OF TREBIZON *and* SORIA, AMYRAS, CELEBINUS,
USUMCASANE; ORCANES *king of Natolia, and the*
KING OF JERUSALEM, *led by soldiers; and others*

TAMBUR.  The stately buildings of fair Babylon,
Whose lofty pillars, higher than the clouds,
Were wont to guide the seaman in the deep,
Being carried thither by the cannon's force,
Now fill the mouth of Limnasphaltis' lake,
And make a bridge unto the batter'd walls.
Where Belus, Ninus, and great Alexander
Have rode in triumph, triumphs Tamburlaine,        70
Whose chariot-wheels have burst th' Assyrians' bones,
Drawn with these kings on heaps of carcasses.
Now in the place, where fair Semiramis,
Courted by kings and peers of Asia,
Hath trod the measures, do my soliders march;
And in the streets, where brave Assyrian dames
Have rid in pomp like rich Saturnia,
With furious words and frowning visages
My horsemen brandish their unruly blades.

*Re-enter* THERIDAMAS *and* TECHELLES,
*bringing in the* GOVERNOR OF BABYLON

Who have ye there, my lords?        80
THERID.  The sturdy governor of Babylon,
That made us all the labour for the town,
And us'd such slender reckoning of your majesty.
TAMBUR.  Go, bind the villain; he shall hang in chains
Upon the ruins of this conquer'd town —
Sirrah, the view of our vermilion tents
(Which threaten'd more than if the region
Next underneath the element of fire
Were full of comets and of blazing stars,
Whose flaming trains should reach down to the earth)
Could not affright you; no, nor I myself,
The wrathful messenger of mighty Jove,
That with his sword hath quail'd all earthly kings,
Could not persuade you to submission,

But still the ports were shut: villain, I say,
Should I but touch the rusty gates of hell,
The triple-headed Cerberus would howl,
And make black Jove to crouch and kneel to me;
But I have sent volleys of shot to you,
Yet could not enter till the breach was made.          100

GOVERNOR Nor, if my body could have stopt the breach,
Shouldst thou have enter'd, cruel Tamburlaine.
'Tis not thy bloody tents can make me yield,
Nor yet thyself, the anger of the Highest;
For, though thy cannon shook the city-walls,
My heart did never quake, or courage faint.

TAMBUR.  Well, now I'll make it quake – Go draw him up,
Hang him in chains upon the city walls,
And let my soldiers shoot the slave to death.

GOVERNOR Vile monster, born of some infernal hag,          110
And sent from hell to tryannise on earth,
Do all thy worst; nor death, nor Tamburlaine,
Torture, or pain, can daunt my dreadless mind.

TAMBUR.  Up with him, then! His body shall be scar'd.

GOVERNOR But, Tamburlaine, in Limnasphaltis' lake
There lies more gold than Babylon is worth,
Which, when the city was besieg'd, I hid:
Save but my life, and I will give it thee.

TAMBUR.  Then, for all your valour, you would save your life?
Whereabout lies it?          120

GOVERNOR Under a hollow bank, right opposite
Against the western gate of Babylon.

TAMBUR.  Go thither, some of you, and take his gold –
                    [exeunt some Attendants
The rest forward with execution.
Away with him hence, let him speak no more –
I think I make your courage something quail –
            [exeunt Attendants with the Governor of Babylon
When this is done, we'll march from Babylon,
And make our greatest haste to Persia.
These jades are broken-winded and half-tir'd;
Unharness them, and let me have fresh horse.          130
            [Attendants unharness the Kings of Trebizon and Soria

So; now their best is done to honour me,
Take them and hang them both up presently.

TREBIZON    Vile tyrant! Barbarous bloody Tamburlaine!

TAMBUR.    Take them away, Theridamas; see them despatch'd.

THERID.    I will, my lord.

                    [exit with the Kings of Trebizon and Soria

TAMBUR.    Come, Asian viceroys; to your tasks a while,
           And take such fortune as your fellows felt.

ORCANES    First let thy Scythian horse tear both our limbs,
           Rather than we should draw thy chariot,
           And, like base slaves, abject our princely minds        140
           To vile and ignominious servitude.

JERUSALEM Rather lend me thy weapon, Tamburlaine.
          That I may sheathe it in this breast of mine.
          A thousand deaths could not torment our hearts
          More than the thought of this doth vex our souls.

AMYRAS    They will talk still, my lord, if you do not
                                                bridle them.

TAMBUR.   Bridle them, and let me to my coach.
                [Attendants bridle Orcanes king of Natolia, and the King of
                    Jerusalem, and harness them to the chariot — the Governor
                        of Babylon appears hanging in chains on the walls

                    Re-enter THERIDAMAS

AMYRAS    See, now, my lord, how brave the captain hangs:

TAMBUR.   'Tis brave indeed, my boy — well done!
          Shoot first, my lord, and then the rest shall follow.   150

THERID.   Then have at him, to begin withal.
                                    [Theridamas shoots at the Governor

GOVERNOR Yet save my life, and let this wound appease
         The mortal fury of great Tamburlaine!

TAMBUR.   No, though Asphaltis' lake were liquid gold,
          And offer'd me as ransom for thy life,
          Yet shouldst thou die — Shoot at him all at once.
                                                    [they shoot

          So, now he hangs like Bagdet's governor,
          Having as many bullets in his flesh
          As there be breaches in her batter'd wall.
          Go now, and bind the burghers hand and foot,        160

           And cast them headlong in the city's lake.
           Tartars and Persians shall inhabit there;
           And, to command the city, I will build
           A citadel, that all Africa,
           Which hath been subject to the Persian king,
           Shall pay me tribute for in Babylon.

TECHELLES  What shall be done with their wives and children, my
           lord?

TAMBUR.    Techelles, drown them all, man, woman, and child;
           Leave not a Babylonian in the town.         170

TECHELLES  I will about it straight – Come, soldiers.

                                    *[exit with Soldiers*

TAMBUR.    Now, Casane, where's the Turkish Alcoran,
           And all the heaps of superstitious books
           Found in the temples of that Mahomet
           Whom I have thought a god? They shall be burnt.

USUMCAS.  Here thy are, my lord.

TAMBUR.    Well said! Let there be a fire presently.  *[they light a fire*
           In vain, I see, men worship Mahomet:
           My sword hath sent millions of Turks to hell,
           Slew all his priests, his kinsmen, and his friends,    180
           And yet I live untouch'd by Mahomet.
           There is a God, full of revenging wrath,
           From whom the thunder and the lightning breaks,
           Whose scourge I am, and him will I obey.
           So, Casane; fling them in the fire –  *[they burn the books*
           Now, Mahomet, if thou have any power,
           Come down thyself and work a miracle:
           Thou art not worthy to be worshipped
           That suffer'st flames of fire to burn the writ
           Wherein the sum of thy religion rests:         190
           Why send'st thou not a furious whirlwind down,
           To blow thy Alcoran up to thy throne,
           Where men report thou sitt'st by God himself?
           Or vengeance on the head of Tamburlaine
           That shakes his sword against thy majesty,
           And spurns the abstracts of thy foolish laws?
           Well, soldiers, Mahomet remains in hell;

He cannot hear the voice of Tamburlaine:
Seek out another godhead to adore;
The God that sits in heaven, if any god,          200
For he is God alone, and none but he.

*Re-enter* TECHELLES

TECHELLES  I have fulfill'd your highness' will, my lord:
Thousands of men, drown'd in Asphaltis' lake,
Have made the water swell above the banks,
And fishes, fed by human carcasses,
Amaz'd, swim up and down upon the waves,
As when they swallow assafoetida,
Which makes them fleet aloft and gape for air.

TAMBUR.  Well, then, my friendly lords, what now remains,
But that we leave sufficient garrison,          210
And presently depart to Persia,
To triumph after all our victories?

THERID.  Ay, good my lord, let us in haste to Persia;
And let this captain be remov'd the walls
To some high hill about the city here.

TAMBUR.  Let it be so – about it, soldiers –
But stay; I feel myself distemper'd suddenly.

TECHELLES  What is it dares distemper Tamburlaine?

TAMBUR.  Something, Techelles; but I know not what –
But, forth, ye vassals! Whatsoe'er it be.          220
Sickness or death can never conquer me.

                                        [*exeunt*


SCENE 2

*Enter* CALLAPINE, KING OF AMASIA, *a Captain and train,*
*with drums and trumpets*

CALLAPINE  King of Amasia, now our mighty host
Marcheth in Asia Major, where the streams
Of Euphrates and Tigris swiftly run;
And here may we behold great Babylon,
Circled about with Limnasphaltis' lake,
Where Tamburlaine with all his army lies,

Which being faint and weary with the siege,
We may lie ready to encounter him
Before his host be full from Babylon,
And so revenge our latest grievous loss,                    10
If God or Mahomet send any aid.

AMASIA     Doubt not, my lord, but we shall conquer him:
The monster that hath drunk a sea of blood,
And yet gapes still for more to quench his thirst,
Our Turkish swords shall headlong send to hell;
And that vile carcass, drawn by warlike kings,
The fowls shall eat, for never sepulchre
Shall grace this base-born tyrant Tamburlaine.

CALLAPINE  When I record my parents' slavish life,
Their cruel death, mine own captivity,                       20
My viceroys' bondage under Tamburlaine,
Methinks I could sustain a thousand deaths
To be reveng'd of all his villany —
Ah, sacred Mahomet, thou that hast seen
Millions of Turks perish by Tamburlaine,
Kingdoms made waste, brave cities sack'd and burnt,
And but one host is left to honour thee,
Aid thy obedient servant Callapine,
And make him, after all these overthrows,
To triumph over cursed Tamburlaine!                         30

AMASIA     Fear not, my lord: I see great Mahomet,
Clothed in purple clouds, and on his head
A chaplet brighter than Apollo's crown,
Marching about the air with armed men,
To join with you against this Tamburlaine.

CAPTAIN    Renowned general, mighty Callapine,
Though God himself and holy Mahomet
Should come in person to resist your power,
Yet might your mighty host encounter all,
And pull proud Tamburlaine upon his knees                    40
To sue for mercy at your highness' feet.

CALLAPINE  Captain, the force of Tamburlaine is great,
His fortune greater, and the victories
Wherewith he hath so sore dismay'd the world
Are greatest to discourage all our drifts;

Yet, when the pride of Cynthia is at full,
She wanes again; and so shall his, I hope.
For we have here the chief selected men
Of twenty several kingdoms at the least;
Nor ploughman, priest, nor merchant, stays at home;
All Turkey is in arms with Callapine;
And never will we sunder camps and arms
Before himself or his be conquered:
This is the time that must eternise me
For conquering the tyrant of the world.
Come, soldiers, let us lie in wait for him,
And, if we find him absent from his camp,
Or that it be rejoin'd again at full,
Assail it, and be sure of victory.

[*exeunt*

## SCENE 3

*Enter* THERIDAMAS, TECHELLES, *and* USUMCASANE

THERID.    Weep, heavens, and vanish into liquid tears!
Fall, stars that govern his nativity,
And summon all the shining lamps of heaven
To cast their bootless fires to the earth,
And shed their feeble influence in the air:
Muffle your beauties with eternal clouds;
For Hell and Darkness pitch their pitchy tents,
And Death, with armies of Cimmerian spirits,
Gives battle 'gainst the heart of Tamburlaine!
Now, in defiance of that wonted love          10
Your sacred virtues pour'd upon his throne,
And made his state an honour to the heavens,
These cowards invisibly assail his soul,
And threaten conquest on our sovereign;
But, if he die, your glories are disgrac'd,
Earth droops, and says that hell in heaven is plac'd!

TECHELLES  O, then, ye powers that sway eternal seats,
And guide this massy substance of the earth,
If you retain desert of holiness,

        As your supreme estates instruct our thoughts,    20
        Be not inconstant, careless of your fame,
        Bear not the burden of your enemies' joys,
        Triumphing in his fall when you advanc'd;
        But, as his birth, life, health, and majesty
        Were strangely blest and governed by heaven,
        So honour, heaven (till heaven dissolved be),
        His birth, his life, his health, and majesty!

USUMCAS. Blush, heaven, to lose the honour of thy name,
        To see thy footstool set upon thy head;
        And let no baseness in thy haughty breast    30
        Sustain a shame of such inexcellence,
        To see the devils mount in angels' thrones,
        And angels dive into the pools of hell!
        And, though they think their painful date is out,
        And that their power is puissant as Jove's,
        Which makes them manage arms against thy state,
        Yet make them feel the strength of Tamburlaine
        (Thy instrument and note of majesty)
        Is greater far than they can thus subdue;
        For, if he die, thy glory is disgrac'd,    40
        Earth droops, and says that hell in heaven is plac'd!

*Enter* TAMBURLAINE, *drawn in his chariot (as before) by*
ORCANES *king of Natolia, and the* KING OF JERUSALEM;
     AMYRAS, CELEBINUS, *and Physicians*

TAMBUR. What daring god torments my body thus,
        And seeks to conquer mighty Tamburlaine?
        Shall sickness prove me now to be a man,
        That have been term'd the terror of the world?
        Techelles and the rest, come, take your swords,
        And threaten him whose hand afflicts my soul:
        Come, let us march against the powers of heaven,
        And set black streamers in the firmament,
        To signify the slaughter of the gods.    50
        Ah, friends, what shall I do? I cannot stand.
        Come, carry me to war against the gods,
        That thus envy the health of Tamburlaine.

THERID. Ah, good my lord, leave these impatient words,

Which add much danger to your malady!

TAMBUR. Why, shall I sit and languish in this pain?
No, strike the drums, and, in revenge of this,
Come, let us charge our spears, and pierce his breast
Whose shoulders bear the axis of the world,
That, if I perish, heaven and earth may fade.          60
Theridamas, haste to the court of Jove;
Will him to send Apollo hither straight,
To cure me, or I'll fetch him down myself.

TECHELLES Sit still, my gracious lord; this grief will cease,
And cannot last, it is so violent.

TAMBUR. Not last, Techelles! No, for I shall die,
See, where my slave, the ugly monster Death,
Shaking and quivering, pale and wan for fear,
Stands aiming at me with his murdering dart,
Who flies away at every glance I give,          70
And, when I look away, comes stealing on –
Villain, away, and hie thee to the field!
I and mine army come to load thy back
With souls of thousand mangled carcasses –
Look, where he goes! But, see, he comes again,
Because I stay! Techelles, let us march,
And weary Death with bearing souls to hell.

I PHYSIC. Pleaseth your majesty to drink this potion,
Which will abate the fury of your fit,
And cause some milder spirits govern you.          80

TAMBUR. Tell me what think you of my sickness now?

I PHYSIC. I view'd your urine, and the hypostasis,
Thick and obscure, doth make your danger great:
Your veins are full of accidental heat,
Whereby the moisture of your blood is dried:
The humidum and calor, which some hold
Is not a parcel of the elements,
But of a substance more divine and pure,
Is almost clean extinguished and spent;
Which, being the cause of life, imports your death:          90
Besides, my lord, this day is critical,
Dangerous to those whose crisis is as yours:
Your artiers, which alongst the veins convey

The lively spirits which the heart engenders,
Are parch'd and void of spirit, that the soul,
Wanting those organons by which it moves,
Cannot endure, by argument of art.
Yet if your majesty may escape this day,
No doubt but you shall soon recover all.

TAMBUR.　Then will I comfort all my vital parts,　　　　100
And live, in spite of death, above a day.

*[alarms within*

*Enter a Messenger*

MESSENGER　My lord, young Callapine, that lately fled from your
majesty, hath now gathered a fresh army, and, hearing
your absence in the field, offers to set upon us presently.

TAMBUR.　See, my physicians, now, how Jove hath sent
A present medicine to recure my pain!
My looks shall make them fly; and, might I follow,
There should not one of all the villain's power
Live to give offer of another fight.

USUMCAS.　I joy, my lord, your highness is so strong,　　　　110
That can endure so well your royal presence,
Which only will dismay the enemy.

TAMBUR.　I know it will, Casane – Draw, you slaves!
In spite of death, I will go show my face.

*[alarms; exit Tamburlaine with all the rest
(except the Physicians), and re-enter presently*

TAMBUR.　Thus are the villain cowards fled for fear,
Like summer's vapours vanish'd by the sun;
And, could I but a while pursue the field,
That Callapine should be my slave again.
But I perceive my martial strength is spent:
In vain I strive and rail against those powers　　　　120
That mean t' invest me in a higher throne,
As much too high for this disdainful earth.
Give me a map; then let me see how much
Is left for me to conquer all the world,
That these, my boys, may finish all my wants.

*[one brings a map*

Here I began to march towards Persia,

Along Armenia and the Caspian Sea,
And thence unto Bithynia, where I took
The Turk and his great empress prisoners.
Then march'd I into Egypt and Arabia;                    130
And here, not far from Alexandria,
Whereas the Terrene and the Red Sea meet,
Being distant less than full a hundred leagues
I meant to cut a channel to them both,
That men might quickly sail to India.
From thence to Nubia near Borno-lake,
And so along the Aethiopian sea,
Cutting the tropic line of Capricorn,
I conquer'd all as far as Zanzibar.
Then, by the northern part of Africa,                   140
I came at last to Graecia, and from thence
To Asia, where I stay against my will;
Which is from Scythia, where I first began,
Backwards and forwards near five thousand leagues.
Look here, my boys; see, what a world of ground
Lies westward from the midst of Cancer's line
Unto the rising of this earthly globe,
Whereas the sun, declining from our sight,
Begins the day with our Antipodes!
And shall I die, and this unconquered?                   150
Lo, here, my sons, are all the golden mines,
Inestimable drugs and precious stones,
More worth than Asia and the world beside;
And from th'Antarctic Pole eastward behold
As much more land, which never was descried,
Wherein are rocks of pearl that shine as bright
As all the lamps that beautify the sky!
And shall I die, and this unconquered?
Here, lovely boys; what death forbids my life,
That let your lives command in spite of death.          160

AMYRAS    Alas, my lord, how should our bleeding hearts,
Wounded and broken with your highness' grief,
Retain a thought of joy or spark of life?
Your soul gives essence to our wretched subjects,
Whose matter is incorporate in your flesh.

CELEBINUS   Your pains do pierce our souls; no hope survives,
            For by your life we entertain our lives.
TAMBUR.     But, sons, this subject, not of force enough
            To hold the fiery spirit it contains,
            Must part, imparting his impressions                  170
            By equal portions into both your breasts;
            My flesh, divided in your precious shapes,
            Shall still retain my spirit, though I die,
            And live in all your seeds immortally —
            Then now remove me, that I may resign
            My place and proper title to my son —
            First, take my scourge and my imperial crown,
            And mount my royal chariot of estate,
            That I may see thee crown'd before I die —
            Help me, my lords, to make my last remove.             180
                                    [they assist Tamburlaine to
                                      descend from the chariot
THERID.     A woful change, my lord, that daunts our thoughts
            More than the ruin of our proper souls!
TAMBUR.     Sit up, my son, [and] let me see how well
            Thou wilt become thy father's majesty.
AMYRAS      With what a flinty bosom should I joy
            The breath of life and burden of my soul,
            If not resolv'd into resolved pains,
            My body's mortified lineaments
            Should exercise the motions of my heart,
            Pierc'd with the joy of any dignity!                   190
            O father, if the unrelenting ears
            Of Death and Hell be shut against my prayers,
            And that the spiteful influence of Heaven
            Deny my soul fruition of her joy,
            How should I step, or stir my hateful feet
            Against the inward powers of my heart,
            Leading a life that only strives to die,
            And plead in vain unpleasing sovereignty?
TAMBUR.     Let not thy love exceed thine honour, son,
            Nor bar thy mind that magnanimity                      200
            That nobly must admit necessity.

|          | Sit up, my boy, and with these silken reins |
|----------|---------------------------------------------|
|          | Bridle the steeled stomachs of these jades. |
| THERID.  | My lord, you must obey his majesty, |
|          | Since fate commands and proud necessity. |
| AMYRAS   | Heavens witness me with what a broken heart |

*[mounting the chariot*

And damned spirit I ascend this seat.
And send my soul, before my father die,
His anguish and his burning agony!

*[they crown Amyras*

TAMBUR.   Now fetch the hearse of fair Zenocrate;              210
          Let it be plac'd by this my fatal chair,
          And serve as parcel of my funeral.

USUMCAS.  Then feels your majesty no sovereign ease,
          Nor may our hearts, all drown'd in tears of blood,
          Joy any hope of your recovery?

TAMBUR.   Casane, no; the monarch of the earth,
          And eyeless monster that torments my soul,
          Cannot behold the tears ye shed for me,
          And therefore still augments his cruelty.

TECHELLES Then let some god oppose his holy power             220
          Against the wrath and tyranny of Death,
          That his tear-thirsty and unquenched hate
          May be upon himself reverberate!

*[they bring in the hearse of Zenocrate*

TAMBUR.   Now, eyes, enjoy your latest benefit,
          And, when my soul hath virtue of your sight,
          Pierce through the coffin and the sheet of gold,
          And glut your longings with a heaven of joy.
          So, reign, my son; scourge and control those slaves,
          Guiding thy chariot with thy father's hand.
          As precious is the charge thou undertak'st             230
          As that which Clymene's brain-sick son did guide,
          When wandering Phoebe's ivory cheeks
                                           were scorch'd,
          And all the earth, like Aetna, breathing fire:
          Be warn'd by him, then; learn with awful eye
          To sway a throne as dangerous as his;
          For, if thy body thrive not full of thoughts

As pure and fiery as Phyteus' beams,
The nature of these proud rebelling jades
Will take occasion by the slenderest hair,
And draw thee piecemeal, like Hippolytus,    240
Through rocks more steep and sharp than
                              Caspian cliffs:
The nature of thy chariot will not bear
A guide of baser temper than myself,
More than heaven's coach the pride of Phaeton.
Farewell, my boys! My dearest friends, farewell!
My body feels, My soul doth weep to see
Your sweet desires depriv'd my company,
For Tamburlaine, the scourge of God, must die.  *[dies*

AMYRAS    Meet heaven and earth, and here let all things end,
For earth hath spent the pride of all her fruit,    250
And heaven consum'd his choicest living fire!
Let earth and heaven his timeless death deplore,
For both their worths will equal him no more!
                                      *[exeunt*

# THE TRAGICAL HISTORY
# OF DOCTOR FAUSTUS

## THE A-TEXT (1604)

# INTRODUCTION TO DOCTOR FAUSTUS
## (1604 AND 1616)

Marlowe's *Doctor Faustus* exists in two distinct versions: an edition published in 1604, eleven years after Marlowe's death (often called the A-text in critical studies), and one published in 1616 (the B-text). Both are printed in this edition. There are several discrepancies between the two. The 1616 version is much longer than that of 1604, containing over 600 additional lines. It contains a number of comic scenes which are not present in the earlier version. It is also more concerned with the visual representation of hell and the devils, perhaps suggesting that it was intended for a theatre where more ambitious staging effects could be achieved. The descending throne in Act 5 is a good example of this use of elaborate stage machinery. We know, from an inventory of props held by the Lord Admiral's Men, that a number of stage properties had been acquired for Marlowe's plays, including, for *Doctor Faustus*, 'one Hell mouth'. It has been argued that the differences between the plays identify the 1604 version as closer to our idea of a tragedy in which individual volition is paramount, whereas the 1616 text has affinities with the didactic medieval form of the morality play, in which virtue is rewarded and vice punished. It could, however, be argued that the 1616 text gives more agency to Faustus as well as, paradoxically, a more sinister and deliberate role to Mephistopheles, who claims, in the later version only, that it was he who made Faustus stray in the first place: ' 'Twas I that, when thou wert i' the way to heaven,/ Damm'd up thy passage; when thou took'st the book/ To view the scriptures, then I turn'd the leaves / And led thine eye'. It has also been suggested that the later text makes explicit and more theologically orthodox actions which are left ambiguous in the 1604 edition. For example, the earlier text ends with Faustus being led off by Mephistopheles, and we are left to imagine the details of his hellish fate. In the 1616 version, an additional scene in which the scholars find his dismembered body graphically illustrates the physical nature of his torment. Most modern editions create a single play as an amalgam or conflation of the two texts according to the editor's personal sense of what is significant about each version. In this edition the two texts are printed separately, so that their differences can be identified and analysed without being effaced by a conflated text.

There has been extensive critical debate about the relative statuses of the two versions of the play, largely concerned to identify which is the 'original'. Since neither version was printed during Marlowe's lifetime, neither can be identified as decisively authorial. The quest to prioritise the two versions may, however, rest on a misapprehension about the role of authors and the status of the text in the early modern theatre industry. Philip Henslowe, the theatrical entrepreneur who owned the Rose theatre, is recorded as paying two writers, William Bird and Samuel Rowley, to write additions to the play in 1602. It has tended to be assumed that these additions are the scenes which appear in the 1616 text but not in 1604, namely the additional comic scenes and the representations of hell, but this cannot be proved, since the dates show that Marlowe's play had been added to before it ever appeared in print. Many scholars have suggested that other writers, too, had a hand in the two texts of the play, either working alongside Marlowe or changing his script after his death. Our own modern stress on the authority of the writer and the reverence for the detail of what he or she has written may blind us to the fact that the Elizabethan theatre was, by its very nature, collaborative. Many, perhaps the majority, of plays were not written by a single author, and all plays were shaped and changed by the processes of rehearsal and performance. Plays were performance scripts and entertainment commodities, not literary works, and in the absence of any legal system of copyright, they belonged not to their author/s, but to the playing company which could alter, elaborate, rewrite or cut them according to the demands of the particular production. What the two versions of *Doctor Faustus* offer us is a chance to see how the play may have looked at different moments in its theatrical history, as well as the opportunity to see how the variations between the text affect the story and our response to it.

*Doctor Faustus* has its immediate source in the English translation, published in 1592, of the German story of Faust, a man who enters into a pact with the devil. Fasutus calls up Mephistopheles and makes a compact to surrender his soul to the devil after twenty-four years, during which time Mephistopheles will supply him with anything he demands. Under this bargain, Faustus travels to Rome and plays some unedifying tricks on the Pope, and he asks Mephistopheles to bring him Helen of Troy. His philosophical questions about the universe remain unanswered, and as the hour approaches for the bargain to be enacted his anguish grows, although he is unable or unwilling to take the advice of others and repent of his sins. He is led into hell by Mephistopheles at the end of the play. The prologue seems to set the play in a conventional morality structure, by which Faustus' desire to 'mount above his reach' is compared to Icarus' doomed attempt to fly, and suffers the same fate. Audiences of *Doctor Faustus* are invited to watch 'The form of Faustus' fortunes, good or bad', suggesting some moral ambiguity about what is to be performed. The prologue identifies him as a man of humble birth who has nevertheless gone to university – perhaps there is an echo of Marlowe himself here – and suggests that it is the logical development of Faustus's pride, or 'self-conceit', which leads him to 'a devilish exercise'. Faustus 'surfeits upon cursed necromancy' and places magic above all else, particularly above the religious observances which ought to form 'his chiefest bliss'. The prologue seems to preempt our responses, as it tells us what is going to happen before we actually see it. Similarly, the play ends with another didactic intervention, an epilogue which rounds off the story by pointing out its moral: the story of Faustus' 'hellish fall' is presented to warn others of the dangers of exceeding the heavenly-ordained limits of knowledge. The last lines of the play exhort its audiences 'only to wonder at unlawful things' – not, that is, to try and fathom them. It is a quietist conclusion, preaching a doctrine of incuriosity and subjection to conventional limitations.

The prologue and epilogue to *Doctor Faustus* thus establish the play as a fable about the dangers of knowledge. The link between knowledge and sin or disobedience is key to the biblical story of the

Fall, where it is the fruit of the Tree of Knowledge which is forbidden to Adam and Eve and which they are tempted to eat. Faustus' story draws on this long association, and also anticipates the scores of amoral scientists from Mary Shelley's Victor Frankenstein to cinematic 'mad scientists' who are developing scientific discovery beyond what is considered humanly right. The phrase 'playing God' is commonly used in the media for those scientific endeavours which seem to us grossly to intervene in natural processes, and it is this same concern which animates the play. The sixteenth century was a time of rapid scientific development and discovery, and much of this new understanding ran counter to religious teaching. The astronomer Galileo, for example, was forced by the Inquisition or Church court to renounce his discoveries which challenged the view that the earth was the centre of the universe. The more humans discovered about their world, the more imperative it was for religion to stress the dangers inherent in the pursuit of knowledge. Antagonism between theology and science was considerable. Faustus represents the interface between them: a man who excelled in 'heavenly matters of theology' but who began to glut on 'learning's golden gifts'. He is the dark side of Renaissance man, or the obverse of the humanist movement's interest in developing all branches of knowledge – a man, like other Marlovian heroes, who so immoderately pursues a goal which is not in itself a bad thing but which is rendered so by the single-minded and excessive nature of the quest. Like Tamburlaine, Faustus wants to break through the barriers of mortality: the words 'yet art thou still but Faustus and a man' are the *cri de coeur* of the great scholar who wants more.

It is because Faustus is such an epitome of Renaissance aspiration that our attitude to the play's central protagonist is always divided. Although Faustus is wrong, he is, like Tamburlaine perhaps, magnificently wrong, and his aspirations, however heretical, have a grandeur about them. The play's sympathies seem to be with Faustus, particularly in the absence of any alternative figure of dramatic or psychological interest. His final anguished, broken soliloquy gives grounds for claiming him as the first character with inner complexity on the Renaissance stage. On the other hand, the play's stern and fearful depiction of the consequences of rebellion – initially that of Mephistopheles, whose torment 'in being deprived of everlasting bliss' poignantly prefigures Faustus' – leaves little room for an alternative interpretation. Faustus' rewards for his great sacrifice are repeatedly shown to be miserable, and the play's uncomfortable yoking of farcical comedy with this tragedy of damnation seems determined to belittle the intellectual status with which he is decorated at the outset. The question, too, of how far he is in control of his actions is one which exists within and between the two versions of the play, and some of the differences between them might be attributed to a desire to make this most crucial aspect of the play more secure. Is Faustus' fate already inevitable – a Calvinist approach to elected salvation – or is he given free will which he fatally misuses? At what point in the play would it be possible to repent? Is it the bond which marks the point of no return, or could sincere repentance, as the Old Man suggests in Act 5, still avert the terrible conclusion? Some critics have attempted to argue for one position or another, but what seems more centrally true of both texts of the play, as well as the interplay between them, is that they are preoccupied with an insistent theological questioning. However orthodox the final punishment of Faustus might be, the means by which this is, or becomes, inevitable, takes up more of the play and more of our energies than the moralistic framework of prologue and epilogue allow.

Faustus seals his bond with the devil in an ironic, blasphemous echo of Christ's words on the cross – Consummatum est – but Christ too wonders why God has forsaken him, and God himself is a notable absence in the play. The devils are much keener for Faustus' soul than God is, and goodness is presented as an act of faith not proof, in a play which can offer only a meek challenge to the wily and attractive Mephistopheles in the persons of the Old Man and the Good Angel. There are contemporary accounts of performances of the play in which a real devil seemed to appear among the actors: the terrifying proximity of Hell to the Elizabethan mind is shared by Doctor Faustus and its audiences, worlds in which God can never be revealed, can only be imagined and hoped for. It is not, ultimately, God who punishes Faustus' sin.

# CHARACTERS IN THE PLAY

THE POPE
CARDINAL OF LORRAIN
THE EMPEROR OF GERMANY
DUKE OF VANHOLT
FAUSTUS
VALDES
CORNELIUS } *friends to* FAUSTUS
WAGNER, *servant to* FAUSTUS
CLOWN
ROBIN
RALPH
VINTNER
HORSE-COURSER
A KNIGHT
AN OLD MAN
SCHOLARS, FRIARS *and* ATTENDANTS
DUCHESS OF VANHOLT
LUCIFER
BELZEBUB
MEPHISTOPHILIS
GOOD ANGEL
EVIL ANGEL
THE SEVEN DEADLY SINS
DEVILS
SPIRITS *in the shapes of* ALEXANDER THE GREAT,
    *of his* PARAMOUR *and of* HELEN
CHORUS

# THE TRAGICAL HISTORY
# OF DOCTOR FAUSTUS

## THE A-TEXT (1604)

*Enter* CHORUS

CHORUS      Not marching now in fields of Thrasymene,
Where Mars did mate the Carthaginians,
Nor sporting in the dalliance of love,
In courts of kings where state is overturn'd;
Nor in the pomp of proud audacious deeds,
Intends our Muse to vaunt her heavenly verse:
Only this, gentlemen – we must perform
The form of Faustus' fortunes, good or bad:
To patient judgments we appeal our plaud,
And speak for Faustus in his infancy.      10
Now is he born, his parents base of stock,
In Germany, within a town call'd Rhodes:
Of riper years, to Wertenberg he went,
Whereas his kinsmen chiefly brought him up.
So soon he profits in divinity,
The fruitful plot of scholarism grac'd,
That shortly he was grac'd with doctor's name,
Excelling all whose sweet delight disputes
In heavenly matters of theology;
Till swoln with cunning, of a self-conceit,      20
His waxen wings did mount above his reach,
And, melting, heavens conspir'd his overthrow;
For, falling to a devilish exercise,
And glutted now with learning's golden gifts,
He surfeits upon cursed necromancy;
Nothing so sweet as magic is to him,
Which he prefers before his chiefest bliss:
And this the man that in his study sits.

         [*exit*

# ACT ONE

## SCENE I

FAUSTUS *discovered in his study*

FAUSTUS   Settle thy studies, Faustus, and begin
To sound the depth of that thou wilt profess:
Having commenc'd, be a divine in show,
Yet level at the end of every art,
And live and die in Aristotle's works.
Sweet Analytics, 'tis thou hast ravish'd me!
*Bene disserere est finis logices.*
Is, to dispute well, logic's chiefest end?
Affords this art no greater miracle?
Then read no more; thou hast attain'd that end:      10
A greater subject fitteth Faustus' wit:
Bid Economy farewell, and Galen come,
Seeing, *Ubi desinit philosophus, ibi incipit medicus:*
Be a physician, Faustus; heap up gold,
And be eternis'd for some wondrous cure:
*Summum bonum medicinae sanitas,*
The end of physic is our body's health.
Why, Faustus, hast thou not attain'd that end?
Is not thy common talk found aphorisms?
Are not thy bills hung up as monuments,      20
Whereby whole cities have escap'd the plague,
And thousand desperate maladies been eas'd?
Yet art thou still but Faustus, and a man.
Couldst thou make men to live eternally,
Or, being dead, raise them to life again,
Then this profession were to be esteem'd.
Physic, farewell! Where is Justinian?
[*reads*] *Si una eademque res legatur duobus, alter rem, alter*
*valorem, rei, etc.*
A pretty case of paltry legacies!      30
[*reads*] *Exhaereditare filium non potest pater, nisi, etc.*
Such is the subject of the institute,

And universal body of the law:
This study fits a mercenary drudge,
Who aims at nothing but external trash:
Too servile and illiberal for me.
When all is done, divinity is best:
Jerome's Bible, Faustus; view it well.
[*reads*] *Stipendium peccati mors est.* Ha! *Stipendium, etc.*
The reward of sin is death: that's hard.     40
[*reads*] *Si peccasse negamus, fallimur, et nulla est in nobis
veritas;* if we say that we have no sin, we deceive our-
selves, and there's no truth in us. Why, then, belike we
must sin, and so consequently die:
Ay, we must die an everlasting death.
What doctrine call you this, *Che sera, sera,*
What will be, shall be? Divinity, adieu!
These metaphysics of magicians,
And necromantic books are heavenly;
Lines, circles, scenes, letters, and characters;     50
Ay, these are those that Faustus most desires.
O, what a world of profit and delight,
Of power, of honour, of omnipotence,
Is promis'd to the studious artisan!
All things that move between the quiet poles
Shall be at my command: emperors and kings
Are but obeyed in their several provinces,
Nor can they raise the wind, or rend the clouds;
But his dominion that exceeds in this,
Stretcheth as far as doth the mind of man;     60
A sound magician is a mighty god:
Here, Faustus, tire thy brains to gain a deity.

*Enter* WAGNER

Wagner, commend me to my dearest friends,
The German Valdes and Cornelius;
Request them earnestly to visit me.

WAGNER     I will, sir.                             [*exit*

FAUSTUS     Their conference will be a greater help to me
Than all my labours, plod I ne'er so fast.

*Enter* GOOD ANGEL *and* EVIL ANGEL

GOOD A.    O, Faustus, lay thy damned book aside,
           And gaze not on it lest it tempt thy soul,          70
           And heap God's heavy wrath upon thy head!
           Read, read the Scriptures – that is blasphemy.

EVIL A.    Go forward, Faustus, in that famous art
           Wherein all Nature's treasure is contain'd:
           Be thou on earth as Jove is in the sky,
           Lord and commander of these elements.

                                               [*exeunt Angels*

FAUSTUS    How am I glutted with conceit of this!
           Shall I make spirits fetch me what I please,
           Resolve me of all ambiguities,
           Perform what desperate enterprise I will?          80
           I'll have them fly to India for gold,
           Ransack the ocean for orient pearl,
           And search all corners of the new-found world
           For pleasant fruits and princely delicates;
           I'll have them read me strange philosophy,
           And tell the secrets of all foreign kings;
           I'll have them wall all Germany with brass,
           And make swift Rhine circle fair Wertenberg;
           I'll have them fill the public schools with silk,
           Wherewith the students shall be bravely clad;      90
           I'll levy soldiers with the coin they bring,
           And chase the Prince of Parma from our land,
           And reign sole king of all the provinces;
           Yea, stranger engines for the brunt of war,
           Than was the fiery keel at Antwerp's bridge,
           I'll make my servile spirits to invent.

*Enter* VALDES *and* CORNELIUS

           Come, German Valdes and Cornelius,
           And make me blest with your sage conference.
           Valdes, sweet Valdes, and Cornelius,
           Know that your words have won me at the last       100
           To practise magic and concealed arts:
           Yet not your words only, but mine own fantasy,
           That will receive no object; for my head

But ruminates on necromantic skill.
Philosophy is odious and obscure;
Both law and physic are for petty wits;
Divinity is basest of the three,
Unpleasant, harsh, contemptible, and vile:
'Tis magic, magic, that hath ravish'd me.
Then, gentle friends, aid me in this attempt;    110
And I, that have with concise syllogisms
Gravell'd the pastors of the German church,
And made the flowering pride of Wertenberg
Swarm to my problems, as the infernal spirits
On sweet Musaeus when he came to hell,
Will be as cunning as Agrippa was,
Whose shadow made all Europe honour him.

VALDES    Faustus, these books, thy wit, and our experience,
Shall make all nations to canonise us.
As Indian Moors obey their Spanish lords,    120
So shall the spirits of every element
Be always serviceable to us three;
Like lions shall they guard us when we please;
Like Almain rutters with their horsemen's staves.
Or Lapland giants, trotting by our sides,
Sometimes like women, or unwedded maids,
Shadowing more beauty in their airy brows
Than have the white breasts of the queen of love:
From Venice shall they drag huge argosies,
And from America the golden fleece    130
That yearly stuffs old Philip's treasury;
If learned Faustus will be resolute.

FAUSTUS    Valdes, as resolute am I in this
As thou to live: therefore object it not.

CORNELIUS    The miracles that magic will perform
Will make thee vow to study nothing else.
He that is grounded in astrology,
Enrich'd with tongues, well seen in minerals,
Hath all the principles magic doth require:
Then doubt not, Faustus, but to be renowm'd,    140
And more frequented for this mystery

Than heretofore the Delphian oracle.
The spirits tell me they can dry the sea,
And fetch the treasure of all foreign wrecks,
Ay, all the wealth that our forefathers hid
Within the massy entrails of the earth:
Then tell me, Faustus, what shall we three want?

FAUSTUS    Nothing, Cornelius. O, this cheers my soul!
Come, show me some demonstrations magical,
That I may conjure in some lusty grove,     150
And have these joys in full possession.

VALDES    Then haste thee to some solitary grove,
And bear wise Bacon's and Albertus' works,
The Hebrew Psalter, and New Testament;
And whatsoever else is requisite
We will inform thee ere our conference cease.

CORNELIUS    Valdes, first let him know the words of art;
And then, all other ceremonies learn'd,
Faustus may try his cunning by himself.

VALDES    First I'll instruct thee in the rudiments,     160
And then wilt thou be perfecter than I.

FAUSTUS    Then come and dine with me, and, after meat,
We'll canvass every quiddity thereof;
For, ere I sleep, I'll try what I can do:
This night I'll conjure, though I die therefore.

*[exeunt*


## SCENE 2

*Enter two Scholars*

I SCHOLAR    I wonder what's become of Faustus, that was wont to
make our schools ring with *sic probo*.

2 SCHOLAR    That shall we know, for see, here comes his boy.

*Enter* WAGNER

I SCHOLAR    How now, sirrah! Where's thy master?

WAGNER    God in heaven knows.

2 SCHOLAR    Why, dost not thou know?

WAGNER    Yes, I know; but that follows not.

I SCHOLAR    Go to, sirrah! Leave your jesting, and tell us where he is.

WAGNER      That follows not necessary by force of argument, that
            you, being licentiates, should stand upon: therefore
            acknowledge your error, and be attentive.

2 SCHOLAR   Why, didst thou not say thou knewest?

WAGNER      Have you any witness on't?

1 SCHOLAR   Yes, sirrah, I heard you.

WAGNER      Ask my fellow if I be a thief.

2 SCHOLAR   Well, you will not tell us?

WAGNER      Yes, sir, I will tell you; yet, if you were not dunces, you
            would never ask me such a question, for is not he *corpus
            naturale*? And is not that *mobile*? Then wherefore should
            you ask me such a question? But that I am by nature
            phlegmatic, slow to wrath, and prone to lechery (to
            love, I would say), it were not for you to come within
            forty foot of the place of execution, although I do not
            doubt to see you both hanged the next sessions. Thus
            having triumphed over you, I will set my countenance
            like a precisian, and begin to speak thus: Truly, my dear
            brethren, my master is within at dinner, with Valdes
            and Cornelius, as this wine, if it could speak, would
            inform your worships: and so, the Lord bless you,
            preserve you, and keep you, my dear brethren, my dear
            brethren!                                      [*exit*

1 SCHOLAR   Nay, then, I fear he has fallen into that damned art for
            which they two are infamous through the world.

2 SCHOLAR   Were he a stranger, and not allied to me, yet should I
            grieve for him. But, come, let us go and inform the
            Rector, and see if he by his grave counsel can reclaim
            him.

1 SCHOLAR   O, but I fear me nothing can reclaim him!

2 SCHOLAR   Yet let us try what we can do.

                                                          [*exeunt*

## SCENE 3

*Enter* FAUSTUS *to conjure*

FAUSTUS  Now that the gloomy shadow of the earth,
Longing to view Orion's drizzling look,
Leaps from th' antarctic world unto the sky,
And dims the welkin with her pitchy breath,
Faustus, begin thine incantations,
And try if devils will obey thy hest,
Seeing thou hast pray'd and sacrific'd to them.
Within this circle is Jehovah's name,
Forward and backward anagrammatis'd,
Th' abbreviated names of holy saints,                    10
Figures of every adjunct to the heavens,
And characters of signs and erring stars,
By which the spirits are enforc'd to rise:
Then fear not, Faustus, but be resolute,
And try the uttermost magic can perform.
*Sint mihi dei Acherontis propitii! Valeat numen triplex
Jehovae! Ignei, aërii, aquatani spiritus, salvete! Orientis
princeps Belzebub, inferni ardentis monarcha, et Demogorgon,
propitiamus vos, ut appareat et surgat Mephistophilis, quod
tumeraris: per Jehovam, Gehennam, et consecratam aquam
quam nunc spargo, signumque crucis quod nunc facio, et per
vota nostra, ipse nunc surgat nobis dicatus Mephistophilis!*

*Enter* MEPHISTOPHILIS

I charge thee to return, and change thy shape;
Thou art too ugly to attend on me:
Go, and return an old Franciscan friar;
That holy shape becomes a devil best.

                                    [*exit Mephistophilis*

I see there's virtue in my heavenly words:
Who would not be proficient in this art?
How pliant is this Mephistophilis,
Full of obedience and humility!                          30
Such is the force of magic and my spells:
No, Faustus, thou art conjuror laureat,

That canst command great Mephistophilis:
*Quin regis Mephistophilis fratris imagine.*

*Re-enter* MEPHISTOPHILIS *like a Franciscan friar*

MEPHISTO. Now, Faustus, what wouldst thou have me do?
FAUSTUS    I charge thee wait upon me whilst I live,
          To do whatever Faustus shall command,
          Be it to make the moon drop from her sphere,
          Or the ocean to overwhelm the world.
MEPHISTO. I am a servant to great Lucifer,          40
          And may not follow thee without his leave:
          No more than he commands must we perform.
FAUSTUS    Did not he charge thee to appear to me?
MEPHISTO. No, I came hither of mine own accord.
FAUSTUS    Did not my conjuring speeches raise thee? Speak.
MEPHISTO. That was the cause, but yet *per accidens*;
          For, when we hear one rack the name of God,
          Abjure the Scriptures and his Saviour Christ,
          We fly, in hope, to get his glorious soul;
          Nor will we come, unless he use such means     50
          Whereby he is in danger to be damn'd.
          Therefore the shortest cut for conjuring
          Is stoutly to abjure the Trinity,
          And pray devoutly to the prince of hell.
FAUSTUS    So Faustus hath
          Already done; and holds this principle,
          There is no chief but only Belzebub;
          To whom Faustus doth dedicate himself.
          This word 'damnation' terrifies not him,
          For he confounds hell in Elysium:          60
          His ghost be with the old philosophers!
          But, leaving these vain trifles of men's souls,
          Tell me what is that Lucifer thy lord?
MEPHISTO. Arch-regent and commander of all spirits.
FAUSTUS    Was not that Lucifer an angel once?
MEPHISTO. Yes, Faustus, and most dearly lov'd of God.
FAUSTUS    How comes it, then, that he is prince of devils?
MEPHISTO. O, by aspiring pride and insolence;
          For which God threw him from the face of heaven.

| | | |
|---|---|---|
| FAUSTUS | And what are you that live with Lucifer? | 70 |
| MEPHISTO. | Unhappy spirits that fell with Lucifer, | |
| | Conspir'd against our God with Lucifer, | |
| | And are for ever damn'd with Lucifer. | |
| FAUSTUS | Where are you damn'd? | |
| MEPHISTO. | In hell. | |
| FAUSTUS | How comes it, then, that thou art out of hell? | |
| MEPHISTO. | Why, this is hell, nor am I out of it. | |
| | Think'st thou that I, who saw the face of God, | |
| | And tasted the eternal joys of heaven, | |
| | Am not tormented with ten thousand hells, | 80 |
| | In being depriv'd of everlasting bliss? | |
| | O, Faustus, leave these frivolous demands, | |
| | Which strike a terror to my fainting soul! | |
| FAUSTUS | What, is great Mephistophilis so passionate | |
| | For being deprived of the joys of heaven? | |
| | Learn thou of Faustus manly fortitude, | |
| | And scorn those joys thou never shalt possess. | |
| | Go bear these tidings to great Lucifer: | |
| | Seeing Faustus hath incurr'd eternal death | |
| | By desperate thoughts against Jove's deity, | 90 |
| | Say, he surrenders up to him his soul, | |
| | So he will spare him four-and-twenty rears, | |
| | Letting him live in all voluptuousness; | |
| | Having thee ever to attend on me, | |
| | To give me whatsoever I shall ask, | |
| | To tell me whatsoever I demand, | |
| | To slay mine enemies, and aid my friends, | |
| | And always be obedient to my will. | |
| | Go and return to mighty Lucifer, | |
| | And meet me in my study at midnight, | 100 |
| | And then resolve me of thy master's mind. | |
| MEPHISTO. | I will, Faustus. | [exit |
| FAUSTUS | Had I as many souls as there be stars, | |
| | I'd give them all for Mephistophilis. | |
| | By him I'll be great emperor of the world, | |
| | And make a bridge thorough the moving air, | |
| | To pass the ocean with a band of men; | |
| | I'll join the hills that bind the Afric shore, | |

And make that country continent to Spain,
And both contributory to my crown:      110
The Emperor shall not live but by my leave,
Nor any potentate of Germany.
Now that I have obtained what I desir'd,
I'll live in speculation of this art,
Till Mephistophilis return again.

                                       *[exit*

## SCENE 4

### *Enter* WAGNER *and Clown*

WAGNER     Sirrah boy, come hither.

CLOWN     How, boy! Swowns, boy! I hope you have seen many boys with such pickadevaunts as I have: boy, quotha!

WAGNER     Tell me, sirrah, hast thou any comings in?

CLOWN     Ay, and goings out too; you may see else.

WAGNER     Alas, poor slave! See how poverty jesteth in his nakedness! The villain is bare and out of service, and so hungry, that I know he would give his soul to the devil for a shoulder of mutton, though it were blood-raw.

CLOWN     How! My soul to the devil for a shoulder of mutton, though 'twere blood-raw! Not so, good friend: by'r lady, I had need have it well roasted, and good sauce to it, if I pay so dear.

WAGNER     Well, wilt thou serve me and I'll make thee go like *Qui mihi discipulus*?

CLOWN     How, in verse?

WAGNER     No, sirrah; in beaten silk and staves-acre.

CLOWN     How, how, knaves-acre! Ay, I thought that was all the land his father left him. Do you hear? I would be sorry to rob you of your living.      20

WAGNER     Sirrah, I say in staves-acre.

CLOWN     Oho, oho, staves-acre! Why, then, belike, if I were your man, I should be full of vermin.

WAGNER     So thou shalt, whether thou beest with me or no. But, sirrah, leave your jesting, and bind yourself presently unto me for seven years, or I'll turn all the lice about thee into familiars, and they shall tear thee in pieces.

CLOWN     Do you hear, sir? You may save that labour; they are
          too familiar with me already: swowns, they are as bold
          with my flesh as if they had paid for their meat and
          drink.

WAGNER    Well, do your hear, sirrah? Hold, take these guilders.
                                                    [gives money

CLOWN     Gridirons! What be they?

WAGNER    Why, French crowns.

CLOWN     Mass, but for the name of French crowns, a man were
          as good have as many English counters. And what
          should I do with these?

WAGNER    Why, now, sirrah, thou art at an hour's warning,
          whensoever and wheresoever the devil shall fetch thee.

CLOWN     No, no; here, take your gridirons again.          40

WAGNER    Truly, I'll none of them.

CLOWN     Truly, but you shall.

WAGNER    Bear witness I gave them him.

CLOWN     Bear witness I give them you again.

WAGNER    Well, I will cause two devils presently to fetch thee
          away – Baliol and Belcher!

CLOWN     Let your Baliol and your Belcher come here, and I'll
          knock them, they were never so knocked since they
          were devils: say I should kill one of them, what would
          folks say? 'Do ye see yonder tall fellow in the round
          slop? He has killed the devil.' So I should be called
          Kill-devil all the parish over.

*Enter two Devils; and the Clown runs up and down crying*

WAGNER    Baliol and Belcher – spirits, away!    [exeunt Devils

CLOWN     What, are they gone? A vengeance on them! They
          have vile long nails. There was a he-devil and a she-
          devil: I'll tell you how you shall know them; all he-
          devils has horns, and all she-devils has clifts and cloven
          feet.

WAGNER    Well, sirrah, follow me.

CLOWN     But, do you hear? If I should serve you, would you
          teach me to raise up Banios and Belcheos?          60

WAGNER    I will teach thee to turn thyself to anything, to a dog,
          or a cat, or a mouse, or a rat, or anything.

CLOWN     How! A Christian fellow to a dog, or a cat, a mouse, or a rat! No, no, sir, if you turn me into anything, let it be in the likeness of a little pretty frisking flea, that I may he here and there and everywhere: O, I'll tickle the pretty wenches' plackets! I'll be amongst them, i'faith.

WAGNER   Well, sirrah, come.

CLOWN     But, do you hear, Wagner?

WAGNER   How – Baliol and Belcher!              70

CLOWN     O Lord! I pray, sir, let Banio and Belcher go sleep.

WAGNER   Villain, call me Master Wagner, and let thy left eye be diametarily fixed upon my right heel, with *quasi vestigiis nostris insistere.*                   *[exit*

CLOWN     God forgive me, he speaks Dutch fustian. Well, I'll follow him; I'll serve him, that's flat.

                                                  *[exit*

# ACT TWO

## SCENE I

FAUSTUS *discovered in his study*

FAUSTUS    Now, Faustus, must
Thou needs be damn'd, and canst thou not be sav'd:
What boots it, then, to think of God or heaven?
Away with such vain fancies, and despair;
Despair in God, and trust in Belzebub:
Now go not backward; no, Faustus, be resolute:
Why waver'st thou? O, something soundeth
                              in mine ears,
'Abjure this magic, turn to God again!'
Ay, and Faustus will turn to God again.
To God? He loves thee not;                                    10
The god thou serv'st is thine own appetite,
Wherein is fix'd the love of Belzebub:
To him I'll build an altar and a church,
And offer lukewarm blood of new-horn babes.

*Enter* GOOD ANGEL *and* EVIL ANGEL

GOOD A.   Sweet Faustus, leave that execrable art.
FAUSTUS   Contrition, prayer, repentance – what of them?
GOOD A.   O, they are means to bring thee unto heaven!
EVIL A.    Rather illusions, fruits of lunacy,
That make men foolish that do trust them most.
GOOD A.   Sweet Faustus, think of heaven and heavenly things.
EVIL A.    No, Faustus; think of honour and of wealth.
                                      *[exeunt Angels*

FAUSTUS   Of wealth!
Why, the signiory of Embden shall he mine,
When Mepistophilis shall stand by me.
What god can hurt thee, Faustus? Thou art safe:
Cast no more doubts – Come, Mephistophilis,
And bring glad tidings from great Lucifer –
Is't not midnight? Come, Mephistophilis,
*Veni, veni Mephistophile!*

*Enter* MEPHISTOPHILIS

|   |   |   |
|---|---|---|

Now tell me what says Lucifer, thy lord?                    30

MEPHISTO.  That I shall wait on Faustus whilst he lives,
So he will buy my service with his soul.

FAUSTUS  Already Faustus hath hazarded that for thee.

MEPHISTO.  But, Faustus, thou must bequeath it solemnly,
And write a deed of gift with thine own blood;
For that security craves great Lucifer.
If thou deny it, I will back to hell.

FAUSTUS  Stay, Mephistophilis, and tell me, what good will my
soul do thy lord?

MEPHISTO.  Enlarge his kingdom.                              40

FAUSTUS  Is that the reason why he tempts us thus?

MEPHISTO.  *Solamen miseris socios habuisse doloris.*

FAUSTUS  Why, have you any pain that torture others?

MEPHISTO.  As great as have the human souls of men.
But, tell me, Faustus, shall I have thy soul?
And I will be thy slave, and wait on thee,
And give thee more than thou hast wit to ask.

FAUSTUS  Ay, Mephistophilis, I give it thee.

MEPHISTO.  Then, Faustus, stab thy arm courageously,
And bind thy soul, that at some certain day            50
Great Lucifer may claim it as his own;
And then be thou as great as Lucifer.

FAUSTUS  [*stabbing his arm*] Lo, Mephistophilis, for love of thee,
I cut mine arm, and with my proper blood
Assure my soul to be great Lucifer's,
Chief lord and regent of perpetual night!
View here the blood that trickles from mine arm,
And let it be propitious for my wish.

MEPHISTO.  But, Faustus, thou must
Write it in manner of a deed of gift.                      60

FAUSTUS  Ay, so I will. [*writes*] But, Mephistophilis,
My blood congeals, and I can write no more.

MEPHISTO.  I'll fetch thee fire to dissolve it straight.     [*exit*

FAUSTUS  Why might the staying of my blood portend?
Is it unwilling I should write this bill?
Why streams it not, that I may write afresh?
*Faustus gives to thee his soul*: ah, there it stay'd!

Why shouldst thou not? Is not thy soul thine own?
Then write again, *Faustus gives to thee his soul.*

*Re-enter* MEPHISTOPHILIS *with a chafer of coals*

MEPHISTO.  Here's fire; come, Faustus, set it on.          70
FAUSTUS    So, now the blood begins to clear again;
                  Now will I make an end immediately.          [*writes*
MEPHISTO.  [*aside*] O, what will not I do to obtain his soul!
FAUSTUS    *Consummatum est*; this bill is ended,
                  And Faustus hath bequeathed his soul to Lucifer.
                  But what is this inscription on mine arm?
                  *Homo, fuge*: whither should I fly?
                  If unto God, he'll throw me down to hell.
                  My senses are deceiv'd: here's nothing writ —
                  I see it plain; here in this place is writ,          80
                  *Homo, fuge*: yet shall not Faustus fly.
MEPHISTO.  [*aside*] I'll fetch him somewhat to delight his mind.
                                              [*exit*

*Re-enter* MEPHISTOPHILIS *with Devils, who give crowns
and rich apparel to* FAUSTUS, *dance, and then depart*

FAUSTUS    Speak, Mephistophilis, what means this show?
MEPHISTO.  Nothing, Faustus, but to delight thy mind withal,
                  And to show thee what magic can perform.
FAUSTUS    But may I raise up spirits when I please?
MEPHISTO.  Ay, Faustus, and do greater things than these.
FAUSTUS    Then there's enough for a thousand souls.
                  Here, Mephistophilis, receive this scroll
                  A deed of gift of body and of soul:          90
                  But yet conditionally that thou perform
                  All articles prescrib'd between us both.
MEPHISTO.  Faustus, I swear by hell and Lucifer
                  To effect all promises between us made!
FAUSTUS    Then hear me read them. [*reads*] *On these conditions*
                  *following. First that Faustus may be a spirit in form and*
                  *substance. Secondly, that Mephistophilis shall be his servant,*
                  *and at his command. Thirdly, that Mephistophilis shall do for*
                  *him, and bring him whatsoever he desires. Fourthly, that he*
                  *shall be in his chamber or house invisible. Lastly, that he shall*
                  *appear to the said John Faustus, at all times, in what form or*

*shape soever he please. I, John Faustus, of Wertenberg, Doctor, by these presents, do give both body and soul to Lucifer prince of the east, and his minister Mephistophilis; and furthermore grant unto them, that twenty-four years being expired, the articles above written inviolate, full power to fetch or carry the said John Faustus, body and soul, flesh, blood, or goods, into their habitation wheresoever. By me, John Faustus.*

MEPHISTO. Speak, Faustus, do you deliver this as your deed?

FAUSTUS Ay, take it, and the devil give thee good on't!          110

MEPHISTO. Now, Faustus, ask what thou wilt.

FAUSTUS First will I question with thee about hell.
Tell me, where is the place that men call hell?

MEPHISTO. Under the heavens.

FAUSTUS                         Ay, but whereabout?

MEPHISTO. Within the bowels of these elements,
Where we are tortur'd and remain for ever:
Hell hath no limits, nor is circumscrib'd
In one self place; for where we are is hell,
And where hell is, there must we ever be:
And, to conclude, when all the world dissolves,          120
And every creature shall be purified,
All places shall be hell that are not heaven.

FAUSTUS Come, I think hell's a fable.

MEPHISTO. Ay, think so still, till experience change thy mind.

FAUSTUS Why, think'st thou, then, that Faustus shall
                                        be damn'd?

MEPHISTO. Ay, of necessity, for here's the scroll
Wherein thou hast given thy soul to Lucifer.

FAUSTUS Ay, and body too: but what of that?
Think'st thou that Faustus is so fond to imagine
That, after this life, there is any pain?          130
Tush, these are trifles and mere old wives' tales.

MEPHISTO. But. Faustus, I am an instance to prove the contrary.
For I am damn'd, and am now in hell.

FAUSTUS How! Now in hell! Nay, an this he hell, I'll willingly be
damn'd here: what! Walking, disputing, etc. But, leaving
off this, let me have a wife, the fairest maid in Germany;
for I am wanton and lascivious, and cannot live without
a wife.

MEPHISTO.  How! A wife! I prithee, Faustus, talk not of a wife.

FAUSTUS  Nay, sweet Mephistophilis, fetch me one, for I will have one.

MEPHISTO.  Well, thou wilt have one? Sit there till I come: I'll fetch thee a wife in the devil's name.          [exit

*Re-enter* MEPHISTOPHILIS *with a Devil drest like a woman, with fireworks*

MEPHISTO.  Tell me, Faustus, how dost thou like thy wife?

FAUSTUS  A plague on her for a hot whore!

MEPHISTO.                              Tut, Faustus,
Marriage is but a ceremonial toy;
If thou lovest me, think no more of it.
I'll cull thee out the fairest courtesans
And bring them every morning to thy bed:
She whom thine eye shall like, thy heart shall have,
Be she as chaste as was Penelope,
As wise as Saba, or as beautiful
As was bright Lucifer before his fall.
Hold, take this book, peruse it thoroughly: [*gives book*
The iterating of these lines brings gold;
The framing of this circle on the ground
Brings whirlwinds, tempests, thunder, and lightning;
Pronounce this thrice devoutly to thyself,
And men in armour shall appear to thee,
Ready to execute what thou desir'st.          160

FAUSTUS  Thanks, Mephistophilis: yet fain would I have a book wherein I might behold all spells and incantations, that I might raise up spirits when I please.

MEPHISTO.  Here they are in this book.          [*turns to them*

FAUSTUS  Now would I have a book where I might see all characters and planets of the heavens, that I might know their motions and dispositions.

MEPHISTO.  Here they are too.          [*turns to them*

FAUSTUS  Nay, let me have one book more – and then I have done – wherein I might see all plants, herbs, and trees, that grow upon the earth.

MEPHISTO.  Here they be.

FAUSTUS  O, thou art deceived.

MEPHISTO.  Tut, I warrant thee.          [*exeunt*

### SCENE 2

*Enter* ROBIN *the Ostler, with a book in his hand*

ROBIN     O, this is admirable! Here I ha' stolen one of Doctor Faustus' conjuring books, and, i'faith, I mean to search some circles for my own use. Now will I make all the maidens in our parish dance at my pleasure, stark naked before me; and so by that means I shall see more than e'er I felt or saw yet.

*Enter* RALPH *calling* ROBIN

RALPH     Robin, prithee, come away; there's a gentleman tarries to have his horse, and he would have his things rubbed and made clean: he keeps such a chafing with my mistress about it; and she has set me to look thee out; prithee, come away.

ROBIN     Keep out, keep out, or else you are blown up, you are dismembered, Ralph: keep out, for I am about a roaring piece of work.

RALPH     Come, what doest thou with that same book? Thou canst not read?

ROBIN     Yes, my master and mistress shall find that I can read, he for his forehead, she for her private study; she's born to bear with me, or else my art fails.

RALPH     Why, Robin, what book is that?       20

ROBIN     What book! Why, the most intolerable book for conjuring that e'er was invented by any brimstone devil.

RALPH     Canst thou conjure with it?

ROBIN     I can do all these things easily with it; first, I can make thee drunk with ippocras at any tavern in Europe for nothing; that's one of my conjuring works.

RALPH     Our Master Parson says that's nothing.

ROBIN     True, Ralph: and more, Ralph, if thou hast any mind to Nan Spit, our kitchen-maid, then turn her and wind her to thy own use, as often as thou wilt, and at midnight.

RALPH     O, brave, Robin! Shall I have Nan Spit, and to mine own use? On that condition I'll feed thy devil with horse-bread as long as he lives, of free cost.

ROBIN     No more, sweet Ralph: let's go and make clean our
          boots, which lie foul upon our hands, and then to our
          conjuring in the devil's name.

                                                    [*exeunt*


                            SCENE 3

                *Enter* FAUSTUS *and* MEPHISTOPHILIS

FAUSTUS      When I behold the heavens, then I repent,
             And curse thee, wicked Mephistophilis,
             Because thou hast depriv'd me of those joys.
MEPHISTO.    Why, Faustus,
             Thinkest thou heaven is such a glorious thing?
             I tell thee, 'tis not half so fair as thou,
             Or any man that breathes on earth.
FAUSTUS      How prov'st thou that?
MEPHISTO.    'Twas made for man, therefore is man more excellent.
FAUSTUS      If it were made for man, 'twas made for me:          10
             I will renounce this magic and repent.
                *Enter* GOOD ANGEL *and* EVIL ANGEL

GOOD A.      Faustus, repent; yet God will pity thee.
EVIL A.      Thou art a spirit; God cannot pity thee.
FAUSTUS      Who buzzeth in mine ears I am a spirit?
             Be I a devil, yet God may pity me;
             Ay, God will pity me, if I repent.
EVIL A.      Ay, but Faustus never shall repent.
                                              [*exeunt Angels*
FAUSTUS      My heart's so harden'd, I cannot repent:
             Scarce can I name salvation, faith, or heaven,
             But fearful echoes thunder in mine ears,          20
             'Faustus, thou art damn'd!' Then swords, and knives,
             Poison, guns, halters, and envenom'd steel
             Are laid before me to despatch myself;
             And long ere this I should have slain myself,
             Had not sweet pleasure conquer'd deep despair.
             Have not I made blind Homer sing to me
             Of Alexander's love and Oenon's death?
             And hath not he that built the walls of Thebes

With ravishing sound of his melodious harp
Made music with my Mephistophilis?                    30
Why should I die, then, or basely despair!
I am resolv'd; Faustus shall ne'er repent –
Come Mephistophilis, let us dispute again
And argue of divine astrology.
Tell me, are there many heavens above the moon?
Are all celestial bodies but one globe,
As is the substance of this centric earth?

MEPHISTO.  As are the elements, such are the spheres,
Mutually folded in each other's orb,
And, Faustus,                                          40
All jointly move upon one axletree,
Whose terminus is term'd the world's wide pole;
Nor are the names of Saturn, Mars, or Jupiter
Feign'd, but are erring stars.

FAUSTUS  But, tell me, have they all one motion, both *situ et tempore*?

MEPHISTO.  All jointly move from east to west in twenty-four hours upon the poles of the world; but differ in their motion upon the poles of the zodiac.

FAUSTUS  Tush,                                         50
These slender trifles Wagner can decide:
Hath Mephistophilis no greater skill?
Who knows not the double motion of the planets?
The first is finish'd in a natural day;
The second thus: as Saturn in thirty years; Jupiter in twelve; Mars in four; the Sun, Venus, and Mercury in a year; the Moon in twenty-eight days. Tush, these are freshmen's suppositions. But, tell me, hath every sphere a dominion or *intelligentia*?

MEPHISTO.  Ay.                                         60

FAUSTUS  How many heavens or spheres are there?

MEPHISTO.  Nine: the seven planets, the firmament, and the empyreal heaven.

FAUSTUS  Well resolve me in this question; why have we not conjunctions, oppositions, aspects, eclipses, all at one time, but in some years we have more, in some less?

MEPHISTO.  *Per inaequalem motum respectu totius.*

FAUSTUS    Well, I am answered. Tell me, who made the world?
MEPHISTO.  I will not.
FAUSTUS    Sweet Mephistophilis, tell me.                        70
MEPHISTO.  Move me not, for I will not tell thee.
FAUSTUS    Villain, have I not bound thee to tell me anything?
MEPHISTO.  Ay, that is not against our kingdom: but this is. Think
           thou on hell, Faustus, for thou art damned.
FAUSTUS    Think, Faustus, upon God that made the world.
MEPHISTO.  Remember this.                                 [exit
FAUSTUS    Ay, go, accursed spirit, to ugly hell!
           'Tis thou hast damn'd distressed Faustus' soul.
           Is't not too late?

              *Re-enter* GOOD ANGEL *and* EVIL ANGEL

EVIL A.    Too late.                                             80
GOOD A.    Never too late, if Faustus can repent,
EVIL A.    If thou repent, devils shall tear thee in pieces.
GOOD A.    Repent, and they shall never raze thy skin.
                                          [*exeunt Angels*

FAUSTUS    Ah, Christ, my Saviour,
           Seek to save distressed Faustus' soul!

        *Enter* LUCIFER, BELZEBUB, *and* MEPHISTOPHILIS

LUCIFER    Christ cannot save thy soul, for he is just:
           There's none but I have interest in the same.
FAUSTUS    O, who art thou that look'st so terrible?
LUCIFER    I am Lucifer,
           And this is my companion–prince in hell.            90
FAUSTUS    O, Faustus, they are come to fetch away thy soul!
LUCIFER    We come to tell thee thou dost injure us;
           Thou talk'st of Christ, contrary to thy promise:
           Thou shouldst not think of God: think of the devil,
           And of his dam too.
FAUSTUS    Nor will I henceforth: pardon me in this,
           And Faustus vows never to look to heaven,
           Never to name God, or to pray to Him,
           To burn his Scriptures, slay his ministers,
           And make my spirits pull his churches down.         100
LUCIFER    Do so, and we will highly gratify thee.
           Faustus, we are come from hell to show thee some

|   |   |
|---|---|
| | pastime: sit down, and thou shalt see all the Seven Deadly Sins appear in their proper shapes. |
| FAUSTUS | That sight will be as pleasing unto me, |
| | As Paradise was to Adam, the first day |
| | Of his creation. |
| LUCIFER | Talk not of Paradise nor creation; but mark this show: talk of the devil, and nothing else – Come away! |

*Enter the* SEVEN DEADLY SINS

|   |   |
|---|---|
| | Now, Faustus, examine them of their several names and dispositions. |
| FAUSTUS | What art thou, the first? |
| PRIDE | I am Pride. I disdain to have any parents. I am like to Ovid's flea; I can creep into every corner of a wench; sometimes, like a perriwig, I sit upon her brow; or, like a fan of feathers, I kiss her lips; indeed, I do – what do I not? But, fie, what a scent is here! I'll not speak another word, except the ground were perfumed, and covered with cloth of arras. |
| FAUSTUS | What art thou, the second?                              120 |
| COVETOUS | I am Covetousness, begotten of an old churl, in an old leathern bag; and, might I have my wish, I would desire that this house and all the people in it were turned to gold, that I might lock you up in my good chest. O, my sweet gold! |
| FAUSTUS | What art thou, the third? |
| WRATH | I am Wrath. I had neither father nor mother: I leapt out of a lion's mouth when I was scarce half an hour old; and ever since I have run up and down the world with this case of rapiers, wounding myself when I had nobody to fight withal. I was born in hell; and look to it, for some of you shall be my father. |
| FAUSTUS | What art thou, the fourth? |
| ENVY | I am Envy, begotten of a chimney-sweeper and an oyster-wife. I cannot read, and therefore wish all books were burnt. I am lean with seeing others eat. O, that there would come a famine through all the world, that all might die, and I live alone! Then thou shouldst see how fat I would be. But must thou sit, and I stand? Come down, with a vengeance!                              140 |

FAUSTUS     Away, envious rascal – What art thou, the fifth?
GLUTTONY    Who I, sir? I am Gluttony. My parents are all dead, and
            the devil a penny they have left me, but a bare pension,
            and that is thirty meals a day, and ten bevers – a small
            trifle to suffice nature. O, I come of a royal parentage!
            My grandfather was a Gammon of Bacon, my grand-
            mother a Hogshead of Claret-wine; my godfathers were
            these, Peter Pickle-herring and Martin Martlemas-
            beef; O but my godmother, she was a jolly gentle-
            woman, and well-beloved in every good town and city;
            her name was Mistress Margery March-beer. Now,
            Faustus, thou hast heard all my progeny; wilt thou bid
            me to supper?
FAUSTUS     No, I'll see thee hanged: thou wilt eat up all my victuals.
GLUTTONY    Then the devil choke thee!
FAUSTUS     Choke thyself, glutton – What art thou, the sixth?
SLOTH       I am Sloth. I was begotten on a sunny bank, where I
            have lain ever since; and you have done me great
            injury to bring me from thence: let me be carried
            thither again by Gluttony and Lechery. I'll not speak
            another word for a king's ransom.
FAUSTUS     What are you, Mistress Minx, the seventh and last?
LECHERY     Who I, sir? I am one that loves an inch of raw mutton
            better than an ell of fried stock-fish; and the first letter
            of my name begins with L.
FAUSTUS     Away, to hell, to hell!                    [exeunt the Sins
LUCIFER     Now, Faustus, how dost thou like this?
FAUSTUS     O, this feeds my soul!
FAUSTUS     O, might I see hell, and return again,
            How happy were I then!                               170
LUCIFER     Thou shalt; I will send for thee at midnight.
            In meantime take this book: peruse it thoroughly,
            And thou shalt turn thyself into what shape thou wilt.
FAUSTUS     Great thanks, mighty Lucifer!
            This will I keep as chary as my life.
LUCIFER     Farewell, Faustus, and think on the devil.
FAUSTUS     Farewell, great Lucifer.     [exeunt Lucifer and Belzebub
            Come, Mephistophilis.
                                                          [exeunt

## ACT THREE

### *Enter* CHORUS

CHORUS    Learned Faustus,
To know the secrets of astronomy
Graven in the book of Jove's high firmament,
Did mount himself to scale Olympus' top,
Being seated in a chariot burning bright,
Drawn by the strength of yoky dragons' necks.
He now is gone to prove cosmography,
And, as I guess, will first arrive in Rome,
To see the Pope and manner of his court,
And take some part of holy Peter's feast,      10
That to this day is highly solemnis'd.

*[exit*

## SCENE I

### *Enter* FAUSTUS *and* MEPHISTOPHILIS

FAUSTUS    Having now, my good Mephistophilis
Pass'd with delight the stately town of Trier,
Environ'd round with airy mountain-tops,
With walls of flint, and deep-entrenched lakes,
Not to be won by any conquering prince;
From Paris next, coasting the realm of France,
We saw the river Maine fall into Rhine,
Whose banks are set with groves of fruitful vines;
Then up to Naples, rich Campania,
Whose buildings fair and gorgeous to the eye,    10
The streets straight forth, and pav'd with finest brick,
Quarter the town in four equivalents:
There saw we learned Maro's golden tomb,
The way he cut, an English mile in length,
Thorough a rock of stone, in one night's space;
From thence to Venice, Padua, and the rest,
In one of which a sumptuous temple stands,

That threats the stars with her aspiring top.
Thus hitherto hath Faustus spent his time:
But tell me now what resting-place is this?        20
Hast thou, as erst I did command
Conducted me within the walls of Rome?

MEPHISTO.    Faustus, I have; and, because we will not be unprovided,
I have taken up his Holiness' privy-chamber for our use.

FAUSTUS    I hope his Holiness will bid us welcome.

MEPHISTO.    Tut, 'tis no matter, man: we'll be bold with his
                                                    good cheer.
And now, my Faustus, that thou mayst perceive
What Rome containeth to delight thee with,
Know that this city stands upon seven hills
That underprop the groundwork of the same:        30
Just through the midst runs flowing Tiber's stream
With winding banks that cut it in two parts;
Over the which four stately bridges lean,
That make safe passage to each part of Rome:
Upon the bridge call'd Ponte Angelo
Erected is a castle passing strong,
Within whose walls such store of ordnance are,
And double cannons fram'd of carved brass,
As match the days within one complete year;
Besides the gates, and high pyramides,        40
Which Julius Caesar brought from Africa.

FAUSTUS    Now, by the kingdoms of infernal rule,
Of Styx, of Acheron, and the fiery lake
Of ever-burning Phlegethon, I swear
That I do long to see the monuments
And situation of bright-splendent Rome:
Come, therefore, let's away.

MEPHISTO.    Nay, Faustus, stay: I know you'd fain see the Pope,
And take some part of holy Peter's feast,
Where thou shalt see a troop of bald-pate friars,        50
Whose *summum bonum* is in belly-cheer.

FAUSTUS    Well, I'm content to compass then some sport,
And by their folly make us merriment.
Then charm me, that I
May be invisible, to do what I please,

Unseen of any whilst I stay in Rome.

*[Mephistophilis charms him*

MEPHISTO.  So, Faustus; now
Do what thou wilt, thou shalt not be discern'd.

*Sound a sennet. Enter the* POPE *and the* CARDINAL
*OF* LORRAIN *to the banquet, with Friars attending*

POPE        My lord of Lorrain, will't please you draw near?

FAUSTUS     Fall to, and the devil choke you, an you spare!          60

POPE        How now! Who's that which spake? Friars, look about.

1 FRIAR     Here's nobody, if it like your Holiness.

POPE        My lord, here is a dainty dish was sent me from the
            Bishop of Milan.

POPE        How now! Who's that which snatched the meat from
            me? Will no man look? My lord, this dish was sent me
            from the Cardinal of Florence.

FAUSTUS     You say true, I'll ha't.          *[snatches the dish*

POPE        What, again! My lord, I'll drink to your grace.

FAUSTUS     I'll pledge your grace.          *[snatches the cup*

LORRAIN     My lord, it may be some ghost, newly crept out of
            Purgatory, come to beg a pardon of your Holiness.

POPE        It may be so – Friars, prepare a dirge to lay the fury of
            this ghost – Once again, my lord, fall to.

*[the Pope crosses himself*

FAUSTUS     What, are you crossing of yourself?
            Well, use that trick no more, I would advise you.

*[the Pope crosses himself again*

            Well, there's the second time. Aware the third;
            I give you fair warning.

*[the Pope crosses himself again, and Faustus hits
            him a box of the ear; and they all run away.*

            Come on, Mephistophilis; what shall we do?

MEPHISTO.  Nay, I know not: we shall be cursed with bell, book,
            and candle.

FAUSTUS     How! Bell, book, and candle – candle, book, and bell –
            Forward and backward, to curse Faustus to hell!
            Anon you shall hear a hog grunt, a calf bleat,

            and an ass bray,

            Because it is Saint Peter's holiday.

*Re-enter all the Friars to sing the dirge*

I FRIAR      Come, brethren, let's about our business with good
           devotion.
           *[they sing]*
               Cursed be he that stole away his Holiness'
                   meat from the table! *Maledicat Dominus!*
               Cursed be he that struck his Holiness a
                   blow on the face! *Maledicat Dominus!*
               Cursed be he that took Friar Sandelo a blow
                   on the pate! *Maledicat Dominus!*
               Cursed be he that disturbeth our holy dirge!
                   *Maledicat Dominus!*
               Cursed be he that took away his Holiness'
                   wine! *Maledicat Dominus!*
               *Et omnes Sancti! Amen!*
                   *[Mephistophilis and Faustus beat the Friars,*
                   *and fling fireworks among than; and so exeunt.*

### SCENE 2

*Enter* ROBIN *and* RALPH *with a silver goblet*

ROBIN      Come, Ralph: did not I tell thee, we were for ever
           made by this Doctor Faustus' book? *Ecce, signum!*
           Here's a simple purchase for horse-keepers: our horses
           shall eat no hay as long as this lasts.

RALPH      But, Robin, here comes the Vintner.

ROBIN      Hush! I'll gull him supernaturally.

*Enter* VINTNER

           Drawer, I hope all is paid; God be with you – Come,
           Ralph.

VINTNER    Soft, sir; a word with you. I must yet have a goblet paid
           from you, ere you go.                      10

ROBIN      I a goblet, Ralph, I a goblet! I scorn you; and you are
           but a, etc. I a goblet! Search me.

VINTNER    I mean so, sir, with your favour.        *[searches Robin*

ROBIN      How say you now?

VINTNER    I must say somewhat to your fellow – You, sir!

ROBIN      Me, sir! Me, sir! Search your fill. *[Vintner searches him]*

Now, sir, you may be ashamed to burden honest men
with a matter of truth.

VINTNER    Well, one of you hath this goblet about you.

ROBIN      [aside] You lie, drawer, 'tis afore me — Sirrah you, I'll
teach you to impeach honest men — stand by — I'll
scour you for a goblet — stand aside you had best, I
charge you in the name of Belzebub — [aside to Ralph]
Look to the goblet, Ralph.

VINTNER    What mean you, sirrah?

ROBIN      I'll tell you what I mean. [reads from a book] Sanctobulorum
Periphrasticon — nay, I'll tickle you, Vintner — [aside to
Ralph] Look to the goblet, Ralph — [reads] Polypragmos
Belseborams framanto pacostiphos tostu, Mephistophilis, etc.

Enter MEPHISTOPHILIS, sets squibs at their backs,
and then exit. They run about

VINTNER    O, nomine Domini! What meanest thou, Robin? Thou
hast no goblet.

RALPH      Peccatum peccatorum! Here's thy goblet, good Vintner.
                    [gives the goblet to Vintner, who exit

ROBIN      Misericordia pro nobis! What shall I do? Good devil,
forgive me now, and I'll never rob thy library more.

Re-enter MEPHISTOPHILIS

MEPHISTO.  Monarch of hell, under whose black survey
Great potentates do kneel with awful fear,
Upon whose altars thousand souls do lie,
How am I vexed with these villains' charms?
From Constantinople am I hither come,
Only for pleasure of these damned slaves.          40

ROBIN      How, from Constantinople! You have had a great
journey: will you take sixpence in your purse to pay
for your supper, and be gone?

MEPHISTO.  Well, villains, for your presumption, I transform thee
into an ape, and thee into a dog; and so be gone! [exit

ROBIN      How, into an ape! That's brave: I'll have fine sport
with the boys; I'll get nuts and apples enow.

RALPH      And I must be a dog.

ROBIN      I'faith, thy head will never be out of the pottage-pot.
                    [exeunt

## ACT FOUR

*Enter* CHORUS

CHORUS    When Faustus had with pleasure ta'en the view
Of rarest things, and royal courts of kings,
He stay'd his course, and so returned home;
Where such as bear his absence but with grief,
I mean his friends and near'st companions,
Did gratulate his safety with kind words,
And in their conference of what befell,
Touching his journey through the world and air,
They put forth questions of astrology,
Which Faustus answer'd with such learned skill    10
As they admir'd and wonder'd at his wit.
Now is his fame spread forth in every land:
Amongst the rest the Emperor is one,
Carolus the Fifth, at whose palace now
Faustus is feasted 'mongst his noblemen.
What there he did, in trial of his art,
I leave untold; your eyes shall see't perform'd.

                                                   [*exit*

## SCENE I

*Enter* EMPEROR, FAUSTUS, *and a Knight, with Attendants*

EMPEROR    Master Doctor Faustus, I have heard strange report of
thy knowledge in the black art, how that none in my
empire nor in the whole world can compare with thee
for the rare effects of magic: they say thou hast a
familiar spirit, by whom thou canst accomplish what
thou list. This, therefore, is my request, that thou let
me see some proof of thy skill, that mine eyes may be
witnesses to confirm what mine ears have heard re-
ported: and here I swear to thee, by the honour of
mine imperial crown, that, whatever thou doest, thou
shalt be no ways prejudiced or endamaged.

KNIGHT    [*aside*] I'faith, he looks much like a conjurer.

FAUSTUS    My gracious sovereign, though I must confess myself far inferior to the report men have published, and nothing answerable to the honour of your imperial majesty, yet, for that love and duty binds me thereunto, I am content to do whatsoever your majesty shall command me.

EMPEROR    Then, Doctor Faustus, mark what I shall say.
As I was sometime solitary set
Within my closet, sundry thoughts arose    20
About the honour of mine ancestors,
How they had won by prowess such exploits,
Got such riches, subdu'd so many kingdoms,
As we that do succeed, or they that shall
Hereafter possess our throne, shall
(I fear me) ne'er attain to that degree
Of high renown and great authority:
Amongst which kings is Alexander the Great,
Chief spectacle of the world's pre-eminence,
The bright shining of whose glorious acts    30
Lightens the world with his reflecting beams,
As when I hear but motion made of him,
It grieves my soul I never saw the man:
If, therefore, thou, by cunning of thine art,
Canst raise this man from hollow vaults below,
Where lies entomb'd this famous conqueror,
And bring with him his beauteous paramour,
Both in their right shapes, gesture, and attire
They us'd to wear during their time of life,
Thou shalt both satisfy my just desire,    40
And give me cause to praise thee whilst I live.

FAUSTUS    My gracious lord, I am ready to accomplish your request, so far forth as by art and power of my spirit I am able to perform.

KNIGHT    [*aside*] I'faith, that's just nothing at all.

FAUSTUS    But, if it like your grace, it is not in my ability to present before your eyes the true substantial bodies of those two deceased princes, which long since are consumed to dust.

| | |
|---|---|
| KNIGHT | [*aside*] Ay, marry, Master Doctor, now there's a sign of grace in you, when you will confess the truth. |
| FAUSTUS | But such spirits as can lively resemble Alexander and his paramour shall appear before your grace, in that manner that they both lived in, in their most flourishing estate; which I doubt not shall sufficiently content your imperial majesty |
| EMPEROR | Go to, Master Doctor; let me see them presently. |
| KNIGHT | Do you hear, Master Doctor? You bring Alexander and his paramour before the Emperor! |
| FAUSTUS | How then, sir?                                          60 |
| KNIGHT | I'faith, that's as true as Diana turned me to a stag. |
| FAUSTUS | No, sir; but, when Actaeon died, he left the horns for you – Mephistophilis, be gone.     [*exit Mephistophilis* |
| KNIGHT | Nay, an you go to conjuring, I'll be gone.     [*exit* |
| FAUSTUS | I'll meet with you anon for interrupting me so – Here they are, my gracious lord. |

*Re-enter* MEPHISTOPHILIS *with Spirits in the shapes of*
ALEXANDER *and his paramour*

| | |
|---|---|
| EMPEROR | Master Doctor, I heard this lady, while she lived, had a wart or mole in her neck: how shall I know whether it be so or no? |
| FAUSTUS | Your highness may boldly go and see.               70 |
| EMPEROR | Sure, these are no spirits, but the true substantial bodies of those two deceased princes.     [*exeunt Spirits* |
| FAUSTUS | Wilt please your highness now to send for the knight that was so pleasant with me here of late? |
| EMPEROR | One of you call him forth.     [*exit Attendant* |

*Re-enter the Knight with a pair of horns on his head*

| | |
|---|---|
| | How now, sir knight! Why I had thought thou hadst been a bachelor, but now I see thou hast a wife, that not only gives thee horns, but makes thee wear them. Feel on thy head. |
| KNIGHT | Thou damned wretch and execrable dog,               80 |
| | Bred in the concave of some monstrous rock, |
| | How dar'st thou thus abuse a gentleman? |
| | Villain, I say, undo what thou hast done! |
| FAUSTUS | O, not so fast, sir! There's no haste: but, good, are you |

remembered how you crossed me in my conference
with the Emperor? I think I have met with you for it.

EMPEROR    Good Master Doctor, at my entreaty release him: he
hath done penance sufficient.

FAUSTUS    My gracious lord, not so much for the injury he offered
me here in your presence, as to delight you with some
mirth, hath Faustus worthily requited this injurious
knight; which being all I desire, I am content to release
him of his horns – and, sir knight, hereafter speak well
of scholars – Mephistophilis, transform him straight.
[*Mephistophilis removes the horns*] – Now, my good lord,
having done my duty, I humbly take my leave.

EMPEROR    Farewell, Master Doctor: yet, ere you go,
Expect from me a bounteous reward.

           [*exeunt Emperor, Knight, and Attendants*

FAUSTUS    Now, Mephistophilis, the restless course
That time doth run with calm and silent foot,     100
Shortening my days and thread of vital life,
Calls for the payment of my latest years:
Therefore, sweet Mephistophilis, let us
Make haste to Wertenberg,

MEPHISTO.    What, will you go on horse-back or on foot?

FAUSTUS    Nay, till I'm past this fair and pleasant green,
I'll walk on foot.

           *Enter a Horse-courser*

COURSER    I have been all this day seeking one Master Fustian:
mass, see where he is – God save you Master Doctor!

FAUSTUS    What, horse-courser! You are well met.     110

COURSER    Do you hear, sir? I have brought you forty dollars for
your horse.

FAUSTUS    I cannot sell him so: if thou likest him for fifty, take him.

COURSER    Alas, sir, I have no more – I pray you, speak for me.

MEPHISTO.    I pray you, let him have him: he is an honest fellow,
and he has a great charge, neither wife nor child.

FAUSTUS    Well, come, give me your money [*Horse-courser gives
Faustus the money*]: my boy will deliver him to you. But
I must tell you one thing before you have him; ride
him not into the water, at any hand.     120

COURSER   Why, sir, will he not drink of all waters?

FAUSTUS   O, yes, he will drink of all waters; but ride him not into the water; ride him over hedge or ditch, or where thou wilt, but not into the water.

COURSER   Well, sir — [*aside*] Now am I made man for ever: I'll not leave my horse for forty: if he had but the quality of hey-ding-ding, hey-ding-ding, I'd make a brave living on him: he has a buttock as slick as an eel — Well, God b'wi'ye, sir: your boy will deliver him me: but, hark you, sir: if my horse be sick or ill at ease if I bring his water to you, you'll tell me what it is?

FAUSTUS   Away, you villain! What, dost think I am a horse-doctor?

[*exit Horse-courser*

What art thou, Faustus, but a man condemn'd to die?
Thy fatal time doth draw to final end.
Despair doth drive distrust into my thoughts:
Confound these passions with a quiet sleep:
Tush, Christ did call the thief upon the Cross;
Then rest thee, Faustus, quiet in conceit.

[*sleeps in his chair*

*Re-enter* HORSE-COURSER, *all wet, crying*

COURSER   Alas, alas! Doctor Fustian, quotha? Mass, Doctor Lopus was never such a doctor: has given me a purgation, has purged me of forty dollars; I shall never see them more. But yet, like an ass as I was, I would not be ruled by him, for he bade me I should ride him into no water: now I, thinking my horse had had some rare quality that he would not have had me know of, I, like a venturous youth, rid him into the deep pond at the town's end. I was no sooner in the middle of the pond, but my horse vanished away, and I sat upon a bottle of hay, never so near drowning in my life. But I'll seek out my doctor and have my forty dollars again, or I'll make it the dearest horse — O, yonder is his snipper-snapper. Do you hear? You, hey-pass, where's your master?

MEPHISTO.   Why, sir, what would you? You cannot speak with him.

COURSER   But I will speak with him.

MEPHISTO.   Why, he's fast asleep: come some other time.

COURSER     I'll speak with him now, or I'll break his glass-windows
            about his ears.

MEPHISTO.   I tell thee, he has not slept this eight nights.

COURSER     An he have not slept this eight weeks, I'll speak with
            him.                                                    160

MEPHISTO.   See, where he is, fast asleep.

COURSER     Ay, this is he – God save you, Master Doctor. Master
            Doctor, Master Doctor Fustian! Forty dollars, forty
            dollars for a bottle of hay!

MEPHISTO.   Why, thou seest he hears thee not.

COURSER     So-ho, ho! So-ho, ho! [*holloas in his ear*] No, will you
            not wake? I'll make you wake ere I go. [*pulls Faustus
            by the leg, and pulls it away*] Alas. I am undone! What
            shall I do?

FAUSTUS     O, my leg, my leg! Help, Mephistophilis! Call the
            officers – My leg, my leg!

MEPHISTO.   Come, villain, to the constable.

COURSER     O Lord, sir, let me go. and I'll give you forty dollars
            more!

MEPHISTO.   Where be they?

COURSER     I have none about me: come to my ostry, and I'll give
            them you.

MEPHISTO.   Be gone quickly.                     [*Horse-courser runs away*

FAUSTUS     What, is he gone? Farewell he! Faustus has his leg
            again, and the Horse-courser, I take it, a bottle of hay
            for his labour: well, this trick shall cost him forty
            dollars more.

                          *Enter* WAGNER

            How now Wagner! What's the news with thee?

WAGNER      Sir, the Duke of Vanholt doth earnestly entreat your
            company.

FAUSTUS     The Duke of Vanholt! An honourable gentleman, to
            whom I must be no niggard of my cunning – Come
            Mephistophilis, let's away to him.

                                                      [*exeunt*

## SCENE 2

*Enter the* DUKE OF VANHOLT, *the* DUCHESS, *and* FAUSTUS

VANHOLT     Believe me, Master Doctor, this merriment hath much
            pleased me.

FAUSTUS     My gracious lord, I am glad it contents you so well –
            But it may be, madam, you take no delight in this. I
            have heard that great-bellied women do long for some
            dainties or other: what is it, madam? Tell me, and you
            shall have it.

DUCHESS     Thanks, good Master Doctor: and, for I see your
            courteous intent to pleasure me, I will not hide from
            you the thing my heart desires; and, were it now
            summer, as it is January and the dead time of the
            winter, I would desire no better meat than a dish of
            ripe grapes.

FAUSTUS     Alas, madam, that's nothing! Mephistophilis, be gone.
            [*exit Mephistophilis*] Were it a greater thing than this, so
            it would content you, you should have it.

            *Re-enter* MEPHISTOPHILIS *with grapes*

            Here they be, madam: wilt please you taste on them?

DUKE        Believe me, Master Doctor, this makes me wonder
            above the rest, that being in the dead time of winter
            and in the month of January, how you should come by
            these grapes.

FAUSTUS     If it like your grace, the year is divided into two circles
            over the whole world, that, when it is here winter with
            us, in the contrary circle it is summer with them, as in
            India, Saba, and farther countries in the east; and by
            means of a swift spirit that I have, I had them brought
            hither, as you see – How do you like them, madam?
            Be they good?

DUCHESS     Believe me, Master Doctor, they be the best grapes
            that e'er I tasted in my life before.                    30

FAUSTUS     I am glad they content you so, madam.

DUKE        Come, madam, let us in, where you must well reward this learned man for the great kindness he hath showed to you.

DUCHESS　And so I will, my lord; and, whilst I live, rest beholding for this courtesy.

FAUSTUS　I humbly thank your grace.

DUKE　Come, Master Doctor, follow us, and receive your reward.

*[exeunt*

## ACT FIVE

### SCENE I

*Enter* WAGNER

WAGNER   I think my master means to die shortly,
For he hath given to me all his goods:
And yet, methinks, if that death were near,
He would not banquet, and carouse, and swill
Amongst the students, as even now he doth,
Who are at supper with such belly-cheer
As Wagner ne'er beheld in all his life.
See, where they come! Belike the feast is ended. [*exit*

*Enter* FAUSTUS *with two or three Scholars, and* MEPHISTOPHILIS

1 SCHOLAR   Master Doctor Faustus, since our conference about fair
ladies, which was the beautifulest in all the world, we
have determined with ourselves that Helen of Greece
was the admirablest lady that ever lived: therefore,
Master Doctor, if you will do us that favour, as to let us
see that peerless dame of Greece, whom all the world
admires for majesty, we should think ourselves much
beholding unto you.

FAUSTUS   Gentlemen,
For that I know your friendship is unfeign'd,
And Faustus' custom is not to deny
The just requests of those that wish him well,          20
You shall behold that peerless dame of Greece,
No otherways for pomp and majesty
Than when Sir Paris cross'd the seas with her
And brought the spoils to rich Dardania.
Be silent, then, for danger is in words.
                    [*music sounds, and Helen passeth over the stage*

2 SCHOLAR   Too simple is my wit to tell her praise,
Whom all the world admires for majesty.

3 SCHOLAR   No marvel though the angry Greeks pursu'd
With ten years' war the rape of such a queen,
Whose heavenly beauty passeth all compare.          30

I SCHOLAR    Since we have seen the pride of Nature's works,
             And only paragon of excellence,
             Let us depart, and for this glorious deed
             Happy and blest be Faustus evermore!

FAUSTUS      Gentlemen, farewell: the same I wish to you.

                                            [*exeunt Scholars*

                         *Enter an Old Man*

OLD MAN      Ah. Doctor Faustus, that I might prevail
             To guide thy steps unto the way of life,
             By which sweet path thou mayst attain the goal
             That shall conduct thee to celestial rest!
             Break heart, drop blood, and mingle it with tears,   40
             Tears falling from repentant heaviness
             Of thy most vile and loathsome filthiness,
             The stench whereof corrupts the inward soul
             With such flagitious crimes of heinous sin
             As no commiseration may expel,
             But mercy, Faustus, of thy Saviour sweet,
             Whose blood alone must wash away thy guilt.

FAUSTUS      Where art thou, Faustus? Wretch, what hast thou done?
             Damn'd art thou, Faustus, damn'd; despair and die!
             Hell calls for right, and with a roaring voice         50
             Says, 'Faustus, come; thine hour is almost come;'
             And Faustus now will come to do thee right.

                                  [*Mephistophilis gives him a dagger*

OLD MAN      Ah, stay, good Faustus, stay thy desperate steps!
             I see an angel hovers o'er thy head,
             And, with a vial full of precious grace,
             Offers to pour the same into thy soul:
             Then call for mercy, and avoid despair.

FAUSTUS      Ah, my sweet friend, I feel
             Thy words to comfort my distressed soul!
             Leave me a while to ponder on my sins.                 60

OLD MAN      I go, sweet Faustus; but with heavy cheer,
             Fearing the ruin of thy hopeless soul.          [*exit*

FAUSTUS      Accursed Faustus, where is mercy now?
             I do repent; and yet I do despair:
             Hell strives with grace for conquest in my breast:
             What shall I do to shun the snares of death?

MEPHISTO. Thou traitor, Faustus, I arrest thy soul
          For disobedience to my sovereign lord:
          Revolt, or I'll in piece-meal tear thy flesh.

FAUSTUS   Sweet Mephistophilis, entreat thy lord          70
          To pardon my unjust presumption,
          And with my blood again I will confirm
          My former vow I made to Lucifer.

MEPHISTO. Do it, then, quickly, with unfeigned heart,
          Lest greater danger do attend thy drift.

FAUSTUS   Torment, sweet friend, that base and crooked age,
          That durst dissuade me from thy Lucifer,
          With greatest torments that our hell affords.

MEPHISTO. His faith is great; I cannot touch his soul;
          But what I may afflict his body with          80
          I will attempt, which is but little worth.

FAUSTUS   One thing, good servant, let me crave of thee,
          To glut the longing of my heart's desire –
          That I might have unto my paramour
          That heavenly Helen which I saw of late,
          Whose sweet embracings may extinguish clean
          Those thoughts that do dissuade me from my vow,
          And keep mine oath I made to Lucifer.

MEPHISTO. Faustus, this, or what else thou shalt desire,
          Shall be perform'd in twinkling of an eye.          90

                    *Re-enter* HELEN

FAUSTUS   Was this the face that launch'd a thousand ships,
          And burnt the topless towers of Ilium?
          Sweet Helen, make me immortal with a kiss –
                                        [*kisses her*
          Her lips suck forth my soul: see, where it flies!
          Come, Helen, come, give me my soul again.
          Here will I dwell, for heaven is in these lips,
          And all is dross that is not Helena.
          I will be Paris, and for love of thee,
          Instead of Troy, shall Wertenberg be sack'd;
          And I will combat with weak Menelaus,          100
          And wear thy colours on my plumed crest;
          Yes, I will wound Achilles in the heel,
          And then return to Helen for a kiss.

O, thou art fairer than the evening air
Clad in the beauty of a thousand stars;
Brighter art thou than flaming Jupiter
When he appear'd to hapless Semele;
More lovely than the monarch of the sky
In wanton Arethusa's azur'd arms;
And none but thou shalt be my paramour!     *[exeunt*

*Enter the Old Man*

OLD MAN    Accursed Faustus, miserable man,
That from thy soul exclud'st the grace of heaven,
And fly'st the throne of his tribunal-seat!

*Enter Devils*

Satan begins to sift me with his pride:
As in this furnace God shall try my faith,
My faith, vile hell, shall triumph over thee.
Ambitious fiends, see how the heavens smile
At your repulse, and laugh your state to scorn!
Hence, hell! For hence I fly unto my God.

          *[exeunt – on one side, Devils,*
             *on the other, Old Man*

## SCENE 2

*Enter* FAUSTUS, *with Scholars*

FAUSTUS    Ah, gentlemen!

I SCHOLAR    What ails Faustus?

FAUSTUS    Ah, my sweet chamber-fellow, had I lived with thee, then had I lived still! But now I die eternally. Look, comes he not? Comes he not?

2 SCHOLAR    What means Faustus?

3 SCHOLAR    Belike he is grown into some sickness by being over-solitary.

I SCHOLAR    If it be so, we'll have physicians to cure him – 'Tis but a surfeit; never fear, man.      10

FAUSTUS    A surfeit of deadly sin, that hath damned both body and soul.

2 SCHOLAR    Yet, Faustus, look up to heaven; remember God's mercies are infinite.

FAUSTUS      But Faustus' offence can ne'er be pardoned: the serpent
             that tempted Eve may be saved, but not Faustus. Ah,
             gentlemen, hear me with patience, and tremble not at
             my speeches! Though my heart pants and quivers to
             remember that I have been a student here these thirty
             years, O, would I had never seen Wertenberg, never
             read book! And what wonders I have done, all Ger-
             many can witness, yea, all the world; for which Faustus
             hath lost both Germany and the world, yea, heaven
             itself, heaven, the seat of God, the throne of the blessed,
             the kingdom of joy; and must remain in hell for ever,
             hell, ah, hell, for ever! Sweet friends, what shall become
             of Faustus, being in hell for ever?

3 SCHOLAR    Yet, Faustus, call on God.

FAUSTUS      On God, whom Faustus hath abjured! On God, whom
             Faustus hath blasphemed! Ah, my God, I would weep!
             But the devil draws in my tears. Gush forth blood,
             instead of tears! Yea, life and soul! O, he stays my
             tongue! I would lift up my hands; but see, they hold
             them, they hold them!

ALL          Who, Faustus?

FAUSTUS      Lucifer and Mephistophilis. Ah, gentlemen, I gave them
             my soul for my cunning!

ALL          God forbid!                                            38

FAUSTUS      God forbade it, indeed; but Faustus hath done it: for
             vain pleasure of twenty-four years hath Faustus lost
             eternal joy and felicity. I writ them a bill with mine
             own blood: the date is expired; the time will come,
             and he will fetch me.

1 SCHOLAR    Why did not Faustus tell us of this before, that divines
             might have prayed for thee?

FAUSTUS      Oft have I thought to have done so; but the devil
             threatened to tear me in pieces, if I named God; to
             fetch both body and soul, if I once gave ear to divinity:
             and now 'tis too late. Gentlemen, away, lest you perish
             with me.                                               50

2 SCHOLAR    O, what shall we do to save Faustus?

FAUSTUS      Talk not of me, but save yourselves, and depart.

3 SCHOLAR    God will strengthen me; I will stay with Faustus.

1 SCHOLAR    Tempt not God, sweet friend, but let us into the next room, and there pray for him.

FAUSTUS    Ay, pray for me, pray for me; and what noise soever ye hear, come not unto me, for nothing can rescue me.

2 SCHOLAR   Pray thou, and we will pray that God may have mercy upon thee.

FAUSTUS    Gentlemen, farewell: if I live till morning, I'll visit you; if not, Faustus is gone to hell.

ALL    Faustus, farewell.

                        *[exeunt Scholars – the clock strikes eleven*

FAUSTUS    Ah, Faustus.
         Now hast thou but one bare hour to live,
         And then thou must be damn'd perpetually!
         Stand still, you ever-moving spheres of heaven,
         That time may cease, and midnight never come;
         Fair Nature's eye, rise, rise again, and make
         Perpetual day; or let this hour be but
         A year, a month, a week, a natural day,         70
         That Faustus may repent and save his soul!
         *O lente, lente currite, noctis equi!*
         The stars move still, time runs, the clock will strike,
         The devil will come, and Faustus must be damn'd.
         O, I'll leap up to my God! Who pulls me down?
         See, see, where Christ's blood streams in the
                               firmament!
         One drop would save my soul, half a drop:
                          ah, my Christ –
         Ah, rend not my heart for naming of my Christ!
         Yet will I call on him: O, spare me, Lucifer!
         Where is it now? 'Tis gone: and see, where God    80
         Stretcheth out his arm, and bends his ireful brows!
         Mountains and hills, come, come, and fall on me,
         And hide me from the heavy wrath of God!
         No, no!
         Then will I headlong run into the earth:
         Earth, gape! O, no, it will not harbour me!
         You stars that reign'd at my nativity,
         Whose influence hath allotted death and hell,
         Now draw up Faustus, like a foggy mist,

Into the entrails of yon labouring clouds,            90
That, when you vomit forth into the air,
My limbs may issue from your smoky mouths,
So that my soul may but ascend to heaven!

*[the clock strikes the half-hour*

Ah, half the hour is past! 'Twill all be past anon.
O God,
If thou wilt not have mercy on my soul,
Yet for Christ's sake, whose blood hath ransom'd me,
Impose some end to my incessant pain;
Let Faustus live in hell a thousand years,
A hundred thousand, and at last be sav'd!            100
O, no end is limited to damned souls!
Why wert thou not a creature wanting soul?
Or why is this immortal that thou hast?
Ah, Pythagoras' metempsychosis, were that true,
This soul should fly from me, and I be chang'd
Unto some brutish beast! All beasts are happy,
For, when they die,
Their souls are soon dissolv'd in elements;
But mine must live still to be plagu'd in hell.
Curs'd be the parents that engender'd me!            110
No, Faustus, curse thyself, curse Lucifer
That hath depriv'd thee of the joys of heaven.

*[the clock strikes twelve*

O, it strikes, it strikes! Now, body, turn to air,
Or Lucifer will bear thee quick to hell!

*[thunder and lightning*

O soul, be chang'd into little water-drops,
And fall into the ocean, ne'er be found!

*Enter Devils*

My God, my God, look not so fierce on me!
Adders and serpents, let me breathe a while!
Ugly hell, gape not! Come not, Lucifer!
I'll burn my books! – Ah, Mephistophilis!            120

*[exeunt Devils with Faustus*

*Enter* CHORUS

CHORUS     Cut is the branch that might have grown full straight,
And burned is Apollo's laurel-bough,
That sometime grew within this learned man.
Faustus is gone: regard his hellish fall,
Whose fiendful fortune may exhort the wise
Only to wonder at unlawful things,
Whose deepness doth entice such forward wits
To practise more than heavenly power permits.

                                                    [*exit*

*Terminat hora diem; terminat auctor opus.*

# THE TRAGICAL HISTORY
# OF DOCTOR FAUSTUS

## THE B-TEXT (1616)

# CHARACTERS IN THE PLAY

CHORUS
FAUSTUS
WAGNER
GOOD ANGEL *and* EVIL ANGEL
VALDES *and* CORNELIUS
MEPHISTOPHILIS
LUCIFER
BELZEBUB
THE SEVEN DEADLY SINS
ROBIN THE CLOWN
DICK
THE POPE
RAYMOND KING OF HUNGARY
ARCHBISHOP OF RHEIMS
BISHOP OF LORRAINE
BRUNO
CARDINALS OF FRANCE *and* PADUA
VINTNER
HORSE-COURSER
CARTER
HOSTESS
MARTINO *and* FREDERICK
BENVOLIO
CHARLES THE GERMAN EMPEROR
DUKE OF SAXONY
ATTENDANTS
DUKE AND DUCHESS OF VANHOLT
HELEN OF TROY
OLD MAN

*Scholars, Cardinals, Bishops, Monks, Friars
Devils, Attendants, Soldiers, Cupids*

SPIRITS *of* ALEXANDER THE GREAT, DARIUS
*and* HIS PARAMOUR

# THE TRAGICAL HISTORY
# OF DOCTOR FAUSTUS

## THE B-TEXT (1616)


*Enter* CHORUS

CHORUS     Not marching in the fields of Thrasymene,
Where Mars did mate the warlike Carthagens;
Nor sporting in the dalliance of love,
In courts of kings where state is overturn'd;
Nor in the pomp of proud audacious deeds,
Intends our Muse to vaunt her heavenly verse:
Only this, gentles – we must now perform
The form of Faustus' fortunes, good or bad:
And now to patient judgements we appeal,
And speak for Faustus in his infancy.         10
Now he is born of parents base of stock,
In Germany, within a town call'd Rhodes:
At riper years, to Wittenberg he went,
Whereas his kinsmen chiefly brought him up.
So much he profits in divinity,
That shortly he was grace'd with doctor's name,
Excelling all, and sweetly can dispute
In th' heavenly matters of theology;
Till swoln with cunning, of a self-conceit,
His waxen wings did mount above his reach,      20
And, melting, heavens conspir'd his overthrow;
For, falling to a devilish exercise,
And glutted now with learning's golden gifts,
He surfeits upon cursed necromancy;
Nothing so sweet as magic is to him,
Which he prefers before his chiefest bliss:
And this the man that in his study sits.

                                              *[exit*

## ACT ONE

### SCENE I

FAUSTUS *discovered in his study*

FAUSTUS    Settle thy studies, Faustus, and begin
To sound the depth of that thou wilt profess:
Having commenc'd, be a divine in show,
Yet level at the end of every art,
And live and die in Aristotle's works.
Sweet Analytics, 'tis thou has ravish'd me!
*Bene disserere est finis logices.*
Is, to dispute well, logic's chiefest end?
Affords this art no greater miracle?
Then read no more; thou hast attain'ed that end:   10
A greater subject fitteth Faustus' wit:
Bid Economy farewell, and Galen come:
Be a physician, Faustus; heap up gold,
And be eternis'd for some wondrous cure:
*Summum bonum medicinae sanitas,*
The end of physic is our body's health.
Why, Faustus, hast thou not attain'd that end?
Are not thy bills hung up as monuments,
Whereby whole cities have escap'd the plague,
And thousand desperate maladies been cur'd?   20
Yet art thou still but Faustus, and a man.
Couldst thou make men to live eternally,
Or, being dead, raise them to life again,
Then this profession were to be esteem'd.
Physic, farewell! Where is Justinian?
[*reads*] *Si una eademque res legatur duobus, alter rem, alter
valorem rei, etc.*
A petty case of paltry legacies!
[*reads*] *Exhaereditare filium non potest pater, nisi, etc.*
Such is the subject of the institute,   30
And universal body of the law:

This study fits a mercenary drudge,
Who aims at nothing but external trash;
Too servile and illiberal for me.
When all is done, divinity is best:
Jerome's Bible, Faustus; view it well.
[reads] *Stipendium peccati mors est.* Ha! *Stipendium, &c.*
The reward of sin is death: that's hard.
[reads] *Si peccasse negamus, fallimur, et nulla est in nobis
veritas;* If we say that we have no sin, we deceive
ourselves, and there is no truth in us. Why, then, belike
we must sin, and so consequently die:
Ay, we must die an everlasting death.
What doctrine call you this, *Che sera, sera,*
What will be, shall be? Divinity, adieu!
These metaphysics or magicians,
And necromantic books are heavenly;
Lines, circles, scenes, letters, and characters;
Ay, these are those that Faustus most desires.
O, what a world of profit and delight,                    50
Of power, of honour, and omnipotence,
Is promis'd to the studious artisan!
All things that move between the quiet poles
Shall be at my command: emperors and kings
Are but obeyed in their several provinces;
But his dominion that exceeds in this,
Stretcheth as far as doth the mind of man;
A sound magician is a demigod:
Here tire, my brains, to gain a deity.

*Enter* WAGNER

Wagner, commend me to my dearest friends,          60
The German Valdes and Cornelius;
Request them earnestly to visit me.

WAGNER    I will, sir.                                    [*exit*

FAUSTUS   Their conference will be a greater help to me
Than all my labours, plod I ne'er so fast.

*Enter* GOOD ANGEL *and* EVIL ANGEL

GOOD. A   O, Faustus, lay that damned book aside,
And gaze not on it, lest it tempt thy soul,

  And heap God's heavy wrath upon thy head!
  Read, read the Scriptures — that is blasphemy.
EVIL A. Go forward, Faustus, in that famous art      70
  Wherein all Nature's treasure is contain'd:
  Be thou on earth as Jove is in the sky,
  Lord and commander of these elements.
               *[exeunt Angels*

FAUSTUS How am I glutted with conceit of this!
  Shall I make spirits fetch me what I please,
  Resolve me of all ambiguities,
  Perform what desperate enterprise I will?
  I'll have them fly to India for gold,
  Ransack the ocean for orient pearl,
  And search all corners of the new-found world    80
  For pleasant fruits and princely delicates;
  I'll have them read me strange philosophy,
  And tell the secrets of all foreign kings;
  I'll have them wall all Germany with brass,
  And make swift Rhine circle fair Wittenberg;
  I'll have them fill the public schools with silk,
  Wherewith the students shall be bravely clad;
  I'll levy soldiers with the coin they bring,
  And chase the Prince of Parma from our land,
  And reign sole king of all the provinces;      90
  Yea, stranger engines for the brunt of war,
  Than was the fiery keel at Antwerp-bridge,
  I'll make my servile spirits to invent.

      *Enter* VALDES *and* CORNELIUS

  Come, German Valdes, and Cornelius,
  And make me blest with your sage conference.
  Valdes, sweet Valdes, and Cornelius,
  Know that your words have won me at the last
  To practise magic and concealed arts.
  Philosophy is odious and obscure;
  Both law and physic are for petty wits:      100
  'Tis magic, magic that hath ravish'd me.
  Then, gentle friends, aid me in this attempt;
  And I, that have with subtle syllogisms
  Gravell'd the pastors of the German church,

And made the flowering pride of Wittenberg
Swarm to my problems, as th'infernal spirits
On sweet Musaeus when he came to hell,
Will be as cunning as Agrippa was,
Whose shadow made all Europe honour him.

VALDES      Faustus, these books, thy wit, and our experience, 110
Shall make all nations to canonise us.
As Indian Moors obey their Spanish lords,
So shall the spirits of every element
Be always serviceable to us three;
Like lions shall they guard us when we please;
Like Almain rutters with their horsemen's staves,
Or Lapland giants, trotting by our sides;
Sometimes like women, or unwedded maids,
Shadowing more beauty in their airy brows
Than have the white breasts of the queen of love: 120
From Venice shall they drag huge argosies,
And from America the golden fleece
That yearly stuffs old Philip's treasury,
If learned Faustus will be resolute.

FAUSTUS     Valdes, as resolute am I in this
As thou to live; therefore object it not.

CORNELIUS   The miracles that magic will perform
Will make thee vow to study nothing else.
He that is grounded in astrology,
Enrich'd with tongues, well seen in minerals,       130
Hath all the principles magic doth require:
Then doubt not, Faustus, but to be renown'd,
And more frequented for this mystery
Than heretofore the Delphian oracle.
The spirits tell me they can dry the sea,
And fetch the treasure of all foreign wrecks,
Yea, all the wealth that our forefathers hid
Within the massy entrails of the earth:
Then tell me, Faustus, what shall we three want?

FAUSTUS     Nothing, Cornelius. O, this cheers my soul!      140
Come, shew me some demonstrations magical,
That I may conjure in some bushy grove,
And have these joys in full possession.

VALDES      Then haste thee to some solitary grove,
            And bear wise Bacon's and Albertus' works,
            The Hebrew Psalter, and New Testament;
            And whatsoever else is requisite
            We will inform thee ere our conference cease.
CORNELIUS   Valdes, first let him know the words of art;
            And then, all other ceremonies learn'd,                150
            Faustus may try his cunning by himself.
VALDES      First I'll instruct thee in the rudiments,
            And then wilt thou be perfecter than I.
FAUSTUS     Then come and dine with me, and, after meat,
            We'll canvass every quiddity thereof;
            For, ere I sleep, I'll try what I can do:
            This night I'll conjure, though I die therefore.
                                                        [exeunt


## SCENE 2

### Enter two Scholars

1 SCHOLAR   I wonder what's become of Faustus, that was wont to
            make our schools ring with *sic probo*.
2 SCHOLAR   That shall we presently know; here comes his boy.

### Enter WAGNER

1 SCHOLAR   How now, sirrah! Where's thy master?
WAGNER      God in heaven knows.
2 SCHOLAR   Why, dost not thou know, then?
WAGNER      Yes, I know; but that follows not.
1 SCHOLAR   Go to, sirrah! Leave your jesting, and tell us where he is.
WAGNER      That follows not by force of argument, which you,
            being licentiates, should stand upon: therefore acknow-
            ledge your error, and be attentive.
2 SCHOLAR   Then you will not tell us?
WAGNER      You are deceived, for I will tell you: yet if you were
            not dunces, you would never ask me such a question;
            for is he not *corpus naturale*? And is not that *mobile*?
            Then wherefore should you ask me such a question?
            But that I am by nature phlegmatic, slow to wrath, and
            prone to lechery (to love, I would say), it were not for

you to come within forty foot of the place of execution, although I do not doubt but to see you both
hanged the next sessions. Thus having triumphed over
you, I will set my countenance like a precisian, and
begin to speak thus — Truly, my dear brethren, my
master is within at dinner, with Valdes and Cornelius,
as this wine, if it could speak, would inform your
worships: and so, the Lord bless you, preserve you, and
keep you, my dear brethren!                    [*exit*

1 SCHOLAR  O Faustus!
Then I fear that which I have long suspected,
That thou art fall'n into that damned art          30
For which they two are infamous through the world.

2 SCHOLAR  Were he a stranger, not allied to me,
The danger of his soul would make me mourn.
But, come, let us go and inform the Rector:
It may be his grave counsel may reclaim him.

1 SCHOLAR  I fear me nothing will reclaim him now.

2 SCHOLAR  Yet let us see what we can do.

                                          [*exeunt*


## SCENE 3

### *Enter* FAUSTUS

FAUSTUS  Now that the gloomy shadow of the night,
Longing to view Orion's drizzling look,
Leaps from th'antarctic world unto the sky,
And dims the welkin with her pitchy breath,
Faustus, begin thine incantations,
And try if devils will obey thy hest,
Seeing thou hast pray'd and sacrific'd to them.
Within this circle is Jehovah's name,
Forward and backward anagrammatis'd,
Th' abbreviated names of holy saints,               10
Figures of every adjunct to the heavens,
And characters of signs and erring stars,
By which the spirits are enforc'd to rise;
Then fear not, Faustus, to be resolute,
And try the utmost magic can perform.     [*thunder*

*Sint mihi dii Acherontis propitii! Valeat numen triplex*
*Jehovae! Ignei, aerii, aquatani spiritus, salvete! Orientis prin-*
*ceps Belzebub, inferni ardentis monarcha, et Demogorgon,*
*propitiamus vos, ut appareat et surgat Mephistophilis Dragon,*
*quod tumeraris: per Jehovam, Gehennam, et consecratam*
*aquam quam nunc spargo, signumque crucis quod nunc facio, et*
*per vota nostra, ipse nunc surgat nobis dicatus Mephistophilis!*

*Enter* MEPHISTOPHILIS

I charge thee to return, and change thy shape;
Thou art too ugly to attend on me;
Go, and return an old Franciscan friar;
That holy shape becomes a devil best.

                                        [*exit Mephistophilis*

I see there's virtue in my heavenly words.
Who would not be proficient in this art?
How pliant is this Mephistophilis,
Full of obedience and humility!                          30
Such is the force of magic and my spells.

*Re-enter* MEPHISTOPHILIS *like a Franciscan friar*

MEPHISTO.  Now, Faustus, what wouldst thou have me do?
FAUSTUS    I charge thee wait upon me whilst I live,
           To do whatever Faustus shall command,
           Be it to make the moon drop from her sphere,
           Or the ocean to overwhelm the world.
MEPHISTO.  I am a servant to great Lucifer,
           And may not follow thee without his leave:
           No more than he commands must we perform.
FAUSTUS    Did not he charge thee to appear to me?          40
MEPHISTO.  No, I came hither of mine own accord.
FAUSTUS    Did not my conjuring speeches raise thee? Speak!
MEPHISTO.  That was the cause, but yet *per accidens*;
           For, when we hear one rack the name of God,
           Abjure the Scriptures and his Saviour Christ,
           We fly, in hope to get his glorious soul;
           Nor will we come, unless he use such means
           Whereby he is in danger to be damn'd.
           Therefore the shortest cut for conjuring
           Is stoutly to abjure all godliness,               50

|  | And pray devoutly to the prince of hell. |  |
|---|---|---|
| FAUSTUS | So Faustus hath |  |
|  | Already done; and holds this principle, |  |
|  | There is no chief but only Belzebub; |  |
|  | To whom Faustus doth dedicate himself. |  |
|  | This word 'damnation' terrifies not me, |  |
|  | For I confound hell in Elysium: |  |
|  | My ghost be with the old philosophers! |  |
|  | But, leaving these vain trifles of men's souls, |  |
|  | Tell me what is that Lucifer thy lord? | 60 |
| MEPHISTO. | Arch-regent and commander of all spirits. |  |
| FAUSTUS | Was not that Lucifer an angel once? |  |
| MEPHISTO. | Yes, Faustus, and most dearly lov'd of God. |  |
| FAUSTUS | How comes it, then, that he is prince of devils? |  |
| MEPHISTO. | O, by aspiring pride and insolence; |  |
|  | For which God threw him from the face of heaven. |  |
| FAUSTUS | And what are you that live with Lucifer? |  |
| MEPHISTO. | Unhappy spirits that fell with Lucifer, |  |
|  | Conspir'd against our God with Lucifer, |  |
|  | And are for ever damn'd with Lucifer. | 70 |
| FAUSTUS | Where are you damn'd? |  |
| MEPHISTO. | In hell. |  |
| FAUSTUS | How comes it, then, that thou art out of hell? |  |
| MEPHISTO. | Why, this is hell, nor am I out of it: |  |
|  | Think'st thou that I, that saw the face of God, |  |
|  | And tasted the eternal joys of heaven, |  |
|  | Am not tormented with ten thousand hells, |  |
|  | In being depriv'd of everlasting bliss? |  |
|  | O, Faustus, leave these frivolous demands, |  |
|  | Which strike a terror to my fainting soul! | 80 |
| FAUSTUS | What, is great Mephistophilis so passionate |  |
|  | For being deprived of the joys of heaven? |  |
|  | Learn thou of Faustus manly fortitude, |  |
|  | And scorn those joys thou never shalt possess. |  |
|  | Go bear these tidings to great Lucifer: |  |
|  | Seeing Faustus hath incurr'd eternal death |  |
|  | By desperate thoughts against Jove's deity, |  |
|  | Say, he surrenders up to him his soul, |  |
|  | So he will spare him four and twenty years, |  |

Letting him live in all voluptuousness;                    90
Having thee ever to attend on me,
To give me whatsoever I shall ask,
To tell me whatsoever I demand,
To slay mine enemies, and to aid my friends,
And always be obedient to my will.
Go, and return to mighty Lucifer,
And meet me in my study at midnight,
And then resolve me of thy master's mind.

MEPHISTO.  I will, Faustus.                                    [*exit*

FAUSTUS   Had I as many souls as there be stars,               100
I'd give them all for Mephistophilis.
By him I'll be great emperor of the world,
And make a bridge thorough the moving air,
To pass the ocean with a band of men;
I'll join the hills that bind the Afric shore,
And make that country continent to Spain,
And both contributary to my crown:
The Emperor shall not live but by my leave,
Nor any potentate of Germany.
Now that I have obtain'd what I desir'd,
I'll live in speculation of this art,
Till Mephistophilis return again.

                                                          [*exit*


SCENE 4

*Enter* WAGNER *and* CLOWN

WAGNER    Come hither, sirrah boy.

CLOWN     Boy! O, disgrace to my person! Zounds, boy in your
          face! You have seen many boys with beards, I am sure.

WAGNER    Sirrah, hast thou no comings in?

CLOWN     Yes, and goings out too, you may see, sir.

WAGNER    Alas, poor slave! See how poverty jests in his naked-
          ness! I know the villain's out of service, and so hungry,
          that I know he would give his soul to the devil for a
          shoulder of mutton, though it were blood-raw.

CLOWN     Not so neither: I have need to have it well roasted, and
          good sauce to it, if I pay so dear, I can tell you.

WAGNER    Sirrah, wilt thou be my man, and wait on me, and I will make thee go like *Qui mihi discipulus*?

CLOWN    What, in verse?

WAGNER    No, slave; in beaten silk and staves-acre.

CLOWN    Staves-acre! That's good to kill vermin: then, belike, if I serve you, I shall be lousy.

WAGNER    Why, so thou shalt be, whether thou dost it or no; for, sirrah, if thou dost not presently bind thyself to me for seven years, I'll turn all the lice about thee into familiars, and make them tear thee in pieces.

CLOWN    Nay, sir, you may save yourself a labour, for they are as familiar with me as if they paid for their meat and drink, I can tell you.

WAGNER    Well, sirrah, leave your jesting, and take these guilders.
                                           *[gives money*

CLOWN    Yes, marry, sir; and I thank you too.

WAGNER    So, now thou art to be at an hour's warning, whensoever and wheresoever the devil shall fetch thee.

CLOWN    Here, take your guilders again; I'll none of 'em.

WAGNER    Not I; thou art pressed: prepare thyself, or I will presently raise up two devils to carry thee away — Banio! Belcher!

CLOWN    Belcher! An Belcher come here, I'll belch him: I am not afraid of a devil.

*Enter two Devils*

WAGNER    How now, sir! Will you serve me now?

CLOWN    Ay, good Wagner; take away the devils, then.

WAGNER    Spirits, away! *[exeunt Devils]* Now, sirrah, follow me.

CLOWN    I will, sir: but hark you, master; will you teach me this conjuring occupation?

WAGNER    Ay, sirrah, I'll teach thee to turn thyself to a dog, or a cat, or a mouse, or a rat, or any thing.

CLOWN    A dog, or a cat, or a mouse, or a rat! O, brave, Wagner!

WAGNER    Villain, call me Master Wagner, and see that you walk attentively, and let your right eye be always diametrally fixed upon my left heel, that thou mayst *quasi vestigiis nostris insistere*.

CLOWN    Well, sir, I warrant you.
                                           *[exeunt*

## SCENE 5

FAUSTUS *discovered in his study*

FAUSTUS    Now, Faustus,
Must thou needs be damn'd, canst thou not be sav'd.
What boots, it, then, to think on God or heaven?
Away with such vain fancies, and despair;
Despair in God, and trust in Belzebub:
No, go not backward, Faustus; be resolute:
Why waver'st thou? O, something soundeth in
                              mine ear,
'Abjure this magic, turn to God again!'
Why, he loves thee not;
The god thou serv'st is thine own appetite,     10
Wherein is fix'd the love of Belzebub:
To him I'll build an altar and a church,
And offer lukewarm blood of new-born babes.

*Enter* GOOD ANGEL *and* EVIL ANGEL

EVIL A.    Go forward, Faustus, in that famous art.
GOOD A.   Sweet Faustus, leave that execrable art.
FAUSTUS   Contrition, prayer, repentance – what of these?
GOOD A.   O, they are means to bring thee unto heaven!
EVIL A.    Rather illusions, fruits of lunacy,
That make men foolish that do use them most.
GOOD A.   Sweet Faustus, think of heaven and heavenly things.
EVIL A.    No, Faustus; think of honour and of wealth.
                           *[exeunt Angels*

FAUSTUS   Wealth!
Why, the signiory of Embden shall be mine.
When Mephistophilis shall stand by me,
What power can hurt me? Faustus, thou art safe:
Cast no more doubts – Mephistophilis, come,
And bring glad tidings from great Lucifer –
Is't not midnight – come Mephistophilis,
*Veni, veni, Mephistophile!*

*Enter* MEPHISTOPHILIS

Now tell me what saith Lucifer, thy lord?

MEPHISTO. That I shall wait on Faustus whilst he lives,     30
            So he will buy my service with his soul.

FAUSTUS Already Faustus hath hazarded that for thee.

MEPHISTO. But now thou must bequeath it solemnly,
            And write a deed of gift with thine own blood;
            For that security craves Lucifer.
            If thou deny it, I must back to hell.

FAUSTUS Stay, Mephistophilis, and tell me, what good will my
            soul do thy lord?

MEPHISTO. Enlarge his kingdom.

FAUSTUS Is that the reason why he tempts us thus?     40

MEPHISTO. *Solamen miseris socios habuisse doloris.*

FAUSTUS Why, have you any pain that torture others?

MEPHISTO. As great as have the human souls of men.
            But, tell me, Faustus, shall I have thy soul?
            And I will be thy slave, and wait on thee,
            And give thee more than thou hast wit to ask.

FAUSTUS Ay, Mephistophilis, I'll give it thee.

MEPHISTO. Then, Faustus, stab thine arm courageously,
            And bind thy soul, that at some certain day
            Great Lucifer may claim it as his own;     50
            And then be thou as great as Lucifer.

FAUSTUS [*stabbing his arm*] Lo, Mephistophilis, for love of thee,
            Faustus hath cut his arm, and with his proper blood
            Assures his soul to be great Lucifer's,
            Chief lord and regent of perpetual night!
            View here this blood that trickles from mine arm,
            And let it be propitious for my wish.

MEPHISTO. But, Faustus,
            Write it in manner of a deed of gift.

FAUSTUS [*writing*] Ay, so I do. But, Mephistophilis,     60
            My blood congeals, and I can write no more.

MEPHISTO. I'll fetch thee fire to dissolve it straight.     [*exit*

FAUSTUS What might the staying of my blood portend?
            Is it unwilling I should write this bill?
            Why streams it not, that I may write afresh?
            *Faustus gives to thee his soul*: O, there it stay'd!
            Why shouldst thou not? Is not thy soul thine own?
            Then write again, *Faustus gives to thee his soul.*

*Re-enter* MEPHISTOPHILIS *with the chafer of fire*

MEPHISTO.   See, Faustus, here is fire; set it on.

FAUSTUS    So, now the blood begins to clear again;         70
           Now will I make an end immediately.         [*writes*

MEPHISTO.   [*aside*] What will not I do to obtain his soul?

FAUSTUS    *Consummatum est*; this bill is ended,
           And Faustus hath bequeath'd his soul to Lucifer.
           But what is this inscription on mine arm?
           *Homo, fuge*: whither should I fly?
           If unto God, he'll throw me down to hell.
           My senses are deceiv'd; here's nothing writ –
           O, yes, I see it plain; even here is writ,
           *Homo, fuge*: yet shall not Faustus fly.         80

MEPHISTO.   [*aside*] I'll fetch him somewhat to delight his mind.
                                                          [*exit*

*Enter Devils, giving crowns and rich apparel to* FAUSTUS.
*They dance, and then depart*

*Enter* MEPHISTOPHILIS

FAUSTUS    What means this show? Speak, Mephistophilis.

MEPHISTO.   Nothing, Faustus, but to delight thy mind,
           And let thee see what magic can perform.

FAUSTUS    But may I raise such spirits when I please?

MEPHISTO.   Ay, Faustus, and do greater things than these.

FAUSTUS    Then, Mephistophilis, receive this scroll,
           A deed of gift of body and of soul:
           But yet conditionally that thou perform
           All covenants and articles between us both!         90

MEPHISTO.   Faustus, I swear by hell and Lucifer
           To effect all promises between us both!

FAUSTUS    Then hear me read it, Mephistophilis.
           [*reads*] *On these conditions following, First, that Faustus may*
           *be a spirit in form and substance. Secondly, that Mephisto-*
           *philis shall be his servant, and be by him commanded.*
           *Thirdly, that Mephistophilis shall do for him, and bring him,*
           *whatsoever he desires. Fourthly, that he shall be in his*
           *chamber or house invisible. Lastly, that he shall appear to the*
           *said John Faustus, at all times, in what shape and form soever*

> *he please. I, John Faustus, of Wittenberg, Doctor, by these*
> *presents do give both body and soul to Lucifer prince of the*
> *east, and his minister Mephistophilis; and furthermore grant*
> *unto them, that, four-and-twenty years being expired, and*
> *these articles above-written being inviolate, full power to fetch*
> *or carry the said John Faustus, body and soul, flesh and blood,*
> *into their habitation wheresoever. By me, John Faustus.*

MEPHISTO.   Speak, Faustus, do you deliver this as your deed?

FAUSTUS     Ay, take it, and the devil give thee good of it!

MEPHISTO.   So, now, Faustus, ask me what thou wilt.          110

FAUSTUS     First I will question with thee about hell.
            Tell me, where is the place that men call hell?

MEPHISTO.   Under the heavens.

FAUSTUS     Ay, so are all things else; but whereabouts?

MEPHISTO.   Within the bowels of these elements,
            Where we are tortur'd and remain for ever:
            Hell hath no limits, nor is circumscrib'd
            In one self-place; but where we are is hell,
            And where hell is, there must we ever be:
            And, to be short, when all the world dissolves,     120
            And every creature shall be purified,
            All places shall be hell that are not heaven.

FAUSTUS     I think hell's a fable.

MEPHISTO.   Ay, think so still, till experience change thy mind.

FAUSTUS     Why, dost thou think that Faustus shall be damn'd?

MEPHISTO.   Ay, of necessity, for here's the scroll
            In which thou hast given thy soul to Lucifer.

FAUSTUS     Ay, and body too; and what of that?
            Think'st thou that Faustus is so fond to imagine
            That, after this life, there is any pain?            130
            No, these are trifles and mere old wives' tales.

MEPHISTO.   But I am an instance to prove the contrary,
            For I tell thee I am damn'd and now in hell.

FAUSTUS     Nay, an this be hell, I'll willingly be damn'd;
            What! Sleeping, eating, walking, and disputing!
            But, leaving this, let me have a wife,
            The fairest maid in Germany;
            For I am wanton and lascivious,
            And cannot live without a wife.

MEPHISTO. Well, Faustus, thou shalt have a wife.                    140

[*Mephistophilis fetches in a Woman-devil*

FAUSTUS    What sight is this?

MEPHISTO. Now, Faustus, wilt thou have a wife?

FAUSTUS    Here's a hot whore, indeed: no, I'll no wife.

MEPHISTO. Marriage is but a ceremonial toy,
           And, if thou lov'st me, think no more of it.
           I'll cull thee out the fairest courtesans,
           And bring them every morning to thy bed:
           She whom thine eye shall like, thy heart shall have,
           Were she as chaste as was Penelope,
           As wise as Saba, or as beautiful                    150
           As was bright Lucifer before his fall.
           Here, take this book, and peruse it well:
           The iterating of these lines brings gold;
           The framing of this circle on the ground
           Brings thunder, whirlwinds, storm, and lightning;
           Pronounce this thrice devoutly to thyself,
           And men in harness shall appear to thee,
           Ready to execute what thou command'st.

FAUSTUS    Thanks, Mephistophilis, for this sweet book:
           This will I keep as chary as my life.                    160

[*exeunt*

# ACT TWO

## SCENE I

*Enter* FAUSTUS, *in his study, and* MEPHISTOPHILIS

FAUSTUS    When I behold the heavens, then I repent,
           And curse thee, wicked Mephistophilis,
           Because thou hast depriv'd me of those joys.

MEPHISTO.  'Twas thine own seeking, Faustus; thank thyself.
           But, think'st thou heaven is such a glorious thing?
           I tell thee, Faustus, it is not half so fair
           As thou, or any man that breathes on earth.

FAUSTUS    How prov'st thou that?

MEPHISTO.  'Twas made for man; then he's more excellent.

FAUSTUS    If heaven was made for man, 'twas made for me:   10
           I will renounce this magic and repent.

*Enter* GOOD ANGEL *and* EVIL ANGEL

GOOD A.    Faustus, repent; yet God will pity thee.

EVIL A.    Thou art a spirit; God cannot pity thee.

FAUSTUS    Who buzzeth in mine ears I am a spirit?
           Be I a devil, yet God may pity me;
           Yea, God will pity me, if I repent.

EVIL A.    Ay, but Faustus never shall repent.    *[exeunt Angels*

FAUSTUS    My heart is harden'd, I cannot repent;
           Scarce can I name salvation, faith, or heaven:
           Swords, poisons, halters, and envenom'd steel   20
           Are laid before me to despatch myself:
           And long ere this I should have done the deed,
           Had not sweet pleasure conquer'd deep despair.
           Have not I made blind Homer sing to me
           Of Alexander's love and Oenon's death?
           And hath not he, that built the walls of Thebes
           With ravishing sound of his melodious harp,
           Made music with my Mephistophilis?
           Why should I die, then, or basely despair?
           I am resolv'd; Faustus shall not repent –   30
           Come, Maphistophilis, let us dispute again,

        And reason of divine astrology.
        Speak, are there many spheres above the moon?
        Are all the celestial bodies but one globe,
        As is the substance of this centric earth?

MEPHISTO.  As are the elements, such are the heavens,
        Even from the moon unto th'empyreal orb,
        Mutually folded in each other's spheres,
        And jointly move upon one axletree,
        Whose termine is term'd the world's wide pole;    40
        Nor are the names of Saturn, Mars or Jupiter
        Feign'd, but are erring stars.

FAUSTUS    But have they all one motion, both *situ et tempore*?

MEPHISTO.  All move from east to west in four-and-twenty hours
        upon the poles of the world; but differ in their motions
        upon the poles of the zodiac.

FAUSTUS    These slender questions Wagner can decide:
        Hath Mephistophilis no greater skill?
        Who knows not the double motion of the planets?
        That the first is finish'd in a natural day;    50
        The second thus; Saturn in thirty years;
        Jupiter in twelve; Mars in four; the Sun, Venus, and
        Mercury in a year; the Moon in twenty-eight days.
        These are fresh-men's questions. But tell me, hath
        every sphere a dominion or *intelligentia*?

MEPHISTO.  Ay.

FAUSTUS    How many heavens or spheres are there?

MEPHISTO.  Nine; the seven planets, the firmament, and the em-
        pyreal heaven.

FAUSTUS    But is there not *coelum igneum et crystallinum*?    60

MEPHISTO.  No, Faustus, they be but fables.

FAUSTUS    Resolve me, then, in this one question; why are not
        conjunctions, oppositions, aspects, eclipses, all at one
        time, but in some years we have more, in some less?

MEPHISTO.  *Per inaequalem motum respectu totius*.

FAUSTUS    Well, I am answered. Now tell me who made the
        world?

MEPHISTO.  I will not.

FAUSTUS    Sweet Mephistophilis, tell me.

MEPHISTO.  Move me not, Faustus.    70

| | |
|---|---|
| FAUSTUS | Villain, have not I bound thee to tell me any thing? |
| MEPHISTO. | Ay, that is not against our kingdom; this is. Thou art damned; think thou of hell. |
| FAUSTUS | Think, Faustus, upon God that made the world. |
| MEPHISTO. | Remember this.                      [*exit* |
| FAUSTUS | Ay, go, accursed spirit, to ugly hell! |
| | 'Tis thou hast damn'd distressed Faustus' soul. |
| | Is't not too late? |

*Re-enter* GOOD ANGEL *and* EVIL ANGEL

| | | |
|---|---|---|
| EVIL A. | Too late. | |
| GOOD A. | Never too late, if Faustus will repent. | 80 |
| EVIL A. | If thou repent, devils will tear thee in pieces. | |
| GOOD A. | Repent, and they shall never raze thy skin. | |

                                    [*exeunt Angels*

| | |
|---|---|
| FAUSTUS | O Christ, my Saviour, my Saviour, |
| | Help to save distressed Faustus' soul! |

*Enter* LUCIFER, BELZEBUB, *and* MEPHISTOPHILIS

| | | |
|---|---|---|
| LUCIFER | Christ cannot save thy soul, for he is just: | |
| | There's none but I have interest in the same. | |
| FAUSTUS | O, what art thou that look'st so terribly? | |
| LUCIFER | I am Lucifer, | |
| | And this is my companion-prince in hell. | |
| FAUSTUS | O Faustus, they are come to fetch thy soul! | 90 |
| BELZEBUB | We are come to tell thee thou dost injure us. | |
| LUCIFER | Thou call'st on Christ, contrary to thy promise. | |
| BELZEBUB | Thou shouldst not think on God. | |
| LUCIFER | Think on the devil. | |
| BELZEBUB | And his dam too. | |
| FAUSTUS | Nor will Faustus henceforth: pardon him for this, | |
| | And Faustus vows never to look to heaven. | |
| LUCIFER | So shalt thou shew thyself an obedient servant, | |
| | And we will highly gratify thee for it. | |
| BELZEBUB | Faustus, we are come from hell in person to shew thee some pastime: sit down, and thou shalt behold the Seven Deadly Sins appear to thee in their own proper shapes and likeness. | |
| FAUSTUS | That sight will be as pleasant unto me, | |
| | As Paradise was to Adam the first day | |

Of his creation.

LUCIFER     Talk not of Paradise or creation; but mark the show –
            Go, Mephistophilis, and fetch them in.

MEPHISTOPHILIS *brings in the Seven Deadly Sins*

BELZEBUB    Now, Faustus, question them of their names and dis-
            positions.                                        110

FAUSTUS     That shall I soon – What art thou, the first?

PRIDE       I am Pride. I disdain to have any parents. I am like to
            Ovid's flea; I can creep into every corner of a wench;
            sometimes, like a perriwig, I sit upon her brow; next,
            like a necklace, I hang about her neck; then, like a fan
            of feathers, I kiss her lips; and then, turning myself to a
            wrought smock, do what I list. But, fie, what a smell is
            here! I'll not speak a word more for a king's ransom,
            unless the ground be perfumed, and covered with
            cloth or arras.                                   120

FAUSTUS     Thou art a proud knave, indeed – What art thou, the
            second?

COVETOUS    I am Covetousness, begotten of an old churl, in a
            leather bag: and, might I now obtain my wish, this
            house, you, and all, should turn to gold, that I might
            lock you in safe into my chest: O my sweet gold!

FAUSTUS     And what art thou, the third?

ENVY        I am Envy, begotten of a chimney-sweeper and an
            oyster-wife. I cannot read, and therefore wish all books
            burned. I am lean with seeing others eat. O, that there
            would come a famine over the world, that all might
            die, and I live alone! Then thou shouldst see how fat
            I'd be. But must thou sit, and I stand? Come down,
            with a vengeance!

FAUSTUS     Out, envious wretch! But what art thou, the fourth?

WRATH       I am Wrath. I had neither father nor mother: I leapt
            out of a lion's mouth when I was scarce an hour old;
            and ever since have run up and down the world with
            this case of rapiers, wounding myself when I could get
            none to fight withal. I was born in hell; and look to it,
            for some of you shall be my father.

FAUSTUS     And what art thou, the fifth?

GLUTTONY   I am Gluttony. My parents are all dead, and the devil a
           penny they have left me, but a small pension, and that
           buys me thirty meals a-day and ten bevers – a small
           trifle to suffice nature. I come of a royal pedigree: my
           father was a Gammon of Bacon, and my mother was a
           Hogshead of Claret-wine; my godfathers were these,
           Peter Pickled-herring and Martin Martlemas-beef; but
           my godmother, O, she was an ancient gentlewoman;
           her name was Margery March-beer. Now, Faustus,
           thou hast heard all my progeny; wilt thou bid me to
           supper?
FAUSTUS    Not I.
GLUTTONY   Then the devil choke thee!
FAUSTUS    Choke thyself, glutton! What are thou, the sixth?
SLOTH      Heigho! I am Sloth. I was begotten on a sunny bank.
           Heigho! I'll not speak a word more for a king's ransom.
FAUSTUS    And what are you, Mistress Minx, the seventh and last?
LECHERY    Who, I, sir? I am one that loves an inch of raw mutton
           better than an ell of fried stock-fish; and the first letter
           of my name begins with L.
LUCIFER    Away to hell, away! On, piper!        [exeunt the Sins
FAUSTUS    O, how this sight doth delight my soul!
LUCIFER    Tut, Faustus, in hell is all manner of delight.
FAUSTUS    O, might I see hell, and return again safe,
           How happy were I then!
LUCIFER    Faustus, thou shalt; at midnight I will send for thee.
           Meanwhile peruse this book and view it throughly,
           And thou shalt turn thyself into what shape thou wilt.
FAUSTUS    Thanks, mighty Lucifer!
           This will I keep as chary as my life.
LUCIFER    Now, Faustus, farewell.
FAUSTUS    Farewell, great Lucifer.     [exeunt Lucifer and Belzebub
           Come, Mephistophilis.
                                                              [exit

## SCENE 2

*Enter* ROBIN, *with a book*

ROBIN   What, Dick! Look to the horses there, till I come again. I have gotten one of Doctor Faustus' conjuring-books; and now we'll have such knavery as't passes.

*Enter* DICK

DICK   What, Robin! You must come away and walk the horses.

ROBIN   I walk the horses! I scorn't, faith: I have other matters in hand: let the horses walk themselves, and they will – [*reads*] *A per se, a; t, h, e, the; o per se, o; Demy orgon gorgon* – Keep further from me, O thou illiterate and unlearned hostler!

DICK   'Snails, what hast thou got there? A book! Why, thou canst not tell ne'er a word on't.

ROBIN   That thou shalt see presently: keep out of the circle, I say, lest I send you into the ostry with a vengeance.

DICK   That's like, faith! You had best leave your foolery; for, an my master come, he'll conjure you, faith.

ROBIN   My master conjure me! I'll tell thee what; an my master come here, I'll clap as fair a pair of horns on's head as e'er thou sawest in thy life.

DICK   Thou need'st not do that, for my mistress hath done it.

ROBIN   Ay, there be of us here that have waded as deep into matters as other men, if they were disposed to talk.

DICK   A plague take you! I thought you did not sneak up and down after her for nothing. But, I prithee, tell me in good sadness, Robin, is that a conjuring-book?

ROBIN   Do but speak what thou'lt have me to do, and I'll do't: if thou'lt dance naked, put off thy clothes, and I'll conjure thee about presently; or, if thou'lt go but to the tavern with me, I'll give thee white wine, red wine, claret-wine, sack, muscadine, malmsey, and whippincrust, hold, belly, hold; and we'll not pay one penny for it.

DICK   O, brave! Prithee, let's go to it presently, for I am as dry as a dog.

ROBIN   Come, then, let's away.

                                        [*exeunt*

## ACT THREE

### SCENE I

*Enter* CHORUS

CHORUS    Learned Faustus,
To find the secrets of astronomy
Graven in the book of Jove's high firmament,
Did mount him up to scale Olympus' top;
Where, sitting in a chariot burning bright,
Drawn by the strength of yoked dragons' necks,
He views the clouds, the planets, and the stars,
The tropic zones, and quarters of the sky,
From the bright circle of the horned moon
Even to the height of *Primum Mobile*;         10
And, whirling round with this circumference,
Within the concave compass of the pole,
From east to west his dragons swiftly glide,
And in eight days did bring him home again.
Not long he stay'd within his quiet house,
To rest his bones after his weary toil;
But new exploits do hale him out again:
And, mounted then upon a dragon's back,
That with his wings did part the subtle air,
He now is gone to prove cosmography,         20
That measures coasts and kingdoms of the earth;
And, as I guess, will first arrive at Rome,
To see the Pope and manner of his court,
And take some part of holy Peter's feast,
The which this day is highly solemnis'd.

                                            *[exit*

## SCENE 2

*Enter* FAUSTUS *and* MEPHISTOPHILIS

FAUSTUS      Having now, my good Mephistophilis,
Pass'd with delight the stately town of Trier,
Environ'd round with airy mountain-tops,
With walls of flint, and deep-entrenched lakes,
Not to be won by any conquering prince;
From Paris next, coasting the realm of France,
We saw the river Maine fall into Rhine,
Whose banks are set with groves of fruitful vines;
Then up to Naples, rich Campania,
Whose buildings fair and gorgeous to the eye,     10
The streets straight forth, and pav'd with finest brick,
Quarter the town in four equivalents:
There saw we learned Maro's golden tomb;
The way he cut, an English mile in length,
Thorough a rock of stone, in one night's space;
From thence to Venice, Padua, and the rest,
In one of which a sumptuous temple stands,
That threats the stars with her aspiring top,
Whose frame is pav'd with sundry-colour'd stones,
And roof'd aloft with curious work in gold.     20
Thus hitherto hath Faustus spent his time:
But tell me now, what resting-place is this?
Hast thou, as erst I did command,
Conducted me within the walls of Rome?

MEPHISTO.  I have, my Faustus; and, for proof thereof,
This is the goodly palace of the Pope;
And, 'cause we are no common guests,
I choose his privy-chamber for our use.

FAUSTUS      I hope his Holiness will bid us welcome.

MEPHISTO.  All's one, for we'll be bold with his venison.     30
But now, my Faustus, that thou mayst perceive
What Rome contains for to delight thine eyes,
Know that this city stands upon seven hills
That underprop the groundwork of the same:
Just through the midst runs flowing Tiber's stream,

           With winding banks that cut it in two parts;
           Over the which two stately bridges lean,
           That make safe passage to each part of Rome:
           Upon the bridge call'd Ponte Angelo
           Erected is a castle passing strong,                                        40
           Where thou shalt see such store of ordnance,
           As that the double cannons, forg'd of brass,
           Do match the number of the days contain'd
           Within the compass of one complete year;
           Beside the gates, and high pyramides,
           That Julius Caesar brought from Africa.
FAUSTUS    Now, by the kingdoms of infernal rule,
           Of Styx, of Acheron, and the fiery lake
           Of ever-burning Phlegethon, I swear
           That I do long to see the monuments                                     50
           And situation of bright-splendent Rome:
           Come, therefore, let's away.
MEPHISTO.  Nay, stay, my Faustus: I know you'd see the Pope,
           And take some part of holy Peter's feast,
           The which, in state and high solemnity,
           This day, is held through Rome and Italy,
           In honour of the Pope's triumphant victory.
FAUSTUS    Sweet Mephistophilis, thou pleasest me.
           Whilst I am here on earth, let me be cloy'd
           With all things that delight the heart of man:                          60
           My four-and-twenty years of liberty
           I'll spend in pleasure and in dalliance,
           That Faustus' name, whilst this bright frame
                                 doth stand,
           May be admir'd thorough the furthest land.
MEPHISTO.  'Tis well said, Faustus. Come, then, stand by me,
           And thou shalt see them come immediately.
FAUSTUS    Nay, stay, my gentle Mephistophilis,
           And grant me my request, and then I go.
           Thou know'st, within the compass of eight days
           We view'd the face of heaven, of earth, and hell;                   70
           So high our dragons soar'd into the air,
           That, looking down, the earth appear'd to me
           No bigger than my hand in quantity;

         There did we view the kingdoms of the world,
         And what might please mine eye I there beheld.
         Then in this show let me an actor be,
         That this proud Pope may Faustus' cunning see.

MEPHISTO. Let it be so, my Faustus. But, first, stay,
         And view their triumphs as they pass this way;
         And then devise what best contents thy mind,    80
         By cunning in thine art to cross the Pope,
         Or dash the pride of this solemnity;
         To make his monks and abbots stand like apes,
         And point like antics at his triple crown;
         To beat the beads about the friars' pates,
         Or clap huge horns upon the cardinals' heads;
         Or any villainy thou canst devise;
         And I'll perform it, Faustus. Hark! They come:
         This day shall make thee be admir'd in Rome.

*Enter the Cardinals and Bishops, some bearing crosiers, some*
*the pillars; Monks and Friars, singing their procession; then the*
POPE, RAYMOND KING OF HUNGARY, *the* ARCHBISHOP
OF RHEIMS, BRUNO *led in chains, and Attendants*

POPE       Cast down our footstool.

RAYMOND                Saxon Bruno, stoop,    90
         Whilst on thy back his Holiness ascends
         Saint Peter's chair and state pontifical.

BRUNO      Proud Lucifer, that state belongs to me;
         But thus I fall to Peter, not to thee.

POPE       To me and Peter shalt thou grovelling lie,
         And crouch before the Papal dignity –
         Sound trumpets, then; for thus Saint Peter's heir,
         From Bruno's back, ascends Saint Peter's chair.
                       *[a flourish while he ascends*
         Thus, as the gods creep on with feet of wool,
          Long ere with iron hands they punish men,    100
         So shall our sleeping vengeance now arise,
         And smite with death thy hated enterprise –
         Lord Cardinals of France and Padua,
         Go forthwith to our holy consistory,
         And read, amongst the statutes decretal,
         What, by the holy council held at Trent,

|            | The sacred synod hath decreed for him |
|------------|---------------------------------------|

The sacred synod hath decreed for him
That doth assume the Papal government
Without election and a true consent:
Away, and bring us word with speed.          110

C. FRANCE We go, my lord. [*exeunt Cardinals of France and Padua*

POPE     Lord Raymond.          [*they converse in dumb show*

FAUSTUS  Go, haste thee, gentle Mephistophilis,
Follow the cardinals to the consistory;
And, as they turn their superstitious books,
Strike them with sloth and drowsy idleness,
And make them sleep so sound, that in their shapes
Thyself and I may parley with this pope,
This proud confronter of the Emperor;
And, in despite of all his holiness,          120
Restore this Bruno to his liberty,
And bear him to the states of Germany.

MEPHISTO. Faustus, I go.

FAUSTUS  Despatch it soon:
The Pope shall curse, that Faustus came to Rome.
                    [*exeunt Faustus and Mephistophilis*

BRUNO    Pope Adrian, let me have right of law:
I was elected by the Emperor.

POPE     We will depose the Emperor for that deed,
And curse the people that submit to him:
Both he and thou shall stand excommunicate,          130
And interdict from church's privilege
And all society of holy men.
He grows too proud in his authority,
Lifting his lofty head above the clouds,
And, like a steeple, overpeers the church:
But we'll pull down his haughty insolence;
And, as Pope Alexander, our progenitor,
Trod on the neck of German Frederick,
Adding this golden sentence to our praise,
'That Peter's heirs should tread on Emperors,          140
And walk upon the dreadful adder's back,
Treading the lion and the dragon down,
And fearless spurn the killing basilisk',
So will we quell that haughty schismatic,

|         | And, by authority apostolical,                     |     |
|---------|---------------------------------------------------|-----|
|         | Depose him from his regal government.             |     |
| BRUNO   | Pope Julius swore to princely Sigismond,          |     |
|         | For him and the succeeding Popes of Rome,         |     |
|         | To hold the Emperors their lawful lords.          |     |
| POPE    | Pope Julius did abuse the church's rights,        | 150 |

POPE    Pope Julius did abuse the church's rights,     150
And therefore none of his decrees can stand.
Is not all power on earth bestow'd on us?
And therefore, though we would, we cannot err.
Behold this silver belt, whereto is fix'd
Seven golden seals, fast sealed with seven seals,
In token of our seven-fold power from heaven,
To bind or loose, lock fast, condemn or judge,
Resign or seal, or what so pleaseth us:
Then he and thou, and all the world, shall stoop,
Or be assured of our dreadful curse,     160
To light as heavy as the pains of hell.

*Re-enter* FAUSTUS *and* MEPHISTOPHILIS, *in the shapes
of the* CARDINALS OF FRANCE AND PADUA

MEPHISTO.   Now tell me, Faustus, are we not fitted well?
FAUSTUS    Yes, Mephistophilis; and two such cardinals
Ne'er serv'd a holy Pope as we shall do.
But, whilst they sleep within the consistory,
Let us salute his reverend fatherhood.
RAYMOND   Behold, my lord, the Cardinals are return'd.
POPE    Welcome, grave fathers: answer presently
What hath our holy council there decreed
Concerning Bruno and the Emperor,     170
In quittance of their late conspiracy
Against our state and papal dignity?
FAUSTUS    Most sacred patron of the church of Rome,
By full consent of all the synod
Of priests and prelates, it is thus decreed –
That Bruno and the German Emperor
Be held as Lollards and bold schismatics,
And proud disturbers of the church's peace;
And if that Bruno, by his own assent,
Without enforcement of the German peers,     180

> Did seek to wear the triple diadem,
> And by your death to climb Saint Peter's chair,
> The statutes decretal have thus decreed —
> He shall be straight condemn'd of heresy,
> And on a pile of faggots burnt to death.

POPE    It is enough. Here, take him to your charge,
> And bear him straight to Ponte Angelo,
> And in the strongest tower enclose him fast.
> Tomorrow, sitting in our consistory,
> With all our college of grave cardinals,       190
> We will determine of his life or death.
> Here, take his triple crown along with you,
> And leave it in the church's treasury.
> Make haste again, my good Lord Cardinals,
> And take our blessing apostolical.

MEPHISTO.   So, so; was never devil thus bless'd before.

FAUSTUS   Away, sweet Mephistophilis, be gone;
> The Cardinals will be plagu'd for this anon.
>         [*exeunt Faustus and Mephistophilis with Bruno*

POPE    Go presently and bring a banquet forth,
> That we may solemnize Saint Peter's feast,       200
> And with Lord Raymond, King of Hungary,
> Drink to our late and happy victory.


## SCENE 3

*A Sennet while the banquet is brought in; and then enter*
*Faustus and Mephistophilis in their own shapes.*

MEPHISTO.   Now, Faustus, come, prepare thyself for mirth:
> The sleepy Cardinals are hard at hand,
> To censure Bruno, that is posted hence,
> And on a proud-pac'd steed, as swift as thought,
> Flies o'er the Alps to fruitful Germany,
> There to salute the woeful Emperor.

FAUSTUS   The Pope will curse them for their sloth to-day,
> That slept both Bruno and his crown away.
> But now, that Faustus may delight his mind,
> And by their folly make some merriment,       10

Sweet Mephistophilis, so charm me here,
That I may walk invisible to all,
And do whate'er I please, unseen of any.

MEPHISTO. Faustus, thou shalt: then kneel down presently,
Whilst on thy head I lay my hand,
And charm thee with this magic wand.
First, wear this girdle; then appear
Invisible to all are here;
The planets seven, the gloomy air,
Hell, and the Furies' forked hair,
Pluto's blue fire, and Hecat's tree,
With magic spells so compass thee,
That no eye may thy body see!
So, Faustus, now; for all their holiness,
Do what thou wilt, thou shalt not be discern'd

FAUSTUS Thanks, Mephistophilis – Now, friars, take heed,
Lest Faustus make your shaven crowns to bleed.

MEPHISTO. Faustus, no more: see, where the Cardinals come!

*Re-enter the* CARDINALS OF FRANCE AND PADUA *with a book*

POPE Welcome, Lord Cardinals; come, sit down –
Lord Raymond, take your seat – Friars, attend,
And see that all things be in readiness,
As best beseems this solemn festival.

FRANCE First, may it please your sacred Holiness
To view the sentence of the reverend synod
Concerning Bruno and the Emperor?

POPE What needs this question? Did I not tell you,
To-morrow we would sit i' the consistory,
And there determine of his punishment?
You brought us word even now, it was decreed
That Bruno and the cursed Emperor
Were by the holy council both condemn'd
For loathed lollards and base schismatics:
Then wherefore would you have me view that book?

FRANCE Your grace mistakes; you gave us no such charge.

RAYMOND Deny it not; we all are witnesses
That Bruno here was late deliver'd you,
With his rich triple crown to be reserv'd

|              | And put into the church's treasury. |    |
|--------------|-------------------------------------|----|
| CARDINALS    | By holy Paul, we saw them not!      |    |
| POPE         | By Peter, you shall die,            | 50 |
|              | Unless you bring them forth immediately! | |
|              | Hale them to prison, lade their limbs with gyves – | |
|              | False prelates, for this hateful treachery | |
|              | Curs'd be your souls to hellish misery! | |

*[exeunt Attendants with the two Cardinals*

| FAUSTUS | So, they are safe. Now, Faustus, to the feast: |    |
|---------|-----------------------------------------------|----|
|         | The Pope had never such a frolic guest.       |    |
| POPE    | Lord Archbishop of Rheims, sit down with us.  |    |
| ARCHB.  | I thank your Holiness.                         |    |
| FAUSTUS | Fall to; the devil choke you, an you spare!   |    |
| POPE    | Who is that spoke? Friars, look about –       | 60 |
|         | Lord Raymond, pray, fall to. I am beholding   |    |
|         | To the Bishop of Milan for this so rare a present. | |
| FAUSTUS | I thank you, sir.              *[snatches the dish* | |
| POPE    | How now! Who snatch'd the meat from me?       |    |
|         | Villains, why speak you not?                  |    |
|         | My good Lord Archbishop, here's a most dainty dish | |
|         | Was sent me from a cardinal in France.        |    |
| FAUSTUS | I'll have that too.            *[snatches the dish* | |
| POPE    | What Lollards do attend our holiness,         |    |
|         | That we receive such great indignity?         | 70 |
|         | Fetch me some wine.                           |    |
| FAUSTUS | Ay, pray, do, for Faustus is a-dry.           |    |
| POPE    | Lord Raymond,                                 |    |
|         | I drink unto your grace.                      |    |
| FAUSTUS | I pledge your grace.            *[snatches the cup* | |
| POPE    | My wine gone too! Ye lubbers, look about,     |    |
|         | And find the man that doth this villainy,     |    |
|         | Or, by our sanctitude, you all shall die!     |    |
|         | I pray, my lords, have patience at this       |    |
|         | Troublesome banquet.                          | 80 |
| ARCHB.  | Please it your Holiness, I think it be some ghost crept | |
|         | out of Purgatory, and now is come unto your Holiness | |
|         | for his pardon.                               |    |
| POPE    | It may be so –                                |    |
|         | Go, then, command our priests to sing a dirge, | |

To lay the fury of this same troublesome ghost.

*[exit an Attendant – the Pope crosses himself*

FAUSTUS How now! Must every bit be spic'd with a cross?
Nay, then, take that.                    *[strikes the Pope*

POPE O, I am slain! Help me, my lords!
O, come and help to bear my body hence!
Damn'd be his soul for ever for this deed!

*[exeunt all except Faustus and Mephistophilis*

MEPHISTO. Now, Faustus, what will you do now? For I can tell
you you'll be cursed with bell, book, and candle.

FAUSTUS Bell, book and candle – candle, book, and bell –
Forward and backward, to curse Faustus to hell!

*Re-enter the Friars, with bell, book, and candle, for the dirge*

I FRIAR Come, brethren, let's about our business with good
devotion.
*[they sing]*

> Cursed be he that stole his Holiness' meat
>     from the table! *Maledicat Dominus!*
> Cursed be he that struck his Holiness a blow
>     on the face! *Maledicat Dominus!*
> Cursed be he that struck Friar Sandelo a blow
>     on the pate! *Maledicat Dominus!*
> Cursed be he that disturbeth our holy dirge!
>     *Maledicat Dominus!*
> Cursed be he that took away his Holiness'
>     wine! *Maledicat Dominus!*

*[Mephistophilis and Faustus beat the Friars,*
*fling fire-works among them, and exeunt*

## SCENE 4

*Enter* ROBIN *and* DICK

DICK      Sirrah Robin, we were best look that your devil can answer the stealing of this same cup, for the Vintner's boy follows us at the hard heels.

ROBIN      'Tis no matter; let him come: an he follow us, I'll so conjure him as he was never conjured in his life, I warrant him. Let me see the cup.

DICK      Here 'tis.          [*gives the cup to Robin*
Yonder he comes: now, Robin, now or never shew thy cunning.

*Enter* VINTNER

VINTNER      O, are you here? I am glad I have found you. You are a couple of fine companions: pray, where's the cup you stole from the tavern?

ROBIN      How, how! We steal a cup! Take heed what you say: we look not like cup-stealers, I can tell you.

VINTNER      Never deny't, for I know you have it; and I'll search you.

ROBIN      Search me! Ay, and spare not – [*aside to Dick, giving him the cup*] Hold the cup, Dick. Come, come, search me, search me.          [*Vintner searches him*

VINTNER      Come on, sirrah, let me search you now.      20

DICK      Ay, ay, do, do – [*aside to Robin, giving him the cup*] Hold the cup, Robin. [*to the Vintner*] I fear not your searching: we scorn to steal your cups, I can tell you.
         [*Vintner searches him*

VINTNER      Never out-face me for the matter; for, sure, the cup is between you two.

ROBIN      Nay, there you lie; 'tis beyond us both.

VINTNER      A plague take you! I thought 'twas your knavery to take it away: come, give it me again.

ROBIN      Ay, much! When, can you tell? Dick, make me a circle, and stand close at my back, and stir not for thy life – Vintner, you shall have your cup anon – Say nothing, Dick – [*reads from a book*] O per se, O; Demogorgon, Belcher, and Mephistophilis!

*Enter* MEPHISTOPHILIS

MEPHISTO.　You princely legions of infernal rule,
　　　　　How am I vexed by these villains' charms!
　　　　　From Constantinople have they brought me now,
　　　　　Only for pleasure of these damned slaves. [*exit Vintner*

ROBIN　　By Lady, sir, you have had a shrewd journey of it! Will
　　　　　it please you to take a shoulder of mutton to supper,
　　　　　and a tester in your purse, and go back again?　　40

DICK　　Ay, I pray you heartily, sir; for we called you but in
　　　　　jest, I promise you.

MEPHISTO.　To purge the rashness of this cursed deed,
　　　　　First, be thou turned to this ugly shape,
　　　　　For apish deeds transformed to an ape.

ROBIN　　O, brave! An ape! I pray, sir, let me have the carrying
　　　　　of him about, to shew some tricks.

MEPHISTO.　And so thou shalt: be thou transformed to a dog, and
　　　　　carry him upon thy back. Away! Be gone!

ROBIN　　A dog! That's excellent: let the maids look well to their
　　　　　porridge-pots, for I'll into the kitchen presently –
　　　　　Come, Dick, Come.　　　　　[*exeunt Robin and Dick*

MEPHISTO.　Now with the flames of ever-burning fire
　　　　　I'll wing myself, and forthwith fly amain
　　　　　Unto my Faustus, to the Great Turk's court.

　　　　　　　　　　　　　　　　　　　　　　[*exit*

# ACT FOUR

## SCENE I

*Enter* MARTINO *and* FREDERICK

MARTINO   What, ho, officers, gentlemen!
Hie to the presence to attend the Emperor –
Good Frederick, see the rooms be voided straight:
His majesty is coming to the hall;
Go back, and see the state in readiness.

FREDERICK   But where is Bruno, our elected Pope,
That on a Fury's back came post from Rome?
Will not his grace consort the Emperor?

MARTINO   O, yes; and with him comes the German conjurer,
The learned Faustus, fame of Wittenberg,          10
The wonder of the world for magic art;
And he intends to shew great Carolus
The race of all his stout progenitors,
And bring in presence of his majesty
The royal shapes and perfect semblances
Of Alexander and his beauteous paramour.

FREDERICK   Where is Benvolio?

MARTINO                         Fast asleep, I warrant you;
He took his rouse with stoops of Rhenish wine
So kindly yesternight to Bruno's health
That all this day the sluggard keeps his bed.     20

FREDERICK   See, see, his window's ope! We'll call to him.

MARTINO   What, ho! Benvolio!

*Enter* BENVOLIO *above, at a window,*
*in his nightcap, buttoning*

BENVOLIO   What a devil ail you two?

MARTINO   Speak softly, sir, lest the devil hear you;
For Faustus at the court is late arriv'd,
And at his heels a thousand Furies wait,
To accomplish whatsoe'er the doctor please.

BENVOLIO   What of this?

MARTINO   Come, leave thy chamber first, and thou shalt see

|            | This conjurer perform such rare exploits,            | 30 |
|            | Before the Pope and royal Emperor,                   |    |
|            | As never yet was seen in Germany.                    |    |

BENVOLIO   Has not the Pope enough of conjuring yet?
He was upon the devil's back late enough:
An if he be so far in love with him,
I would he would post with him to Rome again!

FREDERICK   Speak, wilt thou come and see this sport?

BENVOLIO   Not I.

MARTINO   Wilt thou stand in thy window, and see it, then?

BENVOLIO   Ay, an I fall not asleep i' the mean time.          40

MARTINO   The Emperor is at hand, who comes to see
What wonders by black spells may compass'd be.

BENVOLIO   Well, go you attend the Emperor. I am content, for
this once, to thrust my head out at a window; for they
say, if a man be drunk over night, the devil cannot hurt
him in the morning: if that be true, I have a charm in
my head shall control him as well as the conjurer, I
warrant you.

[*exeunt Frederick and Martino*

## SCENE 2

*A Sennet. Enter* CHARLES THE GERMAN EMPEROR,
BRUNO, DUKE OF SAXONY, FAUSTUS, MEPHISTOPHILIS,
FREDERICK, MARTINO, *and Attendants*

EMPEROR   Wonder of men, renowm'd magician,
Thrice-learned Faustus, welcome to our court.
This deed of thine, in setting Bruno free
From his and our professed enemy,
Shall add more excellence unto thine art
Than if by powerful necromantic spells
Thou couldst command the world's obedience:
For ever be belov'd of Carolus!
And if this Bruno thou hast late redeem'd,
In peace possess the triple diadem,                           10
And sit in Peter's chair, despite of chance,
Thou shalt be famous through all Italy,

|  | And honour'd of the German Emperor. |
| FAUSTUS | These gracious words, most royal Carolus, |
|  | Shall make poor Faustus, to his utmost power, |
|  | Both love and serve the German Emperor, |
|  | And lay his life at holy Bruno's feet: |
|  | For proof whereof, if so your grace be pleas'd, |
|  | The doctor stands prepar'd by power of art |
|  | To cast his magic charms, that shall pierce through 20 |
|  | The ebon gates of ever-burning hell, |
|  | And hale the stubborn Furies from their caves, |
|  | To compass whatsoe'er your grace commands. |
| BENVOLIO | [aside] Blood, he speaks terribly! But, for all that, I do |
|  | not greatly believe him: he looks as like a conjurer as |
|  | the Pope to a costermonger. |
| EMPEROR | Then, Faustus, as thou late didst promise us, |
|  | We would behold that famous conqueror, |
|  | Great Alexander, and his paramour, |
|  | In their true shapes and state majestical, 30 |
|  | That we may wonder at their excellence. |
| FAUSTUS | Your majesty shall see them presently – |
|  | Mephistophilis, away, |
|  | And, with a solemn noise of trumpets' sound, |
|  | Present before this royal Emperor |
|  | Great Alexander and his beauteous paramour. |
| MEPHISTO. | Faustus, I will.  [exit |
| BENVOLIO | Well, Master Doctor, an your devils come not away |
|  | quickly, you shall have me asleep presently: zounds, I |
|  | could eat myself for anger, to think I have been such |
|  | an ass all this while, to stand gaping after the devil's |
|  | governor, and can see nothing! |
| FAUSTUS | I'll make you feel something anon, if my art fail me |
|  | not – |
|  | My lord, I must forewarn your majesty, |
|  | That, when my spirits present the royal shapes |
|  | Of Alexander and his paramour, |
|  | Your grace demand no questions of the king, |
|  | But in dumb silence let them come and go. |
| EMPEROR | Be it as Faustus please; we are content. 50 |
| BENVOLIO | Ay, ay, and I am content too: an thou bring Alexander |

and his paramour before the Emperor, I'll be Actaeon, and turn myself to a stag.

FAUSTUS    And I'll play Diana, and send you the horns presently.

*Sennet. Enter, at one door, the* EMPEROR ALEXANDER, *at the other,* DARIUS. *They meet.* DARIUS *is thrown down;* ALEXANDER *kills him, takes off his crown, and, offering to go out, his* PARAMOUR *meets him. He embraceth her, and sets* DARIUS' *crown upon her head; and, coming back, both salute the* EMPEROR, *who, leaving his state, offers to embrace them; which* FAUSTUS, *seeing, suddenly stays him. Then trumpets cease, and music sounds.*

My gracious lord, you do forget yourself;
These are but shadows, not substantial.

EMPEROR    O, pardon me! My thoughts are so ravish'd
With sight of this renowned emperor,
That in mine arms I would have compass'd him.
But, Faustus, since I may not speak to them,
To satisfy my longing thoughts at full,                          60
Let me this tell thee: I have heard it said
That this fair lady, whilst she liv'd on earth,
Had on her neck a little wart or mole;
How may I prove that saying to be true?

FAUSTUS    Your majesty may boldly go and see.

EMPEROR    Faustus, I see it plain;
And in this sight thou better pleasest me
Than if I gain'd another monarchy.

FAUSTUS    Away! Be gone! [*exit show*] – See, see, my gracious
lord! What strange beast is yon, that thrusts his head
out at window?

EMPEROR    O, wondrous sight! See, Duke of Saxony,
Two spreading horns most strangely fastened
Upon the head of young Benvolio!

SAXONY    What, is he asleep or dead?

FAUSTUS    He sleeps, my lord; but dreams not of his horns.

EMPEROR    This sport is excellent: we'll call and wake him –
What, ho, Benvolio!

BENVOLIO    A plague upon you! Let me sleep a while.

EMPEROR    I blame thee not to sleep much, having such a head of
thine own.

SAXONY      Look up, Benvolio; 'tis the Emperor calls.

BENVOLIO    The Emperor! Where? O, zounds, my head!

EMPEROR     Nay, an thy horns hold, 'tis no matter for thy head, for
            that's armed sufficiently.

FAUSTUS     Why, how now, Sir Knight! What, hanged by the
            horns! This is most horrible: fie, fie, pull in your head,
            for shame! Let not all the world wonder at you.

BENVOLIO    Zounds, doctor, this is your villainy!

FAUSTUS     O, say not so, sir! The doctor has not skill,          90
            No art, no cunning, to present these lords,
            Or bring before this royal Emperor
            The mighty monarch, warlike Alexander.
            If Faustus do it, you are straight resolv'd,
            In bold Actaeon's shape, to turn a stag –
            And therefore, my lord, so please your majesty,
            I'll raise a kennel of hounds shall hunt him so
            As all his footmanship shall scarce prevail
            To keep his carcass from their bloody fangs –
            Ho, Belimoth, Argiron, Asteroth!                       100

BENVOLIO    Hold, hold! Zounds, he'll raise up a kennel of devils, I
            think, anon – Good my lord, entreat for me – 'Sblood,
            I am never able to endure these torments.

EMPEROR     Then, good Master Doctor.
            Let me entreat you to remove his horns;
            He has done penance now sufficiently.

FAUSTUS     My gracious lord, not so much for injury done to me,
            as to delight your majesty with some mirth, hath
            Faustus justly requited this injurious knight; which
            being all I desire, I am content to remove his horns –
            Mephistophilis, transform him [Mephistophilis removes
            the horns] – and hereafter, sir, look you speak well of
            scholars.

BENVOLIO    [aside] Speak well of ye! 'Sblood, an scholars be such
            cuckold-makers, to clap horns of honest men's heads o'
            this order, I'll ne'er trust smooth faces and small ruffs
            more – But, an I be not revenged for this, would I
            might be turned to a gaping oyster, and drink nothing
            but salt water!                                  [exit above

EMPEROR     Come, Faustus: while the Emperor lives,                120

In recompense of this thy high desert,
Thou shalt command the state of Germany,
And live belov'd of mighty Carolus.

[exeunt

### SCENE 3

*Enter* BENVOLIO, MARTINO, FREDERICK, *and Soldiers*

MARTINO     Nay, sweet Benvolio, let us sway thy thoughts
            From this attempt against the conjurer.
BENVOLIO    Away! You love me not, to urge me thus:
            Shall I let slip so great an injury,
            When every servile groom jests at my wrongs,
            And in their rustic gambols proudly say,
            'Benvolio's head was grac'd with horns today'?
            O, may these eyelids never close again,
            Till with my sword I have that conjurer slain!
            If you will aid me in this enterprise,          10
            Then draw your weapons and be resolute;
            If not, depart; here will Benvolio die,
            But Faustus' death shall quit my infamy.
FREDERICK   Nay, we will stay with thee, betide what may,
            And kill that doctor, if he come this way.
BENVOLIO    Then, gentle Frederick, hie thee to the grove,
            And place our servants and our followers
            Close in an ambush there behind the trees.
            By this, I know the conjurer is near:
            I saw him kneel, and kiss the Emperor's hand,   20
            And take his leave, laden with rich rewards.
            Then, soldiers, boldly fight: if Faustus die,
            Take you thy wealth, leave us the victory.
FREDERICK   Come, soldiers, follow me unto the grove:
            Who kills him shall have gold and endless love.

[exit Frederick with Soldiers

BENVOLIO    My head is lighter than it was, by the horns;
            But yet my heart's more ponderous than my head,
            And pants until I see that conjurer dead.
MARTINO     Where shall we place ourselves, Benvolio?

| | | |
|---|---|---|
| BENVOLIO | Here will we stay to bide the first assault: | 30 |
| | O, were that damned hell-hound but in place, | |
| | Thou soon shouldst see me quit my foul disgrace! | |

*Re-enter* FREDERICK

FREDERICK Close, close! The conjurer is at hand,
And all alone comes walking in his gown;
Be ready, then, and strike the peasant down.

BENVOLIO Mine be that honour, then. Now, sword, strike home!
For horns he gave I'll have his head anon.

MARTINO See, see, he comes!

*Enter* FAUSTUS *with a false head*

BENVOLIO                         No words. This blow ends all:
Hell take his soul! His body thus must fall.

                                        [*stabs Faustus*

FAUSTUS [*falling*] O!                                            40

FREDERICK Groan you, Master Doctor?

BENVOLIO Break may his heart with groans! Dear Frederick, see,
Thus will I end his griefs immediately.

MARTINO Strike with a willing hand.
[*Benvolio strikes off Faustus' head*] His head is off.

BENVOLIO The devil's dead; the Furies now may laugh.

FREDERICK Was this that stern aspect, that awful frown,
Made the grim monarch of infernal spirits
Tremble and quake at his commanding charms?

MARTINO Was this that damned head, whose art conspir'd
Benvolio's shame before the Emperor?                          50

BENVOLIO Ay, that's the head, and there the body lies,
Justly rewarded for his villainies.

FREDERICK Come, let's devise how we may add more shame
To the black scandal of his hated name.

BENVOLIO First, on his head, in quittance of my wrongs,
I'll nail huge forked horns, and let them hang
Within the window where he yok'd me first,
That all the world may see my just revenge.

MARTINO What use shall we put his beard to?

BENVOLIO We'll sell it to a chimney-sweeper: it will wear out ten
birchen brooms, I warrant you.

FREDERICK What shall his eyes do?

BENVOLIO    We'll pull out his eyes; and they shall serve for buttons
to his lips, to keep his tongue from catching cold.

MARTINO    An excellent policy! And now, sirs, having divided
him, what shall the body do?      [*Faustus rises*

BENVOLIO    Zounds, the devil's alive again!

FREDERICK    Give him his head, for God's sake.

FAUSTUS    Nay, keep it: Faustus will have heads and hands,
Ay, all your hearts to recompense this deed.      70
Knew you not, traitors, I was limited
For four-and-twenty years to breathe on earth?
And, had you cut my body with your swords,
Or hew'd this flesh and bones as small as sand,
Yet in a minute had my spirit return'd,
And I had breath'd a man, made free from harm.
But wherefore do I dally my revenge –
Asteroth, Belimoth, Mephistophilis?

*Enter* MEPHISTOPHILIS *and other Devils*

Go, horse these traitors on your fiery backs,
And mount aloft with them as high as heaven:      80
Thence pitch them headlong to the lowest hell.
Yet, stay: the world shall see their misery,
And hell shall after plague their treachery.
Go, Belimoth, and take this caitiff hence,
And hurl him in some lake of mud and dirt.
Take thou this other, drag him through the woods
Amongst the pricking thorns and sharpest briers;
Whilst, with my gentle Mephistophilis,
This traitor flies unto some steepy rock,
That, rolling down, may break the villain's bones,
As he intended to dismember me.
Fly hence; despatch my charge immediately.

FREDERICK    Pity us, gentle Faustus! Save our lives!

FAUSTUS    Away!

FREDERICK        He must needs go that the devil drives.
                  [*exeunt Mephistophilis and Devils with
                        Benvolio, Martino and Frederick*

*Enter the ambushed Soldiers*

I SOLDIER    Come, sirs, prepare yourselves in readiness;

Make haste to help these noble gentlemen:
I heard them parley with the conjurer.
2 SOLDIER See, where he comes! Despatch and kill the slave.
FAUSTUS What's here? An ambush to betray my life!
Then, Faustus, try they skill — Base peasants, stand!
For, lo, these trees remove at my command,
And stand as bulwarks 'twixt yourselves and me,
To shield me from your hated treachery!
Yet, to encounter this your weak attempt,
Behold, an army comes incontinent!

*[Faustus strikes the door, and enter a Devil playing on a
drum; after him another, bearing an ensign; and divers
with weapons; Mephistophilis with fire-works — they
set upon the Soldiers, drive them out, and exeunt*

## SCENE 4

*Enter, at several doors, BENVOLIO, FREDERICK, and MARTINO,
their heads and faces bloody, and besmeared with mud and dirt;
all having horns on their heads*

MARTINO What, ho, Benvolio!
BENVOLIO                    Here — What, Frederick, ho!
FREDERICK O, help me, gentle friend — Where is Martino?
MARTINO Dear Frederick, here,
Half smother'd in a lake of mud and dirt,
Through which the Furies dragg'd me by the heels.
FREDERICK Martino, see, Benvolio's horns again!
MARTINO O, misery — How now, Benvolio!
BENVOLIO Defend me, heaven! Shall I be haunted still?
MARTINO Nay, fear not, man; we have no power to kill.
BENVOLIO My friends transformed thus! O, hellish spite!          10
Your heads are all set with horns.
FREDERICK                              You hit it right;
It is your own you mean; feel on your head.
BENVOLIO Zounds, horns again!
MARTINO Nay, chafe not, man; we all are sped.
BENVOLIO What devil attends this damn'd magician,
That, spite of spite, our wrongs are doubled?

FREDERICK  What may we do, that we may hide our shames?
BENVOLIO   If we should follow him to work revenge,
           He'd join long asses' ears to these huge horns,
           And make us laughing-stocks to all the world.          20
MARTINO    What shall we, then, do, dear Benvolio?
BENVOLIO   I have a castle joining near these woods;
           And thither we'll repair, and live obscure,
           Till time shall alter these our brutish shapes:
           Sith black disgrace hath thus eclips'd our fame,
           We'll rather die with grief than live with shame.

                                                    [*exeunt*


## SCENE 5

*Enter* FAUSTUS, *a Horse-courser and* MEPHISTOPHILIS

COURSER    I beseech your worship, accept of these forty dollars.
FAUSTUS    Friend, thou canst not buy so good a horse for so small
           a price. I have no great need to sell him: but, if thou
           likest him for ten dollars more, take him, because I see
           thou hast a good mind to him.
COURSER    I beseech you, sir, accept of this: I am a very poor man,
           and have lost very much of late by horse-flesh, and this
           bargain will set me up again.
FAUSTUS    Well, I will not stand with thee: give me the money.
           [*Horse-courser gives Faustus the money*] Now, sirrah, I must
           tell you that you may ride him o'er hedge and ditch,
           and spare him not; but, do you hear, in any case, ride
           him not into the water.
COURSER    How, sir! Not into the water! Why, will he not drink
           of all waters?
FAUSTUS    Yes, he will drink of all waters; but ride him not into
           the water: o'er hedge and ditch, or where thou wilt,
           but not into the water. Go, bid the hostler deliver him
           unto you, and remember what I say.
COURSER    I warrant you, sir – O, joyful day! Now am I a made
           man for ever.                                          [*exit*
FAUSTUS    What art thou, Faustus, but a man condemn'd to die?
           Thy fatal time draws to a final end;

Despair doth drive distrust into my thoughts:
Confound these passions with a quiet sleep:
Tush, Christ did call the thief upon the Cross;
Then rest thee, Faustus, quiet in conceit.

[*he sits to sleep*

*Re-enter the Horse-courser, wet*

COURSER    O, what a cozening doctor was this! I, riding my horse into the water, thinking some hidden mystery had been in the horse, I had nothing under me but a little straw, and had much ado to escape drowning. Well, I'll go rouse him, and make him give me my forty dollars again – Ho, sirrah Doctor, you cozening scab! Master Doctor, awake, and rise, and give me my money again, for your horse is turned to a bottle of hay, Master Doctor! [*he pulls off Faustus' leg*] Alas, I am undone! What shall I do? I have pulled off his leg.

FAUSTUS    O, help, help! The villain hath murdered me.

COURSER    [*aside*] Murder or not murder, now he has but one leg, I'll outrun him, and cast this leg into some ditch or other.                          [*runs out*

FAUSTUS    Stop him, stop him, stop him – Ha, ha, ha! Faustus hath his leg again, and the Horse-courser a bundle of hay for his forty dollars.

*Enter* WAGNER

How now, Wagner! What new with thee?

WAGNER    If it please you, the Duke of Vanholt doth earnestly entreat your company, and hath sent some of his men to attend you, with provision fit for your journey.

FAUSTUS    The Duke of Vanholt's an honourable gentleman, and one to whom I must be no niggard of my cunning. Come, away!

[*exeunt*

## SCENE 6

*Enter* ROBIN, DICK, *the Horse-courser, and a Carter*

CARTER    Come, my masters, I'll bring you to the best beer in
          Europe – What, ho, hostess! Where be these whores?

*Enter* HOSTESS

HOSTESS   How now! What lack you? What, my old guests!
          Welcome.

ROBIN     Sirrah Dick, dost thou know why I stand so mute?

DICK      No, Robin: why is't?

ROBIN     I am eighteen-pence on the score: but say nothing; see
          if she have forgotten me.

HOSTESS   Who's this that stands so solemnly by himself? What,
          my old guest!                                          10

ROBIN     O, hostess, how do you? I hope my score stands still.

HOSTESS   Ay, there's no doubt of that; for methinks you make
          no haste to wipe it out.

DICK      Why, hostess, I say, fetch us some beer.

HOSTESS   You shall presently – Look up into the hall there, ho!
          [*exit – drink is presently brought in*

DICK      Come, sirs, what shall we do now till mine hostess
          comes?

CARTER    Marry, sir, I'll tell you the bravest tale how a conjurer
          served me. You know Doctor Faustus?

COURSER   Ay, a plague take him! Here's some on's have cause to
          know him. Did he conjure thee too?

CARTER    I'll tell you how he served me. As I was going to
          Wittenberg, t'other day, with a load of hay, he met
          me, and asked me what he should give me for as much
          hay as he could eat. Now, sir, I thinking that a little
          would serve his turn, bad him take as much as he
          would for three farthings: so he presently gave me my
          money and fell to eating; and, as I am a cursen man, he
          never left eating till he had eat up all my load of hay.

ALL       O, monstrous! Eat a whole load of hay!                 30

ROBIN     Yes, yes, that may be; for I have heard of one that has
          eat a load of logs.

COURSER    Now, sirs, you shall hear how villainously he served me. I went to him yesterday to buy a horse of him, and he would by no means sell him under forty dollars. So, sir, because I knew him to be such a horse as would run over hedge and ditch and never tire, I gave him his money. So, when I have my horse, Doctor Faustus bad me ride night and day, and spare him no time; but, quoth he, in any case, ride him not into the water. Now, sir, I thinking the horse had had some quality that he would not have me know of, what did I but rid him into a great river? And when I came just in the midst, my horse vanished away, and I sat straddling upon a bottle of hay.

ALL    O, brave doctor!

COURSER    But you shall hear how bravely I served him for it. I went me home to his house, and there I found him asleep. I kept a hallooing and whooping in his ears; but all could not wake him. I, seeing that, took him by the leg, and never rested pulling till I had pulled me his leg quite off; and now 'tis at home in mine hostry.

ROBIN    And has the doctor but one leg, then? That's excellent; for one of his devils turned me into the likeness of an ape's face.

CARTER    Some more drink, hostess!

ROBIN    Hark you, we'll into another room and drink a while, and then we'll go seek out the doctor.

*[exeunt*

## SCENE 7

*Enter the* DUKE OF VANHOLT, *his* DUCHESS, FAUSTUS,
MEPHISTOPHILIS, *and Attendants*

VANHOLT    Thanks, Master Doctor, for these pleasant sights; nor know I how sufficiently to recompense your great deserts in erecting that enchanted castle in the air, the sight whereof so delighted me as nothing in the world could please me more.

FAUSTUS    I do think myself, my good lord, highly recompensed in that it pleaseth your grace to think but well of that which Faustus hath performed – But, gracious lady, it may be that you have taken no pleasure in those sights; therefore, I pray you tell me, what is the thing you most desire to have; be it in the world, it shall be yours: I have heard that great-bellied women do long for things are rare and dainty.

DUCHESS True, Master Doctor; and, since I find you so kind, I will make known unto you what my heart desires to have; and, were it now summer, as it is January, a dead time of the winter, I would request no better meat than a dish of ripe grapes.

FAUSTUS This is but a small matter – Go, Mephistophilis; away! [*exit Mephistophilis*] Madam, I will do more than this for your content.

*Re-enter* MEPHISTOPHILIS *with grapes*

Here now, taste you these: they should be good, for they come from a far country, I can tell you.

VANHOLT This makes me wonder more than all the rest, that at this time of the year, when every tree is barren of his fruit, from whence you had these ripe grapes.

FAUSTUS Please it your grace, the year is divided into two circles over the whole world; so that, when it is winter with us, in the contrary circle it is likewise summer with them, as in India, Saba, and such countries that like far east, where they have fruit twice a-year; from whence, by means of a swift spirit that I have, I had these grapes brought as you see.

DUCHESS And, trust me, they are the sweetest grates that e'er I tasted. [*the Clowns bounce at the gate, within*

VANHOLT What rude disturbers have we at the gate?
Go, pacify their fury, set it ope,
And then demand of them what they would have.
[*they knock again, and call out to talk with Faustus*

SERVANT Why, how now, masters! What a coil is there! What is the reason you disturb the Duke? 40

DICK [*within*] We have no reason for it; therefore a fig for him!

SERVANT Why, saucy varlets, dare you be so bold?

COURSER    [*within*] I hope, sir, we have wit enough to be more bold than welcome.

SERVANT    It appears so: pray, be bold elsewhere, and trouble not the Duke.

VANHOLT    What would they have?

SERVANT    They all cry out to speak with Doctor Faustus.

CARTER    [*within*] Ay, and we will speak with him.

VANHOLT    Will you, sir? Commit the rascals.        50

DICK    [*within*] Commit with us! He were as good commit with his father as commit with us.

FAUSTUS    I do beseech your grace, let them come in;
They are good subject for a merriment.

VANHOLT    Do as thou wilt, Faustus; I give thee leave.

FAUSTUS    I thank your grace.

*Enter* ROBIN, DICK, *Carter, and Horse-courser*

                   Why, how now, my good friends!
Faith, you are too outrageous: but, come near;
I have procur'd your pardons: welcome, all.

ROBIN    Nay, sir, we will be welcome for our money, and we will pay for what we take – What, ho! Give's half a dozen of beer here, and be hanged!

FAUSTUS    Nay, hark you; can you tell me where you are?

CARTER    Ay, marry, can I; we are under heaven.

SERVANT    Ay; but, Sir Saucebox, know you in what place?

COURSER    Ay, ay, the house is good enough to drink in. Zounds, fill us some beer, or we'll break all the barrels in the house, and dash out all your brains with your bottles!

FAUSTUS    Be not so furious: come, you shall have beer –
My lord, beseech you give me leave a while;
I'll gage my credit 'twill content your grace.        70

VANHOLT    With all my heart, kind doctor; please thyself;
Our servants and our court's at thy command.

FAUSTUS    I humbly thank your grace – Then fetch some beer.

COURSER    Ay, marry, there spake a doctor, indeed! And, faith, I'll drink a health to thy wooden leg for that word.

FAUSTUS    My wooden leg! What dost thou mean by that?

CARTER    Ha, ha, ha! Dost hear him, Dick? He has forgot his leg.

COURSER    Ay, ay, he does not stand much upon that.

FAUSTUS    No, faith; not much upon a wooden leg.        80

CARTER     Good Lord, that flesh and blood should be so frail with
           your worship! Do not you remember a horse-courser
           you sold a horse to?

FAUSTUS    Yes, I remember I sold one a horse.

CARTER     And do you remember you bid he should not ride him
           into the water?

FAUSTUS    Yes, I do very well remember that.

CARTER     And do you remember nothing of your leg?

FAUSTUS    No, in good sooth.

CARTER     Then, I pray you, remember your courtesy.          90

FAUSTUS    I thank you, sir.

CARTER     'Tis not so much worth. I pray you, tell me one thing.

FAUSTUS    What's that?

CARTER     Be both your legs bed-fellows every night together?

FAUSTUS    Wouldst thou make a Colossus of me, that thou askest
           me such questions?

CARTER     No, truly, sir; I would make nothing of you; but I
           would fain know that.

                    *Enter* HOSTESS *with drink*

FAUSTUS    Then, I assure thee certainly, they are.

CARTER     I thank you; I am fully satisfied.          100

FAUSTUS    But wherefore dost thou ask?

CARTER     For nothing, sir: but methinks you should have a
           wooden bed-fellow of one of 'em.

COURSER    Why, do you hear, sir? Did not I pull off one of your
           legs when you were asleep?

FAUSTUS    But I have it again, now I am awake: look you here,
           sir.

ALL        O, horrible! Had the doctor three legs?

CARTER     Do you remember, sir, how you cozened me, and eat
           up my load of . . .          110

DICK       Do you remember how you made me wear an ape's . . .

COURSER    You whoreson conjuring scab, do you remember how
           you cozened me with a ho . . .

ROBIN      Ha' you forgotten me? You think to carry it away with
           your hey-pass and re-pass: do you remember the dog's
           fa . . .

           [*Faustus, in the middle of each speech, charms them dumb*
                                                    [*exeunt Clowns*

HOSTESS    Who pays for the ale? Hear you, Master Doctor; now
           you have sent away my guests, I pray who shall pay me
           for my a . . .                              [exit Hostess
DUCHESS    My lord,
           We are much beholding to this learned man.
VANHOLT    So are we, madam; which we will recompense
           With all the love and kindness that we may:
           His artful sport drives all sad thoughts away.

                                                        [exeunt

# ACT FIVE

## SCENE I

*Thunder and lightning. Enter Devils with covered dishes:*
MEPHISTOPHILIS *leads them into* FAUSTUS'S *study:*
*then enter* WAGNER

WAGNER    I think my master means to die shortly; he has made his
will, and given me his wealth, his house, his goods, and
store of golden plate, besides two thousand ducats
ready-coined. I wonder what he means: if death were
nigh, he would not frolic thus. He's now at supper
with the scholars, where there's such belly-cheer as
Wagner in his life ne'er saw the like: and, see where
they come! Belike the feast is ended.          [*exit*

*Enter* FAUSTUS, MEPHISTOPHILIS, *and two or three Scholars*

I SCHOLAR  Master Doctor Faustus, since our conference about fair
ladies, which was the beautifulest in all the world, we
have determined with ourselves that Helen of Greece
was the admirablest lady that ever lived: therefore,
Master Doctor, if you will do us so much favour as to
let us see that peerless dame of Greece, whom all the
world admires for majesty, we should think ourselves
much beholding unto you.

FAUSTUS    Gentlemen.
For that I know your friendship is unfeign'd,
It is not Faustus' custom to deny
The just request of those that wish him well:          20
You shall behold that peerless dame of Greece,
No otherwise for pomp or majesty
Than when Sir Paris cross'd the seas with her,
And brought the spoils to rich Dardania.
Be silent, then for danger is in words.

*Music sounds.* MEPHISTOPHILIS *brings in* HELEN;
*she passeth over the stage*

2 SCHOLAR  Was this fair Helen, whose admired worth
Made Greece with ten years' war afflict poor Troy?

3 SCHOLAR  Too simple is my wit to tell her worth,
           Whom all the world admires for majesty.                  30
1 SCHOLAR  Now we have seen the pride of Nature's work,
           We'll take our leaves: and, for this blessed sight,
           Happy and blest be Faustus evermore!
FAUSTUS    Gentlemen, farewell: the same wish I to you.
                                              [exeunt Scholars
                       Enter an Old Man

OLD MAN    O gentle Faustus, leave this damned art,
           This magic, that will charm thy soul to hell,
           And quite bereave thee of salvation!
           Though thou hast now offended like a man,
           Do not persever in it like a devil:
           Yet, yet thou hast an amiable soul,                      40
           If sin by custom grow not into nature;
           Then, Faustus, will repentance come too late;
           Then thou art banish'd from the sight of heaven;
           No mortal can express the pains of hell.
           It may be, this my exhortation
           Seems harsh and all unpleasant: let it not;
           For, gentle son, I speak it not in wrath,
           Or envy of thee, but in tender love,
           And pity of thy future misery;
           And so have hope that this my kind rebuke,               50
           Checking thy body, may amend thy soul.
FAUSTUS    Where art thou, Faustus? Wretch, what has thou done?
           Hell claims his right, and with a roaring voice
           Says, 'Faustus, come; thine hour is almost come;'
           And Faustus now will come to do thee right.
                              [Mephistophilis gives him a dagger
OLD MAN    O, stay, good Faustus, stay thy desperate steps!
           I see an angel hover o'er thy head,
           And, with a vial full of precious grace,
           Offers to pour the same into thy soul:
           Then call for mercy, and avoid despair.                  60
FAUSTUS    O friend, I feel
           Thy words to comfort my distressed soul!
           Leave me a while to ponder on my sins.

OLD MAN   Faustus, I leave thee; but with grief of heart,
          Fearing the enemy of thy hapless soul.          [exit

FAUSTUS   Accursed Faustus, wretch, what hast thou done?
          I do repent; and yet I do despair:
          Hell strives with grace for conquest in my breast:
          What shall I do to shun the snares of death?

MEPHISTO.  Thou traitor, Faustus, I arrest thy soul          70
          For disobedience to my sovereign lord:
          Revolt, or I'll in piece-meal tear thy flesh.

FAUSTUS   I do repent I e'er offended him.
          Sweet Mephistophilis, entreat thy lord
          To pardon my unjust presumption,
          And with my blood again I will confirm
          The former vow I made to Lucifer.

MEPHISTO.  Do it, then, Faustus, with unfeigned heart,
          Lest greater dangers do attend thy drift.

FAUSTUS   Torment, sweet friend, that base and aged man,          80
          That durst dissuade me from thy Lucifer,
          With greatest torments that our hell affords.

MEPHISTO.  His faith is great; I cannot touch his soul;
          But what I may afflict his body with
          I will attempt, which is but little worth.

FAUSTUS   One thing, good servant, let me crave of thee
          To glut the longing of my heart's desire –
          That I may have unto my paramour
          That heavenly Helen which I saw of late,
          Whose sweet embraces may extinguish clean          90
          Those thoughts that do dissuade me from my vow,
          And keep my oath I made to Lucifer.

MEPHISTO.  This, or what else my Faustus shall desire,
          Shall be perform'd in twinkling of an eye.

          *Re-enter* HELEN, *passing over the stage between two Cupids*

FAUSTUS   Was this the face that launch'd a thousand ships,
          And burnt the topless towers of Ilium?
          Sweet Helen, make me immortal with a kiss –
                                                    [*kisses her*
          Her lips suck forth my soul; see, where it flies!
          Come, Helen, come, give me my soul again.

Here will I dwell, for heaven is in these lips,   100
And all is dross that is not Helena.
I will be Paris, and for love of thee,
Instead of Troy, shall Wittenberg be sack'd;
And I will combat with weak Menelaus,
And wear thy colours on my plumed crest;
Yea, I will wound Achilles in the heel,
And then return to Helen for a kiss.
O, thou art fairer than the evening air
Clad in the beauty of a thousand stars;
Brighter art thou than flaming Jupiter   110
When he appear'd to hapless Semele;
More lovely than the monarch of the sky
In wanton Arethusa's azur'd arms;
And none but thou shalt be my paramour!

                                              *[exeunt*

## SCENE 2

*Thunder. Enter* LUCIFER, BELZEBUB, *and* MEPHISTOPHILIS

LUCIFER    Thus from infernal Dis do we ascend
To view the subjects of our monarchy,
Those souls which sin seals the black sons of hell;
'Mong which, as chief, Faustus, we come to thee,
Bringing with us lasting damnation
To wait upon thy soul: the time is come
Which makes it forfeit.

MEPHISTO.                    And, this gloomy night,
Here, in this room will wretched Faustus be.

BELZEBUB    And here we'll stay,
To mark him how he doth demean himself.   10

MEPHISTO.    How should he but in desperate lunacy?
Fond worldling, now his heart-blood dries with grief;
His conscience kills it; and his labouring brain
Begets a world of idle fantasies
To over-reach the devil; but all in vain;
His store of pleasures must be sauc'd with pain.
He and his servant Wagner are at hand;

Both come from drawing Faustus' latest will.
See, where they come!

*Enter* FAUSTUS *and* WAGNER

FAUSTUS        Say, Wagner — thou hast perus'd my will —          20
               How dost thou like it?

WAGNER                             Sir, so wondrous well,
               As in all humble duty I do yield
               My life and lasting service for your love.

FAUSTUS        Gramercy, Wagner.                    [*exit Wagner*
               [*enter scholars*]        Welcome, gentlemen.

1 SCHOLAR      Now, worthy Faustus, methinks your looks are chang'd.

FAUSTUS        O gentlemen!

2 SCHOLAR      What ails Faustus?

FAUSTUS        Ah, my sweet chamber-fellow, had I lived with thee,
               then had I lived still! But now must die eternally.
               Look, sirs, comes he not? Comes he not?          30

1 SCHOLAR      O my dear Faustus, what imports this fear?

2 SCHOLAR      Is all our pleasure turn'd to melancholy?

3 SCHOLAR      He is not well with being over-solitary.

2 SCHOLAR      If it be so, we'll have physicians,
               And Faustus shall be cur'd.

3 SCHOLAR      'Tis but a surfeit, sir; fear nothing.

FAUSTUS        A surfeit of deadly sin, that hath damned both body
               and soul.

2 SCHOLAR      Yet, Faustus, look up to heaven, and remember mercy
               is infinite.                                    40

FAUSTUS        But Faustus' offence can ne'er be pardoned: the serpent
               that tempted Eve may be saved, but not Faustus. O
               gentlemen, hear me with patience, and tremble not at
               my speeches! Though my heart pant and quiver to
               remember that I have been a student here these thirty
               years, O would I had never seen Wittenberg, never read
               book! And what wonders I have done, all Germany can
               witness, yea, all the world; for which Faustus hath lost
               both Germany and the world, yea, heaven itself, heaven,
               the seat of God, the throne of the blessed, the kingdom
               of joy; and must remain in hell for ever, hell, O hell, for
               ever! Sweet friends, what shall become of Faustus, being
               in hell for ever?

2 SCHOLAR  Yet, Faustus, call on God.

FAUSTUS    On God, whom Faustus hath abjured! On God, whom
           Faustus hath blasphemed! O my God, I would weep!
           But the devil draws in my tears. Gush forth blood,
           instead of tears! Yea, life and soul! O, he stays my
           tongue! I would lift up my hands; but see, they hold
           'em, they hold 'em?                                    60

ALL        Who, Faustus?

FAUSTUS    Why, Lucifer and Mephistophilis. O gentlemen, I gave
           them my soul for my cunning!

ALL        O, God forbid!

FAUSTUS    God forbade it, indeed; but Faustus hath done it:
           for the vain pleasure of four-and-twenty years hath
           Faustus lost eternal joy and felicity. I writ them a bill
           with mine own blood: the date is expired; this is the
           time, and he will fetch me.

1 SCHOLAR  Why did not Faustus tell us of this before, that divines
           might have prayed for thee?

FAUSTUS    Oft have I thought to have done so; but the devil
           threatened to tear me in pieces, if I named God; to
           fetch me body and soul, if I once gave ear to divinity:
           and now 'tis too late. Gentlemen, away, lest you perish
           with me.

2 SCHOLAR  O, what may we do to save Faustus?

FAUSTUS    Talk not of me, but save yourselves, and depart.

3 SCHOLAR  God will strengthen me; I will stay with Faustus.

1 SCHOLAR  Tempt not God, sweet friend; but let us into the next
           room and pray for him.

FAUSTUS    Ay, pray for me, pray for me; and what noise soever you
           hear, come not unto me, for nothing can rescue me.

2 SCHOLAR  Pray thou, and we will pray that God may have mercy
           upon thee.

FAUSTUS    Gentlemen, farewell: if I live till morning, I'll visit you;
           if not, Faustus is gone to hell.

ALL        Faustus, farewell.                    [exeunt Scholars

MEPHISTO.  Ay, Faustus, now thou hast no hope of heaven;
           Therefore despair, think only upon hell,              90
           For that must be thy mansion, there to dwell.

FAUSTUS    O thou bewitching fiend, 'twas thy temptation

Hath robb'd me of eternal happiness!

MEPHISTO. I do confess it, Faustus, and rejoice:
'Twas I that, when thou were i'the way to heaven,
Damm'd up thy passage; when thou took'st the book
To view the Scriptures, then I turn'd the leaves,
And led thine eye.
What, weep'st thou? 'Tis too late; despair! Farewell:
Fools that will laugh on earth must weep in hell.    100
                                                [exit

*Enter* GOOD ANGEL *and* EVIL ANGEL *at several doors*

GOOD A.    O Faustus, if thou hadst given ear to me,
Innumerable joys had follow'd thee!
But thou didst love the world.

EVIL A.                                  Gave ear to me,
And now must taste hell-pains perpetually.

GOOD A.    O, what will all thy riches, pleasures, pomps,
Avail thee now?

EVIL A.                        Nothing, but vex thee more,
To want in hell, that had on earth such store.

GOOD A.    O, thou hast lost celestial happiness,
Pleasures unspeakable, bliss without end.
Hadst thou affected sweet divinity,                 110
Hell or the devil had had no power on thee:
Hadst thou kept on that way, Faustus, behold
                    [*music, while a throne descends*
In what resplendent glory thou hadst sat
In yonder throne, like those bright-shining saints,
And triumph'd over hell! That hast thou lost;
And now, poor soul, must thy good angel leave thee:
The jaws of hell are open to receive thee.
                        [*exit; the throne ascends*

EVIL A.    Now, Faustus, let thine eyes with horror stare
                            [*Hell is discovered*
Into that vast perpetual torture-house:
There are the Furies tossing damned souls           120
On burning forks; there bodies boil in lead;
There are live quarters broiling on the coals,
That ne'er can die; this ever-burning chair
Is for o'er-tortur'd souls to rest them in;

These that are fed with sops of flaming fire,
Were gluttons, and lov'd only delicates,
And laugh'd to see the poor starve at their gates:
But yet all these are nothing; thou shalt see
Ten thousand tortures that more horrid be.

FAUSTUS    O, I have seen enough to torture me!     130

EVIL A.    Nay, thou must feel them, taste the smart of all:
He that loves pleasure must for pleasure fall:
And so I leave thee, Faustus, till anon:
Then wilt thou tumble in confusion.

                 [*exit; Hell disappears; the clock strikes eleven*

FAUSTUS    O Faustus,
Now hast thou but one bare hour to live,
And then thou must be damn'd perpetually!
Stand still, you ever-moving spheres of heaven,
That time may cease, and midnight never come;
Fair Nature's eye, rise, rise again, and make     140
Perpetual day; or let this hour be but
A year, a month, a week, a natural day,
That Faustus may repent and save his soul!
*O lente, lente currite, noctis equi!*
The stars move still, time runs, the clock will strike,
The devil will come, and Faustus must be damn'd.
O, I'll leap up to heaven! Who pulls me down?
See, where Christ's blood streams in the firmament!
One drop of blood will save me: O my Christ!
Rend not my heart for naming of my Christ;
Yet will I call on him: O, spare me, Lucifer!     150
Where is it now? 'Tis gone:
And, see, a threatening arm, an angry brow!
Mountains and hills, come, come, and fall on me,
And hide me from the heavy wrath of heaven!
No!
Then will I headlong run into the earth:
Gape, earth! O, no, it will not harbour me!
You stars that reign'd at my nativity,
Whose influence hath allotted death and hell,
Now draw up Faustus, like a foggy mist,     160
Into the entrails of yon labouring clouds,

That, when you vomit forth into the air,
My limbs may issue from your smoky mouths;
But let my soul mount and ascend to heaven!
                    [*the clock strikes the half-hour*
O, half the hour is past! 'Twill all be past anon.
O, if my soul must suffer for my sin,
Impose some end to my incessant pain;
Let Faustus live in hell a thousand years,
A hundred thousand, and at last be sav'd!
No end is limited to damned souls.                    170
Why wert thou not a creature wanting soul?
Or why is this immortal that thou hast?
O, Pythagoras' metempsychosis, were that true,
This soul should fly from me, and I be chang'd
Into some brutish beast! All beasts are happy,
For, when they die,
Their souls are soon dissolv'd in elements;
But mine must live still to be plagu'd in hell.
Curs'd be the parents that engender'd me!
No, Faustus, curse thyself, curse Lucifer          180
That hath depriv'd thee of the joys of heaven.
                    [*the clock strikes twelve*
It strikes, it strikes! Now, body, turn to air,
Or Lucifer will bear thee quick to hell!
O soul, be chang'd into small water-drops,
And fall into the ocean, ne'er be found!

                *Thunder. Enter Devils*

O, mercy, heaven! Look not so fierce on me!
Adders and serpents, let me breathe a while!
Ugly hell, gape not! Come not, Lucifer!
I'll burn my books! O Mephistophilis!
                    [*exeunt Devils and Faustus*

### SCENE 3

*Enter Scholars*

1 SCHOLAR  Come, gentlemen, let us go visit Faustus,
For such a dreadful night was never seen;
Since first the world's creation did begin,
Such fearful shrieks and cries were never heard:
Pray heaven the doctor have escap'd the danger.

2 SCHOLAR  O, help us, heaven! See, here are Faustus' limbs,
All torn asunder by the hand of death!

3 SCHOLAR  The devils whom Faustus serv'd have torn him thus;
For, twixt the hours of twelve and one, methought,
I heard him shriek and call aloud for help;      10
At which self time the house seem'd all on fire
With dreadful horror of these damned fiends.

2 SCHOLAR  Well, gentlemen, though Faustus' end be such
As every Christian heart laments to think on,
Yet, for he was a scholar once admir'd
For wondrous knowledge in our German schools,
We'll give his mangled limbs due burial;
And all the students, cloth'd in mourning black,
Shall wait upon his heavy funeral.      [*exeunt*

*Enter* CHORUS

CHORUS  Cut is the branch that might have grown full straight,
And burned is Apollo's laurel-bough,
That sometimes grew within this learned man.
Faustus is gone: regard his hellish fall,
Whose fiendful fortune may exhort the wise,
Only to wonder at unlawful things,
Whose deepness doth entice such forward wits
To practise more than heavenly power permits.

     [*exit*

*Terminat hora diem; terminat auctor opus.*

# THE JEW OF MALTA

# INTRODUCTION

If Faustus and Tamburlaine are offered to us as morally ambivalent central characters, whose will to power is simultaneously attractive and repellent, *The Jew Of Malta* may seem clearer in its effect. Barabas, the eponymous Jew, is, after all, a man who delights in his own cunning and wickedness, who revels 'to walk abroad a-nights,/ And kill sick people groaning under walls;/ Sometimes I go about and poison wells', and claims credit for killing 'friend and enemy with my strategems' in wartime, filling jails with bankrupts ruined by his usury, and driving his victims to insanity and suicide (2,3). Whereas the prologue in *Doctor Faustus* constructs the play within a didactic and controlled framework, presenting itself as the authoritative voice of what might be identified as conventional morality, *The Jew of Malta* opens with the figure of Machiavel. Machiavel represents the popular Elizabethan conception of the Italian political theorist Niccolò Machiavelli, whose reputation as immoral and ungodly was as firmly established as it was ill-deserved. Machiavel is immediately challenging: 'I count religion but a childish toy,/And hold there is no sin but ignorance.' Machiavel presents the play as 'the tragedy of a Jew', and, in a way which by now seems characteristic of the Marlovian prologue, invites the audience to judge him 'as he deserves'. Stage Machiavels in the Elizabethan period were associated with 'policy', with the capacity for malignity motivated only by the enjoyment of plotting, and this solipsistic motivation recurs throughout a play in which most characters have little reason for their excessive actions. Just as the prologue to *Doctor Faustus* introduced the central character in the confined space of his study, so Barabas is introduced in his counting house, praising his money as 'infinite riches in a tiny room'. Money explicitly motivates much of the plot, and more broadly, the themes of payment and repayment, the economics of exchange, are recurrent. In the play, Malta has been required by Turkey to pay tribute, and the Governor of Malta decrees that this expense should be sustained by the Jews of the island. Barabas is a rich Jew who resists the impounding of his assets and the requisitioning of his house as a nunnery. He enacts multiple and bloody revenges for this sequestration, including poisoning his daughter Abigail and ordering the murder of her lover. He betrays Malta to the Turks and is made its Governor by the conquerors. His downfall is due to an elaborate plot to destroy the Turkish commander and his soldiers, by means of a collapsible floor at a banquet, but he is himself betrayed and falls to his death in his own cauldron.

Barabas is, as the play's title makes clear, an outsider, separated by religion and race from the citizens of Malta and by his wealth from his fellow Jews. He is not a character with whom we want to identify, but we may, even if unwillingly, find his vaunted amorality attractive. His dramatic predecessor is the Vice figure of medieval drama, whose charisma could be enjoyed because of the certain knowledge that he would be ultimately undone. We are drawn to him although we know we should not be. His name, after all, recalls the name of the thief whom the people chose over Christ when Pilate offered to free one of the prisoners condemned to crucifixion. His technique of speaking asides to the audience implicates us in his machinations – in the second scene of the play he warns us that we will see 'more of the serpent than the dove; that is, more knave than fool' (1,2) – and we may find a certain pleasure in being on his side. Barabas' power in Malta is the power of theatre and of dissembling, and we witness his actions as various episodes choreographed by his infernal theatrical ingenuity. Crucially, the play proposes no moral alternative to his behaviour, and while Barabas is on one level different from the other characters, a more fundamental concern of the play is to express the similarities between them. Ferneze, in particular, is a figure of considerable ambiguity, whose politic machiavellianism ensures that he is the play's only survivor. Malta is shown to be utterly corrupt, rife with sexual and religious hypocrisy, and for this reason it is a misreading to castigate the play as only, or clearly, anti-semitic, despite those exchanges which report a particularly Elizabethan fantasy of

Jewishness. Barabas is as much representative of his degenerate world as he is marginalised by it by his racial difference. Everyone in Malta, it seems, is devious and deceitful: the play is shot through with cynicism about human motives. Barabas is loyal only to himself, and here he can be seen alongside other Marlovian protagonists whose single-mindedness is a source of strength as well as evil. He cleverly inhabits Maltese traditions in order to destroy his enemies. It is entirely fitting that his final act of betrayal should be presented as an act of hospitality, the culmination of his manipulation of codes of honour and love for his own diabolic purposes.

Other of Marlowe's plays combine comedy and farce with more 'serious' material, but, despite being introduced by Machiavel as a tragedy, *The Jew of Malta* seems more thoroughgoing, and more mordant, in its humour. T. S. Eliot memorably dubbed it 'savage farce'. Rhetoric is constantly deflated, as in Barabas' grandiloquent curse over the porridge pot in Act 3, which is followed by the bathetic riposte from Ithamore: 'was ever pot of / Rice porridge so sauced?' Even the verse is not allowed to aspire to anything noble in this corrupted world. Moments of pathos are savagely undercut. Abigail's death is one such, dying on a declaration of faith and bidding her confessor to convert her father: 'witness that I die a Christian'. Friar Barnardine's remark 'Ay, and a virgin too; that grieves me most' (4,1) symbolises the grubby, anti-heroic ethic of Maltese society. Marlowe is self-parodying, too: the version of his lyric 'Come live with me and be my love' given to the drunken Ithamore in Act 4 is a case in point, and there are numerous speeches in which Barabas mockingly borrows the rhetorical tricks of catalogue and amplification from Tamburlaine. The role of ironic juxtaposition in the play's humour makes for uneasy laughter, particularly as the play manipulates us into finding the most macabre actions funny. Reviewers of the play on the stage in recent times have been somewhat disconcerted by audience's hearty enjoyment of episodes such as the mass poisoning of the nuns. The audience is at times co-conspirator with Barabas, laughing with him at other characters' misfortunes, but the grotesque *Schadenfreude* which is the keynote of Maltese life infects the audience too: we end up laughing as Barabas, our erstwhile collaborator, boils to death in his own cauldron.

## TO MY WORTHY FRIEND,
## MASTER THOMAS HAMMON,
## OF GRAY'S INN, ETC

This play, composed by so worthy an author as Master Marlowe, and the part of the Jew presented by so unimitable an actor as Master Alleyn, being in this later age commended to the stage; as I ushered it unto the court, and presented it to the Cock-pit, with these Prologues and Epilogues here inserted, so now being newly brought to the press, I was loath it should be published without the ornament of an Epistle; making choice of you unto whom to devote it; than whom (of all those gentlemen and acquaintance within the compass of my long knowledge) there is none more able to tax ignorance, or attribute right to merit. Sir, you have been pleased to grace some of mine own works with your courteous patronage: I hope this will not be the worse accepted, because commended by me; over whom none can claim more power or privilege than yourself. I had no better a new year's gift to present you with; receive it therefore as a continuance of that inviolable obligement, by which he rests still engaged, who, as he ever hath, shall always remain,

*Tuissimus*
THO. HEYWOOD

# THE PROLOGUE SPOKEN AT COURT

Gracious and great, that we so boldly dare
('Mongst other plays that now in fashion are)
To present this, writ many years agone,
And in that age thought second unto none,
We humbly crave your pardon. We pursue
The story of a rich and famous Jew
Who liv'd in Malta: you shall find him still,
In all his projects, a sound Machiavill;
And that's his character. He that hath past
So many censures is now come at last
To have your princely ears: grace you him; then
You crown the action, and renown the pen.

## THE PROLOGUE TO THE STAGE
### AT THE COCK-PIT

We know not how our play may pass this stage,
But by the best of poets in that age
*The Malta-Jew* had being and was made;
And he then by the best of actors play'd:
In *Hero and Leander* one did gain
A lasting memory; in *Tamburlaine*,
This Jew, with others many, th' other wan
The tribute of peerless, being a man
Whom we may rank with (doing no one wrong)
Proteus for shapes, and Roscius for a tongue —
So could he speak, so vary; nor is't hate
To merit in him who doth personate
Our Jew this day; nor is it his ambition
To exceed or equal, being of condition
More modest: this is all that he intends
(And that too at the urgence of some friends),
To prove his best, and, if none here gainsay it,
The part he hath studied, and intends to play it.

# CHARACTERS IN THE PLAY

FERNEZE, *governor of Malta*

LODOWICK, *his son*

SELIM CALYMATH, *son to the* GRAND SEIGNIOR

MARTIN DEL BOSCO, *vice-admiral of Spain*

MATHIAS, *a gentleman*

JACOMO  
BARNADINE } *friars*

BARABAS, *a wealthy Jew*

ITHAMORE, *a slave*

PHILIA-BORZA, *a bully, attendant to* BELLAMIRA

TWO MERCHANTS

THREE JEWS

*Knights, Bassoes, Officers, Guard, Slaves,  
    Messenger and Carpenters*

KATHARINE, *mother to* MATHIAS

ABIGAIL, *daughter to* BARABAS

BELLAMIRA, *a courtesan*

ABBESS

NUN

MACHIAVEL *as Prologue-speaker*

*Scene*: MALTA

# THE JEW OF MALTA

*Enter* MACHIAVEL

MACHIAVEL Albeit the world think Machiavel is dead,
Yet was his soul but flown beyond the Alps;
And, now the Guise is dead, is come from France,
To view this land, and frolic with his friends.
To some perhaps my name is odious;
But such as love me, guard me from their tongues,
And let them know that I am Machiavel,
And weigh not men, and therefore not men's words.
Admir'd I am of those that hate me most:
Though some speak openly against my books,          10
Yet will they read me, and thereby attain
To Peter's chair; and, when they cast me off,
Are poison'd by my climbing followers.
I count religion but a childish toy,
And hold there is no sin but ignorance.
Birds of the air will tell of murders past!
I am asham'd to hear such fooleries.
Many will talk of title to a crown:
What right had Caesar to the empery?
Might first made kings, and laws were then most sure
When, like the Draco's, they were writ in blood.
Hence comes it that a strong built citadel
Commands much more than letters can import:
Which maxim had Phalaris observ'd,
H'ad never bellow'd, in a brazen bull,
Of great ones' envy: o' the poor petty wights
Let me be envied and not pitied.
But whither am I bound! I come not, I,
To read a lecture here in Britain,
But to present the tragedy of a Jew,          30
Who smiles to see how full his bags are cramm'd;
Which money was not got without my means.

I crave but this – grace him as he deserves,
And let him not be entertain'd the worse
Because he favours me.

[*exit*

## ACT ONE

### SCENE I

BARABAS *discovered in his counting house,*
*with heaps of gold before him*

BARABAS      So that of thus much that return was made;
And of the third part of the Persian ships
There was the venture summ'd and satisfied.
As for those Samnites, and the men of Uz,
That brought my Spanish oils and wines of Greece,
Here have I purs'd their paltry silverlings.
Fie, what a trouble 'tis to count this trash!
Well fare the Arabians, who so richly pay
The things they traffic for with wedge of gold,
Whereof a man may easily in a day                    10
Tell that which may maintain him all his life.
The needy groom, that never finger'd groat,
Would make a miracle of thus much coin;
But he whose steel-barr'd coffers are cramm'd full,
And all his life-time hath been tired,
Wearying his fingers' ends with telling it,
Would in his age be loath to labour so
And for a pound to sweat himself to death.
Give me the merchants of the Indian mines,
That trade in metal of the purest mould;             20
The wealthy Moor, that in the eastern rocks
Without control can pick his riches up,
And in his house heap pearl like pebble stones,
Receive them free, and sell them by the weight!
Bags of fiery opals, sapphires, amethysts,
Jacinths, hard topaz, grass-green emeralds,
Beauteous rubies, sparkling diamonds,
And seld-seen costly stones of so great price,

As one of them, indifferently rated,
And of a carat of this quantity,      30
May serve, in peril of calamity,
To ransom great kings from captivity.
This is the ware wherein consists my wealth;
And thus methinks should men of judgment frame
Their means of traffic from the vulgar trade,
And, as their wealth increaseth, so inclose
Infinite riches in a little room.
But now how stands the wind?
Into what corner peers my halcyon's bill?
Ha! To the east? Yes. See how stand the vanes –    40
East and by south: why, then, I hope my ships
I sent for Egypt and the bordering isles
Are gotten up by Nilus' winding banks;
Mine argosy from Alexandria,
Loaden with spice and silks, now under sail,
Are smoothly gliding down by Candy-shore
To Malta, through our Mediterranean sea –
But who comes here? [enter a Merchant]
                 How now!

MERCHANT                Barabas,
Thy ships are safe, riding in Malta-road;
And all the merchants with other merchandise    50
Are safe arriv'd, and have sent me to know
Whether yourself will come and custom them.

BARABAS   The ships are safe thou say'st, and richly fraught?

MERCHANT They are.

BARABAS   Why, then, go bid them come ashore,
And bring with them their bills of entry:
I hope our credit in the custom-house
Will serve as well as I were present there.
Go send 'em threescore camels, thirty mules,
And twenty waggons, to bring up the ware.    60
But art thou master in a ship of mine,
And is thy credit not enough for that?

MERCHANT The very custom barely comes to more
Than many merchants of the town are worth,
And therefore far exceeds my credit, sir.

| BARABAS | Go tell 'em the Jew of Malta sent thee, man: |
| | Tush, who amongst 'em knows not Barabas? |
| MERCHANT | I go. |
| BARABAS | So, then, there's somewhat come – |
| | Sirrah, which of my ships art thou master of? 70 |
| MERCHANT | Of the Speranza, sir. |
| BARABAS | And saw'st thou not |
| | Mine argosy at Alexandria? |
| | Thou couldst not come from Egypt, or by Caire, |
| | But at the entry there into the sea, |
| | Where Nilus pays his tribute to the main, |
| | Thou needs must sail by Alexandria. |
| MERCHANT | I neither saw them, nor inquir'd of them: |
| | But this we heard some of our seamen say, |
| | They wonder'd how you durst with so much wealth |
| | Trust such a crazed vessel, and so far. 80 |
| BARABAS | Tush, they are wise! I know her and her strength. |
| | But go, go thou thy ways, discharge thy ship, |
| | And bid my factor bring his loading in. |

*[exit Merchant*

And yet I wonder at this argosy.

*Enter a Second Merchant*

| 2 MERCH. | Thine argosy from Alexandria |
| | Know, Barabas, doth ride in Malta road, |
| | Laden with riches, and exceeding store |
| | Of Persian silks, of gold, and orient pearl. |
| BARABAS | How chance you came not with those other ships |
| | That sail'd by Egypt? |
| 2 MERCH. | Sir, we saw 'em not. 90 |
| BARABAS | Belike they coasted round by Candy-shore |
| | About their oils or other businesses. |
| | But 'twas ill done of you to come so far |
| | Without the aid or conduct of their ships. |
| 2 MERCH. | Sir, we were wafted by a Spanish fleet, |
| | That never left us till within a league, |
| | That had the galleys of the Turk in chase. |
| BARABAS | O, they were going up to Sicily. |
| | Well, go, |
| | And bid the merchants and my men despatch, 100 |

|  | And come ashore, and see the fraught discharg'd. |  |
|---|---|---|
| 2 MERCH. | I go. | [*exit* |
| BARABAS | Thus trolls our fortune in by land and sea, |  |

And thus are we on every side enrich'd:
These are the blessings promis'd to the Jews,
And herein was old Abraham's happiness:
What more may heaven do for earthly man
Than thus to pour out plenty in their laps,
Ripping the bowels of the earth for them,
Making the seas their servants, and the winds     110
To drive their substance with successful blasts?
Who hateth me but for my happiness?
Or who is honour'd now but for his wealth?
Rather had I, a Jew, be hated thus,
Than pitied in a Christian poverty;
For I can see no fruits in all their faith,
But malice, falsehood, and excessive pride,
Which methinks fits not their profession.
Haply some hapless man hath conscience,
And for his conscience lives in beggary.     120
They say we are a scatter'd nation:
I cannot tell; but we have scrambled up
More wealth by far than those that brag of faith:
There's Kirriah Jairim, the great Jew of Greece,
Obed in Bairseth, Nones in Portugal,
Myself in Malta, some in Italy,
Many in France, and wealthy every one;
Ay, wealthier far than any Christian.
I must confess we come not to be kings:
That's not our fault: alas, our number's few!     130
And crowns come either by succession,
Or urg'd by force; and nothing violent,
Oft have I heard tell, can be permanent.
Give us a peaceful rule; make Christians kings,
That thirst so much for principality.
I have no charge, nor many children,
But one sole daughter, whom I hold as dear
As Agamemnon did his Iphigen;
And all I have is hers — But who comes here?

*Enter three Jews*

| | | |
|---|---|---|
| 1 JEW | Tush, tell not me; 'twas done of policy. | 140 |
| 2 JEW | Come, therefore, let us go to Barabas; | |
| | For he can counsel best in these affairs: | |
| | And here he comes. | |
| BARABAS |                 Why, how now, countrymen! | |
| | Why flock you thus to me in multitudes? | |
| | What accident's betided to the Jews? | |
| 1 JEW | A fleet of warlike galleys, Barabas, | |
| | Are come from Turkey, and lie in our road: | |
| | And they this day sit in the council-house | |
| | To entertain them and their embassy. | |
| BARABAS | Why, let 'em come, so they come not to war; | 150 |
| | Or let 'em war, so we be conquerors – | |
| | [*aside*] Nay, let 'em combat, conquer, and kill all, | |
| | So they spare me, my daughter, and my wealth. | |
| 1 JEW | Were it for confirmation of a league, | |
| | They would not come in warlike manner thus. | |
| 2 JEW | I fear their coming will afflict us all. | |
| BARABAS | Fond men, what dream you of their multitudes? | |
| | What need they treat of peace that are in league? | |
| | The Turks and those of Malta are in league: | |
| | Tut, tut, there is some other matter in't. | 160 |
| 1 JEW | Why, Barabas, they come for peace or war. | |
| BARABAS | Haply for neither, but to pass along, | |
| | Towards Venice, by the Adriatic sea, | |
| | With whom they have attempted many times, | |
| | But never could effect their stratagem. | |
| 3 JEW | And very wisely said; it may be so. | |
| 2 JEW | But there's a meeting in the senate-house, | |
| | And all the Jews in Malta must be there. | |
| BARABAS | Hum – all the Jews in Malta must be there! | |
| | Ay, like enough: why, then, let every man | 170 |
| | Provide him, and be there for fashion-sake. | |
| | If anything shall there concern our state, | |
| | Assure yourselves I'll look – [*aside*] unto myself. | |
| 1 JEW | I know you will – Well, brethren 'et us go. | |
| 2 JEW | Let's take our leaves – Farewell, good Barabas. | |
| BARABAS | Farewell, Zaareth; farewell, Temainte.    [*exeunt Jews* | |

And, Barabas, now search this secret out;
Summon thy senses, call thy wits together:
These silly men mistake the matter clean:
Long to the Turk did Malta contribute;                    180
Which tribute all in policy, I fear,
The Turk has let increase to such a sum
As all the wealth of Malta cannot pay;
And now by that advantage thinks, belike,
To seize upon the town; ay, that he seeks.
Howe'er the world go, I'll make sure for one,
And seek in time to intercept the worst,
Warily guarding that which I ha' got:
*Ego mihimet sum semper proximus*:
Why, let 'em enter, let 'em take the town.                190
                                                        [*exit*


## SCENE 2

*Enter* FERNEZE *Governor of Malta, Knights, and Officers;*
*met by* CALYMATH, *and Bassoes of the Turk*

FERNEZE      Now, bassoes, what demand you at our hands?
I BASSO      Know, knights of Malta, that we came from Rhodes,
             From Cyprus, Candy, and those other isles
             That lie betwixt the Mediterranean seas.
FERNEZE      What's Cyprus, Candy, and those other isles
             To us or Malta? What at our hands demand ye?
CALYMATH     The ten years' tribute that remains unpaid.
FERNEZE      Alas, my lord, the sum is over-great!
             I hope your highness will consider us.
CALYMATH     I wish, grave governor, 'twere in my power          10
             To favour you; but 'tis my father's cause.
             Wherein I may not, nay, I dare not dally.
FERNEZE      Then give us leave, great Selim Calymath.
CALYMATH     Stand all aside, and let the knights determine;
             And send to keep our galleys under sail,
             For happily we shall not tarry here –
             Now, governor, how are you resolv'd?
FERNEZE      Thus; since your hard conditions are such

|            | That you will needs have ten years' tribute past, |
|            | We may have time to make collection                20 |
|            | Amongst the inhabitants of Malta for't. |
| I BASSO    | That's more than is in our commission. |
| CALYMATH   | What, Callapine! A little courtesy: |
|            | Let's know their time; perhaps it is not long; |
|            | And 'tis more kingly to obtain by peace |
|            | Than to enforce conditions by constraint. – |
|            | What respite ask you, governor? |
| FERNEZE    |                              But a month. |
| CALYMATH   | We grant a month; but see you keep your promise. |
|            | Now launch our galleys back again to sea, |
|            | Where we'll attend the respite you have ta'en,      30 |
|            | And for the money send our messenger. |
|            | Farewell, great governor, and brave knights of Malta. |
| FERNEZE    | And all good fortune wait on Calymath! |

[*exeunt Calymath and Bassoes*

|            | Go one and call those Jews of Malta hither: |
|            | Were they not summon'd to appear today? |
| I OFFICER  | They were, my lord; and here they come. |

*Enter* BARABAS *and three Jews*

| I KNIGHT   | Have you determin'd what to say to them? |
| FERNEZE    | Yes; give me leave – and, Hebrews, now come near. |
|            | From the Emperor of Turkey is arriv'd |
|            | Great Selim Calymath, his highness' son,            40 |
|            | To levy of us ten years' tribute past: |
|            | Now, then, here know that it concerneth us. |
| BARABAS    | Then, good my lord, to keep your quiet still, |
|            | Your lordship shall do well to let them have it. |
| FERNEZE    | Soft, Barabas! There's more 'longs to't than so. |
|            | To what this ten years' tribute will amount, |
|            | That we have cast, but cannot compass it |
|            | By reason of the wars, that robb'd our store; |
|            | And therefore are we to request your aid. |
| BARABAS    | Alas, my lord, we are no soldiers!                  50 |
|            | And what's our aid against so great a prince? |
| I KNIGHT   | Tut, Jew, we know thou art no soldier, |
|            | That art a merchant and a money'd man; |

|  | And 'tis thy money, Barabas, we seek. |
| BARABAS | How, my lord! My money! |
| FERNEZE | Thine and the rest; |
|  | For, to be short, amongst you't must be had. |
| I JEW | Alas, my lord, the most of us are poor! |
| FERNEZE | Then let the rich increase your portions. |
| BARABAS | Are strangers with your tribute to be tax'd? |
| 2 KNIGHT | Have strangers leave with us to get their wealth?     60 |
|  | Then let them with us contribute. |
| BARABAS | How! Equally? |
| FERNEZE | No, Jew, like infidels; |
|  | For through our sufferance of your hateful lives, |
|  | Who stand accursed in the sight of heaven, |
|  | These taxes and afflictions are befall'n, |
|  | And therefore thus we are determined – |
|  | Read there the articles of our decrees. |
| OFFICER | [reads] First, the tribute-money of the Turks shall all be levied amongst the Jews, and each of them to pay one half of his estate.     70 |
| BARABAS | How! Half his estate! [aside] I hope you mean not mine. |
| FERNEZE | Read on. |
| OFFICER | [reads] Secondly, he that denies to pay, shall straight become a Christian. |
| BARABAS | How! A Christian! [aside] Hum, – what's here to do? |
| OFFICER | [reads] Lastly, he that denies this, shall absolutely lose all he has. |
| JEWS | O my lord, we will give half! |
| BARABAS | O earth-mettled villains, and no Hebrews born! |
|  | And will you basely thus submit yourselves     80 |
|  | To leave your goods to their arbitrement? |
| FERNEZE | Why, Barabas, wilt thou be christened? |
| BARABAS | No, governor, I will be no convertite. |
| FERNEZE | Then pay thy half. |
| BARABAS | Why, know you what you did by this device? |
|  | Half of my substance is a city's wealth. |
|  | Governor, it was not got so easily; |
|  | Nor will I part so slightly therewithal. |
| FERNEZE | Sir, half is the penalty of our decree; |
|  | Either pay that, or we will seize on all.     90 |

BARABAS    *Corpo di Dio!* Stay: you shall have half;
           Let me be us'd but as my brethren are.

FERNEZE    No, Jew, thou hast denied the articles,
           And now it cannot be recall'd.
                          [*exeunt Officers, on a sign from Ferneze*

BARABAS    Will you, then, steal my goods?
           Is theft the ground of your religion?

FERNEZE    No, Jew; we take particularly thine,
           To save the ruin of a multitude:
           And better one want for a common good,
           Than many perish for a private man:                    100
           Yet, Barabas, we will not banish thee,
           But here in Malta, where thou gott'st thy wealth,
           Live still; and, if thou canst, get more.

BARABAS    Christians, what or how can I multiply?
           Of naught is nothing made.

I KNIGHT   From naught at first thou cam'st to little wealth,
           From little unto more, from more to most:
           If your first curse fall heavy on thy head,
           And make thee poor and scorn'd of all the world,
           'Tis not our fault, but thy inherent sin.              110

BARABAS    What, bring you Scripture to confirm your wrongs?
           Preach me not out of my possessions.
           Some Jews are wicked, as all Christians are;
           But say the tribe that I descended of
           Were all in general cast away for sin,
           Shall I be tried for their transgressions?
           The man that dealeth righteously shall live;
           And which of you can charge me otherwise?

FERNEZE    Out, wretched Barabas!
           Sham'st thou not thus to justify thyself,              120
           As if we knew not thy profession?
           If thou rely upon thy righteousness,
           Be patient, and thy riches will increase.
           Excess of wealth is cause of covetousness;
           And covetousness, O, 'tis a monstrous sin!

BARABAS    Ay, but theft is worse: tush! take not from me, then,
           For that is theft, and, if you rob me thus,
           I must be forc'd to steal, and compass more.

| I KNIGHT | Grave governor, list not to his exclaims: |
|---|---|
| | Convert his mansion to a nunnery:       130 |
| | His house will harbour many holy nuns. |
| FERNEZE | It shall be so. |

*Re-enter Officers*

| | Now, officers, have you done? |
|---|---|
| I OFFICER | Ay, my lord, we have seiz'd upon the goods |
| | And wares of Barabas, which, being valu'd, |
| | Amount to more than all the wealth in Malta: |
| | And of the other we have seiz'd half. |
| FERNEZE | Then we'll take order for the residue. |
| BARABAS | Well, then, my lord, say, are you satisfied? |
| | You have my goods, my money, and my wealth, |
| | My ships, my store, and all that I enjoy'd;       140 |
| | And, having all, you can request no more, |
| | Unless your unrelenting flinty hearts |
| | Suppress all pity in your stony breasts, |
| | And now shalt move you to bereave my life. |
| FERNEZE | No, Barabas; to stain our hands with blood |
| | Is far from us and our profession. |
| BARABAS | Why, I esteem the injury far less, |
| | To take the lives of miserable men |
| | Than be the causers of their misery. |
| | You have my wealth, the labour of my life,       150 |
| | The comfort of mine age, my children's hope; |
| | And therefore ne'er distinguish of the wrong. |
| FERNEZE | Content thee, Barabas; thou hast naught but right. |
| BARABAS | Your extreme right does me exceeding wrong: |
| | But take it to you, i' the devil's name! |
| FERNEZE | Come, let us in, and gather of these goods |
| | The money for this tribute of the Turk. |
| I KNIGHT | 'Tis necessary that be look'd unto; |
| | For, if we break our day, we break the league, |
| | And that will prove but simple policy.       160 |

*[exeunt all except Barabas and the three Jews*

| BARABAS | Ay, policy! That's their profession, |
|---|---|
| | And not simplicity, as they suggest. |
| | The plagues of Egypt, and the curse of heaven, |

Earth's barrenness, and all men's hatred,
Inflict upon them, thou great *Primus Motor*!
And here upon my knees, striking the earth,
I ban their souls to everlasting pains,
And extreme tortures of the fiery deep,
That thus have dealt with me in my distress!

1 JEW      O, yet be patient, gentle Barabas!            170

BARABAS    O silly brethren, born to see this day,
Why stand you thus unmov'd with my laments?
Why weep you not to think upon my wrongs?
Why pine not I, and die in this distress?

1 JEW      Why, Barabas, as hardly can we brook
The cruel handling of ourselves in this:
Thou seest they have taken half our goods.

BARABAS    Why did you yield to their extortion?
You were a multitude, and I but one;
And of me only have they taken all.            180

1 JEW      Yet, brother Barabas, remember Job.

BARABAS    What tell you me of Job? I wot his wealth
Was written thus; he had seven thousand sheep,
Three thousand camels, and two hundred yoke
Of labouring oxen, and five hundred
She asses: but for every one of those,
Had they been valu'd at indifferent rate,
I had at home, and in mine argosy,
And other ships that came from Egypt last,
As much as would have bought his beasts and him, 190
And yet have kept enough to live upon;
So that not he, but I, may curse the day,
Thy fatal birthday, forlorn Barabas;
And henceforth wish for an eternal night,
That clouds of darkness may inclose my flesh,
And hide these extreme sorrows from mine eyes;
For only I have toil'd to inherit here
The months of vanity, and loss of time,
And painful nights, have been appointed me.

2 JEW      Good Barabas, be patient.

BARABAS                    Ay! ay!            200
Pray, leave me in my patience. You, that

Were ne'er possess'd of wealth, are pleas'd with want;
But give him liberty at least to mourn,
That in a field, amidst his enemies,
Doth see his soldiers slain, himself disarm'd,
And know no means of his recovery:
Ay, let me sorrow for this sudden chance;
'Tis in the trouble of my spirit I speak:
Great injuries are not so soon forgot.

1 JEW    Come, let us leave him; in his ireful mood          210
Our words will but increase his ecstasy.

2 JEW    On, then: but, trust me, 'tis a misery
To see a man in such affliction –
Farewell, Barabas.          [exeunt three Jews

BARABAS          Ay, fare you well.
See the simplicity of these base slaves,
Who, for the villains have no wit themselves,
Think me to be a senseless lump of clay,
That will with every water wash to dirt!
No, Barabas is born to better chance,
And fram'd of finer mould than common men,          220
That measure naught but by the present time.
A reaching thought will search his deepest wits,
And casts with cunning for the time to come;
For evils are apt to happen every day.

*Enter* ABIGAIL

But whither wends my beauteous Abigail?
O, what has made my lovely daughter sad?
What, woman! Moan not for a little loss;
Thy father has enough in store for thee.

ABIGAIL    Not for myself, but aged Barabas,
Father, for thee lamenteth Abigail:          230
But I will learn to leave these fruitless tears;
And, urg'd thereto with my afflictions,
With fierce exclaims run to the senate-house,
And in the senate reprehend them all,
And rent their hearts with tearing of my hair,
Till they reduce the wrongs done to my father.

BARABAS    No, Abigail; things past recovery

Are hardly cur'd with exclamations:
Be silent, daughter; sufferance breeds ease,
And time may yield us an occasion,                              240
Which on the sudden cannot serve the turn.
Besides, my girl, think me not all so fond
As negligently to forego so much
Without provision for thyself and me:
Ten thousand portagues, besides great pearls,
Rich costly jewels, and stones infinite,
Fearing the worst of this before it fell,
I closely hid.

ABIGAIL    Where, father?

BARABAS    In my house, my girl.                                250

ABIGAIL    Then shall they ne'er be seen of Barabas;
For they have seiz'd upon thy house and wares.

BARABAS    But they will give me leave once more, I trow,
To go into my house.

ABIGAIL                           That may they not;
For there I left the governor placing nuns,
Displacing me; and of thy house they mean
To make a nunnery, where none but their own sect
Must enter in; men generally barr'd.

BARABAS    My gold, my gold, and all my wealth is gone!
You partial heavens, have I deserv'd this plague?    260
What, will you thus oppose me, luckless stars,
To make me desperate in my poverty?
And, knowing me impatient in distress,
Think me so mad as I will hang myself,
That I may vanish o'er the earth in air,
And leave no memory that e'er I was?
No, I will live; nor loathe I this my life:
And, since you leave me in the ocean thus
To sink or swim, and put me to my shifts,
I'll rouse my senses, and awake myself –               270
Daughter, I have it: thou perceiv'st the plight
Wherein these Christians have oppressed me:
Be rul'd by me, for in extremity
We ought to make bar of no policy.

| | |
|---|---|
| ABIGAIL | Father, whate'er it be, to injure them |
| | That have so manifestly wronged us, |
| | What will not Abigail attempt? |
| BARABAS | Why, so. |
| | Then thus: thou told'st me they have turn'd my house |
| | Into a nunnery, and some nuns are there? |
| ABIGAIL | I did. |
| BARABAS | Then, Abigail, there must my girl 280 |
| | Entreat the abbess to be entertain'd. |
| ABIGAIL | How! As a nun? |
| BARABAS | Ay, daughter: for religion |
| | Hides many mischiefs from suspicion. |
| ABIGAIL | Ay, but, father they will suspect me there. |
| BARABAS | Let 'em suspect; but be thou so precise |
| | As they may think it done of holiness: |
| | Entreat 'em fair, and give them friendly speech, |
| | And seem to them as if thy sins were great, |
| | Till thou hast gotten to be entertain'd. |
| ABIGAIL | Thus, father, shall I much dissemble. |
| BARABAS | Tush! 290 |
| | As good dissemble that thou never mean'st, |
| | As first mean truth and then dissemble it: |
| | A counterfeit profession is better |
| | Than unseen hypocrisy. |
| ABIGAIL | Well, father, |
| | Say I be entertain'd, what then shall follow? |
| BARABAS | This shall follow then. |
| | There have I hid, close underneath the plank |
| | That runs along the upper-chamber floor, |
| | The gold and jewels which I kept for thee – |
| | But here they come: be cunning, Abigail. 300 |
| ABIGAIL | Then, father, go with me. |
| BARABAS | No, Abigail, |
| | In this it is not necessary I be seen; |
| | For I will seem offended with thee for't: |
| | Be close, my girl, for this must fetch my gold. |
| | *[they retire* |

*Enter* FRIAR JACOMO, FRIAR BERNARDINE,
*Abbess, and a Nun*

| | |
|---|---|
| FRIAR J. | Sisters, |
| | We now are almost at the new-made nunnery. |
| ABBESS | The better; for we love not to be seen. |
| | 'Tis thirty winters long since some of us |
| | Did stray so far amongst the multitude. |
| FRIAR J. | But, madam, this house                                310 |
| | And waters of this new-made nunnery |
| | Will much delight you. |
| ABBESS | It may be so — But who comes here? |
| ABIGAIL | [*comes forward*] Grave abbess, and you happy |
| | virgins' guide, |
| | Pity the state of a distressed maid! |
| ABBESS | What art thou, daughter? |
| ABIGAIL | The hopeless daughter of a hapless Jew, |
| | The Jew of Malta, wretched Barabas, |
| | Sometime the owner of a goodly house, |
| | Which they have now turn'd to a nunnery.      320 |
| ABBESS | Well, daughter, say, what is thy suit with us? |
| ABIGAIL | Fearing the afflictions which my father feels |
| | Proceed from sin or want of faith in us, |
| | I'd pass away my life in penitence, |
| | And be a novice in your nunnery, |
| | To make atonement for my labouring soul. |
| FRIAR J. | No doubt, brother, but this proceedeth of the spirit. |
| FRIAR B. | Ay, and of a moving spirit too, brother: but come, let |
| | us entreat she may be entertain'd. |
| ABBESS | Well, daughter, we admit you for a nun.        330 |
| ABIGAIL | First let me as a novice learn to frame |
| | My solitary life to your strait laws, |
| | And let me lodge where I was wont to lie: |
| | I do not doubt, by your divine precepts |
| | And mine own industry, but to profit much. |
| BARABAS | [*aside*] As much, I hope, as all I hid is worth. |
| ABBESS | Come, daughter, follow us. |
| BARABAS | [*coming forward*] Why, how now? Abigail! |
| | What mak'st thou 'mongst these hateful Christians? |

| | | |
|---|---|---|
| FRIAR J. | Hinder her not, thou man of little faith, | 340 |
| | For she has mortified herself— | |
| BARABAS | How! Mortified! | |
| FRIAR J. | And is admitted to the sisterhood. | |
| BARABAS | Child of perdition, and thy father's shame! | |
| | What wilt thou do among these hateful fiends? | |
| | I charge thee on my blessing that thou leave | |
| | These devils and their damned heresy! | |
| ABIGAIL | Father, forgive me — | |
| BARABAS | Nay, back, Abigail. | |

[*aside to Abigail in a whisper*]
And think upon the jewels and the gold;
The board is marked thus that covers it —
Away, accursed, from thy father's sight!            350

FRIAR J. Barabas, although thou art in misbelief,
And wilt not see thine own afflictions,
Yet let thy daughter be no longer blind.

BARABAS Blind friar, I reck not thy persuasions —
[*aside to Abigail in a whisper*] The board is marked
thus that covers it —
[*aloud*] For I had rather die than see her thus —
Wilt thou forsake me too in my distress,
Seduced daughter? [*aside to her*] Go, forget not —
[*aloud*] Becomes it Jews to be so credulous?
[*aside to her in a whisper*] Tomorrow early I'll be
at the door —            360
[*aloud*] No, come not at me; if thou wilt be damn'd,
Forget me, see me not; and so, be gone!
[*aside to her in a whisper*] Farewell; remember
tomorrow morning —
[*aloud*] Out, out, thou wretch!

[*exit, on one side, Barabas; exeunt, on the other side, Friars, Abbess, Nan, and Abigail*

*As they are going out, enter* MATHIAS

MATHIAS Who's this? Fair Abigail, the rich Jew's daughter,
Become a nun! Her father's sudden fall
Has humbled her, and brought her down to this.
Tut, she were fitter for a tale of love,

Than to be tired out with orisons;
And better would she far become a bed,                        370
Embraced in a friendly lover's arms,
Than rise at midnight to a solemn mass.

*Enter* LODOWICK

LODOWICK  Why, how now, Don Mathias! In a dump?
MATHIAS   Believe me, noble Lodowick, I have seen
          The strangest sight, in my opinion,
          That ever I beheld.
LODOWICK                        What was't, I prithee?
MATHIAS   A fair young maid, scarce fourteen years of age,
          The sweetest flower in Cytherea's field,
          Cropt from the pleasures of the fruitful earth,
          And strangely metamorphos'd [to a] nun.            380
LODOWICK  But say, what was she?
MATHIAS                        Why, the rich Jew's daughter.
LODOWICK  What, Barabas, whose goods were lately seiz'd?
          Is she so fair?
MATHIAS                And matchless beautiful
          As, had you seen her, 'twould have mov'd your heart,
          Though countermin'd with walls of brass, to love,
          Or, at the least, to pity.
LODOWICK  An if she be so fair as you report,
          'Twere time well spent to go and visit her:
          How say you? Shall we?
MATHIAS   I must and will, sir; there's no remedy.            390
LODOWICK  And so will I too, or it shall go hard.
          Farewell, Mathias.
MATHIAS                        Farewell, Lodowick.
                                            [*exeunt severally*

## ACT TWO

### SCENE I

*Enter* BARABAS, *with a light*

BARABAS    Thus, like the sad presaging raven, that tolls
    The sick man's passport in her hollow beak,
    And in the shadow of the silent night
    Doth shake contagion from her sable wings,
    Vex'd and tormented runs poor Barabas
    With fatal curses towards these Christians.
    The incertain pleasures of swift-footed time
    Have ta'en their flight, and left me in despair;
    And of my former riches rests no more
    But bare remembrance; like a soldier's scar,    10
    That has no further comfort for his maim.
    O Thou, that with a fiery pillar ledd'st
    The sons of Israel through the dismal shades,
    Light Abraham's offspring; and direct the hand
    Of Abigail this night! Or let the day
    Turn to eternal darkness after this!
    No sleep can fasten on my watchful eyes,
    Nor quiet enter my distemper'd thoughts,
    Till I have answer of my Abigail.

*Enter* ABIGAIL *above*

ABIGAIL    Now have I happily espied a time    20
    To search the plank my father did appoint;
    And here, behold, unseen, where I have found
    The gold, the pearls, and jewels, which he hid.
BARABAS    Now I remember those old women's words
    Who in my wealth would tell me winter's tales
    And speak of spirits and ghosts that glide by night
    About the place where treasure hath been hid:
    And now methinks that I am one of those;
    For, whilst I live, here lives my soul's sole hope,
    And, when I die, here shall my spirit walk.    30
ABIGAIL    Now that my father's fortune were so good

As but to be about this happy place!
'Tis not so happy: yet, when we parted last,
He said he would attend me in the morn.
Then, gentle Sleep, where'er his body rests,
Give charge to Morpheus that he may dream
A golden dream, and of the sudden wake,
Come and receive the treasure I have found.

BARABAS *Bueno para todos mi ganado no era:*
As good go on, as sit so sadly thus –                    40
But stay: what star shines yonder in the east?
The loadstar of my life, if Abigail –
Who's there?

ABIGAIL                       Who's that?

BARABAS                                   Peace, Abigail! 'Tis I.

ABIGAIL Then, father, here receive thy happiness.

BARABAS Hast thou't?

ABIGAIL Here. [*throws down bags*] Hast thou't?
There's more, and more, and more.

BARABAS                                     O my girl,
My gold, my fortune, my felicity,
Strength to my soul, death to mine enemy;
Welcome the first beginner of my bliss!                 50
O Abigail, Abigail, that I had thee here too!
Then my desires were fully satisfied:
But I will practise thy enlargement thence:
O girl! O gold! O beauty! O my bliss!   [*hugs the bags*

ABIGAIL Father, it draweth towards midnight now,
And 'bout this time the nuns begin to wake;
To shun suspicion, therefore, let us part.

BARABAS Farewell, my joy, and by my fingers take
A kiss from him that sends it from his soul.
                                    [*exit Abigail above*

Now, Phoebus, ope the eye-lids of the day,               60
And, for the raven, wake the morning lark,
That I may hover with her in the air,
Singing o'er these, as she does o'er her young.
*Hermoso placer de los dineros.*
                                    [*exit*

## SCENE 2

*Enter* FERNEZE, MARTIN DEL BOSCO,
*Knights, and Officers*

FERNEZE       Now, captain, tell us whither thou art bound,
              Whence is thy ship that anchors in our road,
              And why thou cam'st ashore without our leave.

DEL BOSCO     Governor of Malta, hither am I bound;
              My ship, the Flying Dragon, is of Spain,
              And so am I; Del Bosco is my name,
              Vice-admiral unto the Catholic King.

I KNIGHT      'Tis true, my lord: therefore entreat him well.

DEL BOSCO     Our fraught is Grecians, Turks, and Afric Moors;
              For late upon the coast of Corsica,                      10
              Because we vail'd not to the Turkish fleet,
              Their creeping galleys had us in the chase:
              But suddenly the wind began to rise,
              And then we luff'd and tack'd, and fought at ease:
              Some have we fir'd, and many have we sunk;
              But one amongst the rest became our prize:
              The captain's slain; the rest remain our slaves,
              Of whom we would make sale in Malta here.

FERNEZE       Martin del Bosco, I have heard of thee:
              Welcome to Malta, and to all of us!                      20
              But to admit a sale of these thy Turks,
              We may not, nay, we dare not give consent,
              By reason of a tributary league.

I KNIGHT      Del Bosco, as thou lov'st and honour'st us,
              Persuade our governor against the Turk:
              This truce we have is but in hope of gold,
              And with that sum he craves might we wage war.

DEL BOSCO     Will knights of Malta be in league with Turks,
              And buy it basely too for sums of gold?
              My lord, remember that, to Europe's shame,              30
              The Christian Isle of Rhodes, from whence you came,
              Was lately lost, and you were stated here
              To be at deadly enmity with Turks.

FERNEZE       Captain, we know it; but our force is small.

DEL BOSCO  What is the sum that Calymath requires?

FERNEZE  A hundred thousand crowns.

DEL BOSCO  My lord and king hath title to this isle,
And he means quickly to expel you hence;
Therefore be rul'd by me, and keep the gold:
I'll write unto his majesty for aid,                    40
And not depart until I see you free.

FERNEZE  On this condition shall thy Turks be sold –
Go, officers, and set them straight in show –

                                        [*exeunt Officers*

Bosco, thou shalt be Malta's general;
We and our warlike knights will follow thee
Against these barbarous misbelieving Turks.

DEL BOSCO  So shall you imitate those you succeed;
For, when their hideous force environ'd Rhodes,
Small though the number was that kept the town,
They fought it out, and not a man surviv'd                    50
To bring the hapless news to Christendom.

FERNEZE  So will we fight it out; come, let's away.
Proud daring Calymath, instead of gold,
We'll send thee bullets wrapt in smoke and fire:
Claim tribute where thou wilt, we are resolv'd –
Honour is bought with blood, and not with gold.

                                        [*exeunt*


                    SCENE 3

        *Enter Officers, with* ITHAMORE *and other Slaves*

1 OFFICER  This is the market-place; here let 'em stand:
Fear not their sale, for they'll be quickly bought.

2 OFFICER  Every one's price is written on his back,
And so much must they yield, or not be sold.

1 OFFICER  Here comes the Jew: had not his goods been seiz'd,
He'd give us present money for them all.

                    *Enter* BARABAS

BARABAS  In spite of these swine-eating Christians,
(Unchosen nation, never circumcis'd,
Poor villains, such as were ne'er thought upon

Till Titus and Vespasian conquer'd us)                    10
Am I become as wealthy as I was.
They hop'd my daughter would ha' been a nun;
But she's at home, and I have bought a house
As great and fair as is the governor's:
And there, in spite of Malta, will I dwell,
Having Ferneze's hand; whose heart I'll have,
Ay, and his son's too, or it shall go hard.
I am not of the tribe of Levi, I,
That can so soon forget an injury.
We Jews can fawn like spaniels when we please;   20
And when we grin we bite; yet are our looks
As innocent and harmless as a lamb's.
I learn'd in Florence how to kiss my hand,
Heave up my shoulders when they call me dog,
And duck as low as any bare-foot friar;
Hoping to see them starve upon a stall,
Or else be gather'd for in our synagogue,
That, when the offering-basin comes to me,
Even for charity I may spit into't –
Here comes Don Lodowick, the governor's son,   30
One that I love for his good father's sake.

*Enter* LODOWICK

LODOWICK I hear the wealthy Jew walked this way:
I'll seek him out, and so insinuate,
That I may have a sight of Abigail,
For Don Mathias tells me she is fair.
BARABAS [*aside*] Now will I show myself to have more of the
serpent than the dove; that is, more knave than fool.
LODOWICK Yond' walks the Jew: now for fair Abigail.
BARABAS [*aside*] Ay, ay, no doubt but she's at your command.
LODOWICK Barabas, thou know'st I am the governor's son.   40
BARABAS I would you were his father too, sir! That's all the harm
I wish you. [*aside*] The slave looks like a hog's cheek
new singed.
LODOWICK Whither walk'st thou, Barabas?
BARABAS No further: 'tis a custom held with us,
That when we speak with Gentiles like to you,

We turn into the air to purge ourselves;
For unto us the promise doth belong.

LODOWICK  Well, Barabas, canst help me to a diamond?

BARABAS  O, sir, your father had my diamonds:                    50
Yet I have one left that will serve your turn –
[aside] I mean my daughter; but, ere he shall have her,
I'll sacrifice her on a pile of wood:
I ha' the poison of the city for him,
And the white leprosy.

LODOWICK  What sparkle does it give without a foil?

BARABAS  The diamond that I talk of ne'er was foil'd –
[aside] But, when he touches it, it will be foil'd –
[aloud] Lord Lodowick, it sparkles bright and fair.

LODOWICK  Is it square or pointed? Pray, let me know.            60

BARABAS  Pointed it is, good sir, [aside] but not for you.

LODOWICK  I like it much the better.

BARABAS                              So do I too.

LODOWICK  How shows it by night?

BARABAS                              Outshines Cynthia's rays –
[aside] You'll like it better far o' nights than days.

LODOWICK  And what's the price?

BARABAS                    [aside] Your life, an if you have it.
[aloud] O my lord, we will not jar about the price:
come to my house, and I will give't your honour –
[aside] with a vengeance.

LODOWICK  No, Barabas, I will deserve it first.

BARABAS  Good sir,                                                70
Your father has deserv'd it at my hands,
Who, of mere charity and Christian ruth,
To bring me to religious purity,
And, as it were, in catechising sort,
To make me mindful of my mortal sins,
Against my will, and whether I would or no,
Seiz'd all I had, and thrust me out of doors,
And made my house a place for nuns most chaste.

LODOWICK  No doubt your soul shall reap the fruit of it.

BARABAS  Ay, but, my lord, the harvest is far off:              80
And yet I know the prayers of those nuns
And holy friars, having money for their pains,

|  | Are wondrous – [aside] and indeed do no man good – |
|---|---|
|  | And, seeing they are not idles but still doing, |
|  | 'Tis likely they in time may reap some fruit, |
|  | I mean, in fullness of perfection. |
| LODOWICK | Good Barabas, glance not at our holy nuns. |
| BARABAS | No, but I do it through a burning zeal – |
|  | [aside] Hoping ere long to set the house a-fire; |
|  | For, though they do a while increase and multiply, 90 |
|  | I'll have a saying to that nunnery – |
|  | [aloud] As for the diamond, sir, I told you of, |
|  | Come home, and there's no price shall make us part, |
|  | Even for your honourable father's sake – |
|  | [aside] It shall go hard but I will see your death – |
|  | [aloud] But now I must be gone to buy a slave. |
| LODOWICK | And, Barabas, I'll bear thee company. |
| BARABAS | Come, then; here's the market place – |
|  | What's the price of this slave? Two hundred crowns! |
|  | Do the Turks weigh so much?      100 |
| I OFFICER | Sir, that's his price. |
| BARABAS | What, can he steal, that you demand so much? |
|  | Belike he has some new trick for a purse: |
|  | An if he has, he is worth three hundred plates! |
|  | So that, being bought, the town seal might be got |
|  | To keep him for his life-time from the gallows: |
|  | The sessions-day is critical to thieves, |
|  | And few or none escape but by being purg'd. |
| LODOWICK | Rat'st thou this Moor but at two hundred plates? |
| I OFFICER | No more, my lord.      110 |
| BARABAS | Why should this Turk be dearer than that Moor? |
| I OFFICER | Because he is young, and has more qualities. |
| BARABAS | What, hast the philosopher's stone? An thou hast, break my head with it, I'll forgive thee. |
| SLAVE | No, sir; I can cut and shave. |
| BARABAS | Let me see, sirrah; are you not an old shaver? |
| SLAVE | Alas, sir, I am a very youth! |
| BARABAS | A youth! I'll buy you, and marry you to Lady Vanity, if you do well. |
| SLAVE | I will serve you, sir.      120 |

| BARABAS | Some wicked trick or other: it may be, under colour of shaving, thou'lt cut my throat for my goods. Tell me, hast thou thy health well? |
| SLAVE | Ay, passing well. |
| BARABAS | So much the worse: I must have one that's sickly, an't be but for sparing victuals: 'tis not a stone of beef a day will maintain you in these chops — Let me see one that's somewhat leaner. |
| I OFFICER | Here's a leaner; how like you him? |
| BARABAS | Where wast thou born?                                    130 |
| ITHAMORE | In Thrace; brought up in Arabia. |
| BARABAS | So much the better; thou art for my turn. An hundred crowns? I'll have him; there's the coin. |

[gives money

| I OFFICER | Then mark him, sir, and take him hence. |
| BARABAS | [aside] Ay, mark him, you were best; for this is he That by my help shall do much villany — [aloud] My lord, farewell — Come, sirrah; you |

are mine —

As for the diamond, it shall be yours:
I pray, sir, be no stranger at my house;
All that I have shall be at your command.                    140

*Enter* MATHIAS *and* KATHARINE

| MATHIAS | What make the Jew and Lodowick so private? [aside] I fear me 'tis about fair Abigail. |
| BARABAS | [to Lodowick] Yonder comes Don Mathias; let us stay: He loves my daughter, and she holds him dear; But I have sworn to frustrate both their hopes, And be reveng'd upon the — [aside] governor. |

[exit Lodowick

| KATHARINE | This Moor is comeliest, is he not? Speak, son. |
| MATHIAS | No, this is the better, mother; view this well. |
| BARABAS | Seem not to know me here before your mother, Lest she mistrust the match that is in hand:               150 When you have brought her home, come to |

my house;

Think of me as thy father; son, farewell.

| MATHIAS | But wherefore talk'd Don Lodowick with you? |

BARABAS    Tush, man! We talk'd of diamonds, not of Abigail.

KATHARINE  Tell me, Mathias, is not that the Jew?

BARABAS    As for the comment on the Maccabees,
           I have it, sir, and 'tis at your command.

MATHIAS    Yes, madam, and my talk with him was
           About the borrowing of a book or two.

KATHARINE  Converse not with him; he is cast off from heaven —
           Thou hast thy crowns, fellow — Come, let's away.

MATHIAS    Sirrah Jew, remember the book.

BARABAS                                    Marry, will I, sir.
                      [exeunt Katharine and Mathias

I OFFICER  Come, I have made a reasonable market; let's away.
                      [exeunt Officers with Slaves

BARABAS    Now let me know thy name, and therewithal
           Thy birth, condition, and profession.

ITHAMORE   Faith, sir, my birth is but mean; my name's
           Ithamore; my profession what you please.

BARABAS    Hast thou no trade? Then listen to my words,
           And I will teach [thee] that shall stick by thee:
           First, be thou void of these affections,            170
           Compassion, love, vain hope, and heartless fear;
           Be mov'd at nothing, see thou pity none,
           But to thyself smile when the Christians moan.

ITHAMORE   O, brave, master! I worship your nose for this.

BARABAS    As for myself, I walk abroad o' nights,
           And kill sick people groaning under walls:
           Sometimes I go about and poison wells;
           And now and then, to cherish Christian thieves,
           I am content to lose some of my crowns,
           That I may, walking in my gallery,                  180
           See 'em go pinion'd along by my door.
           To practise first upon the Italian,
           There I enrich'd the priests with burials,
           And always kept the sexton's arms in ure
           With digging graves and ringing dead men's knells:
           And, after that, was I an engineer,
           And in the wars 'twixt France and Germany,
           Under pretence of helping Charles the Fifth,
           Slew friend and enemy with my stratagems:

Then, after that, was I an usurer,                    190
And with extorting, cozening, forfeiting,
And tricks belonging unto brokery,
I fill'd the gaols with bankrupts in a year,
And with young orphans planted hospitals;
And every moon made some or other mad.
And now and then one hang himself for grief,
Pinning upon his breast a long great scroll
How I with interest tormented him.
But mark how I am blest for plaguing them –
I have as much coin as will buy the town.             200
But tell me now, how hast thou spent thy time?

ITHAMORE  Faith, master,
In setting Christian villages on fire,
Chaining of eunuchs, binding galley slaves.
One time I was an hostler at an inn
And in the night time secretly would I steal
To travellers' chambers, and there cut their throats.
Once at Jerusalem, where the pilgrims kneel'd,
I strewed powder on the marble stones,
And therewithal their knees would rankle so,          210
That I have laugh'd a-good to see the cripples
Go limping home to Christendom on stilts.

BARABAS  Why, this is something: make account of me
As of thy fellow; we are villains both;
Both circumcised; we hate Christians both:
Be true and secret; thou shalt want no gold.
But stand aside; here comes Don Lodowick.

*Enter* LODOWICK

LODOWICK  O, Barabas, well met;
Where is the diamond you told me of?

BARABAS  I have it for you, sir: please you walk in with me –
What, ho, Abigail! Open the door, I say!

*Enter* ABIGAIL, *with letters*

ABIGAIL  In good time, father; here are letters come
From Ormus, and the post stays here within.

BARABAS  Give me the letters – Daughter, do you hear?
Entertain Lodowick, the governor's son,

With all the courtesy you can afford,
Provided that you keep your maidenhead:
[*aside to her*] Use him as if he were a Philistine;
Dissemble, swear, protest, vow love to him:
He is not of the seed of Abraham –                    230
[*aloud*] I am a little busy, sir; pray, pardon me –
Abigail, bid him welcome for my sake.

ABIGAIL    For your sake and his own he's welcome hither.

BARABAS    Daughter, a word more:
[*aside to her*]        Kiss him, speak him fair,
And like a cunning Jew so cast about,
That ye be both made sure ere you come out.

ABIGAIL    O father, Don Mathias is my love!

BARABAS    [*aside to her*] I know it: yet I say, make love to him;
Do, it is requisite it should be so –
[*aloud*] Nay, on my life, it is my factor's hand;        240
But go you in, I'll think upon the account.
                    [*exeunt Abigail and Lodowick into the house*
The account is made, for Lodovico dies.
My factor sends me word that a merchant's fled
That owes me for a hundred tun of wine:
I weigh it thus much! [*snapping his fingers*] I have
                        wealth enough;
For now by this has he kiss'd Abigail,
And she vows love to him, and he to her.
As sure as heaven rain'd manna for the Jews,
So sure shall he and Don Mathias die:
His father was my chiefest enemy.                    250

               *Enter* MATHIAS

Whither goes Don Mathias? Stay a while.

MATHIAS    Whither, but to my fair love Abigail?

BARABAS    Thou know'st, and heaven can witness it is true,
That I intend my daughter shall be thine.

MATHIAS    Ay, Barabas, or else thou wrong'st me much.

BARABAS    O, heaven forbid I should have such a thought!
Pardon me though I weep: the governor's son
Will, whether I will or no, have Abigail;
He sends her letters, bracelets, jewels, rings.

| MATHIAS | Does she receive them? | 260 |

BARABAS   She! No, Mathias, no, but sends them back;
          And, when he comes, she locks herself up fast;
          Yet through the key-hole will he talk to her,
          While she runs to the window looking out
          When you should come and hale him from the door.

MATHIAS   O treacherous Lodowick!

BARABAS   Even now, as I came home, he slipt me in,
          And I am sure he is with Abigail.

MATHIAS   I'll rouse him thence.

BARABAS   Not for all Malta; therefore sheathe your sword;     270
          If you love me, no quarrels in my house;
          But steal you in, and seem to see him not:
          I'll give him such a warning ere he goes,
          As he shall have small hopes of Abigail.
          Away, for here they come.

                *Re-enter* LODOWICK *and* ABIGAIL

MATHIAS   What, hand in hand! I cannot suffer this.

BARABAS   Mathias, as thou lov'st me, not a word.

MATHIAS   Well, let it pass; another time shall serve.

                                          [*exit into the house*

LODOWICK  Barabas, is not that the widow's son?

BARABAS   Ay, and take heed, for he hath sworn your death.

LODOWICK  My death! What, is the base-born peasant mad?

BARABAS   No, no; but happily he stands in fear
          Of that which you, I think, ne'er dream upon –
          My daughter here, a paltry silly girl.

LODOWICK  Why, loves she Don Mathias?

BARABAS   Doth she not with her smiling answer you?

ABIGAIL   [*aside*] He has my heart; I smile against my will.

LODOWICK  Barabas, thou know'st I have lov'd thy daughter long.

BARABAS   And so has she done you, even from a child.

LODOWICK  And now I can no longer hold my mind.              290

BARABAS   Nor I the affection that I bear to you.

LODOWICK  This is thy diamond; tell me, shall I have it?

BARABAS   Win it, and wear it; it is yet unsoil'd.
          O, that I know your lordship would disdain
          To marry with the daughter of a Jew:

|               | And yet I'll give her many a golden cross, |     |
|---------------|---------------------------------------------|-----|
|               | With Christian posies round about the ring. |     |
| LODOWICK      | 'Tis not thy wealth, but her that I esteem; |     |
|               | Yet crave I thy consent.                    |     |
| BARABAS       | And mine you have; yet let me talk to her — | 300 |
|               | [aside to her] This offspring of Cain, this Jebusite, |     |
|               | That never tasted of the Passover,          |     |
|               | Nor e'er shall see the land of Canaan,      |     |
|               | Nor our Messias that is yet to come;        |     |
|               | This gentle maggot, Lodowick, I mean,       |     |
|               | Must be deluded: let him have thy hand,     |     |
|               | But keep thy heart till Don Mathias comes.  |     |
| ABIGAIL       | What, shall I be betroth'd to Lodowick?     |     |
| BARABAS       | [aside to her] It's no sin to deceive a Christian; |     |
|               | For they themselves hold it a principle,    | 310 |
|               | Faith is not to be held with heretics:      |     |
|               | But all are heretics that are not Jews;     |     |
|               | This follows well, and therefore, daughter, fear not. |     |
|               | [aloud] I have entreated her and she will grant. |     |
| LODOWICK      | Then, gentle Abigail, plight thy faith to me. |     |
| ABIGAIL       | I cannot choose, seeing my father bids:     |     |
|               | Nothing but death shall part my love and me. |     |
| LODOWICK      | Now have I that for which my soul hath long'd. |     |
| BARABAS       | [aside] So have not I; but yet I hope I shall. |     |
| ABIGAIL       | [aside] O wretched Abigail, what hast thou done? | 320 |
| LODOWICK      | Why on the sudden is your colour chang'd?   |     |
| ABIGAIL       | I know not: but farewell; I must be gone.   |     |
| BARABAS       | Stay her, but let her not speak one word more. |     |
| LODOWICK      | Mute o' the sudden! Here's a sudden change. |     |
| BARABAS       | O, muse not at it; 'tis the Hebrews' guise, |     |
|               | That maidens new-betrothed should weep a while: |     |
|               | Trouble her not; sweet Lodowick, depart:    |     |
|               | She is thy wife, and thou shalt be mine heir. |     |
| LODOWICK      | O, is't the custom? Then I am resolv'd:     |     |
|               | But rather let the brightsome heavens be dim, | 330 |
|               | And nature's beauty choke with stifling clouds, |     |
|               | Than my fair Abigail should frown on me —   |     |
|               | There comes the villain; now I'll be reveng'd. |     |

*Re-enter* MATHIAS

| | |
|---|---|
| BARABAS | Be quiet, Lodowick; it is enough |
| | That I have made thee sure to Abigail. |
| LODOWICK | Well, let him go.                    [*exit* |
| BARABAS | Well, but for me, as you went in at doors |
| | You had been stabb'd: but not a word on't now: |
| | Here must no speeches pass, nor swords be drawn. |
| MATHIAS | Suffer me, Barabas, but to follow him.          340 |
| BARABAS | No; so shall I, if any hurt be done, |
| | Be made an accessary of your deeds: |
| | Revenge it on him when you meet him next. |
| MATHIAS | For this I'll have his heart. |
| BARABAS | Do so. Lo, here I give thee Abigail! |
| MATHIAS | What greater gift can poor Mathias have? |
| | Shall Lodowick rob me of so fair a love? |
| | My life is not so dear as Abigail. |
| BARABAS | My heart misgives me, that, to cross your love, |
| | He's with your mother; therefore after him.          350 |
| MATHIAS | What, is he gone unto my mother? |
| BARABAS | Nay, if you will, stay till she comes herself. |
| MATHIAS | I cannot stay; for, if my mother come, |
| | She'll die with grief.          [*exit* |
| ABIGAIL | I cannot take my leave of him for tears. |
| | Father, why have you thus incens'd them both? |
| BARABAS | What's that to thee? |
| ABIGAIL |          I'll make 'em friends again. |
| BARABAS | You'll make 'em friends! Are there not Jews |
| |                              enow in Malta, |
| | But thou must dote upon a Christian? |
| ABIGAIL | I will have Don Mathias; he is my love.          360 |
| BARABAS | Yes, you shall have him – Go, put her in. |
| ITHAMORE | Ay, I'll put her in.          [*puts in Abigail* |
| BARABAS | Now tell me, Ithamore, how lik'st thou this? |
| ITHAMORE | Faith, master, I think by this |
| | You purchase both their lives: is it not so? |
| BARABAS | True; and it shall be cunningly perform'd. |
| ITHAMORE | O, master, that I might have a hand in this! |
| BARABAS | Ay, so thou shalt; 'tis thou must do the deed: |

Take this [*giving a letter*], and bear it to Mathias straight.
And tell him that it comes from Lodowick.                    370
ITHAMORE 'Tis poison'd, is it not?
BARABAS  No, no; and yet it might he done that way:
It is a challenge feign'd from Lodowick.
ITHAMORE Fear not; I will so set his heart a–fire
That he shall verily think it comes from him.
BARABAS  I cannot choose but like thy readiness:
Yet be not rash, but do it cunningly.
ITHAMORE As I behave myself in this, employ me hereafter.
BARABAS  Away, then!                          [*exit Ithamore*
So; now will I go in to Lodowick,                  380
And, like a cunning spirit, feign some lie,
Till I have set 'em both at enmity.
                                         [*exit*

## ACT THREE

### SCENE I

*Enter* BELLAMIRA

BELLAMIRA  Since this town was besieg'd, my gain grows cold:
    The time has been, that but for one bare night
    A hundred ducats have been freely given;
    But now against my will I must be chaste:
    And yet I know my beauty doth not fail.
    From Venice merchants, and from Padua
    Were wont to come rare-witted gentlemen,
    Scholars I mean, learned and liberal;
    And now, save Pilia-Borza, comes there none,
    And he is very seldom from my house;                    10
    And here he comes.

*Enter* PILIA-BORZA

PILIA-B.  Hold thee, wench, there's something for thee to spend.
                                 *[showing a bag of silver*

BELLAMIRA  'Tis silver; I disdain it.

PILIA-B.  Ay, but the Jew has gold,
    And I will have it, or it shall go hard.

BELLAMIRA  Tell me, how cam'st thou by this?

PILIA-B.  Faith, walking the back-lanes, through the gardens, I
    chanced to cast mine eye up to the Jew's counting-
    house, where I saw some bags of money, and in the
    night clambered up with my hooks; and, as I was
    taking my choice, I heard a rumbling in the house; so I
    took only this, and run my way – But here's the Jew's
    man.

BELLAMIRA  Hide the bag.

*Enter* ITHAMORE

PILIA-B.  Look not towards him, let's away. Zoons, what a
    looking thou keepest! Thou'lt betray's anon.
                     *[exeunt Bellamira and Pilia-Borza*

ITHAMORE  O, the sweetest face that ever I beheld! I know she is a
    courtesan by her attire: now would I give a hundred of

the Jew's crowns that I had such a concubine.
Well, I have deliver'd the challenge in such sort,     30
As meet they will and fighting die – brave sport!

[*exit*

## SCENE 2

*Enter* MATHIAS

MATHIAS     This is the place: now Abigail shall see
            Whether Mathias holds her dear or no.

*Enter* LODOWICK

LODOWICK [*looking at a letter*] What, dares the villain write
                                        in such base terms?
MATHIAS     Thou villain, durst thou court my Abigail?
LODOWICK    I did it; and revenge it, if thou dar'st!     [*they fight*

*Enter* BARABAS *above*

BARABAS     O, bravely fought! And yet they thrust not home.
            Now, Lodovico! Now, Mathias! – So;        [*both fall*
            So, now they have show'd themselves to be
                                        tall fellows.
[*cries within*]    Part 'em, part 'em!
BARABAS     Ay, part 'em now they are dead. Farewell, farewell
                                        [*exit above*

*Enter* FERNEZE, KATHARINE, *and Attendants*

FERNEZE     What sight is this? My Lodovico slain!     10
            These arms of mine shall be thy sepulchre.
KATHARINE Who is this? My son Mathias slain!
FERNEZE     O Lodowick, hadst thou perish'd by the Turk,
            Wretched Ferneze might have veng'd thy death!
KATHARINE Thy son slew mine, and I'll revenge his death.
FERNEZE     Look, Katharine, look! Thy son gave mine
                                        these wounds.
KATHARINE O, leave to grieve me! I am griev'd enough.
FERNEZE     O, that my sighs could turn to lively breath,
            And these my tears to blood, that he might live!
KATHARINE Who made them enemies?     20

| | |
|---|---|
| FERNEZE | I know not; and that grieves me most of all. |
| KATHARINE | My son lov'd thine. |
| FERNEZE | And so did Lodowick him. |
| KATHARINE | Lend me that weapon that did kill my son, |
| | And it shall murder me. |
| FERNEZE | Nay, madam, stay; that weapon was my son's, |
| | And on that rather should Ferneze die. |
| KATHARINE | Hold; let's inquire the causers of their deaths, |
| | That we may venge their blood upon their heads. |
| FERNEZE | Then take them up, and let them be interr'd |
| | Within one sacred monument of stone;                30 |
| | Upon which altar I will offer up |
| | My daily sacrifice of sighs and tears, |
| | And with my prayers pierce impartial heavens, |
| | Till they [reveal] the causers of our smarts, |
| | Which forc'd their hands divide united hearts. |
| | Come, Katharine; our losses equal are; |
| | Then of true grief let us take equal share. |

[*exeunt with the bodies*

### SCENE 3

*Enter* ITHAMORE

| | |
|---|---|
| ITHAMORE | Why, was there ever seen such villany, |
| | So neatly plotted, and so well perform'd? |
| | Both held in hand, and flatly both beguil'd? |

*Enter* ABIGAIL

| | |
|---|---|
| ABIGAIL | Why, how now, Ithamore! Why laugh'st thou so? |
| ITHAMORE | O mistress! Ha, ha, ha! |
| ABIGAIL | Why, what ail'st thou? |
| ITHAMORE | O, my master! |
| ABIGAIL | Ha! |
| ITHAMORE | O mistress, I have the bravest, gravest, secret, subtle, bottle nosed knave to my master, that ever gentleman had! |
| ABIGAIL | Say, knave, why rail'st upon my father thus? |
| ITHAMORE | O, my master has the bravest policy! |
| ABIGAIL | Wherein? |

ITHAMORE   Why, know you not?
ITHAMORE   Know you not of Mathias' and Don Lodowick's disaster?
ABIGAIL    No: what was it?
ITHAMORE   Why, the devil invented a challenge, my master writ
           it, and I carried it, first to Lodowick, and *imprimis* to
           Mathias;                                                      20
           And then they met, and, as the story says,
           In doleful wise they ended both their days.
ABIGAIL    And was my father furtherer of their deaths?
ITHAMORE   Am I Ithamore?
ABIGAIL    Yes.
ITHAMORE   So sure did your father write, and I carry the challenge.
ABIGAIL    Well, Ithamore, let me request thee this:
           Go to the new-made nunnery, and inquire
           For any of the friars of Saint Jaques,
           And say, I pray them come and speak with me.                 30
ITHAMORE   I pray, mistress, will you answer me to one question?
ABIGAIL    Well, sirrah, what is't?
ITHAMORE   A very feeling one: have not the nuns fine sport with
           the friars now and then?
ABIGAIL    Go to, Sirrah Sauce! Is this your question? Get ye gone.
ITHAMORE   I will, forsooth, mistress.                          [*exit*
ABIGAIL    Hard-hearted father, unkind Barabas!
           Was this the pursuit of thy policy,
           To make me show them favour severally,
           That by my favour they should both be slain?                 40
           Admit thou lov'dst not Lodowick for his sire,
           Yet Don Mathias ne'er offended thee:
           But thou wert set upon extreme revenge,
           Because the prior dispossess'd thee once,
           And couldst not venge it but upon his son;
           Nor on his son but by Mathias' means;
           Nor on Mathias but by murdering me:
           But I perceive there is no love on earth,
           Pity in Jews, nor piety in Turks –
           But here comes cursed Ithamore with the friar.               50

                 *Re-enter* ITHAMORE *with* FRIAR JACOMO

FRIAR J.   *Virgo, salve.*

ITHAMORE   When duck you?
ABIGAIL    Welcome, grave friar – Ithamore, be gone.

                                                  [*exit Ithamore*

           Know, holy sir, I am bold to solicit thee.
FRIAR J.   Wherein?
ABIGAIL    To get me be admitted for a nun.
FRIAR J.   Why, Abigail, it is not yet long since
           That I did labour thy admission,
           And then thou didst not like that holy life.

ABIGAIL    Then were my thoughts so frail and unconfirm'd   60
           As I was chain'd to follies of the world:
           But now experience, purchased with grief,
           Has made me see the difference of things.
           My sinful soul, alas, hath pac'd too long
           The fatal labyrinth of misbelief,
           Far from the sun that gives eternal life!
FRIAR J.   Who taught thee this?
ABIGAIL                        The abbess of the house,
           Whose zealous admonition I embrace:
           O, therefore, Jacomo, let me be one,
           Although unworthy, of that sisterhood!           70
FRIAR J.   Abigail, I will: but see thou change no more,
           For that will be most heavy to thy soul.
ABIGAIL    That was my father's fault.
FRIAR J.                        Thy father's! How?
ABIGAIL    Nay, you shall pardon me – [*aside*] O Barabas,
           Though thou deservest hardly at my hands,
           Yet never shall these lips bewray thy life!
FRIAR J.   Come, shall we go?
ABIGAIL                        My duty waits on you.

                                                  [*exeunt*

## SCENE 4

*Enter* BARABAS, *reading a letter*

BARABAS    What, Abigail become a nun again!
False and unkind! What, hast thou lost thy father?
And, all unknown and unconstrain'd of me,
Art thou again got to the nunnery?
Now here she writes, and wills me to repent:
Repentance! *Spurca!* What pretendeth this?
I fear she knows — 'tis so — of my device
In Don Mathias' and Lodovico's deaths:
If so, 'tis time that it be seen into;
For she that varies from me in belief,           10
Gives great presumption that she loves me not,
Or, loving, doth dislike of something done —
But who comes here?

*Enter* ITHAMORE

                O Ithamore, come near;
Come near, my love; come near, thy master's life,
My trusty servant, nay, my second self;
For I have now no hope but even in thee,
And on that hope my happiness is built.
When saw'st thou Abigail?

ITHAMORE                Today.

BARABAS                      With whom?

ITHAMORE  A friar.

BARABAS    A friar! False villain! He hath done the deed.

ITHAMORE  How, sir!

BARABAS        Why, made mine Abigail a nun.       20

ITHAMORE  That's no lie: for she sent me for him.

BARABAS    O unhappy day!
False, credulous, inconstant Abigail!
But let 'em go: and, Ithamore, from hence
Ne'er shall she grieve me more with her disgrace;
Ne'er shall she live to inherit aught of mine,
Be bless'd of me, nor come within my gates,
But perish underneath my bitter curse,

|              | Like Cain by Adam for his brother's death. |
|---|---|

ITHAMORE   O master —                                                    30

BARABAS   Ithamore, entreat not for her; I am mov'd,
And she is hateful to my soul and me:
And, 'less thou yield to this that I entreat,
I cannot think but that thou hat'st my life.

ITHAMORE   Who, I, master? Why, I'll run to some rock,
And throw myself headlong into the sea;
Why, I'll do anything for your sweet sake.

BARABAS   O trusty Ithamore! No servant, but my friend!
I here adopt thee for mine only heir:
All that I have is thine when I am dead;                          40
And, whilst I live, use half; spend as myself;
Here, take my keys — I'll give 'em thee anon;
Go buy thee garments; but thou shalt not want:
Only know this, that thus thou art to do —
But first go fetch me in the pot of rice
That for our supper stands upon the fire.

ITHAMORE   [aside] I hold my head, my master's hungry —
I go, sir.                                                          [exit

BARABAS   Thus every villain ambles after wealth,
Although he ne'er be richer than in hope —                       50
But, husht!

*Re-enter* ITHAMORE *with the pot*

ITHAMORE            Here 'tis, master.

BARABAS                     Well said, Ithamore!
What, hast thou brought the ladle with thee too?

ITHAMORE   Yes, sir; the proverb says, he that eats with the devil
had need of a long spoon, I have brought you a ladle.

BARABAS   Very well, Ithamore; then now be secret;
And, for thy sake, whom I so dearly love,
Now shalt thou see the death of Abigail,
That thou mayst freely live to be my heir.

ITHAMORE   Why, master, will you poison her with a mess of rice-
porridge? That will preserve life, make her round and
plump, and batten more than you are aware.

BARABAS   Ay, but, Ithamore, seest thou this?
It is a precious powder that I bought

Of an Italian, in Ancona, once,
Whose operation is to bind, infect,
And poison deeply, yet not appear
In forty hours after it is ta'en.

ITHAMORE How, master?

BARABAS Thus, Ithamore:
This even they use in Malta here — 'tis call'd    70
Saint Jaques' Even — and then, I say, they use
To send their alms unto the nunneries:
Amongst the rest, bear this, and set it there:
There's a dark entry where they take it in,
Where they must neither see the messenger,
Nor make inquiry who hath sent it them.

ITHAMORE How so?

BARABAS Belike there is some ceremony in't.
There, Ithamore, must thou go place this pot:
Stay; let me spice it first.    80

ITHAMORE Pray, do, and let me help you, master. Pray, let me
taste first.

BARABAS Prithee, do. [*Ithamore tastes*] What say'st thou now?

ITHAMORE Troth, master, I'm loath such a pot of pottage should
be spoiled.

BARABAS Peace, Ithamore! 'Tis better so than spar'd.
[*puts the powder into the pot*
Assure thyself thou shalt have broth by the eye:
My purse, my coffer, and myself is thine.

ITHAMORE Well, master, I go.

BARABAS Stay; first let me stir it, Ithamore.    90
As fatal be it to her as the draught
Of which great Alexander drunk, and died;
And with her let it work like Borgia's wine,
Whereof his sire the Pope was poisoned!
In few, the blood of Hydra, Lerna's bane,
The juice of hebon and Cocytus' breath,
And all the poisons of the Stygian pool,
Break from the fiery kingdom, and in this
Vomit your venom, and envenom her
That, like a fiend, hath left her father thus!    100

ITHAMORE  [*aside*] What a blessing has he given't! Was ever pot of
rice-porridge so sauced? What shall I do with it?

BARABAS  O my sweet Ithamore, go set it down;
And come again as soon as thou hast done,
For I have other business for thee.

ITHAMORE  Here's a drench to poison a whole stable of Flanders
mares: I'll carry't to the nuns with a powder.

BARABAS  And the horse-pestilence to boot: away!

ITHAMORE  I am gone:
Pay me my wages, for my work is done.          110

[*exit with the pot*

BARABAS  I'll pay thee with a vengeance, Ithamore.

[*exit*


## SCENE 5

*Enter* FERNEZE, MARTIN DEL BOSCO, *Knights, and Basso*

FERNEZE  Welcome, great basso: how fares Calymath?
What wind drives you thus into Malta-road?

BASSO  The wind that bloweth all the world besides,
Desire of gold.

FERNEZE  Desire of gold, great sir!
That's to be gotten in the Western Inde:
In Malta are no golden minerals.

BASSO  To you of Malta thus saith Calymath:
The time you took for respite is at hand
For the performance of your promise pass'd;          10
And for the tribute money I am sent.

FERNEZE  Basso, in brief, shalt have no tribute here,
Nor shall the heathens live upon our spoil:
First will we raze the city-walls ourselves,
Lay waste the island, hew the temples down,
And, shipping off our goods to Sicily,
Open an entrance for the wasteful sea,
Whose billows, beating the resistless banks,
Shall overflow it with their refluence.

BASSO  Well, governor, since thou hast broke the league          20
By flat denial of the promis'd tribute,

         Talk not of razing down your city-walls;
         You shall not need trouble yourselves so far,
         For Selim Calymath shall come himself,
         And with brass bullets batter down your towers,
         And turn proud Malta to a wilderness,
         For these intolerable wrongs of yours:
         And so farewell.

FERNEZE        Farewell.                       *[exit Basso*
         And now, you men of Malta, look about,       30
         And let's provide to welcome Calymath:
         Close your port-cullis, charge your basilisks,
         And, as you profitably take up arms,
         So now courageously encounter them,
         For by this answer broken is the league,
         And naught is to be look'd for now but wars,
         And naught to us more welcome is than wars.

                                              *[exeunt*

## SCENE 6

*Enter* FRIAR JACOMO *and* FRIAR BARNADINE

FRIAR J.       O brother, brother, all the nuns are sick.
             And physic will not help them! They must die.
FRIAR B.       The abbess sent for me to be confess'd:
             O, what a sad confession will there be!
FRIAR J.       And so did fair Maria send for me:
             I'll to her lodging; hereabouts she lies.       *[exit*

*Enter* ABIGAIL

FRIAR B.       What, all dead, save only Abigail!
ABIGAIL       And I shall die too, for I feel death coming.
             Where is the friar that convers'd with me?
FRIAR B.       O, he is gone to see the other nuns.            10
ABIGAIL       I sent for him; but, seeing you are come,
             Be you my ghostly father: and first know,
             That in this house I liv'd religiously,
             Chaste, and devout, much sorrowing for my sins;
             But, ere I came –
FRIAR B.       What then?

| | |
|---|---|
| ABIGAIL | I did offend high heaven so grievously |
| | As I am almost desperate for my sins; |
| | And one offence torments me more than all. |
| | You knew Mathias and Don Lodowick?                    20 |
| FRIAR B. | Yes; what of them? |
| ABIGAIL | My father did contract me to 'em both; |
| | First to Don Lodowick: him I never lov'd; |
| | Mathias was the man that I held dear, |
| | And for his sake did I become a nun. |
| FRIAR B. | So: say how was their end? |
| ABIGAIL | Both, jealous of my love, envied each other; |
| | And by my father's practice, which is there |

*[gives writing*

| | |
|---|---|
| | Set down at large, the gallants were both slain. |
| FRIAR B. | O, monstrous villany!                    30 |
| ABIGAIL | To work my peace, this I confess to thee: |
| | Reveal it not; for then my father dies. |
| FRIAR B. | Know that confession must not be reveal'd; |
| | The canon-law forbids it, and the priest |
| | That makes it known, being degraded first, |
| | Shall be condemn'd, and then sent to the fire. |
| ABIGAIL | So I have heard; pray, therefore, keep it close. |
| | Death seizeth on my heart: ah, gentle friar, |
| | Convert my father that he may be sav'd, |
| | And witness that I die a Christian!                    *[dies* |
| FRIAR B. | Ay, and a virgin too; that grieves me most. |
| | But I must to the Jew, and exclaim on him, |
| | And make him stand in fear of me. |

*Re-enter* FRIAR JACOMO

| | |
|---|---|
| FRIAR J. | O brother, all the nuns are dead! Let's bury them. |
| FRIAR B. | First help to bury this; then go with me, |
| | And help me to exclaim against the Jew. |
| FRIAR J. | Why, what has he done? |
| FRIAR B. | A thing that makes me tremble to unfold. |
| FRIAR J. | What, has he crucified a child? |
| FRIAR B. | No, but a worse thing: 'twas told me in shrift:                    50 |
| | Thou know'st 'tis death, an if it be reveal'd. |
| | Come, let's away. |

*[exeunt*

# ACT FOUR

## SCENE I

*Enter* BARABAS *and* ITHAMORE. *Bells within.*

BARABAS   There is no music to a Christian's knell:
              How sweet the bells ring, now the nuns are dead,
              That sound at other times like tinkers' pans!
              I was afraid the poison had not wrought,
              Or, though it wrought, it would have done no good,
              For every year they swell, and yet they live:
              Now all are dead, not one remains alive.

ITHAMORE   That's brave, master: but think you it will not be
              known?

BARABAS   How can it, if we two be secret?

ITHAMORE   For my part, fear you not.            10

ARABAS   I'd cut thy throat, if I did.

ITHAMORE                     And reason too.
              But here's a royal monastery hard by;
              Good master, let me poison all the monks.

BARABAS   Thou shalt not need; for, now the nuns are dead,
              They'll die with grief.

ITHAMORE   Do you not sorrow for your daughter's death?

BARABAS   No, but I grieve because she liv'd so long,
              An Hebrew born, and would become a Christian:
              *Cazzo, diabolo!*

ITHAMORE   Look, look, master; here comes two religious cater-
              pillars.            20

*Enter* FRIAR JACOMO *and* FRIAR BERNADINE

BARABAS   I smelt 'em ere they came.

ITHAMORE   God-a-mercy, nose! Come, let's begone.

FRIAR B.   Stay, wicked Jew; repent, I say, and stay.

FRIAR J.   Thou hast offended, therefore must be damn d.

BARABAS   I fear they know we sent the poison'd broth.

ITHAMORE   And so do I, master; therefore speak 'em fair.

FRIAR B.   Barabas, thou hast —

FRIAR J.                  Ay, not that thou hast —

| | |
|---|---|
| BARABAS | True, I have money; what though I have? |
| FRIAR B. | Thou art a – |
| FRIAR J. | Ay, that thou art, a – |
| BARABAS | What needs all this? I know I am a Jew. |
| FRIAR B. | Thy daughter – |
| FRIAR J. | Ay, thy daughter – |
| BARABAS | O, speak not of her! Then I die with grief. |
| FRIAR B. | Remember that – |
| FRIAR J. | Ay, remember that – |
| BARABAS | I must needs say that I have been a great usurer. |
| FRIAR B. | Thou hast committed – |
| BARABAS | Fornication: but that was in another country; |

And besides the wench is dead.

FRIAR B.                                              Ay, but, Barabas,
Remember Mathias and Don Lodowick.

BARABAS   Why, what of them?

FRIAR B.   I will not say that by a forged challenge they met.

BARABAS   [aside to Ithamore] She has confess'd, and we
                                              are both undone,
My bosom inmate! But I must dissemble –
[aloud] O holy friars, the burden of my sins
Lie heavy on my soul! Then, pray you, tell me,
Is't not too late now to turn Christian?
I have been zealous in the Jewish faith,
Hard-hearted to the poor, a covetous wretch,
That would for lucre's sake have sold my soul;
A hundred for a hundred I have ta'en;
And now for store of wealth may I compare
With all the Jews in Malta: but what is wealth?
I am a Jew, and therefore am I lost.
Would penance serve [to atone] for this my sin,
I could afford to whip myself to death –

ITHAMORE   And so could I; but penance will not serve –

BARABAS   To fast, to pray, and wear a shirt of hair,
And on my knees creep to Jerusalem.
Cellars of wine, and sollars full of wheat
Warehouses stuff'd with spices and with drugs,
Whole chests of gold in bullion and in coin,
Besides, I know not how much weight in pearl,

30

40

50

60

|  | Orient and round, have I within my house; |
|--|--|
|  | At Alexandria merchandise untold; |
|  | But yesterday two ships went from this town, |
|  | Their voyage will be worth ten thousand crowns; |
|  | In Florence, Venice, Antwerp, London, Seville, 70 |
|  | Frankfort, Lubeck, Moscow, and where not, |
|  | Have I debts owing; and, in most of these, |
|  | Great sums of money lying in the banco; |
|  | All this I'll give to some religious house, |
|  | So I may be baptiz'd, and live therein. |
| FRIAR J. | O good Barabas, come to our house! |
| FRIAR B. | O, no, good Barabas, come to our house! |
|  | And Barabas, you know – |
| BARABAS | I know that I have highly sinn'd: |
|  | You shall convert me, you shall have all my wealth. |
| FRIAR J. | O Barabas, their laws are strict! |
| BARABAS | I know they are; and I will be with you. |
| FRIAR B. | They wear no shirts, and they go barefoot too. |
| BARABAS | Then 'tis not for me; and I am resolv'd |
|  | You shall confess me, and have all my goods. |
| FRIAR J. | Good Barabas, come to me. |
| BARABAS | You see I answer him, and yet he stays; |
|  | Bid him away, and go you home with me. |
| FRIAR J. | I'll be with you tonight. |
| BARABAS | Come to my house at one o'clock this night. 90 |
| FRIAR J. | You hear your answer, and you may be gone. |
| FRIAR B. | Why, go, get you away. |
| FRIAR J. | I will not go for thee. |
| FRIAR B. | Not! Then I'll make thee go. |
| FRIAR J. | How! Dost call me rogue? *[they fight* |
| ITHAMORE | Part 'em, master, part 'em |
| BARABAS | This is mere frailty: brethren, be content – |
|  | Friar Barnardine, go you with Ithamore: |
|  | You know my mind; let me alone with him. |
| FRIAR J. | Why does he go to thy house? Let him be gone. 100 |
| BARABAS | I'll give him something, and so stop his mouth. |
|  | *[exit Ithamore with Friar Barnardine* |
|  | I never heard of any man but he |
|  | Malign'd the order of the Jacobins; |

But do you think that I believe his words?
Why, brother, you converted Abigail;
And I am bound in charity to requite it,
And so I will. O Jacomo, fail not, but come.

FRIAR J.    But, Barabas, who shall be your godfathers?
For presently you shall be shriv'd.

BARABAS    Marry, the Turk shall be one of my godfathers,    110
But not a word to any of your convent.

FRIAR J.    I warrant thee, Barabas.    [exit

BARABAS    So, now the fear is past, and I am safe;
For he that shriv'd her is within my house:
What if I murder'd him ere Jacomo comes?
Now I have such a plot for both their lives,
As never Jew nor Christian knew the like:
One turn'd my daughter, therefore he shall die;
The other knows enough to have my life,
Therefore 'tis not requisite he should live.    120
But are not both these wise men, to suppose
That I will leave my house, my goods, and all,
To fast and be well whipt? I'll none of that.
Now, Friar Barnardine, I come to you:
I'll feast you, lodge you, give you fair words,
And after that, I and my trusty Turk –
No more, but so: it must and shall be done.

*Enter* ITHAMORE

Ithamore, tell me, is the friar asleep?

ITHAMORE    Yes; and I know not what the reason is,
Do what I can, he will not strip himself,    130
Nor go to bed, but sleeps in his own clothes:
I fear me he mistrusts what we intend.

BARABAS    No, 'tis an order which the friars use:
Yet, if he knew our meanings, could he scape?

ITHAMORE    No, none can hear him, cry he ne'er so loud.

BARABAS    Why, true; therefore did I place him there:
The other chambers open towards the street.

ITHAMORE    You loiter, master; wherefore stay we thus?
O, how I long to see him shake his heels!

BARABAS    Come on, sirrah:    140

Off with your girdle; make a handsome noose –

[*Ithamore takes off his girdle, and ties a noose on it*]

Friar, awake!

[*they put the noose round the Friar's neck*]

FRIAR B. What, do you mean to strangle me?

ITHAMORE Yes, 'cause you use to confess.

BARABAS Blame not us, but the proverb – Confess and be hanged – Pull hard.

FRIAR B. What, will you have my life?

BARABAS Pull hard, I say – You would have had my goods.

ITHAMORE Ay, and our lives too – therefore pull amain.

[*they strangle the friar*

'Tis neatly done, sir; here's no print at all.          150

BARABAS Then is it as it should be. Take him up

ITHAMORE Nay, master, be ruled by me a little. [*takes the body, sets it upright against the wall, and puts a staff in its hand*] So, let him lean upon his staff, excellent! He stands as if he were begging of bacon.

BARABAS Who would not think but that this friar liv'd? What time o' night is't now, sweet Ithamore?

ITHAMORE Towards one.

BARABAS Then will not Jacomo be long from hence.          [*exeunt*

*Enter* FRIAR JACOMO

FRIAR J. This is the hour wherein I shall proceed;          160
O happy hour wherein I shall convert
An infidel, and bring his gold into our treasury!
But soft! Is not this Barnardine? It is:
And, understanding I should come this way,
Stands here o' purpose, meaning me some wrong,
And intercept my going to the Jew –
Barnardine!
Wilt thou not speak? Thou think'st I see thee not;
Away, I'd wish thee, and let me go by:
No, wilt thou not? Nay, then, I'll force my way;          170
And, see, a staff stands ready for the purpose.

[*strikes down the body*

As thou lik'st that, stop me another time!

*Enter* BARABAS *and* ITHAMORE

| | |
|---|---|
| BARABAS | Why, how now, Jacomo! What hast thou done? |
| FRIAR J. | Why, stricken him that would have struck at me. |
| BARABAS | Who is it? Barnardine! Now, out, alas, he is slain! |
| ITHAMORE | Ay, master, he's slain; look how his brains drop out on's nose. |
| FRIAR J. | Good sirs, I have done't: but nobody knows it but you two; I may escape. |
| BARABAS | So might my man and I hang with you for company. |
| ITHAMORE | No; let us bear him to the magistrates. |
| FRIAR J. | Good Barabas, let me go. |
| BARABAS | No, pardon me; the law must have his course: |

       I must be forc'd to give in evidence,
       That, being importun'd by this Barnardine,
       To be a Christian, I shut him out,
       And there he sate: now I, to keep my word,
       And give my goods and substance to your house,
       Was up thus early, with intent to go
       Unto your friary, because you stay'd.     190

| | |
|---|---|
| ITHAMORE | Fie upon 'em! Master, will you turn Christian, when holy friars turn devils and murder one another? |
| BARABAS | No; for this example I'll remain a Jew: |

       Heaven bless me! What, a friar a murderer!
       When shall you see a Jew commit the like?

| | |
|---|---|
| ITHAMORE | Why, a Turk could ha' done no more. |
| BARABAS | Tomorrow is the sessions; you shall to it – |

       Come, Ithamore, let's help to take him hence.

| | |
|---|---|
| FRIAR J. | Villains, I am a sacred person; touch me not. |
| BARABAS | The law shall touch you; we'll but lead you, we:  200 |

       'Las, I could weep at your calamity!
       Take in the staff too, for that must be shown:
       Law wills that each particular be known.

                              *[exeunt*

## SCENE 2

*Enter* BELLAMIRA *and* PILIA-BORZA

BELLAMIRA Pilia-Borza, didst thou meet with Ithamore?

PILIA-B. I did.

BELLAMIRA And didst thou deliver my letter?

PILIA-B. I did.

BELLAMIRA And what thinkest thou? Will he come?

PILIA-B. I think so: and yet I cannot tell; for, at the reading of the letter, he looked like a man of another world.

BELLAMIRA Why so?

PILIA-B. That such a base slave as he should be saluted by such a tall man as I am, from such a beautiful dame as you.

BELLAMIRA And what said he?

PILIA-B. Not a wise word; only gave me a nod, as who should say, 'Is it even so?' And so I left him, being driven to a nonplus at the critical aspect of my terrible countenance.

BELLAMIRA And where didst meet him?

PILIA-B. Upon mine own free-hold, within forty foot of the gallows, conning his neck-verse, I take it, looking of a friar's execution; whom I saluted with an old hempen proverb, *Hodie tibi, cras mihi,* and so I left him to the mercy of the hangman: but, the exercise being done, see where he comes.

*Enter* ITHAMORE

ITHAMORE I never knew a man take his death so patiently as this friar; he was ready to leap off ere the halter was about his neck; and, when the hangman had put on his hempen tippet, he made such haste to his prayers, as if he had had another cure to serve. Well, go whither he will, I'll be none of his followers in haste: and, now I think on't, going to the execution, a fellow met me with a muschatoes like a raven's wing, and a dagger with a hilt like a warming pan; and he gave me a letter from one Madam Bellamira, saluting me in such sort as if he had meant to make clean my boots with his lips; the effect was, that I should come to her house: I

wonder what the reason is; it may be she sees more in
me than I can find in myself; for she writes further that
she loves me ever since she saw me; and who would
not requite such love? Here's her house; and here she
comes; and now would I were gone! I am not worthy
to look upon her.

PILIA-B.      This is the gentleman you writ to.                         40

ITHAMORE   [aside] Gentleman! He flouts me: what gentry can be in
a poor Turk of tenpence? I'll be gone.

BELLAMIRA  Is't not a sweet-faced youth, Pilia?

ITHAMORE   [aside]Again, sweet youth! Did not you sir, bring the
sweet youth a letter?

PILIA-B.      I did, sir, and from this gentlewoman, who, as myself
and the rest of the family, stand or fall at your service.

BELLAMIRA  Though woman's modesty should hale me back, I can
withhold no longer: welcome, sweet love.

ITHAMORE   [aside] Now am I clean, or rather foully, out of the way.

BELLAMIRA  Whither so soon?

ITHAMORE   [aside] I'll go steal some money from my master to
make me handsome – Pray, pardon me; I must go see a
ship discharged.

BELLAMIRA  Canst thou be so unkind to leave me thus?

PILIA-B.      An ye did but know how she loves you, sir!

ITHAMORE   Nay, I care not how much she loves me – Sweet
Bellamira, would I had my master's wealth for thy
sake!

PILIA-B.      And you can have it, sir, an if you please.            60

ITHAMORE   If 'twere above ground, I could, and would have it;
but he hides and buries it up, as partridges do their
eggs, under the earth.

PILIA-B.      And is't not possible to find it out?

ITHAMORE   By no means possible.

BELLAMIRA  [aside to Pilia-Borza] What shall we do with this base
villain, then?

PILIA-B.      [aside to her] Let me alone; do but you speak him fair –
But you know some secrets of the Jew,
Which, if they were reveal'd, would do him harm.   70

ITHAMORE   Ay, and such as – go to, no more! I'll make him send
me half he has, and glad he scapes so too: I'll write unto

              him; we'll have money straight.

PILIA-B.     Send for a hundred crowns at least.

ITHAMORE     Ten hundred thousand crowns! [*writes*] *Master Barabas* –

PILIA-B.     Write not so submissively, but threatening him.

ITHAMORE     [*writes*] *Sirrah Barabas, send me a hundred crowns*.

PILIA-B.     Put in two hundred at least.

ITHAMORE     [*writes*] *I charge thee send me three hundred by this bearer, and
              this shall be your warrant: if you do not* – *no more, but so.* 80

PILIA-B.     Tell him you will confess.

ITHAMORE     [*writing*] *Otherwise I'll confess all* – Vanish, and return in
              a twinkle.

PILIA-B.     Let me alone, I'll use him in his kind.

ITHAMORE     Hang him, Jew!         [*exit Pilia-Borza with the letter*

BELLAMIRA     Now, gentle Ithamore, lie in my lap –
              Where are my maids? Provide a cunning banquet;
              Send to the merchant, bid him bring me silks;
              Shall Ithamore, my love, go in such rags?

ITHAMORE     And bid the jeweller come hither too.

BELLAMIRA     I have no husband; sweet, I'll marry thee.        90

ITHAMORE     Content: but we will leave this paltry land,
              And sail from hence to Greece, to lovely Greece –
              I'll be thy Jason, thou my golden fleece –
              Where painted carpets o'er the meads are hurl'd,
              And Bacchus' vineyards overspread the world;
              Where woods and forests go in goodly green –
              I'll be Adonis, thou shalt be Love's Queen –
              The meads, the orchards, and the primrose-lanes,
              Instead of sedge and reed, bear sugar-canes:
              Thou in those groves, by Dis above,        100
              Shalt live with me, and be my love.

BELLAMIRA     Whither will I not go with gentle Ithamore?

*Re-enter* PILIA-BORZA

ITHAMORE     How now! Hast thou the gold?

PILIA-B.     Yes.

ITHAMORE     But came it freely? Did the cow give down her milk
              freely?

PILIA-B.     At reading of the letter, he stared and stamped, and
              turned aside: I took him by the beard, and looked

upon him thus; told him he were best to send it: then
he hugged and embraced me.                          110

ITHAMORE Rather for fear than love.

PILIA-B. Then, like a Jew, he laughed and jeered, and told me
he loved me for your sake, and said what a faithful
servant you had been.

ITHAMORE The more villain he to keep me thus: here's goodly
'parel, is there not?

PILIA-B. To conclude, he gave me ten crowns.
                              [delivers the money to Ithamore

ITHAMORE But ten? I'll not leave him worth a grey groat. Give me
a ream of paper: we'll have a kingdom of gold for't.

PILIA-B. Write for five hundred crowns.                    120

ITHAMORE [writes] Sirrah Jew, as you love your life, send me five
hundred crowns, and give the bearer a hundred – Tell him I
must have't.

PILIA-B. I warrant, your worship shall have't.

ITHAMORE And, if he ask why I demand so much, tell him I scorn
to write a line under a hundred crowns.

PILIA-B. You'd make a rich poet, sir. I am gone.
                                      [exit with the letter

ITHAMORE Take thou the money; spend it for my sake.

BELLAMIRA 'Tis not thy money, but thyself I weigh:
Thus Bellamira esteems of gold;        [throws it aside
But thus of thee.                      [kisses him

ITHAMORE That kiss again! [aside] She runs division of my lips.
What an eye she casts on me! It twinkles like a star.

BELLAMIRA Come, my dear love, let's in and sleep together.

ITHAMORE O, that ten thousand nights were put in one, that we
might sleep seven years together afore we wake!

BELLAMIRA Come, amorous wag, first banquet, and then sleep.
                                              [exeunt

## SCENE 3

*Enter* BARABAS, *reading a letter*

BARABAS  *Barabas, send me three hundred crowns –*
Plain Barabas! O, that wicked courtesan!
He was not wont to call me Barabas –
*Or else I will confess –* ay, there it goes:
But, if I get him, *coupe de gorge* for that.
He sent a shaggy, tatter'd, staring slave,
That, when he speaks, draws out his grisly beard,
And winds it twice or thrice about his ear;
Whose face has been a grind-stone for men's swords;
His hands are hack'd, some fingers cut quite off,        10
Who, when he speaks, grunts like a hog, and looks
Like one that is employ'd in catzery
And cross-biting; such a rogue
As is the husband to a hundred whores;
And I by him must send three hundred crowns.
Well, my hope is, he will not stay there still;
And, when he comes – O, that he were but here!

*Enter* PILIA-BORZA

PILIA-B.  Jew, I must ha' more gold.
BARABAS  Why, want'st thou any of thy tale?
PILIA-B.  No; but three hundred will not serve his turn.        20
BARABAS  Not serve his turn, sir!
PILIA-B.  No, sir; and therefore I must have five hundred more.
BARABAS  I'll rather –
PILIA-B.  O, good words, sir, and send it you were best! See,
there's his letter.                               [*gives letter*
BARABAS  Might he not as well come as send? Pray, bid him
come and fetch it: what he writes for you, ye shall have
straight.
PILIA-B.  Ay, and the rest too, or else –
BARABAS  [*aside*] I must make this villain away [*aloud*] – Please
you dine with me, sir – [*aside*] and you shall be most
heartily poisoned.
PILIA-B.  No, God-a-mercy. Shall I have these crowns?

| BARABAS | I cannot do it; I have lost my keys. |
| PILIA-B. | O, if that be all, I can pick ope your locks. |
| BARABAS | Or climb up to my counting-house window: you know my meaning. |
| PILIA-B. | I know enough, and therefore talk not to me of your counting-house. The gold! Or know, Jew, it is in my power to hang thee. |
| BARABAS | [*aside*] I am betray'd —                                    40 |
|  | 'Tis not five hundred crowns that I esteem; |
|  | I am not mov'd at that: this angers me, |
|  | That he, who knows I love him as myself, |
|  | Should write in this imperious vein. Why, sir, |
|  | You know I have no child, and unto whom |
|  | Should I leave all, but unto Ithamore? |
| PILIA-B. | Here's many words, but no crowns: the crowns! |
| BARABAS | Commend me to him, sir, most humbly, |
|  | And unto your good mistress as unknown. |
| PILIA-B. | Speak, shall I have 'em, sir?                               50 |
| BARABAS | Sir, here they are —                    [*gives money* |
|  | [*aside*] O, that I should part with so much gold! |
|  | Here, take 'em, fellow, with as good a will — |
|  | [*aside*] As I would see thee hang'd. O, love stops |
|  |                                              my breath! |
|  | Never lov'd man servant as I do Ithamore. |
| PILIA-B. | I know it, sir. |
| BARABAS | Pray, when, sir, shall I see you at my house? |
| PILIA-B. | Soon enough to your cost, sir. Fare you well.    [*exit* |
| BARABAS | Nay, to thine own cost, villain, if thou com'st! |
|  | Was ever Jew tormented as I am?                             60 |
|  | To have a shag-rag knave to come [force from me] |
|  | Three hundred crowns, and then five hundred |
|  |                                              crowns! |
|  | Well; I must seek a means to rid 'em all, |
|  | And presently; for in his villany |
|  | He will tell all he knows, and I shall die for't. |
|  | I have it: |
|  | I will in some disguise go see the slave, |
|  | And how the villain revels with my gold. |
|  |                                              [*exit* |

## SCENE 4

*Enter* BELLAMIRA, ITHAMORE, *and* PILIA-BORZA

BELLAMIRA  I'll pledge thee, love, and therefore drink it off.

ITHAMORE  Say'st thou me so? Have at it! And do you hear –

[*whispers to her*

BELLAMIRA  Go to, it shall be so.

ITHAMORE  Of that condition I will drink it up:
Here's to thee.

BELLAMIRA                    Nay, I'll have all or none.

ITHAMORE  There, if thou lov'st me, do not leave a drop.

BELLAMIRA  Love thee! Fill me three glasses.

ITHAMORE  Three and fifty dozen: I'll pledge thee.

PILIA-B.  Knavely spoke, and like a knight-at-arms.

ITHAMORE  Hey, *Rivo Castiliano!* A man's a man.                    10

BELLAMIRA  Now to the Jew.

ITHAMORE  Ha! To the Jew; and send me money he were best.

PILIA-B.  What wouldst thou do, if he should send thee none?

ITHAMORE  Do nothing: but I know what I know; he's a murderer.

BELLAMIRA  I had not thought he had been so brave a man.

ITHAMORE  You knew Mathias and the governor's son; he and I
killed 'em both, and yet never touched 'em.

PILIA-B.  O, bravely done!

ITHAMORE  I carried the broth that poisoned the nuns; and he and
I – snicle hand too fast – strangled a friar.                    20

BELLAMIRA  You two alone?

ITHAMORE  We two, and 'twas never known, nor never shall be for
me.

PILIA-B.  [*to Bellamira*] This shall with me unto the governor.

BELLAMIRA  [*to Pilia-Borza*] And fit it should: but first let's ha'
more gold –

Come, gentle Ithamore, lie in my lap.

ITHAMORE  Love me little, love me long: let music rumble,
Whilst I in thy incony lap do tumble.

*Enter* BARABAS, *disguised as a French musician,*
*with a lute, and a nosegay in his hat*

BELLAMIRA  A French musician! Come, let's hear your skill.

| | |
|---|---|
| BARABAS | Must tuna my lute for sound, twang, twang, first.    30 |
| ITHAMORE | Wilt drink, Frenchman? Here's to thee with a – pox on this drunken hiccup! |
| BARABAS | Gramercy, monsieur. |
| BELLAMIRA | Prithee, Pilia-Borza, bid the fiddler give me the posy in his hat there. |
| PILIA-B. | Sirrah, you must give my mistress your posy. |
| BARABAS | *A votre commandement, madame.*            [*gives nosegay* |
| BELLAMIRA | How sweet, my Ithamore, the flowers smell! |
| ITHAMORE | Like thy breath, sweetheart; no violet like 'em. |
| PILIA-B. | Foh! Methinks they stink like a hollyhock.    40 |
| BARABAS | [*aside*] So, now I am reveng'd upon 'em all: The scent thereof was death; I poison'd it. |
| ITHAMORE | Play, fiddler, or I'll cut your cat's guts into chitterlings. |
| BARABAS | *Pardonnez moi,* be no in tune yet: so, now, now all be in. |
| ITHAMORE | Give him a crown, and fill me out more wine. |
| PILIA-B. | There's two crowns for thee: play.            [*gives money* |
| BARABAS | [*aside*] How liberally the villain gives me mine own gold!            [*plays* |
| PILIA-B. | Methinks he fingers very well. |
| BARABAS | [*aside*] So did you when you stole my gold.    50 |
| PILIA-B. | How swift he runs! |
| BARABAS | [*aside*] You run swifter when you threw my gold out of my window. |
| BELLAMIRA | Musician, hast been in Malta long? |
| BARABAS | Two, three, four month, madam. |
| ITHAMORE | Dost not know a Jew, one Barabas? |
| BARABAS | Very mush: monsieur, you no be his man? |
| PILIA-B. | His man! |
| ITHAMORE | I scorn the peasant: tell him so. |
| BARABAS | [*aside*] He knows it already.    60 |
| ITHAMORE | 'Tis a strange thing of that Jew, he lives upon pickled grasshoppers and sauced mushrooms. |
| BARABAS | [*aside*] What a slave's this! The governor feeds not as I do. |
| ITHAMORE | He never put on clean shirt since he was circumcised. |
| BARABAS | [*aside*] O rascal! I change myself twice a-day. |
| ITHAMORE | The hat he wears, Judas left under the elder when he hanged himself. |

| | |
|---|---|
| BARABAS | [*aside*] 'Twas sent me for a present from the Great Cham. 70 |
| PILIA-B. | A nasty slave he is – Whither now, fiddler? |
| BARABAS | *Pardonnez moi, monsieur,* me be no well. |
| PILIA-B. | Farewell, fiddler. [*exit Barabas*] One letter more to the Jew. |
| BELLAMIRA | Prithee, sweet love, one more, and write it sharp. |
| ITHAMORE | No, I'll send by word of mouth now – Bid him deliver thee a thousand crowns by the same token that the nuns loved rice, that Friar Barnardine slept in his own clothes; any of 'em will do it. |
| PILIA-B. | Let me alone to urge it, now I know the meaning. 80 |
| ITHAMORE | The meaning has a meaning. Come, let's in. To undo a Jew is charity, and not sin. |

[*exeunt*

# ACT FIVE

## SCENE I

*Enter* FERNEZE, *Knights,* MARTIN DEL BOSCO, *and Officers*

FERNEZE    Now, gentlemen, betake you to your arms,
And see that Malta be well fortified;
And it behoves you to be resolute;
For Calymath, having hover'd here so long,
Will win the town, or die before the walls.

I KNIGHT    And die he shall: for we will never yield.

*Enter* BELLAMIRA *and* PILIA-BORZA

BELLAMIRA    O, bring us to the governor!

FERNEZE    Away with her! She is a courtesan.

BELLAMIRA    Whatever I am, yet, governor, hear me speak:
I bring thee news by whom thy son was slain:    10
Mathias did it not; it was the Jew.

PILIA-B.    Who, besides the slaughter of these gentlemen,
Poison'd his own daughter and the nuns,
Strangled a friar, and I know not what
Mischief beside.

FERNEZE             Had we but proof of this –

BELLAMIRA    Strong proof, my lord: his man's now at my lodging
That was his agent; he'll confess it all.

FERNEZE    Go fetch him straight [*exeunt Officers*]. I always
                             fear'd that Jew.

*Re-enter* Officers *with* BARABAS *and* ITHAMORE

BARABAS    I'll go alone; dogs, do not hale me thus.

ITHAMORE    Nor me either; I cannot out-run you, constable – O,
my belly!

BARABAS    [*aside*] One dram of powder more had made all sure:
What a damn'd slave was I!

FERNEZE    Make fires, heat irons, let the rack be fetched.

I KNIGHT    Nay, stay, my Lord; 't may be he will confess.

BARABAS    Confess! What mean you, lords? Who should confess?

FERNEZE    Thou and thy Turk; 'twas you that slew my son.

ITHAMORE    Guilty, my lord, I confess. Your son and Mathias were

both contracted unto Abigail: [he] forged a counterfeit
challenge.                  30

BARABAS    Who carried that challenge?

ITHAMORE   I carried it, I confess; but who writ it? Marry, even he
that strangled Barnardine, poisoned the nuns and his
own daughter.

FERNEZE    Away with him! His sight is death to me.

BARABAS    For what, you men of Malta? Hear me speak.
She is a courtesan, and he a thief,
And he my bondman: let me have law;
For none of this can prejudice my life.

FERNEZE    Once more, away with him – You shall have law.   40

BARABAS    Devils, do your worst! [aside] I'll live in spite

of you –

[aloud] As these have spoke, so be it to their souls –
[aside] I hope the poison'd flowers will work anon.

[exeunt Officers with Barabas and Ithamore;<br/>Bellamira, and Pilia-Borza

Enter KATHARINE

KATHARINE   Was my Mathias murder'd by the Jew?
Ferneze, 'twas thy son that murder'd him.

FERNEZE    Be patient, gentle madam; it was he;
He forg'd the daring challenge made them fight.

KATHARINE   Where is the Jew? Where is that murderer?

FERNEZE    In prison, till the law has pass'd on him.

Re-enter First Officer

I OFFICER   My lord, the courtesan and her man are dead;      50
So is the Turk and Barabas the Jew.

FERNEZE    Dead?

I OFFICER        Dead, my lord, and here they bring his body.

DEL BOSCO   This sudden death of his is very strange.

Re-enter Officers, carrying BARABAS as dead

FERNEZE    Wonder not at it, sir; the heavens are just;
Their deaths were like their lives; then think

not of 'em.

Since they are dead, let them be buried:
For the Jew's body, throw that o'er the walls,
To be a prey for vultures and wild beasts –

So, now away and fortify the town.                                            60

        *[exeunt all, leaving Barabas on the floor*

BARABAS    [*rising*] What, all alone! Well fare, sleepy drink!
I'll be reveng'd on this accursed town;
For by my means Calymath shall enter in:
I'll help to slay their children and their wives,
To fire the churches, pull their houses down,
Take my goods too, and seize upon my lands.
I hope to see the governor a slave,
And, rowing in a galley, whipt to death.

      *Enter* CALYMATH, *Bassoes, and Turks*

CALYMATH   Whom have we there? A spy?

BARABAS    Yes, my good lord, one that can spy a place          70
Where you may enter, and surprise the town:
My name is Barabas; I am a Jew.

CALYMATH   Art thou that Jew whose goods we heard were sold
For tribute money?

BARABAS                The very same, my lord:
And since that time they have hir'd a slave, my man,
To accuse me of a thousand villanies:
I was imprisoned, but scap'd their hands.

CALYMATH   Didst break prison?

BARABAS    No, no:
I drank of poppy and cold mandrake juice;                                     80
And being asleep, belike they thought me dead,
And threw me on the walls: so, or how else,
The Jew is here, and rests at your command.

CALYMATH   'Twas bravely done: but tell me, Barabas,
Canst thou, as thou report'st, make Malta ours?

BARABAS    Fear not, my lord; for here, against the trench,
The rock is hollow, and of purpose digg'd,
To make a passage for the running streams
And common channels of the city.
Now, whilst you give assault unto the walls,                                   90
I'll lead five hundred soldiers through the vault,
And rise with them i' the middle of the town,
Open the gates for you to enter in;
And by this means the city is your own.

CALYMATH  If this be true, I'll make thee governor.
BARABAS   And, if it be not true, then let me die.
CALYMATH  Thou'st doom'd thyself – Assault it presently.

                                                    [exeunt


                        SCENE 2

        *Alarums within. Enter* CALYMATH, *Bassoes, Turks*
        *and* BARABAS; *with* FERNEZE *and Knights prisoners*

CALYMATH  Now vail your pride, you captive Christians,
          And kneel for mercy to your conquering foe:
          Now where's the hope you had of haughty Spain?
          Ferneze, speak; had it not been much better
          To [have] kept thy promise than be thus surpris'd?
FERNEZE   What should I say? We are captives, and must yield.
CALYMATH  Ay, villains, you must yield, and under Turkish yokes
          Shall groaning bear the burden of our ire –
          And, Barabas, as erst we promis'd thee,
          For thy desert we make thee governor;                10
          Use them at thy discretion.
BARABAS                              Thanks, my lord.
FERNEZE   O fatal day, to fall into the hands
          Of such a traitor and unhallow'd Jew!
          What greater misery could heaven inflict?
CALYMATH  'Tis our command – and, Barabas, we give,
          To guard thy person, these our Janizaries:
          Entreat them well as we have used thee –
          And now, brave bassoes, come: we'll walk about
          The ruin'd town, and see the wreck we made –
          Farewell, brave Jew, farewell, great Barabas!        20
BARABAS   May all good fortune follow Calymath!
                          [*Exeunt Calymath and Bassoes*
          And now, as entrance to our safety,
          To prison with the governor and these
          Captains, his consorts and confederates.
FERNEZE   O villain! Heaven will be reveng'd on thee.
BARABAS   Away! No more; let him not trouble me.
                          [*exeunt Turks with Ferneze and Knights*

Thus hast thou gotten, by thy policy,
No simple place, no small authority:
I now am governor of Malta; true –
But Malta hates me, and, in hating me,                    30
My life's in danger; and what boots it thee,
Poor Barabas, to be the governor,
Whenas thy life shall be at their command?
No, Barabas, this must be look'd into;
And, since by wrong thou gott'st authority,
Maintain it bravely by firm policy;
At least, unprofitably lose it not;
For he that liveth in authority,
And neither gets him friends nor fills his bags,
Lives like the ass that Aesop speaketh of,                    40
That labours with a load of bread and wine,
And leaves it off to snap on thistle tops:
But Barabas will be more circumspect.
Begin betimes; occasion's bald behind:
Slip not thine opportunity, for fear too late
Thou seek'st for much, but canst not compass it –
Within here!

*Enter* FERNEZE, *with a Guard*

FERNEZE          My lord?
BARABAS                              Ay, lord; thus slaves will learn.
Now, governor – stand by there, wait within –
                                        [*exeunt Guard*

This is the reason that I sent for thee:
Thou seest thy life and Malta's happiness                    50
Are at my arbitrement; and Barabas
At his discretion may dispose of both:
Now tell me governor, and plainly too,
What think'st thou shall become of it and thee?
FERNEZE          This, Barabas; since things are in thy power,
I see no reason but of Malta's wreck,
Nor hope of thee but extreme cruelty:
Nor fear I death, nor will I flatter thee.
BARABAS          Governor, good words; be not so furious.
'Tis not thy life which can avail me aught;                    60

Yet you do live, and live for me you shall:
And as for Malta's ruin, think you not
'Twas slender policy for Barabas
To dispossess himself of such a place?
For sith, as once you said, within this isle,
In Malta here, that I have got my goods,
And in this city still have had success,
And now at length am grown your governor,
Yourselves shall see it shall not be forgot;
For, as a friend not known but in distress,       70
I'll rear up Malta, now remediless.

FERNEZE    Will Barabas recover Malta's loss?
           Will Barabas be good to Christians?

BARABAS    What wilt thou give me, governor, to procure
           A dissolution of the slavish bands
           Wherein the Turk hath yok'd your land and you?
           What will you give me if I render you
           The life of Calymath, surprise his men,
           And in an out-house of the city shut
           His soldiers, till I have consum'd 'em all with fire?  80
           What will you give him that procureth this?

FERNEZE    Do but bring this to pass which thou pretendest,
           Deal truly with us as thou intimatest,
           And I will send amongst the citizens,
           And by my letters privately procure
           Great sums of money for thy recompense:
           Nay, more, do this, and live thou governor still.

BARABAS    Nay, do thou this, Ferneze, and be free:
           Governor, I enlarge thee; live with me;
           Go walk about the city, see thy friends:           90
           Tush, send not letters to 'em; go thyself,
           And let me see what money thou canst make:
           Here is my hand that I'll set Malta free;
           And thus we cast it: to a solemn feast
           I will invite young Selim Calymath,
           Where be thou present, only to perform
           One stratagem that I'll impart to thee,
           Wherein no danger shall betide thy life,

And I will warrant Malta free for ever.

FERNEZE    Here is my hand; believe me, Barabas,                    100
I will be there, and do as thou desirest.
When is the time?

BARABAS                    Governor, presently;
For Calymath, when he hath view'd the town,
Will take his leave, and sail toward Ottoman.

FERNEZE    Then will I, Barabas, about this coin,
And bring it with me to thee in the evening.

BARABAS    Do so; but fail not: now farewell, Ferneze —

                                                    [exit Ferneze

And thus far roundly goes the business:
Thus, loving neither, will I live with both,
Making a profit of my policy;                    110
And he from whom my most advantage comes,
Shall be my friend.
This is the life we Jews are us'd to lead;
And reason too, for Christians do the like.
Well, now about effecting this device;
First, to surprise great Selim's soldiers,
And then to make provision for the feast,
That at one instant all things may be done:
My policy detests prevention.
To what event my secret purpose drives,                    120
I know; and they shall witness with their lives.

                                                    [exeunt


## SCENE 3

*Enter* CALYMATH *and Bassoes*

CALYMATH    Thus have we view'd the city, seen the sack,
And caus'd the ruins to be new-repair'd,
Which with our bombards' shot and basilisks
We rent in sunder at our entry:
And, now I see the situation,
And how secure this conquer'd island stands,
Environ'd with the Mediterranean sea,
Strong countermin'd with other petty isles,

And, toward Calabria, back'd by Sicily
(Where Syracusian Dionysius reign'd),        10
Two lofty turrets that command the town,
I wonder how it could be conquered thus.

*Enter a Messenger*

MESSENG. From Barabas, Malta's governor, I bring
A message unto mighty Calymath:
Hearing his sovereign was bound for sea,
To sail to Turkey, to great Ottoman,
He humbly would entreat your majesty
To come and see his homely citadel,        20
And banquet with him ere thou leav'st the isle.

CALYMATH To banquet with him in his citadel!
I fear me, messenger, to feast my train
Within a town of war so lately pillag'd,
Will be too costly and too troublesome:
Yet would I gladly visit Barabas,
For well has Barabas deserv'd of us.

MESSENG. Selim, for that, thus saith the governor –
That he hath in his store a pearl so big,
So precious, and withal so orient,
As, be it valu'd but indifferently,
The price thereof will serve to entertain        30
Selim and all his soldiers for a month;
Therefore he humbly would entreat your highness
Not to depart till he has feasted you.

CALYMATH I cannot feast my men in Malta-walls,
Except he place his tables in the streets.

MESSENG. Know, Selim, that there is a monastery
Which standeth as an out-house to the town;
There will he banquet them; but thee at home,
With all thy bassoes and brave followers.

CALYMATH Well, tell the governor we grant his suit;        40
We'll in this summer-evening feast with him.

MESSENG. I shall, my lord.        [*exit*

CALYMATH And now, bold bassoes, let us to our tents,
And meditate how we may grace us best,
To solemnise our governor's great feast.        [*exeunt*

*Enter* FERNEZE, *Knights, and* MARTIN DEL BOSCO

| | |
|---|---|
| FERNEZE | In this, my countrymen, be rul'd by me: |
| | Have special care that no man sally forth |
| | Till you shall hear a culverin discharg'd |
| | By him that bears the linstock, kindled thus; |
| | Then issue out and come to rescue me,                     50 |
| | For happily I shall be in distress, |
| | Or you released of this servitude. |
| 1 KNIGHT | Rather than thus to live as Turkish thralls, |
| | What will we not adventure? |
| FERNEZE | On, then; be gone. |
| KNIGHTS | Farewell, grave governor. |

> [*exeunt, on one side, Knights and Martin
>     Del Bosco; on the other, Ferneze*

## SCENE 4

*Enter, above,* BARABAS, *with a hammer, very busy; and Carpenters*

| | |
|---|---|
| BARABAS | How stand the cords? How hang these hinges? Fast? |
| | Are all the cranes and pulleys sure? |
| 1 CARPENT. | All fast. |
| BARABAS | Leave nothing loose, all levell'd to my mind. |
| | Why, now I see that you have art, indeed: |
| | There, carpenters, divide that gold amongst you; |

> [*gives money*

| | |
|---|---|
| | Go, swill in bowls of sack and muscadine; |
| | Down to the cellar, taste of all my wines. |
| 1 CARPENT. | We shall, my lord, and thank you. [*exeunt Carpenters* |
| BARABAS | And, if you like them, drink your fill and die; |
| | For, so I live, perish may all the world!                  10 |
| | Now, Selim Calymath, return me word |
| | That thou wilt come, and I am satisfied. |

*Enter Messenger*

| | |
|---|---|
| | Now, sirrah; what, will he come? |
| MESSENG. | He will; and has commanded all his men |
| | To come ashore, and march through Malta-streets, |
| | That thou mayst feast them in thy citadel. |
| BARABAS | Then now are all things as my wish would have 'em; |

There wanteth nothing but the governor's pelf;
And see, he brings it.

*Enter* FERNEZE

                              Now governor, the sum?

FERNEZE    With free consent, a hundred thousand pounds.    20
BARABAS    Pounds say'st thou, governor? Well, since it is
                                        no more,
I'll satisfy myself with that; nay, keep it still,
For, if I keep not promise, trust not me:
And, governor, now partake my policy;
First, for his army, they are sent before,
Enter'd the monastery, and underneath
In several places are field-pieces pitch'd,
Bombards, whole barrels full of gunpowder,
That on the sudden shall dissever it,
And batter all the stones about their ears,    30
Whence none can possibly escape alive:
Now, as for Calymath and his consorts,
Here have I made a dainty gallery,
The floor whereof, this cable being cut,
Doth fall asunder, so that it doth sink
Into a deep pit past recovery.
Here, hold that knife [*throws down a knife*],
                    and, when thou seest he comes,
And with his bassoes shall be blithely set,
A warning-piece shall be shot off from the tower,
To give thee knowledge when to cut the cord,    40
And fire the house. Say, will not this be brave?
FERNEZE    O, excellent! Here, hold thee, Barabas;
I trust thy word; take what I promis'd thee.
BARABAS    No, governor; I'll satisfy thee first;
Thou shalt not live in doubt of anything.
Stand close, for here they come.        [*Ferneze retires*
                              Why, is not this
A kingly kind of trade, to purchase towns
By treachery, and sell 'em by deceit?
Now tell me, worldlings, underneath the sun
If greater falsehood ever has been done?    50

*Enter* CALYMATH *and Bassoes*

CALYMATH  Come, my companion-bassoes: see, I pray,
          How busy Barabas is there above
          To entertain us in his gallery:
          Let us salute him – Save thee, Barabas!

BARABAS   Welcome, great Calymath!

FERNEZE   [*aside*] How the slave jeers at him!

BARABAS   Will't please thee, mighty Selim Calymath,
          To ascend our homely stairs?

CALYMATH                                   Ay, Barabas –
          Come, bassoes, ascend.

FERNEZE              [*coming forward*] Stay, Calymath;
          For I will show thee greater courtesy                    60
          Than Barabas would have afforded thee.

KNIGHT    [*within*] Sound a charge there!

                    [*A charge sounded within: Ferneze cuts the cord;
                        the floor of the gallery gives way, and Barabas
                        falls into a cauldron placed in a pit*

*Enter Knights and* MARTIN DEL BOSCO

CALYMATH  How now! What means this?

BARABAS   Help, help me, Christians, help!

FERNEZE   See, Calymath! This was devis'd for thee.

CALYMATH  Treason, treason! Bassoes, fly!

FERNEZE   No, Selim, do not fly:
          See his end first, and fly then if thou canst.

BARABAS   O, help me, Selim! Help me, Christians!
          Governor, why stand you all so pitiless?                 70

FERNEZE   Should I in pity of thy plaints or thee,
          Accursed Barabas, base Jew, relent?
          No, thus I'll see thy treachery repaid,
          But wish thou hadst behav'd thee otherwise.

BARABAS   You will not help me, then?

FERNEZE                                   No, villain, no.

BARABAS   And, villains, know you cannot help me now –
          Then, Barabas, breathe forth thy latest fate,
          And in the fury of thy torments strive
          To end thy life with resolution –
          Know, governor, 'twas I that slew thy son –              80

I fram'd the challenge that did make them meet:
Know, Calymath, I aim'd thy overthrow:
And, had I but escap'd this stratagem,
I would have brought confusion on you all,
Damn'd Christian dogs, and Turkish infidels!
But now begins the extremity of heat
To pinch me with intolerable pangs:
Die, life! Fly, soul! Tongue, curse thy fill, and die!

[dies

CALYMATH Tell me, you Christians, what doth this portend?

FERNEZE This train he laid to have entrapp'd thy life;          90
Now, Selim, note the unhallow'd deeds of Jews;
Thus he determin'd to have handled thee,
But I have rather chose to save thy life.

CALYMATH Was this the banquet he prepar'd for us?
Let's hence, lest further mischief he pretended.

FERNEZE Nay, Selim, stay; for, since we have thee here,
We will not let thee part so suddenly:
Besides, if we should let thee go, all's one,
For with thy galleys couldst thou not get hence,
Without fresh men to rig and furnish them.          100

CALYMATH Tush, governor, take thou no care for that;
My men are all aboard,
And do attend my coming there by this.

FERNEZE Why, heard'st thou not the trumpet sound a charge?

CALYMATH Yes, what of that?

FERNEZE                          Why, then the house was fir'd,
Blown up, and all thy soldiers massacred.

CALYMATH O, monstrous treason!

FERNEZE                          A Jew's courtesy;
For he that did by treason work our fall,
By treason hath deliver'd thee to us:
Know, therefore, till thy father hath made good          110
The ruins done to Malta and to us,
Thou canst not part; for Malta shall be freed,
Or Selim ne'er return to Ottoman.

CALYMATH Nay, rather, Christians, let me go to Turkey,
In person there to mediate your peace:
To keep me here will naught advantage you.

FERNEZE          Content thee, Calymath, here thou must stay,
                 And live in Malta prisoner: for come all the world
                 To rescue thee, so will we guard us now,
                 As sooner shall they drink the ocean dry,          120
                 Than conquer Malta, or endanger us.
                 So, march away; and let due praise begin
                 Neither to Fate nor Fortune, but to Heaven.

                                                           [*exeunt*

## EPILOGUE SPOKEN AT COURT

It is our fear, dread sovereign, we have bin
Too tedious; neither can 't be less than sin
To wrong your princely patience: if we have,
Thus low dejected, we your pardon crave;
And, if aught here offend your ear or sight,
We only act and speak what others write.

## EPILOGUE TO THE STAGE
### AT THE COCK-PIT

In graving with Pygmalion to contend,
Or painting with Apelles, doubtless the end
Must be disgrace: our actor did not so –
He only aim'd to go, but not out-go.
Nor think that this day any prize was play'd;
Here were no bets at all, no wagers laid:
All the ambition that his mind doth swell
Is but to hear from you (by me) 'twas well.

# EDWARD THE SECOND

# INTRODUCTION

Marlowe's only foray into the history genre so popular during the 1590s, *Edward II*, is remarkable for its intertwining of sexual and national politics. On his accession to the English throne, Edward II recalls from France his banished favourite Piers Gaveston. While Edward is preoccupied with Gaveston, the nobles, led by Mortimer and Edward's estranged queen Isabella, rebel against him, and he is imprisoned, forced to abdicate, and ultimately murdered. It is an extraordinary play, caught between subversion and convention, and one in which clear interpretations of events are hard to sustain.

Framed by the deaths and successions of three kings – Edward I, II and III – the play's structural symmetry is striking. While Edward II is nominally at the play's centre, and it is his own death which concludes the play, his declining fortunes are mirrored in the rise and fall of Gaveston in the early part of the play, of Spenser and Baldock in the middle section, and of Isabella and Mortimer in the third part. The play's concern with shifting power relations is expressed through its structure, in which different players take, then pass on, stage importance. Ultimately, the funeral rituals for Edward at the end of the play reinstate a natural order of succession: the excessive and violent passions expressed both sexually and politically are spent, and the quieter notes of the new boy king's 'grief and innocency' take centre stage. The play opens with Gaveston reading the letter of Edward calling him back to England. It is significant for Edward's subsequent characterisation that his first words in the play are spoken by another: he is struggling to be at the heart of his play, as well as at the heart of government. Both Gaveston and Mortimer seek to control or overpower Edward, and it is their enmity, fuelled by their structural similarity, which motivates the plot. Both are characteristically Marlovian protagonists, asserting themselves above the limitations of their status to take over power and material wealth.

Marlowe's characteristic moral ambiguity is evident in the suspicious and uncertain world of the play. While the relationship between Edward and Gaveston is not explicitly condemned – indeed, it has been claimed as a strikingly positive representation for its time, of same-sex love – nor is it celebrated. Gaveston seems interested largely in luxury and sensual pleasures, and his wish to 'draw the pliant king which way I please' (1,1) suggests that a desire for self-advancement is an important aspect of his relationship with Edward. His interest in erotic entertainment, 'Italian masques [ . . . ] sweet speeches, comedies', in voyeuristic and luxurious pleasures, is established early on, and it is never clear that he returns Edward's fervent devotion. Although his presence close to the king is a source of friction with the nobles, Mortimer senior's surprising admission that 'mightiest kings have had their minions' (1,4) suggests that it is not necessarily the sexual nature of their association that is problematic. Rather, the barons complain about Gaveston on three counts: he is encouraging rash and lavish spending, draining the national coffers; his aesthetic interests promote a foreign influence on the English court; and, most significantly, he is too lowly-born to exercise such power over the king. On all three counts he disturbs the traditional structure of authority in which privilege and influence were the birthright of the landed and inherited native nobility.

Despite the fact that it is not primarily Edward's sexual antics which cost him the throne, the brutal manner of his death, in a terrible parody of the act of sodomy, identifies these behaviours as ultimately fatal. In despatching Edward by such means, the play may seem to endorse the negative constructions of male homosexual acts and to punish them with death – sodomy was, under Elizabethan law, a felony – but in fact deviant or uncontrolled sexuality becomes increasingly identified with heterosexuality as the play progresses. Far from being a distinct contast to Edward, Mortimer, his nemesis, is characterised as an adulterer, and his claims to act for the honour of the state and the maintenance of social order are critically undermined by this unnatural act of sexual, social and political rebellion. By the time Edward is being murdered in prison by the satanically named Lightborn, it is Isabella and Mortimer whose downfall is described as morally justified, evenly divinely sanctioned. The murderous sodomising of Edward literalises the usurpation of his throne by Mortimer, and it is Mortimer who is punished for this act. In a decisive *volte face*, sexual deviance and unnatural rebellion have been manoeuvred on to Mortimer, who claimed to be acting against them. Edward's decentring in the play, presaged by the ventriloquised words of his letter in the opening scene, ironically reaches its height at his death. His tragic status is only ever tentative.

Many comparisons have been made between *Edward II* and Shakespeare's play about usurpation and regicide, *Richard II*. One difference between these fruitfully similar plays is in Marlowe's presentation of Queen Isabella. Elsewhere in his plays, with the notable exception of *Dido Queen of Carthage*, women play minor roles and are acted upon rather than initiating action. Isabella is the play's ultimate image of its major theme of dissembling. Her early protestations of fidelity and attempts to reconcile the breach among the English are thoroughly discredited, and her attempts to play off Edward and Mortimer are deliberate and unsympathetic. The role of her sexuality, however, and her foreignness, is important to the play's underlying themes. The manner of Edward's death underscores how sexuality in the play needs to be understood in political terms. It is not necessary for us to empathise with, or even to believe in, the relationship between Edward and Gaveston, nor to concern ourselves with why Edward seems to transfer these passionate feelings to young Spenser without demur: the issue is not psychological but social. Edward's sexual behaviour, like that of Mortimer or of Isabella, figures political patterns and affiliations rather than personal ones. Mortimer's last speech tries to give control of human destiny to the classical figure of Fortune: 'in thy wheel/There is a point, to which when men aspire/ They tumble headlong down', as if the limits on behaviour are externally and providentially ordered. It is a philosophy at which Tamburlaine cocked a decisive snook. But Tamburlaine controls his play to an extent unachievable by Edward, and perhaps in *Edward II*, a play of competing autonomies and shared limelight, some external authority must be acknowledged. When the play comes to its conclusion, however, there is considerable uncertainty about how to judge its actions and characters. As such, it can claim to be Marlowe's most unresolved work.

# CHARACTERS IN THE PLAY

KING EDWARD THE SECOND
PRINCE EDWARD, *his son, afterwards King Edward the Third*
KENT, *brother to King Edward the Second*
GAVESTON
ARCHBISHOP OF CANTERBURY
BISHOP OF COVENTRY
BISHOP OF WINCHESTER
WARWICK
LANCASTER
PEMBROKE
ARUNDEL
LEICESTER
BERKELEY
MORTIMER *the elder*
MORTIMER *the younger, his nephew*
SPENSER *the elder*
SPENSER *the younger, his son*
BALDOCK
BEAUMONT
SIR JOHN OF HAINAULT
LEVUNE
TRUSSEL
RICE AP HOWEL
ABBOT
MONKS
HERALD
JAMES
MOWER
GURNEY
MATREVIS
LIGHTBORN
*Lords, Poor Men, Champion, Messengers, Soldiers and Attendants*
QUEEN ISABELLA, *wife to King Edward the Second*
NIECE *to King Edward the Second, daughter to the Duke
    of Gloucester*
*Ladies*

# EDWARD THE SECOND

## ACT ONE

### SCENE I

*Enter* GAVESTON, *reading a letter*

GAVESTON   *My father is deceas'd. Come, Gaveston,*
           *And share the kingdom with thy dearest friend.*
           Ah, words that make me surfeit with delight!
           What greater bliss can hap to Gaveston
           Than live and be the favourite of a king!
           Sweet prince, I come! These, these thy amorous lines
           Might have enforc'd me to have swum from France,
           And, like Leander, gasp'd upon the sand,
           So thou wouldst smile, and take me in thine arms.
           The sight of London to my exil'd eyes         10
           Is as Elysium to a new-come soul:
           Not that I love the city or the men,
           But that it harbours him I hold so dear –
           The king, upon whose bosom let me lie,
           And with the world be still at enmity.
           What need the arctic people love star-light,
           To whom the sun shines both by day and night?
           Farewell base stooping to the lordly peers!
           My knee shall bow to none but to the king.
           As for the multitude, that are but sparks,        20
           Rak'd up in embers of their poverty –
           *Tanti* – I'll fawn first on the wind,
           That glanceth at my lips, and flieth away.

*Enter three Poor Men*

           But how now! What are these?
POOR MEN   Such as desire your worship's service.
GAVESTON   What canst thou do?
I POOR MAN  I can ride.
GAVESTON   But I have no horse – What art thou?

2 POOR MAN  A traveller.

GAVESTON  Let me see; thou wouldst do well to wait at my
          trencher, and tell me lies at dinnertime; And, as I like
          your discoursing, I'll have you — And what art thou?

3 POOR MAN  A soldier, that hath serv'd against the Scot.

GAVESTON  Why, there are hospitals for such as you:
          I have no war; and therefore, sir, be gone.

3 POOR MAN  Farewell, and perish by a soldier's hand,
           That wouldst reward them with an hospital!

GAVESTON  [aside] Ay, ay, these words of his move me as much
          As if a goose should play the porcupine,
          And dart her plumes, thinking to pierce my breast. 40
          But yet it is no pain to speak men fair;
          I'll flatter these, and make them live in hope —
          [aloud] You know that I came lately out of France,
          And yet I have not view'd my lord the king:
          If I speed well, I'll entertain you all.

ALL       We thank your worship.

GAVESTON  I have some business: leave me to myself.

ALL       We will wait here about the court.

GAVESTON  Do. [exeunt Poor Men] These are not men for me;
          I must have wanton poets, pleasant wits,
          Musicians, that with touching of a string           50
          May draw the pliant king which way I please:
          Music and poetry is his delight;
          Therefore I'll have Italian masques by night,
          Sweet speeches, comedies, and pleasing shows:
          And in the day, when he shall walk abroad,
          Like sylvan nymphs my pages shall be clad.
          My men, like satyrs grazing on the lawns,
          Shall with their goat-feet dance the antic hay;
          Sometime a lovely boy in Dian's shape,
          With hair that gilds the water as it glides,          60
          Crownets of pearl about his naked arms,
          And in his sportful hands an olive-tree,
          To hide those parts which men delight to see,
          Shall bathe him in a spring; and there, hard by,
          One like Actaeon, peeping through the grove,
          Shall by the angry goddess be transform'd,

And running in the likeness of an hart,
By yelping hounds pull'd down, shall seem to die:
Such things as these best please his majesty —
Here comes my lord the king, and the nobles,     70
From the parliament. I'll stand aside.     [*retires*

*Enter* KING EDWARD, KENT, LANCASTER, *the elder* MORTIMER,
*the younger* MORTIMER, WARWICK, PEMBROKE, *and Attendants*

KING          Lancaster!
LANCASTER My lord?
GAVESTON [*aside*] That Earl of Lancaster do I abhor.
KING          Will you not grant me this? [*aside*] In spite of them
                 I'll have my will; and these two Mortimers,
                 That cross me thus, shall know I am displeased.
ELD. MORT. If you love us, my lord, hate Gaveston.
GAVESTON [*aside*] That villain Mortimer! I'll be his death.
MORTIMER Mine uncle here, this earl, and I myself          80
                 Were sworn to your father at his death,
                 That he should ne'er return into the realm:
                 And now, my lord, ere I will break my oath,
                 This sword of mine, that should offend your foes,
                 Shall sleep within the scabbard at thy need,
                 And underneath thy banners march who will,
                 For Mortimer will hang his armour up.
GAVESTON [*aside*] *Mort Dieu!*
KING          Well, Mortimer, I'll make thee rue these words:
                 Beseems it thee to contradict thy king?          90
                 Frown'st thou thereat, aspiring Lancaster?
                 The sword shall plane the furrows of thy brows,
                 And hew these knees that now are grown so stiff.
                 I will have Gaveston; and you shall know
                 What danger 'tis to stand against your king.
GAVESTON [*aside*] Well done, Ned!
LANCASTER My lord, why do you thus incense your peers,
                 That naturally would love and honour you,
                 But for that base and obscure Gaveston?
                 Four earldoms have I, besides Lancaster —          100
                 Derby, Salisbury, Lincoln, Leicester;
                 These will I sell, to give my soldiers pay,

              Ere Gaveston shall stay within the realm:
              Therefore, if he be come, expel him straight.

KENT      Barons and earls, your pride hath made me mute;
              But now I'll speak, and to the proof, I hope.
              I do remember, in my father's days,
              Lord Percy of the North, being highly mov'd,
              Brav'd Mowbray in presence of the king;
              For which, had not his highness lov'd him well,   110
              He should have lost his head; but with his look
              Th' undaunted spirit of Percy was appeas'd,
              And Mowbray and he were reconcil'd:
              Yet dare you brave the king unto his face –
              Brother, revenge it, and let these their heads
              Preach upon poles, for trespass of their tongues.

WARWICK   O, our heads!

KING      Ay, yours; and therefore I would wish you grant.

WARWICK   Bridle thy anger, gentle Mortimer.

MORTIMER  I cannot, nor I will not; I must speak –        120
              Cousin, our hands I hope shall fence our heads.
              And strike off his that makes you threaten us –
              Come, uncle, let us leave the brain-sick king,
              And henceforth parley with our naked swords.

ELD. MORT. Wiltshire hath men enough to save our heads.

WARWICK   All Warwickshire will leave him for my sake.

LANCASTER And northward Lancaster hath many friends –
              Adieu, my lord; and either change your mind,
              Or look to see the throne, where you should sit,
              To float in blood, and at thy wanton head   130
              The glozing head of thy base minion thrown.

                      *[Exeunt all except King Edward, Kent,*
                              *Gaveston and Attendants*

KING      I cannot brook these haughty menaces:
              Am I a king, and must be over-rul'd!
               Brother, display my ensigns in the field:
              I'll bandy with the barons and the earls,
              And either die or live with Gaveston.

GAVESTON  I can no longer keep me from my lord.

                               *[comes forward*

KING      What, Gaveston! Welcome! Kiss not my hand:

Embrace me, Gaveston, as I do thee.
Why shouldst thou kneel? Know'st thou not who I am?
Thy friend, thyself, another Gaveston:
Not Hylas was more mourned for of Hercules
Than thou hast been of me since thy exile.

GAVESTON  And, since I went from hence, no soul in hell
Hath felt more torment than poor Gaveston.

KING  I know it – Brother, welcome home my friend –
Now let the treacherous Mortimers conspire,
And that high-minded Earl of Lancaster:
I have my wish, in that I joy thy sight;
And sooner shall the sea o'erwhelm my land          150
Than bear the ship that shall transport thee hence.
I here create thee Lord High Chamberlain,
Chief Secretary to the state and me,
Earl of Cornwall, King and Lord of Man.

GAVESTON  My lord, these titles far exceed my worth.

KENT  Brother, the least of these may well suffice
For one of greater birth than Gaveston.

KING  Cease, brother, for I cannot brook these words –
Thy worth, sweet friend, is far above my gifts:
Therefore, to equal it, receive my heart.          160
If for these dignities thou be envied,
I'll give thee more; for, but to honour thee,
Is Edward pleas'd with kingly regiment.
Fear'st thou thy person? Thou shalt have a guard:
Wantest thou gold? Go to my treasury:
Wouldst thou be lov'd and fear'd? Receive my seal,
Save or condemn, and in our name command
What so thy mind affects, or fancy likes.

GAVESTON  It shall suffice me to enjoy your love;
Which whiles I have, I think myself as great          170
As Caesar riding in the Roman street,
With captive kings at his triumphant car.

*Enter the* BISHOP OF COVENTRY

KING  Whither goes my Lord of Coventry so fast?
COVENTRY  To celebrate your father's exequies.
But is that wicked Gaveston return'd?

KING          Ay, priest, and lives to be reveng'd on thee,
              That wert the only cause of his exile.

GAVESTON      'Tis true; and, but for reverence of these robes,
              Thou shouldst not plod one foot beyond this place.

COVENTRY      I did no more than I was bound to do:                    180
              And, Gaveston, unless thou be reclaim'd,
              As then I did incense the parliament,
              So will I now, and thou shalt back to France.

GAVESTON      Saving your reverence, you must pardon me.

KING          Throw off his golden mitre, rend his stole,
              And in the channel christen him anew.

KENT          Ah, brother, lay not violent hands on him!
              For he'll complain unto the see of Rome.

GAVESTON      Let him complain unto the see of hell:
              I'll be reveng'd on him for my exile.                    190

KING          No, spare his life, but seize upon his goods:
              Be thou lord bishop, and receive his rents,
              And make him serve thee as thy chaplain:
              I give him thee; here, use him as thou wilt.

GAVESTON      He shall to prison, and there die in bolts.

KING          Ay, to the Tower, the Fleet, or where thou wilt.

COVENTRY      For this offence be thou accurs'd of God!

KING          Who's there? Convey this priest to the Tower.

COVENTRY      True, true.

KING          But, in the meantime, Gaveston, away,                    200
              And take possession of his house and goods.
              Come, follow me, and thou shalt have my guard
              To see it done, and bring thee safe again.

GAVESTON      What should a priest do with so fair a house?
              A prison may beseem his holiness.

                                                              [exeunt

## SCENE 2

*Enter, on one side, the elder* MORTIMER,
*and the younger* MORTIMER; *on the other,*
WARWICK, *and* LANCASTER

WARWICK 'Tis true, the bishop is in the Tower,
And goods and body given to Gaveston.

LANCASTER What, will they tyrannise upon the church?
Ah, wicked king! Accursed Gaveston!
This ground, which is corrupted with their steps,
Shall be their timeless sepulchre or mine.

MORTIMER Well, let that peevish Frenchman guard him sure.
Unless his breast be sword-proof, he shall die.

ELD. MORT. How now! Why droops the Earl of Lancaster?

MORTIMER Wherefore is Guy of Warwick discontent?     10

LANCASTER That villain Gaveston is made an earl.

ELD. MORT. An earl!

WARWICK Ay, and besides Lord Chamberlain of the realm,
And Secretary too, and Lord of Man.

ELD. MORT. We may not nor we will not suffer this.

MORTIMER Why post we not from hence to levy men?

LANCASTER 'My Lord of Cornwall' now at every word;
And happy is the man whom he vouchsafes,
For vailing of his bonnet, one good look.
Thus, arm in arm, the king and he doth march:     20
Nay, more, the guard upon his lordship waits,
And all the court begins to flatter him.

WARWICK Thus leaning on the shoulder of the king,
He nods, and scorns, and smiles at those that pass.

ELD. MORT. Doth no man take exceptions at the slave?

LANCASTER All stomach him, but none dare speak a word.

MORTIMER Ah, that bewrays their baseness, Lancaster!
Were all the earls and barons of my mind,
We'd hale him from the bosom of the king,
And at the court-gate hang the peasant up,     30
Who, swoln with venom of ambitious pride,
Will be the ruin of the realm and us.

WARWICK Here comes my Lord of Canterbury's grace.

LANCASTER His countenance bewrays he is displeas'd.

*Enter the* ARCHBISHOP OF CANTERBURY, *and an Attendant*

CANTERB.   First, were his sacred garments rent and torn;
           Then laid they violent hands upon him; next,
           Himself imprison'd, and his goods asseiz'd:
           This certify the Pope: away, take horse. [*exit Attendant*
LANCASTER My lord, will you take arms against the king?
CANTERB.   What need I? God himself is up in arms          40
           When violence is offer'd to the church.
MORTIMER  Then will you join with us, that be his peers,
           To banish or behead that Gaveston?
CANTERB.   What else, my lords? For it concerns me near;
           The bishoprick of Coventry is his.

*Enter* QUEEN ISABELLA

MORTIMER  Madam, whither walks your majesty so fast?
ISABELLA  Unto the forest, gentle Mortimer,
           To live in grief and baleful discontent,
           For now my lord the king regards me not,
           But dotes upon the love of Gaveston:          50
           He claps his cheeks, and hangs about his neck,
           Smiles in his face, and whispers in his ears;
           And, when I come, he frowns, as who should say,
           'Go whither thou wilt, seeing I have Gaveston.'
ELD. MORT. Is it not strange that he is thus bewitch'd?
MORTIMER  Madam, return unto the court again:
           That sly inveigling Frenchman we'll exile,
           Or lose our lives; and yet, ere that day come,
           The king shall lose his crown; for we have power,
           And courage too, to be reveng'd at full.          60
CANTERB.   But yet lift not your swords against the king.
LANCASTER No; but we will lift Gaveston from hence.
WARWICK   And war must be the means, or he'll stay still.
ISABELLA  Then let him stay; for, rather than my lord
           Shall be oppress'd with civil mutinies,
           I will endure a melancholy life,
           And let him frolic with his minion.
CANTERB.   My lords, to ease all this, but hear me speak:
           We and the rest, that are his counsellors,

        Will meet, and with a general consent        70
        Confirm his banishment with our hands and seals.

LANCASTER What we confirm the king will frustrate.

MORTIMER Then may we lawfully revolt from him.

WARWICK But say, my lord, where shall this meeting be?

CANTERB. At the New Temple.

MORTIMER Content.

CANTERB. And, in the meantime, I'll entreat you all
        To cross to Lambeth, and there stay with me.

LANCASTER Come, then, let's away.

MORTIMER Madam, farewell.                     80

ISABELLA Farewell, sweet Mortimer, and, for my sake,
        Forbear to levy arms against the king.

MORTIMER Ay, if words will serve; if not, I must.

                                      *[exeunt*


## SCENE 3

*Enter* GAVESTON *and* KENT

GAVESTON Edmund, the mighty prince of Lancaster,
        That hath more earldoms than an ass can bear,
        And both the Mortimers, two goodly men,
        With Guy of Warwick, that redoubted knight,
        Are gone towards Lambeth: there let them remain.

                                      *[exeunt*


## SCENE 4

*Enter* LANCASTER, WARWICK, PEMBROKE, *the elder* MORTIMER,
*the younger* MORTIMER, *the* ARCHBISHOP OF CANTERBURY,
*and Attendants*

LANCASTER Here is the form of Gaveston's exile;
        May it please your lordship to subscribe your name.

CANTERB. Give me the paper.
                  *[he subscribes, as the others do after him*

LANCASTER Quick, quick, my lord; I long to write my name.

WARWICK But I long more to see him banish'd hence.

MORTIMER The name of Mortimer shall fright the king,
        Unless he be declin'd from that base peasant.

*Enter* KING EDWARD, GAVESTON, *and* KENT

| | |
|---|---|
| KING | What, are you mov'd that Gaveston sits here? |
| | It is our pleasure; we will have it so. |
| LANCASTER | Your grace doth well to place him by your side,     10 |
| | For nowhere else the new earl is so safe. |
| ELD. MORT. | What man of noble birth can brook this sight? |
| | *Quam male conveniunt!* |
| | See, what a scornful look the peasant casts! |
| PEMBROKE | Can kingly lions fawn on creeping ants? |
| WARWICK | Ignoble vassal, that, like Phaeton, |
| | Aspir'st unto the guidance of the sun! |
| MORTIMER | Their downfall is at hand, their forces down: |
| | We will not thus be fac'd and over-peer'd. |
| KING | Lay hands on that traitor Mortimer!     20 |
| ELD. MORT. | Lay hands on that traitor Gaveston! |
| KENT | Is this the duty that you owe your king? |
| WARWICK | We know our duties; let him know his peers. |
| KING | Whither will you bear him? Stay, or ye shall die. |
| ELD. MORT. | We are no traitors; therefore threaten not. |
| GAVESTON | No, threaten not, my lord, but pay them home. |
| | Were I a king – |
| MORTIMER | Thou, villain! Wherefore talk'st thou of a king, |
| | That hardly art a gentleman by birth? |
| KING | Were he a peasant, being my minion,     30 |
| | I'll make the proudest of you stoop to him. |
| LANCASTER | My lord – you may not thus disparage us – |
| | Away, I say, with hateful Gaveston! |
| ELD. MORT. | And with the Earl of Kent that favours him. |

[*Attendants remove Gaveston and Kent*

| | |
|---|---|
| KING | Nay, then lay violent hands upon your king: |
| | Here, Mortimer, sit thou in Edward's throne; |
| | Warwick and Lancaster, wear you my crown. |
| | Was ever king thus over-rul'd as I? |
| LANCASTER | Learn, then, to rule us better, and the realm. |
| MORTIMER | What we have done, our heart-blood shall maintain. |
| WARWICK | Think you that we can brook this upstart pride? |
| KING | Anger and wrathful fury stops my speech. |
| CANTERB. | Why are you mov'd? Be patient, my lord, |
| | And see what we your counsellors have done. |

MORTIMER   My lords, now let us all be resolute,
            And either have our wills, or lose our lives.

KING         Meet you for this, proud over-daring peers?
            Ere my sweet Gaveston shall part from me,
            This isle shall fleet upon the ocean
            And wander to the unfrequented Inde.       50

CANTERB.    You know that I am legate to the Pope:
            On your allegiance to the see of Rome,
            Subscribe, as we have done, to his exile.

MORTIMER   Curse him, if he refuse; and then may we
            Depose him, and elect another king.

KING         Ay, there it goes! But yet I will not yield:
            Curse me, depose me, do the worst you can.

LANCASTER Then linger not, my lord, but do it straight.

CANTERB.    Remember how the bishop was abus'd:
            Either banish him that was the cause thereof,    60
            Or I will presently discharge these lords
            Of duty and allegiance due to thee.

KING         [aside] It boots me not to threat; I must speak fair:
            The legate of the Pope will be obey'd –
            My lord, you shall be Chancellor of the realm;
            Thou Lancaster, High-Admiral of our fleet;
            Young Mortimer and his uncle shall be earls;
            And you, Lord Warwick, President of the North;
            And thou of Wales. If this content you not,
            Make several kingdoms of this monarchy,      70
            And share it equally amongst you all,
            So I may have some nook or corner left,
            To frolic with my dearest Gaveston.

CANTERB.    Nothing shall alter us; we are resolv'd.

LANCASTER Come, come, subscribe.

MORTIMER   Why should you love him whom the world hates so?

KING         Because he loves me more than all the world.
            Ah, none but rude and savage-minded men
            Would seek the ruin of my Gaveston!
            You that be noble-born should pity him.      80

WARWICK   You that are princely-born should shake him off:
            For shame, subscribe, and let the lown depart.

ELD. MORT. Urge him, my lord.

CANTERB. Are you content to banish him the realm?

KING    I see I must, and therefore am content:
        Instead of ink, I'll write it with my tears.     [subscribes

MORTIMER The king is love-sick for his minion.

KING    'Tis done: and now, accursed hand, fall off!

LANCASTER Give it me: I'll have it publish'd in the streets.

MORTIMER I'll see him presently despatch'd away.                    90

CANTERB. Now is my heart at ease.

WARWICK                         And so is mine.

PEMBROKE This will be good news to the common sort.

ELD. MORT. Be it or no, he shall not linger here.
                        [exeunt all except King Edward

KING    How fast they run to banish him I love!
        They would not stir, were it to do me good.
        Why should a king be subject to a priest?
        Proud Rome, that hatchest such imperial grooms,
        With these thy superstitious taper-lights,
        Wherewith thy antichristian churches blaze,
        I'll fire thy crazed buildings, and enforce          100
        The papal towers to kiss the lowly ground,
        With slaughter'd priests make Tiber's channel swell,
        And banks rais'd higher with their sepulchres!
        As for the peers, that back the clergy thus,
        If I be king, not one of them shall live.

### Re-enter GAVESTON

GAVESTON My lord, I hear it whisper'd everywhere,
        That I am banish'd and must fly the land.

KING    'Tis true, sweet Gaveston: O, were it false!
        The legate of the Pope will have it so,
        And thou must hence, or I shall be depos'd.         110
        But I will reign to be reveng'd of them;
        And therefore, sweet friend, take it patiently.
        Live where thou wilt, I'll send thee gold enough;
        And long thou shalt not stay; or, if thou dost,
        I'll come to thee; my love shall ne'er decline.

GAVESTON Is all my hope turn'd to this hell of grief?

KING    Rend not my heart with thy too-piercing words:
        Thou from this land, I from myself am banish'd.

| | |
|---|---|
| GAVESTON | To go from hence grieves not poor Gaveston, |
| | But to forsake you, in whose gracious looks     120 |
| | The blessedness of Gaveston remains; |
| | For nowhere else seeks he felicity. |
| KING | And only this torments my wretched soul, |
| | That, whether I will or no, thou must depart. |
| | Be governor of Ireland in my stead, |
| | And there abide till fortune call thee home. |
| | Here, take my picture, and let me wear thine. |

*[they exchange pictures*

| | |
|---|---|
| | O, might I keep thee here, as I do this, |
| | Happy were I! But now most miserable. |
| GAVESTON | 'Tis something to be pitied of a king.     130 |
| KING | Thou shalt not hence; I'll hide thee, Gaveston. |
| GAVESTON | I shall be found, and then 'twill grieve me more. |
| KING | Kind words and mutual talk makes our grief greater: |
| | Therefore, with dumb embracement, let us part. |
| | Stay, Gaveston: I cannot leave thee thus. |
| GAVESTON | For every look, my love drops down a tear: |
| | Seeing I must go, do not renew my sorrow. |
| KING | The time is little that thou hast to stay, |
| | And, therefore, give me leave to look my fill. |
| | But, come, sweet friend, I'll bear thee on thy way. |
| GAVESTON | The peers will frown. |
| KING | I pass not for their anger. Come, let's go: |
| | O, that we might as well return as go! |

*Enter* QUEEN ISABELLA

| | |
|---|---|
| ISABELLA | Whither goes my lord? |
| KING | Fawn not on me, French strumpet; get thee gone! |
| ISABELLA | On whom but on my husband should I fawn? |
| GAVESTON | On Mortimer; with whom, ungentle queen – |
| | I say no more – judge you the rest, my lord. |
| ISABELLA | In saying this, thou wrong'st me, Gaveston: |
| | Is't not enough that thou corrupt'st my lord,     150 |
| | And art a bawd to his affections, |
| | But thou must call mine honour thus in question? |
| GAVESTON | I mean not so; your grace must pardon me. |
| KING | Thou art too familiar with that Mortimer, |

And by thy means is Gaveston exil'd:
But I would wish thee reconcile the lords,
Or thou shalt ne'er be reconcil'd to me.

ISABELLA      Your highness knows, it lies not in my power.

KING          Away, then! Touch me not – Come, Gaveston.

ISABELLA      Villain, 'tis thou that robb'st me of my lord.          160

GAVESTON      Madam, 'tis you that rob me of my lord.

KING          Speak not unto her: let her droop and pine.

ISABELLA      Wherein, my lord, have I deserv'd these words?
Witness the tears that Isabella sheds,
Witness this heart, that, sighing for thee, breaks,
How dear my lord is to poor Isabel!

KING          And witness heaven how dear thou art to me:
There weep; for, till my Gaveston be repeal'd,
Assure thy self thou com'st not in my sight.

                    [exeunt King Edward and Gaveston

ISABELLA      O miserable and distressed queen!                      170
Would, when I left sweet France, and was embarked,
That charming Circe, walking on the waves,
Had chang'd my shape! Or at the marriage–day
The cup of Hymen had been full of poison!
Or with those arms, that twin'd about my neck,
I had been stifled, and not liv'd to see
The king my lord thus to abandon me!
Like frantic Juno, will I fill the earth
With ghastly murmur of my sighs and cries;
For never doted Jove on Ganymede                                      180
So much as he on cursed Gaveston:
But that will more exasperate his wrath;
I must entreat him, I must speak him fair,
And be a means to call home Gaveston:
And yet he'll ever dote on Gaveston;
And so am I for ever miserable.

*Re-enter* LANCASTER, WARWICK, PEMBROKE,
*the elder* MORTIMER, *and the younger* MORTIMER

LANCASTER Look, where the sister of the king of France
Sits wringing of her hands and beats her breast!

WARWICK   The king, I fear, hath ill intreated her.

| | | |
|---|---|---|
| PEMBROKE | Hard is the heart that injures such a saint. | 190 |
| MORTIMER | I know 'tis 'long of Gaveston she weeps. | |
| ELD. MORT. | Why, he is gone. | |
| MORTIMER | Madam, how fares your grace? | |
| ISABELLA | Ah, Mortimer, now breaks the king's hate forth, And he confesseth that he loves me not! | |
| MORTIMER | Cry quittance, madam, then, and love not him. | |
| ISABELLA | No, rather will I die a thousand deaths: And yet I love in vain; he'll ne'er love me. | |
| LANCASTER | Fear ye not, madam; now his minion's gone, His wanton humour will be quickly left. | |
| ISABELLA | O, never, Lancaster! I am enjoin'd To sue unto you all for his repeal: This wills my lord, and this must I perform, Or else be banish'd from his highness' presence. | 200 |
| LANCASTER | For his repeal, madam! He comes not back, Unless the sea cast up his shipwreck'd body. | |
| WARWICK | And to behold so sweet a sight as that, There's none here but would run his horse to death. | |
| MORTIMER | But, madam, would you have us call him home? | |
| ISABELLA | Ay, Mortimer, for, till he be restor'd, The angry king hath banish'd me the court; And, therefore, as thou lov'st and tender'st me, Be thou my advocate unto these peers. | 210 |
| MORTIMER | What, would you have me plead for Gaveston? | |
| ELD. MORT. | Plead for him that will, I am resolv'd. | |
| LANCASTER | And so am I, my lord: dissuade the queen. | |
| ISABELLA | O, Lancaster, let him dissuade the king! For 'tis against my will he should return. | |
| WARWICK | Then speak not for him; let the peasant go. | |
| ISABELLA | 'Tis for myself I speak, and not for him. | |
| PEMBROKE | No speaking will prevail; and therefore cease. | 220 |
| MORTIMER | Fair queen, forbear to angle for the fish Which, being caught, strikes him that takes it dead; I mean that vile torpedo, Gaveston, That now, I hope, floats on the Irish seas. | |
| ISABELLA | Sweet Mortimer, sit down by me a while, And I will tell thee reasons of such weight As thou wilt soon subscribe to his repeal. | |

MORTIMER  It is impossible: but speak your mind.

ISABELLA  Then thus – but none shall hear it but ourselves
                    [*talks to young Mortimer apart*

LANCASTER  My lords, albeit the queen win Mortimer,                          230
                    Will you be resolute and hold with me?

ELD. MORT.  Not I, against my nephew.

PEMBROKE  Fear not; the queen's words cannot alter him.

WARWICK  No? Do but mark how earnestly she pleads!

LANCASTER  And see how coldly his looks make denial!

WARWICK  She smiles: now, for my life, his mind is chang'd!

LANCASTER  I'll rather lose his friendship, I, than grant.

MORTIMER  Well, of necessity it must be so –
                    My lords, that I abhor base Gaveston
                    I hope your honours make no question,                          240
                    And therefore, though I plead for his repeal,
                    'Tis not for his sake, but for our avail;
                    Nay, for the realm's behoof, and for the king's.

LANCASTER  Fie, Mortimer, dishonour not thyself!
                    Can this be true, 'twas good to banish him,
                    And is this true, to call him home again?
                    Such reasons make white black, and dark night day.

MORTIMER  My lord of Lancaster, mark the respect.

LANCASTER  In no respect can contraries be true.

ISABELLA  Yet, good my lord, hear what he can allege.                          250

WARWICK  All that he speaks is nothing; we are resolv'd.

MORTIMER  Do you not wish that Gaveston were dead?

PEMBROKE  I would he were!

MORTIMER  Why, then, my lord, give me but leave to speak.

ELD. MORT.  But, nephew, do not play the sophister.

MORTIMER  This which I urge is of a burning zeal
                    To mend the king and do our country good.
                    Know you not Gaveston hath store of gold,
                    Which may in Ireland purchase him such friends
                    As he will front the mightiest of us all?                          260
                    And whereas he shall live and be belov'd,
                    Tis hard for us to work his overthrow.

WARWICK  Mark you but that, my lord of Lancaster.

MORTIMER  But, were he here, detested as he is,
                    How easily might some base slave be suborn'd

> To greet his lordship with a poniard,
> And none so much as blame the murderer,
> But rather praise him for that brave attempt,
> And in the chronicle enrol his name
> For purging of the realm of such a plague!    270

PEMBROKE   He saith true.

LANCASTER   Ay, but how chance this was not done before?

MORTIMER   Because, my lords, it was not thought upon.
> Nay, more, when he shall know it lies in us
> To banish him, and then to call him home,
> 'Twill make him vail the top flag of his pride,
> And fear to offend the meanest nobleman.

ELD. MORT.   But how if he do not, nephew?

MORTIMER   Then may we with some colour rise in arms;
> For, howsoever we have borne it out,    280
> 'Tis treason to be up against the king;
> So shall we have the people of our side,
> Which, for his father's sake, lean to the king,
> But cannot brook a night-grown mushroom;
> Such a one as my Lord of Cornwall is,
> Should bear us down of the nobility:
> And, when the commons and the nobles join,
> 'Tis not the king can buckler Gaveston;
> We'll pull him from the strongest hold he hath.
> My lords, if to perform this I be slack,    290
> Think me as base a groom as Gaveston.

LANCASTER   On that condition Lancaster will grant.

WARWICK   And so will Pembroke and I.

ELD. MORT.   And I.

MORTIMER   In this I count me highly gratified,
> And Mortimer will rest at your command.

ISABELLA   And when this favour Isabel forgets,
> Then let her live abandon'd and forlorn –
> But see, in happy time, my lord the king,
> Having brought the Earl of Cornwall on his way,   300
> Is new return'd. This news will glad him much
> Yet not so much as me; I love him more
> Than he can Gaveston: would he lov'd me
> But half so much! Then were I treble-blest.

*Re-enter* KING EDWARD, *mourning*

| | |
|---|---|
| KING | He's gone, and for his absence thus I mourn: |
| | Did never sorrow go so near my heart |
| | As doth the want of my sweet Gaveston; |
| | And, could my crown's revenue bring him back, |
| | I would freely give it to his enemies, |
| | And think I gain'd, having bought so dear a friend. 310 |
| ISABELLA | Hark, how he harps upon his minion! |
| KING | My heart is as an anvil unto sorrow, |
| | Which beats upon it like the Cyclops' hammers, |
| | And with the noise turns up my giddy brain, |
| | And makes me frantic for my Gaveston. |
| | Ah, had some bloodless Fury rose from hell, |
| | And with my kingly sceptre struck me dead, |
| | When I was forc'd to leave my Gaveston! |
| LANCASTER | *Diablo*, what passions call you these? |
| ISABELLA | My gracious lord, I come to bring you news. 320 |
| KING | That you have parled with your Mortimer? |
| ISABELLA | That Gaveston, my lord, shall be repeal'd. |
| KING | Repeal'd! The news is too sweet to be true. |
| ISABELLA | But will you love me, if you find it so? |
| KING | If it be so, what will not Edward do? |
| ISABELLA | For Gaveston, but not for Isabel. |
| KING | For thee, fair queen, if thou lov'st Gaveston: |
| | I'll hang a golden tongue about thy neck, |
| | Seeing thou hast pleaded with so good success. |
| ISABELLA | No other jewels hang about my neck 330 |
| | Than these, my lord; nor let me have more wealth |
| | Than I may fetch from this rich treasury. |
| | O, how a kiss revives poor Isabel! |
| KING | Once more receive my hand: and let this be |
| | A second marriage 'twixt thyself and me. |
| ISABELLA | And may it prove more happy than the first! |
| | My gentle lord, bespeak these nobles fair, |
| | That wait attendance for a gracious look, |
| | And on their knees salute your majesty. |
| KING | Courageous Lancaster, embrace thy king; 340 |
| | And, as gross vapours perish by the sun, |
| | Even so let hatred with thy sovereign's smile: |

Live thou with me as my companion.

LANCASTER This salutation overjoys my heart.

KING Warwick shall be my chiefest counsellor:
These silver hairs will more adorn my court
Than gaudy silks or rich embroidery.
Chide me, sweet Warwick, if I go astray.

WARWICK Slay me, my lord, when I offend your grace.

KING In solemn triumphs and in public shows      350
Pembroke shall bear the sword before the king.

PEMBROKE And with this sword Pembroke will fight for you.

KING But wherefore walks young Mortimer aside?
Be thou commander of our royal fleet;
Or, if that lofty office like thee not,
I make thee here Lord Marshal of the realm.

MORTIMER My lord, I'll marshal so your enemies,
As England shall be quiet, and you safe.

KING And as for you, Lord Mortimer of Chirke,
Whose great achievements in our foreign war      360
Deserve no common place nor mean reward,
Be you the general of the levied troops
That now are ready to assail the Scots.

ELD. MORT. In this your grace hath highly honour'd me,
For with my nature war doth best agree.

ISABELLA Now is the king of England rich and strong,
Having the love of his renowmed peers.

KING Ay, Isabel, ne'er was my heart so light –
Clerk of the crown, direct our warrant forth,
For Gaveston, to Ireland!

*Enter* BEAUMONT *with warrant*

Beaumont, fly      370
As fast as Iris or Jove's Mercury.

BEAUMONT It shall he done, my gracious lord.      [*exit*

KING Lord Mortimer, we leave you to your charge.
Now let us in, and feast it royally.
Against our friend the Earl of Cornwall comes
We'll have a general tilt and tournament:
And then his marriage shall be solemnis'd:
For wot you not that I have made him sure
Unto our cousin, the Earl of Gloucester's heir?

LANCASTER Such news we hear, my lord.        380
KING       That day, if not for him, yet for my sake,
           Who in the triumph will be challenger,
           Spare for no cost; we will requite your love.
WARWICK    In this or aught your highness shall command us.
KING       Thanks, gentle Warwick. Come, let's in and revel.
                  [*exeunt all except the elder Mortimer*
                            *and the younger Mortimer*

ELD. MORT. Nephew, I must to Scotland; thou stay'st here.
           Leave now to oppose thyself against the king:
           Thou seest by nature he is mild and calm;
           And, seeing his mind so dotes on Gaveston,
           Let him without controlment have his will.       390
           The mightiest kings have had their minions;
           Great Alexander lov'd Hephaestion,
           The conquering Hercules for Hylas wept,
           And for Patroclus stern Achilles droop'd:
           And not kings only, but the wisest men;
           The Roman Tully lov'd Octavius,
           Grave Socrates wild Alcibiades.
           Then let his grace, whose youth is flexible,
           And promiseth as much as we can wish,
           Freely enjoy that vain light-headed earl;       400
           For riper years will wean him from such toys.
MORTIMER   Uncle, his wanton humour grieves not me;
           But this I scorn, that one so basely-born
           Should by his sovereign's favour grow so pert,
           And riot it with the treasure of the realm,
           While soldiers mutiny for want of pay.
           He wears a lord's revenue on his back,
           And, Midas-like, he jets it in the court,
           With base outlandish cullions at his heels,
           Whose proud fantastic liveries make such show    410
           As if that Proteus, god of shapes, appear'd.
           I have not seen a dapper Jack so brisk:
           He wears a short Italian hooded cloak,
           Larded with pearl, and in his Tuscan cap
           A jewel of more value than the crown.
           While others walk below, the king and he,

From out a window, laugh at such as we,
And flout our train, and jest at our attire.
Uncle, 'tis this that makes me impatient.

ELD. MORT. But nephew, now you see the king is chang'd.    420

MORTIMER Then so am I, and live to do him service:
But, whiles I have a sword, a hand, a heart,
I will not yield to any such upstart.
You know my mind: come, uncle, let's away.

*[exeunt*

## ACT TWO

### SCENE I

*Enter the younger* SPENSER *and* BALDOCK

BALDOCK    Spenser,
Seeing that our lord the Earl of Gloucester's dead,
Which of the nobles dost thou mean to serve?

SPENSER    Not Mortimer, nor any of his side,
Because the king and he are enemies.
Baldock, learn this of me: a factious lord
Shall hardly do himself good, much less us,
But he that hath the favour of a king
May with one word advance us while we live.
The liberal Earl of Cornwall is the man      10
On whose good fortune Spenser's hope depends.

BALDOCK    What, mean you, then, to be his follower?

SPENSER    No, his companion, for he loves me well,
And would have once preferr'd me to the king.

BALDOCK    But he is banish'd; there's small hope of him.

SPENSER    Ay, for a while; but, Baldock, mark the end.
A friend of mine told me in secrecy
That he's repeal'd and sent for back again;
And even now a post came from the court
With letters to our lady from the king;      20
And, as she read, she smil'd; which makes me think
It is about her lover Gaveston.

BALDOCK    'Tis like enough; for, since he was exil'd,
She neither walks abroad nor comes in sight.
But I had thought the match had been broke off,
And that his banishment had chang'd her mind.

SPENSER    Our lady's first love is not wavering;
My life for thine, she will have Gaveston.

BALDOCK    Then hope I by her means to be preferr'd,
Having read unto her since she was a child.      30

SPENSER    Then, Baldock, you must cast the scholar off,
And learn to court it like a gentleman.
'Tis not a black coat and a little band,

A velvet-cap'd cloak, fac'd before with serge,
And smelling to a nosegay all the day,
Or holding of a napkin in your hand,
Or saying a long grace at a table's end,
Or making low legs to a nobleman,
Or looking downward, with your eye-lids close,
And saying, 'Truly, an't may please your honour',    40
Can get you any favour with great men:
You must be proud, bold, pleasant, resolute,
And now and then stab, as occasion serves.

BALDOCK    Spenser, thou know'st I hate such formal toys,
And use them but of mere hypocrisy.
Mine old lord, whiles he liv'd, was so precise,
That he would take exceptions at my buttons,
And, being like pins' heads, blame me for the bigness;
Which made me curate-like in mine attire,
Though inwardly licentious enough,             50
And apt for any kind of villany.
I am none of these common pedants, I,
That cannot speak without *propterea quod*.

SPENSER    But one of those that saith *quando-quidem*,
And hath a special gift to form a verb.

BALDOCK    Leave off this jesting; here my lady comes.

*Enter King Edward's Niece*

NIECE    The grief for his exile was not so much
As is the joy of his returning home.
This letter came from my sweet Gaveston:
What need'st thou, love, thus to excuse thyself?    60
I know thou couldst not come and visit me.
[*reads*] *I will not long be from thee, though I die* –
This argues the entire love of my lord –
[*reads*] *When I forsake thee, death seize on my heart!*
But stay thee here where Gaveston shall sleep.
                     [*puts the letter into her bosom*
Now to the letter of my lord the king:
He wills me to repair unto the court,
And meet my Gaveston: why do I stay,
Seeing that he talks thus of my marriage day?
Who's there? Baldock!                   70

See that my coach be ready, I must hence.

BALDOCK   It shall be done, madam.

NIECE     And meet me at the park-pale presently. *[exit Baldock*
          Spenser, stay you, and bear me company,
          For I have joyful news to tell thee of:
          My lord of Cornwall is a-coming over,
          And will be at the court as soon as we.

SPENSER   I knew the king would have him home again.

NIECE     If all things sort out, as I hope they will,
          Thy service, Spenser, shall be thought upon.          80

SPENSER   I humbly thank your ladyship.

NIECE     Come, lead the way: I long till I am there.

                                                      *[exeunt*


## SCENE 2

*Enter* KING EDWARD, QUEEN ISABELLA, KENT,
LANCASTER, *the younger* MORTIMER, WARWICK,
PEMBROKE, *and Attendants*

KING      The wind is good; I wonder why he stays:
          I fear me he is wreck'd upon the sea.

ISABELLA  Look. Lancaster, how passionate he is,
          And still his mind runs on his minion!

LANCASTER My lord —

KING      How now! What news? Is Gaveston arriv'd?

MORTIMER  Nothing but Gaveston! What means your grace?
          You have matters of more weight to think upon:
          The King of France sets foot in Normandy.

KING      A trifle! We'll expel him when we please.          10
          But tell me, Mortimer, what's thy device
          Against the stately triumph we decreed?

MORTIMER  A homely one, my lord, not worth the telling.

KING      Pray thee, let me know it.

MORTIMER  But, seeing you are so desirous, thus it is;
          A lofty cedar tree, fair flourishing,
          On whose top branches kingly eagles perch,
          And by the bark a canker creeps me up,
          And gets unto the highest bough of all;
          The motto, *Aeque tandem*.          20

KING        And what is yours, my Lord of Lancaster?

LANCASTER   My lord, mine's more obscure than Mortimer's.
            Pliny reports, there is a flying-fish
            Which all the other fishes deadly hate,
            And therefore, being pursu'd, it takes the air:
            No sooner is it up, but there's a fowl
            That seizeth it: this fish, my lord, I bear;
            The motto this? *Undique mors est.*

KENT        Proud Mortimer! Ungentle Lancaster!
            Is this the love you bear your sovereign?        30
            Is this the fruit your reconcilement bears?
            Can you in words make show of amity,
            And in your shields display your rancorous minds?
            What call you this but private libelling
            Against the Earl of Cornwall and my brother?

ISABELLA   Sweet husband, be content; they all love you.

KING        They love me not that hate my Gaveston.
            I am that cedar: shake me not too much;
            And you the eagles: soar ye ne'er so high,
            I have the jesses that will pull you down;        40
            And *Aeque tandem* shall that canker cry
            Unto the proudest peer of Britainy.
            Thou that compar'st him to a flying-fish,
            And threaten'st death whether he rise or fall,
            'Tis not the hugest monster of the sea,
            Nor foulest harpy, that shall swallow him.

MORTIMER   If in his absence thus he favours him,
            What will he do whenas he shall be present?

LANCASTER   That shall we see. Look, where his lordship comes!

*Enter* GAVESTON

KING        My Gaveston!        50
            Welcome to Tynmouth! Welcome to thy friend!
            Thy absence made me droop and pine away;
            For, as the lovers of fair Danaë,
            When she was lock'd up in a brazen tower,
            Desir'd her more, and wax'd outrageous,
            So did it fare with me: and now thy sight
            Is sweeter far than was thy parting hence
            Bitter and irksome to my sobbing heart.

GAVESTON  Sweet lord and king, your speech preventeth mine;
        Yet have I words left to express my joy:        60
        The shepherd, nipt with biting winter's rage,
        Frolics not more to see the painted spring
        Than I do to behold your majesty.

KING  Will none of you salute my Gaveston?

LANCASTER  Salute him? Yes. Welcome, Lord Chamberlain!

MORTIMER  Welcome is the good Earl of Cornwall!

WARWICK  Welcome, Lord Governor of the Isle of Man!

PEMBROKE  Welcome, Master Secretary!

KENT  Brother, do you hear them?

KING  Still will these earls and barons use me thus?        70

GAVESTON  My lord, I cannot brook these injuries.

ISABELLA  [aside] Ay me, poor soul, when these begin to jar!

KING  Return it to their throats, I'll be thy warrant.

GAVESTON  Base, leaden earls, that glory in your birth,
        Go sit at home, and eat your tenants' beef,
        And come not here to scoff at Gaveston,
        Whose mounting thoughts did never creep so low
        As to bestow a look on such as you.

LANCASTER  Yet I disdain not to do this for you.
              [draws his sword and offers to stab Gaveston

KING  Treason! Treason! Where's the traitor?        80

PEMBROKE  Here, here!

KING  Convey hence Gaveston; they'll murder him.

GAVESTON  The life of thee shall salve this foul disgrace.

MORTIMER  Villain, thy life, unless I miss mine aim.
              [wounds Gaveston

ISABELLA  Ah, furious Mortimer, what hast thou done?

MORTIMER  No more than I would answer, were he slain.
              [exit Gaveston with Attendants

KING  Yes, more than thou canst answer, though he live:
        Dear shall you both abide this riotous deed:
        Out of my presence! Come not near the court.

MORTIMER  I'll not be barr'd the court for Gaveston.        90

LANCASTER  We'll hale him by the ears unto the block.

KING  Look to your own heads; his is sure enough.

WARWICK  Look to your own crown, if you back him thus.

KENT  Warwick, these words do ill beseem thy years.

KING        Nay, all of them conspire to cross me thus:
            But, if I live, I'll tread upon their heads
            That think with high looks thus to tread me down.
            Come, Edmund, let's away, and levy men:
            'Tis war that must abate these barons' pride,
                    [*exeunt King Edward, Queen Isabella and Kent*

WARWICK     Let's to our castles, for the king is mov'd.        100
MORTIMER    Mov'd may he be, and perish in his wrath!
LANCASTER   Cousin, it is no dealing with him now;
            He means to make us stoop by force of arms:
            And therefore let us jointly here protest
            To prosecute that Gaveston to the death.
MORTIMER    By heaven, the abject villain shall not live!
WARWICK     I'll have his blood, or die in seeking it.
PEMBROKE    The like oath Pembroke takes.
LANCASTER                              And so doth Lancaster.
            Now send our heralds to defy the king:
            And make the people swear to put him down.       110

                        *Enter a Messenger*

MORTIMER    Letters! From whence?
MESSENGER   From Scotland, my lord.      [*giving letters to Mortimer*
LANCASTER   Why, how now, cousin! How fare all our friends?
MORTIMER    My uncle's taken prisoner by the Scots.
LANCASTER   We'll have him ransom'd, man: be of good cheer.
MORTIMER    They rate his ransom at five thousand pound.
            Who should defray the money but the king,
            Seeing he is taken prisoner in his wars?
            I'll to the king.
LANCASTER   Do, cousin, and I'll bear thee company.          120
WARWICK     Meantime my Lord of Pembroke and myself
            Will to Newcastle here, and gather head.
MORTIMER    About it, then, and we will follow you.
LANCASTER   Be resolute and full of secrecy.
WARWICK     I warrant you.                     [*exit with Pembroke*
MORTIMER    Cousin, an if he will not ransom him,
            I'll thunder such a peal into his ears
            As never subject did unto his king.
LANCASTER   Content; I'll bear my part – Holla! Who's there?

*Enter Guard*

| | | |
|---|---|---|
| MORTIMER | Ay, marry, such a guard as this doth well. | 130 |
| LANCASTER | Lead on the way. | |
| GUARD | Whither will your lordships? | |
| MORTIMER | Whither else but to the king? | |
| GUARD | His highness is dispos'd to be alone. | |
| LANCASTER | Why, so he may; but we will speak to him. | |
| GUARD | You may not in, my lord. | |
| MORTIMER | May we not? | |

*Enter* KING EDWARD *and* KENT

KING                                        How now!
What noise is this? Who have we there? Is't you?
                                        [*going*

MORTIMER  Nay, stay, my lord; I come to bring you news;
          Mine uncle's taken prisoner by the Scots.
KING      Then ransom him.                              140
LANCASTER 'Twas in your wars; you should ransom him.
MORTIMER  And you shall ransom him, or else –
KENT      What, Mortimer, you will not threaten him?
KING      Quiet yourself; you shall have the broad seal,
          To gather for him thoroughout the realm.
LANCASTER Your minion Gaveston hath taught you this.
MORTIMER  My lord, the family of the Mortimers
          Are not so poor, but, would they sell their land
          'Twould levy men enough to anger you.
          We never beg, but use such prayers as these.   150
KING      Shall I still be haunted thus?
MORTIMER  Nay, now you are here alone, I'll speak my mind.
LANCASTER And so will I; and then, my lord, farewell.
MORTIMER  The idle triumphs, masques, lascivious shows,
          And prodigal gifts bestow'd on Gaveston,
          Have drawn thy treasury dry, and made thee weak;
          The murmuring commons, overstretched, break.
LANCASTER Look for rebellion, look to be depos'd:
          Thy garrisons are beaten out of France,
          And, lame and poor, lie groaning at the gates;   160
          The wild O'Neil, with swarms of Irish kerns,
          Lives uncontroll'd within the English pale;
          Unto the walls of York the Scots make road,

            And, unresisted, drive away rich spoils.

MORTIMER    The haughty Dane commands the narrow seas,
            While in the harbour ride thy ships unrigg'd.

LANCASTER What foreign prince sends thee ambassadors?

MORTIMER    Who loves thee, but a sort of flatterers?

LANCASTER Thy gentle queen, sole sister to Valois,
            Complains that thou hast left her all forlorn.       170

MORTIMER    Thy court is naked, being bereft of those
            That make a king seem glorious to the world;
            I mean the peers, whom thou shouldst dearly love;
            Libels are cast again thee in the street;
            Ballads and rhymes made of thy overthrow.

LANCASTER The northern borderers, seeing their houses burnt,
            Their wives and children slain, run up and down,
            Cursing the name of thee and Gaveston.

MORTIMER    When wert thou in the field with banner spread,
            But once? And then thy soldiers march'd like players,
            With garish robes, not armour; and thyself,
            Bedaub'd with gold, rode laughing at the rest,
            Nodding and shaking of thy spangled crest,
            Where women's favours hung like labels down.

LANCASTER And thereof came it that the fleering Scots,
            To England's high disgrace, have made this jig;
               Maids of England, sore may you mourn,
                 For your lemans you have lost at Bannocksbourn –
                   With a heave and a ho!
                 What weeneth the King of England       190
                 So soon to have won Scotland –
                   With a rombelow!

MORTIMER    Wigmore shall fly, to set my uncle free.

LANCASTER And, when 'tis gone, our swords shall purchase more.
            If you be mov'd, revenge it as you can:
            Look next to see us with our ensigns spread.
                       [exit with younger Mortimer

KING         My swelling heart for very anger breaks:
            How oft have I been baited by these peers,
            And dare not be reveng'd, for their power is great!
            Yet shall the crowing of these cockerels       200
            Affright a lion? Edward, unfold thy paws,

|          | And let their lives' blood slake thy fury's hunger. |
|----------|------|
|          | If I be cruel and grow tyrannous, |
|          | Now let them thank themselves, and rue too late. |
| KENT     | My lord, I see your love to Gaveston |
|          | Will be the ruin of the realm and you, |
|          | For now the wrathful nobles threaten wars; |
|          | And therefore, brother, banish him for ever. |
| KING     | Art thou an enemy to my Gaveston? |
| KENT     | Ay; and it grieves me that I favour'd him. |
| KING     | Traitor, be gone! Whine thou with Mortimer. |
| KENT     | So will I, rather than with Gaveston. |
| KING     | Out of my sight, and trouble me no more! |
| KENT     | No marvel though thou scorn thy noble peers, |
|          | When I thy brother am rejected thus. |
| KING     | Away!                               [*exit Kent* |
|          | Poor Gaveston, thou hast no friend but me! |
|          | Do what they can, we'll live in Tynmouth here; |
|          | And, so I walk with him about the walls, |
|          | What care I though the earls begirt us round? |
|          | Here comes she that is cause of all these jars. |

210

220

*Enter* QUEEN ISABELLA, *with Edward's* NIECE, *two Ladies,*
GAVESTON, BALDOCK, *and the younger* SPENSER

| ISABELLA | My lord, 'tis thought the earls are up in arms. |
|----------|------|
| KING     | Ay, and 'tis likewise thought you favour 'em. |
| ISABELLA | Thus do you still suspect me without cause. |
| NIECE    | Sweet uncle, speak more kindly to the queen. |
| GAVESTON | My lord, dissemble with her; speak her fair. |
| KING     | Pardon me, sweet; I forgot myself. |
| ISABELLA | Your pardon is quickly got of Isabel. |
| KING     | The younger Mortimer is grown so brave, |
|          | That to my face he threatens civil wars. |
| GAVESTON | Why do you not commit him to the Tower? |
| KING     | I dare not, for the people love him well. |
| GAVESTON | Why, then, we'll have him privily made away. |
| KING     | Would Lancaster and he had both carous'd |
|          | A bowl of poison to each other's health! |
|          | But let them go, and tell me what are these. |
| NIECE    | Two of my father's servants whilst he liv'd: |
|          | May't please your grace to entertain them now. |

230

| KING | Tell me, where wast thou born? What is thine arms? |
|---|---|
| BALDOCK | My name is Baldock, and my gentry          240 |
| | I fetch from Oxford, not from heraldry. |
| KING | The fitter art thou, Baldock, for my turn. |
| | Wait on me, and I'll see thou shalt not want. |
| BALDOCK | I humbly thank your majesty. |
| KING | Knowest thou him, Gaveston. |
| GAVESTON | Ay, my lord; |
| | His name is Spenser; he is well allied: |
| | For my sake let him wait upon your grace; |
| | Scarce shall you find a man of more desert. |
| KING | Then, Spenser, wait upon me for his sake: |
| | I'll grace thee with a higher style ere long.          250 |
| SPENSER | No greater titles happen unto me |
| | Than to be favour'd of your majesty! |
| KING | Cousin, this day shall be your marriage feast – |
| | And, Gaveston, think that I love thee well, |
| | To wed thee to our niece, the only heir |
| | Unto the Earl of Gloucester late deceas'd. |
| GAVESTON | I know, my lord, many will stomach me; |
| | But I respect neither their love nor hate. |
| KING | The headstrong barons shall not limit me: |
| | He that I list to favour shall be great.          260 |
| | Come, let's away, and, when the marriage ends, |
| | Have at the rebels and their complices! |

*[exeunt*


## SCENE 3

*Enter* KENT, LANCASTER, *the younger* MORTIMER,
WARWICK, PEMBROKE, *and others*

| KENT | My lords, of love to this our native land, |
|---|---|
| | I come to join with you, and leave the king; |
| | And in your quarrel, and the realm's behoof, |
| | Will be the first that shall adventure life. |
| LANCASTER | I fear me, you are sent of policy, |
| | To undermine us with a show of love. |
| WARWICK | He is your brother; therefore have we cause |
| | To cast the worst, and doubt of your revolt. |

KENT        Mine honour shall be hostage of my truth:
            If that will not suffice, farewell, my lords.          10
MORTIMER    Stay, Edmund: never was Plantagenet
            False of his word, and therefore trust we thee.
PEMBROKE    But what's the reason you should leave him now?
KENT        I have informed the Earl of Lancaster.
LANCASTER   And it sufficeth. Now, my lords, know this,
            That Gaveston is secretly arriv'd,
            And here in Tynmouth frolics with the king.
            Let us with these our followers scale the walls,
            And suddenly surprise them unawares.
MORTIMER    I'll give the onset.
WARWICK                      And I'll follow thee.          20
MORTIMER    This tatter'd ensign of my ancestors,
            Which swept the desert shore of that Dead Sea
            Whereof we got the name of Mortimer,
            Will I advance upon this castle walls –
            Drums, strike alarum, raise them from their sport,
            And ring aloud the knell of Gaveston!
LANCASTER   None be so hardy as to touch the king;
            But neither spare you Gaveston nor his friends.
                                                    [exeunt


### SCENE 4

*Enter, severally,* KING EDWARD *and the younger* SPENSER

KING        O, tell me, Spenser, where is Gaveston?
SPENSER     I fear me he is slain, my gracious lord.
KING        No, here he comes; now let them spoil and kill.

            *Enter* QUEEN ISABELLA, *King Edward's* NIECE,
                        GAVESTON *and Nobles*

            Fly, fly, my lords; The earls have got the hold;
            Take shipping, and away to Scarborough:
            Spenser and I will post away by land.
GAVESTON    O, stay, my lord! They will not injure you.
KING        I will not trust them. Gaveston, away!
GAVESTON    Farewell, my lord.
KING        Lady, farewell.          10
NIECE       Farewell, sweet uncle, till we meet again.

| | |
|---|---|
| KING | Farewell, sweet Gaveston: and farewell, niece. |
| ISABELLA | No farewell to poor Isabel thy queen? |
| KING | Yes, yes, for Mortimer your lover's sake. |
| ISABELLA | Heavens can witness, I love none but you. |

                   *[exeunt all except Queen Isabella*

From my embracements thus he breaks away.
O, that mine arms could close this isle about,
That I might pull him to me where I would!
Or that these tears, that drizzle from mine eyes,
Had power to mollify his stony heart,        20
That, when I had him, we might never part!

    *Enter* LANCASTER, WARWICK, *the younger* MORTIMER,
          *and others. Alarums within*

| | |
|---|---|
| LANCASTER | I wonder how he scap'd. |
| MORTIMER |                   Who's this? The queen! |
| ISABELLA | Ay, Mortimer, the miserable queen, |
| | Whose pining heart her inward sighs have blasted, |
| | And body with continual mourning wasted: |
| | These hands are tir'd with haling of my lord |
| | From Gaveston, from wicked Gaveston; |
| | And all in vain; for, when I speak him fair, |
| | He turns away, and smiles upon his minion. |
| MORTIMER | Cease to lament, and tell us where's the king?   30 |
| ISABELLA | What would you with the king? Is't him you seek? |
| LANCASTER | No, madam, but that cursed Gaveston: |
| | Far be it from the thought of Lancaster |
| | To offer violence to his sovereign! |
| | We would but rid the realm of Gaveston: |
| | Tell us where he remains, and he shall die. |
| ISABELLA | He's gone by water unto Scarborough: |
| | Pursue him quickly, and he cannot 'scape. |
| | The king hath left him, and his train is small. |
| WARWICK | Forslow no time, sweet Lancaster; let's march.   40 |
| MORTIMER | How comes it that the king and he is parted? |
| ISABELLA | That thus your army, going several ways, |
| | Might be of lesser force, and with the power |
| | That he intendeth presently to raise, |
| | Be easily suppress'd: therefore be gone. |
| MORTIMER | Here in the river rides a Flemish hoy. |

Let's all aboard, and follow him amain.

LANCASTER The wind that bears him hence will fill our sails;
Come, come, aboard! 'Tis but an hour's sailing.

MORTIMER Madam, stay you within this castle here.        50

ISABELLA No, Mortimer, I'll to my lord the king.

MORTIMER Nay, rather sail with us to Scarborough.

ISABELLA You know the king is so suspicious
As, if he hear I have but talk'd with you,
Mine honour will be call'd in question;
And therefore, gentle Mortimer, be gone.

MORTIMER Madam, I cannot stay to answer you:
But think of Mortimer as he deserves.

*[exeunt all except Queen Isabella*

ISABELLA So well hast thou deserv'd, sweet Mortimer,
As Isabel could live with thee for ever.        60
In vain I look for love at Edward's hand,
Whose eyes are fix'd on none but Gaveston.
Yet once more I'll importune him with prayer:
If he be strange, and not regard my words,
My son and I will over into France,
And to the king my brother there complain
How Gaveston hath robb'd me of his love:
But yet, I hope, my sorrows will have end,
And Gaveston this blessed day be slain.

*[exit*

### SCENE 5

*Enter GAVESTON, pursued*

GAVESTON Yet, lusty lords, I have escap'd your hands,
Your threats, your 'larums, and your hot pursuits;
And, though divorced from King Edward's eyes,
Yet liveth Piers of Gaveston unsurpris'd,
Breathing in hope (*malgrado* all your beards,
That muster rebels thus against your king)
To see his royal sovereign once again.

*Enter* WARWICK, LANCASTER, PEMBROKE, *the younger* MORTIMER,
Soldiers, JAMES, *and other Attendants of Pembroke*

WARWICK Upon him, soldiers! Take away his weapons!

MORTIMER    Thou proud disturber of thy country's peace,
               Corrupter of thy king, cause of these broils,     10
               Base flatterer, yield! And, were it not for shame,
               Shame and dishonour to a soldier's name,
               Upon my weapon's point here shouldst thou fall,
               And welter in thy gore.

LANCASTER                        Monster of men,
               That, like the Greekish strumpet, train'd to arms
               And bloody wars so many valiant knights,
               Look for no other fortune, wretch, than death!
               King Edward is not here to buckler thee.

WARWICK    Lancaster, why talk'st thou to the slave?
               Go, soldiers, take him hence; for, by my sword,    20
               His head shall off – Gaveston, short warning
               Shall serve thy turn: it is our country's cause
               That here severely we will execute
               Upon thy person – Hang him at a bough.

GAVESTON    My lord –

WARWICK    Soldiers, have him away.
               But, for thou wert the favourite of a king,
               Thou shalt have so much honour at our hands.

GAVESTON    I thank you all, my lords: then I perceive
               That heading is one, and hanging is the other,    30
               And death is all.

*Enter* ARUNDEL

LANCASTER                How now, my Lord of Arundel!

ARUNDEL    My lords, King Edward greets you all by me.

WARWICK    Arundel, say your message.

ARUNDEL                     His majesty,
               Hearing that you had taken Gaveston,
               Entreateth you by me, yet but he may
               See him before he dies; for why, he says,
               And sends you word, he knows that die he shall;
               And, if you gratify his grace so far,
               He will be mindful of the courtesy.

WARWICK    How now!

GAVESTON               Renowmed Edward, how thy name
               Revives poor Gaveston!

WARWICK                    No, it needeth not:

Arundel, we will gratify the king
In other matters; he must pardon us in this —
Soldiers, away with him!

GAVESTON                      Why, my Lord of Warwick,
Will now these short delays beget my hopes?
I know it, lords, it is this life you aim at,
Yet grant King Edward this.

MORTIMER                 Shalt thou appoint
What we shall grant? Soldiers, away with him!
Thus we'll gratify the king;
We'll send his head by thee; let him bestow       50
His tears on that, for that is all he gets
Of Gaveston, or else his senseless trunk.

LANCASTER Not so, my lord, lest he bestow more cost
In burying him than he hath ever earn'd.

ARUNDEL   My lords, it is his majesty's request,
And in the honour of a king he swears,
He will but talk with him, and send him back.

WARWICK   When, can you tell? Arundel, no; we wot,
He that the care of his realm remits,
And drives his nobles to these exigents         60
For Gaveston, will, if he seize him once,
Violate any promise to possess him.

ARUNDEL   Then, if you will not trust his grace in keep,
My lords, I will be pledge for his return.

MORTIMER 'Tis honourable in thee to offer this;
But, for we know thou art a noble gentleman,
We will not wrong thee so,
To make away a true man for a thief.

GAVESTON How mean'st thou, Mortimer? That is over-base.

MORTIMER Away, base groom, robber of king's renown!    70
Question with thy companions and mates.

PEMBROKE My Lord Mortimer, and you, my lords, each one,
To gratify the king's request therein,
Touching the sending of this Gaveston,
Because his majesty so earnestly
Desires to see the man before his death,
I will upon mine honour undertake
To carry him, and bring him back again;

Provided this, that you, my Lord of Arundel,
Will join with me.

WARWICK                      Pembroke, what wilt thou do?    80
Cause yet more bloodshed? Is it not enough
That we have taken him, but must we now
Leave him on 'Had I wist', and let him go?

PEMBROKE My lords, I will not over-woo your honours:
But, if you dare trust Pembroke with the prisoner,
Upon mine oath, I will return him back.

ARUNDEL My Lord of Lancaster, what say you in this?

LANCASTER Why, I say, let him go on Pembroke's word.

PEMBROKE And you, Lord Mortimer?

MORTIMER How say you, my Lord of Warwick?        90

WARWICK Nay, do your pleasures. I know how 'twill prove.

PEMBROKE Then give him me.

GAVESTON                   Sweet sovereign, yet I come
To see thee ere I die!

WARWICK               [aside] Yet not perhaps,
If Warwick's wit and policy prevail.

MORTIMER My Lord of Pembroke, we deliver him you:
Return him on your honour – Sound, away!
           [exeunt all except Pembroke, Arundel, Gaveston,
                  James, and other Attendants of Pembroke

PEMBROKE My lord, you shall go with me:
My house is not far hence; out of the way
A little; but our men shall go along.
We that have pretty wenches to our wives,      100
Sir, must not come so near to balk their lips.

ARUNDEL 'Tis very kindly spoke, my Lord of Pembroke:
Your honour hath an adamant of power
To draw a prince.

PEMBROKE             So, my lord – Come, hither, James:
I do commit this Gaveston to thee;
Be thou this night his keeper; in the morning
We will discharge thee of thy charge: be gone.

GAVESTON Unhappy Gaveston, whither go'st thou now?
          [exit with James and other Attendants of Pembroke

HORSE-BOY My lord, we'll quickly be at Cobham.
                            [exeunt

## ACT THREE

### SCENE I

*Enter* GAVESTON *mourning,* JAMES
*and other Attendants of Pembroke*

GAVESTON O treacherous Warwick, thus to wrong thy friend!

JAMES I see it is your life these arms pursue.

GAVESTON Weaponless must I fall, and die in bands?
O, must this day be period of my life,
Centre of all my bliss? And ye be men,
Speed to the king.

*Enter* WARWICK *and soldiers*

WARWICK                     My Lord of Pembroke's men,
Strive you no longer: I will have that Gaveston.

JAMES Your lordship doth dishonour to yourself,
And wrong our lord, your honourable friend.

WARWICK No, James, it is my country's cause I follow –          10
Go, take the villain: soldiers, come away;
We'll make quick work – Commend me to
                                        your master,
My friend, and tell him that I watch'd it well –
Come, let thy shadow parley with King Edward.

GAVESTON Treacherous earl, shall not I see the king?

WARWICK The king of heaven perhaps, no other king –
Away!          [*exeunt Warwick and Soldiers with Gaveston*

JAMES Come, fellows: it booted not for us to strive:
We will in haste go certify our lord.

                                        [*exeunt*

### SCENE 2

*Enter* KING EDWARD, *the younger* SPENSER, BALDOCK,
*Noblemen of the king's side, and Soldiers with drums and fifes*

KING I long to hear an answer from the barons
Touching my friend, my dearest Gaveston.
Ah, Spenser, not the riches of my realm

Can ransom him! Ah, he is mark'd to die!
I know the malice of the younger Mortimer;
Warwick I know is rough, and Lancaster
Inexorable; and I shall never see
My lovely Piers of Gaveston again:
The barons overbear me with their pride.

SPENSER   Were I King Edward, England's sovereign,                    10
Son to the lovely Eleanor of Spain,
Great Edward Longshanks' issue, would I bear
These braves, this rage, and suffer uncontroll'd
These barons thus to beard me in my land,
In mine own realm? My lord, pardon my speech:
Did you retain your father's magnanimity,
Did you regard the honour of your name,
You would not suffer thus your majesty
Be counterbuff'd of your nobility.
Strike off their heads, and let them preach on poles:
No doubt, such lessons they will teach the rest,
As by their preachments they will profit much,
And learn obedience to their lawful king.

KING      Yes, gentle Spenser, we have been too mild,
Too kind to them, but now have drawn our sword,
And, if they send me not my Gaveston,
We'll steel it on their crests, and poll their tops.

BALDOCK   This haught resolve becomes your majesty,
Not to be tied to their affection,
As though your highness were a schoolboy still,               30
And must be aw'd and govern'd like a child.

*Enter the elder* SPENSER *with his truncheon and Soldiers*

ELD. SPEN. Long live my sovereign, the noble Edward,
In peace triumphant, fortunate in wars!

KING      Welcome, old man: com'st thou in Edward's aid?
Then tell thy prince of whence and what thou art.

ELD. SPEN. Lo, with a band of bow-men and of pikes,
Brown bills and targeteers, four hundred strong,
Sworn to defend King Edward's royal right,
I come in person to your majesty,
Spenser, the father of Hugh Spenser there,                    40

Bound to your highness everlastingly
For favour done, in him, unto us all.

KING          Thy father, Spenser?

SPENSER                              True, an it like your grace,
That pours, in lieu of all your goodness shown,
His life, my lord, before your princely feet.

KING          Welcome ten thousand times, old man, again.
Spenser, this love, this kindness to thy king
Argues thy noble mind and disposition.
Spenser, I here create thee Earl of Wiltshire,
And daily will enrich thee with our favour,          50
That, as the sunshine, shall reflect o'er thee.
Beside, the more to manifest our love,
Because we hear Lord Bruce doth sell his land,
And that the Mortimers are in hand withal,
Thou shalt have crowns of us t'outbid the barons;
And, Spenser, spare them not, but lay it on –
Soldiers, a largess, and thrice-welcome all!

SPENSER       My lord, here comes the queen.

*Enter* QUEEN ISABELLA, PRINCE EDWARD, *and* LEVUNE

KING                                        Madam, what news?

ISABELLA      News of dishonour, lord, and discontent.
Our friend Levune, faithful and full of trust,          60
Informeth us, by letters and by words,
That Lord Valois our brother, King of France,
Because your highness hath been slack in homage,
Hath seized Normandy into his hands:
These be the letters, this the messenger.

KING          Welcome, Levune – Tush, Sib, if this be all,
Valois and I will soon be friends again –
But to my Gaveston: shall I never see,
Never behold thee now? Madam, in this matter
We will employ you and your little son;          70
You shall go parley with the King of France –
Boy, see you bear you bravely to the king,
And do your message with a majesty.

PRINCE        Commit not to my youth things of more weight
Than fits a prince so young as I to bear;

|  | And fear not, lord and father – heaven's great beams |
|  | On Atlas' shoulder shall not lie more safe |
|  | Than shall your charge committed to my trust. |
| ISABELLA | Ah, boy, this towardness makes thy mother fear |
|  | Thou art not mark'd to many days on earth!    80 |
| KING | Madam, we will that you with speed be shipp'd, |
|  | And this our son; Levune shall follow you |
|  | With all the haste we can despatch him hence. |
|  | Choose of our lords to bear you company; |
|  | And go in peace; leave us in wars at home. |
| ISABELLA | Unnatural wars, where subjects brave their king: |
|  | God end them once – My lord, I take my leave, |
|  | To make my preparation for France. |

*[exit with Prince Edward*

### Enter ARUNDEL

| KING | What, Lord Arundel, dost thou come alone? |
| ARUNDEL | Yea, my good lord, for Gaveston is dead.     90 |
| KING | Ah, traitors, have they put my friend to death? |
|  | Tell me, Arundel, died he ere thou cam'st, |
|  | Or didst thou see my friend to take his death? |
| ARUNDEL | Neither, my lord; for, as he was surpris'd, |
|  | Begirt with weapons and with enemies round, |
|  | I did your highness' message to them all, |
|  | Demanding him of them, entreating rather, |
|  | And said, upon the honour of my name, |
|  | That I would undertake to carry him |
|  | Unto your highness, and to bring him back.    100 |
| KING | And, tell me, would the rebels deny me that? |
| SPENSER | Proud recreants! |
| KING |                Yea, Spenser, traitors all! |
| ARUNDEL | I found them at the first inexorable; |
|  | The Earl of Warwick would not bide the hearing, |
|  | Mortimer hardly; Pembroke and Lancaster |
|  | Spake least; and when they flatly had denied, |
|  | Refusing to receive me pledge for him, |
|  | The Earl of Pembroke mildly thus bespake: |
|  | 'My lords, because our sovereign sends for him, |
|  | And promiseth he shall be safe return'd,    110 |

              I will this undertake: to have him hence,
              And see him re–deliver'd to your hands.'
KING         Well, and how fortunes it that he came not?
SPENSER     Some treason or some villany was cause.
ARUNDEL    The Earl of Warwick seiz'd him on his way;
              For, being deliver'd unto Pembroke's men,
              Their lord rode home, thinking his prisoner safe;
              But, ere he came, Warwick in ambush lay,
              And bare him to his death; and in a trench
              Strake off his head, and march'd unto the camp.
SPENSER     A bloody part, flatly 'gainst law of arms!
KING         O, shall I speak, or shall I sigh and die!
SPENSER     My lord, refer your vengeance to the sword
              Upon these barons; hearten up your men;
              Let them not unreveng'd murder your friends:
              Advance your standard, Edward, in the field,
              And march to fire them from their starting-holes.
KING         [*kneeling*] By earth, the common mother of us all,
              By heaven, and all the moving orbs thereof,
              By this right hand, and by my father's sword,    130
              And all the honours 'longing to my crown,
              I will have heads and lives for him as many
              As I have manors, castles, towns, and towers!   [*rises*
              Treacherous Warwick! Traitorous Mortimer!
              If I be England's king, in lakes of gore
              Your headless trunks, your bodies will I trail,
              That you may drink your fill, and quaff in blood,
              And stain my royal standard with the same,
              That so my bloody colours may suggest
              Remembrance of revenge immortally       140
              On your accursed traitorous progeny,
              You villains that have slain my Gaveston!
              And in this place of honour and of trust,
              Spenser, sweet Spenser, I adopt thee here;
              And merely of our love we do create thee
              Earl of Gloucester and Lord Chamberlain,
              Despite of times, despite of enemies.
SPENSER     My lord, here's a messenger from the barons
              Desires access unto your majesty.

KING       Admit him near.                             150

*Enter Herald with his coat of arms*

HERALD     Long live King Edward, England's lawful lord!
KING       So wish not they, I wis, that sent thee hither:
             Thou com'st from Mortimer and his complices:
             A ranker rout of rebels never was.
             Well, say thy message.
HERALD     The barons, up in arms, by me salute
             Your highness with long life and happiness;
             And bid me say, as plainer to your grace,
             That if without effusion of blood
             You will this grief have ease and remedy,        160
             That from your princely person you remove
             This Spenser, as a putrifying branch
             That deads the royal vine, whose golden leaves
             Empale your princely head, your diadem;
             Whose brightness such pernicious upstarts dim.
             Say they, and lovingly advise your grace
             To cherish virtue and nobility,
             And have old servitors in high esteem,
             And shake off smooth dissembling flatterers:
             This granted, they, their honours, and their lives,
             Are to your highness vow'd and consecrate.
SPENSER   Ah, traitors, will they still display their pride?
KING       Away! Tarry no answer, but be gone!
             Rebels, will they appoint their sovereign
             His sports, his pleasures, and his company?
             Yet, ere thou go, see how I do divorce
                           *[embraces young Spenser*
             Spenser from me. Now get thee to thy lords,
             And tell them I will come to chastise them
             For murdering Gaveston: hie thee, get thee gone!
             Edward, with fire and sword, follows at thy heels.
                                *[exit Herald*
             My lords, perceive you how these rebels swell?
             Soldiers, good hearts! Defend your sovereign's right,
             For, now, even now, we march to make them stoop.
             Away!
                                *[exeunt*

### SCENE 3

*Alarums, excursions, a great fight and a retreat sounded, within.*
*Re-enter* KING EDWARD, *the elder* SPENSER, *the younger*
SPENSER, BALDOCK, *and Noblemen of the king's side*

KING   Why do we sound retreat? Upon them, lords!
     This day I shall pour vengeance with my sword
     On those proud rebels that are up in arms,
     And do confront and countermand their king.

SPENSER  I doubt it not, my lord: right will prevail.

ELD. SPEN. 'Tis not amiss, my liege, for either part
     To breathe a while; our men, with sweat and dust
     All chok'd well near, begin to faint for heat;
     And this retire refresheth horse and man.

SPENSER  Here come the rebels.

    *Enter the younger* MORTIMER, LANCASTER,
      WARWICK, PEMBROKE, *and others*

MORTIMER        Look, Lancaster, yonder is Edward
     Among his flatterers.

LANCASTER        And there let him be,
     Till he pay dearly for their company,

WARWICK  And shall, or Warwick's sword shall smite in vain.

KING   What, rebels, do you shrink and sound retreat?

MORTIMER No, Edward, no; thy flatterers faint and fly.

LANCASTER They'd best betimes forsake thee and their trains,
     For they'll betray thee, traitors as they are.

SPENSER  Traitor on thy face, rebellious Lancaster!

PEMBROKE Away, base upstart! Brav'st thou nobles thus?  20

ELD. SPEN. A noble attempt and honourable deed,
     Is it not, trow ye, to assemble aid
     And levy arms against your lawful king?

KING   For which, ere long, their heads shall satisfy
     T' appease the wrath of their offended king.

MORTIMER Then, Edward, thou wilt fight it to the last,
     And rather bathe thy sword in subjects' blood
     Than banish that pernicious company?

KING   Ay, traitors all, rather than thus be brav'd,

Make England's civil towns huge heaps of stones,
And ploughs to go about our palace-gates.

WARWICK    A desperate and unnatural resolution!
Alarum! To the fight!
Saint George for England, and the barons' right!

KING    Saint George for England, and King Edward's right!

*[alarums; exeunt the two parties severally*


## SCENE 4

*Enter* KING EDWARD *and his followers, with
the Barons and* KENT *captive*

KING    Now, lusty lords, now not by chance of war,
But justice of the quarrel and the cause,
Vail'd is your pride: methinks you hang the heads;
But we'll advance them, traitors: now 'tis time
To be aveng'd on you for all your braves,
And for the murder of my dearest friend,
To whom right well you knew our soul was knit,
Good Piers of Gaveston, my sweet favourite:
Ah, rebels, recreants, you made him away!

KENT    Brother, in regard of thee and of thy land    10
Did they remove that flatterer from thy throne.

KING    So, sir, you have spoke: away, avoid our presence!

*[exit Kent*

Accursed wretches, was't in regard of us,
When we had sent our messenger to request
He might be spar'd to come to speak with us,
And Pembroke undertook for his return,
That thou, proud Warwick, watch'd the prisoner,
Poor Piers, and headed him 'gainst law of arms?
For which thy head shall overlook the rest
As much as thou in rage outwent'st the rest.    20

WARWICK    Tyrant, I scorn thy threats and menaces;
It is but temporal that thou canst inflict.

LANCASTER    The worst is death; and better die to live
Than live in infamy under such a king.

KING    Away with them, my lord of Winchester!

These lusty leaders, Warwick and Lancaster,
I charge you roundly, off with both their heads!
Away!

WARWICK    Farewell, vain world!

LANCASTER            Sweet Mortimer, farewell!

MORTIMER    England, unkind to thy nobility,        30
Groan for this grief! Behold how thou art maim'd!

KING    Go, take that haughty Mortimer to the Tower;
There see him safe bestow'd; and, for the rest,
Do speedy execution on them all.
Be gone!

MORTIMER    What, Mortimer, can ragged stony walls
Immure thy virtue that aspires to heaven?
No, Edward, England's scourge, it may not be;
Mortimer's hope surmounts his fortune far.

                     [*the captive Barons are led off*

KING    Sound, drums and trumpets! March with me,
                     my friends.    40
Edward this day hath crown'd him king anew.

                     [*exeunt all except the younger*
                     *Spenser, Levune and Baldock*

SPENSER    Levune, the trust that we repose in thee
Begets the quiet of King Edward's land:
Therefore be gone in haste, and with advice
Bestow that treasure on the lords of France,
That, therewith all enchanted, like the guard
That suffer'd Jove to pass in showers of gold
To Danaë, all aid may be denied
To Isabel the queen, that now in France
Makes friends, to cross the seas with her young son
And step into his father's regiment.

LEVUNE    That's it these barons and the subtle queen
Long levell'd at.

BALDOCK            Yea, but, Levune, thou seest,
These barons lay their heads on blocks together:
What they intend, the hangman frustrates clean.

LEVUNE    Have you no doubt, my lords, I'll clap so close
Among the lords of France with England's gold,
That Isabel shall make her plaints in vain,

And France shall be obdurate with her tears.
SPENSER Then make for France amain; Levune, away!     60
Proclaim King Edward's wars and victories.

[exeunt

## ACT FOUR

### SCENE 1

*Enter* KENT

KENT        Fair blows the wind for France: blow, gentle gale,
            Till Edmund be arriv'd for England's good!
            Nature, yield to my country's cause in this!
            A brother? No, a butcher of thy friends!
            Proud Edward, dost thou banish me thy presence?
            But I'll to France, and cheer the wronged queen,
            And certify what Edward's looseness is.
            Unnatural king, to slaughter noblemen
            And cherish flatterers! Mortimer, I stay
            Thy sweet escape. Stand gracious, gloomy night,      10
            To his device!

                    *Enter the younger* MORTIMER *disguised*

MORTIMER                Holla! Who walketh there?
            Is't you, my lord?
KENT                        Mortimer? 'Tis I.
            But hath thy potion wrought so happily?
MORTIMER    It hath, my lord: the warders all asleep,
            I thank them, gave me leave to pass in peace.
            But hath your grace got shipping unto France?
KENT        Fear it not.

                                                    [*exeunt*


### SCENE 2

*Enter* QUEEN ISABELLA *and* PRINCE EDWARD

ISABELLA    Ah, boy, our friends do fail us all in France!
            The lords are cruel, and the king unkind.
            What shall we do?
PRINCE                        Madam, return to England,
            And please my father well; and then a fig
            For all my uncle's friendship here in France!
            I warrant you, I'll win his highness quickly;

'A loves me better than a thousand Spensers.

ISABELLA   Ah, boy, thou art deceiv'd, at least in this,
To think that we can yet be tun'd together!
No, no, we jar too far. Unkind Valois!                    10
Unhappy Isabel, when France rejects,
Whither, O whither dost thou bend thy steps?

*Enter* SIR JOHN OF HAINAULT

HAINAULT   Madam, what cheer?
ISABELLA                          Ah, good Sir John of Hainault,
Never so cheerless nor so far distrest!
HAINAULT   I hear, sweet lady, of the king's unkindness:
But droop not, madam; noble minds contemn
Despair. Will your grace with me to Hainault,
And there stay time's advantage with your son?
How say you, my lord! Will you go with
                                       your friends,
And shake off all our fortunes equally?                    20
PRINCE   So pleaseth the queen my mother, me it likes:
The king of England, not the court of France,
Shall have me from my gracious mother's side,
Till I be strong enough to break a staff;
And then have at the proudest Spenser's head!
HAINAULT   Well said, my lord!
ISABELLA   O my sweet heart, how do I moan thy wrongs,
Yet triumph in the hope of thee, my joy!
Ah, sweet Sir John, even to the utmost verge
Of Europe, on the shore of Tanaïs,                         30
Will we with thee to Hainault — so we will:
The marquis is a noble gentleman;
His grace, I dare presume, will welcome me —
But who are these?

*Enter* KENT *and the younger* MORTIMER

KENT                          Madam, long may you live
Much happier than your friends in England do!
ISABELLA   Lord Edmund and Lord Mortimer alive!
Welcome to France! The news was here, my lord,
That you were dead, or very near your death.
MORTIMER   Lady, the last was truest of the twain:

|  | But Mortimer, reserv'd for better hap, | 40 |
| --- | --- | --- |
|  | Hath shaken off the thraldom of the Tower, |  |
|  | And lives t' advance your standard, good my lord. |  |
| PRINCE | How mean you, an the king my father lives? |  |
|  | No, my Lord Mortimer, not I, I trow. |  |
| ISABELLA | Not, son! Why not? I would it were no worse, |  |
|  | But, gentle lords, friendless we are in France. |  |
| MORTIMER | Monsieur Le Grand, a noble friend of yours, |  |
|  | Told us, at our arrival, all the news — |  |
|  | How hard the nobles, how unkind the king |  |
|  | Hath show'd himself: but, madam, right makes room |  |
|  | Where weapons want; and, though a many friends |  |
|  | Are made away, as Warwick, Lancaster, |  |
|  | And others of our part and faction, |  |
|  | Yet have we friends, assure your grace, in England |  |
|  | Would cast up caps, and clap their hands for joy, |  |
|  | To see us there, appointed for our foes. |  |
| KENT | Would all were well, and Edward well reclaim'd, |  |
|  | For England's honour, peace, and quietness! |  |
| MORTIMER | But by the sword, my lord, 't must be deserv'd: |  |
|  | The king will ne'er forsake his flatterers. | 60 |
| HAINAULT | My lords of England, sith th' ungentle king |  |
|  | Of France refuseth to give aid of arms |  |
|  | To this distressed queen, his sister, here, |  |
|  | Go you with her to Hainault: doubt ye not |  |
|  | We will find comfort, money, men, and friends |  |
|  | Ere long to bid the English king a base — |  |
|  | How say'st, young prince, what think you of |  |
|  | the match? |  |
| PRINCE | I think King Edward will outrun us all. |  |
| ISABELLA | Nay, son, not so; and you must not discourage |  |
|  | Your friends that are so forward in your aid. | 70 |
| KENT | Sir John of Hainault, pardon us, I pray: |  |
|  | These comforts that you give our woful queen |  |
|  | Bind us in kindness all at your command. |  |
| ISABELLA | Yea, gentle brother — and the God of heaven |  |
|  | Prosper your happy motion, good Sir John! |  |
| MORTIMER | This noble gentleman, forward in arms, |  |
|  | Was born, I see, to be our anchor-hold. |  |

Sir John of Hainault, be it thy renown
That England's queen and nobles in distress
Have been by thee restor'd and comforted.          80
HAINAULT   Madam, along; and you, my lords, with me,
That England's peers may Hainault's welcome see.

[*exeunt*

## SCENE 3

*Enter* KING EDWARD, ARUNDEL, *the elder* SPENSER,
*the younger* SPENSER, *and others*

KING        Thus, after many threats of wrathful war
Triumpheth England's Edward with his friends;
And triumph Edward with his friends uncontroll'd!
My Lord of Gloucester, do you hear the news?
SPENSER     What news, my lord?
KING        Why, man, they say there is great execution
Done through the realm — My Lord of Arundel,
You have the note, have you not?
ARUNDEL     From the Lieutenant of the Tower, my lord.
KING        I pray, let us see it [*takes the note from Arundel*] —
                          What have we there?          10
Read it, Spenser.        [*gives the note to young Spenser,
                              who reads their names*
Why, so: they bark'd apace a month ago;
Now, on my life, they'll neither bark nor bite.
Now, sirs, the news from France? Gloucester, I trow,
The lords of France love England's gold so well
As Isabella gets no aid from thence.
What now remains? Have you proclaim'd, my lord,
Reward for them can bring in Mortimer?
SPENSER     My lord, we have; and, if he be in England,
'A will be had ere long, I doubt it not.          20
KING        If, dost thou say? Spenser, as true as death
He is in England's ground: our port-masters
Are not so careless of their king's command.

*Enter a Messenger*

How now! What news with thee? From whence
                              come these?

MESSENGER Letters, my lord, and tidings forth of France,
              To you, my Lord of Gloucester, from Levune.
KING      Read.
SPENSER   [*reading*] *My duty to your honour promised, etc., I have,*
          *according to instructions in that behalf, dealt with the King of*
          *France and his lords, and effected that the queen, all discon-*
          *tented and discomforted, is gone: whither, if you ask, with Sir*
          *John of Hainault, brother to the marquis, into Flanders.*
          *With them are gone Lord Edmund and the Lord Mortimer,*
          *having in their company divers of your nation, and others,*
          *and, as constant report goeth, they intend to give King*
          *Edward battle in England, sooner than he can look for them.*
          *This is all the news of import.*

                              *Your honour's in all service, Levune*

KING      Ah, villains, hath that Mortimer escap'd?
          With him is Edmund gone associate?                         40
          And will Sir John of Hainault lead the round?
          Welcome, o' God's name, madam, and your son!
          England shall welcome you and all your rout.
          Gallop apace, bright Phoebus, through the sky;
          And, dusky Night, in rusty iron car,
          Between you both shorten the time, I pray,
          That I may see that most desired day,
          When we may meet these traitors in the field!
          Ah, nothing grieves me, but my little boy
          Is thus misled to countenance their ills!                  50
          Come, friends, to Bristol, there to make us strong:
          And, winds, as equal be to bring them in,
          As you injurious were to bear them forth!
                                                          [*exeunt*

## SCENE 4

*Enter* QUEEN ISABELLA, PRINCE EDWARD, KENT, *the younger*
MORTIMER, *and* SIR JOHN OF HAINAULT

ISABELLA     Now, lords, our loving friends and countrymen,
Welcome to England all, with prosperous winds!
Our kindest friends in Belgia have we left,
To cope with friends at home; a heavy case
When force to force is knit, and sword and glaive
In civil broils make kin and countrymen
Slaughter themselves in others, and their sides
With their own weapons gor'd! But what's the help?
Misgovern'd kings are cause of all this wreck;
And, Edward, thou art one among them all,       10
Whose looseness hath betray'd thy land to spoil,
Who made the channel overflow with blood
Of thine own people: patron shouldst thou be;
But thou —

MORTIMER          Nay, madam, if you be a warrior,
You must not grow so passionate in speeches. —
Lords, sith that we are, by sufferance of heaven,
Arriv'd and armed in this prince's right,
Here for our country's cause swear we to him
All homage, fealty, and forwardness;
And for the open wrongs and injuries       20
Edward hath done to us, his queen, and land,
We come in arms to wreck it with the sword,
That England's queen in peace may repossess
Her dignities and honours; and withal
We may remove these flatterers from the king
That havock England's wealth and treasury.

HAINAULT    Sound trumpets, my lord, and forward let us march.
Edward will think we come to flatter him.

KENT       I would he never had been flatter'd more!

*[exeunt*

## SCENE 5

*Enter* KING EDWARD, BALDOCK, *and the younger* SPENSER

SPENSER    Fly, fly, my lord! The queen is overstrong;
           Her friends do multiply, and yours do fail.
           Shape we our course to Ireland, there to breathe.
KING       What, was I born to fly and run away,
           And leave the Mortimers conquerors behind?
           Give me my horse, and let's reinforce our troops,
           And in this bed of honour die with fame.
BALDOCK    O, no, my lord! This princely resolution
           Fits not the time: away! We are pursu'd.

                                                        *[exeunt*

## SCENE 6

*Enter* KENT, *with a sword and target*

KENT       This way he fled; but I am come too late.
           Edward, alas, my heart relents for thee!
           Proud traitor, Mortimer, why dost thou chase
           Thy lawful king, thy sovereign, with thy sword?
           Vile wretch, and why hast thou, of all unkind,
           Borne arms against thy brother and thy king?
           Rain showers of vengeance on my cursed head,
           Thou God, to whom in justice it belongs
           To punish this unnatural revolt!
           Edward, this Mortimer aims at thy life;            10
           O, fly him, then! But, Edmund, calm this rage;
           Dissemble, or thou diest; for Mortimer
           And Isabel do kiss, while they conspire:
           And yet she bears a face of love, forsooth:
           Fie on that love that hatcheth death and hate!
           Edmund, away! Bristol to Longshanks' blood
           Is false; be not found single for suspect:
           Proud Mortimer pries near into thy walks.

*Enter* QUEEN ISABELLA, PRINCE EDWARD,
*the younger* MORTIMER, *and* SIR JOHN OF HAINAULT

ISABELLA    Successful battle gives the God of kings
            To them that fight in right, and fear his wrath.    20
            Since, then, successfully we have prevail'd,
            Thanked be heaven's great architect, and you!
            Ere farther we proceed, my noble lords,
            We here create our well-beloved son,
            Of love and care unto his royal person,
            Lord Warden of the realm; and, sith the Fates
            Have made his father so infortunate,
            Deal you, my lords, in this, my loving lords,
            As to your wisdoms fittest seems in all.

KENT        Madam, without offence if I may ask,              30
            How will you deal with Edward in his fall?

PRINCE      Tell me, good uncle, what Edward do you mean?

KENT        Nephew, your father; I dare not call him king.

MORTIMER    My Lord of Kent, what needs these questions?
            'Tis not in her controlment nor in ours;
            But as the realm and parliament shall please,
            So shall your brother be disposed of –
            [*aside to the Queen*] I like not this relenting mood
                                              in Edmund:
            Madam, 'tis good to look to him betimes.

ISABELLA    My lord the Mayor of Bristol knows our mind.      40

MORTIMER    Yea, madam; and they scape not easily
            That fled the field.

ISABELLA                         Baldock is with the king:
            A goodly chancellor, is he not, my lord?

HAINAULT    So are the Spensers, the father and the son.

MORTIMER    This Edward is the ruin of the realm.

*Enter* RICE AP HOWEL *with the elder* SPENSER *prisoner and Attendants*

AP HOWEL    God save Queen Isabel and her princely son!
            Madam, the Mayor and citizens of Bristol,
            In sign of love and duty to this presence,
            Present by me this traitor to the state,
            Spenser, the father to that wanton Spenser,        50
            That, like the lawless Catiline of Rome,

|  | Revell'd in England's wealth and treasury. |
|---|---|
| ISABELLA | We thank you all. |
| MORTIMER | Your loving care in this |
|  | Deserveth princely favours and rewards. |
|  | But where's the king and the other Spenser fled? |
| RICE | Spenser the son, created Earl of Gloucester, |
|  | Is with that smooth-tongu'd scholar Baldock gone, |
|  | And shipp'd but late for Ireland with the king. |
| MORTIMER | [aside] Some whirlwind fetch them back, or sink them all — |
|  | They shall be started thence, I doubt it not.          60 |
| PRINCE | Shall I not see the king my father yet? |
| KENT | [aside] Unhappy Edward, chas'd from England's bounds! |
| HAINAULT | Madam, what resteth? Why stand you in a muse? |
| ISABELLA | I rue my lord's ill-fortune: but, alas, |
|  | Care of my country call'd me to this war! |
| MORTIMER | Madam, have done with care and sad complaint: |
|  | Your king hath wrong'd your country and himself, |
|  | And we must seek to right it as we may — |
|  | Meanwhile have hence this rebel to the block. |
| ELD. SPEN. | Rebel is he that fights against the prince:          70 |
|  | So fought not they that fought in Edward's right. |
| MORTIMER | Take him away; he prates. |

                                *[exeunt Attendants with the elder Spenser*

                          You, Rice ap Howel,

        Shall do good service to her majesty,

        Being of countenance in your country here,

        To follow these rebellious runagates —

        We in mean while, madam, must take advice

        How Baldock, Spenser, and their complices

        May in their fall be follow'd to their end.

                                          *[exeunt*

## SCENE 7

*Enter the Abbot, Monks,* KING EDWARD, *the younger* SPENSER
*and* BALDOCK *(the three latter disguised)*

ABBOT　　Have you no doubt, my lord; have you no fear:
　　　　　As silent and as careful we will be
　　　　　To keep your royal person safe with us,
　　　　　Free from suspect, and fell invasion
　　　　　Of such as have your majesty in chase –
　　　　　Yourself, and those your chosen company –
　　　　　As danger of this stormy time requires.

KING　　Father, thy face should harbour no deceit.
　　　　　O, hadst thou ever been a king, thy heart,
　　　　　Pierc'd deeply with sense of my distress,　　　　10
　　　　　Could not but take compassion of my state!
　　　　　Stately and proud, in riches and in train,
　　　　　Whilom I was, powerful and full of pomp:
　　　　　But what is he whom rule and empery
　　　　　Have not in life or death made miserable?
　　　　　Come, Spenser! Come, Baldock! Come, sit
　　　　　　　　　　　　　　　　　　down by me;
　　　　　Make trial now of that philosophy
　　　　　That in our famous nurseries of arts
　　　　　Thou suck'dst from Plato and from Aristotle –
　　　　　Father, this life contemplative is heaven:　　　　20
　　　　　O, that I might this life in quiet lead!
　　　　　But we, alas, are chas'd – and you, my friends,
　　　　　Your lives and my dishonour they pursue –
　　　　　Yet, gentle monks, for treasure, gold, nor fee
　　　　　Do you betray us and our company.

I MONK　Your grace may sit secure, if none but we
　　　　　Do wot of your abode.

SPENSER　Not one alive: but shrewdly I suspect
　　　　　A gloomy fellow in a mead below;
　　　　　'A gave a long look after us, my lord;　　　　30
　　　　　And all the land, I know, is up in arms,
　　　　　Arms that pursue our lives with deadly hate.

BALDOCK   We were embark'd for Ireland; wretched we,
          With awkward winds and with sore tempests driven,
          To fall on shore, and here to pine in fear
          Of Mortimer and his confederates!
KING      Mortimer! Who talks of Mortimer?
          Who wounds me with the name of Mortimer,
          That bloody man? Good father, on thy lap
          Lay I this head, laden with mickle care.                    40
          O, might I never ope these eyes again,
          Never again lift up this drooping head,
          O, never more lift up this dying heart!
SPENSER   Look up, my lord — Baldock, this drowsiness
          Betides no good; here even we are betray'd.

          *Enter, with Welsh hooks,* RICE AP HOWEL,
                 *a Mower, and* LEICESTER

MOWER     Upon my life, these be the men ye seek.
AP HOWEL  Fellow, enough — My lord, I pray, be short;
          A fair commission warrants what we do.
LEICESTER The queen's commission, urg'd by Mortimer —
          What cannot gallant Mortimer with the queen?              50
          Alas, see where he sits, and hopes unseen
          T'escape their hands that seek to reave his life.
          Too true it is,
          *Quem dies vidit veniens superbum,*
          *Hunc dies vidit fugiens jacentem.*
          But, Leicester, leave to grow so passionate —
          Spenser and Baldock, by no other names,
          I arrest you of high treason here.
          Stand not on titles, but obey th' arrest:
          'Tis in the name of Isabel the queen —                     60
          My lord, why droop you thus?
KING      O day, the last of all my bliss on earth!
          Centre of all misfortune! O my stars,
          Why do you lour unkindly on a king?
          Comes Leicester, then, in Isabella's name
          To take my life, my company from me?
          Here, man, rip up this panting breast of mine,
          And take my heart in rescue of my friends.

AP HOWEL  Away with them!

SPENSER                    It may become thee yet
          To let us take our farewell of his grace.          70

ABBOT     [aside] My heart with pity earns to see this sight;
          A king to bear these words and proud commands!

KING      Spenser, ah sweet Spenser, thus, then, must we part?

SPENSER   We must, my lord; so will the angry heavens.

KING      Nay, so will hell and cruel Mortimer:
          The gentle heavens have not to do in this.

BALDOCK   My lord, it is in vain to grieve or storm.
          Here humbly of your grace we take our leave.
          Our lots are cast; I fear me, so is thine.

KING      In heaven we may, in earth ne'er shall we meet —          80
          And, Leicester, say, what shall become of us?

LEICESTER  Your majesty must go to Killingworth.

KING      Must! It is somewhat hard when kings *must* go.

LEICESTER  Here is a litter ready for your grace,
          That waits your pleasure, and the day grows old.

AP HOWEL  As good be gone, as stay and be benighted.

KING      A litter hast thou? Lay me in a hearse,
          And to the gates of hell convey me hence;
          Let Pluto's bells ring out my fatal knell,
          And hags howl for my death at Charon's shore;          90
          For friends hath Edward none but these,
          And these must die under a tyrant's sword.

AP HOWEL  My lord, be going: care not for these;
          For we shall see them shorter by the heads.

KING      Well, that shall be shall be: part we must;
          Sweet Spenser, gentle Baldock, part we must —
          Hence, feigned weeds! Unfeigned are my woes —
                              [throwing off his disguise
          Father, farewell — Leicester, thou stay'st for me;
          And go I must — Life, farewell, with my friends!
                              [exeunt King Edward and Leicester

SPENSER   O, is he gone? Is noble Edward gone?          100
          Parted from hence, never to see us more!
          Rend, sphere of heaven! And, fire, forsake thy orb!
          Earth, melt to air! Gone is my sovereign,
          Gone, gone, alas, never to make return!

BALDOCK     Spenser, I see our souls are fleeting hence;
We are depriv'd the sunshine of our life.
Make for a new life, man; throw up thy eyes,
And heart and hand to heaven's immortal throne;
Pay nature's debt with cheerful countenance;
Reduce we all our lessons unto this –        110
To die, sweet Spenser, therefore live we all;
Spenser, all live to die, and rise to fall.

AP HOWEL    Come, come, keep these preachments till you come to
the place appointed. You, and such as you are, have
made wise work in England. Will your lordships away?

MOWER      Your lordship I trust will remember me?

AP HOWEL    Remember thee, fellow! What else? Follow me to the
town.

                                                   [exeunt

## ACT FIVE

### SCENE I

*Enter* KING EDWARD, LEICESTER,
*the* BISHOP OF WINCHESTER, *and* TRUSSEL

LEICESTER   Be patient, good my lord, cease to lament.
Imagine Killingworth Castle were your court,
And that you lay for pleasure here a space,
Not of compulsion or necessity.

KING   Leicester, if gentle words might comfort me,
Thy speeches long ago had eas'd my sorrows;
For kind and loving hast thou always been.
The griefs of private men are soon allay'd,
But not of kings. The forest deer, being struck,
Runs to an herb that closeth up the wounds;     10
But when the imperial lion's flesh is gor'd,
He rends and tears it with his wrathful paw,
And, highly scorning that the lowly earth
Should drink his blood, mounts up into the air:
And so it fares with me, whose dauntless mind
Th' ambitious Mortimer would seek to curb,
And that unnatural queen, false Isabel,
That thus hath pent and mew'd me in a prison.
For such outrageous passions cloy my soul,
As with the wings of rancour and disdain     20
Full often am I soaring up to heaven,
To plain me to the gods against them both.
But when I call to mind I am a king,
Methinks I should revenge me of my wrongs,
That Mortimer and Isabel have done.
But what are kings, when regiment is gone,
But perfect shadows in a sunshine day?
My nobles rule, I bear the name of king;
I wear the crown, but am controll'd by them,
By Mortimer, and my unconstant queen,     30
Who spots my nuptial bed with infamy,
Whilst I am lodg'd within this cave of care

Where sorrow at my elbow still attends,
To company my heart with sad laments
That bleeds within me for this strange exchange.
But tell me, must I now resign my crown,
To make usurping Mortimer a king?

WINCH.   Your grace mistakes; it is for England's good,
And princely Edward's right, we crave the crown.

KING     No, tis for Mortimer, not Edward's head;          40
For he's a lamb, encompassed by wolves,
Which in a moment will abridge his life.
But, if proud Mortimer do wear this crown,
Heavens turn it to a blaze of quenchless fire,
Or, like the snaky wreath of Tisiphon,
Engirt the temples of his hateful head!
So shall not England's vine be perished.
But Edward's name survive, though Edward dies.

LEICESTER  My lord, why waste you thus the time away?
They stay your answer: will you yield your crown?

KING     Ah, Leicester, weigh how hardly I can brook
To lose my crown and kingdom without cause,
To give ambitious Mortimer my right,
That, like a mountain, overwhelms my bliss;
In which extreme my mind here murder'd is!
But that the heavens appoint I must obey —
Here, take my crown; the life of Edward too.
                              [taking off the crown

Two kings in England cannot reign at once.
But stay a while: let me be king till night,
That I may gaze upon this glittering crown;          60
So shall my eyes receive their last content,
My head, the latest honour due to it,
And jointly both yield up their wished right.
Continue ever, thou celestial sun;
Let never silent night possess this clime;
Stand still, you watches of the element;
All times and seasons, rest you at a stay,
That Edward may be still fair England's king!
But day's bright beams doth vanish fast away,
And needs I must resign my wished crown.          70

Inhuman creatures, nurs'd with tiger's milk,
Why gape you for your sovereign's overthrow?
My diadem, I mean, and guiltless life.
See, monsters, see! I'll wear my crown again.

*[putting on the crown*

What, fear you not the fury of your king?
But, hapless Edward, thou art fondly led;
They pass not for thy frowns as late they did,
But seek to make a new-elected king;
Which fills my mind with strange despairing thoughts,
Which thoughts are martyred with endless torments,
And in this torment comfort find I none,
But that I feel the crown upon my head;
And therefore let me wear it yet a while.

TRUSSEL    My lord, the parliament must have present news;
And therefore say, will you resign or no?

*[the king rageth*

KING    I'll not resign, but, whilst I live, [be king].
Traitors, be gone, join you with Mortimer.
Elect, conspire, install, do what you will:
Their blood and yours shall seal these treacheries.

WINCH.    This answer we'll return; and so, farewell.    90

*[going with Trussel*

LEICESTER    Call them again, my lord, and speak them fair;
For, if they go, the prince shall lose his right.

KING    Call thou them back; I have no power to speak.

LEICESTER    My lord, the king is willing to resign.

WINCH.    If he be not, let him choose.

KING    O, would I might! But heavens and earth conspire
To make me miserable. Here, receive my crown.
Receive it? No, these innocent hands of mine
Shall not be guilty of so foul a crime;
He of you all that most desires my blood,    100
And will be call'd the murderer of a king,
Take it. What, are you mov'd? Pity you me?
Then send for unrelenting Mortimer,
And Isabel, whose eyes being turn'd to steel
Will sooner sparkle fire than shed a tear.
Yet stay; for, rather than I'll look on them,

Here, here! [*gives the crown*] Now, sweet God
of heaven,

Make me despise this transitory pomp,
And sit for aye enthronised in heaven!
Come, death, and with thy fingers close my eyes, 110
Or, if I live, let me forget myself!

WINCH.     My lord —

KING       Call me not lord; away, out of my sight!
Ah, pardon me! Grief makes me lunatic.
Let not that Mortimer protect my son;
More safety there is in a tiger's jaws
Than his embracements. Bear this to the queen,
Wet with my tears and dried again with sighs:

[*gives a handkerchief*

If with the sight thereof she be not mov'd,
Return it back, and dip it in my blood.            120
Commend me to my son, and bid him rule
Better than I: yet how have I transgress'd,
Unless it be with too much clemency?

TRUSSEL    And thus, most humbly do we take our leave.

KING       Farewell.          [*exeunt the Bishop of Winchester
and Trussel with the crown*

I know the next news that they bring
Will be my death, and welcome shall it be:
To wretched men death is felicity.

LEICESTER  Another post! What news brings he?

*Enter* BERKELEY, *who gives a paper to* LEICESTER

KING       Such news as I expect — Come, Berkeley, come,  130
And tell thy message to my naked breast.

BERKELEY   My lord, think not a thought so villanous
Can harbour in a man of noble birth.
To do your highness service and devoir,
And save you from your foes, Berkeley would die.

LEICESTER  My lord, the council of the queen command.
That I resign my charge.

KING       And who must keep me now? Must you, my lord?

BERKELEY   Ay, my most gracious lord; so 'tis decreed.

KING       [*taking the paper*] By Mortimer, whose name is
written here! 140

|         | Well may I rent his name that rends my heart. *[tears it* |
|         | This poor revenge hath something eas'd my mind: |
|         | So may his limbs be torn as is this paper! |
|         | Hear me, immortal Jove, and grant it too! |
| BERKELEY | Your grace must hence with me to Berkeley straight. |
| KING    | Whither you will: all places are alike, |
|         | And every earth is fit for burial. |
| LEICESTER | Favour him, my lord, as much as lieth in you. |
| BERKELEY | Even so betide my soul as I use him! |
| KING    | Mine enemy hath pitied my estate, |
|         | And that's the cause that I am now remov'd. |
| BERKELEY | And thinks your grace that Berkeley will be cruel? |
| KING    | I know not: but of this am I assur'd, |
|         | That death ends all, and I can die but once – |
|         | Leicester, farewell. |
| LEICESTER | Not yet, my lord. I'll bear you on your way. |

150

*[exeunt*

## SCENE 2

*Enter* QUEEN ISABELLA *and the younger* MORTIMER

| MORTIMER | Fair Isabel, now have we our desire; |
|          | The proud corrupters of the light-brain'd king |
|          | Have done their homage to the lofty gallows, |
|          | And he himself lies in captivity. |
|          | Be rul'd by me, and we will rule the realm: |
|          | In any case, take heed of childish fear, |
|          | For now we hold an old wolf by the ears, |
|          | That, if he slip, will seize upon us both |
|          | And gripe the sorer, being grip'd himself. |
|          | Think therefore, madam, that imports us much |
|          | To erect your son with all the speed we may, |
|          | And that I be protector over him: |
|          | For our behoof, 'twill bear the greater sway |
|          | Whenas a king's name shall be under-writ. |
| ISABELLA | Sweet Mortimer, the life of Isabel, |
|          | Be thou persuaded that I love thee well: |
|          | And therefore, so the prince my son be safe, |
|          | Whom I esteem as dear as these mine eyes, |

10

Conclude against his father what thou wilt,
And I myself will willingly subscribe.                    20

MORTIMER   First would I hear news he were depos'd,
And then let me alone to handle him.

*Enter Messenger*

Letters! From whence?

MESSENGER                              From Killingworth, my lord.

ISABELLA   How fares my lord the king?

MESSENGER   In health, madam, but full of pensiveness.

ISABELLA   Alas, poor soul, would I could ease his grief!

*Enter the* BISHOP OF WINCHESTER *with the crown*

Thanks, gentle Winchester – Sirrah, be gone.
                                        [*exit Messenger*

WINCH.   The king hath willingly resign'd his crown.

ISABELLA   O, happy news! Send for the prince my son.

WINCH.   Further, or this letter was seal'd, Lord Berkeley came,
So that he now is gone from Killingworth;
And we have heard that Edmund laid a plot
To set his brother free; no more but so.
The Lord of Berkeley is so pitiful
As Leicester that had charge of him before.

ISABELLA   Then let some other be his guardian.

MORTIMER   Let me alone; here is the privy-seal –
                              [*exit the Bishop of Winchester*

Who's there? [*to Attendants within*]
                          Call hither Gurney and Matrevis –
To dash the heavy-headed Edmund's drift,
Berkeley shall be discharg'd, the king remov'd,          40
And none but we shall know where he lieth.

ISABELLA   But, Mortimer, as long as he survives,
What safety rests for us or for my son?

MORTIMER   Speak, shall he presently be despatch'd and die?

ISABELLA   I would he were, so 'twere not by my means!

*Enter* MATREVIS *and* GURNEY

MORTIMER   Enough – Matrevis, write a letter presently
Unto the Lord of Berkeley from ourself,
That he resign the king to thee and Gurney;
And, when 'tis done, we will subscribe our name.

| | |
|---|---|
| MATREVIS | It shall be done, my lord. [*writes*] |
| MORTIMER | Gurney — |
| GURNEY | My lord?        50 |
| MORTIMER | As thou intend'st to rise by Mortimer, |
| | Who now makes Fortune's wheel turn as he please, |
| | Seek all the means thou canst to make him droop, |
| | And neither give him kind word nor good look. |
| GURNEY | I warrant you, my lord. |
| MORTIMER | And this above the rest: because we hear |
| | That Edmund casts to work his liberty, |
| | Remove him still from place to place by night, |
| | Till at the last he come to Killingworth, |
| | And then from thence to Berkeley back again;        60 |
| | And by the way, to make him fret the more, |
| | Speak curstly to him; and in any case |
| | Let no man comfort him, if he chance to weep, |
| | But amplify his grief with bitter words. |
| MATREVIS | Fear not, my lord; we'll do as you command. |
| MORTIMER | So, now away! Post thitherwards amain. |
| ISABELLA | Whither goes this letter? To my lord the king? |
| | Commend me humbly to his majesty, |
| | And tell him that I labour all in vain |
| | To ease his grief and work his liberty;        70 |
| | And bear him this as witness of my love.    [*gives ring* |
| MATREVIS | I will, madam.                    [*exit with Gurney* |
| MORTIMER | Finely dissembled! Do so still, sweet queen. |
| | Here comes the young prince with the Earl of Kent. |
| ISABELLA | Something he whispers in his childish ears. |
| MORTIMER | If he have such access unto the prince, |
| | Our plots and stratagems will soon be dash'd. |
| ISABELLA | Use Edmund friendly, as if all were well. |

*Enter* PRINCE EDWARD *and* KENT *talking with him*

| | |
|---|---|
| MORTIMER | How fares my honourable Lord of Kent? |
| KENT | In health, sweet Mortimer — How fares your grace?    80 |
| ISABELLA | Well, if my lord your brother were enlarg'd. |
| KENT | I hear of late he hath depos'd himself. |
| ISABELLA | The more my grief. |
| MORTIMER | And mine. |
| KENT | [*aside*] Ah, they do dissemble! |

| | |
|---|---|
| ISABELLA | Sweet son, come hither: I must talk with thee. |
| MORTIMER | You, being his uncle and the next of blood, |
| | Do look to be protector o'er the prince. |
| KENT | Not I, my lord: who should protect the son, |
| | But she that gave him life? I mean the queen. |
| PRINCE | Mother, persuade me not to wear the crown: |
| | Let him be king; I am too young to reign. 90 |
| ISABELLA | But be content, seeing 'tis his highness' pleasure. |
| PRINCE | Let me but see him first, and then I will. |
| KENT | Ay, do, sweet nephew. |
| ISABELLA | Brother, you know it is impossible. |
| PRINCE | Why, is he dead? |
| ISABELLA | No, God forbid! |
| KENT | I would those words proceeded from your heart! |
| MORTIMER | Inconstant Edmund, dost thou favour him, |
| | That wast a cause of his imprisonment? |
| KENT | The more cause now have I to make amends. 100 |
| MORTIMER | [aside to Queen Isabella] I tell thee, 'tis not meet |
| | that one so false |
| | Should come about the person of a prince – |
| | My lord, he hath betray'd the king his brother, |
| | And therefore trust him not. |
| PRINCE | But he repents, and sorrows for it now. |
| ISABELLA | Come, son, and go with this gentle lord and me. |
| PRINCE | With you I will, but not with Mortimer. |
| MORTIMER | Why, youngling, 'sdain'st thou so of Mortimer? |
| | Then I will carry thee by force away. |
| PRINCE | Help, uncle Kent! Mortimer will wrong me. 110 |
| ISABELLA | Brother Edmund, strive not; we are his friends. |
| | Isabel is nearer than the Earl of Kent. |
| KENT | Sister, Edward is my charge; redeem him. |
| ISABELLA | Edward is my son, and I will keep him. |
| KENT | [aside] Mortimer shall know that he hath wronged me. |
| | Hence will I haste to Killingworth Castle, |
| | And rescue aged Edward from his foes, |
| | To be reveng'd on Mortimer and thee. |

[exeunt, on one side, Queen Isabella, Prince Edward
and the younger Mortimer; on the other, Kent

## SCENE 3

*Enter* MATREVIS, GURNEY, *and Soldiers, with* KING EDWARD

| | |
|---|---|
| MATREVIS | My lord, be not pensive; we are your friends: |
| | Men are ordain'd to live in misery; |
| | Therefore come; dalliance dangereth our lives. |
| KING | Friends, whither must unhappy Edward go? |
| | Will hateful Mortimer appoint no rest? |
| | Must I be vexed like the nightly bird, |
| | Whose sight is loathsome to all winged fowls? |
| | When will the fury of his mind assuage? |
| | When will his heart be satisfied with blood? |
| | If mine will serve, unbowel straight this breast,     10 |
| | And give my heart to Isabel and him: |
| | It is the chiefest mark they level at. |
| GURNEY | Not so, my liege: the queen hath given this charge, |
| | To keep your grace in safety: |
| | Your passions make your dolours to increase. |
| KING | This usage makes my misery increase. |
| | But can my air of life continue long, |
| | When all my senses are annoy'd with stench? |
| | Within a dungeon England's king is kept, |
| | Where I am starv'd for want of sustenance.     20 |
| | My daily diet is heart-breaking sobs, |
| | That almost rent the closet of my heart: |
| | Thus lives old Edward not reliev'd by any, |
| | And so must die, though pitied by many. |
| | O, water, gentle friends, to cool my thirst, |
| | And clear my body from foul excrements! |
| MATREVIS | Here's channel-water, as our charge is given: |
| | Sit down, for we'll be barbers to your grace. |
| KING | Traitors, away! What, will you murder me, |
| | Or choke your sovereign with puddle-water?     30 |
| GURNEY | No, but wash your face, and shave away your beard, |
| | Lest you be known, and so be rescued. |
| MATREVIS | Why strive you thus? Your labour is in vain. |
| KING | The wren may strive against the lion's strength, |

But all in vain so vainly do I strive
To seek for mercy at a tyrant's hand.

> *[they wash him with puddle-water,*
> *and shave his beard away*

Immortal powers, that know the painful cares
That wait upon my poor distressed soul,
O, level all your looks upon these daring men
That wrong their liege and sovereign, England's king!
O Gaveston, it is for thee that I am wrong'd!
For me both thou and both the Spensers died;
And for your sakes a thousand wrongs I'll take.
The Spensers' ghosts, wherever they remain,
Wish well to mine; then, tush, for them I'll die.

MATREVIS 'Twixt theirs and yours shall be no enmity.
Come, come, away! Now put the torches out:
We'll enter in by darkness to Killingworth.

GURNEY How now! Who comes there?

*Enter* KENT

MATREVIS Guard the king sure: it is the Earl of Kent.                    50
KING O gentle brother, help to rescue me!
MATREVIS Keep them asunder; thrust in the king.
KENT Soldiers, let me but talk to him one word.
GURNEY Lay hands upon the earl for his assault.
KENT Lay down your weapons, traitors! Yield the king!
MATREVIS Edmund, yield thou thyself, or thou shalt die.
KENT Base villains, wherefore do you gripe me thus?
GURNEY Bind him, and so convey him to the court.
KENT Where is the court but here? Here is the king,
And I will visit him: why stay you me?                    60
MATREVIS The court is where Lord Mortimer remains:
Thither shall your honour go; and so, farewell.

> *[exeunt Matrevis and Gurney with King Edward*

KENT O, miserable is that common-weal,
Where lords keep courts, and kings are lock'd
                                                    in prison.
I SOLDIER Wherefore stay we? On, sirs, to the court!
KENT Ay, lead me whither you will, even to my death,
Seeing that my brother cannot be releas'd.

> *[exeunt*

## SCENE 4

*Enter the younger* MORTIMER

MORTIMER The king must die, or Mortimer goes down;
The commons now begin to pity him:
Yet he that is the cause of Edward's death
Is sure to pay for it when his son's of age,
And therefore will I do it cunningly.
This letter, written by a friend of ours,
Contains his death, yet bids them save his life;
[*reads*] *Edwardum occidere nolite timere, bonum est,*
*Fear not to kill the king, 'tis good he die.*
But read it thus, and that's another sense:         10
*Edwardum occidere nolite, timere bonum est,*
*Kill not the king, 'tis good to fear the worst.*
Unpointed as it is, thus shall it go.
That, being dead, if it chance to be found,
Matrevis and the rest may bear the blame,
And we be quit that caus'd it to be done.
Within this room is lock'd the messenger
That shall convey it, and perform the rest;
And, by a secret token that he bears,
Shall he be murder'd when the deed is done –       20
Lightborn, come forth!

*Enter* LIGHTBORN

Art thou so resolute as thou wast?
LIGHTBORN What else, my lord? And far more resolute.
MORTIMER And hast thou cast how to accomplish it?
LIGHTBORN Ay, ay; and none shall know which way he died.
MORTIMER But at his looks, Lightborn, thou wilt relent.
LIGHTBORN Relent! Ha, ha! I use much to relent.
MORTIMER Well, do it bravely, and be secret.
LIGHTBORN You shall not need to give instructions;
'Tis not the first time I have kill'd a man:
I learn'd in Naples how to poison flowers;          30
To strangle with a lawn thrust down the throat;
To pierce the wind pipe with a needle's point;

     Or, whilst one is asleep, to take a quill,
     And blow a little powder in his ears;
     Or open his mouth, and pour quick-silver down.
     But yet I have a braver way than these.

MORTIMER  What s that?

LIGHTBORN  Nay, you shall pardon me: none shall know my tricks.

MORTIMER  I care not how it is, so it be not spied.
     Deliver this to Gurney and Matrevis:    *[gives letter*
     At every ten-mile end thou hast a horse:
     Take this *[gives money]*: away, and never see me more!

LIGHTBORN  No?

MORTIMER  No – unless thou bring me news of Edward's death.

LIGHTBORN  That will I quickly do. Farewell, my lord.    *[exit*

MORTIMER  The prince I rule, the queen do I command,
     And with a lowly congé to the ground
     The proudest lords salute me as I pass;
     I seal, I cancel, I do what I will.
     Fear'd am I more than lov'd – let me be fear'd,   50
     And, when I frown, make all the court look pale.
     I view the prince with Aristarchus' eyes,
     Whose looks were as a breeching to a boy.
     They thrust upon me the protectorship,
     And sue to me for that that I desire;
     While at the council-table, grave enough,
     And not unlike a bashful puritan,
     First I complain of imbecility,
     Saying it is *onus quam gravissimum*;
     Till, being interrupted by my friends,     60
     *Suscepi* that *provinciam,* as they term it;
     And, to conclude, I am Protector now.
     Now is all sure: the queen and Mortimer
     Shall rule the realm, the king; and none rule us.
     Mine enemies will I plague, my friends advance;
     And what I list command who dare control?
     *Major sum quam cui possit fortuna nocere:*
     And that this be the coronation-day,
     It pleaseth me and Isabel the queen.   *[trumpets within*
     The trumpets sound; I must go take my place.   70

*Enter* KING EDWARD THE THIRD, QUEEN ISABELLA,
*the* ARCHBISHOP OF CANTERBURY, *Champion, and Nobles*

| | |
|---|---|
| CANTERB. | Long live King Edward, by the grace of God |
| | King of England and Lord of Ireland! |
| CHAMPION | If any Christian, Heathen, Turk, or Jew, |
| | Dares but affirm that Edward's not true king, |
| | And will avouch his saying with the sword, |
| | I am the Champion that will combat him. |
| MORTIMER | None comes: sound, trumpets!       [*trumpets* |
| EDWARD III | Champion, here's to thee.       [*gives purse* |
| ISABELLA | Lord Mortimer, now take him to your charge. |

*Enter Soldiers with* KENT *prisoner*

| | | |
|---|---|---|
| MORTIMER | What traitor have we there with blades and bills? | |
| I SOLDIER | Edmund the Earl of Kent. | 80 |
| EDWARD III | What hath he done? | |
| I SOLDIER | 'A would have taken the king away perforce, | |
| | As we were bringing him to Killingworth. | |
| MORTIMER | Did you attempt his rescue, Edmund? Speak. | |
| KENT | Mortimer, I did: he is our king, | |
| | And thou compell'st this prince to wear the crown. | |
| MORTIMER | Strike off his head: he shall have martial law. | |
| KENT | Strike off my head! Base traitor, I defy thee! | |
| EDWARD III | My lord, he is my uncle, and shall live. | |
| MORTIMER | My lord, he is your enemy, and shall die. | 90 |
| KENT | Stay, villains! | |
| EDWARD III | Sweet mother, if I cannot pardon him, | |
| | Entreat my Lord Protector for his life. | |
| ISABELLA | Son, be content: I dare not speak a word. | |
| EDWARD III | Nor I; and yet methinks I should command: | |
| | But, seeing I cannot, I'll entreat for him – | |
| | My lord, if you will let my uncle live, | |
| | I will requite it when I come to age. | |
| MORTIMER | 'Tis for your highness' good and for the realm's – | |
| | How often shall I bid you bear him hence? | 100 |
| KENT | Art thou king? Must I die at thy command? | |
| MORTIMER | At our command – Once more, away with him! | |
| KENT | Let me but stay and speak; I will not go: | |
| | Either my brother or his son is king, | |

And none of both them thirst for Edmund's blood:
And therefore, soldiers, whither will you hale me?

> [Soldiers hale Kent away,
> and carry him to be beheaded

EDWARD III  What safety may I look for at his hands,
If that my uncle shall be murder'd thus?

ISABELLA  Fear not, sweet boy; I'll guard thee from thy foes.
Had Edmund liv'd, he would have sought thy death.
Come, son, we'll ride a-hunting in the park.

EDWARD III  And shall my uncle Edmund ride with us?

ISABELLA  He is a traitor; think not on him: come.

> [exeunt


## SCENE 5

### Enter MATREVIS and GURNEY

MATREVIS  Gurney. I wonder the king dies not,
Being in a vault up to the knees in water,
To which the channels of the castle run,
From whence a damp continually ariseth,
That were enough to poison any man,
Much more a king, brought up so tenderly.

GURNEY  And so do I, Matrevis: yesternight
I open'd but the door to throw him meat,
And I was almost stifled with the savour.

MATREVIS  He hath a body able to endure                    10
More than we can inflict: and therefore now
Let us assail his mind another while.

GURNEY  Send for him out thence, and I will anger him.

MATREVIS  But stay; who's this?

### Enter LIGHTBORN

LIGHTBORN                    My Lord Protector greets you.

> [gives letter

GURNEY  What's here? I know not how to construe it.

MATREVIS  Gurney, it was left unpointed for the nonce:
*Edwardum occidere nolite timere,*
That's his meaning.

LIGHTBORN  Know you this token? I must have the king.

> [gives token

MATREVIS    Ay, stay a while; thou shalt have answer straight –  20
               This villain's sent to make away the king.
GURNEY    I thought as much.
MATREVIS                 And when the murder's done,
               See how he must be handled for his labour –
               *Pereat iste*! Let him have the king.
               What else? Here is the keys, this is the lake:
               Do as you are commanded by my lord.
LIGHTBORN I know what I must do. Get you away:
               Yet be not far off; I shall need your help:
               See that in the next room I have a fire,
               And get me a spit, and let it be red-hot.       30
MATREVIS    Very well.
GURNEY           Need you anything besides?
LIGHTBORN What else? A table and a featherbed.
GURNEY    That s all?
LIGHTBORN Ay, ay: so, when I call you, bring it in.
MATREVIS    Fear not thou that.
GURNEY    Here's a light to go into the dungeon.
                        *[gives light to Lightborn,*
                        *and then exit with Matrevis*
LIGHTBORN So, now
               Must I about this gear: ne'er was there any
               So finely handled as this king shall be –
               Foh, here's a place indeed with all my heart!     40
KING    Who's there? What light is that? Wherefore
                             com'st thou?
LIGHTBORN To comfort you, and bring you joyful news.
KING    Small comfort finds poor Edward in thy looks:
               Villain, I know thou com'st to murder me.
LIGHTBORN To murder you, my most gracious lord?
               Far be it from my heart to do you harm.
               The queen sent me to see how you were us'd,
               For she relents at this your misery:
               And what eye can refrain from shedding tears,
               To see a king in this most piteous state?        50
KING    Weep'st thou already? List a while to me,
               And then thy heart, were it as Gurney's is,
               Or as Matrevis', hewn from the Caucasus,

     Yet will it melt ere I have done my tale.
     This dungeon where they keep me is the sink
     Wherein the filth of all the castle falls.

LIGHTBORN O villains!

KING   And there, in mire and puddle, have I stood
     This ten days' space; and, lest that I should sleep,
     One plays continually upon a drum;    60
     They give me bread and water, being a king,
     So that, for want of sleep and sustenance,
     My mind's distemper'd, and my body's numb'd,
     And whether I have limbs or no I know not.
     O, would my blood dropp'd out from every vein,
     As doth this water from my tatter'd robes!
     Tell Isabel the queen, I look'd not thus,
     When for her sake I ran at tilt in France,
     And there unhors'd the Duke of Cleremont.

LIGHTBORN O, speak no more, my lord! This breaks my heart.
     Lie on this bed, and rest yourself a while.

KING   These looks of thine can harbour naught but death;
     I see my tragedy written in thy brows.
     Yet stay a while; forbear thy bloody hand,
     And let me see the stroke before it comes,
     That even then when I shall lose my life,
     My mind may be more steadfast on my God.

LIGHTBORN What means your highness to mistrust me thus?

KING   What mean'st thou to dissemble with me thus?

LIGHTBORN These hands were never stain'd with innocent blood,
     Nor shall they now be tainted with a king's.

KING   Forgive my thought for having such a thought.
     One jewel have I left; receive thou this:  [giving jewel
     Still fear I, and I know not what's the cause,
     But every joint shakes as I give it thee.
     O, if thou harbour'st murder in thy heart,
     Let this gift change thy mind, and save thy soul!
     Know that I am a king: O, at that name
     I feel a hell of grief! Where is my crown?
     Gone, gone! And do I [still] remain alive?  90

LIGHTBORN You're overwatch'd, my lord: lie down and rest.

KING   But that grief keeps me waking, I should sleep;

> For not these ten days have these eye-lids clos'd.
> Now, as I speak, they fall; and yet with fear
> Open again. O, wherefore sitt'st thou here?

LIGHTBORN   If you mistrust me, I'll be gone, my lord.

KING       No, no; for, if thou mean'st to murder me,
> Thou wilt return again; and therefore stay.     [*sleeps*

LIGHTBORN   He sleeps.

KING       [*waking*] O, let me not die yet! O, stay a while!    100

LIGHTBORN   How now, my lord!

KING       Something still buzzeth in mine ears,
> And tells me, if I sleep, I never wake:
> This fear is that which makes me tremble thus
> And therefore tell me, wherefore art thou come?

LIGHTBORN   To rid thee of thy life — Matrevis, come!

*Enter* MATREVIS *and* GURNEY

KING       I am too weak and feeble to resist.
> Assist me, sweet God, and receive my soul!

LIGHTBORN   Run for the table.

KING       O, spare me, or despatch me in a trice!     110
>                [*Matrevis brings in a table*

LIGHTBORN   So, lay the table down, and stamp on it,
> But not too hard, lest that you bruise his body.

MATREVIS   I fear me that this cry will raise the town,
> And therefore let us take horse and away.

LIGHTBORN   Tell me, sirs, was it not bravely done?

GURNEY    Excellent well: take this for thy reward.
>                [*stabs Lightborn, who dies*
> Come, let us cast the body in the moat,
> And bear the king's to Mortimer our lord:
> Away!
>                [*exeunt with the bodies*

### SCENE 6

*Enter the younger* MORTIMER *and* MATREVIS

MORTIMER  Is't done, Matrevis, and the murderer dead?

MATREVIS  Ay, my good lord: I would it were undone!

MORTIMER  Matrevis, if thou now grow'st penitent,
    I'll be thy ghostly father; therefore choose,
    Whether thou wilt be secret in this
    Or else die by the hand of Mortimer.

MATREVIS  Gurney, my lord, is fled, and will, I fear,
    Betray us both; therefore let me fly.

MORTIMER  Fly to the savages!

MATREVIS         I humbly thank your honour. [*exit*

MORTIMER  As for myself, I stand as Jove's huge tree,   10
    And others are but shrubs compar'd to me:
    All tremble at my name, and I fear none:
    Let's see who dare impeach me for his death.

*Enter* QUEEN ISABELLA

ISABELLA  Ah, Mortimer, the king my son hath news,
    His father's dead, and we have murder'd him!

MORTIMER  What if he have? The king is yet a child.

ISABELLA  Ay, but he tears his hair, and wrings his hands,
    And vows to be reveng'd upon us both.
    Into the council-chamber he is gone,
    To crave the aid and succour of his peers.   20
    Ay me, see where he comes, and they with him!
    Now, Mortimer, begins our tragedy.

*Enter* KING EDWARD THE THIRD, *Lords, and Attendants*

I LORD  Fear not, my lord; know that you are a king.

EDWARD III  Villain!

MORTIMER  Ho, now, my lord!

EDWARD III  Think not that I am frighted with thy words:
    My father's murder'd through thy treachery:
    And thou shalt die, and on his mournful hearse
    Thy hateful and accursed head shall lie,
    To witness to the world that by thy means   30
    His kingly body was too soon interr'd.

ISABELLA    Weep not, sweet son.

EDWARD III   Forbid not me to weep; he was my father,
             And had you lov'd him half so well as I,
             You could not bear his death thus patiently:
             But you, I fear, conspir'd with Mortimer.

I LORD       Why speak you not unto my lord the king?

MORTIMER   Because I think scorn to be accus'd.
             Who is the man dares say I murder'd him?

EDWARD III   Traitor, in me my loving father speaks,          40
             And plainly saith, 'twas thou that murder'dst him.

MORTIMER   But hath your grace no other proof than this?

EDWARD III   Yes, if this be the hand of Mortimer.     [showing letter

MORTIMER   [aside to Queen Isabella] False Gurney hath
                                 betray'd me and himself.

ISABELLA    I fear'd as much: murder can not be hid.

MORTIMER   It is my hand: what gather you by this?

EDWARD III   That thither thou didst send a murderer.

MORTIMER   What murderer? Bring forth the man I sent.

EDWARD III   Ah, Mortimer, thou know'st that he is slain!
             And so shalt thou be too — Why stays he here?     50
             Bring him unto a hurdle, drag him forth;
             Hang him, I say, and set his quarters up;
             And bring his head back presently to me.

ISABELLA    For my sake, sweet son, pity Mortimer!

MORTIMER   Madam, entreat not: I will rather die
             Than sue for life unto a paltry boy.

EDWARD III   Hence with the traitor, with the murderer!

MORTIMER   Base Fortune, now I see, that in thy wheel
             There is a point, to which when men aspire,
             They tumble headlong down: that point I touch'd,
             And, seeing there was no place to mount up higher,
             Why should I grieve at my declining fall?
             Farewell, fair queen: weep not for Mortimer,
             That scorns the world, and, as a traveller,
             Goes to discover countries yet unknown.

EDWARD III   What, suffer you the traitor to delay?
                        [exit the younger Mortimer with
                         First Lord and some of the Attendants

ISABELLA    As thou receiv'dst thy life from me,

|             | Spill not the blood of gentle Mortimer! |
|-------------|------------------------------------------|

EDWARD III  This argues that you spilt my father's blood;
             Else would you not entreat for Mortimer.          70

ISABELLA  I spill his blood! No.

EDWARD III  Ay, madam, you: for so the rumour runs.

ISABELLA  That rumour is untrue: for loving thee,
          Is this report rais'd on poor Isabel.

EDWARD III  I do not think her so unnatural.

I LORD  My lord, I fear me it will prove too true.

EDWARD III  Mother, you are suspected for his death,
          And therefore we commit you to the Tower,
          Till further trial may be made thereof.
          If you be guilty, though I be your son,          80
          Think not to find me slack or pitiful.

ISABELLA  Nay, to my death; for too long have I liv'd,
          Whenas my son thinks to abridge my days.

EDWARD III  Away with her! Her words enforce these tears,
          And I shall pity her, if she speak again.

ISABELLA  Shall I not mourn for my beloved lord,
          And with the rest accompany him to his grave?

2 LORD  Thus, madam, 'tis the king's will you shall hence.

ISABELLA  He hath forgotten me: stay, I am his mother.

2 LORD  That boots not; therefore, gentle madam, go.          90

ISABELLA  Then come, sweet death, and rid me of this grief!
                 *[exit with Second Lord and some of the Attendants*

*Re-enter First Lord, with the head of the younger* MORTIMER

I LORD  My lord, here is the head of Mortimer.

EDWARD III  Go fetch my father's hearse, where it shall lie;
          And bring my funeral robes. *[exeunt Attendants]*
                      Accursed head,
          Could I have rul'd thee then, as I do now,
          Thou hadst not hatch'd this monstrous treachery!
          Here comes the hearse: help me to mourn, my lords.

*Re-enter Attendants, with the hearse and funeral robes*

          Sweet father, here unto thy murder'd ghost
          I offer up the wicked traitor's head;
          And let these tears, distilling from mine eyes,          100
          Be witness of my grief and innocency.
                            *[exeunt*

# THE MASSACRE AT PARIS

# INTRODUCTION

*The Massacre at Paris* has received relatively little critical attention, perhaps because the shortness of the extant text – only about 1200 lines – has suggested some corruption in its transmission. In addition, it is dependent on a disconnected series of bloody episodes involving a gallery of stereotyped characters, and it is unsurprising that it has hardly ever been revived in the theatre. For modern readers of Marlowe, it is perhaps the least satisfying of his works. For all that, the play deserves our attention, for its recognisably Marlovian features as well as for its unique qualities, not least its extreme topicality. The play is Marlowe's only known treatment of a recent historical event, and tells the story of the infamous massacre of protestants in Paris in August 1572, St Bartholomew's Day. The massacre is depicted through a number of short episodes, and then concludes with the murder of Henry III and the accession of the protestant Henry of Navarre to the French throne. The play was first performed in 1593, only four years after the events with which it concludes. It is Marlowe at his most historically and ideologically immediate, and, notably given the characteristic moral ambiguities of his other works, his nearest approach to propaganda.

For English contemporaries, the St Bartholomew massacre was a byword for Catholic treachery, and news from France circulated in popular pamphlets and in conversation, not least because of the large numbers of protestant refugees from France and other European countries in Elizabethan London. Thus Marlowe's central figure, the Duke of Guise, represents the deceit specifically attributed to Catholics as well as the more general machiavellian enjoyment of plotting and dissembling familiar from *The Jew of Malta*. The Duke of Guise, like Barabas, inspires that typically

Marlovian and contradictory response of loathing and admiration in the audience. This representation of Catholicism as analogous to deceit, however, tumbles over itself in its logical conclusion that Catholicism is itself only deceit: Guise suggests that his religious public presentation is expedience rather than conviction: 'My policy hath fram'd religion' (1,2). However, despite the play's apparently transparent religio-political affiliations, there are considerable uncertainties in it, some of which may result from the divergences between Marlowe's differently partisan sources. At the end, Henry III, a staunch catholic, undergoes a deathbed conversion and professes friendship to 'the Queen of England'. Marlowe's presentation of the king, however, is far from positive: he is shown to be a liar when he denies his involvement in the massacre, and his murder of the Guise is cold-blooded and calculating. His heir, Henry of Navarre, is crowned as a protestant, vowing that 'Rome and all those popish prelates there /Shall curse the time that e'er Navarre was king': a remark which must have resounded hollowly in the Rose theatre in 1593 when Navarre's politic conversion to Catholicism was widely known. The play's events take place over more than a decade, but Marlowe's design seems to have been to suggest an equivalence between the massacre of the protestants which occupies the first part of the play and the murder of the Guise brothers in the econd. This symmetry may have been intended to suggest a poetic, if delayed, justice, by which the later actions are seen as retribution for earlier events. More unsettlingly, the play's apparent sympathy for the murdered Guise brothers suggests that its ideological position is less clear-cut than its status as committed Protestant propaganda might suggest.

# CHARACTERS IN THE PLAY

CHARLES THE NINTH, *King of France*
DUKE OF ANJOU, *his brother, afterwards King Henry the Third*
KING OF NAVARRE
PRINCE OF CONDÉ, *his cousin*
DUKE OF GUISE ⎫
CARDINAL OF LORRAINE ⎬ *brothers*
DUKE DUMAINE ⎭
SON TO THE DUKE OF GUISE, *a boy*
THE LORD HIGH ADMIRAL
DUKE JOYEUX
EPERNOUN
PLESHÉ
BARTUS
TWO LORDS OF POLAND
GONZAGO
RETES
MOUNTSORRELL
MUGEROUN
THE CUTPURSE
LOREINE, *his cousin*
SEROUNE
RAMUS
TALAEUS
FRIAR
SURGEON
ENGLISH AGENT
APOTHECARY
CAPTAIN OF THE GUARD, *Protestants, Schoolmasters,*
  *Soldiers, Murderers, Attendants, etc.*
CATHERINE, *the Queen-Mother of France*
MARGARET, *her daughter, wife to the King of Navarre*
THE OLD QUEEN OF NAVARRE
DUCHESS OF GUISE
WIFE *to Seroune*
MAID *to the Duchess of Guise*

# THE MASSACRE AT PARIS

## ACT ONE

### SCENE I

*Enter* CHARLES *the French King,* CATHERINE, *the Queen-Mother;*
*the* KING OF NAVARRE; MARGARET, *Queen of Navarre;*
*the* PRINCE OF CONDÉ; *the* LORD HIGH ADMIRAL;
*the* OLD QUEEN OF NAVARRE; *with others*

CHARLES     Prince of Navarre, my honourable brother,
            Prince Condé, and my good Lord Admiral,
            I wish this union and religious league,
            Knit in these hands, thus join'd in nuptial rites,
            May not dissolve till death dissolve our lives;
            And that the native sparks of princely love,
            That kindled first this motion in our hearts,
            May still be fuell'd in our progeny.

NAVARRE     The many favours which your grace hath shown,
            From time to time, but specially in this,           10
            Shall bind me ever to your highness' will,
            In what Queen-Mother or your grace commands.

CATHERINE   Thanks, son Navarre. You see we love you well,
            That link you in marriage with our daughter here:
            And as you know, our difference in religion
            Might be a means to cross you in your love –

CHARLES     Well, madam, let that rest –
            And now, my lords, the marriage-rites perform'd,
            We think it good to go and consummate
            The rest with hearing of a holy mass –         20
            Sister, I think yourself will bear us company.

MARGARET   I will, my good lord.

CHARLES     The rest that will not go, my lords, may stay –
            Come, mother,
            Let us go to honour this solemnity.

CATHERINE   [*aside*] Which I'll dissolve with blood and cruelty.

                             [*exeunt all except the King of Navarre,*
                                   *Condé, and the Admiral*

NAVARRE    Prince Condé, and my good Lord Admiral,
           Now Guise may storm, but do us little hurt,
           Having the king, Queen-mother on our sides,
           To stop the malice of his envious heart,                    30
           That seeks to murder all the Protestants.
           Have you not heard of late how he decreed
           (If that the king had given consent thereto)
           That all the protestants that are in Paris
           Should have been murdered the other night?

ADMIRAL    My lord, I marvel that th' aspiring Guise
           Dares once adventure, without the king's consent,
           To meddle or attempt such dangerous things.

CONDÉ      My lord, you need not marvel at the Guise,
           For what he doth, the Pope will ratify,                     40
           In murder, mischief or in tyranny.

NAVARRE    But he that sits and rules above the clouds
           Doth hear and see the prayers of the just,
           And will revenge the blood of innocents,
           That Guise hath slain by treason of his heart,
           And brought by murder to their timeless ends.

ADMIRAL    My lord, but did you mark the Cardinal,
           The Guise's brother, and the Duke Dumaine,
           How they did storm at these your nuptial rites,
           Because the house of Bourbon now comes in             50
           And joins your lineage to the crown of France?

NAVARRE    And that's the cause that Guise so frowns at us,
           And heats his brains to catch us in his trap,
           Which he hath pitch'd within his deadly toil.
           Come, my lords, let's go to the church, and pray
           That God may still defend the right of France,
           And make his Gospel flourish in this land.

                                                          [exeunt

## SCENE 2

*Enter* GUISE

GUISE    If ever Hymen lour'd at marriage-rites,
And had his altars deck'd with dusky lights;
If ever sun stain'd heaven with bloody clouds,
And made it look with terror on the world;
If ever day were turn'd to ugly night,
And night made semblance of the hue of hell;
This day, this hour, this fatal night,
Shall fully show the fury of them all –
Apothecary!

*Enter Apothecary*

APOTHEC.    My lord?                                          10

GUISE    Now shall I prove, and guerdon to the full,
The love thou bear'st unto the house of Guise.
Where are those perfum'd gloves which I sent
To be poison'd? Hast thou done them? Speak;
Will every savour breed a pang of death?

APOTHEC.    See where they be, my good lord; and he that smells
But to them, dies.

GUISE                      Then thou remain'st resolute?

APOTHEC.    I am, my lord, in what your grace commands,
Till death.

GUISE    Thanks, my good friend: I will requite thy love.    20
Go, then, present them to the Queen Navarre;
For she is that huge blemish in our eye
That makes these upstart heresies in France:
Be gone, my friend, present them to her straight.

                                    *[exit Apothecary*

Soldier!

*Enter a Soldier*

SOLDIER    My lord?

GUISE    Now come thou forth, and play thy tragic part.
Stand in some window, opening near the street,
And when thou see'st the Admiral ride by,
Discharge thy musket, and perform his death;    30

And then I'll guerdon thee with store of crowns.

SOLDIER   I will, my lord.                                    [exit

GUISE     Now, Guise, begin those deep-engender'd thoughts
          To burst abroad those never-dying flames
          Which cannot be extinguish'd but by blood.
          Oft have I levell'd, and at last have learn'd
          That peril is the chiefest way to happiness,
          And resolution honour's fairest aim.
          What glory is there in a common good,
          That hangs for every peasant to achieve?                    40
          That like I best, that flies beyond my reach.
          Set me to scale the high Pyramides,
          And thereon set the diadem of France;
          I'll either rend it with my nails to naught,
          Or mount the top with my aspiring wings,
          Although my downfall be the deepest hell.
          For this I wake, when others think I sleep;
          For this I wait, that scorn attendance else;
          For this, my quenchless thirst, whereon I build,
          Hath often pleaded kindred to the king;                     50
          For this, this head, this heart, this hand, and sword,
          Contrives, imagines, and fully executes,
          Matters of import aimed at by many,
          Yet understood by none;
          For this, hath heaven engender'd me of earth:
          For this, this earth sustains my body's weight,
          And with this weight I'll counterpoise a crown,
          Or with seditions weary all the world;
          For this, from Spain the stately Catholics
          Send Indian gold to coin me French ecues;                   60
          For this, have I a largess from the Pope,
          A pension, and a dispensation too;
          And by that privilege to work upon,
          My policy hath fram'd religion.
          Religion! *O Diabole*!
          Fie, I am asham'd, however that I seem,
          To think a word of such a simple sound
          Of so great matter should be made the ground!
          The gentle king, whose pleasure uncontroll'd

Weakeneth his body, and will waste his realm,     70
If I repair not what he ruinates –
Him, as a child, I daily win with words,
So that for proof he barely bears the name.
I execute, and he sustains the blame.
The Mother-Queen works wonders for my sake,
And in my love entombs the hope of France,
Rifling the bowels of her treasury,
To supply my wants and necessity.
Paris hath full five hundred colleges,
As monasteries, priories, abbeys, and halls,     80
Wherein are thirty thousand able men,
Besides a thousand sturdy student Catholics;
And more – of my knowledge, in one cloister keep
Five hundred fat Franciscan friars and priests:
All this, and more, if more may be compris'd,
To bring the will of our desires to end.
Then, Guise,
Since thou hast all the cards within thy hands,
To shuffle or cut, take this as surest thing,
That, right or wrong, thou deal thyself a king.     90
Ay, but, Navarre – 'tis but a nook of France,
Sufficient yet for such a petty king,
That, with a rabblement of his heretics,
Blinds Europe's eyes, and troubleth our estate.
Him will we – [*pointing to his sword*]
                but first let's follow those in France
That hinder our possession to the crown.
As Caesar to his soldiers, so say I –
Those that hate me will I learn to loathe.
Give me a look, that, when I bend the brows,
Pale death may walk in furrows of my face;     100
A hand, that with a grasp may gripe the world;
An ear to hear what my detractors say;
A royal seat, a sceptre, and a crown;
That those which do behold them may become
As men that stand and gaze against the sun.
The plot is laid, and things shall come to pass
Where resolution strives for victory.

                                [*exit*

## SCENE 3

*Enter the* KING OF NAVARRE, QUEEN MARGARET,
*the* OLD QUEEN OF NAVARRE, *the* PRINCE OF CONDÉ,
*and the* ADMIRAL; *they are met by the Apothecary*
*with the gloves, which he gives to the* OLD QUEEN

| | |
|---|---|
| APOTHEC. | Madam, |
| | I beseech your grace to accept this simple gift. |
| O. QUEEN | Thanks, my good friend. Hold, take thou this reward. |
| | *[gives a purse* |
| APOTHEC. | I humbly thank your majesty.          *[exit* |
| O. QUEEN | Methinks the gloves have a very strong perfume, |
| | The scent whereof doth make my head to ache. |
| NAVARRE | Doth not your grace know the man that gave |
| | then you? |
| O. QUEEN | Not well; but do remember such a man. |
| ADMIRAL | Your grace was ill-advis'd to take them, then, |
| | Considering of these dangerous times.          10 |
| O. QUEEN | Help, son Navarre! I am poison'd! |
| MARGARET | The heavens forbid your highness such mishap! |
| NAVARRE | The late suspicion of the Duke of Guise |
| | Might well have mov'd your highness to beware |
| | How you did meddle with such dangerous gifts. |
| MARGARET | Too late it is, my lord, if that be true, |
| | To blame her highness; but I hope it be |
| | Only some natural passion makes her sick. |
| O. QUEEN | O, no, sweet Margaret! The fatal poison |
| | Works within my head; my brain-pan breaks;          20 |
| | My heart doth faint; I die!          *[dies* |
| NAVARRE | My mother poison'd here before my face! |
| | O gracious God, what times are these! |
| | O, grant, sweet God, my days may end with hers, |
| | That I with her may die and live again! |
| MARGARET | Let not this heavy chance, my dearest lord, |
| | (For whose effects my soul is massacred) |
| | Infect thy gracious breast with fresh supply |
| | To aggravate our sudden misery. |
| ADMIRAL | Come, my lords, let us bear her body hence,          30 |

And see it honoured with just solemnity.

                    *[As they are going out, the soldier*
                    *dischargeth his musket at the Admiral*

CONDÉ    What, are you hurt, my Lord High Admiral?

ADMIRAL    Ay, my good lord, shot through the arm.

NAVARRE    We are betray'd! Come, my lords,
And let us go tell the king of this.

ADMIRAL                     These are
The cursed Guisians, that do seek our death.
O, fatal was this marriage to us all.

                *[exeunt, bearing out the body of*
                *the Old Queen of Navarre*

## SCENE 4

*Enter* KING CHARLES, CATHERINE *the Queen-Mother,*
GUISE, ANJOU, *and* DUMAINE

CATHERINE  My noble son, and princely Duke of Guise,
Now have we got the fatal, straggling deer
Within the compass of a deadly toil,
And, as we late decreed, we may perform.

CHARLES  Madam, it will he noted through the world
An action bloody and tyrannical;
Chiefly, since under safety of our word
They justly challenge their protection:
Besides, my heart relents that noblemen,
Only corrupted in religion,          10
Ladies of honour, knights, and gentlemen,
Should, for their conscience, taste such ruthless ends.

ANJOU  Though gentle minds should pity others' pains,
Yet will the wisest note their proper griefs,
And rather seek to scourge their enemies
Than be themselves base subjects to the whip.

GUISE  Methinks my Lord Anjou hath well advis'd
Your highness to consider of the thing,
And rather choose to seek your country's good
Than pity or relieve these upstart heretics.    20

CATHERINE  I hope these reasons may serve my princely son

To have some care for fear of enemies.

CHARLES      Well, madam, I refer it to your majesty,
And to my nephew here, the Duke of Guise:
What you determine, I will ratify.

CATHERINE   Thanks to my princely son – Then tell me, Guise,
What order will you set down for the massacre?

GUISE        Thus madam. They
That shall be actors in this massacre
Shall wear white crosses on their burgonets,          30
And tie white linen scarfs about their arms.
He that wants these, and is suspect of heresy,
Shall die, be he king or emperor. Then I'll have
A peal of ordnance shot from the tower, at which
They all shall issue out, and set the streets,
And then,
The watchword being given, a bell shall ring,
Which when they hear, they shall begin to kill,
And never cease until that bell shall cease,
Then breathe a while.

*Enter the Admiral's Serving-man*

CHARLES                    How now, fellow! What news?  40

SERVANT      An it please your grace, the Lord High Admiral,
Riding the streets, was traitorously shot;
And most humbly entreats your majesty
To visit him, sick in his bed.

CHARLES      Messenger, tell him I will see him straight.
What shall we do now with the Admiral?

CATHERINE   Your majesty were best go visit him,
And make a show as if all were well.

CHARLES      Content; I will go visit the Admiral.

GUISE        And I will go take order for his death.          50

                          [*exeunt Catherine and Guise*

*The* ADMIRAL *discovered in bed*

CHARLES      How fares it with my Lord High Admiral?
Hath he been hurt with villains in the street?
I vow and swear, as I am King of France,
To find and to repay the man with death,
With death delay'd and torments never us'd,

That durst presume, for hope of any gain,
To hurt the nobleman his sovereign loves.

ADMIRAL    Ah, my good lord, these are the Guisians,
That seek to massacre our guiltless lives!

CHARLES    Assure yourself, my good Lord Admiral,                    60
I deeply sorrow for your treacherous wrong;
And that I am not more secure myself
Than I am careful you should be preserv'd —
Cousin, take twenty of our strongest guard,
And, under your direction, see they keep
All treacherous violence from our noble friend,
Repaying all attempts with present death
Upon the cursed breakers of our peace —
And so be patient, good Lord Admiral,
And every hour I will visit you.                                      70

ADMIRAL    I humbly thank your royal majesty.

*[exeunt Charles, etc.*


## SCENE 5

*Enter* GUISE, ANJOU, DUMAINE, GONZAGO, RETES,
MOUNTSORRELL, *and Soldiers, to the massacre*

GUISE      Anjou, Dumaine, Gonzago, Retes, swear,
By the argent crosses in your burgonets,
To kill all that you suspect of heresy.

DUMAINE    I swear by this, to be unmerciful.

ANJOU      I am disguis'd, and none knows who I am,
And therefore mean to murder all I meet.

GONZAGO    And so will I.

RETES      And I.

GUISE      Away, then! Break into the Admiral's house.

RETES      Ay, let the Admiral be first despatch'd.                 10

GUISE      The Admiral,
Chief standard-bearer to the Lutherans,
Shall in the entrance of this massacre
Be murder'd in his bed.
Gonzago, conduct them thither; and then
Beset his house, that not a man may live.

| | |
|---|---|
| ANJOU | That charge is mine – Switzers, keep you the streets; |
| | And at each corner shall the king's guard stand. |
| GONZAGO | Come, sirs, follow me.          [*exit Gonzago with others* |
| ANJOU | Cousin, the captain of the Admiral's guard,          20 |
| | Plac'd by my brother, will betray his lord. |
| | Now, Guise, shall Catholics flourish once again; |
| | The head being off, the members cannot stand. |
| RETES | But look, my lord, there's some in the Admiral's |
| | house. |

*the* ADMIRAL *discovered in bed;*
GONZAGO *and others in the house*

| | |
|---|---|
| ANJOU | In lucky time: come, let us keep this lane, |
| | And slay his servants that shall issue out. |
| GONZAGO | Where is the Admiral? |
| ADMIRAL | O, let me pray before I die! |
| GONZAGO | Then pray unto our Lady; kiss this cross.          [*stabs him* |
| ADMIRAL | O God, forgive my sins!          [*dies* |
| GUISE | Gonzago, what, is he dead? |
| GONZAGO |                                        Ay, my lord. |
| GUISE | Then throw him down. |
| | [*the body of the Admiral is thrown down* |
| ANJOU |                              Now, cousin, view him well: |
| | It may be 'tis some other, and he escap'd. |
| GUISE | Cousin, 'tis he; I know him by his look: |
| | See where my soldier shot him through the arm; |
| | He miss'd him near, but we have struck him now – |
| | Ah, base Chatillon and degenerate, |
| | Chief standard-bearer to the Lutherans, |
| | Thus, in despite of thy religion, |
| | The Duke of Guise stamps on thy lifeless bulk!          40 |
| ANJOU | Away with him! Cut off his head and hands, |
| | And send them for a present to the Pope; |
| | And, when this just revenge is finished, |
| | Unto Mount Faucon will we drag his corse; |
| | And he, that living hated so the Cross, |
| | Shall, being dead, be hang'd thereon in chains. |
| GUISE | Anjou, Gonzago, Retes, if that you three |
| | Will be as resolute as I and Dumaine, |

There shall not be a Huguenot breathe in France.

ANJOU     I swear by this cross, we'll not be partial,      50
But slay as many as we can come near.

GUISE     Mountsorrell, go shoot the ordnance off,
That they, which have already set the street,
May know their watchword; then toll the bell,
And so let's forward to the massacre.

M'SORRELL   I will, my lord.                        [*exit*

GUISE     And now, my lords, let's closely to our business.

ANJOU     Anjou will follow thee.

DUMAINE                 And so will Dumaine.
                [*the ordnance being shot off, the bell tolls*

GUISE     Come, then, let's away.
                                     [*exeunt*

## SCENE 6

*Enter* GUISE, *and the rest, with their swords*
*drawn, chasing the Protestants*

GUISE     *Tuez, tuez, tuez!*
Let none escape! Murder the Huguenots!

ANJOU     Kill them! Kill them!             [*exeunt*

*Enter* LOREINE, *running;* GUISE *and the rest pursuing him*

GUISE     Loreine, Loreine! Follow Loreine! Sirrah,
Are you a preacher of these heresies?

LOREINE   I am a preacher of the word of God;
And thou a traitor to thy soul and him.

GUISE     'Dearly beloved brother' – thus 'tis written.
                      [*stabs Loreine, who dies*

ANJOU     Stay, my lord, let me begin the psalm.

GUISE     Come, drag him away, and throw him in a ditch.   10
                    [*exeunt with the body*

*Enter* MOUNTSORRELL, *and knocks at* SEROUNE's *door*

WIFE     [*within*] Who is that which knocks there?

M'SORRELL   Mountsorrell, from the Duke of Guise.

WIFE     [*within*] Husband, come down; here's one would
                              speak with you,

From the Duke of Guise

*Enter* SEROUNE *from the house*

SEROUNE   To speak with me, from such a man as he?

M'SORRELL  Ay, ay, for this, Seroune; [*showing his dagger*]
                              and thou shalt ha't.

SEROUNE.  O, let me pray, before I take my death!

M'SORRELL  Despatch, then, quickly.

SEROUNE                         O Christ, my Saviour!

M'SORRELL  Christ, villain!
           Why, darest thou to presume to call on Christ,        20
           Without the intercession of some saint?
           *Sanctus Jacobus*, he's my saint; pray to him.

SEROUNE   O, let me pray unto my God!

M'SORRELL  Then take this with you.

                              [*stabs Seroune, who dies;
                              then exit Mountsorrell*


## SCENE 7

*Enter* RAMUS, *in his study*

RAMUS     What fearful cries come from the river Seine,
           That fright poor Ramus sitting at his book!
           I fear the Guisians have pass'd the bridge,
           And mean once more to menace me.

*Enter* TALAEUS

TALAEUS   Fly, Ramus, fly, if thou wilt save thy life!

RAMUS     Tell me, Talaeus, wherefore should I fly?

TALAEUS.  The Guisians are
           Hard at thy door, and mean to murder us:
           Hark, hark, they come! I'll leap out at the window.

RAMUS     Sweet Talaeus, stay.                                   10

*Enter* GONZAGO *and* RETES

GONZAGO   Who goes there?

RETES                    'Tis Talaeus, Ramus' bedfellow.

GONZAGO   What art thou?

TALAEUS.                 I am, as Ramus is, a Christian.

RETES     O, let him go; he is a Catholic.          [*exit Talaeus*

| | |
|---|---|
| GONZAGO | Come, Ramus, more gold, or thou shalt have the stab. |
| RAMUS | Alas, I am a scholar! How should I have gold? |
| | All that I have is but my stipend from the king, |
| | Which is no sooner receiv'd but it is spent. |

*Enter* GUISE, ANJOU, DUMAINE,
MOUNTSORRELL *and Soldiers*

| | | |
|---|---|---|
| ANJOU | Who have you there? | |
| RETES | 'Tis Ramus, the king's Professor of Logic. | |
| GUISE | Stab him. | 20 |
| RAMUS | O, good my lord, | |
| | Wherein hath Ramus been so offensious? | |
| GUISE | Marry, sir, in having a smack in all, | |
| | And yet didst never sound anything to the depth. | |
| | Was it not thou that scoff'dst the Organon, | |
| | And said it was a heap of vanities? | |
| | He that will be a flat dichotomist, | |
| | And seen in nothing but epitomes, | |
| | Is in your judgment thought a learned man; | |
| | And he, forsooth, must go and preach in Germany, | |
| | Excepting against doctors' axioms, | |
| | And *ipse dixi* with this quiddity, | |
| | *Argumentum testimonii est inartificiale.* | |
| | To contradict which, I say, Ramus shall die – | |
| | How answer you that? Your *nego argumentum* | |
| | Cannot serve, sirrah – Kill him. | |
| RAMUS | O, good my lord, let me but speak a word! | |
| ANJOU | Well, say on. | |
| RAMUS. | Not for my life do I desire this pause, | |
| | But in my latter hour to purge myself, | 40 |
| | In that I know the things that I have wrote, | |
| | Which, as I hear, one Scheckius takes it ill, | |
| | Because my places, being but three, contain all his. | |
| | I knew the Organon to be confus'd, | |
| | And I reduc'd it into better form: | |
| | And this for Aristotle will I say, | |
| | That he that despiseth him can ne'er | |
| | Be good in logic or philosophy; | |
| | And that's because the blockish Sorbonnists | |
| | Attribute as much unto their [own] works | 50 |

As to the service of the eternal God.

GUISE     Why suffer you that peasant to declaim?
Stab him, I say, and send him to his friends in hell.

ANJOU     Ne'er was there collier's son so full of pride.

*[stabs Ramus, who dies*

GUISE     My Lord of Anjou, there are a hundred Protestants,
Which we have chas'd into the river Seine,
That swim about, and so preserve their lives:
How may we do? I fear me they will live.

DUMAINE     Go place some men upon the bridge,
With bows and darts, to shoot at them they see,    60
And sink them in the river as they swim.

GUISE     'Tis well advis'd, Dumaine; go see it straight be done.

*[exit Dumaine*

And in the meantime, my lord, could we devise
To get those pedants from the King Navarre,
That are tutors to him and the Prince of Condé –

ANJOU     For that, let me alone: cousin, stay you here,
And when you see me in, then follow hard.

ANJOU *knocketh at the door; and enter the* KING OF NAVARRE
*and the* PRINCE OF CONDÉ, *with their two Schoolmasters*

How now, my lords! How fare you?

NAVARRE     My lord, they say
That all the Protestants are massacred.

ANJOU     Ay, so they are; but yet, what remedy?    70
I have done what I could to stay this broil.

NAVARRE     But yet, my lord, the report doth run,
That you were one that made this massacre.

ANJOU     Who, I? You are deceiv'd; I rose but now.

GUISE, GONZAGO, RETES, MOUNTSORRELL
*and Soldiers come forward*

GUISE     Murder the Huguenots! Take those pedants hence!

NAVARRE     Thou traitor, Guise, lay off thy bloody hands!

CONDÉ     Come, let us go tell the king.

*[exit with the King of Navarre*

GUISE     Come, sirs,
I'll whip you to death with my poniard's point.

*[stabs the Schoolmasters, who die*

| | |
|---|---|
| ANJOU | Away with them both! |

                         *[exeunt Anjou and Soldiers with the bodies*

GUISE       And now, sirs, for this night let our fury stay.      80
              Yet will we not that the massacre shall end:
              Gonzago, post you to Orleans,
              Retes to Dieppe, Mountsorrell unto Rouen,
              And spare not one that you suspect of heresy.
              And now stay
              That bell, that to the devil's matins rings.
              Now every man put off his burgonet,
              And so convey him closely to his bed.

                                          *[exeunt*

## ACT TWO

### SCENE I

*Enter* ANJOU, *with two Lords of Poland*

ANJOU      My lords of Poland, I must needs confess,
      The offer of your Prince Elector's far
      Beyond the reach of my deserts;
      For Poland is, as I have been inform'd,
      A martial people, worthy such a king
      As hath sufficient counsel in himself
      To lighten doubts, and frustrate subtle foes;
      And such a king, whom practice long hath taught
      To please himself with manage of the wars,
      The greatest wars within our Christian bounds –    10
      I mean our wars against the Muscovites,
      And, on the other side, against the Turk,
      Rich princes both, and mighty emperors.
      Yet, by my brother Charles, our king of France,
      And by his grace's council, it is thought
      That, if I undertake to wear the crown
      Of Poland, it may prejudice their hope
      Of my inheritance to the crown of France;
      For, if th' Almighty take my brother hence,
      By due descent the regal seat is mine.           20
      With Poland, therefore, must I covenant thus –
      That if, by death of Charles, the diadem
      Of France be cast on me, then, with your leaves,
      I may retire me to my native home.
      If your commission serve to warrant this,
      I thankfully shall undertake the charge
      Of you and yours, and carefully maintain
      The wealth and safety of your kingdom's right.

1 LORD    All this, and more, your highness shall command
      For Poland's crown and kingly diadem.        30

ANJOU      Then, come, my lords, let's go.

                                         *[exeunt*

## SCENE 2

*Enter two* MEN, *with the Admiral's body*

| | |
|---|---|
| 1ST MAN | Now, sirrah, what shall we do with the Admiral? |
| 2ND MAN | Why, let us burn him for an heretic. |
| 1ST MAN | O, no! His body will infect the fire, and the fire the air, and so we shall be poisoned with him. |
| 2ND MAN | What shall we do, then? |
| 1ST MAN | Let's throw him into the river. |
| 2ND MAN | O, 'twill corrupt the water, and the water the fish, and the fish ourselves, when we eat them! |
| 1ST MAN | Then throw him into the ditch. |
| 2ND MAN | No, no. To decide all doubts, be ruled by me:    10 Let's hang him here upon this tree. |
| 1ST MAN | Agreed. |

*[they hang up the body on a tree, and then exeunt*

*Enter* GUISE, CATHERINE *the Queen-Mother,*
*and the* CARDINAL OF LORRAINE, *with Attendants*

GUISE      Now, madam, how like you our lusty Admiral?
CATHERINE Believe me, Guise, he becomes the place so well
         As I could long ere this have wish'd him there.
         But come,
         Let's walk aside; the air's not very sweet.
GUISE      No, by my faith, madam —
         Sirs, take him away, and throw him in some ditch.
                 *[the attendants bear off the Admiral's body*
         And now, madam, as I understand,
         There are a hundred Huguenots and more,      20
         Which in the woods do hold their synagogue,
         And daily meet about this time of day;
         And thither will I, to put them to the sword.
CATHERINE Do so, sweet Guise; let us delay no time;
         For, if these stragglers gather head again,
         And disperse themselves throughout the realm
                              of France,
         It will be hard for us to work their deaths.
         Be gone; delay no time, sweet Guise.

GUISE        Madam,
             I go as whirlwinds rage before a storm.          [*exit*
CATHERINE    My Lord of Lorraine, have you mark'd of late,          30
             How Charles our son begins for to lament
             For the late night's-work which my Lord of Guise
             Did make in Paris amongst the Huguenots?
LORRAINE     Madam, I have heard him solemnly vow,
             With the rebellious King of Navarre,
             For to revenge their deaths upon us all.
CATHERINE    Ay, but, my lord, let me alone for that;
             For Catherine must have her will in France.
             As I do live, so surely shall he die,
             And Henry then shall wear the diadem.          40
             And, if he grudge or cross his mother's will,
             I'll disinherit him and all the rest;
             For I'll rule France, but they shall wear the crown,
             And, if they storm, I then may pull them down.
             Come, my lord, let us go.
                                                            [*exeunt*


## SCENE 3

*Enter five or six* PROTESTANTS, *with books, and kneel together.*
*Then enter* GUISE *and others.*

GUISE        Down with the Huguenots! Murder them!
I PROT.      O Monsieur de Guise, hear me but speak!
GUISE        No, villain; that tongue of thine,
             That hath blasphem'd the holy Church of Rome,
             Shall drive no plaints into the Guise's ears,
             To make the justice of my heart relent –
             *Tuez, tuez, tuez!* Let none escape.
                                       [*they kill the Protestants*
             So, drag them away.
                                       [*exeunt with the bodies*

## ACT THREE

### SCENE I

*Enter* KING CHARLES, *supported by the* KING OF NAVARRE *and*
EPERNOUN; CATHERINE *the Queen-Mother, the* CARDINAL OF
LORRAINE, PLESHÉ, *and Attendants*

| | |
|---|---|
| CHARLES | O, let me stay, and rest me here a while! |
| | A griping pain hath seiz'd upon my heart, |
| | A sudden pang, the messenger of death. |
| CATHERINE | O, say not so! Thou kill'st thy mother's heart. |
| CHARLES | I must say so; pain forceth me complain. |
| NAVARRE | Comfort yourself, my lord, and have no doubt |
| | But God will sure restore you to your health. |
| CHARLES | O, no, my loving brother of Navarre! |
| | I have deserv'd a scourge, I must confess; |
| | Yet is there patience of another sort      10 |
| | Than to misdo the welfare of their king: |
| | God grant my nearest friends may prove no worse! |
| | O, hold me up! My sight begins to fail, |
| | My sinews shrink, my brains turn upside down. |
| | My heart doth break: I faint and die.     *[dies* |
| CATHERINE | What! Art thou dead, sweet son? Speak to thy mother! |
| | O, no, his soul is fled from out his breast, |
| | And he nor hears nor sees us what we do! |
| | My lords, what resteth there now for to be done, |
| | But that we presently despatch ambassadors     20 |
| | To Poland, to call Henry back again, |
| | To wear his brother's crown and dignity? |
| | Epernoun, go see it presently be done, |
| | And bid him come without delay to us. |
| EPERNOUN | Madam, I will.        *[exit* |
| CATHERINE | And now, my lords, after these funerals be done, |
| | We will, with all the speed we can, provide |
| | For Henry's coronation from Polony. |
| | Come, let us take his body hence. |

*[the body of King Charles is borne out;*
*exeunt all except the King of Navarre and Pleshé*

NAVARRE   And now, Pleshé, whilst that these broils do last,   30
          My opportunity may serve me fit
          To steal from France, and hie me to my home.
          For here's no safety in the realm for me:
          And now that Henry is call'd from Poland,
          It is my due, by just succession;
          And therefore, as speedily as I can perform,
          I'll muster up an army secretly,
          For fear that Guise, join'd with the king of Spain,
          Might seek to cross me in mine enterprise.
          But God, that always doth defend the right,   40
          Will show his mercy, and preserve us still.

PLESHÉ    The virtues of our true religion
          Cannot but march, with many graces more,
          Whose army shall discomfit all your foes,
          And, at the length, in Pampeluna crown
          (In spite of Spain, and all the popish power,
          That holds it from your highness wrongfully)
          Your majesty her rightful lord and sovereign.

NAVARRE   Truth, Pleshé; and God so prosper me in all,
          As I intend to labour for the truth,   50
          And true profession of his holy word!
          Come, Pleshé, let's away whilst time doth serve.

                                                  [exeunt


                           SCENE 2

     *Trumpets sounded within, and a cry of 'Vive le Roi', two or*
     *three times. Enter* ANJOU *crowned as King Henry the Third;*
     CATHERINE *the Queen-Mother, the* CARDINAL OF LORRAINE,
     GUISE, EPERNOUN, MUGERNOUN, *the Cutpurse and others*

ALL        *Vive le Roi, Vive le Roi!*          [*a flourish of trumpets*
CATHERINE  Welcome from Poland, Henry, once again!
           Welcome to France, thy father's royal seat!
           Here hast thou a country void of fears,
           A warlike people to maintain thy right,
           A watchful senate for ordaining laws,
           A loving mother to preserve thy state,

And all things that a king may wish besides;
All this, and more, hath Henry with his crown.
LORRAINE   And long may Henry enjoy all this, and more!          10
ALL        *Vive le Roi, Vive le Roi!*          [*a flourish of trumpets*
HENRY      Thanks to you all. The guider of all crowns
Grant that our deeds may well deserve your loves!
And so they shall, if fortune speed my will,
And yield your thoughts to height of my deserts.
What say our minions? Think they Henry's heart
Will not both harbour love and majesty?
Put off that fear, they are already join'd:
No person, place, or time, or circumstance,
Shall slack my love's affections from his bent:          20
As now you are, so shall you still persist,
Removeless from the favours of your king.
MUGEROUN  We know that noble minds change not their
                                              thoughts
For wearing of a crown, in that your grace
Hath worn the Poland diadem before
You were invested in the crown of France.
HENRY      I tell thee, Mugeroun, we will be friends,
And fellows too, whatever storms arise.
MUGEROUN  Then may it please your majesty to give
Me leave to punish those that do profane          30
This holy feast.
HENRY      How mean'st thou that?
                              [*Mugeroun cuts off the Cutpurse's ear,
                              for cutting the gold buttons of his cloak*
CUTPURSE   O Lord, mine ear!
MUGEROUN  Come, sir, give me my buttons, and here's your ear.
GUISE      Sirrah, take him away.
HENRY      Hands off, good fellow; I will be his bail
For this offence – Go, sirrah, work no more
Till this our coronation-day be past –
And now,
Our solemn rites of coronation done,
What now remains but for a while to feast,          40
And spend some days in barriers, tourney, tilt,
And like disports, such as do fit the court?

Let's go, my lords; our dinner stays for us.

*[exeunt all except Catherine the Queen-Mother*
*and the Cardinal of Lorraine*

CATHERINE My Lord Cardinal of Lorraine, tell me,
How likes your grace my son's pleasantness?
His mind, you see, runs on his minions,
And all his heaven is to delight himself;
And, whilst he sleeps securely thus in ease,
Thy brother Guise and we may now provide
To plant ourselves with such authority                      50
As not a man may live without our leaves.
Then shall the Catholic faith of Rome
Flourish in France, and none deny the same.

LORRAINE Madam, as in secrecy I was told,
My brother Guise hath gather'd a power of men,
Which are, he saith, to kill the Puritans;
But 'tis the house of Bourbon that he means.
Now, madam, must you insinuate with the king,
And tell him that 'tis for his country's good,
And common profit of religion.                              60

CATHERINE Tush, man, let me alone with him,
To work the way to bring this thing to pass;
And, if he do deny what I do say,
I'll despatch him with his brother presently,
And then shall Monsieur wear the diadem.
Tush, all shall die unless I have my will;
For, while she lives, Catherine will be queen.
Come, my lord, let us go seek the Guise,
And then determine of this enterprise.

*[exeunt*

## ACT FOUR

### SCENE I

*Enter the* DUCHESS OF GUISE *and her Maid*

DUCHESS       Go fetch me pen and ink —
MAID                              I will, madam.
DUCHESS       That I may write unto my dearest lord.       [*exit Maid*
              Sweet Mugeroun, 'tis he that hath my heart,
              And Guise usurps it 'cause I am his wife,
              Fain would I find some means to speak with him,
              But cannot, and therefore am enforc'd to write,
              That he may come and meet me in some place,
              Where we may one enjoy the other's sight.

              *Re-enter the Maid, with pen, ink, and paper*

              So, set it down, and leave me to myself.
                                    [*exit Maid; the duchess writes*
              O, would to God, this quill that here doth write,    10
              Had late been pluck'd from out fair Cupid's wing,
              That it might print these lines within his heart!

                            *Enter* GUISE

GUISE         What, all alone, my love? And writing too?
              I prithee, say to whom thou writ'st.
DUCHESS                                    To such
              A one, my lord, as, when she reads my lines,
              Will laugh, I fear me, at their good array.
GUISE         I pray thee, let me see.
DUCHESS       O, no, my lord; a woman only must
              Partake the secrets of my heart.
GUISE         But, madam, I must see.          [*seizes the paper*
              Are these your secrets that no man must know?
DUCHESS       O, pardon me, my lord!
GUISE         Thou trothless and unjust! What lines are these?
              Am I grown old, or is thy lust grown young?
              Or hath my love been so obscur'd in thee,
              That others need to comment on my text?
              Is all my love forgot, which held thee dear,

Ay, dearer than the apple of mine eye?
Is Guise's glory but a cloudy mist,
In sight and judgment of thy lustful eye?                    30
*Mort Dieu!* Were not the fruit within thy womb,
Of whose increase I set some longing hope,
This wrathful hand should strike thee to the heart.
Hence, strumpet! Hide thy head for shame;
And fly my presence, if thou look to live!

                                            [*exit Duchess*

O wicked sex, perjured and unjust!
Now do I see that from the very first
Her eyes and looks sow'd seeds of perjury.
But villain he, to whom these lines should go,
Shall buy her love even with his dearest blood.           40

                                                      [*exit*

### SCENE 2

*Enter the* KING OF NAVARRE, PLESHÉ, BARTUS
*and train, with drums and trumpets*

NAVARRE     My lords, sith in a quarrel just and right
            We undertake to manage these our wars
            Against the proud disturbers of the faith,
            (I mean the Guise, the Pope, and king of Spain,
            Who set themselves to tread us under foot,
            And rent our true religion from this land;
            But for you know our quarrel is no more
            But to defend their strange inventions,
            Which they will put us to with sword and fire)
            We must with resolute minds resolve to fight,     10
            In honour of our God, and country's good.
            Spain is the council-chamber of the Pope,
            Spain is the place where he makes peace and war;
            And Guise for Spain hath now incens'd the king
            To send his power to meet us in the field.
BARTUS      Then in this bloody brunt they may behold
            The sole endeavour of your princely care,
            To plant the true succession of the faith,

           In spite of Spain and all his heresies.

NAVARRE     The power of vengeance now encamps itself     20
           Upon the haughty mountains of my breast;
           Plays with her gory colours of revenge,
           Whom I respect as leaves of boasting green,
           That change their colour when the winter comes,
           When I shall vaunt as victor in revenge.

*Enter a Messenger*

           How now, sirrah! What news?

MESSENGER     My lord, as by our scouts we understand,
           A mighty army comes from France with speed;
           Which are already muster'd in the land,
           And mean to meet your highness in the field.     30

NAVARRE     In God's name, let them come!
           This is the Guise that hath incens'd the king
           To levy arms, and make these civil broils.
           But canst thou tell who is their general?

MESSENGER     Not yet, my lord, for thereon do they stay;
           But, as report doth go, the Duke of Joyeux
           Hath made great suit unto the king therefore.

NAVARRE     It will not countervail his pains, I hope.
           I would the Guise in his stead might have come!
           But he doth lurk within his drowsy couch,     40
           And makes his footstool on security:
           So he be safe, he cares not what becomes
           Of king or country; no, not for them both.
           But come, my lords, let us away with speed,
           And place ourselves in order for the fight.

                                       *[exeunt*


## SCENE 3

*Enter* KING HENRY, GUISE, EPERNOUN, *and* JOYEUX

HENRY     My sweet Joyeux, I make thee general
           Of all my army, now in readiness
           To march 'gainst the rebellious King Navarre:
           At thy request I am content thou go,
           Although my love to thee can hardly suffer't,

Regarding still the danger of thy life.

JOYEUX    Thanks to your majesty: and so, I take my leave –
          Farewell to my Lord of Guise, and Epernoun.

GUISE     Health and hearty farewell to my Lord Joyeux.

                                                    [exit Joyeux

HENRY     So kindly, cousin of Guise, you and your wife        10
          Do both salute our lovely minions.
          Remember you the letter, gentle sir,
          Which your wife writ
          To my dear minion, and her chosen friend?

          [makes horns at Guise]

GUISE     How now, my lord! Faith, this is more than need.
          Am I thus to be jested at and scorn'd?
          'Tis more than kingly or emperious:
          And, sure, if all the proudest kings
          In Christendom should bear me such derision,
          They should know how I scorn'd them and
                                       their mocks.    20
          I love your minions! Dote on them yourself;
          I know none else but holds them in disgrace;
          And here, by all the saints in heaven, I swear,
          That villain for whom I bear this deep disgrace,
          Even for your words that have incens'd me so,
          Shall buy that strumpet's favour with his blood!
          Whether he have dishonour'd me or no,
          Par la mort de Dieu, il mourra!              [exit

HENRY     Believe me, this jest bites sore.

EPERNOUN  My lord, 'twere good to make them friends,        30
          For his oaths are seldom spent in vain.

                        Enter MUGEROUN

HENRY     How now, Mugeroun! Met'st thou not the Guise
          At the door?

MUGEROUN              Not I, my lord; what if I had?

HENRY     Marry, if thou hadst, thou mightst have had the stab;
          For he hath solemnly sworn thy death.

MUGEROUN  I may be stabb'd, and live till he be dead:
          But wherefore bears he me such deadly hate?

HENRY     Because his wife bears thee such kindly love.

MUGEROUN If that be all, the next time that I meet her,
          I'll make her shake off love with her heels.        40
          But which way is he gone? I'll go take a walk
          On purpose from the court to meet with him.   [*exit*
HENRY     I like not this. Come, Epernoun,
          Let us go seek the duke, and make them friends.
                                                       [*exeunt*


### SCENE 4

*Alarums within, and a cry – 'The Duke Joyeux is slain'*
*Enter the* KING OF NAVARRE, BARTUS, *and train*

NAVARRE   The duke is slain, and all his power dispers'd,
          And we are grac'd with wreaths of victory.
          Thus God, we see, doth ever guide the right,
          To make his glory great upon the earth.
BARTUS    The terror of this happy victory,
          I hope, will make the king surcease his hate,
          And either never manage army more,
          Or else employ them in some better cause.
NAVARRE   How many noblemen have lost their lives
          In prosecution of these cruel arms,                 10
          Is ruth, and almost death, to call to mind.
          But God we know will always put them down
          That lift themselves against the perfect truth;
          Which I'll maintain so long as life doth last,
          And with the Queen of England join my force
          To beat the papal monarch from our lands,
          And keep those relics from our countries' coasts.
          Come, my lords; now that this storm is overpast,
          Let us away with triumph to our tents.
                                                       [*exeunt*

## SCENE 5

*Enter a Soldier*

SOLDIER     Sir, to you, sir, that dares make the duke a cuckold, and use a counterfeit key to his privy-chamber-door; and although you take out nothing but your own, yet you put in that which displeaseth him, and so forestall his market, and set up your standing where you should not; and whereas he is your landlord, you will take upon you to be his, and till the ground that he himself should occupy, which is his own free land; if it be not too free – there's the question; and though I come not to take possession (as I would I might!) yet I mean to keep you out; which I will, if this gear hold.

*Enter* MUGEROUN

What, are ye come so soon? Have at ye, sir!

             [*shoots at Mugeroun and kills him*

*Enter* GUISE *and Attendants*

GUISE     [*giving a purse*] Hold thee, tall soldier,

                 take thee this, and fly.   [*exit Soldier*

Lie there, the king's delight, and Guise's scorn!
Revenge it, Henry, as thou list or dare;
I did it only in despite of thee.

          [*Attendants bear off Mugeroun's body*

*Enter* KING HENRY *and* EPERNOUN

HENRY     My Lord of Guise, we understand
That you have gathered a power of men:
What your intent is yet we cannot learn,
But we presume it is not for our good.             20

GUISE     Why, I am no traitor to the crown of France;
What I have done, 'tis for the Gospel's sake.

EPERNOUN   Nay, for the Pope's sake, and thine own benefit.
What peer in France but thou, aspiring Guise,
Durst be in arms without the king's consent?
I challenge thee for treason in the cause.

GUISE     Ah, base Epernoun! Were not his highness here,

Thou shouldst perceive the Duke of Guise is mov'd.

HENRY      Be patient, Guise, and threat not Epernoun,
Lest thou perceive the king of France be mov'd.     30

GUISE      Why, I'm a prince of the Valoyses line,
Therefore an enemy to the Bourbonites;
I am a juror in the holy league,
And therefore hated of the Protestants:
What should I do but stand upon my guard?
And, being able, I'll keep an host in pay.

EPERNOUN   Thou able to maintain an host in pay,
That liv'st by foreign exhibition!
The Pope and King of Spain are thy good friends;
Else all France knows how poor a duke thou art.     40

HENRY      Ay, those are they that feed him with their gold,
To countermand our will, and check our friends.

GUISE      My lord, to speak more plainly, thus it is:
Being animated by religious zeal,
I mean to muster all the power I can,
To overthrow those factious Puritans:
And know, my lord, the Pope will sell his
                                    triple crown,
Ay, and the Catholic Philip, king of Spain,
Ere I shall want, will cause his Indians
To rip the golden bowels of America.               50
Navarre, that cloaks them underneath his wings,
Shall feel the house of Lorraine is his foe.
Your highness needs not fear mine army's force;
'Tis for your safety, and your enemies' wrack.

HENRY      Guise, wear our crown, and be thou king of France,
And, as dictator, make or war or peace,
Whilst I cry *placet*, like a senator!
I cannot brook thy haughty insolence:
Dismiss thy camp, or else by our edict
Be thou proclaim'd a traitor throughout France.    60

GUISE      [*aside*] The choice is hard; I must dissemble —
My lord, in token of my true humility,
And simple meaning to your majesty,
I kiss your grace's hand, and take my leave,
Intending to dislodge my camp with speed.

HENRY          Then farewell, Guise: the king and thou are friends.

                                                    [exit Guise

EPERNOUN   But trust him not, my lord; for, had your highness
               Seen with what a pomp he enter'd Paris,
               And how the citizens with gifts and shows
               Did entertain him,                               70
               And promised to be at his command –
               Nay, they fear'd not to speak in the streets,
               That the Guise durst stand in arms against the king,
               For not effecting of his holiness' will.

HENRY          Did they of Paris entertain him so?
               Then means he present treason to our state.
               Well, let me alone – Who's within there?

                         *Enter an Attendant*

               Make a discharge of all my council straight,
               And I'll subscribe my name, and seal it straight.

                                              [*Attendant writes*

               My head shall be my council; they are false;      80
               And, Epernoun, I will be rul'd by thee.

EPERNOUN   My lord,
               I think, for safety of your royal person,
               It would be good the Guise were made away –
               And so to quite your grace of all suspect.

HENRY          First let us set our hand and seal to this,
               And then I'll tell thee what I mean to do –    [*writes*
               So; convey this to the council presently. [*exit Attendant*
               And, Epernoun, though I seem mild and calm,
               Think not but I am tragical within.               90
               I'll secretly convey me unto Blois;
               For, now that Paris takes the Guise's part,
               Here is no staying for the king of France,
               Unless he mean to be betray'd and die:
               But, as I live, so sure the Guise shall die.

                                                    [*exeunt*

## ACT FIVE

### SCENE I

*Enter the* KING OF NAVARRE, *reading a letter, and* BARTUS

NAVARRE    My lord, I am advertised from France
           That the Guise hath taken arms against the king,
           And that Paris is revolted from his grace.
BARTUS     Then hath your grace fit opportunity
           To show your love unto the king of France,
           Offering him aid against his enemies,
           Which cannot but be thankfully receiv'd.
NAVARRE    Bartus, it shall be so: post, then, to France,
           And there salute his highness in our name;
           Assure him all the aid we can provide                    10
           Against the Guisians and their complices.
           Bartus, be gone: commend me to his grace,
           And tell him, ere it be long, I'll visit him.
BARTUS     I will, my lord.                                    [*exit*
NAVARRE    Pleshé!

*Enter* PLESHÉ

PLESHÉ     My lord!
NAVARRE    Pleshé, go muster up our men with speed,
           And let them march away to France amain;
           For we must aid the king against the Guise.
           Be gone, I say; 'tis time that we were there.           20
PLESHÉ     I go, my lord.                                     [*exit*
NAVARRE    That wicked Guise, I fear me much, will be
           The ruin of that famous realm of France;
           For his aspiring thoughts aim at the crown:
           'A takes his vantage on religion,
           To plant the Pope and Popelings in the realm,
           And bind it wholly to the see of Rome.
           But, if that God do prosper mine attempts,
           And send us safely to arrive in France,
           We'll beat him back, and drive him to his death,       30
           That basely seeks the ruin of his realm.

                                                            [*exit*

## SCENE 2

*Enter the Captain of the Guard, and three Murderers*

CAPTAIN      Come on, sirs. What, are you resolutely bent,
             Hating the life and honour of the Guise?
             What, will you not fear, when you see him come?

1 MURD.      Fear him, said you? Tush, were he here, we would kill
             him presently.

2 MURD.      O, that his heart were leaping in my hand!

3 MURD.      But when will he come, that we may murder him?

CAPTAIN      Well, then, I see you are resolute.

1 MURD.      Let us alone; I warrant you.

CAPTAIN      Then, sirs, take your standings within this chamber; for
             anon the Guise will come.

MURD'ERS     You will give us our money?

CAPTAIN      Ay, ay, fear not: stand close: so; be resolute.

                                            [*exeunt Murderers*

             Now falls the star whose influence governs France,
             Whose light was deadly to the Protestants:
             Now must he fall, and perish in his height.

             *Enter* KING HENRY *and* EPERNOUN

HENRY        Now, captain of my guard, are these murderers
                                                      ready?

CAPTAIN      They be, my good lord.

HENRY        But are they resolute, and arm'd to kill,
             Hating the life and honour of the Guise?             20

CAPTAIN      I warrant ye, my lord.                          [*exit*

HENRY        Then come, proud Guise, and here disgorge
                                                  thy breast,
             Surcharg'd with surfeit of ambitious thoughts.
             Breathe out that life wherein my death was hid,
             And end thy endless treasons with thy death.

                                            [*knocking within*

GUISE        [*within*] Holà, varlet, hé! Epernoun, where is
                                                  the king?

EPERNOUN     Mounted his royal cabinet.

GUISE        [*within*] I prithee, tell him that the Guise is here.

EPERNOUN  An please your grace, the Duke of Guise doth crave
          Access unto your highness.
HENRY                                    Let him come in —
          Come, Guise, and see thy traitorous guile outreach'd,
          And perish in the pit thou mad'st for me.

*Enter* GUISE

GUISE     Good morrow to your majesty.
HENRY     Good morrow to my loving cousin of Guise:
          How fares it this morning with your excellence?
GUISE     I heard your majesty was scarcely pleas'd,
          That in the court I bare so great a train.
HENRY     They were to blame that said I was displeas'd;
          And you, good cousin, to imagine it.
          'Twere hard with me, if I should doubt my kin,          40
          Or be suspicious of my dearest friends.
          Cousin, assure you I am resolute,
          Whatsoever any whisper in mine ears,
          Not to suspect disloyalty in thee:
          And so, sweet coz, farewell.
                                        [*exit with Epernoun*
GUISE     So;
          Now sues the king for favour to the Guise,
          And all his minions stoop when I command:
          Why, this 'tis to have an army in the field.
          Now, by the holy sacrament, I swear,          50
          As ancient Romans o'er their captive lords,
          So will I triumph o'er this wanton king;
          And he shall follow my proud chariot's wheels.
          Now do I but begin to look about,
          And all my former time was spent in vain.
          Hold, sword, for in thee is the Duke of Guise's hope.

*Re-enter Third Murderer*

          Villain, why dost thou look so ghastly? Speak.
3 MURD.   O, pardon me, my Lord of Guise!
GUISE     Pardon thee! Why, what hast thou done?
3 MURD.   O my lord, I am one of them that is set to murder you!
GUISE     To murder me, villain!
3 MURD.   Ay, my lord: the rest have ta'en their standings in the

next room; therefore, good my lord, go not forth.

GUISE     Yet Caesar shall go forth.
          Let mean conceits and baser men fear death:
          Tut, they are peasants; I am Duke of Guise;
          And princes with their looks engender fear.

I MURD.   [*within*] Stand close; he is coming; I know him
                                                 by his voice.

GUISE     As pale as ashes! Nay, then, it is time
          To look about.

                 *Enter First and Second Murderers*

I&2 MURD.              Down with him, down with him!  70
                                          [*they stab Guise*

GUISE     O, I have my death's wound! Give me leave to speak.
2 MURD.   Then pray to God, and ask forgiveness of the king.
GUISE     Trouble me not; I ne'er offended him,
          Nor will I ask forgiveness of the king.
          O, that I have not power to stay my life,
          Nor immortality to be reveng'd!
          To die by peasants, what a grief is this!
          Ah, Sixtus, be reveng'd upon the king!
          Philip and Parma, I am slain for you!
          Pope, excommunicate; Philip, depose          80
          The wicked branch of curs'd Valoyses line!
          *Vive la messe!* Perish Huguenots!
          Thus Caesar did go forth, and thus he died.    [*dies*

                 *Enter the Captain of the Guard*

CAPTAIN   What, have you done?
          Then stay a while, and I'll go call the king.
          But see, where he comes.

          *Enter* KING HENRY, EPERNOUN *and Attendants*

          My lord, see, where the Guise is slain.
HENRY     Ah, this sweet sight is physic to my soul!
          Go fetch his son for to behold his death.
                                          [*exit an Attendant*
          Surcharg'd with guilt of thousand massacres,   90
          Monsieur of Lorraine, sink away to hell!
          And, in remembrance of those bloody broils
          To which thou didst allure me, being alive,

And here in presence of you all, I swear
I ne'er was king of France until this hour.
This is the traitor that hath spent my gold
In making foreign wars and civil broils.
Did he not draw a sort of English priests
From Douay to the seminary at Rheims,
To hatch forth treason 'gainst their natural queen?          100
Did he not cause the king of Spain's huge fleet
To threaten England, and to menace me?
Did he not injure Monsieur that's deceas'd?
Hath he not made me, in the Pope's defence,
To spend the treasure that should strength my land,
In civil broils between Navarre and me?
Tush, to be short, he meant to make me monk,
Or else to murder me, and so be king.
Let Christian princes, that shall hear of this,
(As all the world shall know our Guise is dead)          110
Rest satisfied with this, that here I swear,
Ne'er was there king of France so yok'd as I.

EPERNOUN My lord, here is his son.

*Enter Guise's Son*

HENRY   Boy, look, where your father lies.
SON     My father slain! Who hath done this deed?
HENRY   Sirrah, 'twas I that slew him; and will slay
        Thee too, an thou prove such a traitor.
SON     Art thou king, and hast done this bloody deed?
        I'll be reveng'd.          [*offers to throw his dagger*
HENRY   Away to prison with him! I'll clip his wings          120
        Or e'er he pass my hands. Away with him.
                    [*some of the Attendants bear off Guise's Son*
        But what availeth that this traitor's dead,
        When Duke Dumaine, his brother, is alive,
        And that young cardinal that is grown so proud?
        [*to the Captain of the Guard*] Go to the governor
                                                of Orleans,
        And will him, in my name, to kill the duke.
        [*to the Murderers*] Get you away, and strangle
                                                the cardinal.
                    [*exeunt Captain of the Guard and Murderers*

These two will make one entire Duke of Guise,
Especially with our old mother's help.

EPERNOUN   My lord, see, where she comes, as if she droop'd   130
To hear these news.

HENRY   And let her droop: my heart is light enough.

*Enter* CATHERINE *the Queen-Mother*

Mother, how like you this device of mine?
I slew the Guise, because I would be king.

CATHERINE   King! Why, so thou wert before:
Pray God thou be a king now this is done!

HENRY   Nay, he was king, and countermanded me:
But now I will be king, and rule myself,
And make the Guisians stoop that are alive.

CATHERINE   I cannot speak for grief – When thou wast born,   140
I would that I had murder'd thee, my son!
My son! Thou art a changeling, not my son:
I curse thee, and exclaim thee miscreant,
Traitor to God and to the realm of France!

HENRY   Cry out, exclaim, howl till thy throat be hoarse!
The Guise is slain, and I rejoice therefore:
And now will I to arms – Come, Epernoun,
And let her grieve her heart out, if she will.
                                        [*exit with Epernoun*

CATHERINE   Away! leave me alone to meditate.   [*exeunt Attendants*
Sweet Guise, would he had died, so thou wert here!
To whom shall I bewray my secrets now,
Or who will help to build religion?
The Protestants will glory and insult;
Wicked Navarre will get the crown of France;
The Popedom cannot stand; all goes to wrack;
And all for thee, my Guise! What may I do?
But sorrow seize upon my toiling soul!
For, since the Guise is dead, I will not live.
                                        [*exit*

## SCENE 3

*Enter two Murderers, dragging in the Cardinal*

LORRAINE Murder me not; I am a cardinal.

1 MURD. Wert thou the Pope, thou mightst not 'scape from us.

LORRAINE What, will you file your hands with churchmen's
blood?

2 MURD. Shed your blood! Lord, no! For we intend to
strangle you.

LORRAINE Then there is no remedy, but I must die?

1 MURD. No remedy; therefore prepare yourself.

LORRAINE Yet lives
My brother Duke Dumaine, and many more,
To revenge our death upon that cursed king:
Upon whose heart may all the Furies gripe,
And with their paws drench his black soul in hell! 10

1 MURD. Yours, my Lord Cardinal, you should have said –
[*they strangle him*] So, pluck amain:
He is hard-hearted; therefore pull with violence.
Come, take him away.
[exeunt with the body

## SCENE 4

*Enter DUMAINE, reading a letter; with others*

DUMAINE My noble brother murder'd by the king!
O, what may I do for to revenge thy death?
The king's alone, it cannot satisfy.
Sweet Duke of Guise, our prop to lean upon,
Now thou art dead, here is no stay for us.
I am thy brother, and I'll revenge thy death,
And root Valoyses line from forth of France,
And beat proud Bourbon to his native home,
That basely seeks to join with such a king,
Whose murderous thoughts will be his overthrow.
He will'd the governor of Orleans, in his name,
That I with speed should have been put to death;
But that's prevented, for to end his life,

And all those traitors to the Church of Rome
That durst attempt to murder noble Guise.

*Enter Friar*

FRIAR  My lord, I come to bring you news that your brother
the Cardinal of Lorraine, by the king's consent, is lately
strangled to death.

DUMAINE  My brother the Cardinal slain, and I alive?
O words of power to kill a thousand men!          20
Come, let us away, and levy men;
'Tis war that must assuage this tyrant's pride.

FRIAR  My lord, hear me but speak. I am a friar of the order of
the Jacobins, that for my conscience' sake will kill the
king.

DUMAINE  But what doth move thee, above the rest, to do
                                                the deed?

FRIAR  O, my lord, I have been a great sinner in my days! And
the deed is meritorious.

DUMAINE  But how wilt thou get opportunity?

FRIAR  Tush, my lord, let me alone for that.          30

DUMAINE  Friar, come with me;
We will go talk more of this within.

                                        *[exeunt*


## SCENE 5

*Drums and Trumpets. Enter* KING HENRY,
*the* KING OF NAVARRE, EPERNOUN, BARTUS,
PLESHÉ, *Soldiers and Attendants*

HENRY  Brother of Navarre, I sorrow much
That ever I was prov'd your enemy,
And that the sweet and princely mind you bear
Was ever troubled with injurious wars.
I vow, as I am lawful King of France,
To recompense your reconciled love
With all the honours and affections
That ever I vouchsaf'd my dearest friends.

NAVARRE  It is enough if that Navarre may be
Esteemed faithful to the King of France,          10
Whose service he may still command till death.

| | |
|---|---|
| HENRY | Thanks to my kingly brother of Navarre. |
| | Then here we'll lie before Lutetia walls, |
| | Girting this strumpet city with our siege, |
| | Till, surfeiting with our afflicting arms, |
| | She cast her hateful stomach to the earth. |

*Enter a Messenger*

| | |
|---|---|
| MESSENGER | An it please your majesty, here is a friar of the order of the Jacobins, sent from the President of Paris, that craves access unto your grace. |
| HENRY | Let him come in.                    [*exit Messenger* |

*Enter Friar, with a letter*

| | |
|---|---|
| EPERNOUN | I like not this friar's look:                    20 |
| | 'Twere not amiss, my lord, if he were search'd. |
| HENRY | Sweet Epernoun, our friars are holy men, |
| | And will not offer violence to their king, |
| | For all the wealth and treasure of the world – |
| | Friar, thou dost acknowledge me thy king? |
| FRIAR | Ay, my good lord, and will die therein. |
| HENRY | Then come thou near, and tell what news thou bring'st. |
| FRIAR | My lord, |
| | The President of Paris greets your grace, |
| | And sends his duty by these speedy lines,                    30 |
| | Humbly craving your gracious reply.          [*gives letter* |
| HENRY | I'll read them, friar, and then I'll answer thee. |
| FRIAR | *Sancte Jacobe,* now have mercy upon me! |

[*stabs the King with a knife, as he reads the letter, and then the King gets the knife, and kills him*

| | |
|---|---|
| EPERNOUN | O, my lord, let him live a while! |
| HENRY | No, let the villain die, and feel in hell |
| | Just torments for his treachery. |
| NAVARRE | What, is your highness hurt? |
| HENRY | Yes, Navarre; but not to death, I hope. |
| NAVARRE | God shield your grace from such a sudden death! |
| | Go call a surgeon hither straight.          [*exit an Attendant* |
| HENRY | What irreligious pagans' parts be these, |
| | Of such as hold them of the holy church! |
| | Take hence that damned villain from my sight. |

[*Attendants carry out the Friar's body*

EPERNOUN  Ah, had your highness let him live,
          We might have punish'd him to his deserts!
HENRY     Sweet Epernoun, all rebels under heaven
          Shall take example by his punishment,
          How they bear arms against their sovereign –
          Go call the English agent hither straight:
                              [*exit an Attendant*
          I'll send my sister England news of this,          50
          And give her warning of her treacherous foes.

                    *Enter a Surgeon*

NAVARRE   Pleaseth your grace to let the surgeon search
                                        your wound?
HENRY     The wound, I warrant ye, is deep, my lord –
          Search, surgeon, and resolve me what thou see'st.
                              [*the Surgeon searches the wound*

                    *Enter the English Agent*

          Agent for England, send thy mistress word
          What this detested Jacobin hath done.
          Tell her, for all this, that I hope to live;
          Which if I do, the papal monarch goes
          To wrack, and th' antichristian kingdom falls:
          These bloody hands shall tear his triple crown,     60
          And fire accursed Rome about his ears;
          I'll fire his crazed buildings, and enforce
          The papal towers to kiss the lowly earth.
          Navarre, give me thy hand: I here do swear
          To ruinate that wicked Church of Rome,
          That hatcheth up such bloody practices;
          And here protest eternal love to thee,
          And to the Queen of England specially,
          Whom God hath bless'd for hating papistry.
NAVARRE   These words revive my thoughts, and comfort me, 70
          To see your highness in this virtuous mind,
HENRY     Tell me, surgeon, shall I live?
SURGEON   Alas, my lord, the wound is dangerous,
          For you are stricken with a poison'd knife!
HENRY     A poison'd knife! What, shall the French king die,
          Wounded and poison'd both at once?

| | |
|---|---|
| EPERNOUN | O, that |
| | That damned villain were alive again, |
| | That we might torture him with some new-found death! |
| BARTUS | He died a death too good: |
| | The devil of hell torture his wicked soul!          80 |
| HENRY | Ah, curse him not, sith he is dead! |
| | O, the fatal poison works within my breast! |
| | Tell me, surgeon, and flatter not – may I live? |
| SURGEON | Alas my lord, your highness cannot live! |
| NAVARRE | Surgeon, why say'st thou so? The king may live. |
| HENRY | O, no, Navarre! Thou must be king of France! |
| NAVARRE | Long may you live, and still be King of France. |
| EPERNOUN | Or else, die Epernoun! |
| HENRY | Sweet Epernoun, thy king must die – My lords, |
| | Fight in the quarrel of this valiant prince,          90 |
| | For he's your lawful king, and my next heir; |
| | Valoyses line ends in my tragedy. |
| | Now let the house of Bourbon wear the crown; |
| | And may it ne'er end in blood, as mine hath done! |
| | Weep not, sweet Navarre, but revenge my death – |
| | Ah, Epernoun, is this thy love to me? |
| | Henry, thy king, wipes off these childish tears, |
| | And bids thee whet thy sword on Sixtus' bones, |
| | That it may keenly slice the Catholics. |
| | He loves me not [the most] that sheds most tears,   100 |
| | But he that makes most lavish of his blood. |
| | Fire Paris, where these treacherous rebels lurk – |
| | I die, Navarre; come bear me to my sepulchre. |
| | Salute the Queen of England in my name, |
| | And tell her, Henry dies her faithful friend.          [dies |
| NAVARRE | Come, lords, take up the body of the king, |
| | That we may see it honourably interr'd: |
| | And then I vow so to revenge his death |
| | As Rome, and all those popish prelates there, |
| | Shall curse the time that e'er Navarre was king,   110 |
| | And rul'd in France by Henry's fatal death. |
| | [they march out, with the body of King Henry |
| | lying on four men's shoulders, with a dead |
| | march, drawing weapons on the ground |

# THE TRAGEDY OF DIDO,
# QUEEN OF CARTHAGE

# INTRODUCTION

*Dido, Queen of Carthage* may well be Marlowe's earliest play, written while he was at Cambridge, most likely in collaboration with Thomas Nashe. It was probably written for a private theatre to be performed by children's company, and it has its origins in the university plays on classical subjects which were popular at Cambridge, rather than in the commercial world of the public theatre. Based on books 1, 2 and 4 of Virgil's Latin epic the *Aeneid*, the play tells the story of Dido's failure to persuade her lover Aeneas to stay with her in Carthage and her subsequent suicide. The major innovation of the play is clear from the difference in the titles of the two versions of the story. The *Aeneid* takes its name from its eponymous male protagonist, and it is his wanderings and his destiny which structure the narrative. For Virgil, Aeneas' sojourn in Carthage with Dido is a digression, and while the epic has some sympathy with Dido's tragic position, it is clearly focused on the masculine heroic ethos of Rome and Aeneas' unique destiny. Marlowe's play decisively changes the focus of the story, as his choice of title makes immediately clear. In place of Virgil's male epic he writes a female tragedy, in which Dido is obsessed with an image of a heroic Aeneas, independent of his tired presence in Carthage. The play's sympathies are sometimes with Dido, sometimes with Aeneas, and sometimes satirically or heroically detached.

Dido's passion for Aeneas is set at odds with his divinely appointed ambitions and obligations. Ultimately she must sacrifice her passions for the sake of Aeneas's heroic role, but it is never clear that Aeneas is up to his mythic image. Rooted in the Trojan past, he is preoccupied with memories, of King Priam and the sack of his city. His first words to Dido indicate his deracination: 'Sometime I was a Trojan, mighty Queen;/ But Troy is not; what shall I say I am?' (2,1) His long speeches are nostalgic, reflective rather than active. Rather than a man with a heroic destiny to fulfil, Aeneas takes the commands of Hermes as a man always buffeted by external forces. He is passive in obedience to these demands, lacking the will even consciously to desert Dido. Around this doomed central couple, other stories amplify and ironise the theme, including the framing scenes in which the gods are pictured in their own passions and conflicts, as in Jupiter's flirtation with Ganymede, or the animosity between Venus and Juno.

It is striking that in her distress at Aeneas's desertion, Dido uses the same Icarus imagery as Marlowe uses in the prologue to *Doctor Faustus*. As in the later play, the imagery cuts both ways. Dido's aspiration, even if – perhaps especially as – it is characterised as excessive, is a focus of the play's dramatic and empathetic energies: she is its over-reacher. This reach is ultimately fatal, and yet, as so often in Marlowe's drama, it has a magnificence about it. On a smaller scale, *Dido Queen of Carthage* encapsulates Marlowe's major theme.

# CHARACTERS IN THE PLAY

| | |
|---|---|
| JUPITER | ILIONEUS |
| GANYMEDE | CLOANTHUS |
| HERMES | SERGESTUS |
| CUPID | *Other Trojans* |
| JUNO | IARBAS |
| VENUS | *Carthaginian Lords* |
| AENEAS | DIDO |
| ASCANIUS, *his son* | ANNA, *her sister* |
| ACHATES | *Nurse* |

# THE TRAGEDY OF DIDO,
## QUEEN OF CARTHAGE

## ACT I

### SCENE I

*Here the curtains draw: there is discovered* JUPITER *dandling*
GANYMEDE *upon his knee, and* HERMES *lying asleep*

JUPITER     Come, gentle Ganymede, and play with me;
            I love thee well, say Juno what she will.

GANYMEDE  I am much better for your worthless love,
            That will not shield me from her shrewish blows;
            To day, whenas I fill'd into your cups
            And held the cloth of pleasance whiles you drank,
            She reach'd me such a rap for that I spill'd
            As made the blood run down about mine ears.

JUPITER     What, dares she strike the darling of my thoughts?
            By Saturn's soul, and this earth-threatening hair,     10
            That, shaken thrice, makes nature's buildings quake,
            I vow, if she but once frown on thee more,
            To hang her, meteor like, 'twixt heaven and earth,
            And bind her, hand and foot, with golden cords,
            As once I did for harming Hercules;

GANYMEDE  Might I but see that pretty sport a-foot,
            O, how would I with Helen's brother laugh,
            And bring the gods to wonder at the game;
            Sweet Jupiter, if e'er I pleas'd thine eye,
            Or seemed fair, wall'd-in with eagle's wings,     20
            Grace my immortal beauty with this boon,
            And I will spend my time in thy bright arms.

JUPITER     What is't, sweet wag, I should deny thy youth?
            Whose face reflects such pleasure to mine eyes,
            As I, exhal'd with thy fire-darting beams,
            Have oft driven back the horses of the Night,
            Whenas they would have hal'd thee from my sight.
            Sit on my knee, and call for thy content,

Control proud Fate, and cut the thread of Time:
Why, are not all the gods at thy command,                    30
And heaven and earth the bounds of thy delight?
Vulcan shall dance to make thee laughing sport,
And my nine daughters sing when thou art sad;
From Juno's bird I'll pluck her spotted pride,
To make thee fans wherewith to cool thy face;
And Venus' swans shall shed their silver down
To sweeten out the slumbers of thy bed;
Hermes no more shall show the world his wings,
If that thy fancy in his feathers dwell,
But, as this one, I'll tear them all from him,               40
                    [*plucks a feather from Hermes' wings*
Do thou but say, 'their colour pleaseth me'.
Hold here, my little love: these linked gems,
                                        [*gives jewels*

My Juno ware upon her marriage-day,
Put thou about thy neck, my own sweet heart,
And trick thy arms and shoulders with my theft.

GANYMEDE  I would have a jewel for mine ear,
          And a fine brooch to put in my hat,
          And then I'll hug with you an hundred times.

JUPITER   And shalt have, Ganymede, if thou wilt be my love.

                        *Enter* VENUS

VENUS     Ay, this is it: you can sit toying there,          50
          And playing with that female wanton boy,
          Whiles my Aeneas wanders on the seas,
          And rests a prey to every billow's pride.
          Juno, false Juno, in her chariot's pomp,
          Drawn through the heavens by steeds of
                                        Boreas' brood,
          Made Hebe to direct her airy wheels
          Into the windy country of the clouds;
          Where, finding Aeolus entrench'd with storms,
          And guarded with a thousand grisly ghosts,
          She humbly did beseech him for our bane,           60
          And charg'd him drown my son with all his train.
          Then gan the winds break ope their brazen doors,
          And all Aeolia to be up in arms:

Poor Troy must now be sack'd upon the sea,
And Neptune's waves be envious men of war;
Epeus' horse, to Aetna's hill transform'd,
Prepared stands to wreck their wooden walls;
And Aeolus, like Agamemnon, sounds
The surges, his fierce soldiers, to the spoil:
See how the night, Ulysses-like, comes forth,                70
And intercepts the day, as Dolon erst;
Ay, me! The stars suppris'd, like Rhesus' steeds,
Are drawn by darkness forth Astraeus' tents.
What shall I do to save thee, my sweet boy,
Whenas the waves do threat our crystal world,
And Proteus, raising hills of floods on high,
Intends, ere long, to sport him in the sky?
False Jupiter, reward'st thou virtue so?
What, is not piety exempt from woe?
Then die, Aeneas, in thine innocence,                         80
Since that religion hath no recompense.

JUPITER    Content thee, Cytherea, in thy care,
Since thy Aeneas' wandering fate is firm,
Whose weary limbs shall shortly make repose
In those fair walls I promis'd him of yore.
But, first, in blood must his good fortune bud,
Before he be the lord of Turnus' town,
Or force her smile that hitherto hath frown'd:
Three winters shall he with the Rutiles war,
And, in the end, subdue them with his sword;                  90
And full three summers likewise shall he waste
In managing those fierce barbarian minds;
Which once perform'd, poor Troy, so
                                            long suppress'd,
From forth her ashes shall advance her head,
And flourish once again, that erst was dead.
But bright Ascanius, beauty's better work,
Who with the sun divides one radiant shape,
Shall build his throne amidst those starry towers
That earth-born Atlas, groaning, underprops:
No bounds, but heaven, shall bound his empery,               100
Whose azur'd gates enchased with his name,

Shall make the Morning haste her grey uprise,
To feed her eyes with his engraven fame.
Thus, in stout Hector's race, three hundred years
The Roman sceptre royal shall remain,
Till that a princess-priest conceiv'd by Mars,
Shall yield to dignity a double birth,
Who will eternish Troy in their attempts.

VENUS      How may I credit these thy flattering terms,
           When both sea and sands beset their ships,            110
           And Phoebus, as in Stygian pools, refrains
           To taint his tresses in the Tyrrhene main?

JUPITER    I will take order for that presently –
           Hermes, awake; and haste to Neptune's realm,
           Whereas the wind-god, warring now with fate,
           Beseiges th' offspring of our kingly loins:
           Charge him from me to turn his stormy powers,
           And fetter them in Vulcan's sturdy brass,
           That durst thus proudly wrong our kinsman's peace.
                                              [exit Hermes

           Venus, farewell; thy son shall be our care –           120
           Come, Ganymede, we must about this gear.
                                  [exeunt Jupiter and Ganymede

VENUS      Disquiet seas, lay down your swelling looks,
           And court Aeneas with your calmy cheer,
           Whose beauteous burden well might make you
                                                         proud,
           Had not the heavens, conceived with hell-born
                                                        clouds,
           Veil'd his resplendent glory from your view:
           For my sake pity him, Oceanus,
           That erstwhile issu'd from thy watery loins,
           And had my being from thy bubbling froth.
           Triton, I know, hath fill'd his trump with Troy,     130
           And therefore will take pity on his toil;
           And call both Thetis and Cymodoce
           To succour him in this extremity.

           *Enter* AENEAS, ASCANIUS, ACHATES *and others*

           What, do I see my son now come on shore?
           Venus, how art thou compass'd with content,

The while thine eyes attract their sought-for joys;
Great Jupiter, still honour'd may'st thou be
For this so friendly aid in time of need;
Here in this bush disguised will I stand,
Whiles my Aeneas spends himself in plaints,          140
And heaven and earth with his unrest acquaints.

AENEAS    You sons of care, companions of my course,
Priam's misfortune follows us by sea,
And Helen's rape doth haunt ye at the heels.
How many dangers have we overpass'd;
Both barking Scylla, and the sounding rocks,
The Cyclops' shelves, and grim Ceraunia's seat,
Have you o'ergone, and yet remain alive.
Pluck up your hearts, since Fate still rests our friend,
And changing heavens may those good days return    150
Which Pergama did vaunt in all her pride.

ACHATES   Brave prince of Troy, thou only art our god,
That by thy virtues free'st us from annoy,
And mak'st our hopes survive to coming joys:
Do thou but smile, and cloudy heaven will clear,
Whose night and day descendeth from thy brows.
Though we be now in extreme misery,
And rest the map of weather-beaten woe,
Yet shall the aged sun shed forth his hair,
To make us live unto our former heat,          160
And every beast the forest doth send forth
Bequeath her young ones to our scanted food.

ASCANIUS  Father, I faint; good father, give me meat.

AENEAS    Alas, sweet boy, thou must be still a while,
Till we have fire to dress the meat we kill'd –
Gentle Achates, reach the tinder box,
That we may make a fire to warm us with,
And roast our new found victuals on this shore.

VENUS     [aside] See, what strange arts necessity finds out;
How near, my sweet Aeneas, art thou driven.          170

AENEAS    Hold; take this candle, and go light a fire;
You shall have leaves and windful boughs enow,
Near to these woods, to roast you meat withal –
Ascanius, go and dry thy drenched limbs,

             Whiles I with my Achates rove abroad,
             To know what coast the wind hath driven us on,
             Or whether men or beasts inhabit it.
                             [*exeunt Ascanius and others*

ACHATES    The air is pleasant, and the soil most fit
             For cities and society's supports;
             Yet much I marvel that I cannot find      180
             No steps of men imprinted in the earth.

VENUS      [*aside*] Now is the time for me to play my part –
             Ho, young men! Saw you, as you came,
             Any of all my sisters wandering here,
             Having a quiver girded to her side,
             And clothed in a spotted leopard's skin?

AENEAS    I neither saw nor heard of any such.
             But what may I, fair virgin, call your name,
             Whose looks set forth no mortal form to view,
             Nor speech bewrays aught human in thy birth?   190
             Thou art a goddess that delud'st our eyes,
             And shroud'st thy beauty in this borrow'd shape;
             But whether thou the Sun's bright sister be,
             Or one of chaste Diana's fellow nymphs,
             Live happy in the height of all content,
             And lighten our extremes with this one boon,
             As to instruct us under what good heaven
             We breathe as now, and what this world is call'd
             On which by tempests' fury we are cast:
             Tell us, O, tell us, that are ignorant;      200
             And this right hand shall make thy altars crack
             With mountain-heaps of milk-white sacrifice.

VENUS      Such honour, stranger, do I not affect:
             It is the use for Tyrian maids to wear
             Their bow and quiver in this modest sort,
             And suit themselves in purple for the nonce,
             That they may trip more lightly o'er the lawnds,
             And overtake the tusked boar in chase.
             But for the land whereof thou dost inquire,
             It is the Punic kingdom, rich and strong,     210
             Adjoining on Agenor's stately town,
             The kingly seat of Southern Libya,

            Whereas Sidonian Dido rules as queen.
            But what are you that ask of me these things?
            Whence may you come, or whither will you go?

AENEAS     Of Troy am I, Aeneas is my name,
            Who, driven by war from forth my native world,
            Put sails to sea to seek out Italy,
            And my divine descent from sceptred Jove:
            With twice twelve Phrygian ships I plough'd
                                 the deep, 220
            And made that way my mother Venus led;
            But of all them scarce seven do anchor safe,
            And they so wreck'd and welter'd by the waves,
            As every tide tilts 'twixt their oaken sides;
            And all of them, unburden'd of their load,
            Are ballassed with billows' watery weight.
            But hapless I, God wot, poor and unknown,
            Do trace these Libyan deserts, all despis'd,
            Exil'd forth Europe and wide Asia both,
            And have not any coverture but heaven.         230

VENUS     Fortune hath favour'd thee, whate'er thou be,
            In sending thee unto this courteous coast.
            A' God's name, on! And haste thee to the court,
            Where Dido will receive ye with her smiles:
            And for thy ships, which thou supposest lost,
            Not one of them hath perish'd in the storm,
            But are arrived safe, not far from hence:
            And so, I leave thee to thy fortune's lot,
            Wishing good luck unto thy wandering steps.   *[exit*

AENEAS     Achates, 'tis my mother that is fled;         240
            I know her by the movings of her feet –
            Stay, gentle Venus, fly not from thy son;
            Too cruel, why wilt thou forsake me thus,
            Or in these shades deceiv'st mine eyes so oft?
            Why talk we not together hand in hand,
            And tell our griefs in more familiar terms?
            But thou art gone, and leav'st me here alone
            To dull the air with my discoursive moan.
                                        *[exeunt*

### SCENE 2

*Enter* IARBAS, *followed by* ILIONEUS,
CLOANTHUS, SERGESTUS, *and others*

ILIONEUS    Follow, ye Trojans, follow this brave lord,
              And plain to him the sum of your distress.

IARBAS      Why, what are you, or wherefore do you sue?

ILIONEUS    Wretches of Troy, envied of all the winds,
              That crave such favour at your honour s feet,
              As poor distressed misery may plead:
              Save, save, O save our ships from cruel fire,
              That do complain the wounds of thousand waves,
              And spare our lives, whom every spite pursues;
              We come not, we, to wrong your Libyan gods,    10
              Or steal your household Lares from their shrines;
              Our hands are not prepar'd to lawless spoil,
              Nor armed to offend in any kind;
              Such force is far from our unweapon'd thoughts,
              Whose fading weal, of victory forsook,
              Forbids all hope to harbour near our hearts.

IARBAS      But tell me, Trojans, Trojans if you be,
              Unto what fruitful quarters were ye bound,
              Before that Boreas buckled with your sails?

CLOANTHUS There is a place, Hesperia term'd by us,    20
              An ancient empire, famoused for arms,
              And fertile in fair Ceres' furrow'd wealth,
              Which now we call Italia, of his name
              That in such peace long time did rule the same.
              Thither made we,
              When, suddenly, gloomy Orion rose,
              And led our ships into the shallow sands,
              Whereas the southern wind with brackish breath,
              Dispers'd them all amongst the wreckful rocks:
              From thence a few of us escap'd to land;    30
              The rest, we fear, are folded in the floods.

IARBAS      Brave men-at-arms, abandon fruitless fears,
              Since Carthage knows to entertain distress.

| | |
|---|---|
| SERGESTUS | Ay, but the barbarous sort do threat our steps, |
| | And will not let us lodge upon the sands; |
| | In multitudes they swarm unto the shore, |
| | And from the first earth interdict our feet. |
| IARBAS | Myself will see they shall not trouble ye: |
| | Your men and you shall banquet in our court, |
| | And every Trojan be as welcome here       40 |
| | As Jupiter to silly Baucis' house. |
| | Come in with me; I'll bring you to my queen, |
| | Who shall confirm my words with further deeds. |
| SERGESTUS | Thanks, gentle lord, for such unlook'd-for grace: |
| | Might we but once more see Aeneas' face, |
| | Then would we hope to quite such friendly turns |
| | As shall surpass the wonder of our speech. |

[*exeunt*

# ACT TWO

## SCENE I

*Enter* AENEAS, ACHATES, ASCANIUS, *and others*

| | |
|---|---|
| AENEAS | Where am I now? These should be Carthage walls. |
| ACHATES | Why stands my sweet Aeneas thus amaz'd? |
| AENEAS | O my Achates, Theban Niobe, |
| | Who for her sons' death wept out life and breath, |
| | And, dry with grief, was turn'd into a stone, |
| | Had not such passions in her head as I! |
| | Methinks, |
| | That town there should be Troy, yon Ida's hill, |
| | There Xanthus' stream, because here's Priamus; |
| | And when I know it is not, then I die.            10 |
| ACHATES | And in this humour is Achates too; |
| | I cannot choose but fall upon my knees, |
| | And kiss his hand. O, where is Hecuba? |
| | Here she was wont to sit; but, saving air, |
| | Is nothing here: and what is this but stone? |
| AENEAS | O, yet this stone doth make Aeneas weep! |
| | And would my prayers (as Pygmalion's did) |
| | Could give it life, that under his conduct |
| | We might sail back to Troy, and be reveng'd |
| | On these hard-hearted Grecians which rejoice      20 |
| | That nothing now is left of Priamus! |
| | O, Priamus is left, and this is he! |
| | Come, come aboard; pursue the hateful Greeks. |
| ACHATES | What means Aeneas? |
| AENEAS | Achates, though mine eyes say this is stone, |
| | Yet thinks my mind that this is Priamus; |
| | And when my grieved heart sighs and says no, |
| | Then would it leap out to give Priam life – |
| | O, were I not at all, so thou mightst be – |
| | Achates, see, King Priam wags his hand!           30 |
| | He is alive: Troy is not overcome! |
| ACHATES | Thy mind, Aeneas, that would have it so, |
| | Deludes thy eyesight; Priamus is dead. |

AENEAS     Ah, Troy is sack'd, and Priamus is dead!
           And why should poor Aeneas be alive?
ASCANIUS   Sweet father, leave to weep: this is not he.
           For, were it Priam, he would smile on me.
ACHATES    Aeneas, see, here come the citizens:
           Leave to lament, lest they laugh at our fears.

*Enter* CLOANTHUS, SERGESTUS, ILIONEUS, *and others*

AENEAS     Lords of this town, or whatsoever style        40
           Belongs unto your name? Vouchsafe of ruth
           To tell us who inhabits this fair town,
           What kind of people, and who governs them;
           For we are strangers driven on this shore,
           And scarcely know within what clime we are.
ILIONEUS   I hear Aeneas' voice, but see him not,
           For none of these can be our general.
ACHATES    Like Ilioneus speaks this nobleman,
           But Ilioneus goes not in such robes.
SERGESTUS  You are Achates, or I am deceiv'd.             50
ACHATES    Aeneas, see, Sergestus or his ghost!
ILIONEUS   He names Aeneas; let us kiss his feet.
CLOANTHUS  It is our captain; see, Ascanius!
SERGESTUS  Live long Aeneas and Ascanius!
AENEAS     Achates, speak, for I am overjoy'd.
ACHATES    O Ilioneus, art thou yet alive?
ILIONEUS   Blest be the time I see Achates' face!
CLOANTHUS  Why turns Aeneas from his trusty friends?
AENEAS     Sergestus, Ilioneus, and the rest,
           Your sight amaz'd me. O, what destinies         60
           Have brought my sweet companions in such plight?
           O tell me, for I long to be resolv'd!
ILIONEUS   Lovely Aeneas, these are Carthage walls:
           And here Queen Dido wears th' imperial crown,
           Who for Troy's sake hath entertain'd us all,
           And clad us in these wealthy robes we wear.
           Oft hath she ask'd us under whom we serv'd;
           And, when we told her, she would weep for grief,
           Thinking the sea had swallow'd up thy ships;
           And, now she sees thee, how will she rejoice!   70

SERGESTUS  See, where her servitors pass through the hall
           Bearing a banquet: Dido is not far.
ILIONEUS   Look, where she comes; Aeneas, view her well.
AENEAS     Well may I view her; but she sees not me.

              *Enter* DIDO, ANNA, IARBAS *and train*

DIDO       What stranger art thou, that dost eye me thus.
AENEAS     Sometime I was a Trojan, mighty queen;
           But Troy is not – what shall I say I am?
ILIONEUS   Renowmed Dido, 'tis our general,
           Warlike Aeneas.
DIDO       Warlike Aeneas, and in these base robes –          80
           Go fetch the garment which Sichaeus ware –
                              [*exit an Attendant who brings in the
                                garment, which Aeneas puts on*
           Brave prince, welcome to Carthage and to me,
           Both happy that Aeneas is our guest.
           Sit in this chair, and banquet with a queen:
           Aeneas is Aeneas, were he clad
           In weeds as bad as ever Irus ware.
AENEAS     This is no seat for one that's comfortless:
           May it please your grace to let Aeneas wait;
           For though my birth be great, my fortune's mean,
           Too mean to be companion to a queen.             90
DIDO       Thy fortune may be greater than thy birth:
           Sit down, Aeneas, sit in Dido's place;
           And, if this be thy son, as I suppose,
           Here let him sit – Be merry, lovely child.
AENEAS     This place beseems me not; O pardon me!
DIDO       I'll have it so; Aeneas, be content.
ASCANIUS   Madam, you shall be my mother.
DIDO       And so I will, sweet child – Be merry, man:
           Here's to thy better fortune and good stars.  [*drinks*
AENEAS     In all humility, I thank your grace.           100
DIDO       Remember who thou art; speak like thyself:
           Humility belongs to common grooms.
AENEAS     And who so miserable as Aeneas is?
DIDO       Lies it in Dido's hands to make thee blest?
           Then be assur'd thou art not miserable.

AENEAS     O Priamus, O Troy, O Hecuba!

DIDO       May I entreat thee to discourse at large,
And truly too, how Troy was overcome?
For many tales go of that city's fall,
And scarcely do agree upon one point:            110
Some say Antenor did betray the town;
Others report 'twas Sinon's perjury;
But all in this, that Troy is overcome,
And Priam dead; yet how, we hear no news.

AENEAS     A woful tale bids Dido to unfold,
Whose memory, like pale Death's stony mace,
Beats forth my senses from this troubled soul,
And makes Aeneas sink at Dido's feet.

DIDO       What, faints Aeneas to remember Troy,
In whose defence he fought so valiantly?       120
Look up, and speak.

AENEAS     Then speak, Aeneas, with Achilles' tongue:
And, Dido, and you Carthaginian peers,
Hear me, but yet with Myrmidons' harsh ears,
Daily inur'd to broils and massacres,
Lest you be mov'd too much with my sad tale.
The Grecian soldiers, tir'd with ten years' war,
Began to cry, 'Let us unto our ships,
Troy is invincible, why stay we here?'
With whose outcries Atrides being appall'd,      130
Summon'd the captains to his princely tent;
Who, looking on the scars we Trojans gave,
Seeing the number of their men decreas'd,
And the remainder weak and out of heart,
Gave up their voices to dislodge the camp,
And so in troops all march'd to Tenedos:
Where when they came, Ulysses on the sand
Assay'd with honey words to turn them back;
And as he spoke, to further his intent,
The winds did drive huge billows to the shore,    140
And heaven was darken'd with tempestuous clouds;
Then he alleg'd the gods would have them stay,
And prophesied Troy should be overcome:
And therewithal he call'd false Sinon forth,

A man compact of craft and perjury,
Whose ticing tongue was made of Hermes' pipe,
To force an hundred watchful eyes to sleep;
And him, Epeus having made the horse,
With sacrificing wreaths upon his head,
Ulysses sent to our unhappy town;                    150
Who, grovelling in the mire of Xanthus' banks,
His hands bound at his back, and both his eyes
Turn'd up to heaven, as one resolv'd to die,
Our Phrygian shepherds hal'd within the gates,
And brought unto the court of Priamus;
To whom he us'd action so pitiful,
Looks so remorseful, vows so forcible,
As therewithal the old man overcome,
Kiss'd him, embrac'd him, and unloos'd his bands:
And then – O Dido, pardon me!                         160

DIDO      Nay, leave not here: resolve me of the rest.
AENEAS    O, the enchanting words of that base slave
          Made him to think Epeus' pine-tree horse
          A sacrifice t' appease Minerva's wrath!
          The rather, for that one Laocoon,
          Breaking a spear upon his hollow breast,
          Was with two winged serpents stung to death.
          Whereat aghast, we were commanded straight
          With reverence to draw it into Troy:
          In which unhappy work was I employ'd;        170
          These hands did help to hale it to the gates,
          Through which it could not enter, 'twas so huge –
          O, had it never enter'd, Troy had stood!
          But Priamus, impatient of delay,
          Enforc'd a wide breach in that rampir'd wall
          Which thousand battering-rams could never pierce,
          And so came in this fatal instrument:
          At whose accursed feet, as overjoy'd,
          We banqueted, till, overcome with wine,
          Some surfeited, and others soundly slept.    180
          Which Sinon viewing, caus'd the Greekish spies
          To haste to Tenedos, and tell the camp:
          Then he unlock'd the horse; and suddenly,

From out his entrails, Neoptolemus,
Setting his spear upon the ground, leapt forth,
And, after him, a thousand Grecians more,
In whose stern faces shin'd the quenchless fire
That after burnt the pride of Asia.
By this, the camp was come unto the walls,
And through the breach did march into the streets,
Where, meeting with the rest, 'Kill, kill' they cried.
Frighted with this confused noise, I rose,
And, looking from a turret, might behold
Young infants swimming in their parents' blood,
Headless carcasses piled up in heaps,
Virgins half-dead, dragg'd by their golden hair,
And with main force flung on a ring of pikes,
Old men with swords thrust through their aged sides,
Kneeling for mercy to a Greekish lad,
Who with steel pole-axes dash'd out their brains.   200
Then buckled I mine armour, drew my sword,
And thinking to go down, came Hector's ghost
With ashy visage, blueish sulphur eyes,
His arms torn from his shoulders, and his breast
Furrow'd with wounds, and, that which made
                                        me weep,
Thongs at his heels, by which Achilles' horse
Drew him in triumph through the Greekish camp,
Burst from the earth, crying 'Aeneas, fly!
Troy is afire, the Grecians have the town!'

DIDO        O Hector, who weeps not to hear thy name?   210

AENEAS      Yet flung I forth, and, desperate of my life,
Ran in the thickest throngs, and with this sword
Sent many of their savage ghosts to hell.
At last came Pyrrhus, fell and full of ire,
His harness dropping blood, and on his spear
The mangled head of Priam's youngest son:
And, after him, his band of Myrmidons,
With balls of wild-fire in their murdering paws,
Which made the funeral flame that burnt fair Troy:
All which hemm'd me about, crying, 'This is he!'   220

DIDO        Ah, how could poor Aeneas scape their hands?

| | |
|---|---|
| AENEAS | My mother Venus, jealous of my health, |
| | Convey'd me from their crooked nets and bands; |
| | So I escap'd the furious Pyrrhus' wrath: |
| | Who then ran to the palace of the king, |
| | And at Jove's altar finding Priamus, |
| | About whose wither'd neck hung Hecuba, |
| | Folding his hand in hers, and jointly both |
| | Beating their breasts, and falling on the ground, |
| | He, with his falchion's point rais'd up at once,          230 |
| | And with Megaera's eyes, star'd in their face, |
| | Threatening a thousand deaths at every glance: |
| | To whom the aged king thus, trembling, spoke: |
| | 'Achilles' son, remember what I was, |
| | Father of fifty sons, but they are slain; |
| | Lord of my fortune, but my fortune's turn'd; |
| | King of this city, but my Troy is fir'd; |
| | And now am neither father, lord, nor king: |
| | Yet who so wretched but desires to live? |
| | O, let me live, great Neoptolemus!'          240 |
| | Not mov'd at all but smiling at his tears, |
| | This butcher, whilst his hands were yet held up, |
| | Treading upon his breast, struck off his hands. |
| DIDO | O, end, Aeneas! I can hear no more. |
| AENEAS | At which the frantic queen leap'd on his face, |
| | And in his eyelids hanging by the nails, |
| | A little while prolong'd her husband's life. |
| | At last, the soldiers pull'd her by the heels, |
| | And swung her howling in the empty air, |
| | Which sent an echo to the wounded king:          250 |
| | Whereat he lifted up his bed-rid limbs, |
| | And would have grappled with Achilles' son, |
| | Forgetting both his want of strength and hands; |
| | Which he disdaining, whisk'd his sword about, |
| | And with the wind thereof the king fell down; |
| | Then from the navel to the throat at once |
| | He ripp'd old Priam; at whose latter gasp |
| | Jove's marble statue gan to bend the brow, |
| | As loathing Pyrrhus for this wicked act. |
| | Yet he, undaunted, took his father's flag          260 |

And dipp'd it in the old king's chill-cold blood,
And then in triumph ran into the streets,
Through which he could not pass for slaughter'd men;
So, leaning on his sword, he stood stone still,
Viewing the fire wherewith rich Ilion burnt.
By this, I got my father on my back,
This young boy in mine arms, and by the hand
Led fair Creusa, my beloved wife;
When thou, Achates, with thy sword mad'st way,
And we were round environ'd with the Greeks:     270
O, there I lost my wife; and, had not we
Fought manfully, I had not told this tale.
Yet manhood would not serve; of force we fled;
And, as we went unto our ships, thou know'st
We saw Cassandra sprawling in the streets,
Whom Ajax ravish'd in Diana's fane,
Her cheeks swollen with sighs, her hair all rent;
Whom I took up to bear unto our ships;
But suddenly the Grecians follow'd us,
And I, alas, was forc'd to let her lie!     280
Then got we to our ships, and, being aboard,
Polyxena cried out, 'Aeneas, stay!
The Greeks pursue me; stay, and take me in!'
Mov'd with her voice, I leap'd into the sea,
Thinking to bear her on my back aboard,
For all our ships were launch'd into the deep,
And, as I swom, she, standing on the shore,
Was by the cruel Myrmidons surpris'd,
And, after that, by Pyrrhus sacrific'd.

| | |
|---|---|
| DIDO | I die with melting ruth; Aeneas, leave.     290 |
| ANNA | O, what became of aged Hecuba? |
| IARBAS | How got Aeneas to the fleet again? |
| DIDO | But how scap'd Helen, she that caus'd this war? |
| AENEAS | Achates, speak; sorrow hath tir'd me quite. |
| ACHATES | What happen'd to the queen we cannot show; |

We hear they led her captive into Greece:
As for Aeneas, he swom quickly back;
And Helena betray'd Deiphobus,
Her lover, after Alexander died,

|  | And so was reconcil'd to Menelaus. | 300 |

DIDO  O, had that ticing strumpet ne'er been born!
Trojan, thy ruthful tale hath made me sad:
Come, let us think upon some pleasing sport,
To rid me from these melancholy thoughts.

*[Exeunt all except Ascanius, whom Venus, entering with
Cupid at another door, takes by the sleeve as he is going off*

VENUS  Fair child, stay thou with Dido's waiting maid:
I'll give thee sugar almonds, sweet conserves,
A silver girdle, and a golden purse,
And this young prince shall be thy playfellow.

ASCANIUS  Are you Queen Dido's son?

CUPID  Ay; and my mother gave me this fine bow.    310

ASCANIUS  Shall I have such a quiver and a bow?

VENUS  Such bow, such quiver, and such golden shafts,
Will Dido give to sweet Ascanius.
For Dido's sake I take thee in my arms,
And stick these spangled feathers in thy hat:
Eat comfits in mine arms, and I will sing.

*[sings]*

Now is he fast asleep; and in this grove,
Amongst green brakes, I'll lay Ascanius,
And strew him with sweet-smelling violets,
Blushing roses, purple hyacinths:    320
These milk-white doves shall be his centronels,
Who, if that any seek to do him hurt,
Will quickly fly to Cytherea's fist.
Now, Cupid, turn thee to Ascanius' shape,
And go to Dido, who, instead of him,
Will set thee on her lap, and play with thee:
Then touch her white breast with this arrow head,
That she may dote upon Aeneas' love,
And by that means repair his broken ships,
Victual his soldiers, give him wealthy gifts,    330
And he, at last, depart to Italy,
Or else in Carthage make his kingly throne.

CUPID  I will, fair mother; and so play my part
As every touch shall wound Queen Dido's heart. *[exit*

VENUS     Sleep, my sweet nephew, in these cooling shades,
Free from the murmur of these running streams,
The cry of beasts, the rattling of the winds,
Or whisking of these leaves: all shall be still,
And nothing interrupt thy quiet sleep,
Till I return, and take thee hence again.     340

                                      [*exit*

## ACT THREE

### SCENE I

*Enter* CUPID *as* ASCANIUS

CUPID    Now, Cupid, cause the Carthaginian queen
To be enamour'd of thy brother's looks;
Convey this golden arrow in thy sleeve,
Lest she imagine thou art Venus' son;
And when she strokes thee softly on the head,
Then shall I touch her breast and conquer her.

*Enter* DIDO, ANNA *and* IARBAS

IARBAS    How long, fair Dido, shall I pine for thee?
'Tis not enough that thou dost grant me love,
But that I may enjoy what I desire:
That love is childish which consists in words.    10

DIDO    Iarbas, know that thou, of all my wooers –
And yet have I had many mightier kings –
Hast had the greatest favours I could give.
I fear me, Dido hath been counted light
In being too familiar with Iarbas;
Albeit the gods do know, no wanton thought
Had ever residence in Dido's breast.

IARBAS    But Dido is the favour I request.

DIDO    Fear not, Iarbas; Dido may be thine.

ANNA    Look, sister, how Aeneas' little son    20
Plays with your garments and embraceth you.

CUPID    No, Dido will not take me in her arms;
I shall not be her son, she loves me not.

DIDO    Weep not, sweet boy; thou shalt be Dido's son:
Sit in my lap, and let me hear thee sing.

*[Cupid sings]*

No more, my child, now talk another while,
And tell me where learn'dst thou this preaty song.

CUPID    My cousin Helen taught it me in Troy.

DIDO    How lovely is Ascanius when he smiles!

CUPID    Will Dido let me hang about her neck?    30

| | |
|---|---|
| DIDO | Ay, wag; and give thee leave to kiss her too. |
| CUPID | What will you give me now? I'll have this fan. |
| DIDO | Take it, Ascanius, for thy father's sake. |
| IARBAS | Come, Dido, leave Ascanius; let us walk. |
| DIDO | Go thou away; Ascanius shall stay. |
| IARBAS | Ungentle queen, is this thy love to me? |
| DIDO | O stay, Iarbas, and I'll go with thee! |
| CUPID | An if my mother go, I'll follow her. |
| DIDO | Why stay'st thou here? Thou art no love of mine. |
| IARBAS | Iarbas, die, seeing she abandons thee!     40 |
| DIDO | No, live. Iarbas, what hast thou deserv'd, |
| | That I should say thou art no love of mine? |
| | Something thou hast deserv'd – Away, I say! |
| | Depart from Carthage; come not in my sight. |
| IARBAS | Am I not king of rich Gaetulia? |
| DIDO | Iarbas, pardon me, and stay a while. |
| CUPID | Mother, look here. |
| DIDO | What tell'st thou me of rich Gaetulia? |
| | Am not I queen of Libya? Then depart. |
| IARBAS | I go to feed the humour of my love,     50 |
| | Yet not from Carthage for a thousand worlds. |
| DIDO | Iarbas! |
| IARBAS | Doth Dido call me back? |
| DIDO | No; but I charge thee never look on me. |
| IARBAS | Then pull out both mine eyes, or let me die.     [exit |
| ANNA | Wherefore doth Dido bid Iarbas go? |
| DIDO | Because his loathsome sight offends mine eye, |
| | And in my thoughts is shrin'd another love. |
| | O Anna, didst thou know how sweet love were, |
| | Full soon wouldst thou abjure this single life!     60 |
| ANNA | [aside] Poor soul, I know too well the sour of love: |
| | O, that Iarbas could but fancy me! |
| DIDO | Is not Aeneas fair and beautiful? |
| ANNA | Yes, and Iarbas foul and favourless. |
| DIDO | Is he not eloquent in all his speech? |
| ANNA | Yes; and Iarbas rude and rustical. |
| DIDO | Name not Iarbas: but, sweet Anna, say, |
| | Is not Aeneas worthy Dido's love? |
| ANNA | O sister, were you empress of the world, |

Aeneas well deserves to be your love;          70
So lovely is he, that, where'er he goes,
The people swarm to gaze him in the face.

DIDO       But tell them, none shall gaze on him but I,
           Lest their gross eye-beams taint my lover's cheeks.
           Anna, good sister Anna, go for him,
           Lest with these sweet thoughts I melt clean away.

ANNA       Then, sister, you'll abjure Iarbas' love?

DIDO       Yet must I hear that loathsome name again?
           Run for Aeneas, or I'll fly to him.          [exit Anna

CUPID      You shall not hurt my father when he comes.          80

DIDO       No, for thy sake I'll love thy father well —
           O dull-conceited Dido, that till now
           Didst never think Aeneas beautiful!
           But now, for quittance of this oversight,
           I'll make me bracelets of his golden hair:
           His glistening eyes shall be my looking-glass;
           His lips an altar, where I'll offer up
           As many kisses as the sea hath sands;
           Instead of music I will hear him speak;
           His looks shall be my only library;          90
           And thou, Aeneas, Dido's treasury,
           In whose fair bosom I will lock more wealth
           Than twenty thousand Indias can afford.
           O, here he comes! Love, love, give Dido leave
           To be more modest than her thoughts admit,
           Lest I be made a wonder to the world.

*Enter* AENEAS, ACHATES, SERGESTUS, ILIONEUS, *and* CLOANTHUS

           Achates, how doth Carthage please your lord?

ACHATES    That will Aeneas show your majesty.

DIDO       Aeneas, art thou there?

AENEAS     I understand, your highness sent for me.          100

DIDO       No; but, now thou art here, tell me, in sooth,
           In what might Dido highly pleasure thee.

AENEAS     So much have I receiv'd at Dido's hands
           As, without blushing, I can ask no more:
           Yet, queen of Afric, are my ships unrigg'd,
           My sails all rent in sunder with the wind,

My oars broken, and my tackling lost,
Yea, all my navy split with rocks and shelves;
Nor stern nor anchor have our maimed fleet;
Our masts the furious winds struck overboard: 110
Which piteous wants if Dido will supply,
We will account her author of our lives.

DIDO    Aeneas, I'll repair thy Trojan ships,
Conditionally that thou wilt stay with me,
And let Achates sail to Italy:
I'll give thee tackling made of rivell'd gold,
Wound on the barks of odoriferous trees;
Oars of massy ivory, full of holes,
Through which the water shall delight to play;
Thy anchors shall be hew'd from crystal rocks, 120
Which, if thou lose, shall shine above the waves;
The masts, whereon thy swelling sails shall hang,
Hollow pyramides of silver plate;
The sails of folded lawn, where shall be wrought
The wars of Troy – but not Troy's overthrow;
For ballass, empty Dido's treasury:
Take what ye will, but leave Aeneas here.
Achates, thou shalt be so seemly clad,
As sea-born nymphs shall swarm about thy ships,
And wanton mermaids court thee with sweet songs, 130
Flinging in favours of more sovereign worth
Than Thetis hangs about Apollo's neck,
So that Aeneas may but stay with me.

AENEAS    Wherefore would Dido have Aeneas stay?
DIDO    To war against my bordering enemies.
Aeneas, think not Dido is in love;
For, if that any man could conquer me,
I had been wedded ere Aeneas came:
See, where the pictures of my suitors hang;
And are not these as fair as fair may be? 140

ACHATES    I saw this man at Troy, ere Troy was sack'd.
SERGESTUS    I this in Greece, when Paris stole fair Helen.
ILIONEUS    This man and I were at Olympia's games.
SERGESTUS    I know this face; he is a Persian born:
I travell'd with him to Aetolia.

CLOANTHUS   And I in Athens with this gentleman,
            Unless I be deceiv'd, disputed once.
DIDO        But speak. Aeneas; know you none of these?
AENEAS      No, madam: but it seems that these are kings.
DIDO        All these, and others which I never saw,          150
            Have been most urgent suitors for my love;
            Some came in person, others sent their legates,
            Yet none obtain'd me: I am free from all;
            And yet, God knows, entangled unto one.
            This was an orator, and thought by words
            To compass me; but yet he was deceiv'd;
            And this a Spartan courtier, vain and wild:
            But his fantastic humours pleas'd not me:
            This was Alcion, a musician,
            But, play'd he ne'er so sweet, I let him go:       160
            This was the wealthy king of Thessaly;
            But I had gold enough, and cast him off:
            This, Meleager's son, a warlike prince;
            But weapons gree not with my tender years:
            The rest are such as all the world well knows:
            Yet now I swear, by heaven and him I love,
            I was as far from love as they from hate.
AENEAS      O, happy shall he be whom Dido loves!
DIDO        Then never say that thou art miserable,
            Because, it may be, thou shalt be my love:          170
            Yet boast not of it, for I love thee not —
            And yet I hate thee not — [aside] O, if I speak,
            I shall betray myself — Aeneas, come:
            We two will go a-hunting in the woods;
            But not so much for thee — thou art but one —
            As for Achates and his followers.
                                                        [exeunt

## SCENE 2

*Enter* JUNO *to* ASCANIUS, *who lies asleep*

JUNO        Here lies my hate, Aeneas' cursed brat,
            The boy wherein false Destiny delights,
            The heir of Fury, the favourite of the Fates,
            That ugly imp that shall outwear my wrath,
            And wrong my deity with high disgrace.
            But I will take another order now,
            And raze th' eternal register of Time:
            Troy shall no more call him her second hope,
            Nor Venus triumph in his tender youth;
            For here, in spite of heaven, I'll murder him,        10
            And feed infection with his let-out life.
            Say, Paris, now shall Venus have the ball?
            Say, vengeance, now shall her Ascanius die?
            O, no! God wot, I cannot watch my time,
            Nor quit good turns with double fee down told;
            Tut, I am simple, without mind to hurt,
            And have no gall at all to grieve my foes!
            But lustful Jove and his adulterous child
            Shall find it written on confusion's front,
            That only Juno rules in Rhamnus' town.                20

*Enter* VENUS

VENUS       What should this mean? My doves are back return'd,
            Who warn me of such danger prest at hand
            To harm my sweet Ascanius' lovely life –
            Juno, my mortal foe, what make you here?
            Avaunt, old witch, and trouble not my wits.

JUNO        Fie, Venus, that such causeless words of wrath
            Should e'er defile so fair a mouth as thine!
            Are not we both sprung of celestial race,
            And banquet, as two sisters, with the gods?
            Why is it, then, displeasure should disjoin           30
            Whom kindred and acquaintance co-unites?

VENUS       Out, hateful hag! Thou wouldst have slain my son,
            Had not my doves discover'd thy intent:

But I will tear thy eyes fro forth thy head,
And feast the birds with their blood-shotten balls,
If thou but lay thy fingers on my boy.

JUNO    Is this, then, all the thanks that I shall have
For saving him from snakes' and serpents' stings,
That would have kill'd him, sleeping, as he lay?
What, though I was offended with thy son,    40
And wrought him mickle woe on sea and land,
When, for the hate of Trojan Ganymede,
That was advanced by my Hebe's shame,
And Paris' judgment of the heavenly ball,
I muster'd all the winds unto his wrack,
And urg'd each element to his annoy?
Yet now I do repent me of his ruth,
And wish that I had never wrong'd him so.
Bootless I saw it was to war with fate
That hath so many unresisted friends:    50
Wherefore I chang'd my counsel with the time,
And planted love where envy erst had sprung.

VENUS    Sister of love, if that thy love be such
As these protestations do paint forth,
We two, as friends, one fortune will divide.
Cupid shall lay his arrows in thy lap,
And to a sceptre change his golden shafts:
Fancy and modesty shall live as mates,
And thy fair peacocks by my pigeons perch:
Love my Aeneas, and desire is thine;    60
The day, the night, my swans, my sweets, are thine.

JUNO    More than melodious are these words to me,
That overcloy my soul with their content.
Venus, sweet Venus, how may I deserve
Such amorous favours at thy beauteous hand?
But, that thou mayst more easily perceive
How highly I do prize this amity,
Hark to a motion of eternal league,
Which I will make in quittance of thy love.
Thy son, thou know'st, with Dido now remains    70
And feeds his eyes with favours of her court;
She, likewise, in admiring spends her time,

And cannot talk nor think of aught but him;
Why should not they, then, join in marriage,
And bring forth mighty kings to Carthage town,
Whom casualty of sea hath made such friends?
And, Venus, let there be a match confirm'd
Betwixt these two, whose loves are so alike;
And both our deities, conjoin'd in one,
Shall chain felicity unto their throne.                                    80

VENUS    Well could I like this reconcilement's means;
But much I fear, my son will ne'er consent,
Whose armed soul, already on the sea,
Darts forth her light to Lavinia's shore.

JUNO     Fair queen of love, I will divorce these doubts,
And find the way to weary such fond thoughts.
This day they both a-hunting forth will ride
Into the woods adjoining to these walls;
When, in the midst of all their gamesome sports,
I'll make the clouds dissolve their watery works,           90
And drench Silvanus' dwellings with their showers;
Then in one cave the queen and he shall meet,
And interchangeably discourse their thoughts,
Whose short conclusion will seal up their hearts
Unto the purpose which we now propound.

VENUS    Sister, I see you savour of my wiles;
Be it as you will have it for this once.
Meantime Ascanius shall be my charge;
Whom I shall bear to Ida in mine arms,
And couch him in Adonis' purple down.                        100

                                                            [exeunt


                          SCENE 3

            Enter DIDO, AENEAS, ANNA, IARBAS, ACHATES,
                  CUPID as ASCANIUS, and followers

DIDO     Aeneas, think not but I honour thee,
That thus in person go with thee to hunt:
My princely robes, thou see'st, are laid aside,
Whose glittering pomp Diana's shroud supplies;

|        | All fellows now, dispos'd alike to sport, |
|--------|-------------------------------------------|
|        | The woods are wide, and we have store of game. |
|        | Fair Trojan, hold my golden bow a while, |
|        | Until I gird my quiver to my side – |
|        | Lords, go before; we two must talk alone. |
| IARBAS | [aside] Ungentle, can she wrong Iarbas so?     10 |
|        | I'll die before a stranger have that grace. |
|        | 'We two will talk alone' – what words be these? |
| DIDO   | What makes Iarbas here of all the rest? |
|        | We could have gone without your company. |
| AENEAS | But love and duty led him on perhaps |
|        | To press beyond acceptance to your sight. |
| IARBAS | Why, man of Troy, do I offend thine eyes? |
|        | Or art thou griev'd thy betters press so nigh? |
| DIDO   | How now, Gaetulian! Are you grown so brave, |
|        | To challenge us with your comparisons?         20 |
|        | Peasant, go seek companions like thyself, |
|        | And meddle not with any that I love – |
|        | Aeneas, be not mov'd at what he says; |
|        | For otherwhile he will be out of joint. |
| IARBAS | Women may wrong by privilege of love; |
|        | But, should that man of men, Dido except, |
|        | Have taunted me in these opprobrious terms, |
|        | I would have either drunk his dying blood, |
|        | Or else I would have given my life in gage. |
| DIDO   | Huntsmen, why pitch you not your toils apace,   30 |
|        | And rouse the light-foot deer from forth their lair? |
| ANNA   | Sister, see, see Ascanius in his pomp, |
|        | Bearing his hunt-spear bravely in his hand! |
| DIDO   | Yea, little son, are you so forward now? |
| CUPID  | Ay, mother; I shall one day be a man, |
|        | And better able unto other arms; |
|        | Meantime these wanton weapons serve my war, |
|        | Which I will break betwixt a lion's jaws. |
| DIDO   | What, dar'st thou look a lion in the face? |
| CUPID  | Ay; and outface him too, do what he can.        40 |
| ANNA   | How like his father speaketh he in all; |
| AENEAS | And mought I live to see him sack rich Thebes, |
|        | And load his spear with Grecian princes' heads, |

Then would I wish me with Anchises' tomb,
And dead to honour that hath brought me up.

IARBAS      [aside] And might I live to see thee shipp'd away,
And hoist aloft on Neptune's hideous hills,
Then would I wish me in fair Dido's arms,
And dead to scorn that hath pursu'd me so.

AENEAS      Stout friend Achates, dost thou know this wood?      50

ACHATES     As I remember, here you shot the deer
That sav'd your famish'd soldiers' lives from death,
When first you set your foot upon the shore;
And here we met fair Venus, virgin-like,
Bearing her bow and quiver at her back.

AENEAS      O, how these irksome labours now delight,
And overjoy my thoughts with their escape!
Who would not undergo all kind of toil,
To be well stor'd with such a winter's tale?

DIDO        Aeneas, leave these dumps, and let's away,      60
Some to the mountains, some unto the soil,
You to the valleys – thou unto the house.

                              [exeunt all except Iarbas

IARBAS      Ay, this it is which wounds me to the death,
To see a Phrygian, far-fet o'er the sea,
Preferr'd before a man of majesty.
O love! O hate! O cruel women's hearts,
That imitate the moon in every change,
And, like the planets, ever love to range!
What shall I do, thus wronged with disdain?
Revenge me on Aeneas or on her?      70
On her! Fond man, that were to war 'gainst heaven,
And with one shaft provoke ten thousand darts.
This Trojan's end will be thy envy's aim,
Whose blood will reconcile thee to content,
And make love drunken with thy sweet desire.
But Dido, that now holdeth him so dear,
Will die with very tidings of his death:
But time will discontinue her content,
And mould her mind unto new fancy's shapes.
O God of heaven, turn the hand of Fate      80
Unto that happy day of my delight!

And then – what then? Iarbas shall but love:
So doth he now, though not with equal gain.
That resteth in the rival of thy pain,
Who ne'er will cease to soar till he be slain.

                                              *[exit*

## SCENE 4

*The storm. Enter* AENEAS *and* DIDO
*in the cave, at several times*

| | |
|---|---|
| DIDO | Aeneas! |
| AENEAS | Dido! |
| DIDO | Tell me, dear love, how found you out this cave? |
| AENEAS | By chance, sweet queen, as Mars and Venus met. |
| DIDO | Why, that was in a net, where we are loose; |
| | And yet I am not free – O, would I were! |
| AENEAS | Why, what is it that Dido may desire |
| | And not obtain, be it in human power? |
| DIDO | The thing that I will die before I ask, |
| | And yet desire to have before I die. |

AENEAS    It is not aught Aeneas may achieve?
DIDO    Aeneas! No, although his eyes do pierce.
AENEAS    What, hath Iarbas anger'd her in aught?
              And will she be avenged on his life?
DIDO    Not anger'd me, except in angering thee.
AENEAS    Who, then, of all so cruel may he be
              That should detain thy eye in his defects?
DIDO    The man that I do eye where'er I am,
              Whose amorous face, like Paean, sparkles fire,
              Whenas he butts his beams on Flora's bed.
              Prometheus hath put on Cupid's shape,
              And I must perish in his burning arms:
              Aeneas, O Aeneas, quench these flames!
AENEAS    What ails my queen? Is she faln sick of late?
DIDO    Not sick, my love; but sick I must conceal
              The torment that it boots me not reveal:
              And yet I'll speak – and yet I'll hold my peace.
              Do shame her worst, I will disclose my grief:

10

20

Aeneas, thou art he — what did I say?
Something it was that now I have forgot.          30

**AENEAS** What means fair Dido by this doubtful speech?

**DIDO** Nay, nothing: but Aeneas loves me not.

**AENEAS** Aeneas' thoughts dare not ascend so high
As Dido's heart, which monarchs might not scale.

**DIDO** It was because I saw no king like thee,
Whose golden crown might balance my content;
But now that I have found what to affect,
I follow one that loveth fame 'fore me,
And rather had seem fair in Sirens' eyes,
Than to the Carthage queen that dies for him.          40

**AENEAS** If that your majesty can look so low
As my despised worths that shun all praise,
With this my hand I give to you my heart,
And vow, by all the gods of hospitality,
By heaven and earth, and my fair brother's bow,
By Paphos, Capys, and the purple sea
From whence my radiant mother did descend,
And by this sword that sav'd me from the Greeks,
Never to leave these new-upreared walls
Whiles Dido lives and rules in Juno's town —          50
Never to like or love any but her!

**DIDO** What more than Delian music do I hear,
That calls my soul from forth his living seat
To move unto the measures of delight?
Kind clouds, that sent forth such a courteous storm
As made disdain to fly to fancy's lap!
Stout love, in mine arms make thy Italy,
Whose crown and kingdom rests at thy command:
Sichaeus, not Aeneas, be thou call'd;
The king of Carthage, not Anchises' son:          60
Hold, take these jewels at thy lover's hand,
                              [*giving jewels, etc.*
These golden bracelets, and this wedding-ring,
Wherewith my husband woo'd me yet a maid,
And be thou king of Libya by my gift.
                              [*exeunt to the cave*

# ACT FOUR

## SCENE I

*Enter* ACHATES, CUPID *as Ascanius,* IARBAS *and* ANNA

| | |
|---|---|
| ACHATES | Did ever men see such a sudden storm, |
| | Or day so clear so suddenly o'ercast? |
| IARBAS | I think some fell enchantress dwelleth here, |
| | That can call them forth whenas she please, |
| | And dive into black tempest's treasury, |
| | Whenas she means to mask the world with clouds. |
| ANNA | In all my life I never knew the like; |
| | It hailed, it snow'd, it lighten'd, all at once. |
| ACHATES | I think it was the devil's revelling night, |
| | There was such hurly-burly in the heavens:          10 |
| | Doubtless Apollo's axle-tree is crack'd, |
| | Or aged Atlas' shoulder out of joint, |
| | The motion was so over-violent. |
| IARBAS | In all this coil, where have ye left the queen? |
| ASCANIUS | Nay, where's my warlike father, can you tell? |
| ANNA | Behold where both of them come forth the cave. |
| IARBAS | Come forth the cave! Can heaven endure this sight? |
| | Iarbas, cause that unrevenging Jove, |
| | Whose flinty darts slept in Typhoeus' den, |
| | Whiles these adulterers surfeited with sin –          20 |
| | Nature, why mad'st me not some poisonous beast, |
| | That with the sharpness of my edged sting |
| | I might have stak'd them both unto the earth, |
| | Whilst they were sporting in this darksome cave? |

*Enter, from the cave,* AENEAS *and* DIDO

| | |
|---|---|
| AENEAS | The air is clear, and southern winds are whist. |
| | Come, Dido, let us hasten to the town, |
| | Since gloomy Aeolus doth cease to frown, |
| DIDO | Achates and Ascanius, well met. |
| AENEAS | Fair Anna, how escap'd you from the shower? |
| ANNA | As others did, by running to the wood.          30 |
| DIDO | But where were you, Iarbas, all this while? |

AENEAS  With speed he bids me sail to Italy,
Whenas I want both rigging for my fleet,
And also furniture for these my men.      70
IARBAS  If that be all, then cheer thy drooping looks,
For I will furnish thee with such supplies.
Let some of those thy followers go with me,
And they shall have what thing soe'er thou need'st.
AENEAS  Thanks, good Iarbas, for thy friendly aid:
Achates and the rest shall wait on thee,
Whilst I rest thankful for this courtesy.
                          *[exeunt all except Aeneas*
Now will I haste unto Lavinian shore,
And raise a new foundation to old Troy.
Witness the gods, and witness heaven and earth,    80
How loath I am to leave these Libyan bounds,
But that eternal Jupiter commands!

*Enter* DIDO

DIDO  *[aside]* I fear I saw Aeneas' little son
Led by Achates to the Trojan fleet.
If it be so, his father means to fly —
But here he is! Now, Dido, try thy wit —
Aeneas, wherefore go thy men aboard?
Why are thy ships new-rigg'd? Or to what end,
Launch'd from the haven, lie they in the road?
Pardon me, though I ask; love makes me ask.      90
AENEAS  O, pardon me, if I resolve thee why!
Aeneas will not feign with his dear love.
I must from hence: this day swift Mercury,
When I was laying a platform for these walls,
Sent from his father Jove, appear'd to me,
And in his name rebuk'd me bitterly
For lingering here, neglecting Italy.
DIDO  But yet Aeneas will not leave his love.
AENEAS  I am commanded by immortal Jove
To leave this town and pass to Italy;        100
And therefore must of force.
DIDO  These words proceed not from Aeneas' heart.
AENEAS  Not from my heart, for I can hardly go;
And yet I may not stay. Dido, farewell.

DIDO        Farewell! Is this the 'mends for Dido's love?
            Do Trojans use to quit their lovers thus?
            Fare well may Dido, so Aeneas stay;
            I die, if my Aeneas say farewell.
AENEAS      Then let me go, and never say farewell:
            Let me go; farewell [none]: I must from hence.     110
DIDO        These words are poison to poor Dido's soul:
            O, speak like my Aeneas, like my love!
            Why look'st thou toward the sea? The time hath been
            When Dido's beauty chain'd thine eyes to her.
            Am I less fair than when thou saw'st me first?
            O then, Aeneas, 'tis for grief of thee!
            Say thou wilt stay in Carthage with thy queen,
            And Dido's beauty will return again.
            Aeneas, say, how canst thou take thy leave?
            Wilt thou kiss Dido? O, thy lips have sworn     120
            To stay with Dido! Canst thou take her hand?
            Thy hand and mine have plighted mutual faith;
            Therefore, unkind Aeneas, must thou say,
            'Then let me go, and never say farewell'?
AENEAS      O queen of Carthage, wert thou ugly-black,
            Aeneas could not choose but hold thee dear!
            Yet must he not gainsay the gods' behest.
DIDO        The gods! What gods be those that seek my death?
            Wherein have I offended Jupiter,
            That he should take Aeneas from mine arms?     130
            O, no! The gods weigh not what lovers do:
            It is Aeneas calls Aeneas hence;
            And woful Dido, by these blubber'd cheeks,
            By this right hand, and by our spousal rites,
            Desires Aeneas to remain with her;
            *Si bene quid de te merui, fuit aut tibi quidquam*
            *Dulce meum, miserere domus labentis, et istam,*
            *Oro, si quis adhuc precibus locus, exue mentem.*
AENEAS      *Desine meque tuis incendere teque querelis;*
            *Italiam non sponte sequor.*                     140
DIDO        Hast thou forgot how many neighbour kings
            Were up in arms, for making thee my love?
            How Carthage did rebel, Iarbas storm,

And all the world call'd me a second Helen,
For being entangled by a stranger's looks?
So thou wouldst prove as true as Paris did,
Would, as fair Troy was, Carthage might be sack'd,
And I be call'd a second Helena!
Had I a son by thee, the grief were less,
That I might see Aeneas in his face:      150
Now if thou go'st, what canst thou leave behind,
But rather will augment than ease my woe?

AENEAS    In vain, my love, thou spend'st thy fainting breath:
If words might move me, I were overcome.

DIDO    And wilt thou not be mov'd with Dido's words?
Thy mother was no goddess, perjur'd man,
Nor Dardanus the author of thy stock;
But thou art sprung from Scythian Caucasus,
And tigers of Hyrcania gave thee suck —
Ah, foolish Dido, to forbear this long —      160
Wast thou not wreck'd upon this Libyan shore,
And cam'st to Dido like a fisher swain?
Repair'd not I thy ships, made thee a king,
And all thy needy followers noblemen?
O serpent, that came creeping from the shore,
And I for pity harbour'd in my bosom,
Wilt thou now slay me with thy venom'd sting,
And hiss at Dido for preserving thee?
Go, go, and spare not; seek out Italy:
I hope that that which love forbids me do,      170
The rocks and sea-gulfs will perform at large,
And thou shalt perish in the billows' ways,
To whom poor Dido doth bequeath revenge:
Ay, traitor! And the waves shall cast thee up,
Where thou and false Achates first set foot;
Which if it chance, I'll give ye burial,
And weep upon your lifeless carcasses,
Though thou nor he will pity me a whit.
Why star'st thou in my face? If thou wilt stay,
Leap in mine arms; mine arms are open wide;      180
If not, turn from me, and I'll turn from thee;
For though thou hast the heart to say farewell,

I have not power to stay thee.                    [*exit Aeneas*

                       Is he gone?

Ay, but he'll come again; he cannot go;
He loves me too-too well to serve me so:
Yet he that in my sight would not relent,
Will, being absent, be obdurate still.
By this, is he got to the water-side;
And, see, the sailors take him by the hand;
But he shrinks back; and now, remembering me,   190
Returns amain: welcome, welcome, my love!
But where's Aeneas? Ah, he's gone, he's gone!

*Enter* ANNA

ANNA    What means my sister, thus to rave and cry?
DIDO    O Anna, my Aeneas is aboard,
       And, leaving me, will sail to Italy!
       Once didst thou go, and he came back again:
       Now bring him back, and thou shalt be a queen,
       And I will live a private life with him.
ANNA    Wicked Aeneas!
DIDO    Call him not wicked, sister: speak him fair,   200
       And look upon him with a mermaid's eye;
       Tell him, I never vow'd at Aulis' gulf
       The desolation of his native Troy,
       Nor sent a thousand ships unto the walls,
       Nor ever violated faith to him;
       Request him gently, Anna, to return:
       I crave but this – he stay a tide or two,
       That I may learn to bear it patiently;
       If he depart thus suddenly, I die.
       Run, Anna, run; stay not to answer me.   210
ANNA    I go, fair sister: heavens grant good success.   [*exit*

*Enter nurse*

NURSE    O Dido, your little son Ascanius
       Is gone! He lay with me last night,
       And in the morning he was stoln from me:
       I think, some fairies have beguiled me.
DIDO    O cursed hag and false dissembling wretch,
       That slay'st me with thy harsh and hellish tale!

Thou for some petty gift hast let him go,
And I am thus deluded of my boy –
Away with her to prison presently –                220

*Enter Attendants*

Trait'ress too keen and cursed sorceress!
NURSE   I know not what you mean by treason, I;
I am as true as any one of yours.
DIDO    Away with her! Suffer her not to speak.
                        [*exit Nurse with Attendants*
My sister comes: I like not her sad looks.

*Re-enter* ANNA

ANNA    Before I came, Aeneas was aboard,
And, spying me, hois'd up the sails amain;
But I cried out, 'Aeneas, false Aeneas, stay!'
Then gan he wag his hand, which, yet held up,
Made me suppose he would have heard me speak;  230
Then gan they drive into the ocean:
Which when I view'd, I cried, 'Aeneas, stay!
Dido, fair Dido wills Aeneas stay!'
Yet he, whose heart of adamant or flint
My tears nor plaints could mollify a whit –
Then carelessly I rent my hair for grief:
Which seen to all, though he beheld me not,
They gan to move him to redress my ruth,
And stay a while to hear what I could say;
But he, clapp'd under hatches, sail'd away.      240
DIDO    O Anna, Anna, I will follow him!
ANNA    How can you go when he hath all your fleet?
DIDO    I'll frame me wings of wax, like Icarus,
And, o'er his ships, will soar unto the sun,
That they may melt, and I fall in his arms;
Or else I'll make a prayer unto the waves,
That I may swim to him, like Triton's niece.
O Anna, fetch Arion's harp,
That I may tice a dolphin to the shore,
And ride upon his back unto my love;            250
Look; sister, look! Lovely Aeneas' ships!
See, see, the billows heave 'em up to heaven,

And now down fall the keels into the deep!
O sister, sister, take away the rocks!
They'll break his ships. O Proteus, Neptune, Jove,
Save, save Aeneas, Dido's liefest love!
Now is he come on shore, safe without hurt:
But, see, Achates wills him put to sea,
And all the sailors merry-make for joy;
But he, remembering me, shrinks back again:          260
See where he comes; welcome, welcome, my love!

ANNA        Ah, sister, leave these idle fantasies!
            Sweet sister, cease; remember who you are.

DIDO        Dido I am, unless I be deceiv'd:
            And must I rave thus for a runagate?
            Must I make ships for him to sail away?
            Nothing can bear me to him but a ship,
            And he hath all my fleet – What shall I do,
            But die in fury of this oversight?
            Ay, I must be the murderer of myself –          270
            [aside] No, but I am not; yet I will be straight –
            Anna, be glad; now have I found a mean
            To rid me from these thoughts of lunacy:
            Not far from hence
            There is a woman famoused for arts,
            Daughter unto the nymphs Hesperides,
            Who will'd me sacrifice his ticing relics:
            Go, Anna, bid my servants bring me fire.   [exit Anna

                        Enter IARBAS

IARBAS      How long will Dido mourn a stranger's flight
            That hath dishonour'd her and Carthage both?          280
            How long shall I with grief consume my days,
            And reap no guerdon for my truest love?

                Enter Attendants with wood and torches

DIDO        Iarbas, talk not of Aeneas; let him go:
            Lay to thy hands, and help me make a fire,
            That shall consume all that this stranger left;
            For I intend a private sacrifice,
            To cure my mind, that melts for unkind love.

IARBAS      But, afterwards, will Dido grant me love?

DIDO      Ay, ay, Iarbas; after this is done,
None in the world shall have my love but thou.    290
*[they make a fire*
So, leave me now; let none approach this place.
*[exeunt Iarbas and Attendants*
Now, Dido, with these relics burn thyself,
And make Aeneas famous through the world
For perjury and slaughter of a queen.
Here lie, the sword that in the darksome cave
He drew, and swore by, to be true to me;
Thou shalt burn first; thy crime is worse than his.
Here lie, the garment which I cloth'd him in
When first he came on shore: perish thou too.
These letters, lines, and perjur'd papers, all    300
Shall burn to cinders in this precious flame.
And now, ye gods, that guide the starry frame,
And order all things at your high dispose,
Grant, though the traitors land in Italy,
They may be still tormented with unrest;
And from mine ashes let a conqueror rise,
That may revenge this treason to a queen
By ploughing up his countries with the sword;
Betwixt this land and that be never league;
*Litora litoribus contraria, fluctibus undas*    310
*Imprecor, arma armis; pugnent ipsique nepotes!*
Live, false Aeneas! Truest Dido dies;
*Sic, sic juvat ire sub umbras.*
*[throws herself into the flames*

*Re-enter* ANNA

ANNA      O, help, Iarbas; Dido in these flames
Hath burnt herself; ay me, unhappy me!

*Re-enter* IARBAS, *running*

IARBAS      Cursed Iarbas, die to expiate
The grief that tires upon thine inward soul —
Dido, I come to thee — ay me, Aeneas!
*[stabs himself, and dies*

ANNA      What can my tears or cries prevail me now?
Dido is dead!    320

Iarbas slain, Iarbas my dear love!
O sweet Iarbas, Anna's sole delight!
What fatal Destiny envies me thus,
To see my sweet Iarbas slay himself?
But Anna now shall honour thee in death,
And mix her blood with thine; this shall I do,
That gods and men may pity this my death,
And rue our ends, senseless of life or breath:
Now, sweet Iarbas, stay! I come to thee.

[*stabs herself, and dies*

# WORDSWORTH CLASSICS
# OF WORLD LITERATURE

REQUESTS FOR INSPECTION COPIES Lecturers wishing to obtain copies of Wordsworth Classics, Wordsworth Poetry Library or Wordsworth Classics of World Literature titles on inspection are invited to contact: Dennis Hart, Wordsworth Editions Ltd, Crib Street, Ware, Herts SG12 9ET; E-mail: dennis.hart@wordsworth-editions.com. Please quote the author, title and ISBN of the titles in which you are interested; together with your name, academic address, E-mail address, the course on which the books will be used and the expected enrolment.

Teachers wishing to inspect specific core titles for GCSE or A level courses are also invited to contact Wordsworth Editions at the above address.

Inspection copies are sent solely at the discretion of Wordsworth Editions Ltd.

APULEIUS
*The Golden Ass*

ARISTOTLE
*The Nicomachean Ethics*

MARCUS AURELIUS
*Meditations*

FRANCIS BACON
*Essays*

JAMES BOSWELL
*The Life of Samuel Johnson*
(UNABRIDGED)

JOHN BUNYAN
*The Pilgrim's Progress*

BALDESAR CASTIGLIONE
*The Book of the Courtier*

CATULLUS
*Poems*

CERVANTES
*Don Quixote*

CARL VON CLAUSEWITZ
*On War*
(ABRIDGED)

CONFUCIUS
*The Analects*

CAPTAIN JAMES COOK
*The Voyages of Captain Cook*

DANTE
*The Inferno*

CHARLES DARWIN
*The Origin of Species*
*The Voyage of the Beagle*

RENÉ DESCARTES
*Key Philosophical Writings*

FYODOR DOSTOEVSKY
*The Devils*

ERASMUS
*Praise of Folly*

SIGMUND FREUD
*The Interpretation of Dreams*

EDWARD GIBBON
*The Decline and Fall of the Roman Empire*
(ABRIDGED)

GUSTAVE FLAUBERT
*A Sentimental Journey*

KAHLIL GIBRAN
*The Prophet*

JOHANN WOLFGANG VON GOETHE
*Faust*

HERODOTUS
*Histories*

HOMER
*The Iliad and The Odyssey*

HORACE
*The Odes*

BEN JONSON
*Volpone and Other Plays*

KENKO
*Essays in Idleness*

WILLIAM LANGLAND
*Piers Plowman*

LAO TZU
*Tao Te Ching*

T. E. LAWRENCE
*Seven Pillars of Wisdom*

| | |
|---|---|
| IARBAS | Not with Aeneas in the ugly cave. |
| DIDO | I see, Aeneas sticketh in your mind; |
| | But I will soon put by that stumbling-block, |
| | And quell those hopes that thus employ your cares. |

                                                 [*exeunt*

## SCENE 2

### *Enter* IARBAS *to sacrifice*

| | |
|---|---|
| IARBAS | Come, servants, come; bring forth the sacrifice, |
| | That I may pacify that gloomy Jove, |
| | Whose empty altars have enlarg'd our ills — |

                             [*Servants bring in the sacrifice, and then exeunt*

Eternal Jove, great master of the clouds,
Father of gladness and all frolic thoughts,
That with thy gloomy hand corrects the heaven,
When airy creatures war amongst themselves;
Hear, hear, O hear Iarbas' plaining prayers,
Whose hideous echoes make the welkin howl,
And all the woods Eliza to resound!            10
The woman that thou will'd us entertain,
Where, straying in our borders up and down,
She crav'd a hide of ground to build a town,
With whom we did divide both laws and land,
And all the fruits that plenty else sends forth,
Scorning our loves and royal marriage-rites,
Yields up her beauty to a stranger's bed;
Who, having wrought her shame, is straightway fled:
Now, if thou be'st a pitying god of power,
On whom ruth and compassion ever waits,         20
Redress these wrongs, and warn him to his ships,
That now afflicts me with his flattering eyes.

### *Enter* ANNA

| | |
|---|---|
| ANNA | How now, Iarbas! At your prayers so hard? |
| IARBAS | Ay, Anna: is there aught you would with me? |
| ANNA | Nay, no such weighty busines of import, |
| | But may be slack'd until another time: |
| | Yet, if you would partake with me the cause |

Of this devotion that detaineth you,
I would be thankful for such courtesy.

IARBAS    Anna, against this Trojan do I pray,                    30
          Who seeks to rob me of thy sister's love,
          And dive into her heart by colour'd looks.

ANNA      Alas, poor king, that labours so in vain
          For her that so delighteth in thy pain!
          Be rul'd by me, and seek some other love,
          Whose yielding heart may yield thee more relief.

IARBAS    Mine eye is fix'd where fancy cannot start:
          O, leave me, leave me to my silent thoughts,
          That register the numbers of my ruth,
          And I will either move the thoughtless flint,        40
          Or drop out both mine eyes in drizzling tears,
          Before my sorrow's tide have any stint!

ANNA      I will not leave Iarbas, whom I love,
          In this delight of dying pensiveness.
          Away with Dido! Anna be thy song;
          Anna, that doth admire thee more than heaven.

IARBAS    I may nor will list to such loathsome change,
          That intercepts the course of my desire –
          Servants, come fetch these empty vessels here:
          For I will fly from these alluring eyes,              50
          That do pursue my peace where'er it goes.

                                                            [exit

          *Servants re-enter, and carry out the vessels, etc.*

ANNA      Iarbas, stay! Loving Iarbas, stay!
          For I have honey to present thee with.
          Hard-hearted, wilt not deign to hear me speak?
          I'll follow thee with outcries ne'ertheless,
          And strew thy walks with my dishevell'd hair.

                                                            [exit

## SCENE 3

### *Enter* AENEAS

AENEAS    Carthage, my friendly host, adieu!
Since destiny doth call me from thy shore:
Hermes this night, descending in a dream,
Hath summon'd me to fruitful Italy.
Jove wills it so; my mother wills it so;
Let my Phoenissa grant, and then I go.
Grant she or no, Aeneas must away;
Whose golden fortunes, clogg'd with courtly ease,
Cannot ascend to Fame's immortal house,
Or banquet in bright Honour's burnish'd hall,    10
Till he hath furrow'd Neptune's glassy fields,
And cut a passage through his topless hills –
Achates, come forth! Sergestus, Ilioneus,
Cloanthus, haste away! Aeneas calls.

### *Enter* ACHATES, CLOANTHUS, SERGESTUS *and* ILIONEUS

ACHATES    What wills our lord, or wherefore did he call?
AENEAS    The dream, brave mates, that did beset my bed,
When sleep but newly had embrac'd the night,
Commands me leave these unrenowmed realms,
Whereas nobility abhors to stay,
And none but base Aeneas will abide.    20
Aboard, aboard, since Fates do bid aboard,
And slice the sea with sable-coloured ships,
On whom the nimble winds may all day wait,
And follow them, as footmen, through the deep.
Yet Dido casts her eyes, like anchors, out,
To stay my fleet from loosing forth the bay:
'Come back, come back,' I hear her cry a-far,
'And let me link thy body to my lips,
That, tied together by the striving tongues,
We may, as one, sail into Italy.'    30
ACHATES    Banish that ticing dame from forth your mouth,
And follow your fore-seeing stars in all:
This is no life for men-at-arms to live,

Where dalliance doth consume a soldier's strength,
And wanton motions of alluring eyes
Effiminate our minds, inur'd to war.

ILIONEUS Why, let us build a city of our own,
And not stand lingering here for amorous looks.
Will Dido raise old Priam forth his grave,
And build the town again the Greeks did burn?        40
No, no; she cares not how we sink or swim,
So she may have Aeneas in her arms.

CLOANTHUS To Italy, sweet friends, to Italy!
We will not stay a minute longer here.

AENEAS Trojans, aboard, and I will follow you.

*[exeunt all except Aeneas*

I fain would go, yet beauty calls me back:
To leave her so, and not once say farewell,
Were to transgress against all laws of love.
But, if I use such ceremonious thanks
As parting friends accustom on the shore,        50
Her silver arms will coil me round about,
And tears of pearl cry, 'Stay, Aeneas, stay';
Each word she says will then contain a crown,
And every speech be ended with a kiss:
I may not dure this female drudgery:
To sea, Aeneas! find out Italy!

*[exit*

## SCENE 4

*Enter DIDO and ANNA*

DIDO O Anna, run unto the water side!
They say Aeneas' men are going aboard;
It may be, he will steal away with them:
Stay not to answer me: run, Anna, run!     *[exit Anna*
O foolish Trojans, that would steal from hence,
And not let Dido understand their drift!
I would have given Achates store of gold,
And Ilioneus gum and Libyan spice;
The common soldiers rich embroider'd coats,

And silver whistles to control the winds,                    10
Which Circe sent Sichaeus when he liv'd;
Unworthy are they of a queen's reward.
See, where they come: how might I do to chide?

*Re-enter* ANNA, *with* AENEAS, ACHATES, CLOANTHUS,
ILIONEUS, SERGESTUS *and Carthaginian Lords*

ANNA       'Twas time to run. Aeneas had been gone;
           The sails were hoisting up, and he aboard.
DIDO       Is this thy love to me?
AENEAS     O princely Dido, give me leave to speak!
           I went to take my farewell of Achates.
DIDO       How haps Achates bid me not farewell?
ACHATES    Because I fear'd your grace would keep me here.     20
DIDO       To rid thee of that doubt, aboard again:
           I charge thee put to sea, and stay not here.
ACHATES    Then let Aeneas go aboard with us.
DIDO       Get you aboard; Aeneas means to stay.
AENEAS     The sea is rough, the winds blow to the shore.
DIDO       O false Aeneas! Now the sea is rough;
           But, when you were aboard, 'twas calm enough:
           Thou and Achates meant to sail away.
AENEAS     Hath not the Carthage queen mine only son?
           Thinks Dido I will go and leave him here?           30
DIDO       Aeneas, pardon me; for I forgot
           That young Ascanius lay with me this night;
           Love made me jealous: but, to make amends,
           Wear the imperial crown of Libya,
                              [*giving him her crown and sceptre*
           Sway thou the Punic sceptre in my stead,
           And punish me, Aeneas, for this crime.
AENEAS     This kiss shall be fair Dido's punishment.
DIDO       O, how a crown becomes Aeneas' head!
           Stay here, Aeneas, and command as king.
AENEAS     How vain am I to wear this diadem,                  40
           And bear this golden sceptre in my hand!
           A burgonet of steel, and not a crown,
           A sword, and not a sceptre, fits Aeneas.
DIDO       O keep them still, and let me gaze my fill!

|          | Now looks Aeneas like immortal Jove: |
|----------|--------------------------------------|
|          | O where is Ganymede, to hold his cup, |
|          | And Mercury, to fly for what he calls? |
|          | Ten thousand Cupids hover in the air, |
|          | And fan it in Aeneas' lovely face! |
|          | O that the clouds were here wherein thou fled'st,   50 |
|          | That thou and I unseen might sport ourselves! |
|          | Heaven, envious of our joys, is waxen pale; |
|          | And when we whisper, then the stars fall down, |
|          | To be partakers of our honey talk. |
| AENEAS   | O Dido, patroness of all our lives, |
|          | When I leave thee, death be my punishment! |
|          | Swell, raging seas! Frown, wayward Destinies! |
|          | Blow, winds. Threaten, ye rocks and sandy shelves! |
|          | This is the harbour that Aeneas seeks: |
|          | Let's see what tempests can annoy me now.   60 |
| DIDO     | Not all the world can take thee from mine arms. |
|          | Aeneas may command as many Moors |
|          | As in the sea are little water drops: |
|          | And now, to make experience of my love – |
|          | Fair sister Anna, lead my lover forth, |
|          | And, seated on my jennet, let him ride, |
|          | As Dido's husband, through the Punic streets; |
|          | And will my guard, with Mauritanian darts |
|          | To wait upon him as their sovereign lord. |
| ANNA     | What if the citizens repine thereat?   70 |
| DIDO     | Those that dislike what Dido gives in charge, |
|          | Command my guard to slay for their offence. |
|          | Shall vulgar peasants storm at what I do? |
|          | The ground is mine that gives them sustenance, |
|          | The air wherein they breathe, the water, fire, |
|          | All that they have, their lands, their goods, their lives, |
|          | And I, the goddess of all these, command |
|          | Aeneas ride as Carthaginian king. |
| ACHATES  | Aeneas, for his parentage, deserves |
|          | As large a kingdom as is Libya.   80 |
| AENEAS   | Ay, and, unless the Destinies be false, |
|          | I shall be planted in as rich a land. |
| DIDO     | Speak of no other land; this land is thine; |

Dido is thine, henceforth I'll call thee lord –
Do as I bid thee, sister; lead the way;
And from a turret I'll behold my love.

AENEAS  Then here in me shall flourish Priam's race;
And thou and I, Achates, for revenge
For Troy, for Priam, for his fifty sons,
Our kinsmen's lives and thousand guiltless souls,   90
Will lead an host against the hateful Greeks,
And fire proud Lacedaemon o'er their heads.

            [*exeunt all except Dido and Carthaginian Lords*

DIDO  Speaks not Aeneas like a conqueror?
O blessed tempests that did drive him in!
O happy sand that made him run aground;
Henceforth you shall be our Carthage gods.
Ay, but it may be he will leave my love,
And seek a foreign land call'd Italy:
O that I had a charm to keep the winds
Within the closure of a golden ball;                100
Or that the Tyrrhene sea were in mine arms,
That he might suffer shipwreck on my breast,
As oft as he attempts to hoist up sail!
I must prevent him; wishing will not serve –
Go bid my nurse take young Ascanius,
And bear him in the country to her house;
Aeneas will not go without his son.
Yet, lest he should, for I am full of fear,
Bring me his oars, his tackling, and his sails.

                              [*exit First Lord*

What if I sink his ships? O he will frown!          110
Better he frown than I should die for grief.
I cannot see him frown; it may not be:
Armies of foes resolv'd to win this town,
Or impious traitors vow'd to have my life,
Affright me not; only Aeneas' frown
Is that which terrifies poor Dido's heart:
Not bloody spears, appearing in the air,
Presage the downfall of my empery,
Nor blazing comets threaten Dido's death;
It is Aeneas' frown that ends my days.              120

If he forsake me not, I never die;
For in his looks I see eternity,
And he'll make me immortal with a kiss.

*Re-enter First Lord, with Attendants carrying tackling, etc.*

I LORD      Your nurse is gone with young Ascanius;
         And here's Aeneas' tackling, oars, and sails.
DIDO        Are these the sails that, in despite of me,
         Pack'd with the winds do bear Aeneas hence?
         I'll hang ye in the chamber where I lie;
         Drive, if you can, my house to Italy:
         I'll set the casement open, that the winds       130
         May enter in, and once again conspire
         Against the life of me, poor Carthage queen:
         But, though ye go, he stays in Carthage still:
         And let rich Carthage fleet upon the seas,
         So I may have Aeneas in mine arms.
         Is this the wood that grew in Carthage plains,
         And would be toiling in the watery billows,
         To rob their mistress of her Trojan guest?
         O cursed tree, hadst thou but wit or sense,
         To measure how I prize Aeneas' love,           140
         Thou wouldst have leapt from out the sailors' hands
         And told me that Aeneas meant to go!
         And yet I blame thee not; thou art but wood.
         The water, which our poets term a nymph,
         Why did it suffer thee to touch her breast,
         And shrunk not back, knowing my love was there?
         The water is an element, no nymph.
         Why should I blame Aeneas for his flight?
         O Dido, blame not him, but break his oars!
         These were the instruments that launch'd him forth.
         There's not so much as this base tackling too,
         But dares to heap up sorrow to my heart:
         Was it not you that hoisted up these sails?
         Why burst you not, and they fell in the seas?
         For this will Dido tie ye full of knots,
         And shear ye all asunder with her hands.
         Now serve to chastise shipboys for their faults;

Ye shall no more offend the Carthage queen.
Now, let him hang my favours on his masts,
And see if those will serve instead of sails;      160
For tackling, let him take the chains of gold
Which I bestow'd upon his followers;
Instead of oars, let him use his hands,
And swim to Italy. I'll keep these sure –
Come, bear them in.

                                        *[exeunt*

### SCENE 5

*Enter* NURSE, *with* CUPID *as Ascanius*

| | |
|---|---|
| NURSE | My Lord Ascanius, you must go with me. |
| CUPID | Whither must I go? I'll stay with my mother. |
| NURSE | No, thou shalt go with me unto my house. |

I have an orchard that hath store of plums,
Brown almonds, services, ripe figs, and dates,
Dewberries, apples, yellow oranges;
A garden where are bee-hives full of honey,
Musk-roses, and a thousand sort of flowers;
And in the midst doth run a silver stream,
Where thou shalt see the red-gill'd fishes leap,    10
White swans, and many lovely water-fowls.
Now speak, Ascanius, will you go or no?

| | |
|---|---|
| CUPID | Come, come, I'll go. How far hence is your house? |
| NURSE | But hereby, child; we shall get thither straight. |
| CUPID | Nurse, I am weary; will you carry me? |
| NURSE | Ay, so you'll dwell with me, and call me mother. |
| CUPID | So you'll love me, I care not if I do. |
| NURSE | That I might live to see this boy a man! |

How prettily he laughs! Go to, you wag!
You'll be a twigger when you come to age –    20
Say Dido what she will, I am not old;
I'll be no more a widow; I am young;
I'll have a husband, I, or else a lover.

| | |
|---|---|
| CUPID | A husband, and no teeth! |
| NURSE | O, what mean I to have such foolish thoughts? |

Foolish is love, a toy – O sacred love!
If there be any heaven in earth, 'tis love,
Especially in women of your years –
Blush, blush for shame! Why shouldst thou
                              think of love?
A grave, and not a lover, fits thy age –                    30
A grave! Why, I may live a hundred years!
Fourscore is but a girl's age: love is sweet. –
My veins are wither'd, and my sinews dry:
Why do I think of love, now I should die?

CUPID    Come, nurse.
NURSE    Well, if he come a-wooing, he shall speed:
O, how unwise was I to say him nay!

                                        [exeunt

# ACT FIVE

## SCENE I

*Enter* AENEAS, *with a paper in his hand, drawing the platform of the city;* ACHATES, SERGESTUS, CLOANTHUS *and* ILIONEUS

| | |
|---|---|
| AENEAS | Triumph, my mates; our travels are at end: |
| | Here will Aeneas build a statelier Troy |
| | Than that which grim Atrides overthrew. |
| | Carthage shall vaunt her petty walls no more, |
| | For I will grace them with a fairer frame, |
| | And clad her in a crystal livery, |
| | Wherein the day may evermore delight; |
| | From golden India Ganges will I fetch, |
| | Whose wealthy streams may wait upon her towers, |
| | And triple-wise entrench her round about;          10 |
| | The sun from Egypt shall rich odours bring, |
| | Wherewith his burning beams (like labouring bees |
| | That load their thighs with Hybla's honey-spoils) |
| | Shall here unburden their exhaled sweets, |
| | And plant our pleasant suburbs with their fumes. |
| ACHATES | What length or breadth shall this brave town contain? |
| AENEAS | Not past four thousand paces at the most. |
| ILIONEUS | But what shall it be call'd? Troy, as before? |
| AENEAS | That have I not determin'd with myself. |
| CLOANTHUS | Let it be term'd Aenea, by your name.          20 |
| SERGESTUS | Rather Ascania, by your little son. |
| AENEAS | Nay, I will have it called Anchisaeon, |
| | Of my old father's name. |

*Enter* HERMES *with* ASCANIUS

| | |
|---|---|
| HERMES | Aeneas, stay; Jove's herald bids thee stay. |
| AENEAS | Whom do I see? Jove's winged messenger! |
| | Welcome to Carthage' new-erected town. |
| HERMES | Why, cousin, stand you building cities here, |
| | And beautifying the empire of this queen, |
| | While Italy is clean out of thy mind? |
| | Too-too forgetful of thine own affairs,          30 |
| | Why wilt thou so betray thy son's good hap? |

|  | The king of gods sent me from highest heaven, |
|---|---|
|  | To sound this angry message in thine ears: |
|  | Vain man, what monarchy expect'st thou here? |
|  | Or with what thought sleep'st thou in Libya shore? |
|  | If that all glory hath forsaken thee, |
|  | And thou despise the praise of such attempts, |
|  | Yet think upon Ascanius' prophecy, |
|  | And young Iulus' more than thousand years, |
|  | Whom I have brought from Ida, where he slept,    40 |
|  | And bore young Cupid unto Cyprus' isle. |
| AENEAS | This was my mother that beguil'd the queen, |
|  | And made me take my brother for my son: |
|  | No marvel, Dido, though thou be in love, |
|  | That daily dandlest Cupid in thy arms – |
|  | Welcome, sweet child: where hast thou been this long? |
| ASCANIUS | Eating sweet comfits with Queen Dido's maid, |
|  | Who ever since hath lull'd me in her arms. |
| AENEAS | Sergestus, bear him hence unto our ships, |
|  | Lest Dido, spying him, keep him for a pledge.    50 |

*[exit Sergestus with Ascanius*

| HERMES | Spend'st thou thy time about this little boy, |
|---|---|
|  | And giv'st not ear unto the charge I bring? |
|  | I tell thee, thou must straight to Italy, |
|  | Or else abide the wrath of frowning Jove.    *[exit* |
| AENEAS | How should I put into the raging deep, |
|  | Who have no sails nor tackling for my ships? |
|  | What, would the gods have me, Deucalion-like, |
|  | Float up and down where'er the billows drive? |
|  | Though she repair'd my fleet and gave me ships, |
|  | Yet hath she ta'en away my oars and masts,    60 |
|  | And left me neither sail nor stern aboard. |

*Enter* IARBAS

| IARBAS | How now, Aeneas! Sad? What mean these dumps? |
|---|---|
| AENEAS | Iarbas, I am clean besides myself: |
|  | Jove hath heap'd on me such a desperate charge, |
|  | Which neither art nor reason may achieve, |
|  | Nor I devise by what means to contrive. |
| IARBAS | As how, I pray? May I entreat you tell? |